IN THE
SHADOW
OF PEACE

Printed in Australia

First Printing: May 2022

Shawline Publishing Group Pty Ltd
www.shawlinepublishing.com.au

Paperback ISBN- 9781922701688

Ebook ISBN- 9781922701756

A catalogue record for this book is available from the National Library of Australia

IN THE SHADOW OF PEACE

ADRIAN WEEKS

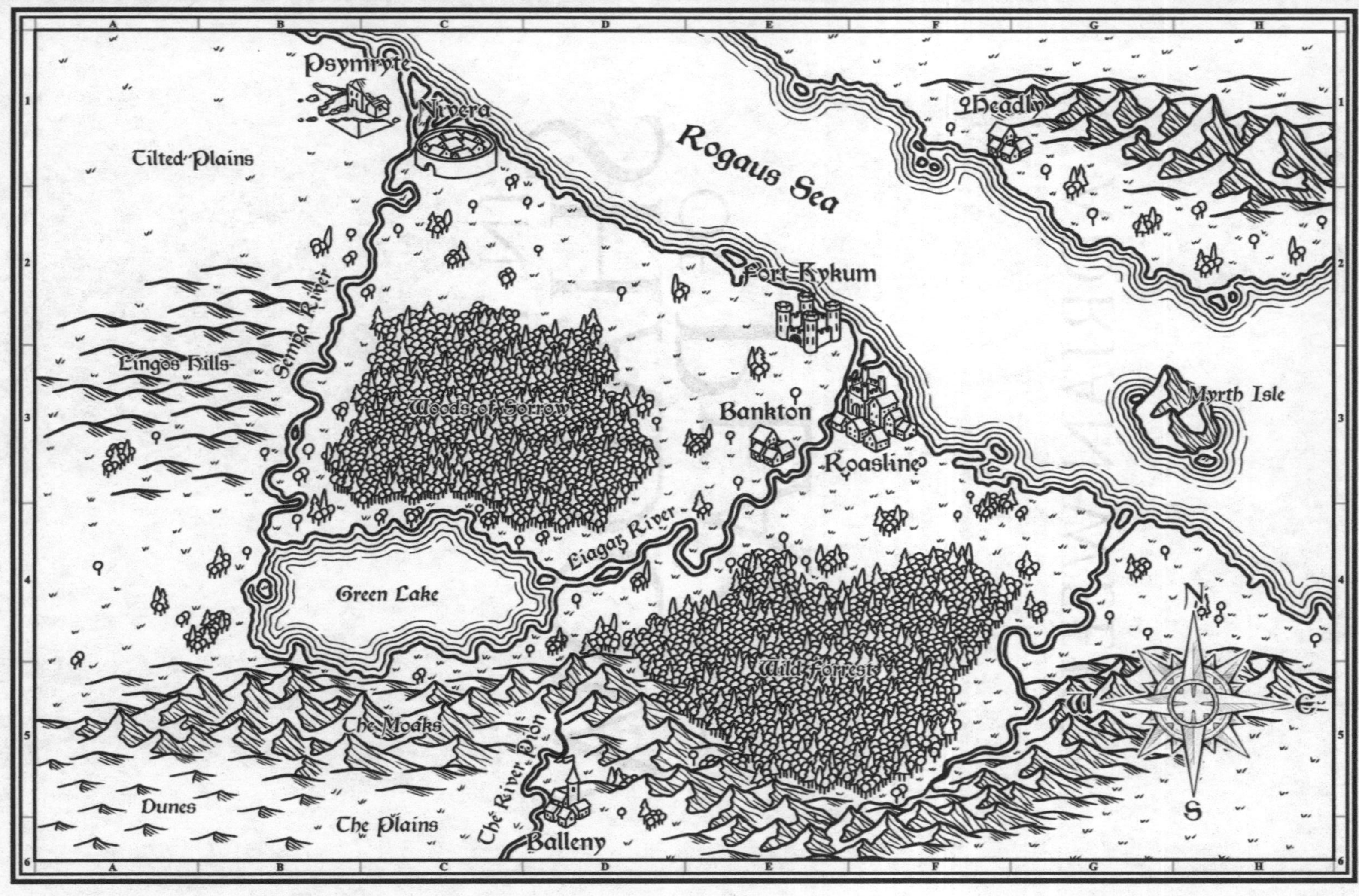

Psymryte
Nivera
Tilted Plains
Rogaus Sea
Headly
Sempa River
Lingos Hills
Woods of Sorrow
Fort Kykum
Bankton
Myrth Isle
Roasline
Green Lake
Liagaz River
Wild Forrest
The Moaks
The River Dion
Dunes
The Plains
Balleny
N
E
W
S

*To my wife, Alice, whose encouragement, support and patience was
(and is) limitless.*

Acknowledgements

I owe thanks to my family; Alice, James and Sophie, for inspiration and patience. To my mum, who proof-read each chapter promptly after it was written. To Veronika Wunderer at www.veronika-wunderer.com and Abbie Jedwab, who created the wonderful map to enable others to visualise this world. To my siblings, in-laws and greater family and friends who have supported me on this journey. Finally, to you, the readers, for allowing me to take you on a journey of turmoil and adventures.

PART 1

1

The first rays of sunlight for the day cut through the ocean breeze to light the crow's nest of a galley of war. The light then crept slowly down her mast to reveal the ship in her entirety. While the main mast was intact, the secondary and tertiary ones were not. The single remaining sail billowed in the wind and drove the ship north east.

From where he stood, Harlorn could make out little more than the ship's outline in the husky light of dawn. The tall, slender man waited patiently as the ship approached his dock. As the vessel got closer, he caught the sound of hardy sailors rushing hither and thither to prepare the ship for docking. Underneath these cries and shouts, he could hear the gentle sound of the high tide lapping only a few feet below the pier. Now and then a large surge of swell struck one of the pylons and sent spray shooting up between the planks to rinse Harlorn's sandaled feet. Above his sandals, Harlorn wore the usual garb of his people: a white robe reaching to just below his knees. A simple leather belt held the robe close against his waist and his sleeves were large and swayed with the breeze.

As the ship drew alongside the dock, Harlorn strode forward to aid in her mooring while reading her name: *Justice*. Meanwhile, two more men clad in white struggled along the dock, pushing a large set of stairs on wheels. Due to the dock's closeness to the water on the high tide, ships of this size needed the stairs to allow access to their decks. Once in place, Harlorn climbed the stairs to meet the ship's captain at the top.

'Captain, welcome to Headly. My name is Harlorn and these are my docks. How may I be of assistance?'

'Good morning Harlorn, I'm Captain Tunley and we seek the services that you provide.'

'How many have you this week, Captain?'

'When we set out from Roasline we had not one more than sixty. But the night before last, we were set on by a pair of the Outcast's ships. In the ferocity of the storm, it was difficult to make them out, but we sunk them nonetheless. It was not until yester-morning that we could take full stock of our damage and I dare say we are lucky to have made it here at all. So, while we set out with sixty, the number grew to seventy-eight before falling to seventy-six early this morning.'

'And I suppose you have the payment for sixty only?'

The captain looked warily at Harlorn. He had heard stories of the harshness of the mysterious people of Headly who dressed in white.

'Unfortunately, that is the case. But I beg you Harlon, the other sixteen were unforeseen, and if you refuse their disembarkation then I fear for their lives.' Tunley took the only bargaining stance he could, and that was to play to the Healer's compassion.

Harlon stood and considered his options for a short while before replying with the authority of his people. 'I see that your need is great. Unfortunately, this falls beyond the specific terms of our agreement with your people and so the decision is placed on my shoulders. If we accept your seventy-six wounded, with only payment for sixty, then our supplies may run short and all those under our care would be affected. If we take only sixty of your charge, then as you say, sixteen may die.' Harlorn rubbed his chin.

'Here is what I will agree to. We will take all of you seventy-six wounded and all of the provisions that you can spare, and *you* will take sixteen that we have here under our care who are close to being healed. We will leave instructions on what is to be done for them, and your healers should be able to bring them back to health, although it will take much longer than if they remained here. Do you agree?'

'I agree.' Tunley clasped his hands behind his back. 'Now there is another matter of which I seek your assistance. While we had planned only to have a short stop here to drop off our wounded, our boat, it seems, is also in need of healing.'

Before Tunley could beg another word, Harlorn replied. 'No. You may not repair your ship here. We have already stretched the agreement between our peoples and to aid you in this matter would overstep our allegiance. I saw you sail here on your own abilities and so I will see you sail out of here on your own abilities, before nightfall.' Harlorn denied Tunley a chance of reply and continued without pause. 'You will remain on your ship. My men and I will make the arrangements and return when we're good and ready.'

Harlorn turned his back on the frustrated captain and returned down the stairs. Once at the base of these, he ordered his men to remove them from the ship's side and to keep watch that none should try to disembark. He then strode from his dock and made off toward the main town of the Healers to prepare his sixteen wounded for transport. Harlorn knew that he would have his way; the ship would not be repaired.

Several days later, another vessel approached Headly. This boat was much smaller than the previous ship and skimmed across the water with magnificent agility.

Harlorn had seen this sloop many times before, but he wondered who the captain might be. Harlorn had come across many an unsavoury captain, but he always managed to remain in command of the trading process. Unlike the people of Roasline, the Outcasts made dedicated trips to Headly to drop off their wounded to be healed. More often than not, their boat would be small and have little room for excess. The smaller boat size allowed them to easily avoid unwanted attention from their enemies en route from the mainland. Those who captained these vessels were well skilled in boating and needed only one or two deck hands to sail on the open seas. On this evening, Harlorn could see the captain going about his docking procedures with a certain type of mechanical efficiency that showed his experience.

After strolling down to where he knew the boat would dock, Harlorn stood and waited. Being a smaller boat than the war ship from several days prior, the embarkation stairs were not needed. The Healer only had to wait a short while before the sloop had glided in next to the pier and was fastened in place.

Captain Ryde leapt from the vessel and landed just in front of Harlorn. The dock master smiled as he recognised the gruesome scar that started where Ryde's prematurely greying hair had begun to recede, passed over his right eye, a glass replacement, and ended where his smile began. Harlorn remembered back to when the Captain had been brought to Headly to be healed himself. The then young man had been an inch from death as the battle wound had become infected and was beginning to rot. His eye had been long gone, but the Healers were still disappointed with their inability to restore his face to its previous mischievous appearance.

The Captain ruefully smiled and thrust out his right hand for Harlorn to shake. The Healer took it warmly and felt the absence of the two digits that Ryde had lost as a child when learning to sail for the first time. The boy of eight had lost his second and fourth fingers when they were wrapped in the running rigging of a small boat and a wave had appeared out of nowhere and sent the boat pitching and the boy flying. His fingers had caught and were mangled beyond repair. His father had swiftly recognised the damage and removed the useless digits entirely.

'Welcome to Headly once more, Captain Ryde. How many do you bring on this journey?'

'Ah Harlorn, it is always straight down to business with you. Can't a seasoned sailor have a kind word first?'

'If you knew I would proceed directly with our business, then must you ask? And besides, you wouldn't recognise a kind word if one was standing right before you in broad daylight.'

Ryde let forth a deep bellied laugh that was short and to the point. Following this, the sound of pained groans reached their ears and both the men's smiles faded.

'I bring fourteen men and women from the military with simple battle wounds and another four civilians. Of these, two have an ongoing fever, one has been hearing voices and one of whom has no feeling from the waist down. The latter is but fourteen years old. And before you ask, we bring the required goods.'

Harlorn took a moment to think before replying. 'Very well. I will have my men help them ashore. In return, we have seventeen of your people fully healed and ready to return to your shores. Ryde, you may not be able to prevent it, but I would prefer if we didn't have to see them on Headly again.'

The men shook hands once more, knowing full well that Captain Ryde had no influence over the Outcasts' policy of war.

'Tell me Harlorn, what would you and your people do if this bloody war was to end tomorrow?'

'First, we would breathe a sigh of relief. And following that, we would recognise that there are sicknesses enough in this world, without those imposed by men. We would fill our time healing those peoples. But Captain, let's not be ignorant, while that would be a much looked for eventuality, this war has been dragging on for close to fifty years; it would be foolish to hope for such a day.'

'Your words are grim, Harlorn.' Both men stood there for a moment in sadness before Ryde broke the silence again. 'As you're a Healer, do you suppose you could heal my thirst while your men work to unload the wounded?'

'Ryde, you know we do not have the kind of drink that you are chasing, but I do have some freshly drawn spring water, to which I have added a hint of wild berries. It is very refreshing. Come and have a cup or two, but after that we should also help with the wounded.'

Harlorn led Captain Ryde to the small hut situated where the pier reached the ground as several other Healers emerged carrying stretchers and pushing carts. These men set about removing the wounded from Captain Ryde's sloop and preparing them for transport to the main healing centre. Before long, Captain Ryde was back aboard his boat and expertly slipping away from the dock.

2

'Are we lost again?'

Dehydration and exhaustion slowed Winter's response to his half-sister, but when it came, there was no uncertainty hidden. 'Once we climb that small rise ahead, we will be no more than a mile from the oasis.'

Without waiting for Winter to continue, Dusk shouldered her bow once more and set off towards the sandy hill ahead. Winter followed more doggedly.

The two siblings scrambled up the dune in what turned out to be quite a challenge. For every three steps forward, they slid back two. Dusk soon became frustrated and started whimpering like a pup, as non-existent tears sprang to her eyes. Winter just kept trudging forward as if in a daze.

Once they finally reached the top of the dune, they both stood with their hands on their hips and sucked the dry air into their dry mouths and down into their dry lungs. Their eyes searched in the spiteful midday sun and soon found what they had been looking for: an oasis. The beauty of it shimmered before their eyes and smiles spread across their cracked lips.

They stood for a moment longer before simultaneously moving forward and loping down the sand dune. When they were half way down, Winter and Dusk mustered all the energy they had and ran towards the oasis as if their lives depended on it.

They raced with their hearts pounding and their breaths rasping in defiance of the increased workload. Then, all of a sudden, they were under the shade of a tree and out of the searing heat. Without speaking, Dusk raised her hand and pointed to a small stream that trickled a few feet ahead. They stumbled towards it and were unable to stop themselves as they splashed into its cooling waters. They both drank deeply and cleaned the desert dirt from their skin. Once refreshed, they scrambled out of the water and sat under what appeared to be a mango tree. The fruit above was green and firm, but to the famished travellers, it tasted as sweet as fresh honey. They both ate their fill before feeling the many days of travel catch them up. Their heads began to nod and they dozed off in the blissful shade.

Dusk was the first to wake, and when she did, her mouth was cracked and sore. She turned to Winter, saw that he was sleeping heavily, and clumsily got to her feet. She only lasted for a moment or two before the weariness within her limbs got the better of her and she sunk to the ground once more. Dusk sat there in a crumpled heap for a while longer before scrambling onto her hands and knees and made her pained way down to the stream. Once there, she drank her fill, soothing her sore mouth.

The cooling waters had an amazing impact on Dusk's energy levels, and she found herself reborn with a new strength of purpose. Leaping to her feet, she raced back to Winter and nudged him firmly with her foot.

'Wake up Winter. It is time we made our next move.'

Winter groaned and stretched his limbs before rousing into a sitting position. 'But sister, I was just having wonderful pain free dreams of berries and hard candy.'

Dusk cast Winter a stern glance that made him look away.

'Oh, very well. Just give me a moment to splash my face and then I will be as ready as you to tackle our next task.'

Once Winter had freshened himself and was ready for whatever lay in store, Dusk suggested they explore the entirety of the oasis. This, they proceeded to do in a methodical fashion. They began where they had entered the oasis and worked their way west. The plants they found consisted of a variety of tropical species with a large proportion bearing fruit. Dusk deemed there would be sufficient fruit for one to live there indefinitely with different plants set to ripen all year round. The oasis itself stretched for a half mile from east to west but no more than a hundred feet from north to south. Dusk and Winter found nothing of note the first time through the oasis and so Dusk suggested they repeat the process in the opposite direction. Not knowing what they were looking for, and with nothing else to do, Winter could hardly argue.

The sun was just dipping below the horizon when Winter broke their long silence. 'Dusk, I think we should get some food, find some shelter and rest for the night. In the morning we can search afresh. I mean, we don't even know what we are looking for. All Father said was to hunt for something that did not belong. I ask you, sister, what does that even mean? Everything here belongs and yet doesn't. All these plants look natural enough, yet who ever heard of a tropical orchard growing in the middle of a desert wasteland *naturally?* None of it belongs if you ask me!'

Dusk was only half listening to Winter's rant as she had found something much more interesting to concentrate on. 'Winter, come and look at this.'

The excitement in her voice sufficed to spark Winter's interest. Dusk heard him approach as she continued to examine what was before her. 'Winter, I think I have found what we are looking for.' Dusk removed her bow from her uninjured shoulder and crouched down. What she saw was a tangled mess of a rosebush.

The plant was growing in the exact centre of the oasis at the base of a gigantic palm tree. 'This plant is not tropical; it does not belong here.'

'What are we to do with this horrible looking bush?'

'I don't know yet.' Dusk remained crouched for a few moments longer before standing and circumnavigating the rose bush. 'Pass me the map, will you? It might hold a clue.'

Winter obeyed and removed his father's ancient map from where he had tied it about his neck for safe keeping. As he passed it to her, he spoke hesitantly. 'Before you try anything rash, I think we should consider our actions carefully.'

Dusk rolled her eyes. 'I'm not going to do anything stupid.' She examined the map as Winter had done many times before. Finding nothing but the land about and the stars imposed upon its surface, she flipped it over to scrutinise the back. She ran her hands over its surface and even tried sniffing it. She raised it to the horizon and the last rays of sun beamed through it. Dusk caught a fleeting glimpse of some lettering hidden within. She stared, but by then the direct rays of the sun were gone and dusk descended.

Her hands shook slightly with excitement. 'Winter! Have you ever seen any writing on this map?'

'No, other than the letter "N" to symbolise north.'

'When I held it up to the sun's rays, I thought I saw a wispy series of letters. Quick, gather some of those dry palm fronds and light a fire. Make it bright.'

Dusk continued to stare at the map as Winter scurried about building a fire. Once the blaze was going, Dusk sat closer than was wise and held up the map with the flames flickering behind.

'It's working, I can see some writing! It's hard to make out but I believe it says: 'Only those who are ready will find that which lies beneath that what does not belong.'

Dusk dropped her hands as a sense of confusion, excitement, and curiosity passed through her. She raced over to the rosebush once more. Dusk proceeded to reach forward and grab the bush. She instantly let out a sharp yelp of pain. She spun around and faced Winter, holding her right hand close to her chest. Blood ran freely from her hand, sliced in many places. She sank to her knees and slowly looked down to see her little finger had been severed just above its base.

Winter swung into action and ripped a portion of cloth from his sleeve. Through her pain, Dusk heard him instructing her to hold the cloth firmly to her hand as he removed a lace from his boot. He quickly tied this securely around the stump to her finger and Dusk let out another yelp of pain.

Winter guided Dusk to the fireside, where she sat while he fetched some water from the stream and put it on the fire to heat. Once warmed, he tore another length of cloth from his shirt and washed it in the warm water. He used this to cleanse the wound and then bind it firmly.

Winter went to gather some food to keep Dusk's spirits up while the poor girl sat by the fire whimpering. After eating some scavenged berries, she leant against Winter while he soothed her with stories of their childhood and the pranks the two of them would play on their three siblings.

Dusk wanted to sleep, but the throbbing pain in finger kept her awake. She shivered with cold and wiped dried tear-salt from her cheeks. The stars above were beautifully abundant yet the fire had gone out. Using her uninjured left hand as a prop, she clambered to her feet and stood still for a moment as a wave of dizziness passed over her. Leaving Winter to his dreams, she fumbled in the moonlight to where the rosebush sat.

She gazed at the beast but could not find her little finger or indeed any of her blood on it. She cursed the bush and spat at it. Her hand continued to throb and her head spun once more. She sat down in front of the bush and repeated the words from the map in her head: *Only those who are ready will find that which lies beneath that what does not belong.* It was clear to her that what they sought was hidden beneath the bush, but what did it mean by *only those who are ready?*

'Ready for what?' she murmured to no one. After much more thinking, she concluded that if one was ready, then they should be able to move the bush.

By that stage, the moon had moved across the sky and a gentle hint of dawn caressed the eastern horizon. She got to her feet and roused Winter gently.

'Good morning.' She greeted her half-brother. 'Once you are ready, I would like you to take another look at my hand and see what damage there is.'

He grunted in dissatisfaction at being woken. 'It's still night time, go to sleep.' He rolled over and turned his back to her.

Dusk knew her brother well and instead of trying again, rebuilt the fire and put some water to boil. She felt anxious to be active and the rosebush kept gnawing at her mind. *The quickest way to get him going will be to soothe him with breakfast.*

Once the water was hot and Dusk had gathered fruit that looked somewhat like an apple, but was larger and softer, she woke Winter again.

'I have food and hot water for you and I want you to look at my finger.' She spoke kindly but firmly and she would not accept his refusal this time.

Winter grumpily cut up the fruit and shared the flesh that was white with a hint of yellow and tasted sweet.

After they had eaten, Dusk asked Winter to remove her bandage and assessed her wounds. The cuts on her palm were deep but clean. Most had clotted well, while a few oozed a clear fluid. Dusk knew that these cuts would heal given time and care, but what concerned her was the little finger stump. Blood continued to seep from the end, despite the tourniquet. On the hand-side of the bootlace, the remaining finger had swollen drastically.

Dusk looked Winter directly in the eyes. 'You must cauterise it.'

'I fear you are right, but it will hurt more than you can imagine.'

'Not as much as if I lose all of my blood, or if my hand becomes infected and has to be removed as well. And besides, the finger is numb; the bootlace has made sure of that. I'm just lucky that the whole bone came out and doesn't have to be removed too.'

'Very well. I will use one of my sai. While that heats in the fire, I will re-dress your main bandage.' As Winter went about tying Dusk's dressing, they sat in silence. Dusk cast her mind back to many of the painful encounters she had experienced and yet none of them seemed to be so planned and calculated as what she was about to undertake.

'It is time. Lie on you back and bite down on this stick. Look up at the sky and think of the time when we first received our weapons from Father. You were so brave; you stuck that arrow into your flesh with no hesitation at all; just as he told you to. And then you were so young; you are much stronger now.'

Dusk lay back, chomped down on the stick offered to her, and thought back to when the blood had oozed out of her arm and onto the arrowhead. A wave of joy had passed through her then as her bow had shimmered and turned a deep red colour. That specific arrow she still kept and had nev—. A searing pain shot through her hand and up her arm. All her thoughts raced to the pain and she tried to withdraw her arm. A gurgled scream escaped her mouth and still the pain continued. Her whole body tensed and became rigid. And then the pain subsided. Dusk felt a weight lift from her arm as Winter released her and she sat up. The stick fell from her mouth and Winter handed her a water skin to wash out the remaining bits of wood. The water was cool in her mouth before she spat it out and looked down to her hand. Winter had been swift; he had not only cauterised the wound, but had dressed the stump as well. All that Dusk could see was her hand wrapped in a conglomerate of cloth. And then the throbbing began. Dusk instantly hated the pulsing pain and wanting a distraction, she stood. 'Let us have another look at that bush.'

The two made their way over to the rosebush and stared at it for a few moments. Winter drew his sai and took a slash at the prostrate tangled mess. The weapon passed straight through the bush unharmed, but did not damage the bush either.

'Fire.' At Dusk's command, Winter strode to their fire and removed the largest burning palm frond he could find. Returning to the bush, he plunged the stick straight into the centre of the rosebush. Sparks flew in every direction, with several finding their way to Winter's hands. With a grunt of pain, he dropped the branch to shake off the embers. Dusk cried out in dismay as the bush refused to ignite and instead had chopped the burning frond into many pieces.

'Perhaps we need to try and think our way through this.'

'It would appear that we have no other choice.'

Dusk and Winter moved into the shade of a nearby tree and sat down to think. Dusk's tired mind could not focus as her hand pained her too much. She couldn't stop her thoughts returning to her lost finger. She closed her eyes and tried to imagine the bush.

Weariness swept over her and she found herself walking in strange dreams where purple horses ran free through tall grass and green chickens clucked about her feet incessantly. Thunderous clouds rolled over her head, plunging her into near darkness. From the clouds came a bolt of lightning which struck one of the chickens. It squawked and turned into a rosebush. The remaining chickens all turned to her and laughed a wicked cackling laugh. Another bolt of lightning struck the rosebush and the power of the thunder threw her to the ground. Dusk gingerly got to her feet and the rosebush was no more, but in its place stood her Father: Avgar. He stood tall in a dark cloak and she noticed that his right hand was missing. She raced to him and knelt before him even as he began to speak.

'Rise child. The task which lies before you is beyond your skill to achieve. You are younger than I had hoped you would be when I set you on this journey, and your real training was yet to begin. I see now that you were thrust into this too early; albeit by circumstances outside my control.

'You must now abandon this road and I will set you on a new one. Once your strength is recovered, you must make your way directly north to the Moaks. You will receive further directions once there. You both must come to me!' Avgar's final words boomed with the authority of thunder and Dusk was thrown onto her back once more.

Dusk woke from her dream with hope kindling within her and she turned to Winter. A moment later he too roused and stared at Dusk with purpose.

'We must go north.'

3

Captain Tunley brought his ship, *Justice*, to a gentle halt amidst the hustle and bustle of the Roasline docks. While there were lengthy queues of fishing boats waiting for the opportunity to offload their haul, Tunley's ship of war had its own reserved space. As he guided his vessel past the many boats and into the docks, several cheers went up from the waiting fishermen. There was much support from the public for the valiant sailors and soldiers who risked their lives fighting the barbaric Outcasts.

The instant *Justice's* side touched the timber pier, Captain Tunley leapt ashore and was greeted by two waiting soldiers. 'Good evening, sir. We are instructed to escort you to wherever you desire to go.'

'Good, good. Take me directly to the Admiral.'

'Right away, sir.'

The two soldiers about-turned and led Captain Tunley at a brisk pace through the crowded docks. Tunley liked the pace set by the soldiers, but it forced him to abandon his Captain's *swagger*, as he liked to call it, and march more rigidly. As he followed the soldiers, he knew his ship was already being unloaded of the freshly healed and that shipwrights were in consultation about how to mend the damage as speedily as possible. He trusted his first-mate fully and thought no more on the matter. Instead, his eyes flickered over the soldiers in their plain boiled leather tunics and infantry sashes. The unadorned grass green wool of the sash hung from its clasp on the right shoulder and joined at the midpoint between the left hip and armpit. This positioning still allowed a swift drawing of one's sword. Tunley approved of the soldier's presence as it reminded the masses that he was someone of importance and not to be hawked.

Captain Tunley himself wore a finely knitted wool tunic and pants, both stained heavily with sea salt. Atop this, he wore his heavy leather coat for appearances, despite the lack of an evening chill. He displayed his sea captain's sash with pride and always ensured that it was spotless when coming ashore.

As the stench of the unwashed masses assaulted his nostrils, he stroked the sea-blue wool and ran his fingers over the fine single gold chain that was sewn within its centre to indicate his captaincy. His lifelong dream of having the three gold chains of the admiralty swiftly flashed before his eyes. This dream was not unrealistic to him either: he had recently received the unofficial nod that before the year was out, he would obtain his next chain and rise to the rank of Ship Master. Of these, there were only two others in all the fleet and they were constantly being sent on dangerous missions. It would not take much for one of these missions to turn sour; all sorts of things could happen at sea. And then there would only be the Admiral, or as the Ship Masters were permitted to call him, the Old Sea Dog. A smile spread across Tunley's unshaven face at the thought.

The march from the docks to the Admiral's chambers was all uphill and took longer than it should have. By the time Tunley arrived, he was both red faced and puffing slightly. After his elevation to captaincy, he had been able to maintain his rope-like arms and legs, but his middle has only grown out. He put this down to the unavoidable fact that he was not growing younger, while the reality lay in the increased amount of rich food and wine he had been consuming.

The final insult to Tunley's fitness came in the form of a lengthy staircase. Upon reaching the top, he paused for a moment and dismissed the two soldiers. Once his breath was caught, the captain swaggered his way down the wide hallway to stop before a solid mahogany door. He pounded on this thrice and waited for a reply.

'Come.'

He entered. The admiral's chamber was perhaps not as large as that of the infantry general's; however, its furnishings were magnificent to the captain's eyes. Each of these resembled various ship parts, but what Captain Tunley desired most was the huge solid desk. This was no ordinary desk, for in its top, underneath a heavy piece of glass, was a map of the lands and oceans. The map was wrought with valuable metals with gems in-set to represent the various cities. Roasline was represented by a light pink diamond that the admiral himself had retrieved from distant lands when he was a much younger man.

The Admiral was now old and he beckoned his underling to stand at attention in the centre of the room. He rose from his chair at the desk and made his slow way over to the captain. Tunley saw the limp, but not a hint of the pain that he knew was shooting through the admiral's leg. Seeing the old man limping, Captain Tunley was reminded how frail he was, this perception was shattered the instant he heard the admiral speak. The voice that escaped those old lips held a strength built over a lifetime. Although great strength was present, it was not a loud voice and Tunley found he was straining to hear what was being said. Experience told him that this was as the admiral wished it to be.

'You have returned, Captain Tunley. You have returned without fulfilling your duty. Your inconsistency displeases me, Captain. What am I to do with you now?'

When Captain Tunley replied, he found his own voice quivering with uncertainty. 'Sir, my ship was attacked by surprise. We took a heavy battering before defeating the Outcast scum. We took more casualties and so pushed on to Headly. We exchanged our wounded for the healed, but they would not let us repair *Justice*.'

The Admiral walked behind Tunley's back. 'What of my nephew? Did he make it to Headly?' The poorly hidden concern within the Admiral's voice gave strength to Tunley and he took control of the conversation.

'Your nephew was delivered safely.' To take further control, he quickly added, 'But he looked rather sickly. That one is not made for sea travel.' Tunley seized his advantage and switched the topic.

'Sir, I have a proposal that if successful, might see us victorious over the Outcasts.' The Admiral moved in front of Tunley and raised a wary eyebrow. 'Let me take the vast majority of the fleet, fill it with skilled soldiers, and attack Nivera outright. Most of the Outcast troops are on our doorstep. They need only cross the Liagar River and they could overrun us. With my fleet, we can take Nivera and all the fertile lands around her. The soldiers can then move in behind the Outcasts and drive them into the Liagar to drown like the pigs they are. Let me do this and the war will be over in months.'

But Captain Tunley had underestimated his opponent. The voice that erupted from the Admiral was no longer laced with concern, but was as strong as a turning tide.

'Captain, you go too far. You either take me for a fool or are as stupid as an ox. You cannot even fulfil the simple task of capturing some prisoners and yet you want me to entrust *my* fleet to you? You want to use force, and yet where was your stomach when you were on Headly? Why was *Justice* not repaired there? And don't you even think about giving me the fishermen's stories about the magical powers of the Healers.

'And, as for your plan of war… the quickest way to get the Outcasts to cross the Liagar and attack us directly would surely be to attack them from behind. And you have not thought of your north-west border. Once in Nivera and many miles from home, the scum of Psymryte need only leap across the Sempa River and *you* are the one who would be surrounded. *Captain*, you will not again come to me with these half-cooked ideas of ending this war that has been raging for close to fifty years!' The Admiral's face was stern.

'As your Admiral, I am commanding you to remain ashore until you have repaired *Justice*. Once that is done, I will think of a task more fitting to your abilities. You are dismissed now, Captain Tunley.'

Turning on his heels, the red-faced Captain marched from the room, swaggering no more.

The admiral returned to his seat at the desk, but before he could return to his work, he thought he heard a slight scratching sound coming from the wall to his right. He had often heard this scratching sound, although it made no sense to him. He would have supposed that birds might be scratching on the wall outside, except that his tower was made of thick stone. Puzzled, he rose and made his way into the hallway; if he was not in his chambers to hear the sound, then he could not be hearing the impossible.

As he opened his beloved mahogany door, he saw the back of the limping form of Guflinkov. The Admiral liked not the old man who, for the most part, kept to himself. He had no official position in the government, although had the ear of the High Chancellor.

'Guflinkov, stop there. What are you doing in this part of my building?'

The wispy old man slowly turned to face his inquisitor and took a swig from his waterskin. From the rumours he had heard, the Admiral guessed that there was no water in that skin and supposed the old man drunk.

Guflinkov bowed his head before speaking with a slight slur, confirming the admiral's suspicions. 'Admiral Sir, I am on official blusiness that I am alfraid must be klept secret.' The word secret he drew out slowly before exclaiming the *t*. The odd use of speech unsettled the Admiral, and he nodded to Guflinkov and returned to his chambers. Regardless of the time of day, the Admiral thought it was high time for a strong drink.

Guflinkov continued to limp down the hallway before reaching the stairs. He made his way slowly down these, one at a time, before stumbling on the final step to fall to his knees. Groaning in pain, he waited for a passing sailor to help him to his feet.

'Guflinkov, are you injured?'

'Nufink another fouthmul won't fix.' The old man shrugged the sailor's hand from his shoulder and drained his water-skin. He continued to stumble out of the building and back towards his chambers. These used to be situated directly above the High Chancellor's chambers, however, the apparent endless stairs had defeated him several years past. His chambers were now on the ground floor adjacent to the kitchens. Guflinkov liked this positioning for its glorious smells, endless gossip and accessibility to midnight snacks. Thinking on this, the old man changed his plans and headed for the kitchens.

The kitchen staff greeted him as they might a cheeky child who kept trying to pinch apple pies. While his speech was now lucid, his favourite wench, Prahum saw the glazed look in his eyes and knew at once that he had been drinking.

'Guflinkov, you cheeky young man, you've been into your wicked drink again, haven't you?'

'I don't know what you're talking about, Prahumumum.'

Giggling, she brandished a wooded spoon and replied. 'I told you not to call me that. Now, if you behave yourself, then I may be able to get you some lovely, fresh, warm beef and kidney stew, but if you continue to misbehave, then I will chase you from here a hungry man.'

Guflinkov bowed so low that he almost toppled over, 'I am sorry my Lady. May you see it within your heart to forgive an old man his foolishness and honour him with a sample of your wondrous stew?'

Prahum waved the spoon at him once more. 'You're as devilish as my five-year-old nephew, you are. Now take your stew and be off, before I change my mind.' Prahum giggled a good deal more as she helped Guflinkov through the door and out of the kitchens.

Upon returning to his room, Guflinkov sat at his scattered desk and ate his stew. He barely noticed how tasty it was for his mind was swimming as the effects of his distilled barley, honey and lemon mix from his water-skin finally began to take effect.

4

The High Chancellor had received the letter twenty-three days past. She had read the parchment dozens of times, yet was still unsure of its truth. Was it simply a ploy to see the end of her; a trap, or was it genuine in its intentions? After all these years, could the dirty scum from across the river really want peace? Her instincts told her not to trust the letter; to destroy it, but her heart told her it must be true. As she stood under the full moon, she brought forth the letter once more and read it to the shadows around her.

To the High Chancellor of the people of Roasline and the surrounding lands,

I wish to meet with you to discuss that which has eluded our people for far too long: a peaceful resolution to this war.

I know that you have no reason to trust me; I would not if I were in your position. To help remove this doubt, I have arranged one of the Healers, Jacov, to mediate. I met with him in Headly two moons past and he agreed. I would advise sending a messenger to the Healers to confirm this for yourself.

Jacov has arranged to sail in a vessel from Headly and is bringing with him the protection of his people and that land. On the evening in question, we cannot be harmed while travelling to and from his vessel as well as for the time we spend on board his boat. As proof of this, before you set out, try and harm yourself, you will be unable to.

The date that I have chosen will be the next full moon. The vessel will first collect me from Fort Kykum before crossing the Liagar to collect you from Roasline's docks at midnight. We will then make our way into the middle of the river where we will be able to conduct our meeting in private.

To confirm your attendance, shoot a single flaming arrow from the south most dock of Roasline five days before the full moon. I hope that this will be the first step on the road to peace between our peoples.

Resvon, Leader of the Outcasts

Kathsum had done as she was requested and sent a secret messenger to Headly. He had recently returned with the confirmation that she had hoped for. Other than this single messenger, she had only confided in one other; her friend and history tutor of old; Guflinkov. She dared not tell others for fear that they would use this potential opportunity to attempt the assassination of Resvon and remove all hope of peace.

The full moon shone down on Kathsum as she paced back and forth in her courtyard. Shakily, she withdrew a small dagger from her sleeve and made to nick the back of her hand. She felt the pressure of the blade, but found that it would not penetrate her flesh. Smiling, she returned the blade to its sheath, raised her hood over her head and made her way towards the courtyard gate.

The High Chancellor nodded to the pair of armed guards as she passed through the gate, indicating that she was to be meeting a friend and would not require their services. As she made her way down the slope towards Roasline's docks, she noticed the streets to be largely empty. The few drunkards she passed gave her a wide berth as her loose-fitting cloak, hanging over her broad shoulders, gave her the appearance of a hardened man. The deep hood that hid her auburn hair and casted her face into shadow added to the masquerade.

While it took the High Chancellor a decent amount of time to make her way onto the south most dock, the time passed quickly for Kathsum. The oil lamps and full moon meant she had little difficulty in finding her way.

Upon her arrival at the docks, she made sure that she was alone and then withdrew her hood. The fresh breeze passing through her long free hair was refreshing after the confines of the hooded clock. She ran her fingers though it before fastening it back with a wooden clasp. Ready, she looked around for a boat.

She did not have to wait long before she spied her boat approaching. Coming from the north-west, the small skiff made little sound through the flowing stream. As it approached the dock, she first saw the man who must have been Jacov the Healer. He was garbed in pure white robes and as the breeze blew about him, she could make out his muscular frame. He appeared to be of similar age to her, yet his face held no love. Even from the distance of many yards she could make out the sternness of his features. And while she may have found his unrobed body to be handsome, his face was not.

As Jacov moved to the gunwale of the boat in preparation of docking, Kathsum achieved her first glance of Resvon. He was huddled under an unusually heavy brown travelling cloak, which Kathsum found odd given the mid-spring weather. He raised his head as the boat approached the docks, removed his hood and looked inquisitively at Kathsum. Remaining seated, he smiled kindly at her. She returned his smile, but could not help but stare at his missing left ear. The darkness hid the disfigurement for the most part, yet the lop-sided appearance unsettled the High Chancellor somewhat. From his ear, she passed her gaze over the rest of his face. His hair was short, thinning and grey and she guessed him to be in his mid-fifties. His face looked rough and yet not scarred. It reminded her of a rocky mountain that had weathered many storms. Her gaze then wandered to his eyes. It wasn't until the boat was nigh on docking that she could really make out his eyes. And they saddened her. As she looked into Resvon's dark brown irises, she saw there a soul that could not remember joy. She immediately thought of parents who had lost their children to the wickedness of illness. Seeing those eyes removed any warmth within her and her hope of a happy peace dimmed.

Instinctively, her right hand reached to the loose necklace about her neck. This had been given to her by her father on the twentieth year of her birth. It was fashioned as a gold chain with five pendants dangling a short way down her chest. The two outside pendants were made of garnet, the next two of the mysterious moonstone, each an inch in diameter. The centre pendant was another, larger, garnet. The central garnet would have measured two inches in height and the depths of its red were endless. Her father had given her this necklace, which had been her mother's before her untimely death. Kathsum knew it had descended many generations on her mother's side and the necklace always reminded her of the fragility of life and that while people pass in and out of the world, it continues to be.

Kathsum's thoughts were drawn away from her father as Jacov beckoned her aboard. She stepped onto the skiff and felt it drop under her weight. The High Chancellor looked about the boat, deciding where to sit.

'You will sit while I take us out to the centre of the river. Then you may begin your discussions.' The gruff voice and bluntness of Jacov's speech startled the High Chancellor; it had been too long since she had thus been spoken to. Kathsum sealed her lips and sat on the opposite side to Resvon. He cast her a knowing glance.

Jacov skilfully took them out of Roasline's docks and directed them into the main current. Kathsum felt a light salty spray on her face and noticed the tide was coming in. The breeze provided ample power for the sail and before long, the small vessel had reached its destination. As the Healer dropped the anchor overboard, Kathsum felt a thrill of nervous excitement and her palms became clammy with sweat.

The High Chancellor and the Leader of the Outcasts looked across the boat at each other and waited for Jacov to be seated. Kathsum could already feel the discomfort of the wooden bench creeping through her buttocks and knew that she must show no signs of weakness.

'I have been asked here as a mediator between the two of you. No Healer has interfered with the matters of those from the mainland in all of our long history.

And now we do not do so lightly. We have only agreed to this as a means to end this bloody war that has raged on for too long. My fellow Healers grow tired of healing battle wounds and are hoping that with the end of the war we may put our skills to enhancing people's health above that of mere survival.'

Jacov continued with a business-like tone. 'The arrangement that we have in place, including your protection, will occur on every full moon until an agreement can be reached. Should I deem this unachievable, I will call a halt to these meetings and the Healers of Headly will see no more victims of war. Your own healers will have to bear the full burden of your shameful violence. This is not negotiable.'

Shock and terror swept through Kathsum's bones; she knew that this chance of peace sounded too simple to be true. She felt like a trapped beast, where the only escapes was to jump across a deep gorge. If a peace agreement could not be reached, many of her people will die. Having little choice, she looked the Healer squarely in the eyes. 'Very well Jacov, we best get started.' Jacov opened his palms to the pair of them and nodded.

Resvon spoke first. 'High Chancellor, I will get straight to the point.' Resvon's voice came as a surprise to Kathsum; it was soft, such that it could only just be heard over the lapping of the river against the bow. 'Your armies have fought valiantly and done my people great harm. Our current stalemate has held us at the Liagar River for close to fifteen years. We have farmed these lands and put our resources into developing them. I request that our peace agreement resolve with our current land holdings. In return, the Liagar will also be yours and all of the lands east and south. We only request sufficient water from the Liagar for crops and consumption. The lake where the Liagar begins will be ours to fish. We both shall have land suited to both crops and animals and within time, trading may open between our peoples. What say you?'

'There was once a time when the High Chancellor of Roasline ruled the lands as far west as the Sempa River. And you want us to just gift you those extremely plentiful lands?' Despite her best efforts, Kathsum found her voice laced with displeasure.

'And if you go back even further, you will find that the colony of Psymryte was started by the Rulers of Roasline. High Chancellor, if you think about it enough, we are really just fighting our own kin. In fact, as far as I know, the only people on the mainland not related to each other are the peaceful monks of the Moaks.' He shook his head. 'But we cannot settle the debts of all of our forefathers or we will end up where we started: at war.'

The truth of this gave Kathsum reason to pause. She pursed her lips and before she could fully form a reply, a plop in the water caught her attention. She felt a sudden shift in the skiff's weight and sensed a presence before she could see anyone.

Hauling his thin body clean out of the water in one leap came a man. His gaunt body dripped with water as he wore nothing but short breeches. Before Kathsum had time to think of what was happening, the lank man drew a knife, yanked back Resvon's head by his hair and ran his knife over Resvon's throat from ear to ear.

The scream that followed was not Resvon's, but the assassin's. His throat opened up and blood gushed out. As he sank to his knees, his gurgling voice uttered a final threat. 'You are weak, Resvon. Others will come for you. The war must continue. My Master will not fail.' And with his last ounce of strength, he flung himself from the boat and into the gushing Liagar.

Jacov lunged to catch the leg of the corpse as it passed over the gunwale, but missed by inches. Cursing, he faced the two leaders. 'I am glad that the powers of the Healers have spared your life Resvon, but for tonight we are done.'

As he hauled up the anchor and unfurled the sail, Kathsum sat shaking gently. When she finally raised her eyes from the bottom of the boat, she saw Resvon rubbing his neck and breathing deeply. He looked across at her, gave her a wry smile, but said no more.

Kathsum did not remember the journey back to Roasline and then to her bedchamber, but once there, she sent for Guflinkov and some of his strong whisky with lemon and honey. She needed this drink to settle her shaking hands and his old mind to talk slowly through the events of her evening.

5

Dusk woke with a start as the morning sun washed over her. Her first thought went straight to her missing little finger. Five days had passed and the wound was healing well. They had tried to keep it damp with a bandage, but the desert heat had sapped away all the moisture. She opened her mouth to lick her lips, but her tongue proved too dry for that. Her lower lip pained her, for it was swollen and scabbing as a result of a fall the previous day.

For four days she had led them north into the blistering desert, but they had not been unprepared. Before setting out, they had fashioned baskets for their backs from sticks and palm leaves. They had filled one of these with as much fruit as they could carry and the other with coconuts that they had found on the western edge of the oasis. The coconuts served the purpose of providing both food and drink. They had also filled their water-skins to bursting point and drunk until their urine was clear before to departing the oasis.

When they first set out, it was in the cooler temperature of the evening and they had walked long into the night. They then found a slight divot to lie in out of the wind and slept for a spell. Dusk had then consulted the map with the stars to ensure that they continued north and walked until the sun became hot. They had then rested through the main heat of the day. This routine they had repeated until Dusk had woken that morning. They had slept longer than they should have and so Dusk roused Winter hurriedly.

'Is it that time already, sister?' Winter's voice was cracked with dryness.

'We have overslept, Winter. Let us now share a coconut and the last of the green mangoes and be off before the sun becomes too hot.'

'You always did like to push yourself to your limits. I agree we should eat, but please can you give me some time to rouse myself first? A few moments won't delay us much, and besides, the extra rest may lengthen my strides.'

Anger and frustration flared within Dusk. 'No! We will leave now and eat while we walk. The distraction will do us good.'

'Very well, have it your way,' grumbled Winter.

This quick submission from Winter annoyed Dusk more than the delay. She turned her back on her brother and readied herself to set out. Over the last few days, she had noticed herself getting angrier and angrier. She knew not the reason, but it frustrated her that she could not control this emotion.

At her angriest times, she took her frustration out on Winter, but this in turn made her feel ashamed, which then cycled back to fuel her anger. Winter himself had been a cause for her frustration at times. He seemed too relaxed for her liking and his constant mantra seemed to be that everything would work out in the end. For the most part, he had taken her abuse, although once he had slapped her face to make her stop yelling at him. Dusk felt that if only they could reach the Moaks and have a bit of a rest from the scorching sun, then she would be able to gain control of her emotions.

As Dusk fastened her almost empty pack on to her back, the predictable feeling of shame swept over her. While she knew that she should apologise to Winter, her only surviving sibling, there was no way that she would give him the satisfaction. Instead, she stomped off towards the haze in the north, not checking to see if Winter was ready and following her.

They marched all through that day, Dusk always keeping half a pace in front of Winter. As the afternoon began to wear away, Dusk noticed that the sand of the desert became more soil like. She saw plants peeking from under rocks and thin wispy grasses beginning to take hold. The change continued until, after several miles, Dusk found herself waist deep in thick grass. She plucked a strand to examine it and ran her thumb up and down its edge. The blade spiked her thumb as she slid it down the shaft and she tossed the leaf aside. As they continued to walk, she became annoyed at the grass. Where first it had been wonderful and cooling about her legs, it soon became stifling and kept catching at her clothes. *This whole, stupid adventure is annoying; why didn't Father let us help more in the defence of his city? Then my siblings wouldn't be dead and we wouldn't be in this stupid place.*

The two trudged north day after day until a haze on the horizon took shape; they were nearing the Moaks. After the gentle rolling hills of the grasslands, the Moaks seemed enormous. Dusk thought that they jutted into the air like a bottom set of teeth. The lower half appeared all greens and browns while the top half appeared to be as white as one of the exotic swans Dusk had heard about in tales. But Dusk paid little heed to their colours; it was the size that impressed her the most. Although she had seen the Moaks before, for some reason the late afternoon deep blue sky made them look as if they could reach the moon itself.

The ground beneath their feet soon began to rise, as did Dusk's mood. The tall grass began to lessen and shrubs and trees began to take hold. Small rabbits could be seen licking the dew from the morning grass and that night they feasted on rabbit cooked over their first fire since the oasis. The rabbit tasted even sweeter to Dusk as she was the one wo caught it.

Just as the rabbit had melted in her mouth, Dusk found that her mood towards Winter melted too. They began chatting about things of no importance and guessing at what the future might have in store for them. Dusk found herself expecting the worst; that they would die hopelessly in the Moaks, whereas Winter could not guess what was to come, but in his usual fashion, knew that everything would be all right in the end.

As they rose higher into the foothills of the Moaks they found streams and many edible berries and leaves. They had long finished their food from the oasis, but their packs they retained, albeit reinforced with more comfortable sticks and leaves.

It wasn't until they were well and truly into the Moaks that Dusk got anxious. Their father had told them to come this far, but nothing more. The siblings knew that if they continued much further into the mountains, animals of a vicious nature would be after their flesh. With spring well progressing, new pups, cubs and kittens would be born to leave their mothers territorial and aggressive. It was with this heightened sense of anxiety that Dusk deemed it necessary for night-time watches. She knew that the lesser sleep would slow them during the day, but with nowhere in particular to go, there was no need for haste.

During the second night of watches, Dusk found herself a soft patch of young heather and lay down to sleep. The instant her head hit the ground, she was whisked away to blissful dreams of a simple life. She found herself a simple farmer's daughter where she started her day with nothing more straining than milking her goat. After three squirts from the udder, the goat turned to face her and bleated. She kept on pulling, but the goat kept on bleating. It wasn't until she stared into its black eyes and asked it to calm down that it bleated in a language that she understood.

'I wiiiillll seeennnddd yyyoouuuu a gooaattt. Fooolllllloooowwww iiittt aannndd iitttt wiilllll lleeaadddd yyooouuu tthhhrrroough the Mmoooaakksss. Mmmiiilllkkk iitttt for mmiiilllkkkk, cut iitttssss ffuuurrrrrrrrr for wwaarrmmmmthhhh. I wwiiiillll sseeeee yoouuu sooooooooonn chilllddd.'

Dusk woke with a start and leapt to her feet. 'Winter. A goat. Have you seen a goat?'

'What are you talking about?'

'A goat. He will send us a goat!'

'Who will? Are you quite right Dusk?'

'Our father! I dreamt it. He was a goat and I was milking him and he said that he was going to send a goat to us. It will lead us to him through the Moaks.'

'Are you sure it was him? Are you sure it wasn't just a dream?'

'It was him. I am sure of it. It had *his* eyes!' Dusk saw Winter's eyes twitch and she knew that he was remembering back to their childhood and the fear that the cold black eyes of Avgar always brought.

Before either of them had a chance to discuss more, a raspy bleat emitted from behind a nearby bush. Then, walking out from behind it came the woolliest, most spindly legged goat that Dusk had ever seen.

6

Captain Ryde was to meet Eyp, the Commander of Ships, on the docks of Fort Kykum. Being the main defensive stronghold for the Outcasts, the docks were behind a massive stone wall that jutted significantly out into both the Liagar River and the Rogaus Sea. The only way in and out of the docks was through a large gate that opened outwards into the mouth of the Liagar. This had originally been made of wood, but under the order of Eyp, it had been replaced by iron a foot thick. It was constructed such that, even on the lowest tide, the bottom of the gate reached several feet below the surface of the water. As a result, it took an enormous effort to open and close, with many oxen required to turn the myriad of pullies and cogs. For this reason, it was mainly left wide enough for a single vessel to pass through during the day, but fully closed at night to ensure security and maintain its ability to seal completely.

Captain Ryde never much liked the gate and always felt like a prisoner when he sailed through her clutches to return home. He was looking at this giant steel contraption and pondering Commander Eyp as he heard the man approach.

The Commander came alone with the exception of a single guard who stopped and stood to attention well out of earshot. Captain Ryde found this odd, for the Commander usually travelled with four guards, especially at this time of day when the sun was setting and the shadows lengthening.

Captain Ryde went to one knee as the Commander reached him. This was one of the Commander's idiosyncrasies that he had instigated upon his appointment. Ryde supposed him insecure about his worth and too loving of the power of his position.

As he knelt before him, Ryde tried to imagine the missing toes on Eyp's left foot that rumour had assured him didn't exist.

'Rise Captain.' The only thing that Ryde did like about his superior was his voice. It was deep and strong and lurking just beneath its surface rested anger and lust. It reminded the Captain of the ocean.

As Ryde stood, he was frowned at how much smaller than Eyp he was. His remaining left eye was level with the Commander's chin and his shoulders were nowhere near as broad. He acknowledged how easy it would be for this man to crush him.

'Commander, how may I be of service?'

A grim smile spread across Eyp's hard features. 'You will be of great service. But first tell me, how is your sister and her two children?'

Ryde became immediately troubled. Why was the Commander asking after his family? He had never mentioned them before; why now?

'They are doing just fine, sir. The children are as playful as children of eight and eleven tend to be, but Prie still morns the loss of her husband, albeit eight moon cycles since he died. She is grateful though, to have me to care for her.'

'I am sorry for her and your loss.' The Commander paused long enough for his smile to disappear. 'But now to business. Leader Resvon has seen it in his infinite wisdom to send a ship of wool, silk and some precious gems across to Roasline in an effort to buy peace. I don't know why, but he has commanded that you captain this ship.'

'Thank you, sir, this will be a great honour.'

'It would, if you were going to do just that. But you will not be going directly to Roasline. You will leave just before the harbour gate is closed and take this ship of bounty to Psymryte. There, you will meet someone sympathetic to *our* cause to unload the top two cargo holds. You will then take the remaining cargo to Roasline as Resvon desires.'

'And Resvon knows nothing of this... deviation?'

'That is not your concern, *Captain*.'

'But, sir, what you are suggesting... it's treason!'

'And what *you* are about to do *will be* treason.'

Captain Ryde tried to look his commander directly in the eye. 'I will not do your dirty work Eyp.'

'You will do as I command, or there will be... consequences.'

'Whatever you do to me will be nothing to what Resvon will do to you when you are discovered. You're nothing more than a filthy traitor!' The anger boiling within Ryde was too much. He spat straight into his commander's face. The blow came swiftly and Ryde found himself face-down on the wooden docks, his jaw throbbing.

'They told me you might be difficult, so I have taken precautions. Your sister, Prie, she is quite a beauty to look on, don't you think?'

'You dare touch her and I will destroy you! I will rip every limb from your body and you will know more pain than even *you* can imagine.'

The Commander knelt down beside Ryde's head, grabbed him by the hair and brought his lips to within an inch of Ryde's ear and whispered. 'But Captain Ryde, I do dare. At least if you don't do my bidding. If you refuse the task before you, in any way, for even a fraction of a moment, then I will touch her... a lot. Do not fear, I will not disturb her beauty. At least not at first, not until I am done with her. You see, I will make her mine. I will make her mine every night until she is with child. Once that happens, she will lose her eyes. I hear it is a wonderful thing to see your children grow into adults. But how will the beautiful Prie help her children grow into adults if she can't even see them? She might not even notice if they all of a sudden *disappeared*. Ha, with another on the way, she might even be grateful.'

The anger within Ryde boiled to icy shards. With every fibre of his body, he hated this man. It took immense resolve within him to stop himself from reaching up and ripping the throat from the man above. In the end, his sense won over his emotions. The voice that came to Ryde's lips however, was laden with sadness of the inevitable. 'When do I leave?'

'You leave now. Once you clear the gates, they will close. When the watchmen see you turning north, I will be forced to send out ships after you. After all, you are committing treason.' A grin spread across Eyp's greedy face. 'Should they catch you, think not of yourself, but of the sweet, sweet Prie.

'Once aboard, should you think of deceiving me, know that amongst your crew will be my eyes and my ears. And again, think once more of Prie.'

Ryde gritted his teeth. 'I will not fail you. But once I return, if she so much as has a scratch on her, you will feel my wrath.'

'Touching, very touching.' Eyp stood and jerked Ryde to his feet. 'Now be gone, scum!' He threw Ryde sprawling on the ground once more, turned on his heels and strode away.

Captain Ryde lay on the ground for what seemed like an age. Eventually, he dragged himself to his feet and made his slow way to the vessel moored close by. She was a mixture of cargo ship and war galley: no cannons rested within her, but the hull was made for strength and speed. Eyp had given him a good ship at least.

As he boarded, the crew greeted him with many a 'Captain' and they looked a mixture of experience and muscle. He found himself trying to pick foe from friend but could not. He soon sought the first-mate, a man that he had never seen before, and ordered him to prepare for their immediate departure.

'Would you like oars, or just the sails, Captain?'

'The fore sails will suffice until we are through the gate. Then half the oars until we are in the ocean proper. Then we shall unfurl our speed and see what this piece of wood can do.'

'Yes, sir.' The man scurried away to prepare the ship for departure. Despite his predicament, Ryde felt good to have the planks of a ship beneath his feet once more. As he grasped the wheel, he uttered to the dying sun: 'If some of these men are Eyp's, then I will row them raw.' His mind then turned to Prie and her children, and while he did not weep, he hungered for their safety.

The journey to Psymryte took several days. Captain Ryde encountered little resistance from the crew. The rowers grumbled about the constant rowing and their hands were long past raw. They had been organised into long shifts, and while the initial power had soon dropped, they still made good speed. On the first dawn, they had sighted a vessel from Fort Kykum following them, but they soon lost her as the wind picked up and the sea became rough. Ryde loved the fierceness of the high seas and had swiftly taken his ship well out into the Rogaus away from prying eyes that might be lingering on the shore. If this filthy task must be done, then he was going to do it his way.

They came at Psymryte directly from the north. On that particular morning, the city was under its usual thick haze. While Psymryte had once been the main city of the Outcasts, it had long sunk into filth and corruption. Captain Ryde had rarely visited it and, on the occasions that he had, he needed a good scrub down on departure to remove the grime from his skin.

Upon their approach that morning, Captain Ryde smelt the city before he saw her. His nostrils burned at the smell, until the wind shifted the haze to reveal the docks. They were completely in disrepair, but it was clear where he was to moor by the men-at-arms that awaited his arrival. These men, who put down their spears to remove the cargo, were as strong as the rowers and Ryde found the goods were gone in a timely manner. During this process, he remained in his cabin and dealt only with his first-mate. As he sat there, he brooded on how much he hated this city and hated the man who had sent him there. His mind strayed to ways that he could make Eyp suffer and thought hard on how he was to capture him. Ryde was not a stupid man and he knew that upon his return he would likely be killed. Being a loyal follower of Resvon he knew that Eyp could not afford to keep him around. He thought about jumping ship before docking at the Fort, but was unsure of where that would leave his younger sister; probably to a fate worse than death. By the time the goods were gone from his ship, Ryde had decided that there was nothing he could do for the moment and that he would have to wait and see what surprises awaited him. He was willing to sacrifice his life for Prie and her children, but he wanted so much to kill Eyp.

After finishing a half jug of wine, Captain Ryde set out once more. As the city disappeared from view, he saw a single hooded man standing on the docks watching him go, no doubt a pawn of Eyp. Captain Ryde was glad to have the loathsome city behind him.

The oarsmen were forced to put their backs into the work once more and Ryde set a course for Roasline. For this he planned to cross the Rogaus, skirt Headly and approach from the north east.

The shoreline of Headly was free from other vessels as the cargo ship from Fort Kykum passed it by. The main dock itself had only one boat moored, which appeared to be a small skiff flying the colours of the Healers. Satisfied with this, Captain Ryde turned the ship south towards Roasline.

For most of this journey the Captain kept to himself but for his first-mate, whose company he began to enjoy. He was always alert and careful with him though, as there was no way to tell if the man was to be trusted or was a flea of Eyp's.

Ryde planned his approach to Roasline such that he would arrive there well before dawn. This meant that there would be fewer people about both at the docks and on the water. As he approached, he ran the white flag of parley high up the mast and brought in the oars.

A good wind was blowing, but the sky was heavy with cloud which made for a dark approach. It wasn't until they were almost atop the docks that Ryde was hailed from the shore. 'Ahoy there! What be your business?'

The first-mate replied in a gruff voice. 'We come bearing gifts for the High Chancellor from our leader Resvon. Do we have leave to dock?'

'Aye, but remain aboard until you have permission to come ashore.'

Captain Ryde had an ill feeling about this. He played anxiously with his glass eye in the darkness as he wondered why it had been so easy to make it to the docks. Roasline had to have some defences or she would have been conquered long ago, but what they were Ryde could not see. At least the dock steward had a reasonable level of suspicion, although it was clear to see that he had little idea of how to handle the peculiar situation. Ryde knew that he may be spending quite some time still aboard his ship.

It was a surprise for him then, when in no time at all, a regiment of soldiers wearing green sashes approached his ship and commanded that the crew come ashore. He had little choice but to obey. His mood turned sour when steel cuffs closed shut around his wrists. He glared at the soldier. 'Is this any way to treat someone bearing the white flag?'

'It is a precaution, Captain, until we can ensure your intent is genuine. Do not resist if you want your crew to live.'

Although the captain cared not for the scum of the crew that belonged to Eyp, he wanted Resvon's peace message to go untainted. 'Very well. Lead on.'

Captain Ryde found himself being led through the old streets of Roasline. He marvelled at her age and beauty. The narrow streets of white marble twisted and turned and he soon found himself lost. The two, three and sometimes four-story buildings seemed to lean inwards over the alleys in which he was led. If there were no clouds above, few stars would have been visible between the houses. Rounding a bend, the party emerged from the small streets onto a larger thoroughfare.

There were few people about as the grey light filled the sky, but the captain noticed whiffs of baking bread and horse stables. He was led up the main road of Roasline and before long he beheld a citadel upon a hill. From where he walked, the road ran as straight as an arrow to the base of the hill where it continued at a steep angle up the slope to a levelled off area and then a series of steep steps. The citadel at the top of these had three spires made of entirely white marble. Ryde was surprised to see many wealthy looking dwellings lining the slopes of the hill. These were clearly not built with the defence of the citadel in mind. As the sun broke the horizon, the citadel was cast into a silhouette which Ryde took as an ill omen.

With his fellow crewmen, he was marched right up to the main doors, but instead of entering, was turned to the right. They followed a paved path around the citadel before entering a dirty granite structure. From the outside, it appeared to be nothing more than a small hut, but once inside, steps descended in all directions. Captain Ryde was taken down one of these flights and rather roughly thrust into a cell. As the solid oak door slammed shut behind him, Ryde examined his cell. The floor was cold stone covered in a thin layer of damp straw. High on the back wall was an empty window no bigger than a foot wide and half a foot high and in the corner was a hole in the floor of similar size. From the smell, he realised what this was for. Scraping some of the straw together, he made a pile and sat down with his back against the door, closed his eyes and waited.

The light through the window changed as the day passed and still Ryde waited. His stomach began to rumble, so he got to his feet to stretch his cramping legs. Just as he had decided to relieve himself, the lock of the door clanged open. The door swung in and two guards entered with drawn swords. A man followed, dressed in a finely knitted wool tunic and breeches. These Ryde ignored as his eyes were drawn to the blue sash the hung from his shoulder with a single gold chain woven within it. The man looked down his nose at Ryde and spoke with a voice that stank of arrogance. 'What's your name?'

The captain thought about resisting this man, but decided against it. 'Captain Ryde.'

'Well *Captain*, my name is Captain Tunley. If you behave well, then this process will be over swiftly and you will not be unduly punished. Should you resist, hhhmmm, well, I'm sure I can think of something that would be fitting to a captain of our enemy. Do you understand?'

'I do.' Captain Ryde couldn't help himself from resenting this man, with his potbelly and crisp clean uniform, and fought to hide his disgust.

'Good. Then perhaps you can tell me what is in the cargo hold of your ship?'

'You haven't searched it yet?'

'Yes, of course we have, but I want to hear it from your own mouth.'

'I am sorry Captain, but I don't know.'

'Ha, you expect me to believe that? You are a captain, are you not? What kind of a captain doesn't know every last detail of his ship's manifest? A captain of the Outcasts, it seems.' Tunley laughed at his own wit.

Captain Ryde detested the insult, but remained silent.

'You know, when the Admiral gave me the task of interrogating you, I thought he was punishing me. Quite the contrary, it would appear. I'm going to enjoy this very much indeed.'

Captain Ryde ignored this last statement and instead answered Tunley's question. 'The type of captain who was forced to take control of a ship against his will.'

'Is that the best you can come up with?'

'It is the truth!'

Captain Tunley nodded to the guard to his right, who stepped forward and rammed the hilt of his sword into Ryde's stomach. The Outcast Captain doubled over, caught his breath for a moment, and then stood up straight.

'Captain Ryde, you seem like a tough man, but even tough men break, eventually. Let me tell you about a poison we have here in Roasline.' Tunley started pacing in front of Ryde. 'It is sweet in taste but sour in disposition. Just a single mouthful leaves the consumer paralysed. But that is not all. Oh no, that is not all.' Tunley's eyes tinkled. 'This particular poison still allows the consumer to breathe. If I feed you this sweet concoction, you will find yourself lying on your back, unable to move or make any noise. You will not even be able to blink. My dear Ryde, the bitterness of this poison lies not in its ability to paralyse you, but in its ability to leave you receptive to pain. I could do anything at all to you and all that you could do in response would be to lie there consumed by the pain. Of course, the poison takes away the joy of hearing you scream, but the results that this can produce are equal to none.' He stopped pacing and stared at Ryde. 'So, I ask you again, what was in your cargo hold?'

Captain Ryde hid his fear and maintained eye contact with his interrogator. 'When I set out from Fort Kykum, there were all sorts of wools, silks and gems. These were taken from my ship at Psymryte. The lowest hold of my ship, as you know, was locked. I chose not to break it open. Had I done so, I would more than willingly tell you what lies beneath. I swear it on my mother's grave.'

Ryde's jaw exploded in pain as the hilt of the guard's sword struck it. Falling to the floor, he spat out a mouthful of blood followed by a single tooth. When he turned to look back at Tunley, it was to find the cell door closing with a snap. Captain Ryde rolled onto his back and massaged his swelling jaw.

After a full day in his cell, Ryde received a heel of stale bread and a small bowl of onion broth. After that first meal, the days began to blur together for the captain. He was bored, frustrated and angry, but controlled his thoughts by thinking of Prie and her family. What he would do to Eyp if he got the chance fuelled his being and he promised to do whatever he could to stay alive.

The prisoner received infrequent visits from Tunley that always ended with him on the floor massaging a new hurt. Tunley himself had not lain a finger on Ryde, but the threat of the paralysing poison was ever evident.

On what seemed like the seventh night to Captain Ryde, he heard the familiar clang of the door being opened and retreated to the far wall, wondering which part of him was about to be attacked. But instead of Tunley with his two guards, a different man entered his cell. The man was old and leaning heavily on a cane. His thin grey hair hung down to his shoulders and in his beard, Ryde could see crumbs of bread and stains of drink. The voice that spoke to Ryde was fragile, and the sea captain wanted nothing more than to help the old man to a seat.

'Good evening to you, Captain Ryde. I hope that you're enjoying your lodgings. I am sorry that they are not more comfortable. Here, have a drink.'

The old man extended a hand with a leather water-skin. Captain Ryde took a long gulp, disregarding the risk of poison and hoping to find water. Instead, he almost spat out the sweet burning liquid. For an instant, he thought he had been tricked and that he was about to lose his ability to move. But then he felt the familiar warmth of alcohol seep through his limbs. 'What is this drink?'

'Do you like it, Captain? It is a spirit of my own concoction. Very similar to whisky; triple distilled, with lemon and honey from Headly added for sweetness. It keeps you warm far better than any fire could, but can leave the novice drinker befuddled.'

Ryde stared at the old man long and hard. Try as he might, he could not make out his purpose. 'Have you come to get me drunk so that Tunley can beat me some more?'

'Oh no Captain. I have come to hear the truth from you.'

'I have told Tunley time and time again; I don't know what was in my cargo hold.'

'And I believe you. But many do not, or chose not to. You see, Ryde, there are those who would find it more convenient if that shipment had come from Resvon himself. What I want to find out is who *did* send you on your voyage? Tell me this, and you may yet live.'

A loud gong sounded inside Ryde's head. Of course, Eyp had never meant for him to return to Kykum. He had planned on the people of Roasline to do his dirty work for him. 'Tell me what was on my ship and I will tell you everything.'

'Bones, Captain. Your ship was full of human bones.' Captain Ryde froze for a moment as the news sunk in. His mouth went momentarily as dry as salt. He took another swig of the sweet whisky and found his tongue loosened as he told Guflinkov all about Eyp. He found Guflinkov an attentive listener and the old man was soon gone with his whisky. Ryde sat down in the corner and for the first time in many days, found himself smiling.

The next morning, Ryde woke with a start. His door clanged open and Tunley stood there with his two guards once more. For a change, Tunley drew his own curved blade and pressed it to Ryde's neck. The Captain found his head pushed back and a goblet brought to his lips. Tunley pinched his nose and said as sadistically as he could: 'drink.'

Ryde had no choice but to swallow the sickly sweet substance and, by the time the sword was removed from his throat, he had collapsed on the floor and was unable to move. He felt a sharp jabbing pain shoot through his lower leg as he felt his left ankle twist. He found himself being straightened out onto his back and saw Tunley's fist crunch into his nose. The taste of blood instantly filled his mouth. His thoughts flew to what could be waiting in store for him as Tunley pressed the blade just below Ryde's remaining eye.

'Would you like it Ryde, if I took your only eye? Oh, that's right, you cannot speak. Maybe I could make that permanent and take your tongue instead. What's it to be, an eye or a tongue?' Captain Ryde heard Tunley laugh a terrible cackle. 'If you don't answer me, I will have to take both!'

All that Ryde could see was the roof above and Tunley's sneering face, but he heard shuffling feet and a cane. Captain Tunley left Ryde's view, but could still be heard.

'What are you doing down here, old man?'

'I have come to make sure that the prisoner is ready.' Guflinkov's voice was sterner than Ryde remembered, but was glad to hear it nonetheless.

'You have no place here, drunk. He is a Captain of a ship; the Admiral has responsibility for him. And the Old Sea Dog has given him over to me.'

'Unless I am mistaken, Captain, the High Chancellor commands the Admiral, and it is on her orders that I am here. You see, she will be here before long and she will want a word with this here Captain.'

A tense silence emerged before Tunley spoke again. 'Then he is yours... for now.'

Captain Ryde heard Tunley leave with his guards and the door closed behind them. The old man came into his range of sight and smiled ruefully. 'That one is a bit too sure of himself, don't you think?'

Guflinkov slowly bent over Ryde, drew something out of his pocket and all of a sudden, the Captain's head spun. A pungent smell broke through his blood clogged nose and he found himself cramping. Instinctively, he curled into a ball and then it struck him; he could move again. 'Thank you.'

'I did not do this for you, Captain. The High Chancellor wants to speak with you and you will tell her everything that you told me and anything else that she commands. If you do not, then Tunley can do as he wants with you. Now clean yourself as best you can, she will be here soon.'

As Ryde watched Guflinkov leave, he saw in the corner of his cell a steaming basin of water. He crawled over to it and began to prepare himself for the High Chancellor's visit.

7

'Baaaaa!'

Dusk woke with a start as the gangly goat stood over her. The sun was just breaking the horizon, and Winter had fallen asleep during his watch. Again. Furious, Dusk kicked him awake. They had followed the goat higher up into the hills beneath the mountainous Moaks and Dusk felt the extra chill. She huddled her arms close around her chest and looked at the stirring Winter.

'Brother, we are going to have to trim this beast of her nice warm-looking wool soon. The higher we get, the colder it becomes. Our clothes aren't warm enough; my very bones are beginning to ache with the cold.'

Winter's sleepy voice came to her ears. 'We'll be fine for a few more days. Just jump around a bit to warm up. Besides, at the pace that goat sets, we'll be warm in no time.'

Dusk ignored this advice and went to nibble some berries and chew some cold hare that was cooked the night before. Two nights past they had camped close to a long-dead soldier pine and Dusk had found ample straight branches to make into arrows. They were nowhere near as good as the steel tipped ones for her days in Balleny, but once she shaped them and hardened their tips over coals, she could kill rabbits, hares and other small creatures easily enough.

As she swallowed the hare, she readied herself for another day of strenuous walking and climbing. The paths that the goat had chosen were by no means easy and many a time, she wondered how the gnarly creature managed to leap from rock to rock. Some of the paths they tread could not be seen until they were walking them, while others were two feet wide. For the most part, they had been travelling north and up into the Moaks, albeit in a meandering fashion, but occasionally they would turn west for a while before heading back north. As they negotiated their way up slopes and down valleys, following the shaggy beast, their pace varied from a brisk walk to a slow shuffle.

Dusk patted the goat while her thoughts wandered the mountains until Winter finally stated that he was ready to leave. Dusk muttered something rude under her breath as the goat took the lead once more with a spring in her step.

They had milked the goat twice so far and Dusk found the milk sour on her tongue. She imagined that as they climbed into the snowy peaks, the milk would provide both sustenance and warmth where there would be little food and less flowing water.

They followed the goat all through the morning and by midday they found themselves in need of a break. The goat had brought them to a mountain stream with its water only just warmer than ice. But with the sun on their heads and sweat on their brows, the cold water was very welcome as it trickled down Dusk's parched throat.

At every stream they came across, and there were many, Dusk marvelled at the clearness of the water. Growing up, she had only known the River Pion, whose massive girth was clouded and, more often than not, murky.

She splashed her face and trickled a few droplets of the chilly water down the back of her neck before dividing up the remainder of the hare and some leaves that were bitter to the taste, but filled up the belly.

Just as they were beginning to recover and cool down, the goat began to bleat incessantly. 'Our woolly friend wants to be on the move again, Winter.'

Winter sighed and got to his feet. 'Very well then, although, hopefully tonight she will give us a bit of time for hunting. I don't much like the idea of eating those bitter leaves for dinner as well.'

'I agree. Did you hear that goat? We need more food.' The only reply that Dusk got was a toothy *bbbaaaa* before the goat turned and trotted away.

They continued to climb for the rest of the day, which left little time for hunting in the evening. Dusk was lucky enough to find a bird's nest and was thankful that it was spring as she plucked three eggs from within. These were quickly devoured.

The following day, the goat started early and led them to a small mountain lake. Dusk braved the near freezing water to wade up to her knees in search of fish. She skewered two little ones and one large one with her arrows before her feet became painfully numb. They set a small fire to warm her toes and cook the meat to prevent it from spoiling. They shared one of the small fish for lunch and then continued on their way, saving the others for later.

By this stage, they had wound into the Moaks such that they could no longer see the desert plains behind them. To either side of them rose massive mountains with slopes too sheer for trees to grow on. To Dusk, it looked as though their path ahead led on for a short while before being squished between two such mountains.

Dusk found that the valley was unpleasantly cold for most of the day. It was only when the sun was at either side of midday that warmth spread through the damp valley. At these times Dusk sighed, relishing the warmth and couldn't help but smile. These times, however, were never as long as the young lady would have liked and before much time had passed, she found herself in the shade once more.

As she expected, the goat continued to lead them up the valley with the occasional rock scramble upwards. As they neared the end of the valley, Dusk noticed they were getting rather close to the top of the tree line. It intrigued her how the trees grew so tall and strong and then suddenly stopped growing. She had asked Winter about this and he supposed that in winter the snow came down to the point where the trees stopped. Dusk was thankful that it was not winter, but despite it being late spring, she shivered as an icy wind whipped through the valley. Without much difficulty, Dusk was able to convince Winter that it was time to shave the goat.

The poor beast put up no fight at all as Winter roughly cut its wool with his sai. He had kept the blades sharp and before long the goat was standing in the cold, looking motley and shivering. Not knowing why, Dusk muttered her apologies to the goat.

Not having the equipment to make garments, the two divided up the wool and stuffed it under their tunics and against their skin. After they had finished, barely a moment had passed before the rain began to fall. The clouds had descended with dusk to just above the tree line, but had waited until the two humans were just getting warm before unleashing their icy downpour and chilling them once more. Dusk acted swiftly and soon had a fire going under the shelter of a tall and bushy pine tree. Although the smoke came back down with the rain, the flickering flames gave them some warmth as steam rose from their sodden clothes.

After a quick supper of fish, Dusk took the first watch and, as Winter slept, the goat came over to her side to keep her company. 'You are a funny sort of creature, aren't you? Come and warm yourself by the fire.'

The goat made no reply but nibbled at some of the bitter leaf poking out of Dusk's pocket. 'Oh, go on, have the lot.' Dusk took the rest of the leaves out and fed it to the goat. She then snuggled down into the still dry pine needles and tried to keep the now drizzling rain off her face.

The night passed slowly and a near full moon rose into the gap between the mountains. Although she could not see it through the pine tree, the ground around her became brighter. She thought it time for Winter to do some watching so that she might sleep and moved her stiff legs into a crouching position. As she reached out a hand to Winter's shoulder, she froze. There, beyond the edge of the pine tree, she saw two enormous eyes reflecting the flickering firelight. The eyes rose high into the air and then she heard a deep, guttural growl.

As quick as a flash of lightning, she shoved Winter awake and grabbed her bow and arrows. Winter woke with a start and leapt to his feet. He picked up a sturdy burning branch just as the black mountain bear tore into the pine tree. Winter thrust the flaming branch in the brute's face as Dusk sent an arrow into his chest. The arrow penetrated deep, but this just seemed to enrage the beast further. With a giant paw, it smashed Winter aside and he nearly landed in the fire. As Dusk released another arrow, she heard the goat grunt and charge. Its horns caught the bear unawares in the side, but then the goat was knocked aside too. The bear rounded on the goat and advanced to crush it. Dusk shot another arrow and kept on shooting. The bear was covered in blood as he smashed a paw onto the goat's head. But the quick goat had just enough time to manoeuvre its horns and the bear's paw impaled itself. The goat cried out as its horn was snapped and the bear stood up furiously.

Dusk only had one arrow left. She stooped, picked up a stone and threw it at the bear's head. The beast turned and faced her. And that was his downfall. Dusk's final arrow flew and it pierced the bear's eye and sunk deep into his brain. The beast let out a final wail and collapsed next to the goat.

Dusk sank to her knees and crawled to where Winter lay, tears already streaming down her cheeks in mourning. But as she reached his foot, he roused and sat up groggily.

'Winter, are you hurt?'

'Not badly, although my head feels as though a stake has been driven into it. Where is the beast? Did you kill it?'

'Yes, with help from the goat.'

Dusk helped Winter to his feet and they made their way over to where the goat lay bleating quietly. Its left horn had been snapped at the base, but otherwise she appeared uninjured. It shakily got to its feet and shook its head. It wandered over to the fire and lay down to rest. Dusk shot Winter a puzzled look. 'Let's see this bear then.'

The bear had seven arrows buried deep within its flesh and one in its eye. Blood flowed freely from the entry points. The goat's horn was still impaled through its right paw and Dusk decided to leave it there. Dusk felt a wave of tiredness wash over her as she stared at the carcass and wanted nothing more than to lie down and sleep. When Winter spoke, his voice sounded muffled to Dusk and she had to shake her head and ask him to repeat what he had said.

'We should cut him up. The meat will keep us for many days and the fur will warm us in the snow.'

Dusk could only utter a quiet 'yes'.

She continued to stare at the bear and was vaguely aware of Winter rustling around behind her. She felt heat on the back of her legs and supposed that he must have built up the fire. It took for Winter to force a sharp knife into the palm of her hand before Dusk finally snapped out of her daze. She sank to her knees by the bear and began to remove its skin. Winter did most of the work, although he never asked his sister to work harder.

Dusk sat by the fire cooking the meat while Winter dug a hole to bury the entrails and unusable bits. Dusk looked up through the pine tree and noticed that the rain had stopped falling. She knew not when this had happened, but was grateful for the change in their fortunes.

Once the meat was cooked and cooled, they packed it away in their harnessed bags and Winter bid Dusk to sleep. As she lay down her head, she saw the greyness of dawn creeping through her surrounds and thought she heard a distant howl. Her eyes closed and she let her exhaustion take her away to sleep.

Dusk opened her eyes as Winter shook her vigorously by the shoulder. 'Wake up, Dusk.'

Dusk looked about and saw her surrounds faintly coloured. 'Is it dusk already? You shouldn't have let me sleep all day.'

'You have only been asleep for a short while. But we must leave this place.'

Dusk detected the urgency in his voice and sat up alert. 'What is it?'

Winter didn't need to answer, for just then a blood chilling howl cut through the morning air. 'Wolves or dogs?'

'Wolves. And by the sound of them, there are many, and they're getting closer.'

Dusk cursed. If it had been the wild dogs of the Moaks, they might have been able to talk their way to freedom as friends of Neclant, but wolves had not the intelligence of speech that their cousins did and were far more savage.

Dusk leapt to her feet and grabbed her pack, now heavy with her share of the meat and fur: Winter had been busy while she slept. She looked to the goat and found her bleating urgently a few yards out from under the tree.

Dusk gulped some water from her skin and then they were off. She knew the chase would be long and hard and as she ran after the sure-footed creature, she hoped it would lead them to a defensible place, perhaps a cave.

The light in the sky became brighter and brighter, and the clouds lifted a bit. The ground underneath alternated between mushy mud and slippery rocks. She preferred the rocks for their greater speed and lesser chance that they would leave a trail for the wolves to follow. These rocky sections did not seem to deter their pursuers though, as the howls grew closer.

As midday approached, she scrambled along the top of a gorge. The valley had dwindled to only nine yards across, but was deeper than Dusk could see. A sheer rock face rose to their left. This they grasped with now-bloody fingers to prevent themselves toppling into the unknown depths to their right. As they continued along this narrow path, sounds of a river greeted them from the chasm. Dusk looked and saw gushing white water only several yards below.

She returned her eyes to the path before them and found it widened out a little before coming to an abrupt stop. The sheer rock face to their left curved around and cut off their path. As she took in this obstruction, the howls of the wolves echoed up the gorge behind them, above even the noise of the rushing river. The goat continued to scamper down the path ahead of them and then she saw it: lying across the chasm was a fallen tree. Dusk could not imagine how it had got there, unless a vicious storm had thrown it down the mountainside, but it seemed too well placed to be an act of nature. As they approached the makeshift bridge, she saw on the other side of the gorge the path continued.

'If we cross this log, then we can cast it down into the river and the wolves will be stuck on this side.'

Before Dusk could answer, the goat was scrambling across the piece of wood. Dusk knew Winter was afraid of heights and saw him steady his nerves before running across. At one place, his foot slipped through a rotten section and he almost fell, but at the last moment he steadied himself and scurried across the remainder of the log.

Then it was her turn. As she stepped up onto the tree, she saw just how rotten it really was. Bits of moss and fungi covered the tree and she felt it dip under her weight. She slowly put one foot in front of the other, being careful not to make the same mistake as Winter. She also held her arms out at either side of her for balance. Just as she was taking her sixth step, she heard the wolves enter the widened section of the path behind her. The colour drained from her face as she turned to look at them. Fear spread through her entire body as she saw the sharp teeth of the massive wolves. Not thinking, she shuffled her right foot slightly and then it slipped. She felt herself falling and grasped at the log. Her chin struck it, as did her upper arms. Chunks of the rotten log came away and she failed to get a grip. She fell backwards towards the river, her stomach left behind. In the moments before she hit the water, she saw the goat ramming the remaining log fragments in after her. Then the water took her. The cold clasped its fingers around her and she sucked in a breath of air an instant before she was dragged under. She didn't even get a chance to scream.

8

As dusk descended over Roasline, Captain Tunley stood before the Admiral's magnificent desk looking down at the withered old man. The Admiral looked to be getting more and more haggard as the days passed him by and although Tunley was mocking inside; he was all courtesy and pleasantries to the Admiral's face.

After the formalities of greetings were passed, it was the Old Sea Dog who set the agenda. 'Captain Tunley, I have asked you here to make you an offer. You have proven yourself faithful to me in the interrogation of the prisoner Ryde and I regret he has been taken out of your hands. If you prove this same loyalty to me tonight, I will grant that which you have long desired. Should you successfully fulfil your mission, I will make you a Master of Ships before the week is out.'

The Admiral paused for Tunley to respond but the captain was not sure if he detected a hint of discomfort in the old man's voice at these words.

Ignoring this feeling, he smiled and answered. 'That would be a great honour, sir. I will do whatever you command.'

'Good. You must speak of this to no one as long as you shall live.'

'Not even my pillow will hear of it.' Tunley felt excited.

'Excellent. The General and I have been led to believe that our honourable High Chancellor has been meeting in secret with none other than Resvon, the leader of the Outcasts.'

This revelation took the Captain aback. He knew Kathsum wanted peace, but if she was meeting with Resvon, then that would provide the perfect opportunity for her to put an end to his life. In his mind, conquering decisively was always better than back-and-forth peace negotiations. And if Kathsum had not the strength to kill Resvon, then surely, the Outcast would kill her first. From all that Tunley had heard, Resvon was a hard man who did what had to be done.

'But sir, how can this be? How could she treat with that filthy scum from across the Liagar? Does she really expect to whittle a peace deal out of him?'

'And that, Captain, is why you are here tonight. I know not what goes on in these meetings and I am disappointed at not being informed. But that will change with you.' The Admiral eyed Tunley over steepled fingers. 'Tonight, under the full moon, she will be meeting Resvon again. My information tells me she is collected in a small boat from the south most pier and taken somewhere out of sight. I want you to follow her and hear all that you can. Will you do this?'

'I will.'

'And Captain, do not harm Resvon. If we are close to reaching peace, then that would surely throw us back into the heat of war.'

'I will restrain myself as best I can.'

The old man pursed his lips at Tunley's comment. 'So, we have an understanding.' The Admiral did not wait for Tunley to reply. 'You may go now Captain, and see to the boating arrangements as you require. And Tunley,' the Admiral called after the Captain, a glint in his eyes, 'should you be captured, I will deny any knowledge of this arrangement. You will be treated as if the crime was yours alone.'

Captain Tunley bowed and left the office with a mischievous grin stretched across his clean-shaven face.

The full moon shone down on the ragged hat of a dirty, potbellied man as he sat in a slender row boat with only one other. Dirt was smeared all over Tunley's face and his clothes were black as night and smelt of old sweat. Sitting low in the water, the boat for two was painted ash black, her rowlocks had been muffled with thick black felt and the oars painted the same as the hull. The boat had no name, just like her owner.

Facing Tunley, the man handled the oars skilfully and stared intently at the Captain. Tunley had specifically chosen this man for his skill with a boat at night and his inability to hear; Tunley didn't want anyone else listening in on what he may discover. To instruct the deaf man, Tunley had learnt several hand gestures that would serve his purpose.

As they sat waiting patiently in the Liagar, Tunley could clearly see the hooded figure of what he assumed was Kathsum waiting on the south most dock. He did not have to wait long before a small skiff swung in from the north with two men on board. Tunley saw his High Chancellor step aboard and the skiff turned out into the flowing river and was off. Tunley signalled to his rower who began to row with a quiet speed that the ship captain could scarce believe.

Although the rowing was fast, the skiff was faster. With the west wind blowing, Tunley found Kathsum gaining away. Just as she was on the edge of his sight, the skiff stopped and dropped anchor. Tunley breathed a sigh of relief and signalled to his rower to take his boat downwind. Looking to the sky, Tunley was pleased to see thick clouds passing in from the west and by the time that they had reached within earshot, the clouds obscured the moon and cast the river into near total darkness. At that moment, Tunley could not have been more pleased with the weather than if he had control of it himself. He signalled to his rower to hold their positioning and closed his eyes to listen to the voices wafting across the water to where he sat.

'Resvon, this is our third meeting and you are still not budging on your initial proposal. When people negotiate, it is usually a two-way discussion. I need to think of my people too, you know. I will be more placated if we can have access to the Green Lake as well. Aside from the monks and Olswerth, it is seldom used at the moment and I don't see why we can't share this extensive fishery.'

'Hhhmmmm, there would most likely be strife among those who reside there; Olswerth for one is a stubborn man. It will take many years and more before our two peoples are trusting of each other enough to live side-by-side. We do not want to bring the land peace, only for it to be shattered by fishermen having at each other.'

'Then let Roasline take all of the Green Lake and we will have an agreement.'

'Ha, and would you like the Woods of Sorrow thrown in for good measure? Kathsum, let the Outcasts have the lake and we will send you an agreed payment at each turn of the moon. I have already sent you a ship full of valuable items; has that not won your trust a little?'

Captain Tunley only just caught the last comment from Resvon and chuckled to himself as he heard the silence seeping out of Kathsum. He thought of the ship of bones and wondered what would happen when Kathsum shoved this in his face.

'Valuables, you say? Yes, I suppose they would be valuable to the families in which they once belonged.'

'High Chancellor, do you propose I stole all of those jewels, wool and other such things?' The indignation in Resvon's voice came thick and fast to Tunley's ears.

'I know not of that which you sent, but only that which arrived. Bones, Resvon. Your Captain brought me a ship of bones.'

Tunley relished the moment as it was Resvon's turn to be silent, but the leader of the Outcasts did not. Instead, he heard Resvon curse and spit out a single word: 'Ryde'.

'Oh yes, I have your Captain Ryde, deep within my dungeons.'

'That traitor! I had heard rumours he had made a detour north, but my ships could not find him and so I did not believe them. Captain Ryde came highly recommended for his loyalty. I have clearly been deceived!' Resvon sounded angry. 'I am sorry for this treachery, Kathsum. If he were in my hands, he would die a most painful death.'

'Then you would have killed a near innocent man. I have spoken with Ryde myself, Resvon, and he tells of a sickness within your ranks that goes deep and high. He was forced to steal my goods under a threat to his family. And he has told me who was behind it.'

Resvon took a sharp intake of breath. 'Tell me, for the sake of peace between us, you must tell me who has betrayed me!'

'Yes, I suppose I must, but only if you agree to allow my people to fish the Green Lake.'

'Is the lake that important to you, that you would risk peace between us by ransoming those who wish to thwart us? That is a dangerous game Kathsum, and I hope you are prepared to lose. I will dig these traitors out myself if I must.' There was a momentary pause. 'Jacov, take Kathsum home. Our negotiations are done for this evening.'

'Jacov, wait, we are not finished just yet.' Kathsum's voice sounded strained. 'Give me access to the lake and I will make sure that those who settle there are trustworthy, peace-loving folk. And, I will not only tell you who your traitor is, but I will bring Captain Ryde back to you at our next meeting.'

Tunley held his breath as he waited for Resvon's reply. A moment ago, he was certain that the war would continue for many more years, but now he was not so sure. When Resvon spoke, his voice could barely be heard across the water.

'Very well Kathsum, you will have access to the lake. Now, who must I strike down?'

'Eyp, Commander Eyp is your traitor. Ryde knows of several others, but I cannot recall their names.'

'Thank you, High Chancellor. I will see that justice is done. Jacov, take us home. Kathsum, bring papers to our next meeting outlining our agreed conditions of peace. At the next full moon, we will finalise our peace.'

Captain Tunley heard the familiar sound of someone hauling in an anchor, the unfurling of sails and the skiff start to move. Over this noise, he heard no more speech. Tunley turned to his rower and signalled that they should return to shore. With the soft plop, plop of oars to soothe him, Captain Tunley wondered what life would be like with no more battles to fight. He also wondered what the Admiral would think. Would he be pleased to see peace so near his death or would he be outraged at not being consulted for such an important part of Roasline's history?

9

The only sound Winter could hear was the thumping of the veins in his neck. Before him lay a rotting log that crossed over a ferocious river. Winter had been afraid of heights ever since he was a little boy, and the gorge that fell away below him brought these fears storming to his mind. Numb, Winter felt himself instructing Dusk that they should follow the goat and cross the log to avoid being caught by the wolves. It made sense in his head, but his fear had hold of his legs. And they were refusing to obey.

The frightened young man looked straight into Dusk's eyes and saw there his fear reflected back at him. Winter loved his sister and now was a time when he had to be the strong one: he had to confront his fears and he had to defeat them. Winter pictured his sister in his mind's eye and steadied his breathing. Only then did the young man step out onto the log. The first few steps were the worst; Winter could not breathe, and his mouth filled with the fearful taste of stomach acid. Swallowing, he continued to put one foot in front of the other. At one stage, he almost slipped into the river below and his blood drained from his face. Despite this, he continued over the log, each step sinking slightly into the rot and sending his fear aflutter once more. He clenched his jaw tightly and watched as the far bank moved closer and closer. With fear chasing him, he ran the last few steps to reach the solid ground.

He smiled at the goat and then turned to Dusk. She had just started to cross when, out of the corner of his eye, Winter caught sight of an enormous black wolf leading four smaller wolves. As the beasts spied their prey, they let out a howl of victory.

In the blink of an eye, Winter watched as Dusk turned to the wolves, lost her footing and fell. Winter's heart leapt into his mouth as he made to move across the log, but it too was falling into the churning water below. Winter yelled out in anguish as he prepared his mind for the icy water that would soon be surrounding him, as he made to jump into the river. But the goat had other ideas. She rounded on him, knocked him off his feet, and pinned him to the ground. The goat had to use all the strength within her to hold the wild beast that Winter had become. He thrashed and swore, bit and hit, but the goat remained in control.

Winter soon felt the goat pressing heavily on his chest and his breaths shortened. Colours flashed in front of his eyes and before he knew what was happening, blackness took him.

When Winter woke, it was cold and dark. The goat was lying close, shielding him from the wind that raced up the valley. As the noise of the gushing river reached his ears, the events of the day came crashing back to Winter. He jumped to his feet and raced to the edge of the gorge. His fear of heights forgotten; Winter strained his eyes in the darkness for any sign of Dusk. Seeing none, he paced to and fro on the edge of the ravine and pondered his options. Time and time again, he kept coming back to the goat. Winter turned to the scrawny animal and felt his pale face flush with anger.

The voice that came to his lips was one filled with anger, loss, and sadness. As his words spilled forth, he felt them quavering despite his best efforts to keep them strong. 'Why did you stop me going in after her? She's my sister! I'm a strong swimmer. I could have saved her! But no, you shoved that great big log right in after her. You killed her! *You* led us here and then, when there was still time to save her, *you* let her go. I hate you, you stupid goat!'

Winter noticed that the goat had made her way over to him and was looking at him unblinkingly.

'Be gone! I don't want you with me anymore. LEAVE!'

But the goat didn't leave. Instead, she came closer still and bowed her head, licking Winter's left hand. Winter flinched at the touch and shoved the goat backwards. As the goat fell to the ground, so did Winter. His hands trembled so hard that he could barely wipe away the burning tears that rolled down his cheeks. In his despair, he curled up into a tight ball and sobbed Dusk's name. Winter didn't notice it, but the goat settled herself against him and shielded him from the wind once more.

When Winter woke the next time, it was to the early light of dawn. His muscles ached and cracked as he straightened out. He reached for his face and felt a thick covering of crusted dirt on his cheeks and dried drool on his chin. He sensed the pain of hunger in his stomach, but pushed that from his mind; the pain in his heart was much more severe. Winter curled back into his tight ball and wept for Dusk, once more.

The morning passed in a cloud of fog for Winter as images of Dusk falling faded from the young man's mind. Matters of survival were pressing. He straightened his limbs and felt the pain of cramps shoot through his entire body. He relished this pain, and as it slowly dissipated, he wished it back. Craving the physical pain once more to distract him, Winter curled up into his ball again.

The goat, however, had other ideas. It had been watching Winter stretch and then re-curl, and as he did so, she moved over and nudged him gently with her nose. Wanting to be left alone, Winter slapped the goat away, but she continued to nudge. After a short while of nudging and slapping, Winter was forced to uncurl and face the goat. When he saw her, he felt an immediate sensation of hatred. He prepared to curse her but, before his sluggish mind could form the words, saw at her feet a pile of berries and his cooked bear meat. Winter turned his back on the goat and curled up once more.

An instant later, he felt her nudging him again, this time with her remaining horn. 'All right, all right, I'll eat.'

When the first juicy berry passed Winter's lips, he realised just how hungry he was and wolfed the remainder of the food down. As Winter gulped a mouthful of water, a feeling of intense guilt swept through his body. How could he sit there eating the offerings of his sister's murderer while her body lay washed up and mangled on some rocky river bank? The thought sickened him and he had to control his mind to stop himself from vomiting. And then his thoughts were once more on Dusk's body as she fell from the log and into the churning river. Winter curled up into his ball yet again and, this time, the goat let him sleep.

Winter shivered as he rolled onto his back and groaned in pain. His upper legs cramped sharply and his back ached dully. He lay like that for a while, allowing himself to become accustomed to the pain and cold. His stomach groaned, so he crawled his way over to his bag and rummaged for some food. An encouraging nudge told him that the goat would not be allowing him to wallow anymore, so he turned and sat with his back against his rucksack.

Winter found himself in a small clearing covered by thin grass and pebbles in the mid-afternoon. From where the log had been positioned, an old path ran northward up the side of the gorge for a short while before disappearing behind a rocky outcrop. Apart from the river, all other sides of the clearing were blocked by sheer cliffs that looked both sharp and difficult to climb. For Winter, there was only one way out of that clearing.

In a fit of haste, an urgency grasped hold of Winter's thoughts and he ran frantically towards the river. As he was just about to leap into the abyss, he felt a sharp pain in his side as the goat collided into him and sent him sprawling in the dirt. Winter's frustration and anger burst out of him as he screamed with all of his might. Scrambling to his feet once more, he made towards the gorge, but again the goat stopped him. This time, Winter landed on his face and tasted blood. From where he lay, he spat it at the goat. She let the spit and blood hit her before cleaning it off. All sorts of new physical pains filled Winter, the sharpest being his swelling tongue. Feeling this with his fingers, he discovered a chunk of the front part, dangling by a thin strand. He ripped the small chunk off, held it up for the goat to see and tossed it into the river.

'Ath leath parth offf me can be wifth Dusk.' At that thought, a fit of laughter took control of Winter and he thrashed about in the dirt. The laughter soon turned to sobs of grief before Winter fell into a fitful sleep where he was visited by nothing but pain.

A dull ache throbbed in the back of Winter's skull as he slowly opened his eyes. These he swiftly shut again as the late afternoon seemed too bright. He felt a funny sensation scraping his back and noticed that his arms were above his head. Confused, he tried to roll onto his side, but was unable to. Winter opened his eyes carefully and tried to look about. He sat up painfully and what he saw took him completely by surprise. The goat had his left foot hooked into her right horn, along with his rucksack, and she had his right foot firmly in her mouth. Slowly, but surely, she was waddling backwards, dragging him along. The dull ache that he felt in his head was from it being dragged across rocks and stones. He kicked out savagely at the goat and scrambled to his feet. Winter stood there breathing heavily as he stared straight at the goat that was staring right back at him.

With a sigh, Winter slumped his shoulders and looked at the ground. He stood like this for a while before raising his head and looking about. The skinny path ahead wound around a corner and was flanked by towering black rocks. Winter tried to think and almost immediately noticed the silence. There was no birdlife, no wind and what Winter noticed the most, was that there was no churning of the river.

He turned to the goat as a trickle of silent tears rolled down his cheeks. 'Damn you.'

The goat bleated gently in reply.

Winter turned to face the way he had been dragged and uttered to the sky. 'I love you sister Dusk. I will never forget you. Goodbye.' Turning to face the path ahead, Winter picked up his rucksack and followed the goat onwards.

Darkness descended quickly upon the Moaks and with it came a light fluttering of snow. The man and the goat camped in a small alcove that night, and they were sheltered from the gusting northerly wind. Winter managed to find sufficient wood to build a small fire and wrapped his new bearskin around his shoulders. The freshly shorn goat shivered by the fire, but Winter refused to let her huddle close to his warmth. As the fire died down, the young man curled up and wept until sleep took him.

The dawn that came to Winter and the goat was neither warm nor hopeful. The wind had developed into a constant force, but the snow had abated. Winter quickly ate some food before preparing himself to face a day of walking. The way he saw it, he had two choices; to continue his journey by following the goat, or to stop where he was and give up. *What would Dusk want me to do?* He smirked. *Do I even need to ask? Go on, of course.*

The goat led the way once more as they left their alcove and crumpled over the now icy snow. Winter had never seen snow before, and in normal circumstances he would have marvelled at it. On this day, however, he could only hate the world and himself. *I should have let her go first across the log. She's dead because of me. And now all four are dead; my poor brothers and sisters and I am all alone.*

Winter stumbled along behind the goat as they left any chance of shelter behind. What faced them now was a series of tall hills, whose sides were a mixture of sheer cliffs, and a scrum of boulders and rocks. Their rounded white snow-capped tops contrasted the blackness of the damp rock. Nothing grew here except moss and the odd purple thistle. The goat paused now and then to nibble on these, but Winter didn't notice; his thoughts were left well behind with the falling body of his sister.

The steep work of the day began to take its toll on the young man. He stumbled and fell and before long his numb hands were cut and bleeding from striking the hard ground so often. But he didn't care. He just got back up and kept following the goat. His falls became more frequent, as the light began to fade and Winter couldn't be bothered looking where he should be putting his feet.

As the snow fell once more, the path became slippery and, exhausted, Winter fell heavily. He stretched out his hands and as he landed on his left wrist, a sharp pain shot up his arm. Defeated, he lay on the ground sobbing.

The goat nudged him, and Winter forced himself to his feet once more. The goat then ran ahead and Winter watched in dazed confusion. When the goat was just on the edge of his vision, she stopped. Winter strained his eyes and saw nestled under a black cliff several dots of white. The bleating of sheep reached his ears and he struggled forward once more. As he got closer to the goat, he saw something else: a shack. It was not big, but looked sturdy. The walls were made of rock, with an old timber roof sitting upon them.

Ignoring his wrist, Winter laboured the final distance. After unlatching the door, he went in, closely followed by the goat. A damp smell reached his nostrils. He ignored that and stared at the fireplace where a ready-made fire sat, begging to be lit. As he sent sparks shooting from his flint stone, he noticed the dust and cobwebs on the wood and realised that this fire had been prepared several months before. The fire soon began to crackle and Winter forced some food down his throat while basking in the flames' warmth.

The next few weeks passed in a haze for Winter. His wrist swelled and then went down. It hurt constantly, but as the days passed, he found he could use it gently. He explored the hut and found a wood pile. This ensured that his fire never went out. To add to his comfort, he also found coarse woollen blankets that he used to sleep in by the fire. Snow and rain came in fits and bursts, but the wind never stopped and the sun was never seen.

Whenever the wind blew up the gully, it swirled around the hut and sang to Winter. He heard many things on it, but ever present was the sound of Dusk's voice. On these days, he would not eat, but lay by the fire and weep.

By night, he often heard howling in the distance and was convinced that the wolves that had chased Dusk to her death had found her carcase and were tearing it to shreds. No tears came at these times, but neither did sleep.

The days following these sleepless nights, Winter sought the goat, and when he could find her, he beat her. She never fought back, and without exception, after her blood mingled with his tears, Winter held her close and begged for forgiveness. At these times, Winter confided in his companion of the many times that Avgar had beaten him for his closeness to Dusk.

As the days continued to pass, Winter's mood continued to fluctuate. Some days, he had moments of mild happiness. On these days, he explored the area and made many discoveries, one of which was that the path that they had followed stopped at the hut and went no further.

On other days, he hated so deeply that he wanted to end his life. But he always found the goat was there to stop him.

On one of his good days, Winter noticed that his food supply was diminishing rapidly. The morning after he finished the bear meat, he made up his mind. He sought out the goat and asked her a question. 'Can you lead me through the Moaks?' The goat nodded and licked his hand. 'Then, the day after tomorrow, we will leave this place.'

The remainder of the day and the next, he set about preparing to depart. He slaughtered two of the wandering sheep and cooked their meat. Their skin he dried and made a vest for himself and a coat that he could drape over the goat. When he put this on her, she seemed pleased and nestled down for a sleep. He also crafted two bags, joined by a rope that would sit astride the goat to carry some supplies. He then sharpened his sai with his whetstone before building up the fire for his last night in the shack and went peacefully to sleep.

10

The full moon had come two nights past and Marlvon had since been harvesting his olives several miles outside the walls of Fort Kykum. By way of tradition, these particular olives could only be harvested in the five days following the full moon. In Marlvon's view, this was an annoying oddity, but if he had any chance of selling them to the olive pressers, then he had to adhere to the old ways.

As he climbed a ladder into his fourteenth tree for the night and started dropping the olives into the basket below, a hooded figure approached. Remaining in his tree, Marlvon hailed the stranger.

'Good evening to you sir, you are far from any path. Mayhap you are lost on this peaceful night?'

A soft voice climbed up the tree to reach the young man's ears. 'Good Marlvon, you are always so polite. Perhaps you can scramble down your olive tree and greet your uncle face to face.'

'Resvon, my apologies, I did not recognise you with your hood drawn so tight.'

'That would be the point, young one.'

Marlvon promptly descended his tree and soon stood before his uncle. While Resvon was not a tall man, Marlvon was shorter still. A sense of unease crept through him as he looked up into his uncle's sad brown eyes. 'You have not come to help with the harvest, have you Uncle?'

'Ah, if I had the time, then I would like nothing more than to find peace in your olive grove. But alas no, I have come seeking your assistance.'

Already knowing the answer, Marlvon asked anyway. 'Will it take long? I have many olive trees still to strip and the nights are passing me by.'

Resvon looked down at his nephew and saw a likeness of his younger self. 'I hate myself for asking this of you, Marlvon, but for this task, there is simply no one else that I can trust. If your father was still alive, then it would be him and not you, that I would be asking.'

'Well, he's not. And he hasn't been for four years. So, hurry up and ask of me what you will, and remember, I am *not* your brother.' At the mention of his father, Marlvon found anger flare within him. He loved the memory of his father, but was in no mood to discuss it tonight.

When Resvon spoke, the young man heard the sadness in his voice and regretted his flash of anger immediately. 'Marlvon, I know that you're not Larvon, but I love you just as much.' Resvon reached out and gently squeezed his nephew's shoulder. He then straightened and stared into Marlvon's eyes. 'Do you know Commander of Ships, Eyp?'

'I have seen him once or twice. Brutish sort of fellow and strong, very strong.'

'Hmmm, yes. As well as that, he's an excellent sailor and has a cunning mind. Well, it may, or may not, as it seems, shock you to hear he has betrayed me.'

'Uncle! Can you be sure of this? His position, his power… He controls the fleet!'

'Calm Marlvon, I know his position only too well. I was the one who put him there.'

'Have you hung him yet? Or at least locked him up? You need to make an example of him.'

'Calm yourself, nephew. Justice will be served.' His manner was calm and the statement had its desired effect on Marlvon, who fell silent. 'That is where you come in. While you may hide it from everyone else, I know the skills my brother passed on to you. I know how dangerous you are.'

Marlvon cut in. 'So, you want me to kill this Eyp for you? Is that it? Or maybe you want me to torture him for information?' Marlvon felt sick in his stomach at the thought.

'No, at least not yet. It is your skill of stealth that I require most. Tomorrow night I will tell him, as well as others, of a deal that I have reached with Roasline. A deal of peace.'

Marlvon felt his heart leap. 'How can that be? *Peace.* I… I cannot imagine what that would be like.'

'It would be like a cleansing rain after a lifetime of drought. But not everyone likes the rain. Eyp has risen in war and remains powerful as long as it continues. He will not like the news. That is where you come in.' Marlvon felt Resvon's stare focus on him and he shifted uneasily.

'I want you at our meeting. Not as my nephew, but in disguise as his cupbearer. You will pour for Eyp and watch him. When he leaves, so will you. I ask that you follow him wherever he goes. Watch him as he goes to those he trusts and remember their faces. When he finally rests, capture him. You do not have to be gentle; you do not have to be nice. But keep him alive.'

Marlvon could see the sense behind this action. Capturing Eyp outright and torturing him may provide little results. Those under pain will name whoever they think needs to be named to ease their suffering.

Marlvon's mind was already racing with the preparation that would need to be done. 'People may notice my absence when I am not picking my olives tomorrow.'

'That is true; I will find someone of similar appearance and set them to work as you. You will still get your harvest. Will you do this task for me?'

'You know I hate this part of me, Uncle.'

'And yet you maintain your training.'

Marlvon resolutely set his jaw. 'If this will help bring about peace, then you have my word that I will perform this task to the fullest of my abilities.'

'Thank you. It will be best if you disguise yourself before entering the fort. Seek out Burban in the kitchens, she will tell you which wines the Commander likes and she'll garb you as a bearer. Forego your real name and call yourself Mantly. Yes, that should do. Marlvon, I will see you tomorrow, although I will not acknowledge it. Good luck.'

His uncle embraced him before he turned and disappeared amongst his olive trees. Marlvon shook his head before climbing his tree once more; his subconscious already forming his plan as he finished the tree he had started.

Marlvon spent the warm, cloudy morning preparing a series of knives which were already sharp enough to shave with before he had even begun with his whetstone. Once satisfied with the knives, he applied a series of pastes and tinctures to disguise his features. For this he used an exotic mixture of ingredients such as coal tar, demure coloured stamen from various flowers and a fine soil that came from the hills upon Headly. When mixed with the juice of a colourless wild berry, the coal tar lost its stench but retained its staining ability. Marlvon applied this creation to his entire body, slightly darkening his natural skin tone to that of a sun-tanned farm servant. He added a fresh-looking scar close to his left ear and wrinkled crow's feet more fitting someone twice his age. He added white ash to his short pepper hair around the ears and the back of his head. He garbed himself in a simple cloth tunic and worn leather sandals as befitting a seasoned farmer.

After finishing his lunch, he tied his sheathed blades in various concealed spots around his body and went out to the stables. Once there, he chose not the fine black stallion, but the ageing work horse, Nal. His father had left her behind when he passed and Marlvon saddled her lovingly. Marlvon concealed within her fastenings a short dirk, but hoped that he would not have to draw it. He then began the slow trot off his land and towards Fort Kykum.

It was a tired man in his mid-fifties with salt and pepper hair who entered the steaming kitchens at Fort Kykum. His skin was tanned to leather and the rasp in his voice matched the years that he had spent toiling in the fields.

'Burban. Where's Burban?' His voice passed through the kitchen and was directed at everyone and no one.

A voice like a whip came cracking back from a nearby potbelly stove. 'I am. Who's asking?'

'Mantly's my name and I'm here under the request of our *great* leader, Resvon.' Marlvon inflected the final words to show a distaste of their mutual master.

'You best be careful to keep that lash of a tongue silent when in his presence, or you may find he'll whip it out. But I best have a look at you and find some more suitable clothes for you to serve in.'

The thin woman came close and sized Marlvon up and down. 'When they said our leader got a new servant as a debt payment, I thought that you'd have been younger.' There was no kindness hidden in Burban's voice.

'Yea, well, it's my master's debt I'm repaying. He should've known better than to borrow so heavily from someone or other who had borrowed from someone else. They in turn gambled against Resvon. Six months in his service. That's what I have to do. I should be out there, tending my master's crops, not cooped up in some fort like a prisoner.'

'Well, like it or not, you're here. And when you're here, you will do as you're told. So, stop complaining or you'll find a lash across your back.'

Marlvon pitied the woman; he knew she must have worries greater than his fabricated ones, yet he had to play his part.

Burban left for a few moments, only to return with an armful of clothes. 'You can keep your sandals, but these'll replace the rest. Why they insisted on an untrained farmer serving the most powerful men alive, I'll never understand.' She dumped the clothes into his arms and pointed him toward a quiet corner for him to change in.

'Probably to humiliate the Treasurer; it was him who lost the debt to Resvon.' Burban nodded her understanding and left Marlvon to get changed.

It took great skill and speed for Marlvon to change in full view of anyone who cared to look without revealing his weapons, but once he was done, he felt comfortable in the three-quarter length trousers and full sleeve fine wool shirt. While the wool was warm, it was soft on his skin and itched little.

When Marlvon re-presented to Burban, he noted the fleeting look of surprise on her face. 'If you're not careful Mantly, you might almost look like you belong here.'

Marlvon had planned his disguise perfectly. Once he'd donned the black outfit, he'd known he would look like he had quality serving experience. He purposefully removed the final resemblance of the old farmer by altering his expression from that of a defeated servant to a man at peace with his situation. Now he looked as if he belonged.

'Come, it is getting dark and the food will soon be served. I best tell you of your duties.'

Marlvon found himself being led out of the bustling kitchens, through the servant's passageways and into a bare room with naught but a dark ash table set for six.

'At the head will be Resvon. To his immediate right will be the Commander of Men, to Resvon's left will be the Commander of Ships. At the bottom of the table will be the Defender of Kykum, the Treasurer of the Outcasts and the Commander of Civilians will fill the other two seats. You have the honour of serving wine to the Commander of Ship. Be careful Mantly, for the last servant to spill wine over Eyp lost his hand for it.'

'I will be careful.'

'Come, let me show you the cellars and the wines that Eyp prefers.' Marlvon followed quietly, taking in every detail.

As Resvon and his Commanders entered the dining room, Marlvon allowed Mantly's nervousness come to the fore to really consolidate his disguise. With his hand shaking ever-so-slightly, he poured Commander Eyp a rich pale-gold variety of wine that shimmered in the Commander's personal golden chalice. Marlvon observed as Eyp sniffed the wine, took a half mouthful, swirled it around his mouth and spat it back into his chalice. He then licked his lips and drained the cup. The Commander shook the chalice at Marlvon, who promptly filled it once more. This time, the Commander sipped while conversing with the Defender of Kykum about his newly commissioned war galley: *Woe*. Eyp managed all of this without even glancing in Marlvon's direction. Resvon's nephew stepped back to the wall and watched Eyp intently as he seated himself and devoured the dark grapes that had been strewn about the table as decoration, whilst others, including Resvon, remained standing.

Marlvon tried not to look at his uncle when Resvon advised them they should be seated. By this stage, Eyp had finished his second chalice and indicated to Marlvon that he would not drink the golden wine anymore, but would prefer to move on to the clear wine that came from grapes grown on Headly. With this, the first food arrived, mussels and scallops harvested fresh that morning. As these were delivered, Marlvon watched as the Commander pinched the serving girl firmly on the buttocks and drain his cup. Marlvon was there in a heartbeat to refill the golden chalice but found that the Commander was ready to move on to a richer wine, the hue of which reminded Marlvon of his mother's garnet marriage band.

In a blink of an eye, the empty plates were cleared and the second serving was being placed down. This consisted of seared ox tongue in a broth of peas and ham. Marlvon noticed Eyp's wandering hands once more and felt for the poor serving girl who was powerless in the situation. As the Commander finished his broth, he sought a refill of wine, happy to stay with the garnet drop.

The plates were cleared and the third course consisted of a duck drumstick surrounded by artichokes stuffed with olives and thick, doughy bread. This time, as the meals were being served, Marlvon moved to fill his Commander's cup and, instead of the serving girl finding herself the attention of Eyp's wandering hand, Marlvon did. The Commander of ships looked at his wine server, squeezed his buttocks hard and gave him a wink. Marlvon would have liked nothing more than to draw a blade from under his arm and stab it though the Commander's groping hand, but he resisted, returned Eyp's wink and returned to his place by the wall.

It was at this point that Resvon pushed his chair back and got to his feet.

'Gentlemen, gentlemen, I hope you are enjoying the food and wine tonight?'

Nods and murmurs of trained agreement rose from all on the table except Eyp, who merely nodded his approval.

Resvon continued, 'I have brought you here for this dinner to make an announcement. For the past three months I have been meeting in secret with the Chancellor of Roasline.' Resvon paused momentarily as the enormity of his claim sank in. He then ploughed on, 'And over this time we have come to an agreement. We have agreed on peace!'

The expected silence followed the announcement, and Marlvon watched Eyp closely. The first thing that the Commander of Ships did was to push the golden chalice away. He then looked straight at Resvon and asked: 'How could you? They are our foes; they are the enemy!'

While most of the others would not have noticed, Marlvon detected the venom in Eyp's words and he was sure that Resvon would have heard it too.

The Leader turned to face Eyp directly. 'Commander Eyp, would you prefer to have an enemy or a friend?'

'I would prefer to defeat my enemies and have friends I can trust.'

The tension between the two emanated throughout the room before the thin voice of the Treasurer broke it. 'And what have you promised them in return for this peace?'

All eyes in the room, except Marlvon's, snapped towards Resvon, wary of his response. 'All the lands south of the Liagar, including the southern shore of the Green Lake.'

Eyp's leer came slurred, but fast. 'They are rich lands, Resvon. Are you getting so old that you are afraid of war?'

'You forget your place, Commander. I am not here to ask your permission; I'm here to *tell* you what has transpired.'

Eyp hesitantly backtracked. 'Forgive me Leader; the wine speaks for me.' Marlvon saw through this thin excuse. 'Now, if you'll excuse me, I shall leave before the wine makes me say anything else uncalled for.' Eyp pushed back his chair and staggered to his feet. He wobbled his way to the door and as he was about to leave, turned and spoke once more. 'Congratulations on your peace, Leader Resvon.'

With that, Marlvon watched as he stumbled out. In the blink of an eye, Resvon glanced at Marlvon who swivelled and hastened through the servant's door.

As soon as Marlvon was through the door he broke into a run down the servant's passageway. He brushed past Burban with her *where-do-you-think-you're-going* look and, instead of returning to the kitchens, made his way through a series of doors and curtains until he found himself in the entrance of the Fort's main keep. As he hid himself in the shadows created by the open doors, he heard the hurried footsteps of long strides. Commander Eyp strode straight out of his passageway and without so much as a sideways glance at the door wardens, exited the keep. With his silent soft leather sandals, Marlvon followed.

Once he had exited the building, Eyp veered to the right and towards the stables. Not wanting to follow the Commander directly, Marlvon headed in a straight line and had his first pang of fear: while a horse offered little benefit of speed within the Fort that housed thousands, if Eyp left the city's protective walls, then Marlvon would have no hope of following him.

The varying possibilities of Eyp's route were endless and all that Marlvon could do was wait just outside the keep's inner wall for him. In his mind, he sifted through the outlay of the Fort and tried to calculate the Commander's most likely route.

The inner keep of Fort Kykum had been built long ago by the rulers of Roasline. As the need grew bigger, so did the number of dwellings surrounding the keep. At this point, the Outcasts had swept down upon her and taken her with heavy casualties. The then-Leader of the Outcasts was ever fearful of a retribution attack and so built an outer wall to encompass all of the dwellings and stretch as far as the banks of the Liagar. As feared, an attack came and was only just repelled. The Leader of the Outcasts grew more fearful and so built a third and final wall. Since its construction, hovels had overtaken the land between the two outer walls. Crime there was rife after dark and nobody who had a choice would live there. To avoid those who had positions of power passing through the stinking slums when they left the Fort, a pathway had been built with high stone walls on either side between the second wall and the outside. It was through this well-kept corridor that Marlvon had come that afternoon and expected Eyp to canter out on this now dark night.

Marlvon's thoughts were broken by the sound of hooves on cobblestones. This preceded Eyp cloaked in full black, trotting under the inner keep's wall. The

Commander passed the guards at the gate and entered the dwindling flow of foot traffic that was heading down the main road. Marlvon jogged after the Commander, keeping to the shadows and making sure that his feet fell in time with Eyp's horse.

The Commander did not follow the main road for long, but slowed to a walk as he entered a poorly lit side street. The traffic down here was less and Marlvon had to be careful in his pursuit. He hung his head and stumbled like a drunkard heading home for the night. The guise could not be kept up for long, as Eyp weaved through many laneways and alleys. Marlvon resorted to light footfalls and keeping his distance instead.

While they weaved about incessantly, Marlvon soon saw a pattern in the Commander's path and realised that they were heading towards the harbour. For the second time that night, the young man felt a pang of fear; if Eyp decided to set sail, there would be no way that he could follow. *For the sake of peace, I must prevent that.*

The waning moon rose, only to be obscured by thick clouds, and before long, the two men reached the harbour. Instead of heading for a ship, as Marlvon had expected, Eyp reined up his horse and dismounted. A cloaked figure that Marlvon had not seen a moment ago emerged from the shadows and whispered something inaudible to the Commander. Eyp, on the other hand, could not restrain his booming voice. 'Take this to your aviary, find your fastest pigeon, and send it to *him*.' Eyp handed the man a tiny piece of parchment and then the man leapt upon the Commander's horse and was gone at a gallop.

The sudden sound of the hooves startled Marlvon and he exhaled louder than he should have. Eyp appeared to hear and raised his head and looked deeply into the shadows away to Marlvon's right. He lost any chance of following the messenger on the horse in that moment of folly.

The commander lowered his gaze, withdrew a flask from within his coat and drank deeply. Marlvon saw the Commander cringe after swallowing, before making his way up the hill once more.

With Eyp coming directly towards him, Marlvon carefully retraced his steps until he found a stack of empty crates to crouch behind. The commander passed him by and continued up the hill. Supposing Eyp to be heading to his lodgings, Marlvon followed at a safe distance once more. But the Commander's feet did not take him home; instead Marlvon found himself following Eyp towards the closest gate that led from the civilised part of town and into the slums.

Before reaching the gate however, Eyp drained his flask and entered the nearest tavern. There were a few patrons slumped in their chairs after a night of heavy drinking and smoke hung thick about their heads. Marlvon watched through the grimy window as the still hooded commander ordered a full wineskin and a goblet of mead. The latter he finished in one gulp, paid the bartender, and left with the wine skin under his arm.

Marlvon kept his smile to himself as he saw the Commander stumble slightly as they approached the guarded gateway.

The pursuer watched from the shadows as the guards haled Eyp as he ducked under the bar that blocked his path. 'Good fortunes to you in there, stranger. I'm sure you'll find a nice place to lie.' Eyp responded with a grunt.

Marlvon waited a moment before following with a drunken meander. The guards sized him up and down before uttering, 'Be careful in there, servant. The girls can be mighty feisty.'

Marlvon slurred his reply. 'That's what I'm hoping for.' And he chuckled to himself. The guards let the drunkard pass and, while patting him on the back, reminded him that none are allowed back until dawn.

The first thing that Marlvon noticed as he passed into the slums was the stench. This reminded him sharply of where he was and he withdrew his longest blade from its sheath under his arm. The blade flickered in the candlelight of nearby taverns as he located Eyp striding away down a side street. Marlvon held the knife by his leg and followed the Commander.

Dust soon covered Marlvon's sandals which became quashed by the damp earth that pervaded the streets beneath the gutters and windowsills. Shanty houses rose on either side of him and men, women and children slept in the street; homeless. As well as following the strong Commander, Marlvon had to keep an eye out for those who might want to attack him; luckily, he was not troubled by anyone.

The stench continued to thicken and Marlvon followed Eyp in the shadows. The Commander continued to drink from his wineskin and cared not when he trod in urine and faeces.

Marlvon's attention was sharpened as an old man leapt out of the shadows and tried to grasp the Commander's wine. Eyp grabbed the man's hand and snapped his arm without even thinking. As the man fell screaming, the Commander kicked him in the head and he lay silent. The Commander continued his brisk pace around the next corner. Marlvon followed and was just in time to see Eyp slip through a doorway and close the door behind him.

Marlvon raced to the door and sized the building up. It was a two-story house made of cheap brown brick with the mortar eroding away. The door was solid wood, but in dire need of a paint. Up above, on the second floor, was a single small window with the shutters open and mouldy curtains flapping out. Marlvon looked back at the door and placed his hand on the latch. He tried lifting it. It squeaked slightly, but would not open.

He cursed under his breath as he saw he had no other choice but to climb into the window. He sheathed his blade, rubbed the sweat off his hands, and began his ascent. The young man knew beyond a doubt that he could make the climb easily. His only concern was that the old bricks would give way under his weight. Nevertheless, he put hand over hand into the gaping mortar.

When he was halfway up, a deep slurred voice gushed forth from the window above and a candle flared to life. He had no doubt that the voice belonged to Eyp.

'Good evening, Prie.'

Marlvon did not know who Prie was or how she fitted into Eyp's rebellion, but he heard her fearful groan at the sound of Eyp's voice.

'Commander, no! You were here last night. You promised it would be at least a week before you came here again. No, please no.'

'Why do you shake, woman? Are you cold?' Eyp paused and after receiving silence as an answer continued on. 'I have heard some very distasteful news tonight and I have need of you.'

'No, not again, please.' Marlvon heard the plea followed by sobs. He then heard a thump and a sharp cry.

'It is not for you to deny me. Now shut your mouth and open your legs or I will gag you.'

At the sound of the whack, Marlvon was snapped out of his trance and raced with all of his speed up the rest of the wall. As he reached the window, he withdrew his knife once more and leapt through the flapping curtains.

As he landed on the wooden floor, his breath was stolen from him by what he saw. A woman was lying on a mouldy mattress, tied to the bed frame. She was naked but for the galaxies of bruises covering her body. Eyp stood over her, draining the last of his wineskin and unlacing his breeches.

The Commander heard Marlvon land and spun around to face the intruder. In a heartbeat, Marlvon had leapt across the room, slashed through the Commander's left hand and was bringing his glistening blade towards the Commander's naked throat. But Eyp was a man of war. With his bleeding hand, he grabbed hold of Marlvon's knife-hand and twisted it sharply. Marlvon's many years of training stepped in and he twisted with his arm, jumping at the same time to complete the circle. As he landed, he struck out with his foot and caught the inside of Eyp's right knee. The knee dislocated and the Commander fell with a grunt. In a flash, Marlvon withdrew another knife and stabbed it clean through Eyp's other hand. He then smashed the Commander in the head and just as Eyp was beginning to rise, slammed down his longest knife through the Commander's foot and into the rotting floorboards beneath. Eyp gasped in pain and Marlvon withdrew another, smaller knife, and slashed expertly across the Commander's chest.

These cuts were not meant to kill the big man, but rather were designed to drain away part of his blood, leaving him weak. But the Commander was strong and drew the blade out of his foot. Marlvon had to act quickly. The smaller man stabbed the Commander quickly in both shoulders and both knees. As Marlvon sliced across Eyp's Achilles tendon, the man yelled out in pain and slumped to the floor unconscious.

Marlvon hastily cut the bonds that held Prie, picked her up gently from the bed and placed her on the floor. He then moved the bed-frame to sit on top of Eyp. He tied the big man firmly to the four posts before relaxing and turning to find Prie huddled in the corner.

The olive farmer collected Eyp's black cloak, draped it about Prie's sobbing shoulders and sat down next to her. He put his arm around her and rocked her gently back and forth.

'Shhhh, sshhhh. You're safe now. Eyp cannot hurt you anymore, it's all over. Sshhhh.'

In between sobs, Prie managed to ask. 'Wwhhooo aa-are you?'

Cursing his disguise, Marlvon replied. 'My name is Mantly, and I'm a friend.'

The woman sobbed for a short while longer before falling into an exhausted sleep, nestled in Marlvon's arms. Marlvon eased himself free, put the straw mattress on the floor and shifted her onto it. He let her sleep as the first grey of dawn crept into the room.

Marlvon turned his attentions back to the bloody mess of Commander Eyp lying on the dusty floor, under the bed frame. He strode over to the man, squatted and prodded him until he roused.

'Ah Commander of Ships, welcome back. It seems to me that your brutish luck has come to an end.'

'I don't know who you think you are, but you are going to die a very painful death!'

'I think not, Commander. And I wouldn't make threats if I were you.' Marlvon pressed his thumb sharply into the fresh knife wound on Eyp's shoulder. The Commander involuntarily cried out in pain.

'Now, lie still, you swine. I will be back before you know I am gone.'

Marlvon raced out of the room, down the stairs and into the laneway. He quickly retraced his steps from the night before until he found himself at the gate that led out of the slums.

'What have we here? In a hurry to get home before you wife wakes up?' The guard elbowed his colleague in the ribs, trying to elicit a response.

'No, I merely have a message for you to deliver.'

'Do I look like a messenger boy to you? I'll tell you where you can stick your message.'

'I can make it worth your while.'

'It's worth my while to stay at my post. If I'm caught not bein' here, then I'll lose me job, I will.'

'Have you heard of Commander of Ships Eyp?'

'Of course. What do you take me for, a simpleton?'

'Well, you are to get a message to Resvon, the Leader of the Outcasts, that the Commander will be here at midday, with me.'

'And who are you?'

'My name is Mantly. Resvon knows who I am.'

'And whats if I say no?'

'Then, when the Commander arrives here and the Leader is absent, I will tell him you refused to obey his orders. I'm not sure if you have seen the Commander when he is angry, but I have. And the last time that happened, a man ended up dead.'

The guard who had been doing all of the talking, fell silent as the threat hung in the air. He looked towards his companion. The second guard, who had not spoken thus far, sized Marlvon up and down with servant's garb and aged face.

'I will do this for the Commander. But if you play me false old man, then I will be the one causing the pain.'

Marlvon breathed a sigh of relief. 'Thank you. I shall be back with the Commander at midday.'

The guard saluted, turned and jogged up the hill. Marlvon watched him until he was satisfied that the message would reach his uncle and then ran back with haste into the stink of the slums.

The way was winding, but it did not take Marlvon long to reach his destination. He re-entered the house and leapt up the stairs to the bedroom. Just as he entered the room, he saw Prie with her hands about Eyp's throat. Gargling pleas for help escaped Eyp's mouth and Marlvon was there in an instant to ease Prie off her victim.

'Prie, no. We need him alive.'

'I don't care. I want him dead!'

'I cannot let you do that. I just can't. Please, do not make me restrain you.'

Prie slumped to the floor and began to sob. Marlvon quickly checked that Eyp was in no threat of dying before comforting the poor woman once more. He cradled her in his arms and let her cry some of her pain away. Once the sobs began to dry up, Marlvon cupped her face in his hands and looked her straight in the eyes.

'I am going to have to ask Eyp a few questions now. He will not want to answer them and I will have to hurt him. It might be better if you waited outside in the hallway. Is that all right with you?'

'No. I will stay. Watching him in pain will bring me some relief.'

'Very well. But if you stay, then you must remain silent, and in the corner, where he cannot be distracted by you or try to manipulate you. You must not interfere. Can you do that?'

'Yes.' Prie stood and, still wrapped in the Commander's cloak, went and sat in a corner where Eyp would not be able to see her.

Marlvon turned from Prie, and in a show of great strength, flipped the simple bed frame on its end and dragged it up against the wall with the Commander tied between the wall and the frame. Marlvon used his knives as levers and removed several of the slats in the bedframe, allowing him access to the front of Eyp's body. Without uttering a word to the Commander, Marlvon cut his clothes off completely and removed his boots.

'Commander, I hope you are not too cold standing there all exposed.' No response was forthcoming from Eyp.

'Oh well, we must press on regardless. Now, before you think that this will all be over soon, there are a few things that I should tell you.' He ticked off the facts on his fingers as he spoke. 'Nobody knows where you are. They may notice that you are not up at the keep this morning, but then, you did have quite a few drinks last night. And when they do start looking, why would anyone think to look here, in the slums? No, I think that this is just about the last place that they will search.'

Eyp looked Marlvon directly in the eyes and spat at his face.

'Now that wasn't very nice, was it?' He wiped the spit from his face with his sleeve. 'Secondary to my primary point is that I know what you are. And by that, I don't mean a raping, murdering bastard. I mean I know that you are a traitor. I know that you are plotting and planning to overthrow Resvon.'

For a fleeting moment Eyp's eyes widened with fear. Marlvon smiled to himself and pointed his knife at Eyp. 'What I don't know, is that which you are about to tell me; who was the man you gave your message to? To whom did he send his pigeon with your message of treachery, and who else is working with you?'

Eyp grinned at Marlvon. 'You will not hear me utter a single name.'

Marlvon sighed. 'Very well, so it must be. But tell me, do you like your testicles?'

Anybody walking past the laneway with the door-that-needed-paint that morning heard hideous screams. Some shook their heads and thought that they heard the cries of a tormented hog, others hurried past feeling sick in the stomach. For Commander Eyp, it felt like he was in pain for an entire lifetime. For Marlvon, it felt like two.

After the morning was almost over, Marlvon cut the Commander down from the bedframe and Eyp crumpled in a bloody mess.

'Prie, I'll be back in a moment.' Prie moved out from the corner and looked out the window while Marlvon made his way down the stairs to the front door.

He used his razor-sharp knives to cut through the rotting wood around the door hinges and removed the door from its frame. He lay it in the street and went to fetch what was left of the Commander.

'Prie, you can stay if you like, but it would be better if you came with me. We can get those injuries tended to and find someone to look after you.' With tears streaming down her face, she followed.

Once downstairs, Marlvon tied Eyp to the door, naked and face down, and with a trail of blood dripping behind them, began to drag him out to the laneway. Many eyes stared as they passed, but more averted their gaze. The slog to the gate was hard, but Marlvon was strong and relished the burn in his tired muscles.

As Marlvon and Prie approached the gate, the guards saw what was being dragged and lowered their spear shafts. 'Halt! Come no further!'

Just as the guards were advancing on Marlvon, the sound of horse's hooves clip-clopped out from behind them. The guards turned and saw five riders in full armour approaching. Between them came Resvon himself. The Leader stopped at the gate and dismounted. Racing forward, he grasped Marlvon on the shoulder. 'You have done well.'

Marlvon dropped the door and wiped his brow with a bloody sleeve.

'No, I have not. After leaving the dinner, he went to the dock. Once there, he sent a message to someone. Who the man was, or where the message was headed, I could not discover. After that he came here and was about to perform a disgusting act, before I stopped him. Despite my best efforts, he would not utter a name. Resvon, you know my skills, you know he will never talk. There is now only one thing that he would be good for: dying.'

'I will consider this. Thank you again for your service. You may go.'

'Before I do, please look after this woman. Her name is Prie and I found her at the mercy of Eyp. She will need to be cared for.'

'I will,' promised Resvon.

Marlvon bid farewell to Prie, turned his back on Eyp and began the long walk up the hill to the keep.

Soon after leaving Resvon behind, Marlvon's surroundings turned to a blur as tears came to his eyes and flowed down his face. When he could see his way no longer, he turned down a side street and collapsed into a ball of shaking sobs.

The day passed into evening before Marlvon could gather himself and begin to walk once more. This time, he made it to the stables of the keep and, saddling his horse, headed straight onto the path for home.

Four days passed and Eyp, the ex-Commander of Ships, found himself aware of his world again. His world, that had once been so full of desires and satisfactions, had turned into a world of meagre eating, breathing hard and troubled sleeping. He noticed not that his cell was no bigger than a well's circumference, only that he could feel the thin soup within his mouth.

A sharp bang at the door made the once proud man jump and spill his soup. The bolt drew back and Resvon entered Eyp's world.

'Good evening, Eyp. I hope you are enjoying your soup. Are you aware of whom I am?'

Eyp answered quickly and at the sound of his own voiced found some of his old pride returning. 'Yes, you are the Leader of the Outcasts.'

'Good, good. Now, would you like to tell me who is rebelling against me?'

To this, Eyp smiled and shook his head. 'I have nothing to say.'

'Very well. Tonight, then, you will die.'

Eyp watched with curiosity as two burly guards entered his cell and dragged him to his feet. Once standing, the ex-Commander collapsed to the ground. 'I'm sorry; my feet don't work so well after that man with his knives cut me up.'

With a guard on each side, Eyp found himself being dragged out of his cell, though a series of tunnels and into the night air. The freshness of the sea breeze after the confines of his cell woke in Eyp the desire to be free again. He breathed deeply and cursed under his breath.

A moment in the fresh breeze was all that Eyp was allowed before he was shoved into an enclosed cart and chained to the floor. The clip-clop of the horse drawing his cart began and he wondered where he would take his final breath.

The next thing Eyp knew, the horse stopped walking and he was greeted by the sea breeze once more. Hauled out of the cart, Eyp was carried down a small jetty and placed into a small boat.

Eyp saw Resvon climb into the boat as well. 'Come to join me on this adventure, Resvon?'

No reply was forthcoming.

Eyp lay in the bottom of the boat and looked up at the sky. There were no stars out that night and the clouds even hid the moon. A few gentle specks of rain kissed his face as the oarsman began to row rhythmically.

It was not long before the rowing stopped and Eyp felt their small boat knock against something. Eyp saw Resvon's hard face above him and realised that the man was smiling.

'I hope you are ready to die, traitor. Your death will not be quick and painless as you no doubt are dreaming of, but prolonged and no doubt anticlimactic. We are just off Kykum's commercial port and we have stopped at a mooring post to which you will be *moored*. The tide is at her low point and is on her way in. You will watch as she creeps up your legs, over your torso and down your throat. But that in itself would be predictable and you would be able to prepare yourself for the end. So, to add to this, you will have the threat of sharks.'

Eyp suddenly felt a sharp pain searing up his left calf and Resvon held something in front of his face.

'This is a sea urchin. It comes from the waters around Myrth Isle. It has many spikes, as you can see. The urchin has less now, as many of its spikes are impaled in your leg. As your blood mixes with the juices within the spines, you will experience much pain and anguish. Tell me Eyp, do sharks prefer to hunt on cloudy nights?'

Eyp did not reply as he felt himself being lifted from the boat and watched as Resvon tied him to the mooring post. The pain in his left leg eased slightly as he was tied with the waves lapping about his knees. He smiled to himself, happy that he would be going to a watery grave; what better place was there for a sailor to die?

'You will not win, Resvon.'

'Oh, but I have.'

With that, Eyp heard the small boat push away and splash its way back to shore.

In the near total darkness, Eyp could see little but the water before him. The fear of a shark attacking him, that at first gripped his throat, began to fade. The pain in his leg rapidly intensified. His energy waned and he soon rested his head against the post. Eyp thought of his violent life as the waves rose higher. The rain strengthened and he shivered with cold as the water reached his nipples. The rain became heavier still, bringing with it a thick, unnatural fog. Eyp soon lost all sight as the droplets stung his eyes. He smiled to himself as, at the end, nature was denying Resvon his spectacle of the ex-Commander's death.

Eyp soon found the waves reaching his neck and his breathing quickened to frightful bursts. A wave splashed him full in the face and Eyp coughed and spluttered, knowing that his time was about to end. As the next wave hit his face, the ropes about his body suddenly loosened. Another wave hit him and he found himself floating in the now rolling seas. As the darkness of death began to take him, a hand reached under his arms and lifted him lightly out of the water and dropped him into the bottom of a boat.

Eyp rolled over, coughed up a lungful of sea water, and turned to his saviour. He looked at the hooded man and gave him a smile of gratitude. As Eyp clasped the man by the forearm and he realised that the hooded stranger had no right hand.

11

When Winter woke at dawn, he was surprised to find that there was no wind howling down the valley. He took the lack of wind as a sign that it was the right time to leave. He swiftly prepared his clothing, loaded himself and the goat with supplies, and left the hut behind.

All morning he followed the crevice of the valley northwards until the sun shone weakly down atop his head. In need of rest, they briefly paused by a trickling stream for a bite to eat, then continued to press further up the treeless valley. After this quick lunch, the incline steepened and Winter found his breath short and his head spinning.

He had long been cast into shadow by the towering peaks, when the climb plateaued out and before him lay a small tarn. With his head throbbing, Winter slumped down with his back against a cold rock and closed his eyes. Sleep took the weary man.

Much later, Winter woke with a start and found he was shivering with cold. Night had settled in and drifting down from above came the soft touch of snowflakes. The goat lay next to him and made noises similar to those of snoring. Winter took a mouthful of the water from the lake and lay down close to the goat for warmth. Sleep would not come immediately, so Winter gazed at the drifting snow and thought how Dusk would have loved to have seen the innocence of the flakes. With images of Dusk passing through his mind, he drifted off to sleep once more with a smile upon his face.

The next time Winter woke, a complete whiteness greeted his eyes. Everywhere he looked, he saw some shade of white: the ground before his feet was a pristine powdery white, similar to the slopes nearby. The sky showed a touch more grey and the water of the tarn was a hard white tinged by blue. Despite these variants, all was essentially white.

The goat shook off her layer of snow and after a quick breakfast of moss from a nearby rock, nudged Winter. It was only then that he realised their valley had come to an end. The only direction that they could take was around the tarn and up a frightfully steep slope.

At first, the climb turned out to be more of a scramble over shale; requiring both hands as well as feet. The thin layer of snow and ice on the mud-rock slope proved extremely slippery under Winter's weight, and he longed to have sturdy hooves like the goat. It was not long before Winter found his fingers aching with cold and cut in several places. He grimaced at how quickly his blood stained the pure snow and thought of Dusk once more. Unable to continue in this way, Winter used some of the bear's skin to fashion a pair of makeshift mittens to protect his hands. The hide worked well, but Winter missed the dexterity of his fingers and found that he slipped more often.

It was not long after this that Winter's head throbbed and knees ached. Yet he continued to climb after the agile goat. The snow soon began to turn to slush and finally Winter could see the top of the hill. As he neared the lip of his climb, a sense of dismay washed through his body: before him lay a span of no more than six feet before the slope continued up once more. Winter slumped on the flat ground and rested his limbs.

Winter's shoulders ached, his fingers throbbed, and his head was foggy with exhaustion. His clothes were also soddened from the snow melted by his warmth. He remained in a heap on the small ledge for the short time it took him to open his water skin and swallow two mouthfuls of ice-cold water. With his head still in a haze and his body shivering, Winter continued up the slope.

Instead of going before him, the goat now followed behind and gave Winter a gentle nudge here and there to keep him moving forward. The sun passed across the sky, yet Winter barely noticed the changing of the brightness.

Looking up, he could not see the hilltop, yet looking down, in all the whiteness, he could not see the tarn. He shivered and clung to the rock face. In this he found a little strength and continued to place one hand in front of the other, one leg higher than it had been, and slowly he made his way up the hill which had almost turned into a cliff.

The light continued to fade and Winter lost sight of his own hands. He groped around above his head for the next hand-hold, found it and hoisted himself up. This process continued slowly and painfully.

Winter eventually pulled himself over a gentle lip and onto flat ground once more. He lay there for a moment more and then reached his hand forward and dragged himself along the now horizontal ground. He continued doing this until the goat scampered around in front of him and blocked his path.

To Winter, this made no sense at all, for in his mind he was still climbing vertically. He clung to the ground as if it were a cliff-face and it wasn't until his hands cramped and he could hold on no longer that he resigned himself to a falling white death of cold bitterness. Then he let go, and despite remaining on flat ground, Winter felt himself fall. He tried to scream, but could not. He tried to flay his arms, but could not. He tried to prepare himself for an impact that would never come, but could not.

The goat moved to Winter's side and prodded him kindly with her foot. He jerked with fear, and he could not make sense of his world. For a moment he cried out in pain until he was taken, not by whiteness, but by blackness. And he felt warm and happy and he slept.

Winter's teeth chattered together and he could not still his shivering muscles. Wanting nothing more than to warm himself, he stood. The goat scampered to her feet and nudged Winter from behind. Turning, he saw her twist her body and expose her teats. Taking the hint, Winter got down on all fours and suckled like a kid. The taste was at once acidic and repulsive, but the warmth of the goat's milk was soothing and wonderful. *Where does she get her energy? She barely eats.* After drinking all he felt was wise, Winter stood once more and took in his surrounds.

The cliff that he had come up looked as steep as it had felt the evening before. The small flat area that he had slept on was thick with snow. It turned out to be more than just a bed as it was a path that ran beneath an even steeper cliff-face than the one he had climbed. His eyes followed it until it disappeared around a corner. In the grey morning light, Winter had no other choice but to follow this path.

He placed one leg in front of the other and felt as stiff as an arthritic elder. Clenching his jaw, he moved his other leg rigidly forward and felt the same stiffness. He moved his legs one after the other until he felt the stiffness ease slightly and warmth creep back into his muscles. Focusing now on the path before him, he rounded the corner.

Where he had slept, the level ground had been wide enough for him to lie across the path. As the track turned the corner, this rapidly became no wider that his foot was long. Winter maintained his balance by running a mitten covered hand along the cliff-face next to him. Every ten steps or so, the young man would slip on a snow-covered rock and find himself within inches of an unbalanced drop into whiteness. This constant fear of death kept his heart pumping fast and warm blood passing through his legs. In this manner, he whiled away the greyness of morning and was greeted with a mid-morning blue sky. The sun had not yet breached the mountains to the east, yet Winter was happy that it was not snowing.

As the morning passed into noon, the sun peaked over the crest of a mountain, the height of which Winter could not possibly guess, and shone down upon him. With the coming of the sun came a new danger: the snow beneath Winter's ever ascending feet glistened and sparkled. And while he was too high for the snow to melt in the weak sun, the brightness that existed in every direction, almost blinded him. He had to squint until his eyes were like slits cut with a sharp knife, and still the brightness pained him.

Shortly after the sun reached her zenith, Winter rested his legs and went to drink some of his water, only to find that his water-skin was frozen solid. Smiling resignedly to himself, he glanced at the goat. With little space to manoeuvre, Winter drank from the goat once more and ate a small portion of the supplies that he had brought sharing a small portion with the goat. After his fill, he continued along the path.

The track continued to hug the cliff, but became significantly steeper. Now and then, Winter was forced to scramble on all fours in an effort to continue forward and not slip off the side. By mid-afternoon his whole body ached, his head most of all, and he vomited up the scant contents of his stomach. His head soon began to spin and he could not tell which was way was forwards or backwards.

Winter lay down on the skinny track and shook, not with the cold, but with fear. With his head as dizzy as it was, he dared not continue on, yet without moving forward, he knew he was sure to freeze to death. Close to despair, Winter closed his eyes and wept icy tears.

The sun passed behind a mountain and he was once more cast into shadow. The change in light through his closed lids focused his mind and sharpened his senses. He opened his eyes, rolled on to his side and dry retched over the side of the cliff. Winter's head cleared somewhat, and he staggered to his feet.

He followed the path beneath a rock jutting from the cliff above. As Winter came out from under the rock, he saw a changed landscape before him. The valley to his left climbed steeply out of the depths below to a saddle between his mountain and another only five-hundred feet distant. The saddle was a touch above Winter's height and the path led straight towards it and over it.

Winter pressed on and, as he reached the midpoint of the narrow saddle, he looked to his right and away from the way that he had come. A vicious wind whipped up behind him and threatened to topple him forward. But Winter noticed this little as the view he beheld stole his breath.

Galloping away from him in leaps and bounds, a hilly cliff descended. Some two-thousand feet below him, the ground plateaued out to a green oasis of life. Fir trees grew tall and birds flew aplenty. Halfway up the right cliff of the valley, a waterfall sprang from nowhere and fell into a rocky pool below. As the wind caught the fall, spray filtered through the nearby trees hiding the ground from Winter's sight. The wind lulled, and Winter could once more see the waterfall's base with its hue of deep azure. He followed this with his eyes until he lost it amongst the trees. Movement caught his attention and, straining his sight, Winter saw three large stags trot to the water's edge, dip their heads and drink.

An odd feeling grew in Winter and he longed to be down in that haven of warmth, away from the bitterness of the mountains. He gazed at the border of the valley and saw peaks surpassing his imagination enclosed it on all sides. Indeed, the saddle on which he stood was the lowest point of the bountiful valley. Seeing that there was no way down without a grisly end, Winter grudgingly dragged his eyes back to the path of ice and snow and plodded forward once more.

After he crossed the saddle, his path led him into a steep climb with a valley falling away to his left. The wind continued up the valley and, before Winter knew what was coming, found that a thick band of clouds had closed in below him. Pausing at a bend in the path, he sat down and rested.

With nothing else to do, Winter counted his woes. His head throbbed like thunder and spun like a top. His neck and back were stiff and sore. Overused, his shoulders and arms ached and his cut fingers were sweaty in their mittens and yet ice cold. Winter's entire legs screamed out in pain and his knees felt as creaky as an old door hinge. The only part that didn't hurt were his feet; they were numb and felt like useless blocks of wood. And his face; oh, how that stung with the cold. His lips were cracked from side to side and his nose dripped incessantly. As he sat there, he wondered if it would be better to throw himself from the path and into the beautiful valley many miles below. *What's the point of continuing up this deathly path? I've lost Dusk, and everything else. What's the point?*

As if reading his mind, the goat bleated loudly and vigorously nudged him.

'I suppose I still have you, don't I?' She *baaahhhed* in response.

'Very well. Let's continue this little journey of ours until I fall down exhausted and can rest in peace.' With that, Winter stood and continued on his way.

While light remained, Winter climbed his frozen path that led to nowhere that he knew. When the light faded, he found the best little nook that he could and used the goat as his shelter. As he lay drifting off to sleep, he realised she had really not eaten in days and yet did not appear to be failing in strength. *Father's magic is in her.*

Winter's dreams were troubled with the goat featuring throughout. At first, she told him he had only travelled into the foothills of the Moaks and that many miles of up and down lay before him. He was then feeding from her, but her milk was red and tasted like metal. The dream then changed and she was suckling *his* nipples. He woke from his dreams to a cloud covered sky, rolled over and drifted back to sleep protecting his nipples with his mitted hands.

The next morning, he woke to a grey dawn and scrambled onto all fours. After a quick feed of the sour milk, he stood and stumbled forward. Three steps he managed before tumbling flat onto his face. He stood once more and this time made it seven steps before falling over. Winter shivered and shook, exhausted. He resigned himself to crawling along on all fours. After a short while of this, Winter found his knees bloody and stinging and his arms unable to hold his weight.

Winter stood fully one last time, stumbled fifteen steps, then fell down once more, rolled onto his back, and did not get up.

The goat came and nudged him, yet he remained motionless. She nuzzled him and bit his cheek, yet still he did not move. Cold death crept into his face, so she stretched out on top of him and bleated feebly. And, as the snow began to fall, Winter lay still.

12

Kathsum stood in her courtyard with her eyes closed. She breathed in deeply and found the familiar early summer smell of sweet, sweet jasmine. The scent entangled its tendrils around her mind and dragged her through happy memories of long past years.

She opened her eyes, smiling and, in the fading light, looked at the jasmine vine as it interwove through the lattice arch that led from the courtyard to her back terrace. She looked closer and saw the jasmine was outdoing itself, sneaking its way towards her beloved wisteria vine. In the jasmine's defence, the wisteria was not helping matters by making its own sly way towards the jasmine.

A distant flash of lightning out of the corner of Kathsum's eye dragged her attention away from her sneaking vines. As she had done since she was a child, Kathsum counted under her breath and listened keenly for the approaching thunder. Her mind wandered when she got to fifty and she lost count.

She thought about the night that awaited her. A trickle of sweat rolled down her back and her arms did an involuntary twitch. Her stomach turned with nerves as she heard footsteps approaching. Guflinkov entered the courtyard and Kathsum's stomach stopped its summersaults;

she always felt more relaxed in the old man's presence.

'Guflinkov, my old friend, it is good to see you this evening.'

'Is it Kath?' The High Chancellor had never been able to stop Guflinkov shortening her name to Kath. 'Well, that is nice to hear. Although I don't think much of this weather; this sticky heat makes everyone stink like a sty, and when those thunder clouds arrive, I'm sure they'll keep me awake most of the night.'

Kathsum found Guflinkov's pessimism to only be half-hearted, and she couldn't stop herself from smiling. 'But then you will take a long drink from your skin and you'll be asleep in no time.'

'You know me well, Kath.'

'I'm sure that you know me better still. Would you like a drink? I have opened my best bottle of wine, made by the Monks of the Day and Night Gods.'

'I'm sorry Kath, you know my rule.'

'I thought you trusted me.'

'I do, but you did not make the wine and I doubt you opened the bottles yourself.'

'That I did not. Very well, I will quench my thirst with *Dawn's Light*.' She poured the golden liquid into her cup.

'Good. And as you do, perhaps you can tell me why you are so nervous? It is unlike you.'

Kathsum avoided the gaze of the old man. 'But how could you know that?'

'Kathsum, Kathsum. You forget I was your history teacher in your youth. Your nervous tells are the same now as they were when I was grilling you on the names of past leaders.'

Kathsum smiled as she remembered back to long days trapped in Guflinkov's musty study with the only possibility of escape being her remembering random names, dates and events.

Guflinkov pointed at her neck. 'You fondle the centre stone on your necklace with your left, non-dominant hand; although it was a different necklace back then. You also shuffle your feet, whether sitting or standing, and your eyelids twitch slightly. And, although I cannot see it from this angle, sweat beads behind your right ear. Not your left, just your right.'

Without thinking, Kathsum felt behind both ears and found her right one to be moist with sweat. She shook her head in amazement and poured herself some wine from one of the bottles sitting open on the table in the courtyard.

'Very well, Guflinkov, you win. I am nervous in anticipation of tonight's meeting. I have called the High Council here tonight to inform them of my closest kept secret. I will not speak of it in the open air, but I'm sure you know of which secret I speak.'

Guflinkov nodded in acknowledgement. 'You don't know how the Council members will react to your news. You are concerned that although you have been High Chancellor for five years, they will not agree to your commands.'

Guflinkov rubbed his chin. 'You have been planning and hoping against all hope for this moment all of your life. Yet, you still have so far to go. And, to get where you want to, you must first cross a frozen lake where the layer of ice is very thin indeed. One false step and you will fall through the ice. You have every right to be nervous!'

The High Chancellor stared into the distant storm with glazed eyes.

'You have to trust yourself, Kath. Listen to your senses; trust your instincts. You are an excellent leader and I trust you to handle this situation as delicately as you would a young seedling.'

'Guflinkov, you always know what to say to calm me. I thank you. But I did not ask you here for reassurance; I asked you here to act as a spy.'

Guflinkov grinned mischievously.

'When the council members arrive, I will greet them here before taking them inside to inform them of my secret. I will do this in the gallery off to the right.

For your spying, I ask that you go upstairs to the room above the gallery. There, near the centre of the room, you will find a knot in the floorboards the size of your thumb. Next to this, I have left a fishing hook that can be used to extract the knot. From your vantage point, you will have a view of most of the room.

'While you will not be able to hear most of what is being said, you will be able to see every person. You know these people and you are cunning and wise. You will be able to read them as if they were talking directly to you.'

Kathsum turned to face Guflinkov. 'Will you spy for me?'

The old man stepped forward. 'I will. I may even enjoy it. Is there any chance that they will see me?'

Kathsum noted an excited twinkle in Guflinkov's eyes. 'Highly unlikely; if you have no flames lit in your room, then the roof downstairs will be cast into shadow by the beams. I have positioned my lamps to ensure that this is the case. The attention of the council members will also be directed at me.'

'Very good. When are your guests due to arrive?'

'Shortly. In fact, you had best make your way upstairs now, so as not to be seen.'

Guflinkov bowed his head to Kathsum and hobbled his way in to the house. As Kathsum watched him go, she could not help but wonder how long the old man had left to live. She did not know his age, but as each day passed, he looked that bit frailer. This saddened her; Guflinkov had been a constant her whole life. He had been like a second father to her, or perhaps, rather, a close uncle; stern when he needed to be and yet always loving, even if he was a bit aloof. She respected the old man and loved him deeply. Raising her pewter goblet, she drank to his health. She put her cup down and just as her nerves began to return, she heard another set of footsteps approaching.

Before she saw him, Kathsum knew the footsteps belonged to The Admiral; the gait from his limp was unmistakable.

'Fair evening to you, High Chancellor.' The Admiral's strong voice, followed by his appearance, confirmed Kathsum's guess.

'Fair evening to you, Admiral.'

The Admiral bowed his head.

Kathsum began to feel an uneasy silence develop between them and repressed a shudder. 'Would you like some wine, Admiral? I have just tasted this lively *Dawn's Light*; it is very refreshing.'

'Yes, thank you.'

They stood there, sipping their wine and sizing each other up through narrowed eyes. Kathsum could feel the silence deepen once more. Eager to start the night well, she searched her mind for a topic of conversation that would show the Admiral that she was interested in his life. After discarding a few, she found one that she thought hit the mark.

'Have you had word from Headly regarding your nephew's healing?'

When the Admiral replied, he spoke softly and Kathsum needed to step closer to hear what he was saying. A flicker of a wry smile crossed her mind as she realised that the cunning Old Sea Dog had just asserted his power over the conversation.

'He is healing slowly, but he's is on the right track. The Healers report he will be ready for collection in a week's time. I plan to send one of my Ship Masters to collect him.'

Kathsum noted he did not seek her approval in this odd decision, but rather appeared to be daring her to challenge his authority over his sailors.

'I do not blame you for wanting to send one of your best sailors. You love your nephew very much and I understand that you do not want to trust his life with a less skilled man.' Kathsum was clever; she knew that she now had the power back. 'Indeed, it is good that he is not on the water tonight: the storm that approaches appears to be a ferocious one.'

'That is true.' The Admiral cocked his head. 'But tell me, do you not find this house to be a little too roomy; living here all by yourself?'

Kathsum noted the jibe at her choice not to take a husband, despite the many suitors.

'On the contrary, I find the space refreshing. And besides, I have my servants about to ensure I'm not alone.' Kathsum knew the Admiral would disapprove of this last statement; he viewed his servants as slaves, rather than as company. 'In truth, Admiral, I spend very little time here at all; due to my many responsibilities as High Chancellor.'

After this little joust with the Admiral, Kathsum found her nerves had been replaced by excitement. She felt her stare regain its familiar piercing nature and she straightened her already wide shoulders to assert her physical presence.

'I believe, Admiral, that the remainder of our council has arrived.'

Five men and one woman came into the flickering light of the courtyard torches. The General came first with his orange moustache upon a stern looking face. He was followed by the Head of Order, who was a plain-looking man of medium build with no distinguishing features. Shortly thereafter, chatting together, came two Aldermen and one Alderwoman. These represented the merchants, the producers, and the farmers. Last of all came the Chief Quaestor, who was a weasel of a man responsible for the purse strings of Roasline.

'Welcome to my home. Please, help yourself to some wine.'

As the men filed past Kathsum to the wine table, she heard the General utter his dissatisfaction at having to pour his own wine.

'General, I am sorry that my servants are not here to pour the wine out of the bottle and into your goblet, but I sent them away this evening so that no one but the Council members could hear what I have to say. I'm sure that you will cope just fine pouring your own wine.' The General huffed as he poured himself a full beaker of a rich red wine.

Kathsum left the Admiral and made her way over to where the three Alderm were standing. Aside from herself, these were the only three members of the council that were elected to their positions, albeit by a subset of the population.

'Fair evening to you all.'

'Fair evening to you, High Chancellor.' The Alderman of the Merchants spoke for all three. He was a man of medium height with greying black hair. As he spoke to Kathsum, she noticed he rested his left hand on his gut while swirling his wine in his right.

'We were just discussing the new tax proposed by the Quaestor on beer and wine. We all agree that the farmers will be worse off as people will buy less drink, the brewers will need to reduce production and the merchants will have less stock to trade. It appears to us that the only beneficiary of the new tax will be the balance book of the Quaestor.'

The other Aldermen nodded in agreement. 'What do you think, Chancellor?'

A flash of lightning caught Kathsum's attention. *One, two, three, four, five, six, sev*—BOOM! Thunder shook the sky above them.

Kathsum snapped her mind back to those before her. 'While it will be hard on many, the benefit will depend on how we choose to spend the revenue raised. But alas, now is not the time for discussions of this sort; I fear the rain will soon be upon us.'

Kathsum raised her voice to address everyone present. 'The storm draws nigh. Fill your goblets and follow me into the shelter of my gallery. There, we may discuss why I have invited you all here tonight.'

Kathsum filled her own cup from a jug of spring water and then led the council members into her house.

The room she had chosen had been cleared of excess furniture to accommodate the eight people. A mantle ran along one wall with an empty fireplace in the centre. Mounted on the wall above the fireplace were two antique swords in a crossed formation. Kathsum chose this as her backing as she thought it would invoke an image of strength.

Each of the council members filed into the room and positioned themselves before her. It did not surprise the High Chancellor to see the General stand directly in front of her. She also noticed the Admiral stood the closest to the door, while the Quaestor stood in the darkest corner.

'Gentlemen and gentlewoman, I have asked you all here tonight to inform you I have been meeting Resvon, the Leader of the Outcasts, in private.'

An angry shout of protest burst from the Chief of Order and the General threw his full goblet to the carpeted floor in a fit of rage.

Kathsum raised her voice and spoke over the furore. 'With Resvon, I have reached an agreement of peace!'

Silence filled the room.

'Gentlemen, this bloody war that has raged on for too many years is the closest that it has ever been to ending!'

The General stepped forward and cut over Kathsum. 'You stupid, naïve woman!'

The High Chancellor cut him off before he could go any further. 'Shut your mouth, General! If you speak to me that way again, I'll have you thrown in the dungeons!' Kathsum glared daggers at the General; daring him to step across the line. The General's face contorted into a hideous snarl. The building tension was broken by the thin voice of the Quaestor. 'Please, High Chancellor, tell us more of your dealings with Resvon.'

Kathsum proceeded to tell the six men and one woman all that had transpired in the last three months. Once her story was complete, she looked to the future.

'I know that the peace deal is a shaky prospect and attempts have already been made to keep this war going, but I am trusting each of you to get behind me on this.'

'I do not like that you have kept your plans secret from us until now, Kathsum, but the prospect of peace is a juicy one.' Kathsum was pleased to see the Alderman of the Farmers stand by her.

The Admiral cleared his throat to get everyone's attention. 'How do you know it is not just a rouse to get us to lower our defences and welcome the enemy with open arms, only to be stabbed in the gut as our reward?'

'Hear, hear,' grumbled the General.

'I cannot. And while I believe Resvon is genuine in his intentions, I am not stupid.' At this comment, she glared at the General for a moment. 'That is why I am putting provisions in place. Admiral, I want you to gather the majority of your fleet. I want them to be filled with supplies and troops and taken to the shores south of Myrth Isle.

'General, you will command half of your troops to be sent with the fleet and almost all of the remainder sent east up the Liagar River.

'I want multiple fast horses waiting at several points throughout the city ready to send messages if needed.

'Aldermen, please assist in arranging supplies for both the fleet and the army. Quaestor, I want our gold and gem reserves moved to Headly. I have arranged for a Healer to collect this at the next full moon. I want you to go with it and watch over it.

'Chief, your task will be to ensure that order is kept in Roasline. There will no doubt be fights aplenty when those from across the river first arrive.

'Does everybody understand their roles?'

Kathsum looked at each man and woman with her piercing stare until she elicited a nod from everyone.

'Good. This will remain a secret between us until the treaty is signed with the Outcasts. If word of this gets out, then it would have come from one of you. So, keep your tongues checked. We all have work to do, so I will ask you all to waste no time in going about it.' Kathsum raised her goblet. 'To peace!' and she drained her cup.

The men were hesitant to leave so abruptly, but Kathsum would allow them to stay no longer: she remained in charge.

As she watched the last of the men leave her house, she relaxed her shoulders and went in search of more wine. Back in the courtyard, she found Guflinkov waiting.

'Well Kath, the storm has passed, the ground is wet and what remains of your last bottle of *Dawn's Light* is ruined.'

Kathsum couldn't help but feeling unreasonably sad at the loss of her open bottles of expensive wine.

'I will just have to go without.' She felt a great tiredness wash over her body. 'Guflinkov, tell me how you fared from your vantage point. What did you see?'

'For the most part, predictable and uninteresting behaviour.'

'How so?'

'The Aldermen were generally excited by the prospect of peace and will back you unquestioningly. The General was displeased but will easily be subdued if given tasks that allow him to exercise his power over others. The Quaestor was difficult to see in the shadows, but was already counting the profits from a new tax that could be reaped with the newcomers. As I say, these reactions were predictable; I could have told you of these if I were blind. There was, however, one interesting reaction: The Admiral's. I expected this stubborn man to react somewhat as the General did, yet he did not. It took me a little while to understand his body language as it seemed at odds with his character, but I got there in the end'

Kathsum found herself getting terse with the old man. 'Guflinkov, I am exhausted and I have a lot of work to do. Please get to the point.'

'As you wish, High Chancellor. The Admiral knew you had been meeting Resvon and that you have been working on a peace deal together.'

This revelation struck Kathsum like a cold wind.

Guflinkov continued regardless. 'He is yet undecided as to if he will support you. I think that if he were twenty years younger, he would fight you on this and challenge your leadership. But as we age, we desire a more peaceful life and less of a warring one. I believe he will come out on your side in the end.'

Kathsum rubbed her brow thoughtfully before responding. 'Thank you, Guflinkov. You have been of great service to me. If it is all right with you, I will leave it there for tonight. Come and find me tomorrow morning after you have broken your fast and we will talk more about this. I need some time to process.'

'As you wish.'

Kathsum remained where she was and Guflinkov left her courtyard. The High Chancellor absentmindedly poured herself a cup of wine and it wasn't until she swallowed a mouthful that she realised that it was half rainwater.

Another wave of tiredness swept through her limbs as her mind slowly began to work through the evening. When she got to Guflinkov's revelation her heart sank with disappointment.

Had the Admiral been spying on me? Does he not trust me? I thought I had earned his trust a long time ago. I know we don't like each other, but I thought that we still trusted each other.

Her mind then turned from disappointment to fear.

If the Admiral has been spying on me, what was his purpose? Is he looking to overthrow me? And if so, who else is in league with him? Can I trust anyone anymore?

This last thought brought with it a sense of loneliness. She wished she had not sent Guflinkov away or that her servants were still about. To rid herself of this feeling, she sat down, closed her eyes and breathed deeply through her nose. The sweet smell of bruised jasmine greeted her once more and a happy melancholy feeling passed through her body. She remained in her courtyard for a good while more, relishing the raw sensation.

13

The first sensation that Winter was aware of was pain; a hard, throbbing pain pounding deep within his head. Following this, Winter could feel. He could *feel* a thick woollen blanket draped over his naked length, and he could feel that he was lying on his back. He tried to open his eyes, but he could not. Instead, he breathed deeply through his nostrils. A faint hint of smoke mixed with a spicy smell that he did not recognise greeted his senses. Winter listened with his ears and heard the soft crackle of a mature fire. Stretching his ears further, he heard the faint sound of people talking and birds chirping outside. He tried to open his eyes once more. This time, he was successful.

Winter was lying in the centre of a small, dark room. He could not tell if there were any windows, but he immediately noticed that he was surrounded by twenty or more lit candles. In the corner was a small fire smouldering and was the only other source of light for the room. As he sat up shakily, a shadowy figure rose from a chair and firmly pushed him back into the lying position.

The young man was wearing a black robe and had a shaved head. Winter could just make out a marking on his forehead in the shape of a crescent moon. The man spoke slowly and calmly, and his voice rose and fell in a melodic fashion.

'You are safe, my son. The danger has passed and you are in a place of peace and healing. You may relax.'

Winter struggled with his voice and croakily managed to ask: 'Where am I?'

'The village is called Ocrill, but more than that, I will not say. I will, however, tell you how you got here. After that, you must rest some more.'

Winter felt a momentary flash of anger at being told what to do, but pushed this aside and nodded in submission.

'Myself and four others were traveling in the Moaks, returning from a pilgrimage, when we happened across your unconscious body. We dusted the snow from you but you would not rouse. We carried you for many miles and many days; over mountains, down valleys, through tunnels and across rivers. While we walked, we chanted prayers for your and our survival.

'Once we arrived home, we lay you where you now lie and prayed day and night for you to wake. We fed you nourishing drinks in your moments of half-waking, but food you would not take. For eleven days we have done so and as each day passed, the mountain sickness was lifted little by little from your body by the Gods. And now you are there and I am here and we are together.'

Winter's mind swam with confusion. 'I don't understand. What is a god?'

The monk chuckled to himself and brought forth a bowl of liquid. 'This is a mixture of honey, lemon juice and a spirit we make from barley. It will help cleanse your body from the mountain sickness.'

Winter had little choice as the bowl was pressed to his mouth and the monk poured the warm concoction down his throat. Heat spread to all of Winter's limbs and he felt himself fall once more into a deep sleep.

When Winter woke the next time, he felt his forehead was wet. A monk leaned over him and wiped it with a cool cloth. The pain in his head had gone, but he felt damp and cold all over with sweat.

'You are safe, my Son.'

The new monk at Winter's side was older than the last and robed in pristine white. Winter looked into his eyes and saw kindness there. He tried to relax himself and let the monk mop his forehead once more.

'Since last waking, you have slept for two and a half days. Over the last two, a fever of evil spirit has entered your body. The spice of the cinnamon candles is helping to drive it away. With the help of the Gods it will have left your body by tomorrow's sunrise.'

Winter looked at the monk's wrinkled face and saw a marking on his forehead similar and yet different to that of the last monk; instead of a moon there was the shape of a full sun.

'Where am I?'

'You are in a room that many have lived in and many have died in. The room is part of a building that can house a score of sick or injured people. As there is no one else needing this type of care at the moment, you have been fortunate enough to be put in one of two smaller single rooms.' After a short pause, the monk continued. 'This building is one of many that we use to honour the Gods. It is positioned just below the summer snow line on the north side of the Moaks and not far from our main temple.'

Winter thought hard about this. His mind was sluggish and he still shook with fever. 'Did you just say that we are on the north side of the Moaks?'

'That is what I said. Now you are in need of rest, for your body must expel the fever from within.'

Winter only half heard what the monk had said. The monk had spoken the word *God* again and Winter had never heard this term before.

'What does *God* mean?'

The white monk chuckled to himself while he brought the bowl of warm liquid to Winter's lips.

'This is the same draught that you drank before, only with the addition of the cinnamon spice.

Drink it and rest, my Son.'

As Winter was forced to drink once more, he felt the chill lift a little.

'Why won't you answer my question?'

'Ssshhh, you must rest now. All answers will come in time.'

Two more days passed before Winter woke again. This time he felt completely different from when he had previously woken. His fever had abated and for the first time he felt energy throughout his body. He sat up swiftly and found the candles around him had burnt low and the embers of the fire had all but gone out. As he looked about the room, he saw no windows. In the half-light he could just make out a monk sitting in the corner on the packed dirt floor. This monk was robed in white cloth and sat with his legs crossed and eyes closed.

Winter moved to the edge of the straw mattress and stood up. As he did, he realised he was completely naked. Without opening his eyes, the monk spoke. 'There is a robe by the fire.'

Winter tentatively stepped around the low bed to the fire and found a black robe folded neatly on the floor. He gently bent down and gathered the robe up. The wool felt coarse to the touch, but he slid it over his head regardless. After tying the provided rope around his waist as a belt, he looked up to see the monk standing before him waiting.

Without a word, the monk turned and led Winter out of the room. They passed into a large rectangle room with many straw mattresses on the floor by the two longest walls. This room did not have windows either, but had a large empty fireplace. The monk led Winter down the centre of the room and out into the brilliant sunshine.

Winter blinked furiously in the brightness as his eyes slowly adjusted to the light. The monk ignored Winter's discomfort and continued walking. Winter followed half blind. In addition to the pain in his eyes, Winter winced as he felt sharp little stones under his bare feet. He tried to walk as lightly as he could, but found this difficult.

The two men followed a well-worn path that sloped down and away from the building that he had recovered in. Winter walked between densely growing pine trees that stretched up to the heavens above with lush green branches. After walking along the path for a short while, the trees thinned out and a clearing appeared ahead.

Instead of continuing downhill to the clearing, the monk turned left off the path and led Winter through the trees. Winter filled his lungs with the refreshing smell of the pine trees and felt strengthened. After a short distance, Winter heard the unmistakable bubble of a stream. It was not much further before they found themselves at the water's edge.

The mountain stream was but ten yards wide and no more than three feet deep at the centre point. The water was crystal clear and Winter could see many small fish battling the downward current.

'Drink, my Son.'

Winter stepped into the shallows with his bare feet and almost leapt out again as the icy water engulfed his calves.

'It comes straight from the Moaks and will bring you strength and vitality.' Winter ignored his cold feet and drank deeply. The cold water ran playfully down his throat and Winter felt a coolness permeate through his limbs.

Upon returning to the bank, Winter found the monk sitting on the soft earth with his legs crossed so each foot sat upon the opposite knee. Winter attempted to do likewise, but found that his inflexible joints prevented this. Instead, he sat on a nearby rock and gazed into the clear river.

As Winter sat there in silence, a myriad of questions popped into his mind. Uncertain which to ask first, he began with what he thought was the simplest.

'Who are you?'

'You may call me Zin. I am a monk of the order who worships the God of Day.'

'My name is Winter.' After pausing for a moment, he continued. 'Several times now I have heard the word *God*. What does it mean?'

'You ask a difficult question Winter, and the answer is not simple. But I will try to explain a little. There are two Gods: The God of Day and the God of Night. Between them, they control all that occurs. Together they made the land, the mountains, the animals, the sky and the people. The God of Day brings life to all. He has granted the earth light and warmth by making his son watch over us. His son, or *the* sun, gives warmth, makes plants grow and allows us to see. Without him, all would be in darkness.

'The God of Night, on the other hand, allows everyone and everything a time to rest. Even the sun. The God of Night sends his daughter to watch down upon us as we rest. However, she is mischievous and disappears every few weeks. But she always returns, shortly after.

'The Gods of Day and Night work together and complement each other. They created everything and so can take everything away. They are watching all and are always present.'

At this burst of information, Winter was dumbfounded. He had never considered how the world had been created or what had created it; he merely thought that it had always been. As he processed this knowledge, it all seemed to make sense to him. He had always wanted there to be something more powerful than man, and here was the perfect answer.

'When did they create the earth?'

'We do not know. The monks of Day and Night have been worshiping in this place for over a thousand years, so sometime before that. Most of us believe the Gods created the earth many thousands of thousands of years ago. But there is no record of this.'

Winter was intrigued by this talk. 'How did they create it all?'

'They are Gods. It is not our place to understand their methods.'

'How many... *monks*... if that's what you called yourself... are there?'

'Yes, we are monks. We serve the Gods and devote our lives to their worship. How many? In this small township, there are a few hundred. And there are many smaller villages dotted around this valley and the northern foothills of the Moaks. Each village serves a different purpose; some grow apples and make cider, some keep livestock for meat, some further downhill on the flatter ground grow crops of wheat and barley, and there are others that produce other foods and goods. This town takes care of the sick, has many beehives to make honey and has the main temple of our order.'

Finding Zin to be free with his answers, Winter pressed with more questions. 'Do you have a leader?'

'We have two, a monk of the Day God and a monk of the Night God. These two oversee this town and all the worshipping villages. Each village has their own two leaders who manage the everyday running of the people. Solar and Lunar, as our leaders are called, are responsible chiefly for the spiritual wellbeing of their people.'

'You seem well organised, and in all honesty, I am a bit surprised you are so willing to share your knowledge so freely with an outsider.'

'We are a peaceful people. We have no reason not to trust you. The Gods will protect us against any mischief that you may cause.' With a sidewards smile, Zin went on. 'We have also saved your life, so you should find it difficult to go against us.'

Winter was astonished at the trust placed in him. 'But if I was wicked, I would have no hesitation in abusing that trust.'

'That may have been the case, yet we do not detect any evil spirits within you. And we do not trust you wholly. The weapons we found on you have been removed and we have made a sacrifice to the God of Day to protect us against you.'

'A sacrifice? What kind of sacrifice?'

'The goat you came with was full of evil spirits. She followed you here and, on your arrival, we offered the blood of her neck to the God of Day. He was pleased and gave us several days of glorious sunshine in return. We took the flesh of the goat as payment for the care that we have given you. It was tough, but full of flavour.'

Winter was taken aback. The goat had saved his life on several occasions and he had grown to like her. 'But… she was my friend. She helped me to survive; she wasn't evil.' Winter felt sadness enter his weakend body.

'I see that this does not please you, Winter. Come; let us return to your room. There we shall find some food, and you can rest some more.'

'You're right, this does not please me.' Winter stood despite his feelings. *With the death of Dusk, the goat was the closest thing I had to family. She even had the essence of my father in her.*

The monk led the way back to Winter's quarters. As Winter entered the building once more, he found the air to be stuffy and close. He desired to return to the fresh air with the smell of the pines, but his stomach said that he needed food.

Waiting on Winter's straw mattress was a wedge of dense bread and a jug of fresh water. To go with the bread was a small plate of oozing honeycomb. The two men shared this small meal in silence. The bread was fresh with a grainy flavour and the honeycomb was blissfully sweet. Once the honey was all gone, Winter chewed on the wax thinking about his poor goat.

Once the bread was finished, Zin spoke. 'You will rest now. You may continue to wear your robe or sleep under the rug naked.'

Winter's body was tired but his mind raced with the new ideas that Zin had imbedded in him and the sadness of losing his four-legged friend. Winter spat the wax into the fire and lay down on the bed in the black robe still on. The monk left the room for a moment and then returned with a bowl of the spiced liquor. 'Drink'

Winter drank and found his mind began to slow. Before he knew what was happening, he fell asleep once more.

When Winter next woke, he found the room much the same. New candles had been lit and as these burned, they smelt sweet like the honeycomb. The fire had all but gone out, yet Winter did not feel cold. Zin had gone and, in his place, sat a young monk dressed in a black robe; the style of which was the same as the one that Winter himself was wearing.

As Winter sat up, the monk's eyes opened and Winter realised that he was a *she*.

'You are the first girl monk I've seen.'

'The Gods do not discriminate on whether we are male or female. They made us all and so we may all worship equally. My name is Sister Sor and I'm a monk of the God of Night. I have been told that your name is Winter and I'm glad to see that you are healing; the Gods have been merciful to you.'

'I feel confined in here Sor, can we go outside?'

'We may. You will find it to be night time outside and while it is summer, there is a cool breeze gently blowing from the ever snowy Moaks.'

Sor led Winter from the room and he noticed that, like him, she wore no shoes.

The night was dark; the moon was hiding behind the Moaks and the trees blocked out the stars. To prevent him from stumbling, Sor held on to Winter's hand as they walked through the wood. To Winter, her hand reminded him of Dusk's: callused from hard work. Winter thought sadly of his sister as they made their way to the place where he had sat with Zin by the stream.

Together they rested in silence for a while as Winter let the breeze play across his unshaven face. The sound of the stream chattered away, soothing his mind and allowing him to stop thinking about Dusk.

'So far, I have met four monks. Two have worn white and two have worn black. What do the different colours mean?'

'That is very observant of you, my Son. Did you also notice that those with black robes had a tattoo of a crescent moon on their foreheads while those in white had a blazing sun?'

'Now that you mention it, yes.'

'Those robed in black, as I am, worship the God of Night, whereas those in white, the God of Day.'

'How do you choose which God you worship?' Winter watched Sor as she talked.

'*You* do not choose; the Gods do. When we are born, we get a temporary mark on our forehead of either the moon or the sun. The symbol we get depends on if we are born during the day or the night. When we come of age and have proven our devotion to our God, the branding becomes permanent. From this point onwards, we perform our duties in the respective day or night and sleep in the other.'

'So, you were born at night?' Winter asked.

'That is correct. During the night I work as a Healer, tend to the beehives and pray. During the day, I sleep. For the periods of dawn and dusk, both Day and Night monks eat together, pray together and then go our separate ways.

'There are a select few who are an exception to the day-night ruling: those born at dawn or dusk. Those born at dawn will have the marking of a moon followed by a sun and those born at dusk will have a sun and then a moon. The dawn people are awake from midnight to midday and those of dusk from midday to midnight. These few people wear black and white robes depending on if it is night or day. Does that all make sense?'

'Yes, I think so.' Winter thought for a moment. 'Why am I robed in black?'

'You first awoke amongst us at night and were hence *born* to us at night.' After a short pause, Sor continued. 'Do not fear, you have not been branded and your fate has yet to be decided by Lunar and Solar.'

Winter did not like the idea of someone else controlling his fate, but said nothing of these thoughts. Instead, he thought of his life growing up with his four siblings and his father as Emperor and how different it would have been if he had been born here. This led him to wonder how the Gods communicate their wishes to the monks.

'Do these Gods talk to you?' Winter asked.

'Not as you and I are doing now. But the monks meditate every day and as we move deep within ourselves, we sometimes discover the Gods have hidden hints in our being on how they want us to live.'

Winter crossed his arms while he mulled this over before asking his next question. 'Do you ever doubt that there are Gods?'

Sor smiled ruefully. 'Some of the young doubt. Those that do are encouraged to discuss their doubts with the more senior monks openly. After working through these concerns, very few doubt again.'

'The idea that there are Gods is so very interesting to me; I have so many more questions.'

'You may ask one more, for the night is soon to be dawn and you must rest.'

Winter thought hard before coming up with the question that stuck in his mind the most. 'If the Gods created the land and rule it, do they control all that goes on?'

'Your questions intrigue me. They signify you are mature beyond your apparent years. The answer to your question is both yes and no. The Gods control the weather, the seasons and the big changes that occur. They do not concern themselves with individuals and the daily tribulations of people's lives.'

Sor gestured to the Moaks. 'An example of this may be that the Gods may cause an avalanche in the mountains or they might make a town prosper by granting a fine season for crop growth, but they would not be concerned about a single person's angst at why a woman doesn't love a man who desires her. It takes many devout worshippers to please the Gods and have them grant us a pleasant life.' Sor stood. 'Now you must go to bed. Tomorrow at dawn you will be brought before Lunar and Solar and your fate will be decided.'

Sor led Winter back to his room with his mind racing with all that he had learnt. As he dozed off to sleep, after more of the draught, he realised that had not even had a chance to think about what may befall him at dawn.

Winter was shaken awake from his half-sleep. His room was as dark as always and he could just make out the bald head of Sor. He realised that Sor was the first young woman he had seen close up with no hair on her head. In his dreamy state, he looked over her face and found her to be not unattractive. As a smile spread across his face, she shook him once more.

'You must rise, my Son. Dawn will soon be upon us and we have been summoned to eat with Lunar and Solar for our dawn meal.'

'Please give me a moment, my head is still thick with sleep.'

Sor left the room and Winter slowly roused himself. Once ready, he found her waiting patiently outside.

'I'm ready now.'

In the grey of first light, Sor led Winter down the same path that they had trodden earlier that night. Instead of turning to go to the stream, they continued down the hill to a clearing. In the clearing, Winter found many wooden buildings of various sizes. He supposed these to be dwellings and places of trade.

Winter was led through the town and to a shallow ford in the stream. The river at which he had previously drunk must have curved to the right, for it passed close to the lower side of the town. Here they passed many monks of the Night and Day Gods filling jugs with water in preparation to break their fast. None of these spoke, but a few were humming to themselves as they went about their tasks; several nodding to Sor as she passed. In the subtle light, it was hard to tell the male monks from the female monks and Winter had to stop himself from staring.

As Winter crossed the stream, he felt how icy it was and his feet were soon numb. After crossing the stoned ford, the path branched in several directions. Winter found their path curved to the right and up a steep incline.

The trees soon became thick about them and they found themselves alone on the path. They continued up the steep hill at a fair pace and Winter became quite short of breath. He noted that Sor did not seem to have the same issue.

As she strode ahead, the path turned to the left and, after walking through a doorway in a thick hedge, Winter was confronted by a truly amazing structure: a temple.

To his left, a cliff-face of jagged dark grey rock rose high into the air. The temple of the monks hugged this cliff and almost looked as if part of it had been chiselled out of the rock itself. Ascending three stories high were two towers of a seven-sided design. Atop one of the two seven sided towers was a golden sun, while the other held a white crescent moon. These were lifted above the main rooftop by solid dark wooden beams.

The front of the building was a wall with no windows and only one massive door. This door was wide open and Winter could see the flicker of candles within.

On entering a small foyer, the two were greeted by a man in white robes who led them through a side door and into a large room. In the centre of the room sat two monks on plush cushions with their legs crossed.

The hazy light of dawn filled the room and caught wisps of smoke from burning candles and incense sticks. Winter had never smelt such a range of herbs and unknown things before. His nostrils tingled with excitement as he followed Sor into the centre of the room to be seated facing the two monks already there.

'Welcome, my Son, to the Temple of Day and Night. I am Lunar and here beside me is Solar.'

Winter was struck by how much like the other monks they looked. His surprise was not missed by Solar. 'We do not need lavish clothes to honour the Gods: they do not need impressing with displays of earthly possessions.' Winter bowed his head in acknowledgment.

A single monk in black brought into the room their breakfast. Much the same as Winter had eaten the previous day, it consisted of dense bread and honeycomb. In addition, there were also slithers of salted pork and wild berries. They all ate together and Winter savoured every morsel; he had not realised just how hungry he was.

After several moments of eating in silence, Lunar spoke with his melodic voice. 'You have come to us from afar, my Son. Some say that the God of Night has sent you, others that the Moon did, for you to cause mischief among us. I believe neither of these are true; the Gods would not waste their time on a single man.'

Solar then spoke with the voice of an old woman. 'It is good to see that your body has healed well. The Gods have been kind to you. However, I sense that while your body is all but healed, there is a black mark on either your mind or your heart; I cannot tell which.'

Winter immediately thought of Dusk, but he did not want to talk to these strangers about his grief for her. 'I'm sorry; I do not know what you mean.'

'I think you do. Although I will not force you to speak of it against your will.'

Lunar spoke once more. 'You have learned a little of our way of life since arriving amongst us, and I believe that this has aided in your healing. But now we must decide what is to be done with you. What would you like to do?'

Winter was caught off guard at being asked this question so openly. 'Honestly, I have thought little of my future since arriving.'

'Would you like to stay amongst us?'

Winter did not have to think for long. 'I think I would, for a little while at least. The goat I was with was acting somewhat like a guide for me and I had planned to keep following her. She was deeply connected to my father; she might have even been taking me to him.' The words sounded foolish in his ears. 'Now that she is dead,' Winter said spitefully, 'I am not sure where I would go.'

The four of them sat in silence for a few moments, Winter trying to imagine what life would be like here, the others letting him.

'Very well. As you are not fully healed in the mind or heart, you may stay with us until you are mended. You will be under the direct supervision of Sor here and you will conform to the rights and rules of those who worship the God of Night.'

Lunar directed his gaze at Sor. 'You will care for this man kindly, answer his questions and instruct him to your way of life as you see fit. Trust him as you would a novice and teach him the ways of the Gods.'

Sor bowed her head. 'I will, Mother and Father. He will learn all that I can teach of the Gods and together we will heal his heart and mind.'

'Very good. And now, my Son and Daughter, you must go to bed; the sun is breaking the horizon.'

Winter walked in an exhausted haze as Sor led him back to his quarters. His slow mind had so much to think about that he only managed one question as he arrived by his bed.

'Why does everyone call me *Son*?'

'It is just the way we are. We call those less spiritually advanced as ourselves, sons and daughters and those more so, mother and father. Those on a similar level are called brother and sister.

'Now, good-day my *Son*, may you sleep well.'

Sor left the room and Winter drifted off to a dreamless sleep.

14

The old Admiral's bones ached. He was coming up to sixty-eight years of age and felt every year acutely. Acknowledging he had led a full life, he was disgruntled nonetheless. He despised getting old and resented the pain that came with it. *If only I had been struck down in my prime, instead of limping through these final years. Perhaps that would have been better.* Despite the obviousness of his constant struggle with pain, the Admiral complained to no one; he was a stubborn, hard old man.

The Old Sea Dog poured himself a stiff drink and sat down in a huff as he rubbed his throbbing big toe. Out of all of his pains, this one irked him the most, for it was not obtained in valour, but came about by old age alone. He hoped that his drink would numb the pain soon when a hurried banging on the door stole his attention.

'Enter.'

A young sailor came bursting into the room, panting hard. 'Sir, you must come to the docks at once! Master Tunley's ship has exploded and the Master has not yet been found.'

The Admiral was on his feet at once. 'Exploded? Explain yourself at once!'

'Exploded; blew up; is on fire. It happened shortly after the Ship Master set sail.'

'Enough! Ready my horse. I will see this for myself.'

The Admiral limped his way outside as quickly as he could and found a horse ready for him.

He was once more in agony as he mounted the horse and made his way through the white streets of Roasline and down to the docks. As he rode with haste, the Admiral thought of the missing Ship Master Tunley and how he was a man that the Admiral couldn't quite figure out. He used to find Tunley rash, irritating and arrogant, but over the last few weeks, Tunley had grown on him. The new Ship Master had shown great loyalty and a willingness to adhere to the Admiral's ways. And yet, there was something about him that put the Admiral on edge: was it his eagerness to inflict pain on others? Or the glint in his eyes that said *I know more than you*? Or was it his swagger that oozed arrogance? The Admiral couldn't quite put his finger on it. Despite all of this, the Admiral couldn't deny that Tunley was an excellent sailor and commanded a ship well. And that is why he chose him to retrieve his nephew from the Healers that very morning.

Once at the docks, he found himself in a scene of chaos. The water was littered with chunks of wood and a mast protruded from the sunken remains of Tunley's ship. Several small vessels were navigating the wreckage and fishing any bodies out of the water that they could find. On the shore, people were running hither and thither, some with purpose, others not knowing what to do.

The Admiral dismounted and, as he made his way to the water's edge, heard the pained growl of Tunley. The Old Sea Dog followed his ears and soon found Tunley being tended to by the naval chief barber. As the Admiral looked more closely, he saw a shard of wood a foot long sticking out of Tunley's right thigh. The barber poured some warm wine on the entry point and with a firm yank, pulled the shard out. He poured more wine into the wound to clean it and wrapped it tightly. Tunley grabbed the remaining wine from the barber and took a big gulp.

'Master Tunley, what have you done with my ship?' The Admiral felt little sympathy for the man now sitting before him.

'Humph! I haven't done anything. Someone has tried to kill me!' The Admiral noted the anger in Tunley's voice and tried a different tack.

'Then tell me, sailor, what happened?'

'I prepared my ship with supplies for Headly as ordered. We cast off and began taking her out of the docks. Four hundred yards had hardly passed when the timber beneath my feet trembled and before I knew what was happening, I was flung into the air and overboard.

'I was submerged for a long time. When I re-surfaced there were flames and smoke all around me. The ship, she was no more. I doubt many of the crew would have survived. I was lucky enough to be standing aft at the gunwale when the blast hit.

'Admiral, it was as if all of the cannons in the navy fired at once; the force was truly amazing.'

The Admiral looked keenly at Tunley. *Could someone really have wanted him dead, or was there a bigger picture to this?*

'Tunley, I want to know who has done this and why. And I want to know soon!'

Tunley bent over, coughed, and sat back up. 'I will find those responsible and make them pay for the attempt on my life.'

He coughed again and a splatter of blood mixed with the dirt on the ground. The barber looked at Tunley and prodded his back and ribs. The Admiral watched on as Tunley winced in pain. The barber turned to the Admiral.

'I'm sorry, sir; Master Tunley will be off his feet for a few days at least. I suspect he has broken ribs and possibly damaged lungs.'

The Admiral sighed. 'Very well, I will find someone else for the task.'

He strode back to his horse and mounted her. He dug his heels into her flanks and sped away from the docks and off to find Kathsum.

Who would do this? I don't believe for a moment that whoever did this wanted to kill Tunley, that arrogant fool. The Admiral thought some more. *Resvon! That's who it will be. That scheming arse of a man!* These thoughts and many others passed through the Admiral's mind as he climbed the streets of Roasline.

The Admiral found Kathsum eating her lunch by herself in the courtyard of her house. He barged straight in and marched right up to where she was sitting.

'Kathsum, Resvon is attacking us! He has blown up one of our ships!'

'Admiral, stop right there.' The Admiral obeyed, halting his approach. 'Now explain to me what has transpired. I want the facts, none of this conjecture.'

The old man pursed his lips in frustration and then spoke as calmly as he could. He told Kathsum all he had seen down at the docks and all that Tunley had told him. A small part of the Admiral was satisfied to see the High Chancellor shocked, scared and a bit lost for words.

'It is Resvon, I know it is. I will strike him back with the full force of the fleet.'

'No, you won't, Admiral.' Kathsum squared her chin. 'You will do nothing.'

The Admiral felt his anger boil once more. 'If you think I'm going to let this go unanswered, then you're greatly mistaken.'

'Calm yourself, Admiral!'

The Admiral heard the strength of his Chancellor and let her continue.

'Why would Resvon do this? He desires peace. He would not risk inflaming the current delicate balance. That put aside, if he did not want peace, then he would just wait until the deal was signed and let our guard down in welcoming him to Roasline. That is when he would strike. *That* is our greater risk from Resvon.'

The Old Sea Dog could see reason in this and calmed his temper.

'No Admiral, it is more likely that this attack came from those who do not wish peace to be attained. And that is why we shall not strike at Resvon.' Kathsum stood. 'But rest assured, we will not remain idle. With one hand we will use all of our available resources to thrash out the truth, while with our other, more subtle hand, we will pick and we will poke, we will push and we will pull and with both hands working hard, we will get to the bottom of this. Whether those plotting against us come from across the Liagar or sit at our council table, we will find them and dispose of them.

'Admiral, you probe those under your command and I will set my most trusted subjects the task of doing likewise.'

It was moments like these that the Admiral remembered the trust that he had gained in his Chancellor when she first took command. He felt mildly ashamed that he had recently lost some of that trust.

'As you wish, High Chancellor.' The Admiral left the courtyard with a determination that pushed all of his old age pains away.

15

The sun was only a short while from going to bed when Marlvon was preparing his evening meal. He had just returned from the market at Bankton, half a day's ride up the Liagar, and his hunger was great.

As he prepared his meal of fresh green tomatoes, pickled onions, a slither of smoked ham and a heel of dark rye, his mind wandered to the town of Bankton. Or more precisely, it wandered to one of its inhabitants: Islonda.

The girl of his thoughts was seven years his junior, having recently turned eighteen, and was the blacksmith of Bankton's daughter.

He had first met her, when he needed his farm horse reshod nine months past. Marlvon had been chatting casually with Jault, the blacksmith, as he worked on the custom request horse shoes, when a young lady came striding into the workshop and went straight up to her father.

'Mother says you won't let me take the trap to Fort Kykum tomorrow.'

The blacksmith spoke without slowing his work. 'It is not that I won't let you take the trap; it's that I won't let you go to the Fort at all. Now, mind your tone child, we have a customer.'

Marlvon still remembered how the girl's dress fanned out and his heart quicken as she twirled in a huff and stormed out of the workshop.

Marlvon made some excuse for leaving and hurried out of the workshop in pursuit of the girl. He followed her all the way down Main Street, but kept his distance as she turned down a side lane and headed for the bank of the Liagar. The young man watched her from a safe distance as she sat under a shady chestnut tree and gazed out over the water.

He soon saw the tension ease from her shoulders; she was slowly beginning to relax. It was then he approached her.

'You've chosen a beautiful spot to sit in. And, if I may be so bold to say, it is made even more so by you being here.' He knew he sounded ridiculous, but he couldn't help himself.

She turned to face him with a dubious expression. 'And who are you to be so bold?'

'I am Marlvon,' he smiled. 'What name do you go by?'

'I am the daughter of the blacksmith, Jault.' She got to her feet. 'And that is all that you need to know.'

As she strode past him, Marlvon caught the subtle scent of lavender.

'It was a pleasure to meet you, daughter of Jault.' She did not respond.

Marlvon grinned to himself. *I think I'll order a new axe head from Jault next week.*

Marlvon brought himself back to the present and continued to chop his tomatoes. He looked down at the knife slicing through the red flesh. His hand jerked back and he dropped the knife. *No!* His vision blurred for a moment and in his mind, he was no longer slicing a tomato, but was slicing through Eyp's flesh. He heard the man scream and Marlvon dropped to his knees. *No!* Marlvon sat against the wall and hugged his knees while he watched as his brain re-lived the torture of Eyp, one slow cut after another. *No!*

Tears streamed down his face and he banged his head backwards into the stone wall. Stars sparkled in his vision and he desperately tried to control his thoughts. *Islonda, Islonda, think of Islonda. You didn't tell me your name until the third time we met.* Prie lay before him, tied to the bed. *Eyes, Islonda's eyes.* 'You look at me with eyes so intelligent and secretive. How do they know everything about me?' Marlvon forced his mind to focus on what he wanted. 'I had to find a job, every week, a job for Jault, so I could see, you, Islonda. Axe head, horseshoe, fileting knife, what else, what else, focus, um… fire poker, log splitter, more, I'm sure there were more.' Marlvon's breathing calmed and his mind returned to his kitchen. He felt the cold floor with his hands, the solid wall behind his back. *I am here, in my house.*

Since capturing Eyp eight days prior, Marlvon had been drawn into reliving the horrendous experience. Each time he had been sucked back to that house in the slums, Marlvon had to force his mind to happier thoughts; the most powerful of these being his courtship of Islonda. As a result, he had taken to thinking about her most of the time in an attempt to stop the visions before they even began.

He stood up at the chopping board once more and, before he picked up the knife, firmly held an image of Islonda in his head. She was an odd girl. She was definitely not pretty, but had her own beauty in the way that she held herself. Her nose was a touch off centre, but this she countered by hanging her black hair down over one side of her face. Islonda's smile, like her nose, was a bit askew, but said nothing except happiness when it was there.

And the girl was stubborn. A trait she inherited from her father that scared away many of the men her age. They did not want to be argued with or disobeyed, they wanted to be praised and doted on. Marlvon, however, found this exciting and enjoyed the challenge of getting to know her better.

Marlvon's heart quickened as he recalled the first time that he had touched Islonda. It was nothing more than simply helping her up after she had fallen over a jutting cobblestone, but as his hand clasped hers, an excitement spread over his entire skin.

She had swiftly shrugged off his help, but it was too late; contact had been made.

As the months passed, Marlvon had noticed a change in Islonda: her demeanour became less frosty and she smiled when he approached her. The young lady began to like him and then began to like him a lot. And then, after nine months of courting, she had allowed him to kiss her.

Oh, how the thrill, then fear, then pure pleasure, had started at his lips and swept through his body like a crashing wave. And then he felt her kiss him back and the passion with which she did stole all the thoughts from his mind. He was there, in that moment, and it lasted for an eternity.

BANG, BANG, BANG, BANG!

Marlvon was yanked out of his most pleasurable memory and into the present. Instinct kicked in and he grabbed a sharp filleting knife on his way to the front door.

He peeked through a purpose made hole and saw a grim-looking man clad in chain mail and holding a spear. Marlvon pocketed his knife and drew a broad, two handed sword that he kept hidden in a crevice built into the wall by the door.

Once prepared, he slid back the bolt and yanked open the door in one swift motion. As the door swung inwards, he leapt back into the shadows and out of range of the spear.

The soldier looked surprised, but not as surprised as Marlvon as he took in the scene before him. The soldier he had seen in the peep-hole was one of four, all clad alike. Marlvon dismissed them quickly as he saw who they were guarding.

'Resvon! Are you trying to knock my door off its hinges with this brute here?'

'Marlvon, that's no way to greet your leader and uncle.'

Marlvon replied with sarcasm. 'I'm sorry Sire, please come in and I will fetch my best wine and tastiest cheese for you to enjoy.'

'Be careful, or I might take you up on that offer. But for now, I think I'll be satisfied with a mug of ale.'

'Very well, but *they*,' Marlvon pointed at the soldiers with his sword, 'wait out here.'

'As you wish.'

Marlvon led the way into his kitchen, filled two mugs with ale and lit four candles; the sun was going to bed after another day had ended. Resvon took a long gulp.

Marlvon paced impatiently. 'Well Resvon, out with it. Why are you here?'

Marlvon saw Resvon's eyes sadden and he regretted his harshness. 'I'm sorry uncle; your arrival interrupted some deep thinking. How have you been?'

'In truth, worried. I am fearful Marlvon, fearful for my life.' Resvon paused and took another mouthful of ale. 'Ever since agreeing to a peace deal with Kathsum, attempts have been made on my life almost daily. And that is why I have come here.' He paused and took a deep breath, as if he was going underwater. 'I want you by my side. I want you to lead my personal guard. I trust you, Marlvon, like no other man alive, and I trust your skills of protection.'

Marlvon felt troubled. 'Resvon, I have a life here. I have a farm to tend to, stock to manage.'

'I know. I can provide men to care for it while you are gone.'

'While I am gone? How long do you expect this to take? Surely if your life is in danger now, then it will be for years to come.'

'I know.' Resvon looked at his feet. 'I believe it will be in danger until peace is reached and becomes the new way of life and the prospect of returning to war is unimaginable.' The Leader of the Outcasts paused and took a swig of ale. 'I know that I am asking lot.'

Marlvon felt frustration build within him. 'I cannot do it Resvon. I will not do it. I do not want to live a life of violence. You know that, uncle.'

'And yet you still answer the door with a sword in your hand.'

'No, Resvon, my answer is no.' Marlvon crossed his arms.

'Believe me when I say that this is not for me. I would not ruin your life to prolong mine. This is for peace. This is to end the war that has gone on for far too long. This is to save countless lives.'

Marlvon knew Resvon would use this argument and he sighed.

'You have other warriors just as capable as me to protect you. Surround yourself with them and you will be as safe as possible. I know that this might sound self-centred, but I will not ruin the essence of who I am on the off chance that it *may* prevent some future attack on your life. And I'm sorry, I truly am, but that is my answer.'

Marlvon was surprised at himself for being so firm. He craved peace as much as Resvon, but his last foray into violence had taken a significant toll on him. He felt his eyes welling at the mere thought of it. 'I still have nightmares of that poor woman and… visions of horror from when I tortured Eyp to within an inch of his life. I am sorry Resvon, but I can't do that anymore.'

'I understand, nephew. I'm sorry for putting you through that and for what I'm about to tell you.' He put down his cup and rested a hand on Marlvon's shoulder. 'Yesterday morning Prie drank a skin-full of whisky and threw herself out of a window. She was showing all the signs of overcoming the terrors of her attack. We were wrong. I'm sorry, but at last she will suffer no more.' As an afterthought, he added, 'Her children will be looked after.'

Marlvon felt as if a horse had kicked him in the guts. 'Get out,' he rasped.

Resvon rose and left quietly with his head bowed. Marlvon sat in silence and wondered why life was so cruel. A short while ago, he had been the happiest man in all the lands and now, he had been stripped bare of all that happiness, while Prie was dead and gone from this world.

'Islonda, oh how I wish you were here with me now.'

16

The cacophony of both Day and Night monks sharing their meal in the dining room greeted Sor as the kind brother Zin bustled over towards her.

'Sister Sor, good evening to you. May I have a quick word with you?'

'Of course, brother.'

'I am concerned for our newest member, Brother Winter. I have just been talking with some of those that share his dormitory and they tell me that for a decent portion of his sleep time, he screamed while he was asleep. They say it was as if he were in great pain.' Zin's eyes opened wide.

'Again?' Sor felt a pang of sadness in her heart.

'It would seem so. And then when I approached him about it this evening, he said that he did not feel like eating and was going to make his way directly to the temple for prayer. He said that he wanted to make the walk alone, too.'

'Thank you, Zin.' Sor turned and left the room with a confused Zin staring after her.

Sor quickly made her way through the village paying little attention to her surroundings; her thoughts were with the tormented Winter. *You poor man, how much pain you must be in to feel it while you are asleep.*

She raced across the river and, as she turned onto the path leading to the temple, she saw him. He wore the black robe of the night monks and his now bald head shone in the dying light. His shoulders were slumped and his sandalled feet fell heavily.

'Winter, please wait.'

The monk kept walking. Sor continued her jog and was soon side by side with him. 'Brother Winter, I looked for you at breakfast, but you were not there.' Winter gave no response and kept walking.

'Winter, your brothers and sisters are worried for you. They tell me that you were crying out in your sleep again.'

Winter grunted.

'Winter, I want to help you, please can you tell me what troubles you?'

'I am fine, Sister Sor. Now, may I please walk in peace?'

Sor was silent for a moment as she caught her breath. She had noted the obvious pain in Winter's voice.

'Winter, you have been with us now for four weeks. You are learning our ways quickly and are fast becoming a true monk, yet your sleep has become riddled with night terrors. When will you let me help you?'

'I said I am fine. Now, I would like to walk *alone*, please.'

Sor stopped walking and let Winter continue. As he got further away, she cried out. 'Winter, the Gods teach us we need to release our burdens, both past and present. Only then can we be at peace with both ourselves and the world. When you are ready, I will help you release yours, as best I can.'

Winter did not reply.

Sor felt hurt at being rejected so coldly by someone she called a friend. She made her slow, lonely way to prayer and positioned herself far from Winter. The young lady only half listened as Lunar's melodic voice told a story of forgiveness of other people's sins: her mind was still focused on Winter.

After prayers had finished, Sor waited in the candlelight for the room to empty. Her task for the evening was to scrub the floor of the prayer room. Winter was to join her.

Together they moved the furniture, mainly benched seats, to the sides of the room in a stiff silence. Sor watched as Winter collected two wooden buckets and scrubbing brushes with coarse bristles. He sulkily handed her a set.

'Brother Winter, I find that scrubbing the floors by candlelight gives one a good opportunity to contemplate one's path.' She received a non-committal grunt in reply.

Winter slunk to the opposite side of the room to Sor, got down on all fours, and started scrubbing. Feeling hurt for the second time that evening, Sor likewise started scrubbing. She soon found herself unable to take her own advice on contemplating one's path and instead thought of Winter and how she might break through the resistance that he was presenting. She remembered that when he had first come to the village, he had been so inquisitive; never ceasing with his questions. Then, as the weeks passed by, he became more closed off and subdued. Upon reflection, Sor realised that this change had coincided with the beginning of his night terrors.

The poor man. He must be in so much pain. But why won't he let me in? Why won't he let me help him? She scrubbed at the stones with fervour, as if by doing a quick job would enable her to help Winter.

After a long period of solid scrubbing, she took a break. She fetched two cups of water and took them to where Winter was resting.

'I'm going to do some scrubbing near you for a while. We still have a long way to go and I'm getting a bit lonely all the way over there.'

Winter grunted in reply.

'I've never quite been able to figure out how this great hall gets so dirty.' Sor tried to sound casual.

Winter grunted again.

'If that's all you've got to say, then we best get back to cleaning.' Winter complied with another grunt.

They continued to scrub in silence, and the floor slowly became cleaner. Sor was just thinking about another rest, to give her shoulders and knees a break, when Winter broke the silence with a croaky voice.

'You were right, Sor. When you said that scrubbing is a good time to contemplate one's path. You were right.'

Sor remained silent and continued scrubbing for fear of discouraging Winter from continuing.

'My mind is in turmoil.' Winter's voice cracked.

Sor heard Winter's strain and emotion so acutely that she felt it herself.

'The path that I have taken to get to this point … there is so much violence … so much pain. It is hard to think about … harder to talk about.'

'Take your time Winter, there is no rush.' Sor tried to sound gentle.

'The nightmares … I never had nightmares before coming to this place. When they started, they were of my sister falling … always falling… I miss her so much.' Winter's fingers pressed into his brow. 'But more recently they have been of my childhood … of when I was beaten … of when I was cut … of when …' Winter trailed off into sobs.

Sor stopped her scrubbing and went to put an arm around Winter's heaving shoulders. This was worse than she had imagined. She didn't know what to say; so she let him cry.

'All my life, I've sought to obey and please my father. The same man that used to…' Winter began to cry afresh. When his sobbing eased, Sor heard the plea in his voice. 'Please … talk to me about something else. I don't want to think about this.'

'What do you want to talk about?' Sor could think of little else but what Winter had just told her.

'I don't know, just make sure it's interesting.' There was a moment of silence. 'Why don't you tell me about yourself?' Winter's mouth twitched.

Sor frowned and uttered modestly. 'Nothing about me is interesting.' *Or at least nothing I'm ready to share with you… yet.*

'Or… you could tell me about the cities north of the Moaks? Tell me about their history; I always liked history.'

'Well, you already know about the monks and their villages, so I'll tell you about the great cities near the ocean.'

Sor seated herself facing Winter with her legs crossed and her hands on her knees. She wasn't quite sure where to begin, so she began at home.

'If you travel down the river that flows through our village, you will soon come to Green Lake. So named from the lush reeds that grow in its shallows. This lake is vast and one side cannot be seen from the other. There is much to be said about the lake, but I will not linger there now.'

Winter appeared to be calming a little, so Sor continued.

'There are two rivers out of Green Lake, the Sempa River directly to the north and the Liagar River which flows slightly north of east. If the Sempa River is followed, it flows into the Rogaus Sea at a city called Psymryte. Its delta also passes near the city of Nivera.

'The other river, the Liagar, enters the Rogaus Sea at the grand city of Roasline and the military stronghold of Fort Kykum. The Liagar River is currently a border between two warring peoples.'

Sor paused for a breath and to reach back into her memories of the history she had been taught.

'Hundreds of years ago, the leader of Roasline, don't ask me his name, for I have forgotten that, found that his gaols were full. He emptied them by shipping the prisoners away from Roasline and started a penal colony far away over the Sempa River. Psymryte was the name given to the colony. He sent all sorts of criminals there; from young boys who stole bread to keep from starving, to murderers, to those who spoke out against him and his regime.' Sor scowled at the thought.

'Over the years, people loyal to Roasline began to live closer and closer to the Sempa River. The leader, a different one from that which set up the colony, closed the prison and set the prisoners free. To a point.

'He gave them the lands from the Rogaus all the way to the Lingos Hills north and west of the Sempa River.' Sor waved her arms to indicate the vastness of this area. 'The ex-prisoners were confined to this region and the river was guarded against their crossing it.

'It is told that there was much warring, fighting and general brutality amongst the prisoners at this point. This continued until a single leader emerged. His first act as leader was to deem that there would be no laws within his borders.'

Winter frowned, 'Surely that would cause chaos.'

'You might think so, but at first this seemed to work better than most had hoped. The prisoners seemed to respect those more powerful than themselves; a hierarchy of strength, if you will. Then, after several years of this pseudo-peace, murders and rapes started to become commonplace. Many of the more vulnerable prisoners saw their fate and unsuccessfully tried to flee across the guarded river.

'Meanwhile, back in Roasline, several leaders had come and gone until the regime of the time re-established the sending of prisoners to Psymryte. But the leader of Roasline did not stop there. He also sent beggars and people with disabilities as well.' Sor turned her mouth up at the thought.

'Apparently, they used to put them in small boats off the coast at Psymryte as the tide was coming in and sail away, leaving the boats to be washed ashore. It was during this time that the colony became known as the colony of the Outcasts.'

'That sounds horrible.'

Sor was pleased that Winter was focusing on what she was saying and not his past.

'Yes, it does. But then, in the lawless state of the Outcasts, the leader was murdered. Historians often enjoy the irony in that.

'The new leader immediately set up laws against many crimes and enforced these severely. He was a man of insight and set his people to farming, fishing, building, producing and other similar activities. And the Outcasts began to progress. Slowly, but surely, they moved out of the filth that they had been and began to prosper.

'That leader of the Outcasts ruled for nearly forty years before dying of a disease that addled his brain. His successor was not as competent and the Outcasts slid backwards once more. To compensate for his inadequacies, he fuelled hatred within his people against those who lived across the Sempa and those of Roasline; blaming them for his people's hardship. This resentment blossomed amongst the Outcasts and over the years the leader used this hatred to establish the beginnings of an army.' Sor smiled wryly at the cunning of the man.

'Leaders for the Outcasts came and went. Some only stayed in power for a few days, while others governed successfully for many years. Although the leaders changed often, one mantra continued to grow in intensity: a deep-seated hatred of those across the Sempa.

'Then, one day, the hatred of the Outcasts leapt forth and in a coordinated attack, they crossed the river to take the more prosperous lands. Revenge and anger burned fiercely in the Outcasts, and Nivera fell early on.

'The war then raged for close to thirty years, with many stalemates and many, many deaths. Over that time, the Outcasts managed to advance all the way to the Liagar. A stalemate has existed for fifteen years or so and the current leaders of Resvon and Kathsum seem content with the status quo.' Sor shrugged. 'The Outcasts have also conquered all the way to the Green Lake, but thankfully through the will of the Gods, Olswerth, the leader of the region, has left us well alone.

'It may be hard to believe, but there are many Outcasts who live respectable lives well away from the battlefront. These are often the children or grandchildren of previous prisoners and outcasts, and not criminals themselves. There are many prosperous farmers and the city of Nivera is a wondrous place to visit, or so I've been told. Psymryte, on the other hand, is a derelict city full of sin and filth. That is where the most depraved live.' Sor shivered at the stories she had heard and moved on. 'We pray often for the war to end, but even Lunar and Solar have little faith that it will be in their lifetimes. No, many more people will die needlessly.'

Sor sat in a sorrowful silence as she prayed for the lives of all those who may die in the war. She was surprised when Winter's cracked voice disrupted her prayers.

'I've skirted around the edge of a war and killed many men in the process, but that now seems like a minor battle in comparison to what you're telling me.'

Sor's heart saddened at the revelation that Winter had killed before. She knew that there were demons in his past, but to have killed *many men* .... what would the Gods think?

'You have an evil past, Brother. The Gods teach us that all killing is a sin and that no one should die at the hand of another person.'

'I did not know about the Gods before coming here. I did not think on my actions. I only followed the commands of the Emperor, my father.' Sor could detect fear in Winter's tone.

'Will the Gods punish me for doing what I was told?'

'It is not for me to say what the Gods will or will not do. It may depend on how you lead the rest of your life. Regardless, I will pray that your sinful past may be forgiven and that the Gods may consider your coming here as a re-birth. They may listen, or they may not. They may choose to punish you during this life or in the afterlife. Maybe they punished you when you were a child for sins committed later in life. Maybe they will wait until you are dead and will take your mind to the dark side of the moon, where it will be tormented for all eternity. No one can know.'

Sor saw a fearful look in Winter's face and her heart softened. *He is so young to be battling such demons.*

'Sor, I no longer want to be that sinful, killing man anymore.'

'Good, then you have taken the first steps to redemption. But you must remember, it is easy to say that you will change; it is another thing to actually change.' Winter nodded.

Sor felt her heart quicken and could hear its pulse in her ears. She knew she shouldn't do what she was about to, but for a moment she lost control of her heart and mind. She looked Winter directly in the eyes and held his gaze. 'By the God of Night, I promise to stay with you and help you make that change, however long that may be.'

Winter's eyes widened in surprise. 'Thank you, Sister Sor.'

Sor reached out and touched Winter's knee. 'But for now, we need to keep scrubbing. There is still a lot of floor to clean and the night goes on.'

They both started scrubbing once more and Sor thought about her promise to the Gods. *What have I done? In the emotions of our talk, have I committed my life to this man I hardly know? What if he doesn't change; will the gods punish me for failing? Oh, what have I done?*

17

Ship Master Tunley felt a dull ache in his right thigh as he limped his way along the water's edge. It had been twelve days since the attempt on his life, and while his ribs had healed well, his leg wound was proving much more stubborn. The pain in itself he could put up with, but the specific location in his upper leg prevented him from walking with his usual swagger. This made him far grumpier than the pain ever could. This grumpiness he took out on all those around him, usually in the form of verbal abuse.

Since his ship had exploded, Tunley had surrounded himself with six guards whenever he was in public. Aside from the added protection, he relished the status that having an armed escort brought. As he walked along the docks that morning, he noticed how the merchants and hawkers parted to let him through, and he was delighted.

A fair breeze blew in his face and with it came the smell of sea salt. The sailor's morning hunger became aroused. Tunley signalled to one of his guards and asked the man to bring him an oyster seller. *What better way to break my fast than with half a dozen fresh oysters?*

The guard promptly returned with an old man carrying a tray laden with oysters and the usual flavourings: lemon, vinegar, sea salt and sugar grains. The man bowed as he approached the Ship Master.

'Master Tunley, I hear you are hungry for some oysters. You are in luck, for I am selling the finest oysters on the docks this morning.'

Tunley raised an eyebrow; he doubted the old man's claim, but the oysters did look good.

The oyster seller continued despite the look from Tunley. 'I'm selling six oysters for five coppers or twelve for nine. But for you, Master, I will do six for four coppers or twelve for seven: a bargain to be sure.'

'Do I look like I'm seeking a bargain, old man?'

'No sir, I meant no offence.' He bowed his head.

'I will take six with no added flavour.'

'Very good, Sir.' The man prepared the oysters and handed them to Tunley one by one.

Tunley felt the bulging mass of the first oyster enter his mouth and slide over his tongue and down his throat. The man was right; they were very delicious indeed. He proceeded to consume the next five oysters in quick succession. He wiped a dribble of oyster juice from his chin and looked at the old man.

'They are bitter.' Tunley lied. 'I will pay you two coppers. And you should be honoured by receiving my business.'

He threw the coins on the ground at the man's feet.

'Guards, remove this beggar from my presence.' As the guards hurried the poor man aside, Tunley continued his walk.

Much better; a stomach full of oysters. Now I'm ready to deal with that useless Admiral.

Tunley passed out of the bustling commercial docks and entered the secure naval section. He passed few sailors, but those he did showed him the appropriate level of both respect and fear.

Tunley's day was starting out nicely.

He soon found the Admiral at the end of the longest pier waiting for him. 'Good morning, Admiral. I hope you are well this morning.'

The Admiral nodded in reply.

'I see that most of the fleet has departed already,' said Tunley.

'They left before daybreak. As you can see, there are only the slower cargo ships that remain as well as Ship Master Strugen to protect the rear.'

'He is a fine Ship Master, well respected by the men.'

'He has much experience, as does Ship Master Jip. He led the fleet's departure.'

Both men watched side-by-side as Strugen's massive war ship pulled anchor and unfurled her many sails.

'That is a fine vessel that Strugen commands, Admiral.'

'*The Beast*, aye she is. Her hull is the strongest in the fleet and she has the firepower to out-blast any other ship.'

Tunley let the Admiral pause, knowing that he would speak again.

'I know you wish you were part of the fleet that has left today. You take it as a slight against your pride. But a good Ship Master knows his place, is confident in his place, and doesn't wish that he was elsewhere.'

'I only wish that I were out at sea, riding this fair breeze.' This was not entirely true, but the Admiral didn't need to know how badly Tunley wanted to be sailing with the fleet. No, not sailing; leading the fleet.

The Admiral smiled. 'Ah Tunley, you're a true sailor.'

Tunley smiled back. 'Thank you, Sir.'

'Ship Master, I've brought you here to tell you I'm going to commission the construction of a new ship for you. My three Ship Masters should each have a ship worthy of their rank. Strugen has *The Beast*, Jip has *Victory* and you will soon have your own ship to name.

'As this new vessel will be your ship, I want you to help with her design. Make her to suit who you are. Strugen's ship is strong and powerful, but easily out sped, much like it's Master. *Victory* is fast and has a surprisingly keen bite to her cannons, but her hull could be stronger. Design your ship to suit your battle tactics. You shall meet with the shipwright's guild this afternoon to begin your designs. Make quick decisions. Ships take months to build and I feel yours will be needed soon.'

Tunley was amazed; he could not believe his luck. To make a ship to his own design was every sailor's dream.

'Thank you, sir; I am truly honoured.'

The Admiral grunted; not one to be praised. 'And Tunley, don't pine too much for being with the fleet. It's more than likely that they sit and wait for war or peace, with nothing much to do.'

Before Tunley could answer, the Admiral had turned and had begun his slow limp along the pier.

Tunley remained behind and watched until *The Beast* rounded the headland and left his sight. *Today is going to be a very good day.*

'Tunley, you must give my compliments to your cook; this tuna is delicious, a perfect lunch meal.'

'I will do that, Admiral. She will be most pleased to hear your praise.' Ship Master Tunley had no intention of passing on the old man's praise; his cook got paid for doing her job, that was all she needed.

'I've seen your designs for your galleon. Very impressive; you must have paid the shipwrights handsomely to get the drawings done in only five days.'

Or the fear of death, thought Tunley.

'I see you've added a fourth mast for speed and the figure of a mermaid on the beak. I also noticed the larger than usual captain's cabin. I suppose we all like a bit of comfort when we can have it. Very nice indeed.

'I have approved these designs and the men have begun construction on her keel today. While we have some stock of hardwoods, lumberjacks have been sent to gather more for the hull and deck. The pine masts should not be a problem, either.

'As for your firepower, I like the mix of demi-culverin with their eight-pound shots and the demi-cannons with their thirty-two pounders to cover a range of about 1500 feet. Your ship will be a master of the sea.'

'Thank you, Admiral. I thought long and hard on her design and—'

BANG, BANG, BANG!

Tunley's front door quivered under the force of the bangs. His man-servant hastened to the door and opened it swiftly.

Tunley and the Admiral looked at each other as they stopped talking and listened to the exchange.

'Can I help you, sir?'

'I have an urgent message for the Admiral. I was told that he was here.'

'Let the man in.' The Admiral growled from the dining room.

The sailor that entered the room was wearing the sash of a captain and was weather stained with an unshaven face.

'My apologies for the interruption, Sirs.' The captain bowed to both the Ship Master and the Admiral.

Tunley began to get impatient. 'Get on with it, man!'

'Admiral, I have come directly from the fleet with the greatest speed I could muster. It happened the night before last and three days after we set out. Ship Master Strugen's ship exploded! And then moments later, so did Ship Master Jip's.'

Tunley glanced at the Admiral and saw his face turn grey. Tunley's flushed red with adrenalin as his thoughts flashed to battle. Both men took large gulps of wine.

The captain continued. 'It was horrible, sir. I was in the vessel closest to Strugen's mighty ship and I felt a powerful wave of heat as the noise struck. It almost knocked me off my feet; I knew that there could be no survivors. The wreckage was strewn about the choppy water while the bulk of *The Beast* sunk quickly. Regardless, we did search but found only dead men.

'I did not witness the explosion of Jip's ship, but the reports from those that did sounded very similar to the demise of *The Beast*.'

Tunley regained his composure before the ageing Admiral. 'Were there any enemy vessels about? Were there any shots fired?'

'The night was dark with clouds, but no one saw any ships or heard any shots.'

The Admiral spoke next with a croaky voice. 'How far had the fleet travelled before this happened?'

'We had a strong tail wind for most of the voyage and were nearing Myrth Isle. A strange place, they say curses lie on that place.'

'Enough of that talk, sailor. Is there anything else you can tell me?'

'Not of great consequence. It was decided to send three separate messengers back to Roasline, clearly, I'm the first to arrive. The fleet continued their voyage as planned. No other ships have befallen the same fate.'

'Who commands the fleet now?'

'No one, sir. It was jointly decided that each captain would remain in charge of their vessel until orders had come from you, sir.'

'Good, good.' The Admiral ran his hand through his hair.

Tunley got a wave of excitement as he realised what was coming next.

'Thank you, captain. You may go now and rest.' The Admiral turned to Tunley. 'Ship Master Tunley, I am commanding you to take charge of the fleet. You will leave at first light tomorrow.'

'Thank you, sir. I won't let you down.'

'Be careful Tunley, it may be that someone tries to kill you again.'

'Yes, sir. I will, sir.'

'I'm going to see the High Chancellor. It seems that the people who tried to kill you are more elusive and dangerous than we first thought.'

As the Admiral stood and limped out of the room, Tunley was already relishing in the prospect of a long night of preparations followed by a swift morning departure. He would soon have command of the fleet.

As night descended, a thick band of low clouds drifted across Roasline. The darkness swiftly swallowed the shadowy figures that roamed the streets holding dull lamps.

Midnight came and went, and a light fog descended. The figures on the streets grew less and less until the streets became empty but for stray dogs and cats.

A broad-shouldered cloaked figure made his way through the back alleys, ever climbing the hill towards the council chambers. When he was a few streets away from his destination, he discarded his low lamp and pulled his hood lower over his face. Excitement and fear ran through his body, but his footing was calm and deliberate. When he was almost at the hilltop, he deviated his course and made his way towards the Admiral's residence.

The Admiral's home was a large, two storied, half-timbered building. While the Admiral's bedroom was upstairs, he seldom slept in his bed, but rather slept on a chaise lounge in the main parlour. The cloaked man knew this and was grateful that he would not have to negotiate a creaky staircase.

He arrived at the Admiral's house and couldn't believe his luck to find the front door unlocked. The Admiral either had a lot on his mind or had consumed a lot of drink. Or perhaps both.

The man lifted the latch and pushed the door gently. A subtle creak escaped the hinge, but was not loud enough to wake anyone. The cloaked man exhaled with relief as he entered the sleeping house.

Walking with great care, the man felt his slow way to the parlour. The shutters were open, but no light came into the room. Low fire embers glowed secretly from the far side of the room to the entrance. An eerie orange glow cast enough light for the cloaked man to see the sleeping form of the old Admiral snoring gently.

The intruder removed his hood and made his way over to the fireside. He was tempted to pick up a fire-poker, but instead selected a firm cushion. He leant over the old man and whispered, 'Wake up Admiral.'

The Admiral's eyes opened partially.

'Tunley, what are you doing here?'

Still whispering, Tunley answered. 'I'm here to kill you, sir.' Tunley leapt onto the old man and gripped him tightly. The Ship Master felt the old man struggle, but his strength was pitiful. Both men realised this and the Admiral stopped struggling.

'Why?'

'I despise you, old man. I despise you and your inability to make firm decisions. I will make a much better Admiral.'

Tunley saw the cogs slowly turning in the Admiral's mind. 'You killed Strugen and Jip. I don't know how, but you killed them.'

'Yes, I did.'

'And you nearly killed yourself?'

'I was never going to die in that explosion. Although, the splinter in the leg was less than pleasant. You see, I had to divert the blame elsewhere before Strugen and Jip were to die. I couldn't have people suspecting me.'

'But how did you do it? You never left Roasline.'

Tunley couldn't help but gloat. '*The Beast* and *Victory* were both double hulled ships. They both recently underwent repairs. During these repairs, I packed oil and gunpowder in the space between the hulls. A lot of it. I snaked a fuse through the woodwork of the ships. A very long fuse. I lit it before they set sail. A risky plan, I agree, but if that plan had failed, then I had assassins on both vessels ready to kill both Strugen and Jip on the fourth night after setting sail. These men knew nothing of my explosive plan.

'And now, Admiral, to finish my plan and secure my position next to the Chancellor as Admiral, I will kill you by suffocating you with your own cushion.'

Unable to move under Tunley's heavy weight, the Admiral spat in his face. 'You will be caught and hung for your crimes.'

Tunley left the spittle on his cheek and smiled. 'No, I won't. I will be praised and honoured as the only surviving Ship Master and will be an easy choice to replace you as Admiral. As for you, you are an old man who has been under a great deal of stress. It will be no surprise to anyone that your heart gave out in your own home. Goodbye, old man!'

Tunley thrust the cushion onto the Admiral's face. He felt the Admiral violently struggle and pressed harder. As the Admiral's strength faded, pure glee crept into Tunley's mind. When the Admiral finally lay still, a wave of excited happiness washed over the Ship Master. Tunley continued to hold the cushion over the Admiral's face for several moments more, just for the fun of it.

The assassin stood and looked down at the corpse and smiled. Not forgetting where he was, Tunley replaced the cushion in its rightful place and then positioned the Admiral as if he had been clutching his chest. The look of pain that was already disfiguring the Admiral's face was the perfect touch. Tunley admired his work once more, pulled his hood over his face and left in the same stealthy way in which he had arrived.

Everything was going according to his plan.

18

Marlvon woke to three firm knocks on the door of his room at the Bankton Inn. The head of a plump woman in her forties poked its way into his dark room.

'Sir, you asked to be woke before first light wif breakfast.'

Marlvon rolled out of bed and onto the wooden floor with a thud. He clumsily heaved himself to his knees.

'Thank you. Can you please set it down on the table by the bed?'

The innkeeper's wife entered the room carrying a tray laden with food and an oil lamp and set it on the small wobbly table.

'As ordered: hot porrie wif honey an' apple an' a mug o' half strengf cider.'

'Thank you.'

The woman turned to leave. 'Is there anyfing else you want?'

'Actually, yes. Can you please see that my horses are saddled and ready to go? I shall be leaving shortly.'

'I'll see to it.'

The woman left Marlvon to his breakfast. As the sweet porridge passed his lips, his mind wandered to the night before when he has arrived in Bankton. After running a few errands, he had collected a parcel in a box three feet long and two wide. This he had tied a deep red ribbon around and added the following note.

Dear Islonda,
A gift for you to wear tomorrow. I'll be waiting at the break of first light out the front of your house. You should look forward to a day of fun and adventure away from Bankton.

Marlvon

Marlvon couldn't help but smile at the look of surprise, and then intelligent recognition, that he imagined would have crossed Islonda's face when she opened her gift.

As he washed down the last of his porridge with the last of the cider, he felt a mixture of excitement and nerves. Leaping to his feet, he shaved his stubble and dressed in his riding pants and a loose-fitting tunic. He collected his bags with lunch supplies pre-packed and smiled to himself as he left the dingy room.

Marlvon made his purposeful way from the Bankton Inn to the blacksmith's workshop and the adjoining house. He led his two horses through the town and delighted at the splendour of the predawn day.

The streets were, for the most part, empty. Silence hung in the air and the gentle warm breeze promised a hot summer's day ahead. He passed the bakery and smelt the delicious wafts of baking bread. He also passed through the Town Square, with its bronze sculpture of Resvon. This brought a cheeky smile to his face, to think that the town idealised his uncle.

Marlvon arrived at Islonda's house at his planned time and waited patiently for the young lady to appear. It was not long before he heard a creaking door and his heart skipped a beat with excitement. Marlvon saw Islonda emerge from the doorway only a few feet away and couldn't help but grin at the sight.

'Good morning to you, Islonda.'

'Horses? You didn't say anything about horses!'

Marlvon was taken aback. 'What's wrong with horses? You can ride, I've seen you.'

'There's nothing wrong with horses in themselves. I was just expecting a cart to go with them.'

Marlvon relaxed his tense shoulders. 'Oh. Well, I apologise for not being able to provide the level of comfort that you desire, but no cart can travel where we are going.'

Marlvon sensed Islonda's interest bubble up by the lifting of her chin. 'Where *are* we going?'

'You will just have to wait to find out.' Marlvon liked to leave Islonda intrigued. 'Now, do you like your gift?'

Islonda looked down at her body. 'The dress is a beautiful deep sky-blue and the fabric feels nice and light, but it seems to have lots of buttons and flaps that I can't quite figure out. I wondered if this could be the new fashion from Fort Kykum, but somehow, I don't think it is.'

Marlvon smirked with satisfaction. 'I've seen you riding side-saddle, as is appropriate for any young woman, but am I right in guessing that you can also ride with your legs astride the horse?'

'You are. I learnt at a young age and practice when no one else was around. But I cannot ride like that in a dress.'

'Yes, well, as it turns out, you are not actually wearing only a dress. You see, the extra buttons, flaps and ribbons allow this garment to create two leg holes, like trousers. There are also other buttons that allow the extra fabric to be held back or even removed entirely. In fact, if the right buttons are manipulated, it can be turned into a pair of tight riding pants attached to a shirt-like garment.' Marlvon grinned. 'It is my own design. What do you think?'

'Incredible, if it actually works as you say it does.' Marlvon detected scepticism. 'Allow me to demonstrate the marvels of my design.'

Marlvon took a step towards Islonda with mischief in his eyes.

She put up her hands. 'If you think that I'm going to let you fondle me in the public just so I can ride a horse, then you can stop right there.'

'I was only going to instruct you.' Marlvon said with mock innocence. 'As you wish, I will stay where I am, though you will have to follow my directions closely.

'Start by putting your fingers on your waist and find the seam that runs vertically.' Islonda nodded when she found the seam.

'If you follow that seam downwards, you will find a series of square buttons. Undo them.' In the fading starlight, Marlvon saw Islonda cock an eyebrow.

'Don't worry, you will not be exposed.'

Marlvon watched as Islonda fumbled to undo the odd shaped buttons on either side of the dress. As she did, two sections of fabric swung down in front of her to hang loose. If it wasn't for the quantity of cloth, a large slit would have exposed Islonda right down the centre, from groin to feet.

Marlvon continued to explain the complicated process to Islonda while trying to hide his cheeky smirk. Eventually she stood back and held out her arms for him to see.

Marlvon clapped his hands once. 'And now, the process is complete.'

'So it is. I'll admit that I had little faith in it working, but I feel almost like I'm wearing trousers. Or what I imagine trousers to feel like.' Islonda blushed in the first grey light of dawn.

Marlvon smiled. He may have sounded confident to Islonda, but he was not without his own reservations about whether the dress conversion would work at all. Supressing this, he glanced to the east and noticed the growing light. 'It is best that we get moving. It would be good to get most of the riding done before the day gets too hot. And besides, then we will have more time at our destination.' Malvorn smiled with anticipation and led the young lady to one of the horses.

'Today you will be riding this fine horse, Nal. Nal, may I introduce Islonda.' Marlvon watched as Islonda looked at the horse, her lips pursed.

'This old thing? She looks just about ready to keel over! She'll never last on a hot day like today's going to be.'

'Don't you listen to her, Old Nal; you've still got strength and spirit to last a good while yet.' Marlvon patted the old nag's soft nose and she snorted in response.

'Nal will treat you well. She is a kind old lady and knows our path well. And besides, I don't want you racing away from me.'

At that, Marlvon stepped back and exposed his horse; a strong chestnut mare in the prime of her youth.

'Now, no more arguing and on you get.'

Not wanting to wait for more complaints, Marlvon mounted his own steed. He did, however, allow himself a cheeky laugh as Nal nickered when Islonda climbed onto her.

The sun was just breaching the horizon as Marlvon and Islonda left the outskirts of Bankton on the northward road. Marlvon delighted in the growing light and the gentle warmth on his flank and he breathed a sign of pleasure.

'So Marlvon, where are we actually going today?'

Marlvon was pleased to see that Islonda had only taken a short while to recover from her sulk about her designated horse.

'We will be journeying for twelve miles, toward the woodland and then start our climb of those hills you see yonder. We will be riding for most of the morning before tackling the final ascent on foot. When we reach our destination, you will be glad of the toil, trust me.'

'You mean we will be leaving the road? But those woods are inhabited by outlaws, vagabonds and even cannibals, if the tales be true. Will we be safe?' Islonda sounded genuinely concerned.

Marlvon had heard such stories and had even seen evidence of camps within the woods, but he had never met another person in all of his visits there.

'We will be safe.' Although he made his voice confident for Islonda's sake, inside he was annoyed at himself for getting caught up in the excitement of spending the day with Islonda and had not thought of the dangers that faced them. He mentally ran through the weapons that he always kept concealed in the saddle of his mount: two small dirks and one hunting knife. They would have to do.

His thoughts were broken by the knowing look that Islonda was giving him. 'Are you sure?'

'Yes, I'm certain,' he promptly replied.

'If you say so.'

Marlvon wanted to change the topic to avoid his concerns from growing.

'How is your father?'

Marlvon saw Islonda was not convinced by his diversion tactics, but she chose not to pursue the subject further.

'My father is doing well. His business is busy and he is ever grateful for the amount of work that you have brought him over the months. I think you're now his best customer.'

Marlvon knew Islonda didn't much like open displays of affection, but he couldn't help himself.

'The only reason I gave him so much business was to give me a chance to see you more.'

'Hmmm, you have mentioned that once or twice before, you know.'

'Don't get me wrong, your father's blacksmithing abilities are quite good. I just think that his best creation was you.' Marlvon cringed as he said it. *Why could I never properly express myself in her presence?*

'If you keep going on like this, Marlvon, I will turn around and head straight home.'

Marlvon knew that the threat was empty, but he received the message nonetheless.

The young man soon felt relief as Islonda helped him out of the awkward situation. 'The sun sure has some warmth to her. Why don't we put a bit of speed on and shorten the distance to the shady woods?'

Marlvon watched as Islonda urged Old Nal into a fast trot and he admired her riding form. He let her get one hundred or so yards ahead before chasing her down at a canter. He pulled up beside her with a smile and they trotted side-by-side in silence.

The stillness of the landscape they passed through was beautiful. Brown fields of nearly mature grain spread out to both sides and there was not a cloud in the sky. Directly in front of them, and a little to the left, stood a series of rambling hills covered with trees and an odd granite boulder poking up here and there. From their current viewpoint, the hills looked gentle, but Marlvon knew they were far from kind.

As the day wore on, the couple passed several travellers and farmers who all greeted them politely, despite Islonda's odd deep sky-blue outfit. For the most part, the two enjoyed the scenery in silence. This silence was interspersed with soft conversations about the happenings at Bankton or Marlvon's farm or even the delightful prospect of peace.

The further they travelled from Bankton, the more Marlvon felt himself relax. He noticed this and realised that it was not so much about being away from the town itself, but more about being outside in the open space with next to nobody around. He sighed audibly with pleasure and Islonda glanced over at him. He tried to convey his feelings by simply smiling back at her; better, he thought, than stumbling over words again.

The young woman raised a comical eyebrow that Marlvon took to mean *you're an odd man* and he felt a flutter of joy to think how lucky he was to be able to spend the entire day with someone who didn't mind if he was odd.

A short while later, they came across a big old dead tree. The way it stood with its dry grey arms out on either side made it look a bit like an old man shrugging his shoulders and putting his hands up in the air in uncertainty. Marlvon loved this tree and would have spent half a day just staring at it.

'This is where we leave the road. But before we do, let's have a quick drink.'

Marlvon passed a water-skin to Islonda, who drank deeply. The now hot morning had made them both parched.

'Care for a tomato too?'

'Yes, please.'

Marlvon passed her a couple of small red tomatoes. 'These are from my neighbour's farm. They are a little small, but that just intensifies the flavour. Be careful, the juice often squirts when you bite into them.'

Marlvon delicately bit into his own tomato. The hot sun on the saddlebags had made the fruit lusciously warm. He savoured the flavour of each mouthful before swallowing.

After eating a few, Marlvon took another gulp of water and looked at Islonda with playfulness in his eyes. 'And soon we will plunge into the glorious shade of the woods and avoid getting ambushed by outlaws.'

Marlvon guided his horse off the road, rode over a short open grassed expanse, and into the woodland.

If Marlvon had found joy in the open fields, then he found love amongst the trees. These were not hugely tall, but still reached far above the traveller's heads. The sun filtered through the leaves that were gently blowing in the breeze to dance upon the trunks of the nearby trees. This excited Marlvon as his eyes chased the ever-changing spectacle. As his vision darted about, he realised that every time he came here, he marvelled at the sheer variety of plant life; from the little purple wild flowers to the hardy shrubs and grasses, all the way to the tallest trees with their smooth skin-like bark and long thin leaves. He breathed in the freshness of the forest and delighted in the slight citrus scent that his favourite tree gave off. While Marlvon was a quick learner in most subjects, he found it almost impossible to learn the names of the abundant flora. His inability to *tame* the plants with names only intensified his love of the area.

The young man turned to Islonda and was pleased to see her looking around in amazement with a subconscious smile spread across her face. He realised, perhaps for the first time, that her life in Bankton really had been confined. He felt genuinely grateful for having had a much less sheltered life.

The road they had been on continued north, whereas the wilderness they were now in spread out to cover a series of not-quite-mountainous hills that rambled off to the west. These hills had unpredictably undulating slopes with a red clay soil strewn with boulders and rock formations jutting through. The uneven ground made for slow riding for Marlvon and Islonda, but as they weaved between the trees, they cared not.

Marlvon led Islonda on a path known only to him. It crossed several small creeks, wove here and there, but led them ever upwards. They passed through dense fern valleys and over open rocky ground where no plants could grow. They chatted to each other and pointed out things of interest that they saw. Marlvon showed Islonda his favourite birds and those that he had seen eating snakes or small rodents. At one point, the couple paused for a short while as Islonda marvelled to see a yellow chested small bird gathering sticks and leaves to build a nest.

As the morning wore on, they found themselves quite high on a hillside and heating up. The wonderful shade of the lower slopes had thinned, allowing the sun to kiss them once more. Marlvon felt himself sweating and knew that Islonda must be hotter than he was in her outfit.

The hill soon levelled off and before them, and on either side, rose a slope too steep for the horses to climb.

'It's time to dismount and journey the last section on foot.'

Marlvon climbed off his horse and helped the saddle-sore Islonda down from Old Nal.

The young man shared another water-skin and, as Islonda sat on a granite rock, Marlvon unloaded his horse's saddlebags. He re-packed most of these goods into a bag for his back and turned to face Islonda.

'It will be worth the effort, I promise you.'

He held out his hand and helped the young lady to her feet. As his hand touched hers, he felt the familiar wave of excitement pass through his body. Marlvon led Islonda to the slope and scrambled up the loose soil. It was hard going and he soon felt dirt sticking to his sweaty body. Despite the challenging climb, Islonda kept close behind him and did not complain once; she was too proud for that.

As they rose higher, the slopes on either side diminished until theirs was the only one remaining. Then, just as Marlvon's legs began to burn, their slope eased off and he stood on flat ground once more.

While Marlvon knew the view behind him to be wonderful, he instead looked at the clump of huge boulders directly before him. Marlvon heard Islonda come panting up behind him and found himself momentarily distracted as she stood close to him to avoid herself sliding back down the hill.

'The view is nice Marlvon, but I'm not sure it was worth that climb.'

'Perhaps not, but we are not there yet.'

Marlvon shimmied his way along the rock-face and found what he was looking for. 'Islonda, where we are about to go; only I have ever been before. Follow me and have faith.'

He turned from his love and squeezed his way into a crack in the rock before him that was hidden behind an old wiry bush. The hole was dark and close, but he pushed forward, knowing where it would lead. He soon heard the drip-drip-plop of water and before long, felt the passageway widening. Light emerged both above and in front of him, and a trickle of water could be seen at his feet. The crack quickly widened further and he emerged from the boulder. Before allowing himself to take in the scenery, he bounded down a few steps that were naturally built into the rock and turned to wait for Islonda's arrival. She was close on his heels, yet before bounding down the steps, she paused and took an audible intake of breath.

'Oh, Marlvon, it's wonderful!'

She carefully made her way down the stairs and rewarded Marlvon with an uncharacteristic hug and a passionate kiss.

From a crack in the rock formation, bubbled a tiny spring-fed creek. It too, leapt down the steps before widening into a deep-water hole. This was close to ten feet wide and ran for thirty feet or so across a flat stretch of rock before tumbling over a rocky cliff and falling many hundreds of feet into a valley below. As the pool approached the waterfall, it became shallow before passing over the ledge. At the end of summer, when the flow of water had eased, no water fell over the cliff. As it was now in the midst of summer, only a small trickle found its way to the land below.

To the right of the waterhole, the same flat rock spread out before it too fell far below. For the fortune of Marlvon and Islonda, to the left of the waterhole, a thin strip of dirt had built up and with the continuous supply of water, had allowed stunted leafy trees to grow. These trees would shade the entire rock outcrop as the sun moved west. In the midday sun however, there was little shade to be found and the rock was warm to the touch.

While the immediate surrounds were lovely, what really made the place wonderful was the view. 'Islonda, you are now facing due north. If you look over there, you can just make out an extension of the road that we were on earlier today. And if you look far over there, north-east, you can just see the sparkling water of the Rogaus Sea. It's truly amazing how far one can see when they have a clear line of sight on a fine summer's day. Looking nearer, you can see our bit of wilderness go on for maybe fifty miles before turning into farmland once more. Now, if you look far away over to your left, you will see a haze on the horizon; that's the Woods of Sorrow. Not somewhere that I would recommend you to go.'

'It's wonderful, all of it! And the difficult climb makes it all the more beautiful.'

Marlvon smiled to himself. 'Yes, is does.'

The happy young man came up behind Islonda and put his arms around her waist.

'Now, I'm all hot and dirty and would like a swim in that cool waterhole to freshen myself up. It is quite safe, and that rock ledge means you cannot easily be washed over the waterfall. If you would like a swim too, then I will take my swim first to show you that it is safe.' He kissed the back of her neck and pulled away.

'You make sure that you just keep looking out at the wondrous view, while I take my clothes off. Once I'm in, I'll let you know. After I've had a quick swim, I'll take in the view and you can have a go.'

As Marlvon undressed, he thought to himself: *If there's one way to make Islonda do something, it's to tell her to do the opposite.* And he was right. As he slid his last item of clothing off and made a dash to the pool, he saw Islonda sneaking a peak out of the corner of her eye.

The cool water enveloped Marlvon's body and he instantly felt relief from the day's heat. He quickly washed the dirt from his skin and submerged himself to wash his filthy hair. He stayed under as long as his breath would allow; soaking the coolness into his bones. As he resurfaced, he saw a white blur of legs and arms as Islonda splashed in to the pool next to him. His amazement at how quickly she had undressed was chased from his mind as her sun heated lips pressed firmly against his mouth. He immediately felt himself react and passionately kissed her back.

Initially, only her lips had made contact, but as he kissed her, he felt the rest of her naked body press against his. While his skin had cooled in the water, hers was still warm. He wrapped his arms around her and held her close.

'This is hardly proper behaviour for such a fine young lady as yourself.' He grinned and kissed her again.

'I can always stop and get out if you would prefer,' she smiled playfully.

'Oh, no you don't.' He cheekily kissed her again.

Despite the water having cooled his skin, he felt his body reacting and his skin heating once more. 'Come here and kiss—'

Islonda needed no beckoning and was kissing him well before he had finished his request.

He ran his fingers across her shoulders and down her spine. He found her lower back and pulled her to him. His hands continued to wander over her contours, and he soon felt her do likewise. He moved his mouth from her lips down to her collarbones and Islonda shuddered with pleasure. As he continued to explore her body, he moved so that he stood firmly on the bottom of the pool.

Marlvon could not believe what was happening and before he realised, he felt Islonda wrap her legs around his waist and eased herself onto him. All of his other senses were lost and he felt pure pleasure. Marlvon felt Islonda move on him and it was not long before they both lost control and screamed out in ecstasy to the emptiness around them.

Afterwards, they remained in the pool in a loving embrace until Marlvon's legs began to cramp with the cold.

'Would you like some lunch, my beautiful Islonda?'

'Mmmm, that sounds lovely; we've certainly worked up an appetite.' Islonda gave Marlvon a cheeky smile and a light kiss.

Marlvon pulled himself out of the pool and became embarrassed by his nakedness. He hurried to his clothes and dressed promptly.

Islonda followed, but instead of being shy like Marlvon, she remained undressed and lay down on the blanket that Marlvon had put out.

'Well, this is a side of you I haven't seen before.'

'It's nice to be free and do as I please. Bankton can be so stifling and restrictive.' Islonda closed her eyes. 'Is my lunch ready yet?'

'Yes, it is, but I won't let you eat anything until you put some clothes on; you're distracting me and I can't think straight.'

'Are you telling me what to do?'

'I believe I am. Now, do you want lunch or not?' Marlvon chuckled as Islonda hastily put her dress-pants on.

Marlvon had laid out a deliciously inviting spread of aged cheeses, preserved olives from his farm, a rich dark rye bread, some tomatoes and thin slices of ham. His stomach was rumbling by the time Islonda was ready, but before starting, he poured himself and Islonda a cup of wine from a flask. There was silence for a few moments while the hungry lovers ate Marlvon's produce.

Thinking about what had happened, Marlvon had a question that he wanted to ask Islonda, but felt awkward about asking it. He put it off for a few moments, until his curiosity got the better of him. 'That wasn't your first time, was it?'

Islonda looked keenly at Marlvon. 'I am a lady of eighteen years who knows what she wants and isn't afraid to take it.' She paused before continuing firmly. 'There are also things in my past that are going to stay there.'

Marlvon felt uncomfortable and regretted asking Islonda what he now realised was a deeply personal question. 'I'm sorry. I… I just didn't expect that to happen. There still seems to be a lot that I need to learn about you.'

'Ha! And there always will be.'

Without knowing how, Marlvon noticed that somehow Islonda had made the mood light once more; and it brought a smile to his face.

'Do you like the food?'

'Mmmm, the olives and ham especially. Presenting this kind of food makes it seem like you're doing quite well for a simple olive farmer.'

Marlvon chuckled. 'It helps having your uncle as the mighty Leader of the Outcasts. I'm glad that you like the olives though. They are last season's best pickings and the oil is pressed from my olives by myself.'

'The bread dipped in the oil is most delicious.'

'Mmm, I could eat it all day. And I find the freshness of the tomatoes helps to lift the saltiness of the olives and the richness of the cheese.'

The two picked at the food in silence and soon found their stomachs filled. After washing the food down with the remainder of the wine, the two felt relaxed and at ease. Marlvon packed up what was left of the food and sat down with his feet dangling into the cool water.

Islonda came to join him and lay with her head in his lap. As Marlvon ran his fingers through her now dry hair, he felt utterly and completely happy. He bent down and kissed her gently on her nose. She smiled up at him, then closed her eyes to avoid the sun's glare.

'Islonda, there's something that I want to ask you, but before I do, I want to tell you something about my past and who I am.'

Islonda opened her eyes. 'You sound almost nervous, Marlvon.'

'Do I? I suppose that's because I have done some terrible things and I'm afraid that by telling you about them, you won't want to be with me anymore. Yet, I don't feel like I can move forward with you while keeping secrets from you.'

Islonda reached up and stroked the back of Marlvon's head.

'Marlvon, one of the great things about meeting someone new is that you can start afresh. You don't know their past and they don't know yours. You are not tied down by a shared history and so can be exactly who you want to be; not who you were. There are things in my past that I hope to never revisit, and if there are things in yours that you would rather forget, then forget them.'

'I'll never be able to forget what I've done.'

'Marlvon, what I'm trying to say is that I don't care who you were. I want to discover who you are and who you're going to be. Marlvon, I didn't fall in love with the man you were many years ago; I am in love with the man you are today. And he is gentle and kind and caring. Do not dwell on the past, but look to the future; look to our future.'

Marlvon felt a lump in his throat. Islonda had never expressed her true love for him and he was touched deeply by her words.

'I want to look to the future. In fact, I want to build a future with you. Islonda, I want to spend the rest of my life with you. Islonda, will you wed me?'

Islonda pulled Marlvon's head down and kissed him strongly. 'Yes, I will.' And she kissed him again.

Joy washed through his heart and body and he wanted to leap about and scream to the sky above. Instead, he picked Islonda up in a loving embrace and jumped into the waterhole with her, clothes and all. She squealed with the shock of the cold water and playfully pushed his head under.

They frolicked around in the water before emerging sodden and cold. In silent agreement, they both stripped off and lay their wet clothes on the hot rock in the sun to dry. They lay down side-by-side on Marlvon's blanket and stared into each other's eyes.

It wasn't long before they heated in the afternoon sun and sadness crept into Marlvon's heart.

'Marlvon, are you all right? You look sad.'

'I've just realised that if we are to make it back to Bankton before dark, then we had best leave soon. Yet, I just want to stay here in this place with you forever.'

'Do we have to go? Couldn't we just stay here for the night?'

'From a practical point of view, we could. We have clean water, the night will be warm, but a fire would be nice too. It's true that we don't have much food, but we wouldn't die of starvation. What concerns me more is your father. What would Jault think of you staying out all night with a young man? Aside from that, he would worry about where you are. I promised to have you back home today and he will be concerned for you if you are not.'

Islonda's firm response shocked Marlvon. 'I'm not a child! He can't tell me what to do, and neither can you. If I want to stay out here tonight, then I'm going to stay out here tonight.'

'Islonda, I'm not trying to tell you what to do. I'm just sharing my concerns with you.'

Marlvon placed a reassuring hand on Islonda's bare shoulder and he felt the tension leave her body.

'*Do* you want to stay here tonight?'

Islonda averted her gaze. 'I don't know.'

Marlvon flicked the corner of his mouth into a smile. 'What happened to the young lady who knows what she wants?'

'Be careful Marlvon, or I might take back what I said before.'

Marlvon detected the cheek behind the words, but chose to err on the side of caution.

'I'm sorry. Do you want me to decide what we should do?'

'No, I'll decide. But in the meantime, I want you to give me a kiss.'

Marlvon obliged without a moment's hesitation. After a short kiss, Marlvon felt Islonda pull back; he saw a mischievous glint in her eyes.

'You know, the night might get quite cool with no cloud cover. We might have to lie close to keep each other warm.'

Marlvon felt his heart quicken at the thought. 'That is very true, Islonda. Does that mean that you've made your decision?'

'If you promise to keep me warm tonight, then I want to stay right here.'

'What about your father?'

'We can tell him we got lost and that you protected me stoically. A lie, it is true, but one that will harm no one.'

'How can I possibly refuse a proposition like that?' Marlvon knew it was not quite the right thing to do, but he simply couldn't help himself. 'Very well, I promise to keep you warm tonight.'

Marlvon watched as Islonda purposefully edged her way closer to him, raised her naked body over his and for the second time that day, they made love.

The sun had moved across the sky and Marlvon woke with his head in the cool shade. He kicked himself for having fallen asleep, but the urge had been too strong. He extracted himself from Islonda's arms and hastily dressed. As Islonda continued to doze, Marlvon left the rocky ledge in search of some wood for a fire. It was quite difficult carrying it through the fissure in the rock, but it wasn't too long before he had sufficient supplies for the night.

As he kindled a blaze, Islonda woke and rose to sit by the flames. The sun soon dipped below the horizon and Marlvon divided up the rest of their food, making sure he gave more to Islonda than to himself.

After they had eaten the meagre meal, they lay down on Marlvon's blanket once more and watched as the stars twinkled into existence one by one.

A sense of melancholy stirred within Marlvon. 'They are so beautiful, the stars, and yet, they sadden me. While they may change from season to season, they remain ever present and, whether you're having the worst day of your life or the best day you've ever had, they remain. They care not for the flow of human existence. They care not for life and death, for heedless, they remain. What are they? I could not even guess. What is their purpose? Who knows? But I'd bet my life that it is not for our enjoyment. And yet, they are enjoyed.'

Marlvon felt Islonda reach over and clasp his hand. 'I know what you mean, but it is hard to verbalise the feelings that they stir within. They seem to make me both happy and sad at the same time; if that is even possible. It's not often that I get to look up and admire them, but every time I do, I'm moved beyond words.'

The two remained silent as more stars emerged, as well as a thin waxing moon. The night deepened, the fire crackled merrily and the two lovers fell asleep as they cuddled close, happy with the world.

19

'Sister Sor, Sister Sor, wait.' Winter chased after the young monk as she headed to the breakfast hall from her place of sleep. Winter had woken early and headed to the female dormitory to catch Sor as she left. As it was, he only just arrived as she was leaving.

'Sister Sor, it has happened again.'

Sor turned to the pale-skinned young man. 'What has happened again?'

'I've had another dream of my father. This is the fourth in a row, assuming that the first one was of him as a boy in an archery competition where he came second and his parents weren't happy. They seem to be in chronological order. The second one was of him conquering Balleny, a city on the far side of the Moaks and where I was raised. The third was a dream of pure elation as he made an epiphany about some black crystal. Don't ask me what that epiphany was; that wasn't part of the dream.'

Sor cut off his excited babble. 'I know all this, Winter; we have gone through it at length. Just hurry up and tell me what your latest dream was so that we can go to breakfast.'

Winter failed to notice Sor's lack of enthusiasm and continued at a rapid pace. 'Well, dream number four was about his downfall as Emperor, and defeat at the hands of Balton. But as with the other dreams, it was not filled with clear vision and logical order. No, it was more about feeling it. I mean, I think I felt exactly what my father must have felt at the time. Anger, he felt such anger, but also deep-seated sadness at having failed and being defeated. And pain; not so much physical pain, even though his hand got cut off, but a deep pain which pierced to the very essence of his being. And, for the first time ever, I think I felt sorry for him.'

Sor looked at Winter with her mouth agape. 'You felt sorry for him? For the man that effectively tortured you your entire life? You felt sorry for *him*?'

'Yes. He is, after all, my father, and he was in so much pain.' Winter smiled, but Sor shook her head and walked towards the dining hall.

'Wait … Sor.' He reached out and grabbed her arm.

Sor shrugged him off. 'Winter, leave me.'

'What have I done? Sor, I … I think I'm beginning to heal. I've stopped having nightmares and I've been less angry and frustrated these last few days. I feel like

I'm on the path to forgiving my father for what he did to me.' Winter stopped talking. Before saying those words, he had not even realised that was how he felt.

Winter composed himself and spoke with a soft voice. 'Sor, can't you be happy for me?' Winter looked pleadingly at her.

'I am happy that you have started your journey to recovery. I really am. But Winter, going from the place you were four nights ago, to forgiving that horrible man, will take time and effort. A lot more time and a lot more effort. You can't expect to have four dreams and then all of a sudden, everything is fixed. You need to think about your past, think about what happened to you; confront it, accept it, and conquer it. And, as I pledged, I'm going to help you with that, but you will also need to pray to the Gods, both Day and Night Gods.

'Winter, you need to calm down and take things slowly and cautiously. You should be wary of these dreams. They may *seem* harmless, even helpful, but they may make everything a lot worse. You cannot know the purpose of them, if they even have a purpose at all, not yet.' Sor turned away from Winter.

'Sister, what if the dreams have been put into my mind by the Gods, to help me heal? I know that they have been put there for a reason. I just know it.'

As Sor turned back to face Winter, the not-quite-monk saw thoughtful conflict on her face.

'You know more about the Gods than I do, Sor. Do they have power to manipulate my dreams? Is it possible that they want me to feel what my father has felt? Perhaps, to understand him better?'

'The power? Yes, they could manipulate your dreams or anyone else's dreams. But the interest? I doubt it. I believe they would prefer you to discover the answers yourself. Hhmmm, but it is an interesting prospect that you raise. I will pray that we get an answer soon.'

'Thank you, Sister. Even if they are not shaping my dreams, the Gods are at the least allowing me to have them. And I take comfort in that.'

Winter noticed that Sor's body was less tense and she seemed less irritable than a moment before. He decided he wanted to keep her in this better mood.

'Now, Sister, would you like some breakfast? I'm starving.'

She smiled at him. 'Yes, I would, thank you.'

The two worshippers of the Night God made their way, side by side, towards the hall to break their fast.

Winter found himself in a room of mist. He could see no walls, windows or doors, but saw before him an empty chair. It was a simple wooden chair and there was nothing remarkable about it. Then Winter blinked and suddenly there was a man sitting on the chair. The man looked old to Winter and as the mist shifted, he noticed that the man was tied to the chair. His wrists and ankles were fastened by a thin rope that was cruelly tight. The man was slouched forward and, as blood dripped out of his mouth, Winter realised the prisoner was naked.

The fog shifted again and a tall man appeared, to stand over the seated figure. Winter immediately knew that the standing man was his father and that he had been torturing the other man for information. Not a word was spoken between the unmoving figures, but Winter felt a thin veil of happiness develop as his father got the information that he wanted. Winter looked beneath this superficial happiness and found there a deep pit of anguish, self-loathing and fear. Mixed in with these, he also sensed a cry for help. He felt so keenly that his brutal, vicious, terrifying father was pleading with everything in existence to be saved; saved from himself and the inevitable path of destruction that had begun many, many years ago.

Winter gasped for breath as the enormous weight of complex emotions washed over him in the misty room. He tried to cry out to his father, but his voice would not work. He tried to reach out to his father, but he found he had no body to reach with. The mist closed in. His vision of the two men became obscured. All he could see was white mist. Then his eyes snapped open and he saw the candlelight flickering on the roof above his bed. He sucked in several deep breaths and calmed his quivering body.

A moment later, Winter's mind was made up: *I'm going to find my father, and with the help of the Gods, I'm going to save him.*

Several nights had passed since Winter had decided to seek out his father and, during that time, he had been busy gathering supplies for his departure. He had not had any further dreams since the vision of the misty room, and this solidified his resolve. *The Gods must have shown me all that I needed to see.*

It had been hard telling Sor that he was going to leave, but he had still sought her out as soon as was possible. She had not taken his resolution well. Her reaction had shocked Winter, perhaps not in its intention, but definitely in its severity. At first, she was silent. This had transitioned to frustration and then ended in anger with the monk uncharacteristically raising her voice and storming off.

Winter had felt saddened by Sor's reaction, but his decision had remained the same. Since then, Winter had been busy preparing himself for his departure and after five nights, he was prepared.

The sun was just rising after a sticky late-summer's night and Winter found himself seated alone, bathing his feet in the cold water of the stream that ran through the village. He chose this spot as it was the same section of the forested stream that Brother Zin had taken him to when he had first arrived with the monks. The water felt just as icy as it had those many weeks ago, but Winter felt like a completely different man. He smiled at the change.

The creek gurgled and plopped and Winter failed to hear the footsteps of Sor as she approached him from behind. She coughed to make her presence known, and Winter sat upright and turned his torso towards her. *She is quite a handsome woman, or would be if her hair was allowed to grow.* Winter looked closely at Sor's face. *She's been crying, her eyes are puffy, but she has that stubborn look about her jaw that she gets when she's digging her heels in to argue. All I wanted was to leave her on a happy memory; it looks like that won't be happening now.*

'Brother Winter, the sun is rising. Isn't it time that you and I were asleep?'

Winter smiled wryly. 'For you, yes. For me, I will sleep no more while the sun shines. Sister Sor, I'm leaving today.'

Winter saw her eyes flash briefly with angst.

'So, you still mean to follow this foolish path?'

'I mean to find my father and try to save him from himself.'

'And what about your path to becoming a monk? What about everything that we've given you, taught you?'

'I value everything that I have been taught immensely. I take those learnings with me; they are what will help me save him, my learnings and the will of the Gods. Sor, I will not change my mind.'

'You're not allowed to leave. You're training to become a monk, Lunar and Solar won't allow it.' Winter felt pity for Sor. *She is clasping for ways to stop me leaving.*

'I have made no pledge or oath to the order of the monks that can force me to stay. And I've already spoken to Lunar and Solar. While they would prefer me to stay, they can see no good in forcing me to remain. They have even been kind enough to provide me with provisions to last for several days, a blanket to sleep under, and coins to help me along. While they were clear that I was not to wear either the black or white robes of the monks, they have permitted me to wear this grey one. It symbolises that I am not yet a monk, but worship the Gods. So, you see Sor, there is nothing to stop me from leaving.'

Sor spoke with a shaky whisper. 'What about me? What about our friendship?'

Winter stood and faced Sor. Placing his hands on her shoulders, he looked into her eyes. 'Sor, I value our friendship very much, but saving my father is bigger than that. This will be the first sacrifice of many that I'll have to make.'

'But why is he more important than you, more important than me?'

Winter thought for a moment. 'I don't fully know. It's this feeling that I have. Maybe part of me becoming a better man is to try to help the man who made me the disgusting person I was. As I say, I don't fully understand, but it feels like the will of the Gods to me.'

Sor raised an eyebrow before her face hardened into an expression of determination. 'I can now see that you won't be convinced to stay, so that leaves me no choice: Winter, I am coming with you.'

'What? No, you can't! You must stay here with you fellow monks.' Winter felt anger and fear building within him.

'Winter, I made a promise to the Night God to help you change into a better person and leave behind your sinful ways. This path that you've chosen will be full of temptation for you to slip backwards. You have come so far, and yet have so much further to go before you've really changed. I cannot help you by staying here. So, in order to keep my promise to the Night God, I must accompany you.'

'But Lunar and Solar…'

'Before you continue, they have granted me permission to join you. They recognise my promise to the God of Night as binding and encourage me to do everything in my power to fulfil that promise. While we journey, I will also continue your education in our ways, so that once you have come to your senses, we can return and you can become a proper monk.'

Winter felt his fear rising. 'No. I won't allow it. It will be too dangerous for you.' The young man thought of his sister and how he had lost her crossing the river. 'I'm going to be visiting some horrible places, meeting with nasty people. I… I don't want to lose you like I lost Dusk.' Winter felt a lump growing in his throat.

'You won't lose me, Winter. I know it will be dangerous, for me and for you, but I'm coming with you. So, now that's been decided, when do we leave? And don't try giving me the slip, because I'm not leaving your side, not for a moment.'

It would be good to have her with me. But the risk to her life is far too great. I could run away from her; I'm probably faster, but my pack is not fully ready to take. I could tie her up, but then she may not be found for days. Winter felt trapped.

'I'm not happy with you, Sor. You're forcing me to do something against my will.'

He looked up at the now light sky. *How long has it been since I saw real daylight? Many weeks, I suppose.*

'If you're coming, then we do things my way. I'm in charge and you'll do exactly as I say. Once we leave the monks and the surrounding towns, you will be outside of your reckoning; not many people will treat you as the monks do.

You must have your wits about you and trust no one. Treat everyone as if they're trying to get the better of you. Beyond the safety of the monk towns, the world is a different place: beware!'

'You make the world sound like a horrible place.'

'That's because a lot of it is; especially for those unwary of its dangers. Now, once we have gathered supplies for you to carry, we will leave. Already the day is progressing quickly.'

'It's so bright, isn't it? I cannot remember seeing the risen sun.' Sor looked from the sky to Winter. 'But where exactly are we going?'

'We will follow this stream to Green Lake. I'm sure you can help guide us to start with. Once there, we will make more plans. Our general aim is to make our way to the place where the filth of humanity is drawn. From what you've told me, that place is Psymryte.'

Sor nodded; her determined expression remaining.

She is foolish to want to come with me; foolish and naïve.

Winter sighed to himself before whispering a heart-felt prayer. 'Please, Gods of both Night and Day, let no harm come to her while we travel.' *Amen.*

20

Kathsum sat at a large marble table with her palms face down on the surface. The white marble with its veins of green felt cool on the warm summer night. She often wondered why marble always felt cooler than the air, no matter how hot or cold the day was, but had never found a satisfying answer. These thoughts did not trouble her mind tonight, though.

Between her hands lay two rolled up scrolls that were fastened with the High Chancellor's official wax seal. She valued these documents almost more than her life; they held so much promise and excitement for her people.

Sitting back in her chair, she subconsciously ran her fingers through her auburn hair as she thought about the night ahead of her. Before she could move on to the excitement that awaited her at midnight, she first had to deal with the unpleasant new Admiral. She disliked the man already; her own intuition told her he was not to be trusted. Guflinkov had reinforced these feelings with his own advice to be wary of the man. Her old teacher was usually an accurate judge of character.

Where is that Tunley? He should have been here by now. Tardiness, another reason to dislike the man.

She looked about the room while she waited. *I've spent many days of my life in this room, arguing and persuading councillors to my way of thinking. And hasn't it been great! Listen to yourself, Kathsum, you are thinking like someone who is about to retire. Just because peace is looming doesn't mean that there won't be a lot of work to do.* Kathsum sighed. *There is always a lot of work to do.* Then a smile spread across her face. *Peace; it is so close. And I have the power to achieve it right here in my hands.* She paused to look at the scrolls before her. *It's funny to think that I've been working towards this for most of my life, and yet, I don't even know what peace will be like.*

Ah, peace. Just the word sounds so inviting. Kathsum ran her fingers through her hair again, pressing firmly on her scalp. *Less people will die, that will be good. Almost everyone in Roasline has lost at least one son, daughter, brother or sister to this war. There has been so much pain. But despite the deaths, the city is nearly full of people; it's certainly very crowded. With less people dying, the population will grow more rapidly. Where will they all live?* Kathsum frowned to herself. *How can you think like that: the positives of people being killed! But… housing will be a problem.* Kathsum sighed audibly. *Nothing is ever simple.*

Her thoughts were swiftly broken by the opening of the door at the far end of the table. Kathsum sat up stiffly and her right hand habitually went to the moonstone on her necklace.

Admiral Tunley strode into the room with a slight limp, paused, and smiled at Kathsum. He ambled his way over to where she sat, his eyes darting about the room.

I shouldn't be sitting. He has all the power of height and being free to move about the room while I remain static.

'Good evening High Chancellor. So, this is the fabled room where the fate of many is decided. Cosy. I particularly like the portraits watching over everyone's shoulders. It's good to know that someone is monitoring proceedings.' He chuckled to himself.

Kathsum observed Tunley as he made his way to her and stood uncomfortably close. Her nostrils flared at the smell of fish on the Admiral's breath.

'Good evening to you, Admiral Tunley. Please, have a seat.'

Kathsum watched as Tunley yanked back a chair and sat on her right. She couldn't help a grimace of disgust as Tunley rocked back in his seat and put his dirty boots on the beautiful white marble tabletop.

'So, is this where I'll be sitting for the council meetings? I like it; it's comfortable.'

'No, that is where the Quaestor sits.' Kathsum was tart in her response.

'Oh, well.'

'Speaking of the Quaestor, I would like to thank you for organising safe passage for him to Headly with our coffers.'

'Thanks is not needed. I am the Admiral; I control all movement in and out of our docks. He would not have been able to leave without me. Thanking me for this service would also imply that I had some sort of choice in the matter.' Tunley scowled at Kathsum as he clipped the last few words of his statement.

How dissatisfying. That's not what I wanted to get out of thanking him. Well, there's no point going down that path; better to be direct.

'I did not ask you here to thank you for performing your duty, but to inform you of the outcome from tonight's council meeting.'

Tunley took his feet off the table and sat up.

'As of now, and as your new title dictates, you are a member of the Council of Roasline.' The corner of her mouth twitched up. 'But you will not begin your tenure with voting rights at council meetings.'

Tunley leapt to his feet, but before he could verbalise his protest, Kathsum continued to speak firmly. As she did so, she slowly rose to her full height and made use of her broad shoulders to appear as physically formidable as she could.

'After six months in this position, the council will vote again on whether to grant you full council membership. This is the decision of the council and it is final.'

By the time the High Chancellor had finished, Tunley was red in the face and fuming.

'This is an outrage! It is unheard of! I'll tell you what is going to happen: I will be on the council and I will vote as every Admiral before me has!'

'No, you won't. You will watch and you will learn, and if you mature enough, then you will be granted the power to vote in six months' time. Remember Admiral, at not even forty years of age, you are the youngest member of the council.'

Tunley brushed this comment aside. 'Who voted against me, Kathsum? You? The three Aldermen? Who?'

'The voting is privy to the current council members only.'

Tunley stepped closer to Kathsum. She could smell his breath and feel his spittle against her cheek when he spoke.

'I will find out who voted against me and I can assure you, they will not be voting the same way next time.'

Tunley brushed past the High Chancellor and stormed towards the doorway. When he was at the threshold, he turned with a nasty smile.

'I will be Admiral until I die, but tell me Kathsum, when are you next up for election?' The Admiral didn't wait for her to reply before he left and slammed the door behind him.

Kathsum felt exhaustion wash over her and slumped in her seat. *He is right. He will outlast me in a position of power. The best I can do is minimise his impact while I'm still High Chancellor.* She sighed once more. *Guflinkov was right; that man is going to be problematic. I should have listened to my old friend and appointed someone else as Admiral.*

The tired High Chancellor looked down at her shaking hands and put them on the table. Her eyes caught sight of the two scrolls sitting there. A smile crept its way into her face and her heart quickened with excitement once more. She pushed the unpleasantness of Tunley from her mind and focused on the prospect of peace. *It is time for me to make my way down to the docks. Jacov and Resvon will almost be there, and tonight of all nights, I don't want to keep them waiting.*

The High Chancellor of Roasline stood, picked up the two identical peace treaties signed by the council, and with full composure strode from the council room.

Kathsum made her way to the docks as the full moon broke through a part in the clouds. The hurried walk was uneventful, with the usual bumps and knocks that any busy street would bring. She arrived just as the small skiff carrying Resvon and Jacov was pulling up to the pier. She shivered with excitement and smiled to see the familiar shaved head of Jacov and the thinning grey hair of Resvon. *They came. One step closer to peace.* She carefully stepped into the boat with the aid of Jacov's firm grip.

'Good evening, gentlemen.'

Jacov only grunted, but Resvon returned her smile. 'Yes, it is, Kathsum.'

Once seated, Jacov pushed off from the dock and began steering the boat out into the current of the Liagar. Kathsum looked back at the shore and saw the new admiral watching her. She shivered and turned away from the foreboding figure.

'Resvon, I trust that your Captain Ryde reached you safely?'

'Yes, he did.'

'Good, good. And did you have any trouble getting your council to approve the peace deal? Mine were a bit troublesome, but the simple prospect of peace in our time convinced them in the end.'

Despite his words, Resvon spoke softly. 'I am the Leader of the Outcasts. I require the approval of no one. Some of my council may not be happy with peace, but they will abide my authority. We do not live in the bureaucracy of a democracy on my side of the river.' Kathsum knew Resvon was a dictator, but his willingness to seek peace and his logical way of thinking had brought her to the conclusion that he was a *good* dictator.

'The people of Roasline may take a while to become accustomed to the idea of dealing with an undemocratic society.' *I imagine the idea of democracy may appeal to Resvon's people. We will need to develop strategies to prevent an influx of these outcasts to Roasline. It would be best though, to wait until after the peace treaty is signed to discuss this with Resvon. I don't want to scare him off at the last moment.*

'I'm sure your people will cope. Now, let's get down to business. Do you have your treaties ready, Kathsum?'

'I do.' Kathsum took out her two identical scrolls from within her light summer coat and passed them to Resvon. He broke the seal and inspected them closely by the light of a paraffin lamp. Kathsum watched keenly as he signed them both next to the signatures of her council members and handed one back to her. Resvon extracted two scrolls from under his seat and handed them to the High Chancellor.

She broke the seals and inspected them as closely as Resvon had done to hers.

'Everything seems to be correct.'

She signed them both next to Resvon's sole signature and handed one back to him.

'Now we both have a copy of each of the treaties.'

Before Kathsum could continue, Jacov spoke with a direct tone. 'I should sign all the documents as well; as a witness.'

'Very good.'

After the Healer had made his mark on all four treaties, he handed Kathsum and Resvon two each.

Kathsum smiled from ear to ear. 'So, does this mean that we are no longer at war; that we are finally at peace?'

The sad eyes of Resvon looked at her. 'Technically, yes. Although, practically speaking, we're the only ones who know it.'

Kathsum felt too much joy to listen to Resvon's negative slant on the situation.

'I've been thinking about celebrations for my people to mark this momentous feat. I'm going to hold a festival at the Citadel of Roasline and provide everyone who attends with food and drink for the day. I will do this in four days' time and I will make a speech to my people. I think it would strongly confirm our new friendship if you could be there, to stand by my side. We can also use the occasion to discuss the finer points of our agreement, such as the trading of goods and the passage of people between our two nations.'

Kathsum could see Resvon thinking before he replied.

'It would be a risky venture, so soon after such a long war, but I believe you are right; it would show the people that we are all in this together.'

'Then it is settled. I will arrange an escort on the water and guards to protect you as you make your way to the Citadel. You should also bring your own guards, as an example of our ability to work together.'

'As you wish. And then I'm sure that you will reciprocate the gesture and visit Fort Kykum afterwards?'

Kathsum hesitated. *I didn't think of that. Of course, I'll have to, but what is stopping Resvon from taking me prisoner or killing me? There are so many criminals on that side of the river. Hang on; has this been Resvon's plan all along? Either way, I suppose I don't really have a choice.*

She hid her concern from Resvon. 'I will.'

'It will be good, Kathsum, to start an era of peace with two significant displays of trust.'

Kathsum nodded. For reasons unknown, Kathsum felt ill at ease and wanted this meeting to be over.

'Shall we go our separate ways then? Jacov, can you please take me ashore? And thank you for the part that you have played in bringing about peace and especially for the healing protection that you have given us. You will soon be able to go back to treating illnesses instead of patching up war wounds'

'We, the Healers and I, are all very much looking forward to the change in our patient types. Now, your respective protection will be lifted once you each step ashore.'

The Healer guided the boat skilfully back towards Roasline's docks. Kathsum sat there pensively watching the shore line draw closer and was relieved when she noticed Tunley was not waiting for her. *At least I don't have to deal with him again tonight.*

Once ashore, she watched the small boat disappear into the darkness. When she was all alone, she turned to climb the hill to the citadel and with each step she took, more and more joy and happiness spread through her. *Finally, we are at peace!*

21

Tunley slammed the door of the council chambers, with Kathsum alone inside. *Stupid woman, why does she have to be so obstructive? I suppose she sees me as a threat to her power.* 'Ha!' The Admiral exclaimed aloud.

Tunley strode away from the chambers feeling a mixture of glee, at having put the High Chancellor in her place, and frustration at not being given voting rights at council meetings.

He left the Citadel of Roasline and wandered the streets under the light of the full moon. As he walked, his mind kept returning to the confrontation with Kathsum. *Why had they even voted to block me? Shouldn't I have just been granted membership? Someone doesn't want me there, that much is clear.* His swift mind immediately thought of Kathsum. *That bitch, it has to be her. No one else would even consider the prospect of a non-voting member. But she would not have won the vote alone. Who does she have on her side? Who does she have in her pocket?*

Tunley sighed audibly. *I need to find out more about the council members. How could I be so stupid not to have found out more about them already?* Tunley ran through the members as he counted them on his fingers. *Kathsum, the General, the Head of Order, the Chief Quaestor, the Alderman of Farmers, the Alderman of Merchants and the Alderman of Producers; or rather the Alderwoman of Producers.*

His thoughts were interrupted as he almost walked straight into someone. He gave them a firm but unaggressive shove. In the busy street he didn't think anything more of it at first, until he recognised the broad shoulders of the High Chancellor walking away from him. *Now, what is she doing out and about?*

Seizing the opportunity, the Admiral decided to follow her. *It's not like our fair leader to be out this late at night with no protection.* Tunley repeated that phrase aloud. 'No protection…' He mused. *Could I? Should I? Why did I leave my dirk at home? I could take her unawares; but that would cause a commotion. If only it were a bit later, there wouldn't be so many people about.*

Tunley continued to stalk her at a safe distance as Kathsum made her way towards the docks.

Would it even be to my benefit to kill her? Who would she be replaced by? Certainly not me; not yet anyway. It would probably be a man. Men are harder to manipulate than women. No, better that she remains alive, for the time being. But what is she doing out here?

It was not long before the two reached the docks and Tunley watched from the shadows as Kathsum climbed into a boat with two men. *Of course! The stinking traitor is meeting with Resvon again. If only I had my sword, I could run the bastard in. What a blow to the Outcasts that would be.*

As the small boat left the shore, Tunley made his way to the edge and watched with loathing until he could see them no more. *I need a drink.*

Tunley left the area and headed for a nearby tavern that he used to frequent in his youth: *The Sea Spray.* The establishment was a few streets back from the commercial docks and it did not take the Admiral long to find it. Being late at night, he knew that the public house would have quietened down and, when he entered the smoky dim room, there were many seats for him to choose from. He ordered a mug of dark ale and found the least lit corner to sit in.

The beer was rich, smoky and strong; just the way the Admiral liked it. *Why don't I drink beer more often? It always seems to be wine these days. I think I'll have another.* Tunley ordered another and returned to his seat.

Mmmmm, that's good. Now, how am I going to get voting rights on the council? I'm certainly not going to let Princess Kathsum walk all over me.

The solid man sat there thinking as the beer relaxed his wound-up mind and tense muscles. *I need to force a re-vote. But before I do that, I need to make sure that I can win. If only I knew who voted against me.* Tunley drained his ale and this time ordered a half strength pale version. It was not as pleasant, but the scheming man needed to stay alert to think. *Who would know? Records must be kept somewhere of what goes on at those meetings. But do I really want to stoop as low as to ferret around for pieces of paper? If all else fails, I suppose I'll have to.* Tunley paused for a moment. *What I need is an ally. The General; now he's likely to see eye to eye with me. But will he tell me confidential details?*

Perhaps. Hmmm, I think I'll pay the good General a visit. Tunley drained his drink and stood. He soon found himself a little bit wobbly on his feet. *Perhaps I should visit him tomorrow, when I have a clear head.* The Admiral grinned to himself before leaving the old tavern.

As he passed out of the door, he noticed an old man sipping cautiously on a hip flask, watching him. In his intoxicated state, he failed to realise that the old man was Guflinkov. The Admiral even nodded to him in greeting, thinking him an old sailor.

Admiral Tunley stood naked and stretched his hands above his head. He threw open the curtains as his man-servant brought in a basin of steaming water. The Admiral ignored the man as the basin was placed on a table next to a rare and expensive full body mirror. When the man had left, Tunley made his way over to stand in front of his reflection.

'Mmmm, what a man!' Tunley spoke under his breath to himself. He sucked in his ample gut, and in doing so bulged out his barrel chest. The sailor flexed his arms and smiled at their strength. The scar on his right thigh stood out and he and shrugged his shoulders in dismissal of it. After washing himself, he moved the wash basin to the floor in front of the mirror and relieved a forceful stream of night-water into it. He gave his member a decent shake, oblivious to the droplets of urine flying around the room.

'I really am a handsome man.' *But I cannot stay here all day, I'd better get dressed.*

The Admiral collected a pair of fine silk breeches and pulled them on. The close fitting, bone coloured pants did nothing to hide his manhood and he fastened the buttons and ribbon below the knee and stood to look at himself once more. Unlike the fashion of the time, he liked to keep his lower legs bare; to show the world his shaved muscular calves. He pulled a fine wool tunic over his head, made sure his chest hairs were visible and slipped on the Admiral's blue sash with three gold chains woven through it. Tunley pulled on soft leather ankle boots and ran his fingers through his long dark brown hair; fastening it into a ponytail with a length of silk that matched his Admiral's sash.

Before leaving the room, he took a few coins from a money pouch and threw them on the bed.

'Make sure you're not here by the time I get back.' He did not wait for a reply from the prostitute before leaving his bed chamber.

Once outside in the heating day, the Admiral began to sweat as he walked. Tunley wanted to speak to the General and he knew that he would either be in the officer's barracks or in his headquarters in the citadel. Wanting to speak with the military man in private, Tunley hoped that he was at the citadel, and so he headed there first.

The climb up the hill soon had Tunley puffing and red in the face. He reached the citadel at mid-morning, but before entering, stood in the shade to cool down and recompose his physical appearance.

I miss a nice spray of sea water on these hot days.

As he began to cool down, he saw an old man making his slow way up the path that the Admiral himself had taken. *What's that old Guflinkov doing here? I really don't trust him; always lurking about. The last thing I want is to have to talk to him.*

The Admiral entered the stone building and made his way to the west section, where the General's headquarters were positioned. He climbed a flight of well-worn stairs and walked along a short passageway before reaching the open doorway that he was after.

As Tunley entered, the General was standing bent over a table with a map of Roasline and the surrounding lands on it. He was concentrating intently on the map and as he breathed through his moustached nose, a whistling sound escaped.

The Admiral knocked on the open door. The General looked up.

'Admiral, I assume you're here to discuss the news. It came as a bit of a shock to me and the High Chancellor certainly hasn't given us much time to prepare.'

Tunley felt stupid. He didn't like feeling stupid.

'Which particular item of news is this, General?'

The General raised his eyebrows. 'Then you haven't heard? No, of course, you weren't at the council meeting last night; you weren't a member till after that meeting.'

Tunley felt his face redden and pursed his lips. *I need this man on my side, calm yourself.*

'Kathsum signed the peace treaty with Resvon last night. And what's more, I've been informed this morning that he's coming here in four days' time, *and*, there's going to be a festival. That woman is really pushing me to my limits. Four days! She could at least have given us a week.'

Tunley was a bit taken aback; he knew that peace was on the way, but did not realise that it was so close. 'That's outrageous. And with the better part of the fleet miles down the coast. What was the old Admiral thinking by sending them so far away and leaving us so exposed?'

'I quite agree, Admiral. We all acted on Kathsum's advice. But now it seems foolish. It's not just the fleet that's miles away, either; most of the army is too.'

A thought crossed Tunley's devious mind. 'Do you think General, that Kathsum might be letting Resvon in? Could she be working for him?'

The General looked sternly at Tunley. 'We need to be careful where this line of thought will take us.' He lowered his voice so that Tunley could only just hear him. 'Treason is not a palatable thought.'

Tunley whispered back. 'But, if she *is* working for Resvon, then that is much, much worse than treason.' The Admiral looked closely at the bald General. *He is not strong enough for such ideas.*

'But, good General, I am not suggesting that we overthrow Kathsum. Oh no, I would never do that.' He saw the General's shoulders relax. 'But given the state of things, do you think it would be prudent to recall our ships and troops?' Tunley gave the General a smile. 'You have more experience that I at fighting this war. What would your counsel be?'

'The High Chancellor did order the fleet and troops away, so we would be going against a direct order.' He paused long enough for Tunley to feel dirty at having had Kathsum give orders to *his* fleet.

Tunley rubbed his chin. 'Perhaps General, we could bring the army and fleet closer, should they be needed. Say, a half a day's sail away. That way, we are not going against the High Chancellor's orders to have them away from the city; but they would be close if needed. Even if I sent word this instant, they wouldn't reach the city for at least five days. So, there would be little harm in starting the process, whereas, if we're caught unawares… well, that could be disastrous. What do you think, General?'

The orange moustache smiled. 'Well done, Tunley. I like the way you think. Besides, we don't want Kathsum ordering us around too much.' The General gave Tunley a rueful wink. 'Now, if you didn't come here to discuss the news, why did you come to see me?'

'I need your help, General. The High Chancellor informed me last night that while I will have a seat on the council, I won't have the right to vote. While I don't take this as a personal slight, it disturbs me that the navy won't have a voice where it really matters. As a result of this, the armed forces will have a diminished presence. At a vital time like this, we cannot allow Roasline to be crippled. Just looking at the position Kathsum has placed us in today shows that we clearly need more of a voice, not less.' Tunley took a deliberate breath. 'Given the information we've shared this morning, I am even beginning to wonder if Kathsum is excluding me so that she has more power.' Tunley watched as this thought sunk in to the General.

'I agree that the navy should have a vote on the council, but the decision has been made; the voting has been done. I don't know what you want of me.'

'I would like to know who voted against the navy, so that I might discuss their concerns and my point of view with them.'

'You should know that those details are confidential. I'm sorry, Admiral, but I cannot tell you that.'

'I understand that General. Perhaps, if I mused my thoughts out loud, you could hear me out.' 'Very well, but my lips will remain sealed.'

'Thank you. The way that I see it, Kathsum clearly voted against me, whereas a sensible man such as yourself would have voted for the navy.' The General remained motionless. 'The Head of Order is a man who loves strength; he would have voted likewise. The Aldermen and Alderwoman bunch together and as a group detest the necessity of a military, they would have voted with Kathsum.' The Admiral paced around the mapped table with his hands behind his back as he spoke. 'So that is four against and two for. Then there is the Quaestor. I don't know much about the man, but I've never trusted anyone who loves the feel of coins as much as he does.' Tunley rubbed his fingers together and looked out of the corner of his eyes at the General. 'My guess is that he would side with the power and that is Kathsum.' At this last comment, he stopped and stared at the General. The moustached man was good; he only smiled a half a fraction, but a half a fraction was all that the sharp admiral needed.

'So, there are five against the navy and two for the navy.'

'You are a shrewd man, Admiral. Although I'm not sure how you knowing this will help your plight.'

'General, I'd like to ask a favour. I don't usually ask favours, but when I do, I remember them and pay them back with interest. General, I would like you to ask for a re-vote.'

The General looked a touch confused. 'That is most irregular, Admiral.'

'I know.' Tunley paused. 'I don't want you to do this just yet, either. I want you to wait for the right time. I don't know when that will be; days or weeks, but when I ask, are you able to do that for me?'

The General was silent except for his whistling nose.

'General, I only ask this for the sake of the navy and the people of Roasline.' Tunley did his best to sound and look sincere.

The General responded grudgingly. 'I will do as you ask, Admiral, for the people of Roasline. Don't forget that. My key priority is the defence of Roasline and the lands held by us; I align myself with no one individual.'

'I thank you for your support in this.' Tunley found himself standing by the man over ten years his senior. He struck out his hand and the General shook it with a nod. Tunley released his grip and wiped his sweaty palm subtly on his thigh.

'General, what can you tell me about the other members of the council? I feel like I know so little of those I'll be working closely with.' The Admiral smiled, but his friendliness was not returned in kind by the General.

'Admiral Tunley, I have a lot to do to prepare for the coming of Resvon. I've given you all the time that I can spare today.'

Tunley feigned a relaxed manner. *The man knows his boundaries.* 'Of course, General, I apologise. I too have much to do. Good luck with your preparations.'

The General nodded and Tunley felt his eyes watching him closely as the Admiral left the General's headquarters.

Admiral Tunley spent the rest of that day and the next finding out as much as he could about his fellow council members. He sought details of who they were and how they had got to be on the council. Most of the information was minutia, while what he really craved was weaknesses that each might have. He wanted ways to persuade the members to his way of thinking. The information was difficult to find and he became frustrated with those unwilling to help him. His main prize would have been to find a way to manipulate Kathsum, but despite being in the public eye more than any of the others, he could find little to use against her.

The Admiral had more luck with the Quaestor who, despite being chosen by the council, seemed liked or trusted by no one. Tunley saw the man as a rat and knew for the right price, his vote could be bought. Tunley was not a wealthy man, but he knew of a rare pink diamond that resided in the map on his desk that should fetch the required sum. But the Admiral could not yet put this plan into action, for the Quaestor was visiting Headly and would not be back for at least ten days. Still, with one extra vote for the Admiral, the balance sat at three¬ for Tunley and four against.

He then set his mind to the Aldermen and Alderwoman and gathered what information he could. Tunley planned to meet two of them before Resvon's visit, starting the evening after he met with the General, and then the final Alderman once the hype had reduced. He had gathered some useful information, but he wanted more. While he knew he may not be able to convince any of them yet, he could at least get their measure.

He wanted to start with, in his opinion, a *soft* target. For this meeting, Tunley chose to wear a similar outfit to that he wore to the General's, but instead of light-coloured breeches, chose a dark green pair; so as not to intimidate them with his manhood. He requested to meet his first target in the council chambers; a neutral ground would remove a propensity to defence on their part. He was not yet sure if he would be required to woo them or use *persuasion* to confirm his view and wanted to leave both options open.

The Admiral arrived before the Alderwoman and waited patiently in his designated council seat. The woman shortly arrived and Tunley was saddened to see she had a tired, yet firm expression on her face. She was of medium build, being neither slender nor plump. Her brown hair was tied back in a plait, and she wore a simple dress of light fabric that ballooned at her hips and fell to her ankles. Tunley tried to guess her age and placed her at about forty-five, almost ten years older than he was.

Tunley only had a moment to take her in before she spoke with a crisp voice that held an element of energy and wit.

'Hello, Admiral Tunley. We finally meet alone. I've been looking forward to this ever since your messenger came requesting a meeting. I want to see if you live up to your reputation.'

Tunley stood and spoke in a pleasant tone. 'And what reputation would that be, Alderwoman?'

She smiled. 'Please, call me Jaid.' Her smile broadened. 'If you need to ask me what your own reputation is, then you won't get far in this arena.'

Tunley felt annoyed at being placed in the ignorant position of less power. *Has this woman just refused me a direct question?* He smiled despite himself.

'Of course not, I just wanted to gauge your thoughts on it.' *Which reputation does she mean?*

'My thoughts, I will keep to myself, if you don't mind.' Her smile faded.

Tunley felt her close gaze scrutinising his reaction. 'As you wish.' He walked casually around the table. 'Jaid, I'm meeting with everyone on the council who voted against the navy having a voice on the council. I wanted to start with you, as I thought your logical mind might reconsider once you've heard the benefits of allowing me to vote.'

Jaid looked at Tunley sharply; her crisp voice matching her stare. 'Who told you I voted against you?'

Tunley shrugged. 'Who is the only one with the authority to do so?'

Tunley knew he was taking a risk; he wasn't even sure if anyone had that authority.

'The High Chancellor?' Jaid's eyes opened wide. 'She wouldn't. She detests you.'

'And yet, here we stand.' *The seeds of distrust are planted.*

'But let us not dwell on Kathsum. Have a seat and let us talk about the value of the navy.' Tunley smiled warmly at the Alderwoman. She scowled back.

'Admiral Tunley, I will not sit here and listen to you trying to buy, bully or blackmail me into supporting you.' She straightened her back. 'I can see through your thin veil of mock friendliness to that which lies beneath; and it is an ugly sight to behold.'

Before Tunley could respond, Jaid swept from the room and slammed the door behind her.

Tunley felt his hackles rise and frustration sneak its grimy claws around his throat. *Bitch! Stupid, ugly whore.*

The Admiral stormed from the room in search of a strong drink. In his younger days, he would have sought out a fight, but he retained enough composure to stop himself doing that. *An Admiral should not look like he's been fighting.* With one vote lost, he would have to work a lot harder on the remaining Aldermen.

⌘

The day before the arrival of Resvon to Roasline had dawned. Admiral Tunley had done little preparation for the significant event, past ordering the fleet's movements. He continued to focus his energies on his inability to vote and those restricting him. He was to meet with the Alderman of the Farmers that morning and he was hopeful of a positive outcome. The Alderman had been elected to a position that he was ill suited for. His inability to make decisions and his desire to have every last bit of information, had hampered his influence as an Alderman and put the farmers on a negative standing. Tunley knew all of this as well as other important information that he planned to use to convince the Alderman to his way of thinking.

The Admiral planned to meet the man in his own house and when the Alderman arrived, Tunley supplied him with a strong wine. Despite the time of day, the Alderman accepted.

'Thank you for meeting me today. I know we're all very busy preparing for tomorrow.'

'Indeed we are. It's such an amazing feat that our High Chancellor has managed to achieve. Peace, who would have thought?'

'I quite agree Alderman, but I didn't ask you here to discuss our wonderful leader.' The Admiral kept all sarcasm out of his voice. 'No, I asked you here to discuss why you voted against me and against the navy having a vote on the council.'

The Alderman almost spat out his wine in surprise. His cheeks quickly became red and he swallowed hard.

The Alderman confusedly asked. 'How did you know?'

'Let's just say that the High Chancellor's lips are not as tightly sealed as some think. Especially when she's in the presence of a man such as myself… and especially after we…' The Admiral deliberately trailed off.

'You and the High Chancellor? Surely Kathsum would never. But I suppose even the High Chancellor must have desires. I just never thought that they would be someone like you; a military man.'

'Alderman, I think I've said too much. I wouldn't want to give you the wrong impression about our leader.' Tunley winked at the Alderman. 'So, Alderman, why did you vote against me and how can we change your mind?'

The Alderman's smile faded. 'I voted against you because the risk of having you voting was greater than the risk of you not voting. Us three Aldermen all decided to vote the same way, which I'm sure you already know. In terms of changing my mind, that's unlikely. The situation remains the same; there is more risk in you having a vote than not. And Kathsum knows who voted as she did, and those who did not.' The Alderman fell silent and Tunley sipped his own wine.

'Tell me, Alderman, how is your family? Your sister, is she managing her farm well?'

The Alderman pursed his lips. 'They are fine, and yes, she is.'

'I understand that she has a strapping son to help her in the absence of her husband. Her second son though, he's in the navy, isn't he? Your nephew, what's his name again?'

'Druin'

'Yes, that's right. Quite a good sailor too, from what I hear. Rumour has it that he's wanting to captain his own ship one day.' Tunley had kept his voice conversational, but he could not help but feel glee at the Alderman's suspicious look.

'It's a shame that your mind cannot be changed. Alderman, I generally like to promote good sailors. Imagine that, young Druin, a captain with a gold chain in his sash.' Tunley's voice became hard. 'Quite a different picture to that of a bloated corpse that has been floating in the Rogaus for several days, isn't it? But, if your vote cannot be changed, I suppose that's where young Druin will end up. And then I suppose that I'll have to be the one to tell your sister. That *will* be hard on her, especially without a husband to comfort her. Who knows, maybe I'll have to comfort her. Tell me Alderman, is she good looking?'

'You filthy swine!' The Alderman slammed down his cup, spilling some wine.

'All I want is your support should there be a re-vote of the navy having a vote on the council. That is all. Grant me that and you'll have a young captain in the family.'

The Alderman spat on the floor. 'You have my vote, *Admiral*.'

'Excellent. And I'm sure that I don't need to remind you to keep our little arrangement private. You know, for Druin's sake.'

'I will speak of it to no one.'

'Excellent, now would you like another wine?'

The Alderman scrunched up his face. 'You disgust me,' he growled and left the room.

The Admiral poured himself another glass of wine and drank it in one motion. *Excellent. One extra vote secured. Much easier than dealing with that woman, Jaid. Now only to convince the Alderman of Merchants after this excitement with Resvon passes and then I'll buy the Quaestor's vote as a security and then I will be where I should rightfully be.* He grinned from ear to ear. *Admiral Tunley. I still like the sound of that.*

22

It had come: the day Kathsum had been aiming towards for most of her life had finally dawned. The High Chancellor lay in her bed as the darkness gave way to a dull greyness and then to real light. Sleep had evaded her through the night; she'd been both nervous and excited and had been waiting impatiently for dawn. Rising, she climbed out of bed and pulled a robe about her. She then made her way out to her courtyard, where she intended to at least try to eat some breakfast.

The morning was warm and moist with a clear sky. Forceful rays of heat evaporated the rain that had fallen well before dawn. A servant wiped a seat for Kathsum and she sat and waited for her breakfast to arrive.

Resvon is coming to Roasline. Small butterflies flew inside her stomach. *This is the first real act to show that we are in a time of peace. Wow, we are in a time of peace!* Large butterflies flew within her and her heart rate quickened. Kathsum may have felt like runny gravy on the inside, but she maintained a strong external disposition.

Her breakfast soon arrived on a tray consisting of a green honeydew cut in half with the seeds removed. In their place was a mound of blackberries. Accompanying the fruit was a jug of water with fresh lemon juice squeezed into it. Kathsum did not feel like eating, but knew that she would need the strength, so began picking at the plump blackberries.

She was only a few mouthfuls in when she heard the familiar footsteps and cane of Guflinkov approaching her from behind. She remained seated as the old man made his slow way around to stand before her. Unlike his usual neutral face, Guflinkov had a broad smile on display.

'Good morning, High Chancellor. I'm sorry to interrupt your meal, but what a wonderful day this is going to be. A historic moment in time that will be remembered forevermore.'

Kathsum couldn't help but smile back. 'And let us hope for all the right reasons. Guflinkov, it is good to see you in high spirits. Would you like anything to eat?'

'I thank you, but no. I ate before the sun rose. My childlike excitement was too much to allow me to sleep.'

'I know exactly how you feel.' Kathsum took a mouthful of the lemon-water. 'Guflinkov, I find your presence calming and reassuring. I'd like you to be by my side today.'

Kathsum watched as Guflinkov's grey eyebrows rose. 'High Chancellor, surely that position is reserved for the council and your guards.'

Kathsum smiled knowingly. 'Oh, stop being coy. You know I value you and your opinion more than the whole council combined. And don't tell me you came here just to wish me good luck, you cunning old fox.'

Guflinkov grinned ruefully. 'Me? A hidden agenda? I can't for the life of me think what you might mean… but now that you mention it, I would greatly covet a place by your side today.'

'I thought you might. Now, go make yourself respectable. I'll not have riffraff representing the people of Roasline to Resvon.' She shoed him away with a wave of her hand. Chuckling to herself, she felt a lot less nervous and ate the rest of her breakfast while thinking about the strange old man.

Kathsum soon rose from her seat and made her way into the house to wash and dress. While she had been eating breakfast, her maid had laid out the clothes that Kathsum had requested. The occasion was formal, so she had decided to wear a corset. She seldom wore a corset in the summer months, but felt that the dignity of the day demanded it. And so, after washing the heat of the night from her skin, she slipped the expensive whale bone bodice around her body and her handmaiden helped fasten it. Despite what most men thought, corsets were not uncomfortable and even suited Kathsum's body shape; a thin waist with broad shoulders. It was not long on, however, before Kathsum felt the first beads of sweat trickle down her back.

Kathsum's handmaid picked up a dress and presented it to the High Chancellor. 'It's a beautiful dress, my lady. And the colour suits you well.'

'Thank you. You would never know it was made so quickly too.' Kathsum had requested the dress to be made for the occasion and she loved it. The overall colour was moss green with fine gold threading woven throughout. The bodice opened out in a 'v' from the waist with the chest covered in fine cream silk with lace edging at the bosom. A simple clasp held the waist in and the dress flowed over Kathsum's hips and buttocks to the floor like water over a waterfall. The sleeves were close fitting to the elbow and then flared out. These wide cuffs were earth brown in hue and allowed for practical use of the hands. As always, Kathsum wore her three stoned necklace that rested at the compressed meeting of her breasts. Her hair was braided out of her face, but allowed the back to fall down over her shoulders in an auburn curtain. On her feet, she wore simple leather sandals in an attempt to keep her feet cool.

Once she was ready, she paused for a few moments to settle her nerves. As she exited the house, she almost ran into Guflinkov, who was about to knock. 'Guflinkov, your timing is excellent.'

She took a step back and looked at her friend wearing an old uniform. His thinning grey hair was slicked back with some sort of oil and his black uniform looked a bit shabby to Kathsum's eyes. On his left hip, he wore a sword and, on his right, a short wooden truncheon.

'You're looking rather handsome.' Kathsum lied. 'What uniform is this? I'm not familiar with it.'

'It was my father's uniform from when he was part of the High Chancellor's personal guard; from a time when the leaders of Roasline were somewhat more paranoid.'

'You have a sword. I didn't know you knew how to fight.'

Guflinkov smiled. 'Wearing a sword is quite different from being able to wield one. And besides, it's part of the uniform.' Guflinkov winked at her.

He thinks he's playing some game. 'Indeed.' Kathsum pointed in the citadel's direction. 'Shall we make our way up the hill?'

Kathsum walked with Guflinkov at her side and found his slow pace irritatingly mismatched to her heightened level of excitement. She did not show this to the old man, who had started a long ramble of the history of the High Chancellor's personal guards.

Kathsum's attention couldn't be held and she attempted to distract herself by assessing the six guards that were escorting them the short distance. The sunlight sparkled off their polished helmets and breastplates while their eyes twitched hither and thither. Similarly, Kathsum's mind twitched away from them and onto the day before her.

All she had to do was to make her way to the steps in front of the citadel before Resvon arrived. She had planned it such that Admiral Tunley and the General would meet Resvon and a small contingent at the docks and escort them with armed soldiers and sailors to the citadel. The Head of Order was to organise security to keep back the crowds on route, as well as before the citadel steps. Once Resvon arrived, he would stand by Kathsum's side and they would each give a brief speech to the people of Roasline. From there, they would enter the citadel for a lunchtime feast, while the people outside would be fed and entertained.

After the feast, Resvon would return to his ship in much the same manner as he was to arrive in. The finer details of the peace treaty were to be worked through at a later date. For safety reasons, it was deemed that Resvon should only remain for a short while in Roasline. His visit was primarily meant as a symbolic gesture to the people that peace had arrived.

It was thought, and Kathsum quite agreed, that a longer stay would provide a greater opportunity for those not happy with the newfound peace to cause unrest. The High Chancellor paused for a moment in her thoughts and marvelled at the reality of peace. She smiled broadly and felt excitedly happy before she was brought back to the present by Guflinkov.

'It's an odd thing to smile at, Kathsum, the murder of High Chancellor Cindred, albeit 156 years past.'

'I'm sorry, Guflinkov, my thoughts had wandered slightly.'

The old man smiled. 'Of course. This should be a day of smiles, laughter and joy. Tomorrow may be a day for a sober reflection on what peace really means.'

'We shall see. I think I should like to walk in peace for a little while, if that's all right with you.'

'Of course it is. I will speak no more; after all, I need all of my breath to climb this hill.'

As the two progressed slowly up the hill, Kathsum noticed more and more people on the streets. As these recognised who she was, they stopped what they were doing and watched her go by. She waved politely to them and began to regret her choice to walk. *Why didn't I take the litter?*

The citizens continued to mill and the High Chancellor felt nervousness prickle at her skin. They continued at their slow pace and the gathering people turning into a crowd. The crowd was not hostile, rather they all seemed happy and excited, but the sheer number of the people was what worried Kathsum. Then the crowd parted and a dozen more guards appeared, coming down the hill from the citadel. Kathsum breathed a sigh of relief and realised then that she was rather close to the citadel, after all. She glanced at Guflinkov and saw the old eyes darting about the place while his left hand rested on the pommel of his basket-hilted broadsword. She felt his tension ease as the new soldiers arrived, and it wasn't long before a smile crossed his face again.

The pair only had to walk a short distance before they broke free from the excited crowd and could make their easy way to the base of the steps at the citadel. Kathsum felt a pleasant breeze as she climbed the steps and realised just how stifling the press of bodies had been. Despite wanting nothing more than to plunge herself into the shadows of the citadel stone, on the top step, she turned and waved generously to the amassed people. She then stepped through the massive doors into the coolness. Already waiting for her were the council members, with the exception of Admiral Tunley and the General.

The Head of Order stepped forward to greet his High Chancellor. 'It is good to see you on this momentous day, High Chancellor. We were afraid for a moment that you would not be able to penetrate the masses in the streets with your own guards.'

'Thank you for your concern. I was never in danger though.'

'The crowds have now gathered and my men are easily holding them back. I'm sure you've noticed that the sun has risen brilliantly and Resvon should be arriving shortly.'

Kathsum was a bit taken aback at this last comment. 'Is it that late already?' *The walk with Guflinkov took longer than I'd planned and I spent too long getting dressed this morning.*

'It is. We should make our way outside; a messenger arrived just before you reporting that Resvon was but a few streets away.'

Kathsum felt a flush of nerves. *I wish I had more time to compose myself.* 'Yes, we should. Is everyone ready?' She looked at everyone in turn and they each smiled broadly back.

'We are.'

'Then let's make history.' Kathsum turned and strode out into the blazing sun once more.

Standing on the top step with the council members behind her and Guflinkov off to the side, the High Chancellor felt alone and exposed. She glanced at her feet and noticed for the first time the series of red rugs that had been placed on each step. Her eyes followed these to near the edge of the held-back people. The crowd itself was made up of people of all types: rich, poor, fat, thin, old, young, women, men, and children. She was happy to see this variety and felt a surge of pride in her people.

She looked over the crowd and down the hill to the city proper of Roasline. It was a beautiful city, with many of the roads and older buildings made up of white limestone and marble. The streets were spacious and many homes on the northern and western sides of the hill enjoyed views of the Rogaus Sea or the Liagar River. Standing where she was now, Kathsum could see the twinkle of the sun on both of the bodies of water. From there, her gaze was drawn back to the foreground as a commotion stirred.

The crowd suddenly parted and a column of soldiers came forth. The soldiers formed a path to the base of the stairs and Resvon marched proudly forth. Behind him came the Admiral and the General.

Resvon climbed the steps with four members of his personal guard and stood facing the High Chancellor at the top. Out of the corner of her eye, Kathsum saw Tunley and the General file in behind her. She then looked the Leader of the Outcasts directly in the eyes. Where these had previously looked sorrowful and forlorn, today they sparkled with joy. He bowed to her and she curtsied to him.

'I welcome you and your people to Roasline.'

'Thank you. She is a beautiful city.'

The two leaders turned from each other and faced the crowd. A silence fell over the thousands gathered, and Kathsum felt her stomach butterflies once more. She raised her chin and took a deep breath.

'We have all come here today in the name of peace. You have come from your homes just as Resvon, the Leader of the Outcasts, has come from his. Never, in all of history, has a leader of the Outcasts, what used to be the colony, stepped foot in Roasline. Resvon does today, in peace.'

A thunder of cheers broke forth from the crowded people. Kathsum put her hand up for silence, but as she did, time seemed to slow. She saw a flicker of a shadow cross the sun and she turned to Resvon. He smiled encouragingly. She then saw a blur of colours as Guflinkov flew from the shadows towards the Leader of the Outcasts. In one fluid motion, he drew his sword with his right hand and bringing it in a sweeping upward arc, struck a flying arrow a foot from Resvon's face. The arrow deviated from its course in splinters. As Guflinkov finished his graceful manoeuvre with his sword, his left hand shot out and he caught a second arrow in mid-air that would have pierced Resvon's unarmoured chest. Continuing to move like water, Guflinkov grabbed Kathsum by the arm and yanked her to the ground.

By the time she hit the stone surface, Resvon's guards were surrounding him as human shields. She saw the guards deflect two more arrows with their round shields. The High Chancellor looked to Resvon and saw fear in his face.

As Kathsum lay on the ground breathing heavily, she saw another blur of movement and blinked. When her eyes opened, she saw a harpoon, steel tipped and many feet long, pierce through the plate armour of Resvon's guard. The weapon passed through the guard's body and stabbed the Outcast's leader in the lower chest. Resvon let out a grunt of pain and fell to the ground, pinned to his guard by the harpoon. Kathsum could just see his face; it grimaced briefly, smiled and then fully relaxed in death.

The next thing Kathsum knew, she was being carried by her own guards into the safety of the citadel. She stood and leaned against a pillar for support as the corpses of Resvon and his guard were dragged within a few feet of her.

People were yelling at her, but she couldn't hear them at first. She stood stiffly and held out a hand for silence. Everyone immediately obeyed. With the doors closed, Kathsum could still make out the screams of chaos from the amassed people and hoped that none of them would be hurt.

She composed her mind in the manner of a true leader and focused on the situation before her. 'Our actions must be swift.' As she heard herself speak, strength and confidence spread through her.

'Admiral, you must recall our fleet to protect Roasline. General, you must do the same with your soldiers, but leaving enough at your garrisons so that they may still be defended. Head of Order, deploy all of your guards. No one is to leave this city without a council member's express permission. Aldermen and Alderwoman speak to your contacts; we must find out who was responsible for this atrocity. We will meet in the council chambers as the sun sets. Now, go and be swift.'

The High Chancellor looked down at Resvon as the council scattered.

'Guflinkov, peace died with that man. I want you to look at the weapons used and search the area for a possible firing location. Meet me in the chambers before sunset; we have much to discuss, old man.'

Kathsum looked at her old teacher, who now stood straight and tall without the aid of a stick.

'Who will care for the body, Kathsum? It should be sent back across the Liagar in a token of good will; the path to peace will need to be started anew.'

'Quite right. I will send the appropriate people to help Resvon's guards prepare the corpse.' She turned to the weeping guards. 'Look over him. He was a great leader and his body will be respected.'

They nodded their thanks. Kathsum looked once more at Guflinkov, trying to figure him out, before turning and striding off to prepare for what may come.

23

So, Resvon is dead! This day is turning out better than I would have thought. Admiral Tunley stood outside the citadel and watched the two Aldermen walking down the hill, side-by–side. Tunley had followed Kathsum's orders and had dispatched one of his sailors to hail the fleet and bring them home. The day was hot and he sucked in the humid air deeply. He had much to do to prepare for the fleet arriving, but thought that he had time enough to follow the Alderman of Merchants.

The meeting tonight will provide the perfect opportunity for me to get my vote. The need of a strong navy will be clear in their minds. But I do still wish that the Quaestor was back. Just to make sure of it and put Kathsum back in her place.

Tunley started down the hill after the Aldermen. He followed the pair for a short while before the Alderman of Farmers turned off and made his way off east. Tunley quickened his pace and, despite profuse sweating and panting, soon gained on the Alderman of Merchants.

'Alderman, wait.'

The man with salt and pepper hair stopped and turned to face Tunley, his expression passive. On seeing the Admiral, the corners of his mouth twitched in a suppressed smile.

'Are you all right, Admiral? It's just, you seem to be breathing rather heavily.'

'I'm fine, fine.' The Admiral noticed the slight, but forced himself to smile. 'Might I have a quick word with you? We can walk as we talk if you like. I know how busy we are this afternoon.'

'As you wish. How may I help?'

'In the interest of time, I'll get straight to the point. Tonight, at the council meeting, there is going to be a re-vote on allowing the navy to be appropriately represented on the council with voting rights. With what has happened this afternoon, it is vitally important that Roasline has a strong navy. You are a sensible man, Alderman. Can I count on you to support the defence of this great city?'

Tunley breathed deeply and silence fell betwixt them for a moment longer than the Admiral would have liked.

'I understand your concern, Admiral. And your proposition is nobly put.' Silence again. 'I will consider your request.'

Not happy with this response, Tunley took another approach. 'I'm not sure if you're aware, Alderman, but the Quaestor is planning to increase taxes on imports by boat. I can only imagine how much of a blow that would be to the traders and merchants that you represent. If I had the power to vote, then as Admiral, I could force the issue of taxes to a vote. If that were the case, it would be useful to have my vote on your side.'

There was more lie than truth in what Tunley said. He had no idea whether the Quaestor had any plan to raise taxes. But it was plausible, and that's all that mattered at the moment.

The Alderman stopped walking and looked the Admiral in the eye. 'So, you want me to help you so that you can help me?'

Yes, that's exactly what I want. 'I want you to help Roasline, so that she remains strong and as payment for your help, I will help your merchants.'

The Alderman pursed his lips. 'That seems like a reasonable business proposition.' His shoulders relaxed. 'You know, Admiral, you're shrewder than you age implies. Very well, I will do what's best for Roasline. Now, unless you're coming into this warehouse with me, this is where we part.'

'Thank you, Alderman. I will see you tonight at the meeting.' The two parted ways and Tunley felt a spring in his step.

So, that's four votes for and two votes against. This day really does just keep getting better and better.

During the remaining time before sunset and the council meeting, Tunley set about doing what the Admiral should have been doing in just such a situation: preparing for the arrival of his fleet and planning the water-based defences of Roasline. Tunley had no doubt that his navy would rebuke an attack from the Outcasts once it had returned; his ships were simply much better as defensive vessels than the smaller, faster crafts of the Outcasts. The real danger was an attack before his fleet arrived in two days' time. As a result, Tunley ordered all remaining naval vessels to sail. Many of these were barely seaworthy, but he wanted the numbers on his side. He set about commandeering many merchant ships to bolster his apparent force. If it came to a fight, he planned to use these as simple ramming ships. The owners were not at all pleased with the forceful acquisition of their property and so Tunley promised compensation should their ships not be returned. It was a desperate manoeuvre and he knew it, but the Outcasts could simply not be allowed to take Roasline and the lands behind her.

Before Admiral Tunley realised, the sun had sunk low and a servant reminded him of the meeting. He uncharacteristically thanked the man and set off from the docks for the citadel.

When he arrived, most of the council members were already present, but not the High Chancellor. Tunley signalled to the General who left the milling men and came over to the Admiral. Not wanting to waste time, Tunley got straight to the point.

'General, I want you to propose a re-vote at tonight's meeting.'

Tunley was disappointed to see the General stare blankly back at him. Tunley raised his eyebrows. 'As we had discussed the other day in your headquarters.'

Recognition showed on the General's face at last. Then his brows furrowed. 'Tonight? But there are so many more important things to discuss.'

Tunley became frustrated and his face reddened. 'You gave me your word, General, that when I asked, you would do this for me. Is your word worthless?'

The General pursed his lips and his eyes narrowed. Tunley felt the anger they conveyed. The next words from the General came in a bellicose whisper. 'You would use the tragic events from today for your own gain?'

Tunley's response came with equal force. 'I will use whatever events I can to strengthen Roasline!'

The General appeared to placate somewhat. 'Of course, of course. I will do as I promised. And don't you ever forget it.'

'Thank you, General' Tunley put forth all signs of being grateful, but felt dirty. *I hate having to rely on this pompous fool to gain power.* He smiled outwardly at the General.

The General's moustache twitched. 'Are we done here, Admiral? I see Kathsum has arrived and everyone's going in.'

'Yes, we are.'

As they walked towards the door, Tunley continued talking. 'Did you notice, General, that just before Resvon was killed, the High Chancellor raised her hand? Was it for the crowd to silence, or was it as a signal to someone?'

The Admiral had been skilful in his timing: both men entered the silent room, instantly ceasing any further possibility of conversation.

That will give the silly, moustached man something to stew on.

The door was closed by Tunley and everyone took their seats. Six sets of eyes looked expectantly at the High Chancellor. Tunley thought that she looked sad, but resolute. She had not changed her clothing since earlier, and she held her body well.

Perhaps she is more of a leader than I've given her credit for.

She eyed everyone quickly, pressed her fingers together before her and then spoke. 'Right, let's get straight to business. I want a brief report from everyone. Head of Order, we'll start with you.'

The non-descript man sat forward and reported that the city was in lockdown. The presence of his guards had meant that no more unruly behaviour had resulted in harm, past the handful of people injured in the immediate aftermath of Resvon's assassination.

Kathsum nodded and then turned to each of the Aldermen and Alderwoman in turn. Tunley noticed that they all seemed to have nothing of substance to report. *Fools! They are out of their depth.*

The High Chancellor then turned to the General. Tunley made sure that the military man saw the Admiral's nod of instruction.

'In conjunction with the Admiral, my troops have been called back. Tunley has been quite helpful, considering his inexperience.' He paused for a moment. 'And, I know that this might not be the right time for this, but I would like to purpose a re-vote to allow the navy to have a real voice on this council and the ability to vote as a member.'

Tunley watched the reactions around the table: The Head of Order looked interested, the two Aldermen looked at Kathsum, the Alderwoman glared at the General, and the High Chancellor looked stone faced.

'You are right, General: it is not the right time. But if someone else seconds your motion, then we will vote nonetheless.'

Tunley froze for a moment; his hearing became fuzzy. *Second? Nobody told me that a motion had to be seconded. How could I have been so stupid?*

He needed not fear, for a moment later the Head of Order raised his hand. 'I'll second the motion.'

Tunley exhaled loudly.

The High Chancellor spoke crisply. 'I don't like repeating history, but if we must, then let's make this prompt. Admiral Tunley will need a majority to win. With the Quaestor absent, he will need four of the six votes for success. Should he lose, then I will expect this matter to be laid to rest and not be revisited. Should he win, then he will have voting powers effective immediately. I believe that we all are familiar with the arguments for and against, so let's get underway.'

This is happening rather quickly. The sudden queasiness in the pit of his stomach surprised Tunley. *Get a grip on yourself, man.*

'General, how do you vote?'

'For.'

'Head of Order?'

'For.'

'Alderwoman of Producers?'

'Against!'

'Alderman of Farmers?'

'For.'

'For? Did I hear you correctly?'

'Yes, High Chancellor; for.' The voice of the blackmailed alderman was shaky. Admiral Tunley's excitement grew, his nerves forgotten.

'As you wish. Alderman of Merchants?'

'Against.'

Tunley froze for the second time that night. He couldn't help but speak. 'Against, are you sure?' 'Quite sure, Admiral.'

The sneaky bastard. He will pay for this.

Silence followed. The High Chancellor looked around the table before speaking.

'Well, Admiral Tunley, your fate lies with me and my vote. Is there anything brief that you would like to say?' She smiled grimly at him.

'You are a leader who clearly cares for her people. Vote in the way that will benefit them and the defence of them.'

Tunley showed a face of restrained pleading while feeling defeated, deflated and angry within.

The High Chancellor frowned slightly at him. 'I vote: for. You may have your vote, but remember, we are stronger united; a bickering council at odds with itself is a terrible punishment for the innocent citizens that it represents. Now, can we get on with the business of the day?'

Tunley couldn't believe it; High Chancellor Kathsum had voted to give him his vote; give him his power. His cynical mind leapt to the fore. *What does she want? How much will this vote cost me? Still, if I hadn't pushed and pulled, then the vote wouldn't have even happened and I would still be a useless spectator here. Well manoeuvred, Admiral.*

Tunley smiled at the table at large and delivered his report of the fleet's movements. He noticed Kathsum was pleased by how soon the fleet would arrive and also noticed that she didn't press on why the fleet was closer than previously expected.

Once he was finished, it was time for the High Chancellor to give her report. For this, she stood up and spoke with intent.

'Following the brutal assassination of the Leader of the Outcasts, amongst others, I asked Guflinkov to investigate. He quickly deduced from the fletching of the arrows that the killer was from Roasline, or at least, familiar with our weapons and therefore made to look like they were from here. He searched the nearby buildings that might have been within firing range. Much to our delight, he found the culprit at the likely scene. His name is Flarg, and he is one of our most skilled archers. Oddly, he was found standing stock still on the rooftop of a nearby house in a daze. Before him rested his bow and alongside him was a harpoon firing device. The harpoon itself was one typically used by the giant squid hunters of a century ago; not in regular use today.

'Guflinkov has spent much time with Flarg interrogating him. The soldier's story is that he was following orders; orders that supposedly came directly from me. He claims to have met myself and the General on several occasions and that these plans had been in the making since peace was a realistic prospect. In addition to this, he cannot remember anything past three days ago where he was lured to a private residence by a message to meet me. Once there, he met a hooded man, had a drink, and then his memory went blank.

'At first it sounded like a poorly thought out story, but Guflinkov believes Flarg is telling the truth as he sees it. Although I trust Guflinkov, I think it prudent for you, General, to speak with *your* soldier. Guflinkov, after all, is not trained in torture as a military man might be and more digging needs to be done.'

Kathsum paused for a moment before continuing. 'I hate that this has come from our own ranks! Once word of this crosses the Liagar, there will be next to no chance of peace forming. But we must at least try. To that end, I mean to return Resvon's body with his guards unharmed with a treaty of peace addressed to whoever will claim leadership. I *would* send a representative from Roasline as well, but I fear that their life would be short. Unless there are any volunteers from this room, I will consider that option closed.'

Kathsum planted her hands on the table and leant forward. 'Thinking closer to home, we must shore up our defences as best we can. I will leave this in the hands of the General, Admiral and Head of Order to work together to ensure that our shores are not breached.'

Tunley noticed how everyone sat and passively absorbed what Kathsum was saying.

'The only real decision for us to make now is the fate of Flarg. It is not lost on me that had he killed Resvon a week ago, he would have publicly been hailed a hero. But alas, now I feel nothing short of death will suffice.' Kathsum shook her head sadly. 'The poor man thinks he deserves a medal.'

Tunley couldn't help but interrupt. 'This Flarg clearly wants to kill Outcasts. I say we send him with an attacking force across the Liagar.'

Tunley watched as everyone looked at their hands and Kathsum gave him a patronising smile.

'And Admiral, what if he is an agent for whoever wants to take control of the Outcasts? We would be returning their hero to them.'

Tunley shut his mouth, feeling foolish.

'No, I feel that once all information can be extracted from him, he should be publicly executed. Is there anyone else that disagrees with this plan?'

Everyone was silent, and the Admiral realised just how much control Kathsum had and how reluctant the council members were to speak out against her. The memory of bumping into her in the middle of the night returned to him. *I should have killed her then, when I had the chance.*

The Admiral paid little attention to the rest of the council proceedings and was glad when he could leave the room and find himself a solitary drink. The next few days, weeks and months were going to be crucial in Roasline's history and the young Admiral planned to play an integral part.

PART 2

24

A muggy dusk descended over Fort Kykum with heavy clouds rolling in from the west. Fat, slow droplets of rain splashed into the water down at the docks; disturbing the tranquil appearance of the surface. The great gate at the mouth of the docks was just about to be closed when a single ship bearing the Outcast's flag from Psymryte was seen approaching. In a slight break from procedure, she was allowed to enter. After all, she was flying the current passcode. She cut through the rain-soaked water and entered the man-made bay. Shortly after her stern passed the closing gate, she was locked within the secure walls of Fort Kykum.

The rain grew heavier and the ship dropped anchor away from the mooring stations. A small party of twelve men boarded a landing boat and rowed ashore. As they climbed onto the wooden dock, they were greeted by two sailors on dock duty.

'Ahoy, we're not expecting any vessels from Psymryte. Who are you and what is your business here?'

'Our business is up at the Fort.' Came a muffled voice from a hooded man. 'We are here on behalf of Resvon.'

The two soldiers looked at each other and shrugged. 'If that is your purpose, then we will escort you to the Fort.'

'No, you won't.'

Two sailors from the landing party stepped forwards and drove long bladed swords into the sailor's stomachs.

'We make that journey alone. Eyp, signal for the others to come ashore.'

'Yes, sir.' Ex-commander of Ships, Eyp, lit a torch and waved it back and forth six times.

'Fan out and secure these buildings,' the hooded man commanded.

The party from Psymryte spread out and left behind the two dead sailors, whose blood dripped between the planks of the pier to the water below. The invaders then waited for fifty more soldiers to join their ranks before starting the short but steep climb to the Fort.

The docks where the party landed were located within the inner circle of the city and a wide, well-maintained road led straight to the keep's gates. The hooded man led his troops firmly up this road. They met no resistance until they arrived at the closed gates. These were made from solid hardwood with a portcullis protecting their outside. One of the gate's guards slid back a peephole and looked out to see a hooded face shrouded in darkness taking up his entire field of view.

'Who are you?' The guard blurted out in surprise.

The reply that the guard heard was as sweet as honey and gentle in his ears. 'I am the Commander of Psymryte. I have been summoned here in great haste. Before you ask, I do not have any official paperwork; the message came by bird. Please, can you admit me? I have urgent business!'

The guard felt his hand rise to give the signal to open the gate, but he paused. 'I want to let you in, I really do, but how do I know you are who you say you are?'

The guard tried to lower his arm, but found it rising instead. He went to cry out an alarm, but found his voice out of his control and speaking of its own accord. 'Open the gate. They're friends.'

The portcullis creaked into motion and when it was raised; the gates swung open. The army from Psymryte swept into the courtyard as the hooded man's voice echoed about.

'Kill any soldiers or those who resist. Capture the rest. Find any commanders and bring them to me in the war chambers.' The hooded man turned to Eyp. 'Send out those you trust to the lodgings of the commanders. Have them brought here alive.'

The clang of sword on sword sounded around the courtyard as the leader from Psymryte made his way across it. By the time he reached the entrance to the keep itself, the sounds of swords were replaced by cries of pain and death: the intruders had quickly gained the upper hand.

The man entered the building with six close soldiers and Eyp limping along behind. 'Eyp, take me to the war chambers and send for some food and drinks to be brought there.'

Eyp ordered a soldier away to the kitchens and led the small party up several flights of stairs. They met a few servants in their night gowns who shrunk into the shadows as they approached and scampered away in fear when they had passed.

They reached the chambers and the hooded man sat down in the empty room at his leisure and waited for the food and his guests to arrive. The room was not large, but easily fit a table for twelve in its centre with ample room around it. Two fire places sat empty along the wall opposite the door. Above these were swords crossed atop a round shield, while on the remaining walls hung drab tapestries depicting battles and war. Between the fireplaces hung another tapestry, but unlike the others, this showed a map of the lands about Fort Kykum. The hooded man glanced interestedly at the map and then closed his eyes.

His food came first; ham on the bone, small tomatoes on the vine and bread. He could have had more, but declined. While he devoured his meal without talking, Eyp sat next to him and massaged his left calf. Resvon's sea urchin wound still pained the old Commander of Ships.

When the first commander arrived, the hooded man stood and slowly paced around the table in silence. It didn't take long before the rest of the commanders were assembled: Commander of Men, Commander of Civilians, Defender of Kykum, the Treasurer of the Outcasts and the new Commander of Ships.

Still, the hooded man paced. His audience looked at each other uncomfortably. Many moments passed before all of their ten eyes couldn't resist but to follow the pacer. That is when he stopped.

He faced them all and removed his hood. One or two of the men before him sucked in an audible breath, while the others just stared. The bald head of the man was completely squid-ink black from repeated tattooing. He smiled to reveal pearl-white teeth which shone against his black lips.

'I am here to tell you that Resvon is dead. He was killed in the day just passed by a soldier of Roasline. His attempt at peace was foolish and died with him. It will not be repeated. My name is Avgar and I'm now the Leader of the Outcasts.'

Only the new Commander of Ships tried to object.

Avgar silenced him with an icy stare. 'Eyp here… I know that you're all familiar with him… has until morning to determine which of you will be useful and loyal, and those who will not. Loyalty to Resvon and his ideals will not work in your favour.'

Avgar turned to the now standing Eyp. 'Before you start work on this pitiful lot, send out the word: relatives of Resvon and all those loyal to him will be put to death.'

Avgar faced the Commanders once more and sneered. 'Have a pleasant evening becoming reacquainted with Eyp.'

Avgar left the room, summoned four of his personal guards and was led to a bedchamber by a young servant boy from the Fort. He entered the basic room, sent the boy away and ordered his guards to keep watch outside his door. Once inside and alone, Avgar heaved a heavy wardrobe to lean against the door; no one would disturb him tonight.

The room he was in had a comfortable bed with a thin summer blanket. A small window was closed by a heavy shutter. Hard, stone floor was softened by a cow's brown skin and a single wooden chair sat by a small empty fireplace. Before the servant boy had left, he had lit three candles on the mantle, which had dried wax cascading down their sides. Dim, flickering light filed the room, just how Avgar liked it.

Avgar sat on the side of the bed and became fearful of the night ahead. He rubbed the stump where his right hand had once been as he thought of what awaited him. Sighing, he withdrew from a concealed pocket in his robe, a pouch of herbs, a short pipe and a bottle of thick liquid. He stood up and placed these on the small mantle. To him, this combination of herbs and viscous concoction was his medicine. Without these ingredients, Avgar would not find peaceful sleep.

He stood with his hand resting on the mantle and closed his tired eyes. He could already feel his punishment starting.

Avgar lay on his back staring up into the youthful eyes of Balton. Hate spread through Avgar and he went to raise his right hand to perform a spell. He brought it up as quickly as he could, but the cold steel of Moon Song in Balton's hand was swifter. Pain seared up his arm as his hand was cut off at the wrist.

Avgar screamed. Looking back at Balton, he realised that he could not win.

'You are defeated Avgar; your eyes tell me so. Surrender to me now and I may think twice about ending your worthless life.'

Avgar saw swift movement from behind Balton and suddenly there was a man standing beside his attacker, telling him to kill Avgar. But Balton refused. Avgar felt a sudden urge of glee bubble up within and he let out a hideous cackle.

As he caught his breath, Avgar felt Balton's body sway back and forth before it was flung across the room. A moment later, he felt a strong wind swirl about him and it lifted him into the air like a giant hand. He couldn't help but keep laughing as he was tossed about the room. Then the fun stopped; the tossing became violent and he felt as if he would be torn apart. Avgar's laughter turned to screams of pain and his senses became overwhelmed. In the blink of an eye, Avgar found himself swept out of the window of Mirny and over the city of Balleny. The pain had plateaued at an unbearable level such that his mind could not cope. All he could do was observe and scream as he was carried between two armies and off towards the mountainous Moaks. His mind could take no more and he blacked out for a while as he was flown over fields and desert.

Avgar woke once more as he ascended up the southern slopes of the Moaks. The pain had been replaced by a cold numbness, but as he flew higher and higher, his ears burst with the sudden pressure change and he began to freeze. His breathing became hurried and urgent as the air got thinner and thinner. His chest hurt, his heart raced, and his head pounded. All he wanted to do was die. Long forgotten was his desire to find out what lay beyond the Moaks. Then darkness took him, not the comforting black hand of death, but merely a state of unconsciousness.

These images came to Avgar as if they were happening to him at that very moment. He gasped a huge breath of air and wiped the sweat from his brow with his left forearm. His fingers shook as he grasped for the thick medicine; fearful of what was still to come. Avgar unstoppered the cork and took a big gulp of the brown liquid.

He fumbled with his herbs; only being able to loosely pack them into his pipe. Using one of the candles to light the pipe, he sucked in a lungful of smoke. Calming his nerves, he went and lay on the bed, smoking. He waited impatiently for the drugs to take effect; hoping they would work before his next round of visions.

Avgar was in luck tonight; he felt his mind calm from the smoke. His whole body felt like it sunk into the mattress as he continued to pull the sweet smoke into his lungs. He just finished his pipe and rested in on the bed beside him when, out of the corner of his eye, he saw the flames of the candles flicker. He looked straight at them and the flame on the right flared bright and tall. As it shrunk back to its usual height, the middle candle flared and then the one on the left did likewise. They repeated this pattern and Avgar stared, amazed. Then the middle flame turned blue and suddenly, out popped a multi-coloured butterfly. Not knowing why, Avgar giggled at this.

The mesmerising butterfly flew around the room before it burst into a shower of sparks over Avgar's head. He rubbed his eyes to clear the sparks and looked down at his fingers. They were not only wavy and bendy, but they bulged in odd ways. Avgar shook his hand to straighten them out, only to find that that made them elongated and thin, like young willow branches. He wiggled his fingers slowly and they appeared to bend and sway as if in a gentle breeze. Avgar looked through his fingers and down to his bent knees…

He was back, descending down the north slopes of the Moaks. His ears and head throbbed with the change in height, but instead of being disturbed by this, he glanced to his right and saw a flock of pink geese flying next to him; honking as they went. Avgar looked down at the stump at the end of his right arm. The blood on the open wound had frozen into crystals when he had passed over the top of the Moaks. The rays of the now setting sun caught the crystalline blood and Avgar marvelled at the infinite reflections of light entering his eyes. The frozen blood started to melt as he was flown lower and lower.

His body was no longer being tossed hither and thither like a leaf in a gale, but he was flying face down and smoothly. In this calm flying state, he gazed around at the lands that he was passing. He flew over a giant lake with green borders and then passed up a river with hills and plains on one side and a massive expanse of woodland on the other. Then the sun set and darkness swept across the land. Avgar had been flying for a full day, and yet to him it felt both like his entire existence and no more than an instant at the same time.

The stars popped into being and Avgar playfully rolled onto his back to take in their beauty. Is this how it happened those many months ago? He could not tell.

With the stars shining gloriously about, Avgar looked to his left and saw himself being violently tossed back and forth. The man he saw was screaming in pain, but no noise reached his ears. That can't be me, for I am here. *He slowly thought some more.* But if I'm there and not here, then who am I that is here? Maybe I am there as well as here… but that can't be, for I am there. Maybe there's two of me, here and there… maybe there's more of me who's not here or not there, but somewhere else altogether. *Then he stopped thinking, but flew and numbly watched the other him being tossed and turned.*

After a while, Avgar took his eyes off his other self and looked once more to the shadow of the ground below him. His speed had slowed and his height had dropped and to his right he saw the vague shadow of a city.

No more than a moment later, he saw the stars below him, or rather, the stars reflected up at him. He wondered at this briefly before being thrust into a swirling spiral of descent. He passed over land, then over water, then over land, then over water and so on and so on until he landed in a sprawling heap on a sandy beach. He looked for his other self but could not find him. A realisation dawned on him. I was him, but now I'm me again.

Avgar heaved himself onto his knees and looked about. He found himself on a long beach halfway between sand dunes and constant waves. The sand beneath him was fine, but cold to the touch. He went to stand up, but before he could, found himself surrounded by a circle of men and women. They were garbed in strange attire and were not completely solid. Avgar could see several stars shining through the heads of many of the people.

When they spoke, they spoke as one, yet none of their mouths moved. 'Avgar, you are full of evil and are a hateful man.'

Avgar tried to speak, but found himself unable.

'We have brought you here not out of desire, but out of necessity. By law, we do not dabble in the affairs of others, but one of our own has deceived us. The man you saw in Mirny with Balton is a sorcerer of great power. He claimed to have looked into your future, which breaks one of our most sacred laws. He claimed that if you were allowed to live, that you would bring much death and sorrow to those who live south of the Moaks. When we would not act, he sought to use Balton to kill you. When that was on the brink of failure, he was prepared to risk our wrath and kill you himself. This would have broken our oldest law. We were watching closely and this we could not allow. As a collective, we intervened and carried you across the Moaks, fighting our adversary every foot of the way. We brought you here and we were victorious against him. We have banished this sorcerer to reside south of the Moaks from where he originally came. He will not enter our territory again.'*

Avgar found himself craving to know more.

'But you will not go unpunished for your crimes. Oh no. Until you vanquish your evil ways and set yourself on a path of love and kindness, every night, before you find sleep, you will relive your defeat at the hand of Balton and your painful journey across the Moaks. In addition to this, we will extract your crystal's power from your essence. Your magical abilities will be minimal and unpredictably dangerous to your life. This process will not be reversible.'

Avgar felt his entire body scream out in pain as his enmeshed crystal fibres were torn from his being. When the pain eventually subsided, he felt an immense sense of loss. He looked up from his knees and the people were gone, but a single voice spoke again.

'Do not seek us out.'

Avgar emerged from his punishment, drenched in sweat. He could still feel the calming effect of his smoked herb, but the mind-altering effects of his tonic were no more. An absent tear rolled down his black cheek and he still felt an overwhelming sense of melancholy loss. He grimaced to himself and closed his eyes for what he knew would be a short, yet calm, sleep.

25

Winter woke with the sun, after a less than restful night. His body was still adjusting to the hard ground and to sleeping during the darkness of night and not during the daylight. As hard as it was for him, he knew it was tenfold harder for Sister Sor, who had slept during the day since she was sixteen years of age. On this morning, she lay perfectly still and he knew she was not asleep.

The young man sat up and looked about their camp. The fire from the previous night had died out and the grey ashes lay cold. Winter's belongings lay at his feet, bundled up tightly. Above and around him were tall lush fir trees that gave cover from both the weather and prying eyes that might be passing on the path. The smell of the morning was fresh with the essence of a warm day ahead.

It had been five days since the two had left the monks. They had followed the mountain path next to the stream that ran through Sor's village; Ocrill. On this path, they had passed through two monk communities that were both smaller than Ocrill. Here, they had been well received and were provided for during their stays. Prayers had been said at their departures for their safe journeys.

The walking had been easy and downhill, yet Winter's knees were protesting under the constant strain. He knew they must be a day or two from Green Lake and he craved the flatter ground. As they had continued to descend, Winter had noticed a stark difference in the weather. The nights were milder and the days warmer the lower they travelled. Again, this was harder on Sor than it was on Winter, but she didn't complain.

Sister Sor was pleasant to travel with. She would talk sometimes; educating him on various matters, would diligently help and would sometimes sing to herself. While Sor was a stable companion, despite her poor sleep, Winter's mood had flipped back and forth. The resolve that he had when setting out was showing cracks. He kept these misgivings to himself and put them down to his sore knees and disturbed sleep cycles.

Winter now sat in a low mood as the sun peeked through the trees and glanced at Sor's still body. *What have I done? I should never have let her come. This journey will prove too much for her; a kind, sheltered monk. She knows nothing of how evil people can be. I suppose I'll have to protect her,* he thought selfishly.

Winter sighed deeply and threw the blanket off his legs before standing. He stretched his arms above his head and swayed from side to side to get his back moving. Already dressed, he passed through the line of trees downhill to relieve himself.

When he came back, Sor was preparing a breakfast of hard bread and water. Winter went over to roll up his blanket and froze. He tried to scream, but all that came out was a strangled yelp. His legs started quivering violently as Sor raced to his side.

'Winter, what is it? What's wrong?'

Winter could barely raise his hand to point at the large, hairy spider that sat atop his blanket. He then turned and ran to the other side of the clearing. Once safe behind a tree, he looked back and saw Sor laughing. She bent down, let the spider crawl onto her knife and held it up. The blade was only short and the beast the size of Winter's palm was making its slow way towards the handle.

'Is this what you're afraid of?'

Sor rolled the knife so that the spider had to cling on. He nodded and she laughed once more and, with a flick of her wrist, flung the spider far away into the bushes.

'You can come back now; the danger has passed.'

Winter didn't much like the mocking tone of her voice, but returned shaking and with a very pale face.

Sor's smile faded. 'You really are petrified, aren't you?' Winter nodded again.

'Sit down and I'll make you some breakfast and a cup of hot water to calm your nerves.'

Winter nodded once more and managed to croak a reply. 'Thank you.'

Once sitting on a low log, Winter hugged his knees while Sor started a new fire to heat some water. Typically, they didn't have a fire in the morning, but the need justified the effort required.

With a cup of warm water in his hands, Winter felt blood return to the rest of his body. With this came a sense of embarrassment and an urge to justify his behaviour.

'I've never liked spiders much; they've always given me the creeps. I could live with this when I was young, I avoided them where I could. But then my father found out.' Winter looked grim. 'He wanted strong children with no weaknesses. I was thirteen at the time, and once he started, he would not stop.' Winter cast his mind back to his childhood.

'At first it was harmless enough, I suppose. He would show me different types of spiders and point out which ones were venomous, which ones had a sharp bite with no poison and which were harmless.'

He paused and looked at Sor's sorrowful face.

'I know that the spider you just released would have done no harm to me, but it still scared the wits out of me.' Winter shuddered. 'Anyway, as I was saying, it started off innocent enough, but when my fear remained, he escalated things. I started finding spiders in my chambers, in my bed, even crawling out of the privy.

That is when my fear became a true phobia. To Avgar, this was unacceptable. He resorted to locking me in small rooms, naked, with spiders. He would not let me out until I had killed them all.'

Winter felt Sor put an arm around his shoulders. He looked at her and smiled wryly.

'That was pleasant compared to what came next.' Winter shook at the memory and sipped his warm water to calm his nerves.

'You don't have to go on, Winter. Forget it and let's talk about the day ahead. I think we might be able to make it to Green Lake if we push on into the evening.'

Winter held up his hand to silence her. 'No, I will finish this; I need to.'

He took a deep breath. 'I would eventually kill the spiders in the rooms, sometimes quickly, other times it took me days. My father wanted to press harder, so he did. His next form of torture was to tie me down and release spiders onto my stomach, my chest and my face. He was careful about which spiders he chose, never selecting ones that could be fatal.

'The first time was the worst; I soiled myself and was bitten by a small black spider. The pain was extreme, the sweats unbearable. But I recovered, and that was his point: to man, most spiders are insignificant. But my fear was so innate, so primal, that reason could not touch it.

'I said that the first time was the worst. That was for the simple reason that from that point onwards, whenever I was strapped down and saw the spiders, my mind would give up and I'd pass out.'

Winter sipped his water again and found himself feeling surprisingly calm. He tried to make sense of his feelings to Sor. 'To heal myself and live a life true to the gods, I believe I need to find my father and forgive him for what he did to me. His actions with the spiders is just one of many that I'll have to confront.'

Sor nodded. 'Thank you for telling me this, Winter. I keep forgetting your past is filled with darkness.'

Winter shook the last thought from his mind and smiled. 'But my future is filled with light, thanks to the Gods.'

He saw a crease of a smile on Sor's face and felt her shove him playfully. He stood up and drank his remaining water.

'Let us go, Sister Sor. We have much ground to cover and I long for the sight of this fabled lake.'

Sor stood too. 'It will not be long before we will round a bend and then we will be able to see her vastness.' She looked up at the sky. 'It might even make a good lunch spot, provided we can find some shade.'

Sor held up her bare arms and Winter was reminded of her paleness and how burnt she was. A lifetime out of the sun would take a long time to be corrected, he mused.

They soon gathered their belongings, put out the fire and set off down the path, with Sor leading the way.

They walked all morning before reaching the bend in the path that Sor had mentioned. She stopped leading and made Winter be the first to round the corner. He walked out from the tree line and followed the track over a rocky section. A short cliff fell away before him and the view opened out in front of him. He could see far and wide, but his eyes were drawn to the massive expanse of water directly in front of him.

Winter looked roughly east and down the six hundred odd miles of Green Lake. To say that it was longer than it was wide was irrelevant as its width spanned close to five hundred miles. The water was so vast that there was no way that he could see the far bank in either direction. At the closest shore, some twenty miles from where he stood, Winter saw a few wooden huts and stone buildings. He also saw several vessels on the sparking water moving slowly in the gentle wind. Green Lake, it was called, and Winter could see why. All along the edge were tall green reeds swaying back and forth in the breeze. These stretched several hundred feet into the water, and the only way the boats could access the shore was via a long pier that stretched well past the line of the late summer reeds.

Only after taking in the marvellous spectacle did Winter realise how bright the sun was. He turned to see Sor blinking furiously. As much as he would have loved to sit in the hot sun and soak up the view, he thought better of it.

'Sor, I think we should keep going and eat lunch while we walk.'

Sor nodded and smiled at his considerate suggestion. They continued walking and soon were covered by the trees once more.

When darkness had fallen, Winter and Sor stopped for a quick discussion about whether to continue walking, or to stop for the night. They continued, both eager to reach Green Lake where they would be able to sleep under a roof. With the full moon overhead, Sor could easily follow the path and Winter trailed closely behind.

They walked on into the night and when they were about five miles out from their destination, they heard voices ahead.

The monks paused for a moment before continuing more cautiously. The voices grew louder and before long they saw the flickering of a fire in the middle of the path. Standing with their backs to the night were two men with strong looking bodies. Winter and Sor edged closer to get a better look before Winter nudged Sor and whispered in her ear.

'Let's go around them.'

Sor nodded and just before they left the path, they were startled by a loud gruff voice right behind them. 'What have we got here? Boys, I've found a couple of spying monks.'

The man carried a crude club and poked Winter in the chest. 'Come over to the fire you two.'

Winter and Sor obeyed without talking. When they entered the light, the same man spoke again. 'Looks like we got a girl monk. It's always hard to tell with their heads all shaved.'

He smiled a toothy grin at Sor. Winter felt rage build within him, and he stepped between Sor and the oaf. He wished that he had his sai, but his fists would have to do.

'Don't even think about touching her.' Winter spoke calmly, but firmly.

The man laughed. 'A feisty one. That's not very *godly* of you.' He looked over Winter's head at the two other men, who were chuckling to themselves.

'Grab her.'

He looked back down at Winter and shoved him in the chest again. 'I've already thought about touching her, and a lot more, too. But first, I'm going to deal with you.'

Winter heard a commotion behind him as the man before him swung the club at his head. Winter ducked and leapt into his attacker's space. He jabbed a right fist into the man's face and a left into his stomach. The big man stepped back. Winter saw the man grin and come at him with the club again. Winter turned and stepped back, but the club caught his cheek and sent him sprawling. He sprang to his feet before the attacker could advance.

I'm better than this. He wiped the blood from his face and clenched his jaw. Both men ran at each other. Winter ducked the club again and swept his foot at the man's moving legs. The big man fell with a thud, but he rose before Winter could capitalise. The man threw his club away and advanced in a full-frontal stance. The blows came fast, and while Winter deflected the first few, the big, heavy man just kept coming. All Winter could do was raise his arms to protect his head as the punches found their marks.

Winter's head spun, he saw stars in front of his eyes and he sank to his knees. His eyes started to close as he fell to the ground. The end was near. Two or three more punches or kicks and it would be over. His vision turned misty and he searched for Sor. Instead, he saw two large bodies lying next to the fire. A hazy figure raced towards his attacker and felled him with a series of twirling kicks and pinpoint punches. He searched for Sor again, but couldn't find her. He couldn't understand what was happening and then, as his eyes closed over, he realised he must have been delirious.

When Winter woke, his head spun and his thoughts were confused. *Where am I? What's happening? Why does my head throb so much?*

He tried to open his eyes, but only his left eyelid would move. He brought his hands up and felt his swollen face. Winter winced as he touched his closed right eye and could only imagine what he must look like. He sat up slowly and groaned from a sharp pain in his ribs. The sound brought footsteps. Winter wondered who it would be that approached. To his great relief and surprise, Sor came into his view in her usual black robe.

'Sor? Where are we? How did we escape those brutes? Who was the warrior that saved us?'

'Calm Winter, calm. First things first; where does it hurt?'

Winter briefly laughed and then cringed at the pain in his ribs. 'Everywhere.' Sor shot him a stare that said; *come on, be more helpful.*

'My head and face, my ribs, forearms, stomach and lower legs. My ribs and my head are the worst. I must look an ugly sight.'

Winter's thoughts began to form into order. 'How long was I unconscious for?'

Sor dipped a cloth into a bucket of cool water and pressed it to his right eye. 'Hold this here. You were out for two days.'

'What? Two whole days? That can't be right.'

'It is. Winter, with the beating you sustained, you're lucky to be alive. As it is, you have severely damaged ribs and bruising on most of your body. The swelling on your face will soon go down, but your ribs will take many weeks before they are back to full strength. I recommend you rest in bed for several days more.'

'I don't want to rest.' Winter suddenly had a strong desire to get up. He went to stand and found his balance was out of kilter. He fell back on to the bed with a thud.

'You will rest, Brother Winter.'

With Sor's gentle help, Winter lay back down painfully.

'If I must lie here, can you at least answer my questions?'

'Of course. You're not confined to solitude and silence.'

Winter relaxed a bit. *Perhaps it is best if I rest.* 'Good. Can you tell me where we are and how we got from being captured to being here… please?'

'Certainly. We're on a boat.'

'A boat?'

'Yes, a boat. Now, what do you last remember?'

'I remember the two thugs gabbing you, me fighting the big oaf and getting pounded.' Winter closed his eyes and thought hard. 'As I was passing out, I saw a warrior leap to save me from certain death.'

Sor didn't respond immediately, but looked at Winter as if weighing him up.

'Your memory is not quite accurate. While you were fighting the big fellow, the other two men tried to grab me. They were unsuccessful and soon found themselves unconscious. By the time you were on the ground and nearing your end, the big man was focused on you and didn't see me coming. It wasn't hard to take him unawares with a kick to the back of the head, and a series of punches for good measure.'

Winter tried to process this information. *Sor was the warrior?*

'After making sure that you were going to live, I tied each of the men to separate trees, threw their boots into the bushes and broke their big toes.'

Winter looked amazed at the young monk.

'I heaved you onto my shoulders and carried you the last five miles to Green Lake. Once there, I sought help from fellow monks who patched you up skilfully. Not wanting to meet the ruffians again, I begged for a boat. For a small fee, the monks were generous and arranged a boat and crew to sail us over Green Lake to the Sempa River. So, that is why we are on a boat.'

Winter didn't know what to say.

'Don't worry, Brother, the men will live. There is daily traffic on that path, so they will only have to wait a night and a morning, at the most, before they are found. I didn't want to kill them; that is sinful, but I couldn't just let them free to hunt us down.'

Winter finally found his voice. 'But... you're a monk.'

'Yes, I am.'

'But... you can fight.'

'Winter, the world is not always as it seems. It is not always as simple as our black and white robes. I will now share with you a secret, but then you must rest.'

Winter nodded.

'All monks can fight. To worship the Gods, you must understand yourself and find harmony with your body and the world around you. Being able to defend yourself is natural; all animals do so in their own fashion. Being part of nature brings you closer to the Gods. As we learn the moves to defend ourselves, we search, we meditate and we find peace.'

Winter again found himself confused and speechless.

'There are only a few outside of the monks who know this secret. Please do not share it with anyone. Now, you must rest.'

Winter found a croaky voice. 'Teach me... please.'

Sor smiled kindly. 'That is not my intention. We do not teach those who are not yet sworn to the Gods. Now rest, I must go to my prayers where I will ask for your swift recovery.'

Winter watched Sor leave and then closed his eyes. Sleep, he could not find, but rest he did, as he thought of Sor's fluid movements that had saved his life.

26

Crunch, crunch.

Marlvon woke from his shallow slumber to the sound of many heavy footsteps on the gravel path that led to his house. His eyes snapped open, but he lay motionless. The steps were marching together, but they were not highly disciplined, for he could count at least twelve people. Marlvon slipped out of bed and quickly pulled the covers to make it look as though it had not been slept in.

The crunching got closer to his front door, then stopped. Marlvon grabbed a short dagger from his bedside table and stood poised. The feet started moving again and he realised they were surrounding his house. Marlvon had only his nightshirt on and there was no time to dress. He got down on the floor and pulled himself under his bed.

BANG! His front door shuddered. *BANG!* it splinted.

Marlvon thanked that the night had been warm and he hadn't needed a fire. He pressed himself close to the stone floor and felt a chill run over his skin. His hands groped around in the dark and he soon found the specific stone he was looking for.

BANG! His front door gave way and heavy boots entered his house.

Marlvon pressed the stone with his bare hands. Nothing happened. The boots were just outside his bedroom. He pressed harder, and with a grunt from the stone, it swung downwards. His bedroom door crashed open and he slithered down into the black hole. Marlvon landed on the dirt floor with a muffled thud. Lucky for him, those above were not employing stealth. He swivelled around in the hole that was no deeper than five feet and, resting his shoulder against the stone trapdoor, heaved it back up. Marlvon was in luck; the hinge made little noise. He balanced the weight of the stone on his back and placed a sweaty hand on a bolt; ready to slide it into place when a noise from above would give him cover.

The boots stomped about his room and paused at his wardrobe. The man jerked the door open. The door creaked, as it always did, but Marlvon's reflexes were not quick enough. If the men above turned his bed over in their search, they would likely see were his stone was not quite at the same level as the others. Only once the bolt was in place would Marlvon feel sure that only the most expert searcher would find his safe-hole.

The door of the wardrobe slammed shut, but again Marlvon missed the chance to lock his stone. Sweat was dripping from his face and down his back as the feet above walked around his room. And then they suddenly left and closed his door with a bang. As close as he could get to match the timing, Marlvon rammed the bolt home. He slumped to the pitch-black floor and sucked in the stale, stuffy air.

When Marlvon had built this secret place, he had hoped that he would never need to use it. Now that he was lying under his bedroom floor, he thanked his paranoia of many years before. Although he hadn't been down there in a long time, he could still visualise the layout. The room was roughly five feet high, five feet wide, and eight feet long. The small size was a deliberate decision so that when in the pitch-black room, he could easily find his way around.

The hole that he had come down was no bigger than three feet wide and up one end of the chamber. At the other end was a low tunnel. If the chamber seemed small, the tunnel was tiny. At the entrance of the tunnel was a simple cart: a plank of wood with four small wheels. When lying flat, the plank of wood measured from Marlvon's nipples to his knees. But Marlvon would not climb onto the trolley just yet. Instead, he sat, crossed his legs, and listened to the muffled feet above. He counted each footfall and followed the dozen men in his mind's eye as they stamped around his house, searching for him. They all converged on his kitchen, stayed there for a short while and then six of the men left the house. Marlvon thought for a while and decided that six likely armed men would be a bit hard for him to defeat. Even if he decided to challenge the men and won, then what would he do? He would have to deal with six corpses and the others would surely return before too long. No, this was a time for flight, not fight. He would have to use his escape tunnel.

Marlvon got down on all fours on the dirt floor and felt his blind way to the tunnel. Sure enough, his trolley was sitting there where he had placed it long ago. He felt the rough wood and a soft leather knapsack on top. This contained some clothes, a sharp hunting knife and a small sum of coppers; enough to get by for a week.

Marlvon pulled the trolley out of the tunnel entrance and lay on it face down. The knapsack he flattened as best he could and put it under his stomach. He then pulled himself forward to the tunnel's entrance. He felt around in the dirt until his fingers found a rope. The rope ran the length of the tunnel and was fastened at either end and at several points along the way. Marlvon would use the rope to pull himself along the tunnel. In the absolute darkness, this rope would be his lifeline. He tugged at the rope and the trolley moved forward. The wheels creaked slightly, but had been well greased many moons ago.

Although Marlvon could see nothing, he felt the tunnel close in around him. He lifted his head and it brushed the roof, sending a shower of loose dirt down his neck.

Why didn't I dig the tunnel bigger? Marlvon cursed his paranoia that a large man might be trying to follow him. He groaned at the job before him and began heaving himself with one hand over the other along the tunnel.

The tunnel ran several hundred yards from Marlvon's house to his stables. He had not gone a hundred of those yards before he started having true misgiving about his course of action. *I haven't been down here in years. What if the roof ahead has collapsed? Would I be able to get back?* His breathing quickened. *What if the roof collapses on me now?* He stopped pulling himself along. He tried to look back the way that he had come and instead knocked his head on the side of the tunnel. This triggered a cascade of dirt. He snapped his head back forwards and hurriedly heaved himself along the rope once more. After a short while, he slowed. There had been a muffled sound behind him. In the total blackness, it was impossible to say if the tunnel had collapsed or if just a few clods of dirt had come away.

Marlvon closed his eyes and breathed through his nose. *Calm yourself. You're not going to get out of this early grave by panicking.*

It only took a few short moments before Marlvon calmed himself and was able to continue his dogged journey.

Time seemed to warp for the man. His shoulders and arms soon began to ache and then started to burn. His hands blistered and bled, but there was nothing for it but to keep going and hope that his tunnel remained open.

Thud. Marlvon's head hit something hard. He put his hands out and felt a wall blocking his path. He also felt where the rope had been fastened to a stone embedded within the dirt. He rolled off the trolley in relief and lay on the spacious floor of another chamber. This chamber was just as dark as the tunnel, but Marlvon still knew its simple layout. It was larger than the chamber under his house and, once rested, Marlvon was able to stand up straight. He did so and felt around for the ladder that would be his escape. He climbed the two rungs and hunched under another trap door. Unlike the other, this was made of wood and had already been bolted from the inside. He found the bolt and slid it back with a screech that sent a chill through his body. Instead of folding down, this trapdoor opened up and out into one of the horse's stalls. He knew that a scattering of hay would be on the top of the trapdoor and he just hoped that Old Nal the horse wasn't lying down on it too.

He gave the trapdoor a shove and peeked out into the stall. It was dark, but not as dark as his hole was. He could see the old mare standing in the corner slowly munching some hay; ignoring her surroundings.

Marlvon could see little else, but more importantly, he could hear nothing that caused him alarm. He pushed the door open further and slithered out into the horse's stall with his small bag from the trolley. The fresh open air splashed across his face after the stale air below ground. He went to Old Nal and gave her a calming pat to alert her to his presence. He then removed his clothing from his nap-sack. He stealthily dressed in the corner of the stall to be clad in soft leather pants, boots and a thin wool tunic over his nightshirt.

The stables themselves were a wooden structure with an earthen floor. There were six stalls; three on each side of a walkway. The entrance was on the corner closest to Marlvon's house. Down the back was a small workshop with tools used for leatherwork, horse shoeing and other carpentry jobs unrelated to horses. Marlvon mused that if someone was in the stables, they would either be in the workshop or patrolling around. Although Marlvon had six stalls in his stables, he only had four horses: Old Nal, a sturdy young Clydesdale, a mare who Marlvon thought of as an all-rounder and his favourite, strong, fast, chestnut mare.

Marlvon peeked over the door of his stall and down the walkway. He saw nothing alarming; no soldiers, no light from a torch, and nothing out of place. He closed his eyes and listened keenly. At first, he heard nothing, but then he thought he heard a light footfall just by the entrance. It could have been the draft horse in the stall closest to the doorway, or it may have been something more sinister.

He ducked back into Nal's stall and listened once more; this time with his eyes open. There… another noise. Was it a swoosh of a tail, or cloth rubbing against wood? Marlvon reassured himself that it was probably a tail; the men were probably wearing full armour.

Marlvon stood motionless and weighed up his two options. He could either leave his stall and seek any men that may be lurking, or stay where he was and draw them into a trap. He promptly chose the former and, clasping his knife in his right hand, crawled under the door of the stall. Once standing on the other side, he made his way down the walkway towards the workshop.

Just outside the door, he crouched down and poked his head around the corner. It was empty. He exhaled silently, only just realising that he had been holding his breath.

Before he could stand, Marlvon heard what sounded like a footstep near the entrance to the stables. Without needing to think, he darted into the workshop and listened intently. Then he heard it again; definite human footsteps. And not one set of footfalls, but two. Marlvon listened closely as the two men advanced down the walkway. Marlvon peeked around the doorframe and saw two sizeable men in chain mail shirts with drawn swords. He ducked back and, knowing his workshop, quietly grabbed a sharp chisel the length of his forearm. He peeked at the men again as they got closer. The brief glance in the dark told Marlvon that the men looked wary, but not nervous; they trod with caution and held their swords firmly.

The footsteps came closer. Marlvon believed he could defeat them both. He had no choice but to believe that, though he was concerned the other men would be within shouting distance. Not only that, but Marlvon wanted one of the men alive; he had to find out what in the name-of-all-that-is-good was going on.

Marlvon remained crouching and forced his mind clear of these thoughts. The steps grew closer. Marlvon rocked to the balls of his feet. They were level with the last stall. A few more steps and they would be at the workshop door. One… two… three… a head poked around the doorframe and Marlvon leapt into the man. He brought the chisel up in his left hand and drove it into the soft underside of the man's chin. As the man fell dead, Marlvon shoved him aside and sliced at the outstretched sword hand of the second man with his knife. His blow glanced off the chain mail but left the man with a jarred arm. Marlvon was quick. The man was just opening his mouth to yell when Marlvon brought the hilt of his knife in a sideward arc and struck the man's temple. He fell with a sickening groan and landed on top of the other man.

There was no time to lose: Marlvon didn't know who else might be patrolling. He dragged the corpse of the first man into the corner of the workshop and piled rags and bits of leather on top of him. He dragged the other man, the one who was still breathing, back to Nal's stall. The old horse smelt the blood and stomped around unsettled. Marlvon spoke to her soothingly, but it didn't seem to help much.

Marlvon quickly tied the man's wrists and ankles with bits of leather from the workshop. He then opened the trapdoor and shoved the unconscious man down into the darkness. He heard the unmistakable sound of a bone breaking and hoped it wasn't the man's neck.

Marlvon then set about saddling up Old Nal and his favourite speedy steed. He was well practiced at this, and the moonlit darkness didn't slow him down. Once the two beasts were ready, Marlvon opened the trapdoor and climbed into the total darkness once more.

The decision to interrogate the man was not an easy one for Marlvon to make. While he felt an urge to flee while he still could, the information that he could gather in a few moments with the man could be invaluable. This desire to understand the situation won out and Marlvon committed himself to this path.

Marlvon paused at the trapdoor before descending and closed his eyes for a moment. He took a deep, steady breath to calm himself and a second one to prepare himself for what was to come. He pushed the thoughts of his peaceful desires out of his mind before they took hold and instead filled his mind with what was needed.

Marlvon pulled open the trapdoor and lowered himself into the darkness. He closed the door before feeling around for the unconscious man. He found him lying in a heap and breathing gently. With a great effort, Marlvon pushed and pulled him to be lying on the trolley. His legs dangled over the end and Marlvon ensured that these were tied together. The man's left foot was dangling loosely; the crack he heard was explained. He also tied the man's wrists in front of him with a loop under the cart to restrict his arm movements. As a final precaution, he looped the man's neck with leather and fastened it under the trolley. All this he did in the total darkness. He paused to smile at his own skills.

Marlvon spoke to himself. 'Right, you bastard, it's time to wake you up.' Marlvon slapped the man on the face. No response. He grabbed his little finger; snap.

'Aaahhhhh!'

Marlvon stepped back and let the man discover his situation. 'What the damnation is going on? My foot… aaarrrhhh… my foot! What the heck is this?' Then silence. The man rasped. 'Hello?'

Marlvon turned and faced away from the man to diffuse his voice about the chamber and barked, 'Who are you? What are you doing at my house?' Marlvon heard a sharp intake of breath.

'I'm not going to tell you nothing.'

Marlvon turned at random intervals so that his voice would sound like it came from multiple directions. 'Yes, you will. You may try to resist, but you will tell me what I want to know.'

The man laughed.

'You don't seem to understand your situation. I'll only ask nicely once more. What are you doing at my house?'

'Go on farmer, do your worst.'

Marlvon pulled a flint out of his pocket and sent a simple shower of sparks falling. He used this fleeting light to measure the distance of every aspect of the chamber. He also saw the man blink furiously.

'As you wish.' Marlvon stepped towards him and broke his right thumb.

The man screamed.

'I can cut off a finger, an ear, or your nose. Which would you like to lose?'

'Oh Mother, you're a butcher.'

'What's that? All three?'

'No, no, no, no. None. I beg you, please.'

'Then tell me what you're doing here.'

The man was silent for a moment; a moment too long. Marlvon flicked his skilful wrist and removed the man's left ear.

'Aaahhh! Curse you!' The man began sobbing.

Marlvon spoke conversationally to the man. 'The key to torture, the real key, is to follow through on your promises. Now, I'm in a bit of a hurry and I need answers quickly. Marlvon changed his tone. 'I like the number three.' He then shouted out the next three words fiercely. 'FINGER, NOSE, EYE?'

'You! We're here for you.'

'Explain.'

The man sobbed, but said no more.

'FINGER, NOSE, EYE!'

'Resvon was killed. Two days ago. The new leader, Avgar, has ordered that all relatives, friends, and those aligned to Resvon must be killed. You though—he wants you alive. He's put a price on your capture; a big price. He's only been in power for one night and one day and they say he's soon going to put out posters with your likeness on them. We wanted to get in first.' The man fell into a series of sobs.

'That wasn't so hard, was it? Now, how many of you are there?'

'A dozen. My friend and I came to the stables, but the rest went to your house.' The man found some confidence. 'But there will soon be many more roaming the countryside.'

This struck a nerve with Marlvon. He itched to escape the blooded chamber. He knew he should kill the man, but his hatred of violence seeped into his being.

'When you wake, you will not be tied down. Your hands and feet will still be fastened, though. I can't have you coming after me too quickly. If you can find your way out of here in this darkness, then good luck to you.'

'What… when I wake?'

Marlvon cracked the man across the skull; knocking him out. After untying him from the trolley, Marlvon found the ladder and climbed his way out of the blood stinking chamber. As he escaped into the air above, he could feel his hands shake. He stumbled out of Nal's empty stall and found his prepared horses waiting for him. Touching their soft noses and smooth necks calmed him greatly.

Marlvon untied them and ensured that Nal was fastened to Thunder with a length of rope. He leapt upon his favourite steed and cautiously walked him out of the stables. The waning moon was out with only patchy clouds to obscure it.

Marlvon looked over to his house and saw four men leaning against his wall. One of them spotted him and let out a yell. The time for stealth was over. Marlvon kicked Thunder into a canter and Nal followed behind.

Nal was old, but Marlvon knew her and knew that she could maintain that pace for only a short while. But that was all he needed; the soldiers were horseless and once he was away from the immediate danger, he would take the slower back roads. As he put distance between himself and his attackers, Marlvon's mind roamed to the one place where he wanted to go; needed to go. Marlvon was heading to Bankton; to Islonda.

An old horse clip-clopped its way through Bankton pulling a rickety old two-wheel, sprung cart. The cart was laden with a few bales of hay, some tired-looking vegetables and a farmer who looked to match the vegetable's sorry state and the horse's age.

The farmer made his way through the main square, where there was a great commotion going on about the statue of Resvon. He showed little interest in that and continued on his way to the blacksmith's workshop.

He pulled the horse in and the cart came to a creaking stop. He looked across the street at the closed door of the blacksmith's shop. Standing out the front were two men of arms wearing plate armour and swords by their sides. The old farmer sighed and painfully climbed down from his cart. He gripped his walking stick and made his slow way across the cobbled stone. He was not yet across the street when one of the guards hailed him.

'You there, old man. I hope you're not thinking of comin' this way.'

The farmer stopped and looked up at the man who spoke. The guard looked away. The farmer was expecting this, for he was ugly; the kind of ugly that made people avert their gaze in embarrassment. The old man replied with the unrefined accent of a peasant.

'As a matter of fac' I do. This here blackie promise me a new hoe by tha end-a last moon. My fields a-awaitin' to be worked over while this lazy sow take-a his time makin me hoe. I come 'ere to get me hoe.'

'You're out of luck, old man. You ain't getting any hoe today. Now, be off with you.'

The old man took two steps forward. 'I travelled half-a day to get 'ere. I ain't leavin withough me hoe.'

'Oh yes, you will. This here blackie is dead and you'll be next if you don't turn around now.'

The farmer clenched his jaw. 'I can see he cheated the wrong sort, as well as me. Well, can I see his wife… or his daughter, so as I can get me money back? I done paid half upfront.'

'You're a heartless, stubborn old man, ain't ya? His poor wife's grieving and I'm sure his daughter would be too if she were here.'

The old man's eyes twinkled.

'Now leave.' The guard unsheathed his sword.

'All righ', all right. No need to get yourself all worked up.'

The old man lowered his gaze in submission. As he did, something out of place caught his vision. He stooped down unsteadily and picked it up.

'What have you got there, man?' asked a guard.

'Ha, here I was thinkin' I found me a coin. All it was is a square button. Good day to you both.'

With head bowed once more, the youthful eyes of Marlvon darted over the cobblestones in search of another button. He soon spied one a few feet up the road. Instead of picking this one up, he made his slow way back to his cart with heart beating rapidly. He clambered up and set Old Nal off at an ambling pace. While his eyes searched for more of the unique buttons that he had given Islonda as part of her changeable dress-pants. He found the trail and followed it. The buttons became more spaced apart and Marlvon racked his mind trying to remember how many buttons were on the dress.

The buttons led down the first alleyway he came to. Ensuring that he remained as the old farmer, Marlvon climbed off his cart gingerly and made his slow way down the lane. About halfway down the alley, the trail ended in a pile of five buttons leaning against a wooden post of someone's fence. Marlvon's eyes roamed over the post and quickly found what he was looking for.

His made-up face smiled at the simple genius of Islonda. There, scratched into the post, was a basic picture that told him all that he needed to know. The picture was of two stick-men holding hands underneath a few stars. Below the people was an etching of a moon, a half-waned moon. Marlvon not only know where Islonda was planning to go, but it was clear from the light shavings of wood upon the cobblestone, she had completed the picture recently. Islonda cannot have been hotly pursued from Bankton, as she had time and composure enough to leave the trail of buttons and etch the picture into the post. With the rush of the welcome news, Marlvon almost forgot his disguise and leapt with glee. Instead, he made his slow way back to Nal and then what felt like his even slower way out of Bankton and towards his lookout where he had taken Islonda for their private day together.

27

Kathsum entered the dusty old classroom where she had received most of her schooling. She had not been there for many years, and the room seemed to have shrunk with the passing of time. The small room was set up exactly as she remembered and it had been unused for many years; the pupil numbers had grown too great. This was as a result of Kathsum, as High Chancellor, placing an increased focus on education.

As she paced around the room, she ran her fingers through the dust on the five student desks and one teacher's desk. She gazed out the simple cloudy window, then looked at the tattered map of the lands on the far wall. She felt a mixture of both happiness and sadness at being in this room again. Walking slowly, she finally made her way over to the teacher's desk and, feeling rather naughty, sat down.

As soon as her backside touched the seat, Guflinkov stepped through the door. Kathsum leapt to her feet as a reflex.

'You've been sprung, High Chancellor. I had better run the cane over your knuckles.'

Kathsum involuntarily rubbed her hands. 'That always hurt more than I expected; every single time.'

'But did it teach you your lesson?'

'In a way; it taught me not to get caught.'

'Ha, the mischievous young Kath returns.'

Guflinkov had made his way over to his old desk and sat down on a creaky chair.

Kathsum wanted to get straight to the point of why she had arranged the meeting. 'I am not the only one who has learnt to conceal things, Guflinkov. It appears that you've been deceiving us all for years.'

'Whatever do you mean, High Chancellor?' Guflinkov asked innocently.

'I'll only have the truth, Guflinkov, or it will be I who will be wielding the cane.' Guflinkov smiled like a cheeky boy and Kathsum continued. 'I saw the way you moved when Resvon was attacked. Only a highly trained person can seamlessly deflect an arrow with their sword and catch another mid-flight.'

Guflinkov looked sad. 'But I could not save Resvon.'

'No, but neither could his guards. Do not be too hard on yourself. Now, as your High Chancellor, and as your friend, please explain yourself and who you really are.'

Guflinkov sighed audibly. 'You had better sit down, Kath.' The old man went silent for a short while before mumbling to himself. 'Where to start?'

When he began speaking, Guflinkov had a distant look in his eyes. 'I was not born in Roasline. I was not even born in the lands that are governed by Roasline. I was born on an island.'

He stopped and pointed to the map on the wall. 'What is beyond the edge of that map, Kath? Have you ever wondered?'

Kathsum realised that while she used to ponder this often, she had not thought about it for many years.

Guflinkov continued before she could respond. 'I was born beyond the edge of that map. If you follow the coastline past Fort Kykum, past Nivera and Psymryte, you will eventually get to my home. I was born into a simple fishing village on one of many small islands. It was a happy life, or so my childhood memories tell me. Then, when I was four or five, our village was set upon by a ship of slave traders. The men of my village who did not submit were killed and the women raped. I was thrust into the belly of a ship with the other children. With little food and no daylight, I could not tell how long I was there for, or where we were going. I later discovered that we had been travelling south.

'Then, one day after a storm had passed, our ship was attacked. I don't know who by, but a hole was blown clear in the side of our cell. Without a second thought, I forced my way out through the inward gushing water and swam to the surface. Even at five, I was a strong swimmer. When I reached fresh air, there was turmoil all around me: cannons, fire and screams. I found a piece of wood and clung to it for dear life. The fighting soon died down and both of the ships sank.'

Kathsum clasped her hand over her mouth in shock.

'I floated there for a day and a night before another ship came. This was a vessel from Roasline. We were eventually taken back to the city and I was fortunate enough to be given into the care of a wealthy family who were unable to have their own children. I was even raised and schooled as if I was their own son. But I never forgot my real parents and my brothers.

'My adoptive parents died when I was a young man and left their wealth entirely to me. They desired that I manage their business and lands.' Guflinkov smiled wryly. 'But being a young man with significant wealth, I wanted to explore the world. I bought a ship, hired a crew and set my sights on the borders of the maps.' Guflinkov closed his eyes and looked as if he was taken back to those youthful days. 'I sailed many seas, visited many lands, learnt much about the world and about men. There is a bigger world out there than you can possibly imagine.'

Kathsum croaked a question. 'Why did you return to Roasline?'

'When I was travelling, I met a group of people, an alliance you might call it. There were representatives from many cities, but none from Roasline. After spending many months with them, I joined their ranks to further their cause. The lands were at war, and not just the skirmish between Roasline and the Outcasts, but lands and peoples that you've never even heard of.

'The purpose of this collection of people was, and is, to bring about peace; to stop the fruitless killing of so many humans.

'I was tasked with Roasline and a rather young Resvon with the Outcasts. And we were close to achieving peace, so close, painfully close.' Guflinkov clenched his fist and brought it down on the desk in frustration.

'Wait, are you claiming that you brought about the treaty with Resvon?' Kathsum felt a bit indignant. 'I did all of that work; it was to be my victory.'

'Kath, do you really think that my education of you was purely for your benefit? I taught you, and others, the values that you hold dear; the kindness that you have deep within you.' Guflinkov paused to let that sink in. 'And surely, the victory was to be for the people of Roasline and not for you alone.'

Kathsum stopped herself. *Of course it was.* She nodded.

'That is now a moot point anyway.'

'Yes, it is.'

'Kath, with Resvon dead, we need to reassess the situation. I need to gather information and I need to meet with the Alliance. I'm going to be leaving Roasline for a time, but I am satisfied that you can manage here without my guidance. In reality, you haven't needed that for many years.' Guflinkov smiled.

Kathsum was silent for a few moments, not knowing what to say. A thought tugged at her. 'Why the charade? Why not speak more openly? Why not confide in me?'

Guflinkov sighed what sounded like a tired sigh. 'That has been one of the hardest parts of playing this role. I wanted to tell you, I really did. It wasn't that I didn't trust you; it was that I wanted you to believe this success was as a result of your actions. The aim of the Alliance is to be covert and not come across as being a manipulating power. That would draw more conflict to the lands. All I wanted to be was a shadow. Can you understand that? Can you forgive me?'

Kathsum didn't know quite what to feel. She felt anger at being deceived and manipulated, love for the old man who was trying to give her success and confusion at the story that she had just been told.

Kathsum stood and her chair fell over. 'Can I forgive you? Not today. I thought we had a bond, a trust, as strong as father and daughter, and now I find that you've been lying to me... for my entire life.' She pointed at him. 'Worse still, you've been manipulating me. You used me like a puppet.' Anger won out. 'Guflinkov, I'm finding out that the rock that I've been leaning on is made of sand. I don't know who you are anymore.'

Guflinkov looked hurt; Kathsum felt a pang of regret. She found herself backtracking and crossed her arms. 'I cannot forgive you today, but I may tomorrow, or the day after.'

Guflinkov nodded. 'That is fair.'

Kathsum walked to the dusty window, thinking through what had been said. She turned back to Guflinkov. 'If Resvon is in your Alliance, why did it take him so long to reach out to me for a treaty?'

Guflinkov smiled like he did when Kathsum was at school and she asked a question that she should have known the answer to. 'Come Kathsum, think about his position. Do you think he would have survived a single day if he had suggested peace *before* he could groom the Outcasts? Even after years of planning, he was still killed for his peaceful persuasions, or so I assume.'

Kathsum felt foolish. 'Of course, of course.' She turned back to the window. Her thoughts rested on the old man. 'Do you really have a limp?'

'No.'

She continued to stare out of the window. 'You can wield a sword. How skilled are you?'

'Very.'

'But you look so frail.'

'And so, everyone dismisses me as an old, drunk, harmless oddity and they tolerate me.'

'Are you frail at all?'

'I'm not as young as I used to be, but I'm not as old as I look.'

'Where did you learn to fight?'

'On my many travels I visited many peoples, learnt from many people. Some of these were Healers, some were historians, and many were fighters. I picked little bits from this person, other bits from that tribe and put them all together in a way that makes sense to me; that's suited to me. And practice. I do a lot of practice and training; so much so that my skills have become reflexes.'

Kathsum was silent.

'Do you have any more questions about me? I sail at dawn.'

The High Chancellor turned back to face him. 'Will you return to me?'

Guflinkov smiled. 'I will try.'

Kathsum nodded. 'Then on your return, I will forgive you.'

The old man stood and walked smoothly over to Kathsum. He spread his arms and invited a hug. She couldn't resist.

'Strive for peace, Kath, and it shall come.'

'Safe travels, Guflinkov.'

Kathsum remained in the room after Guflinkov had left and thought about the many years that she had spent learning from him. She hoped with all of her heart that she would see him again, if for no other reason than to forgive him.

28

Avgar woke with a throbbing head and the sound of someone pounding on his door. From his bed, he yelled out to the disturber of his peace. 'What?!'

A muffled voice replied. 'Sir, you asked to be woken at dawn.'

Curse myself. Avgar stumbled out of bed. 'Fetch me some black sausage and a mug of strong ale.'

He shook his head to try and clear it, but that only made the throbbing worse. Since Avgar had started using his nightly *medicine*, he had not found it easy to wake the next day. At least this morning, he didn't feel as nauseous as he usually did.

Needing a great effort, Avgar managed to rouse his spirits, adjust the clothes that he had slept in, and unlock the door all before his breakfast arrived. He took a big gulp of ale, devoured the salty sausage, and then finished his drink. Only then did he feel ready to face the day.

Avgar made his way down to a lower balcony overlooking the courtyard. He leaned against a parapet and waited for Eyp. The air was already warm and sticky and Avgar longed for the cooler months. Avgar looked down and saw there were two gallows set up below that had already claimed their first victims for the day. *Hanging, it really is a clean form of execution; no blood.* Avgar mused on the benefits of a good hanging. Two more people were executed before Eyp arrived and by that time, Avgar had his full wits about him.

Avgar heard his second-in-command approach from behind and spoke before he was addressed. 'I see they've started early today.'

'No point in delaying, my lord. And there are so many to get through; Resvon seemed to have had a lot of followers.'

'Not the least being *all* the commanders.' Avgar spoke with a hint of dry sarcasm.

'Better to have a clean slate, I say.' Eyp responded with a smile.

'Yes, it is; as long as we can trust their replacements.'

Avgar doubted that all the commanders were behind Resvon, but he chose not to press the point further. Instead, he made a mental note to ensure that the new batch of commanders were foremost loyal to him, not Eyp. He had no reason to doubt Eyp's loyalty. The man owed him his life after all, but he vowed to keep a wary eye on him nonetheless.

'Have you caught Resvon's nephew, Marlvon, yet?'

Eyp sounded frustrated in his reply. 'Not yet. He was last seen heading in the direction of a town west of here called Bankton. And then he seemed to disappear. My sources tell me that his woman lives there. But she has vanished too.'

'And what are you doing to rectify the situation?' Avgar gave his sharp reply.

'All that we can. There is a hefty bounty on his head and we have soldiers combing the countryside.'

'Place a price on her head too.'

'Yes, my lord.'

'And burn Bankton to the ground.'

Eyp smiled wickedly. 'Certainly, my lord. There will be no survivors.'

Avgar felt an urge to know more about this evasive man. 'Have you met this Marlvon? What is he like?'

Avgar saw that anger in Eyp's eyes. 'My sources tell me he is a man who is skilled in the art of disguise; that he can make himself appear as if he were someone else. I have heard a list of the names that he has used in the past, and there are many. My lord, you asked if I have met him before? I have, when he was disguised as another; as a man called Mantly. My lord, Marlvon, was the man who captured me, tortured me and disfigured me. I will not stop pursuing him until he is caught. When that happens, if he is still alive, I will inflict so much pain on him that he will scream for death.'

Avgar smiled to himself. 'I have faith in you, Eyp. You will catch this man or no one will.' They both looked into the courtyard as the next man swung from the noose.

'I want you to organise a meeting between the leaders of the major cities of the Outcasts. I want the leaders from Nivera, Psymryte and any other city or large town that you deem strategically important. I want them to meet here in Fort Kykum as soon as can be arranged.'

'It will be done, my lord.'

Something had gnawed away at Avgar for the past month and played on his mind more and more as he learnt about the Outcast's history. He understood the Outcasts to have spawned from outlaws and outcasts. From that, he could understand their propensity towards violence and war. What he couldn't quite reconcile was how such scum had raised a navy of the quality that they had. Avgar acknowledged that while it didn't have the brute strength and firepower of Roasline's navy, there were skilful sailors and crafty ships designs within the Outcast's navy. He was a novice when it came to war on the open seas, but he could clearly see that the Outcasts played to their strengths. With his leadership secure, and Eyp loyal, Avgar thought this a good time to ask his question.

'Eyp, how did the Outcasts come to be masters of ship building?'

The ex-Commander of Ships gave Avgar a knowing look before answering.

'My lord, you know our history of where our ancestors came from. As you can imagine, there were sailors amongst those who first arrived in Psymryte and many more came later. But sailors don't know how to build ships. That particular craft blossomed shortly after the Outcasts crossed the Sempa and took Nivera. That was, and is, a city of great skill in many areas. And they are proud of it; too proud.

'Since then, our naval ability has ebbed and flowed depending on the leader at the time. That was Resvon's only redeeming quality; he valued the navy and strengthened her.'

Avgar mused. *That makes sense.*

'Is there anything else, my lord?' Eyp enquired.

'No, that is all.' Avgar nodded and Eyp was dismissed. The second in command left the leader of the Outcasts to watch the next hanging alone.

Avgar thought of Nivera and her leader and although he disliked the prospect of alliances, he knew that he would have to make ties with the other leaders; his following just wasn't big enough to control all the lands north of the Liagar. The thought of this made him hungry, and he went to find some more food.

Avgar was halfway through his lunch of bread, ham, pickles and cheese when he heard footsteps approach him. Still chewing, he addressed the intruder behind him. 'What?'

The man stood there and said nothing. Avgar waited for a reply and after a few tense moments slammed his knife down on the table and turned, full of rage. Staring back at him was the steely face of Jacov the Healer.

'So, you're the one they've been calling the new Leader of the Outcasts?' Jacov's voice was calm, yet firm.

Avgar had no idea who this man was, dressed in a simple white robe with sandals, and he didn't really care. He grabbed his cutting knife from the table and swiftly brought it to rest against Jacov's bare throat.

Avgar spat out his reply. 'I'm not going to ask who you are, for I already know; you're a corpse who's still standing.'

Jacov smiled and responded assertively. 'Aren't we all? I am also known as Jacov, a Healer from Headly. You want to kill me? Go on, try.'

The Healer waited for a moment and when Avgar didn't move, put the thumb of his left hand on the blade and pushed it firmly enough to draw blood. Only it didn't. Instead, Avgar drew back his hand as a sharp pain bit into his thumb. He looked down and saw blood, *his* blood, seeping out of a fresh cut. He looked at Jacov, confused.

'What kind of sorcery is this?' He whispered.

'There is a protective power over me. I cannot be harmed. All those who try to harm me will be harmed themselves.'

This was the first magic that Avgar had seen since that fateful meeting on the beach where his powers were stolen from him. He had assumed that no one else on this side of the Moaks had any magical powers at all. He felt a sudden thirst to know more.

'Yes, I've heard rumours about the Healers, but I did not believe them to be true. Who grants this protective power, yourselves? Or someone else?'

Jacov looked at him sternly. 'I did not come here to discuss our secrets with you. I came here to tell you our terms regarding the peace treaty between the Outcasts and the people governed by Roasline.'

Heavy clouds rolled across Avgar's mood at the mention of peace.

Jacov continued talking. 'Resvon, on behalf of the Outcasts, had signed a peace deal with the High Chancellor of Roasline. You will honour this agreement or we will cease treating your wounded soldiers, effective immediately.'

'You dare threaten me?'

'I am not threatening you; I am outlining what is going to occur. If you continue to war, and Roasline honours the agreement, then we will continue to treat her wounded. I'm sure that someone in your position needs no reminding how important numbers can be in war.'

Avgar stood there stone-faced, staring at Jacov.

The Healer smiled.

Avgar admitted to himself that he didn't know much about the Healers of Headly. All he really knew was that boats often carried wounded men to Headly and returned with men ready to fight once more. He could not deny that not having the Healers on his side would be a significant disadvantage.

He forced a smile onto his face. 'I will need time. I've only been the leader for five days and I need to consult with the leaders of Psymryte and Nivera and others besides. After all, you would not want new peace to be ruined by civil war amongst the Outcasts. The good news is that I'm shortly to be meeting those leaders.'

'You have two moon cycles to decide, then I'll be back. If there are any breaches of the agreement in the meantime, then your people will no longer be treated by us.'

Avgar couldn't see anyway past the firm man. 'So be it.'

Jacov nodded and left the room. Avgar took his knife and slammed it into the tabletop, where it stood quivering while he stormed from the room.

29

Marlvon left Bankton behind him, changed his posture and urged Old Nal forward at a faster pace. By straightening his back and lifting his chin, he had wiped ten years off his disguised persona. Now he looked like a seasoned farmer wanting to get to his destination in a timely manner. But the pace of Nal still felt too slow for Marlvon and he wanted nothing more than to hold Islonda safely in his arms.

It was late afternoon by the time that Marlvon reached the spot where he needed to turn off the main road. The journey had been uneventful, except for being stopped once by a patrol of soldiers that had searched his cart for the fugitive Marlvon. But his disguise had prevailed, and the soldiers soon ordered the ugly farmer on his way.

Marlvon led Nal off the road and gave her as much rest as it took for him to take her harness off and hide the cart under some bushes and branches. Just to be certain that no one would find the cart, Marlvon backtracked and checked from the viewpoint of the road. When all was in place, Marlvon searched the ground to see if he could find any tracks of Islonda. He soon found some broken twigs and a footprint. He smiled to himself and pulled Nal away from her meal of grass to follow Islonda's trail. The rugged terrain meant he couldn't go fast, but he knew that he would be going faster than Islonda and therefore, should be gaining on her.

Marlvon covered a decent distance before the light began to fade and then he realised his dilemma: was he to push on, or stop for the night? Marlvon had no doubt that he could find his lookout by the light of the moon and stars, but what if Islonda couldn't remember the way? In fact, he doubted very much that she would have remembered the exact way that they had come last time. But could she still find her way there, knowing to which peak she was headed? *Maybe, but these hills are riddled with sneaky gullies and impossibly fiendish ridges. But then, she is clever and persistent.* There was a fair chance that she had made it and an equally fair chance that she was lost somewhere in the foothills. Marlvon cursed, uncharacteristically frustrated.

After much to-ing and fro-ing, he decided that a night of inaction was more than his nerves could take. And so, after a quick bite of tired vegetables, he set off following the rough path that he had taken with Islonda.

The sun had set and the air cooled somewhat. Had it been under different circumstances, Marlvon would have enjoyed the solitary night-time walk. But it was not, and so he fretted and worried that the worst had befallen his love.

The moon moved across the sky and the repetitive nature of the hard walking eventually calmed Marlvon. He pushed himself all the way to the base of the steep hill that Nal could not climb before taking a break. Marlvon felt as tired as Old Nal looked, but he only rested for a short while before beginning his ascent. The night was growing old as he made his way through his secret crevice, earnestly hoping to see Islonda soon. Eventually, he was through. He leapt down the natural stairs apprehensively and found emptiness; Islonda was not there.

'No.' Marlvon sank to his knees and put his face in his hands. 'Islonda, where are you?' he asked to the night sky.

Luckily for Marlvon, at this point his mind and extensive training dominated his thoughts. *You're exhausted. There's nothing else you can do while it's still night. Rest, sleep if you can, and tomorrow start the search again.* Marlvon's mind told him to rest, but his heart wanted to start searching. Marlvon's heart had already won once that night, but this time it was the logic of exhaustion that was victorious. He curled up, away from the cliff's edge, and it didn't take long for sleep to come.

The sun rose and so did Marlvon. His body ached from having slept on rocks and his tummy grumbled for food. He ignored both of these and, after a quick drink from the pool, set off in haste. He flew down the slope and passed Old Nal; leaving her where she was. Not having to lead her allowed Marlvon more freedom in his choice of path and the speed that he wanted to travel at. The journey downhill and in full daylight was much quicker than the previous night, and Marlvon soon found himself where he had rested at dusk the previous day. While he caught his breath, he searched for signs of Islonda's path. He soon found what he was looking for and raced after her.

The path he followed zigged and zagged, wound and twisted, and even did a full circle here and there. His anxiety grew as he realised that the path that Islonda had taken appeared to have no clear direction or purpose.

As the day wore on, and the heat rose, Marlvon didn't just start worrying about what state Islonda must be in, but he also started to worry about himself. He had only had a shadow of sleep in the past day and a half and he had eaten little. With water, he had done better; crossing several flowing creeks and utilising each one, but his energy and focus waned. Again, he found himself with a dilemma: to continue the pursuit, stop to rest, or hunt and forage for some food. After much circling of these thoughts, his heart won out again and he pressed on.

The hot afternoon was passing rapidly and Marlvon's hopes diminished. Islonda's path, which was easy to follow, had long left his lookout behind and continued west along the base of the hills. Marlvon wondered how Islonda had travelled so far alone, but this gave him hope; for it implied that she was well fed and strong.

As the young man followed her trail, he kept an eye out for any signs of outlaws. While the hills were vast and the outlaws few, the last thing that Marlvon wanted was for either himself or Islonda to come across a bunch of desperate men. In years gone by Marlvon had heard rumours of cannibal outlaws further west and he desperately hoped that these were nothing more than fire-side stories.

As well as keeping an eye out for outlaws, Marlvon had been searching for edible plants. His attentiveness had not gone unrewarded as he had found small snacks of bitter juniper berries and sour uncooked yams. These kept him going, but they certainly didn't fill his stomach.

As the afternoon wore into dusk, Marlvon followed the trail along the edge of a dangerously steep slope. He decided that once the light was gone, he would stop for the night.

The last light left the sky and Marlvon moved away from the precipice and found a groove to lie in. He lay down to rest, closed his eyes and listened to the nightly noises. He heard the daytime birds quieten down and the nocturnal ones take their place. A few large insects and moths flew around, and hungry bats chased after them. Small animals scrummaged around nearby and somewhere distant a wild dog howled. Closer to hand, but down the slope, a sickly animal made a groaning whimper and then stopped. Marlvon was just dozing off to sleep when the same animal cried out once more. This time the noise was pained, not sickly, and drawn out. *Poor thing,* he thought, *it won't last till morning.*

He rolled onto his side to get more comfortable and the cry continued. The pained noise turned into a wail of grief and Marlvon thought, *that almost sounds human.* His eyes snapped open. 'Human!'

He leapt to his feet, quickly gathered his few belongings and made his way to the slope's edge. 'Islonda?' he yelled. Then he waited. A moment later, he heard what his heart desired.

'Marlvon, help.'

Relief swept through his entire body and, despite the circumstances, he smiled. *She's alive.*

'Islonda, I'm here. Keep talking so I can follow your voice.'

'Marlvon, please help me. I'm here, down this hill. I'm stuck.'

Islonda kept talking and Marlvon raced along the edge of the slope for a few hundred yards until he was level with her voice. Marlvon had to be very careful in the minimal light and had already found himself almost slipping once or twice.

He could soon see clearly where Islonda had fallen down the slope; the loose topsoil had been swept away and broken shale could be seen underneath.

'Islonda, I'm going to come down and get you.'

'Be careful, it's slippery.'

Marlvon paced one way and then the other, trying to find the best spot to descend. It would have been easier to go down where Islonda had, but he didn't want to risk falling on her or bringing a cascade of debris down upon her head. He eventually decided on a spot and began the downward climb.

He sat on his bottom and slowly shuffled his way down, crawling like a crab. Whenever he felt the soil giving way, he dug his heels in and spread his weight out. Slowly, bit by bit, he made his way down the not-quite-cliff. He reached the bottom and stood up triumphantly. 'Islonda, I'm coming.'

Marlvon stood in a dark, narrow gully. He took two steps towards Islonda and tripped over a branch, or a rock; he couldn't see to tell which. With bloodied hands, he continued on all fours, ever speaking so that Islonda knew where he was. It wasn't long before he reached her and when he did, he clumsily flung his arms around her and held her close. She wept into his shoulder and he kissed her head.

'I thought I had lost you.' It could have been either of them speaking, but it was Marlvon's voice that spoke.

They held each other for a while before Islonda responded, still teary. 'When *they* came to Bankton, I was walking home. They only cared about finding you. I was careful and didn't go home, but watched and listened from a distance. I realised that if I was captured that they would use me to get to you. They were checking everyone and so I fled. I laid my trail of buttons for you to follow, but doubted that you would even reach Bankton. Then, when I got lost in these hills, I didn't care. You were dead, my family likely dead, so what was the point of persisting?'

Marlvon clasped her to his chest. 'I'm here now, and so are you.'

A loving silence rested between them until. Marlvon broke it. 'Islonda, are you hurt? That was no small hill you fell down.'

'I'm fine. You're here now and so I'm fine.'

Marlvon detected a quaver in her voice. 'Islonda, where are you hurt?'

He pulled back and tried to look at her face in the darkness, but could see little. He felt her body tense for a moment and then relax.

'My right ankle is swollen and I can't put weight on it.'

'Let me feel it.' Marlvon ran his hand down her leg and stopped mid-calf. Islonda took a sharp breath of pain. Marlvon was confused for a moment at what he felt and then he understood.

'Islonda, is there a stick in your leg?'

She replied with a nod which Marlvon sensed more than saw. He continued to feel gently around the wound. The stick was not a think one but was covered in oozy blood.

'I wanted to take it out, but every time I pulled it a little, my head spun and I felt sick.'

Marlvon kissed her forehead. 'How long have you been here?'

'Since midday.'

'Islonda, I need to see this clearer. I'm going to try to light a fire; I dare not wait for dawn.'

Marlvon had his flint stone with him, and he could use his hunting knife to strike a spark. However, he was uncertain if he would be able to obtain the rest of the material needed to light a fire. Luckily, when Islonda had fallen down the slope, she had brought all manner of twigs, leaves and branches with her. Marlvon didn't have to go far to get enough fuel for a fire. The only thing he lacked was the essential material that would turn a spark into a flame. He fumbled around in the dark for what felt like an age before he settled for a dry type of bark that he meticulously shredded into a bunch of fuzzy threads. He sent his sparks into the midst of this and caressed his small flame by blowing gently until it was stable enough to catch on the larger fuel. He continued to care for the fire until it was established enough that it could be left alone.

Marlvon turned to Islonda and smiled at her, but she startled. 'Your face, what's wrong with your face?'

Marlvon thought for a moment and then laughed. 'I was using a disguise; an ugly old man, actually, to avoid being captured. I expect I look quite the sight after days and nights of hard toil.'

'Well, you have looked better.'

Marlvon smiled and thought, *And so have you.*

Islonda looked pale and wan. Her hair was all over the place and she looked like a sick, frightened wild animal. Marlvon looked past that and saw his strong Islonda and smiled at her. 'Right, let's have a look at that leg.'

Marlvon helped Islonda move closer to the fire so that the light on her leg was brighter. The stick that was poking out of the side of her calf was not as big as Marlvon had feared. The extent of the wound could not be determined as half-congealed blood, mixed with dirt, covered Islonda's lower leg.

'First, I'm going to clean the area. This may sting a little, but it has to be done. I just wish I had a pot to boil water in.'

Marlvon pulled out his half-full water skin and poured it on Islonda's leg. She clenched her teeth, but remained silent. Marlvon took a burning branch and went to refill his skin in a nearby brook that he could hear bubbling away. When he returned, he found Islonda dozing. He roused her, removed his shirt and used it with the water to wipe the mess off Islonda's leg. Again, Islonda remained silent as Marlvon worked away.

After several more trips to the creek, Islonda's leg was clean enough to satisfy Marlvon. The stick was half the width of Marlvon's little finger and Marlvon was surprised that it had even penetrated Islonda's leg. He gave it a gentle tug and Islonda let out a yelp of pain. Marlvon thought her response was a bit extreme; she did, after all, have a high pain tolerance. He searched nearby and found a stick as wide as his thumb and handed it to Islonda.

'There's no easy way around this and this is all I can offer you for the pain. I'm sorry, but this will hurt.'

Islonda lay back and bit down on the stick. Marlvon grasped the protruding stick firmly and, with one strong action, ripped it out of Islonda's leg. Islonda screamed through the clenched stick for a moment and then passed out. Marlvon was grateful that she had, for following the stick came a gush of blood. Marlvon grabbed his shirt and pressed firmly on the wound. As he held back the flow, the seasoned warrior looked down at the stick and saw why it had caused so much grief. The sharp tip had snapped off a larger branch and about an inch from the end was an angled nob, like a blunt barb. This had allowed the stick to enter Islonda's flesh easily while preventing it from sliding out; somewhat like an arrowhead. As Marlvon had withdrawn the shaft, the nob had widened Islonda's wound, resulting in the free-flowing blood. Marlvon wished he had been more careful when extracting the stick, but what was done was done and the pragmatic man did not dwell on it.

Marlvon took a peek at the wound after a while and the blood flow had slowed to an ooze. He tied his shirt around Islonda's leg and left her briefly to wash himself in the brook. When he returned, he lay down next to Islonda with the aim of keeping her warm and getting some sleep himself. By that stage, she was breathing gently and sleeping peacefully, and he had no immediate fears for her.

Marlvon slept until his instincts woke him to the sound of soft footsteps some hundred yards up the gully. He peaked under his eyelids and saw the soft grey of dawn.

Marlvon rustled around as if in sleep to position himself so that he was holding his knife. He also noted that the sharp stick from Islonda's leg was close by. Two people approached and Marlvon heard them whispering.

'What have we got here? That one looks like he could provide us with a bit of fun; or at the very least, a few good meals. I do love a nice bit of fresh meat.'

Marlvon had to stop himself from leaping up and attacking the men immediately, as he realised the men were not just outlaws, but cannibal outlaws. He felt sick in the stomach, but his mind was in control and it knew what had to be done: they had to be killed.

The other man then spoke. 'You can have him all you want, but her, the lads and I are going to—' The man gurgled and spluttered as Marlvon's hunting knife pierced his neck. Marlvon was on his feet and had thrown his knife at the cannibal. He now faced the remaining man with no greater weapon than the stick from Islonda's leg. His opponent had a rusty long sword that he clasped firmly in both hands. *I shouldn't have thrown my knife.*

The man smiled a toothy grin and licked his lips. 'Ooooo, a feisty one; yum.'

He lunged and Marlvon stepped aside. He lunged again, Marlvon jumped backwards. Marlvon had to figure out how he could get nice and close to the man without being skewered by the sword. He also had to make sure that he stayed between the man and Islonda. Marlvon could sense the man realising that he had the advantage in the duel and so Marlvon would have to end this quickly. He stepped closer to the man, who swung the sword. Marlvon leapt backwards. He did this a few more times until the man got frustrated and advanced step after step, chasing Marlvon. As he over-lunged, Marlvon changed direction, ducked the blade and dived at the man's ankles. They both tumbled down in a tangled mess on the ground. Marlvon was prepared and so was the first to recover. He quickly stabbed the flailing man in one eye and then the other before driving the bloody stick into the man's neck. The cannibal gurgled, spluttered and writhed around on the ground for a few moments before dying.

As the tension in Marlvon's body eased, he felt his stomach churn with disgust. Before he became incapacitated with revolt, Marlvon searched the two bodies for anything useful. Aside from the rusty sword, he found a poorly made knife, a handful of nuts, and two copper coins. He turned to Islonda and saw her staring at him with an unreadable expression on her face.

'It had to be done.' Marlvon found he couldn't look at her eyes. 'I need to wash. I'll be back shortly.' He didn't wait for a reply.

Marlvon made his way to the river and washed himself before he started to vomit and shake. The urge not to leave Islonda alone was the only reason Marlvon was able to make it back to his love. Without that purpose, Marlvon would have lain down by the water as thoughts of horror took him. Luckily for him, he just made it back to Islonda and the burnt-out fire before he collapsed. He closed his eyes and wept, barely aware of Islonda holding him tightly.

The morning had passed before Marlvon escaped from his state of paralysis and he found that Islonda had fallen asleep with her arms about him. He lay there for many moments, drawing strength from her loving embrace until he could push away the thoughts of horror and could think clearly once again.

Then he felt hunger strike in the pit of his stomach. In trying to wriggle out of Islonda's cuddle, he woke her up. She still looked pale, but smiled at Marlvon.

'I like you with no shirt on.'

Marlvon rubbed his hand over his chest. 'I'd forgotten that I wasn't wearing a shirt.' He smiled back at her. 'Would you like a bite to eat?'

'Yes, please.'

Marlvon gave her most of the nuts and ate some himself. He wanted to find something more and so scrummaged around nearby until he found some wild purple carrots. Their deformed shape proved fibrous to eat, but there were enough to mostly fill their stomachs.

'Islonda, I'd like to move from this place as soon as we're able.' He looked sideways at the corpses. He didn't much fancy wearing one of their shirts. 'But first I need to look at your leg.'

Marlvon felt her intense gaze rest on him. 'I now have a bit more of an understanding of the past you don't want to think about. I will not ask you to talk about it except to say that without it, we would both be dead, or worse.'

Marlvon nodded. The thought had also occurred to him. Even so, he didn't want to discuss it. 'Let me have a look at your wound.' Marlvon requested more gruffly than he had intended.

Marlvon undid the bandage which had partially stuck to the dried blood. The wound itself looked red and angry, but there was no pus and Marlvon knew that was good. Marlvon had seen many wounds heal, but he had also seen simple cuts fester and become putrid. As far as he could tell, it was a matter of keeping the wound clean and luck that determined the outcome. Marlvon cut a length of cloth from one of the corpse's shirts, washed it in the brook, and retied the wound. Before washing his own shirt, he also noticed that Islonda's ankle was swollen. He only then remembered her mentioning it the night before. He had a feel around and, not noticing anything gravely amiss, decided that it should be back to normal in a few days' time.

Marlvon put his wet shirt on and gazed at his surrounds. He looked concernedly up at the steep slope. *How am I going to get Islonda up there?*

'Islonda, we need to go up there.' He pointed to where she had dragged the topsoil down the cliff in her fall. 'But first we need to see if you can stand.' Islonda nodded her head.

Marlvon squatted down next to her and pulled one of her arms around his shoulders. With Marlvon taking as much weight as he could, they both stood together. Islonda swayed, but Marlvon held her tightly. After a few moments, she regained her balance.

'Are you all right?'

She nodded. 'Yes, just a little dizzy.'

'How does the leg feel? Can you put weight on it?'

'It's throbbing where the wound is. I don't know if it will take my weight.'

She gingerly shifted her weight to try the leg out. She attempted a small step forward and winced. 'That hurt!'

'Do you think you could walk on it?'

'Walk? Slowly, maybe. Climb that slope? Not today.'

Marlvon was disappointed but not surprised. He now faced another difficult choice of how to proceed. The last thing he wanted was to stay where they were. Their other options were to wander slowly up or down the gully searching for an easier spot to climb, leave Islonda and search for an easier way out by himself, or try to carry Islonda up the hill. He doubted they could cover much ground in Islonda's shape, and he dared not leave her alone with cannibal outlaws around.

With his mind made up, there was nothing for it but to try the climb. He examined the slope as he spoke to Islonda. 'We're going up that hill. You're going to hold on to my back. We'll rest where we can and try our hardest not to fall back down.' They smiled wryly at each other.

With the morning wearing away, there was nothing else to do but to get on with it. The slope was steep enough in places so that Marlvon would have to use his hands to scramble up. When Islonda had fallen down, most of the topsoil had come with her. This exposed unstable reddish-brown shale with many grooves and crumbling ledges. Marlvon knew that the climb was going to be hard work, but that didn't bother him. What did concern him was the chance of sliding back down and severely injuring them both. What he really wanted was a nice piece of rope, but that was not to be. And so Islonda shuffled over to the slope, put her arms around his neck and hugged his waist with her legs. 'Well, here goes.'

Marlvon felt the muscles in his legs surge as he put one foot higher than the previous and made his way up the treacherous slope. He thanked the stars that Islonda had carried no belongings as it made her lighter to carry.

More than once during the ascent, Marlvon put his foot on an unsteady ledge and had to cling tightly to stop a rapid descent. But he pushed on and Islonda took care of herself. He could sense that she was in great pain, but she said nothing except words of encouragement. And he thanked her for that later.

When he was on the slope, Marlvon could afford Islonda little thought; he had to concentrate on where to put his hands and feet, not to mention, pushing aside his growing pain and exhaustion. Despite all of this, he pushed himself and pushed himself and eventually they made it to the top.

Marlvon was not happy to rest there, but made them find a place of modest shelter away from the ledge. Only then did he allow himself to lie down and relax.

For the rest of that day, they took it easy with Marlvon foraging around for food. He didn't bother making snares, but managed to skewer a lizard with his knife. As dusk set, he lit a fire, cooked the meat and then extinguished the flames. That night they both slept in a small depression under an overhang of leafy branches.

When they woke, Marlvon was faced with another choice: to leave Islonda and fetch Nal to carry her, walk with Islonda slowly back to his hideaway, or remain where they were until her leg healed. He quickly dismissed the first option, as he had the day before. While he was tempted by the third possibility, he couldn't bear to sit doing nothing in an outlaw infested forest. And so, once again, he chose action.

He knew Islonda would be slow and would tire easily and so decided to walk for half the morning, then rest and forage over the heat of the day. If Islonda was up to it, they would then continue for a short while and search for a place to stay for the night. This routine they maintained for several days. The going was slow, but Marlvon enjoyed the opportunity to spend time alone with his future wife; although the possibility of marriage now seemed as distant as the moon.

Many days had passed and Marlvon and Islonda finally found themselves in the relative safety of Marlvon's hideaway. The first thing that they did when they arrived on a hot and sticky day was to take a swim. The cool, crisp water washed the dirt and blood away and the two felt born afresh.

While Marlvon found great comfort just being at his *home*, he knew their stay would be short. The days were still hot, but the nights were beginning to cool and Marlvon dared not light a fire. He was, after all, a wanted man. He still wanted to stay on his hill, at least until Islonda's leg had healed enough for her to be able to walk with no pain, even if she limped a bit. So Marlvon came up with a plan.

He felt nervous at telling Islonda his plan and so he put it off for a few more days until her leg had healed further. He wanted to wait until the time was just right. That time came during one sunset where there were no clouds in the sky and the air was warm. The two of them sat with their feet in the pool, having just finished a meagre meal.

'Islonda, it's been over a full moon cycle since we left Bankton and I think it's time we left this place.' She nodded for him to continue. 'We need to live normal lives in civilisation.' She nodded again, but more slowly. 'I can't see us being able to live anywhere near Fort Kykum or Bankton, though.' Islonda stopped nodding. 'I just don't think we would be safe there. I also don't want to cross the Liagar; I don't know what the people of Roasline are like.'

Islonda raised her eyebrows at him. 'Then where can we go?'

'There is a place across the Rogaus called Headly. The people there are Healers, and the land is outside the reach of the Outcasts.'

Marlvon neglected to mention that there was a small chance that they may not be welcome at Headly. He didn't want to trouble Islonda with that thought.

'That sounds nice. How do we get there?' she asked.

'Hire a ship and a sailor and we sail there.'

'Hire a ship? That sounds expensive.'

'Yes, it would be. I have that covered though. The harder part is finding someone to take us who is trustworthy.'

'You don't know how to sail?' Marlvon couldn't quite tell if Islonda was being sarcastic or not.

'I could fumble around on a lake or a calm river, but cross the Rogaus, not a chance.'

'Then how do we find a sailor?'

'There are a few taverns in Kykum where we might may find such a man.'

'What, in Fort Kykum?' Islonda sounded shocked.

'That's right.'

Islonda stared at Marlvon. 'Won't everyone there be looking for us?'

'Possibly. Although, some time has passed since we were first hunted. The search for us might have cooled down a bit.'

'*Might* have cooled down? Marlvon, this sounds dangerous and poorly thought out.'

'Everywhere we go now is likely to be dangerous. The people of Kykum might be looking for us, but I can disguise us so that we no longer look like us… at least for a short while.'

Islonda pursed her lips. Marlvon could see that she didn't much like his plan, but she knew that there was little other choice.

'Okay, say we go through with this, how are we going to pay for a ship?'

Marlvon smiled ruefully. *She's in.* He then took off his clothes and jumped into the pool. The water was freezing, but he held his breath and searched around the bottom in the deepest part. When he surfaced, he was carrying two leather bags that were sealed with wax. He put these next to Islonda and dived again. This time he brought up another bag as well as a long, thin package. Islonda looked on in surprise as Marlvon broke the wax seal and poured out a small fortune of silver pieces, gold pieces, and precious gems. In another bag he had a mixture of pastes and other items that could be used for disguising oneself.

'This is how we pay for a ship.' He then unwound the long package to reveal a sword in a scabbard. 'And this is how I protect us.'

The water tight bags had stopped the goods from ageing and they were as good as the day that Marlvon had put them in the pool.

'Marlvon, that's more wealth than I've ever seen.'

He smiled at her and thought of the other five bags still at the bottom of the water. 'It's more than most men see in a lifetime.'

'Where did you get it all from?'

'Here and there; I am the nephew of the ex-leader.'

He didn't know why, but he had the desire to conceal the truth of their origins from Islonda. He had, in fact, stolen them when he had gone on raids across the Liagar River during the chapter of his life he would rather forget. The look she gave him suggested she suspected something was not quite in order.

Marlvon averted her gaze by taking out the sword and the whetstone that was tied to the scabbard and started to sharpen the blade.

'Marlvon, I still don't feel comfortable with your plan; just to leave our life behind. I mean, what about my mother?'

Marlvon looked at her again and thought. *She is right, of course, if Islonda's mother still lives, we can't just leave her behind.*

'Would it make it better if we took her with us?'

'Yes, I think I'd like that. I can't imagine how she is feeling having lost her husband and not knowing where I am.'

'Okay, then tomorrow we'll go to Bankton and then to the Fort. In the morning, I will need to take some time to disguise us, but we should reach Bankton by nightfall.'

Islonda smiled and looked happy. 'Well, if this is to be our last night alone, we should make the most of it.'

Marlvon smiled and his heartbeat quickened. 'I'm glad you're back to your old self.'

He was unable to say anything else as Islonda kissed him passionately. Marlvon found it easy to push the thoughts of their uncertain future to the back of his mind as he settled into Islonda's loving embrace.

30

The sun set on another day and night time spread across Green Lake. As the light of day faded and the stars began to twinkle, the wind that had been blowing strong for many days abated and a gentle calmness settled on the water.

Winter sat on the gunwale of a boat and gazed not at the stars above, but at the stars below. The perfectly still glass surface of the lake acted as a mirror to reflect the billions of celestial beacons that glowed in the heavens above. They dazzled Winter's mind and tickled his heart as he marvelled at their beauty. Yet, in that joy, there lay an inkling of sadness; a hidden sense of loneliness.

Winter picked up a pebble that he had found on the deck and dropped it over the side of the boat. A gentle *plop* was followed by smooth ripples that set the reflected stars dancing. The ripples fanned out over the lake gracefully, and Winter looked about the deck for another stone. Before he found one, he saw Sor making her way towards him. She had a smile on her face, which annoyed Winter as he had been enjoying the solitude. She came and sat down next to him, a bit close for his liking, so he shuffled back.

'Great news, Winter. I've just been speaking to the captain about our progress. He said that the wind that has been at our tail for days has pushed us far. He said that in the morning a new breeze should blow and by midday we should reach a dock. This is the dock closest to the Sempa and where we'll go ashore.'

Winter rubbed his ribs. They still hurt. His bruises had turned yellow and he yearned for when the ribs would stop paining him. 'I have enjoyed this boat ride; can't we pay the captain to take us down the Sempa?' *If we're walking with packs, my ribs will keep aching.*

'A boat of this size can't pass into the Sempa. The captain was saying that the Sempa starts more as marshland with high reeds. The water is too shallow for anything greater than a two-person vessel to pass. Even then, navigation would be difficult.'

'I don't suppose we could steal the landing boat from the side of this one?'

Sor raised an eyebrow. 'No.'

'Well, I suppose that's that then.' Winter bit his lip and wanted to capitalise on Sor's good mood. 'Sor, when we're alone again, could you teach me to fight like you do?'

She looked at him tiredly. 'Winter, you know my answer; it is the same every time you ask me. I am only permitted to teach monks who have taken their vows.'

Winter sighed. Sor was annoying him. He turned back to the water and stared at the reflected stars again. Sor took the hint and stood, placing her hand on his shoulder briefly and then left him alone.

The captain was wrong. Winter woke to an unseasonal fog about the vessel, although he couldn't see it from his windowless cabin. And, just like the fog, Winter's mood was thick and sullen.

I suppose I should say my morning prayers. Winter had been sharing a cabin with Sor and he looked over and saw that she was already on her knees, praying with her eyes closed. This prickled Winter, though he didn't know why.

He rolled out of bed gingerly and quickly got dressed into his grey robe while Sor's attention was elsewhere. He then knelt by his bunk and hastily said his prayers. The two monks finished at the same time, stood, turned, and almost bumped into each other in the small cabin.

'Good morning, Winter.'

Winter mumbled his response. 'Good morning.'

'Have you prayed this morning?'

Winter nodded, and a sudden thought struck him. 'Sor, there's something that you said to me many moons ago that I want to clarify. You said that the Gods are all knowing; omniscient. Is that true?'

Winter could see Sor thinking. 'Yes.'

'Well, if they're omniscient, why do we have to pray?'

'I don't understand.' Sor looked confused.

'If they know everything, then they know what we're thinking. If they know what we're thinking, then they know what we want; what our prayers are. Indeed, they probably know it better than we do.' He smiled at Sor.

Sor looked as though she was contemplating his proposal as she responded slowly. 'Prayer is not just to communicate your desires to the Gods. Praying allows the gods to see that you have thought about your wants and prioritised them. *And* that you're taking the time and effort to request help from them. And that's not to mention the sense of humility that comes with prayer.'

Winter still felt that he was right, but could sense the dogmatic side of Sor emerging. He decided it was futile to continue to push his point; no good would come of it.

'I will think on it more, Sister Sor.'

She nodded and he saw the tension leave her shoulders. 'Let us go and see what the weather is doing.'

'And find some food.' Winter added.

A slight breeze blew and the fog gradually lifted. By late morning, Winter and Sor's boat was underway, albeit slowly. By early afternoon, the post-fog clear blue sky became crowded with clouds that descended ominously as the wind increased. When the afternoon was half gone, the clouds opened their bellies and a constant rain fell. The boat bumped vigorously in the waves and Winter closed his eyes and tried to keep his lunch down. He rested uncomfortably against the side railing and put his head between his knees. The cold rain and wind were unpleasant, but not nearly as unpleasant as his windowless cabin.

Winter pitied himself. After a long time, he felt an arm around his shoulders and Sor squatted down beside him. He lifted his head and she put a small yellow nob into his hand.

She spoke close to his ear so that he could hear her. 'Chew this; it's ginger. The crewmen say it will settle the stomach.'

Without argument, Winter popped the ginger into his mouth and felt a spicy burn as he chewed. If nothing else, the flavour distracted him from his churning belly.

A short while later, the wind and waves eased, but the rain continued. Winter was able to stand now and he did; staring at the reedy shore. He heard the heavy footsteps of the captain behind him and he turned to face the stocky man.

The captain held up his looking glass. 'We're getting close to our destination, but something's not quite right. He paused, still looking through his glass.

'What is it?' Winter asked.

'The pier where we're headin' is long, several hundred yards long. To get past all the reeds, you see.'

Winter nodded

'Because of this, there's a shelter on the end of the pier for a watchman.' His voice firmed. 'I think it would be best if you and the sister stayed hidden on the starboard side, away from the dock, until we know all is fine.'

'Why should we hide?'

'For your safety. Something's amiss. Who knows what it is.'

'But that's no reason for us to hide.'

The captain pursed his lips and rubbed his brow. 'I see Sister Sor hasn't told you.'

Winter felt suspicious. 'Told me what?'

'You were unconscious when she brought you aboard and we set sail as soon as we were able. But supplies had to be gathered and a price negotiated.' The captain looked sheepish. 'A sailor has to live, you know. Anyway, shortly after we set sail, a commotion was brewing. We couldn't hear what they were yelling, but there was a lot of pointing in our direction and three angry looking men hobbling around.'

Winter remembered the three men they had met in the night and how Sor had broken their toes.

'I almost turned back, but good Sister Sor convinced me otherwise. It seems that you have three nasty men after you.'

'I suppose we should stay out of sight, then.' Winter finally saw sense in hiding and so he nodded to the captain and went to find Sor.

Winter found her sheltering from the rain in their room. She was sitting on her bed with her eyes closed.

'Sister, we're approaching our dock and the captain says that we should stay out of sight. Something is *not-quite-right,* he says.'

Sor opened her eyes and smiled. 'I'm sure it is nothing. Why don't we find some cover on deck so we can keep an eye on what's happening?'

Winter frowned. He now felt like the timid one. He bristled and wanted to be bold. 'Why didn't you tell me about the men chasing us?' He crossed his arms. Sor looked taken aback.

'You were unconscious, remember? And then, well, I suppose I forgot.'

Winter didn't believe her, but didn't want to go as far as accusing her of lying; monks should always be truthful.

'Now, if you'll excuse me, Winter, I'm going on deck.' Sor brushed past him on her way out.

Winter sighed and then plodded out after her. *I'm meant to be the leader.*

Winter had forgotten that it had been raining and when he went outside, his shoulders slumped under the pounding cold. He followed Sor to a pile of boxes stacked near the single mast. Before he squatted down next to these, he glanced over the portside bow and saw the pier jutting into the lake. He could see no one there, but felt as if he was being watched. He ducked down next to Sor and she pulled a sheet of canvas over their heads to stop the rain.

'From here, Winter, we can peek over the boxes under cover and see what's going on when we dock.'

Winter acknowledged this with a grunt. He then noticed that Sor's leg was pressed firmly against his and he wasn't sure how to feel. 'There's not much room under this canvas.'

'Yes, it's nice and cosy, isn't it? Much nicer than being out in the cold rain,' Sor replied cheerily.

Winter soon felt the water on his robe evaporating and stuck his head out of the canvas for a gulp of fresh air and a peek at their progress. They had gained quickly on the pier and the captain stood portside, ready to jump ashore. Winter mused that one of the crew must have been steering.

Coiled ropes were soon thrown over the gunwale to soften the impact of the boat against the pier and the boat's speed was retarded. The pier came alongside the vessel and the captain leapt ashore; expertly looping ropes about the bollards to secure his boat. Winter looked down the length of the pier and spied two armed men at the far end marching purposefully towards them.

They had only got halfway down the pier before the captain was finished and he stood waiting for them with crossed arms.

Winter noticed that the wind had ceased and the rain now came straight down. Over the noise of the drip-drops on the canvas, he could just hear the captain call to the approaching men before they had a chance to speak.

'What do you two want, and where is the usual watchman?' Winter admired the bravery of the short captain.

'We're here to search your boat.'

'You'll do no such thing without good reason.'

One of the men drew his sword and casually rested it on his chainmail shoulder. 'We're searching for two monks who went and attacked Lord Olswerth's nephew.'

'Done broke his toes, they did.' The other man spoke. 'Way down near the mountains. They were seen sailing away on a boat kind of like this one. Lord Olswerth wants the monks found and brought to justice.'

'Well, they ain't on my boat; we've come across the lake to trade otter-skin coats.'

The first man scoffed gruffly, 'We're still going to search your boat. Now, get your crew up on deck.' The man tapped the hilt of his sword threateningly.

The captain stiffened. 'Of course, when you put it like that.'

Winter froze for a moment before leaping into action. 'We can't stay here. We need to go over the side.' He whispered urgently to Sor. He grabbed her by the scruff and pushed her head down. 'Stay low and in the line of these boxes.'

Together, they scampered to the starboard side and slithered over the edge just as the men were boarding. The monks lowered themselves into the water, the chilled waves making Winter's breath catch.

The gunwale was five feet above the surface and lucky for Winter and Sor, a ridge ran around the outside of the boat at water level. This they could just cling on to with cold, numb fingers.

Sor came close to Winter and whispered in his ear. 'Our luggage in our cabin; the men will find it.'

Winter cursed to himself. 'Nothing we can do about that now.' He whispered back.

Winter's heart beat rapidly and he kept his gaze fixed on the side of the boat above; hoping to see the captain leaning over to tell them that the men had gone. Instead, he saw the head of one of the armed men looking out across the lake. Winter held his breath and closed his eyes; wishing that he and Sor were invisible.

Then Winter heard a splash. Sor's hands had become numb; her fingers slipped on the wood of the boat and almost sent her under water. She quickly regained her grip, but the damage was done.

Winter's eyes snapped open to see the grin of recognition spread across the face of the man looming above. As he stared at Winter and Sor, he called to his colleague to bring the captain.

Winter watched the three men as the soldier spoke with glee. 'Captain, get your crew to fish those two rats out of the lake. Then you and I are going to have a little talk.'

The captain turned to his three crewmen. 'Lads, we've got some fishing to do. Just like we did when old Four Fingers went over.'

Winter's mind raced. *How can we get out of this? Swim? To where? Fight? I doubt even Sor could beat those two with their mail and swords.* Then the captain's head disappeared from above and the two soldiers continued to grin at Winter and Sor.

A commotion followed and, the two armed men went flying overboard. They landed a yard or so from Winter where they thrashed around vigorously before their heavy armour dragged them under. Two ropes were thrown over, and Winter and Sor were hoisted back on deck.

The captain greeted them. 'It always surprises me how quickly chainmail can drag a man down. So heavy in water.' He shook his head in mock sorrow. 'Get inside, get dry and get warm. Then we'll talk about what I'm going to do with you two fugitives.'

Winter led Sor into their cabin where they undressed, facing away from each other, and redressed in the spare robes Sor had insisted they bring on their journey. Winter was now grateful for the first time that they had.

Once dressed and dry, Winter felt some warmth spread through his limbs again. He turned to leave, but Sor stopped him and gave him a hug.

'That was close.' She spoke into his shoulder, her words muffled. 'We haven't even made it past Green Lake and our lives have been in danger twice.' Winter held her close, realising that despite her bravery in fighting, she still feared for her safety.

'Three times. You forgot that spider I found.' Sor gave a short laugh. Winter continued more seriously. 'It's all right, we're safe now.'

'But for how long?'

Winter held her firmly by the shoulders, and looked into her eyes. 'Let's go talk to the captain and make a plan to stay alive.'

She nodded and together they made their way to the captain's cabin.

The clouds had descended and darkness clung to them. The rain fell in a steady flow as night closed in. The captain's room was lit by two paraffin lamps and the captain himself sat at a small desk, deep in thought.

As Winter and Sor entered, he looked up with a grim expression on his face. He remained seated while the monks stood before him.

'What am I going to do with the two of you?' They remained silent.

'I have half a mind to send you ashore and let you fend for yourselves.'

Winter butted in. 'Then let us pack our things and be gone.'

'But that would be heartless. The lands will be crawling with Olswerth's men; you wouldn't last more than a day. Do you even know who Olswerth is? Do you know who you've unwittingly antagonised?'

They shook their heads.

'I thought as much. Typical monks, getting involved in things that are too big for them.'

Winter bristled and took a step forward, but Sor spoke first. 'Mind your tongue, captain; you know not of what you speak.'

Winter looked at Sor, who had been woken from her state of shock and was red in the face.

'Calm down, Sister.' The captain spoke in a reasonable tone. 'I like the monks; they are kind to me and *generally* don't cause me too much trouble.'

Winter observed as Sor flushed redder with embarrassment.

The captain continued. 'Let me enlighten you. Lord Olswerth holds the power in these lands. And that power is strong and absolute. He's the only reason why the Outcasts of Psymryte haven't raped and pillaged you monks. Although he doesn't protect you for *your* sake, he's not that generous, it's simply better for him to have a peace-loving neighbour on one border. He is calculating and ruthless when required. And, most importantly for you, is that he won't permit a bad word to be spoken against him or his family… let alone an actual injury.' The captain paused for a moment and shook his head. 'The only way for you to escape his reach is to leave the lands that he controls.'

Winter found his voice before the captain could continue.

'And where do his lands end?'

The captain rubbed his cheek. 'They stretch from a touch north of the town where I picked you up, run around the green lake and pass a few miles up the

Sempa. The lake is his southern border and he controls many miles north from here.'

Sor spoke next. 'We're near the Sempa, so we must be near his border. Can't we sneak our way out of his lands?'

The captain sniggered. 'His men are searching for you and his border will be well watched. No, the two of you couldn't sneak past his men.'

'But we must get to Psymryte. Could you sail us up the Sempa?' Winter asked.

'Not in this boat. It is true that a few miles east of here, the Sempa begins its journey, but it is not as simple as that. The Sempa starts off in a swamp of shallow water and high reeds. A boat this deep would run aground in no time. That's not to mention the thick reeds that stifle all winds except the most vigorous. So no, I cannot sail you up the Sempa.

'And before you ask about being dropped on the far bank, the swamp stretches for a hundred miles east and there are no docks.'

Winter's shoulders slumped and he felt trapped.

'But with no wind to blow us away from this dock, I need you, and all trace of you, gone from my boat. If more men come, I won't be able to protect you again. So, to help us both, I am going to be generous. I am going to give you my landing boat. She is designed to split reeds and should be shallow enough that you can row her across the marsh. You say that you want to get to Psymryte? Well, you simply have nowhere else to go except down the Sempa and the only way you can do that, without getting caught, will be to row through miles and miles of reedy marshland until the river starts proper and you are out of Olswerth's reach.'

'Thank you for being generous. The gods will look kindly on you.' Sister Sor bowed her head respectfully.

'I am loth to see my landing boat gone, but it is a price worth paying to stay out of Olswerth's mind. Now, while I am being generous, I am not being kind. The journey that you have to make will not be an easy one. The swamp is tricky; you will get lost easily and go crazy with the never ending reeds. You must keep your heads straight and keep pointing north or north east. The water will taste foul to drink, but won't harm you, and there are plenty of eels and small fish to catch. Of course, you won't be able to cook them, but you will not starve.'

Winter felt his stomach churn at the mere thought of eating raw eels.

'If I was a betting man, I would say that we should expect more armed men to come before midnight, so you two had better pack your things and be gone from my vessel.'

Winter thanked him and turned to leave, but Sor was still standing, staring at the captain. 'You shouldn't have killed those men.'

He looked straight back at her. 'You're right. I should have let them take the two of you; I should have let them rape you and carry you off to Olswerth, who would have picked you apart piece by piece. Sometimes, Sister, you have to get your hands dirty to do the right thing. Now leave, before I change my mind about my landing boat and throw you overboard, too.'

The captain's jaw clenched and he looked serious; Sor was taken aback. Winter, on the other hand, saw through the act and saw a kind man not wanting to be seen being kind.

Winter inclined his head. 'We should go Sor.' He left the captain's cabin with Sor in tow.

It was still raining heavily when they pushed off from the larger boat. They could not see where they were going in the darkness, but the captain had left a lamp hanging on the bow of his boat. They used this to paddle in a straight line until the lamp was faint. Then they turned to paddle with the light on their portside until they hit the reeds. By this stage it was edging midnight and the two monks were soaked through and exhausted. The excitement had worn off and a sense of dread and fear seeped into their bones. They turned their small boat and paddled with the reeds beside them for a good while more before Sor asked that they stop for the night. They turned into the reeds and soon became invisible from the lake.

On departure, they had secured a sheet of canvas over their boat to prevent the rain flooding them and, when they stopped, they pulled this over the entire boat, leaving a small hole for breathing. They lay down wet in the muggy summer air and drifted off to sleep, listening to the heavy pitter-patter of the rain just above their heads.

Winter woke drenched in sweat and gasping for air. He sat up and hit his head on the canvas that was covering the boat. Sor stirred next to him, then went back to sleep. In the night, she had made her way next to him and had nuzzled in close. *Why did she do that? Now I'm all sweaty. She surely didn't do it for warmth.* Then Winter thought back to the previous day and their circumstances. *I suppose they were the first people she's seen killed by another person. She must be so scared. Poor thing, she should never have come.* Winter wriggled his way over to the opening in the canvas and poked his head out. He gulped down the fresh morning air.

The rain had stopped, but the clouds still loomed. A gentle breeze blew that Winter heartily welcomed.

He sat with his torso out of the covering and inspected the boat for the first time. The boat was long, but what struck Winter was just how skinny it was.

Sitting on one of the two seats, you could paddle on either side of the boat. The hull looked as if it was a single piece carved out of a giant tree trunk. Winter reckoned that eight men could fit down the length, but there were only two seats; one at either end. Between the seats was ample space to house their small packs. This is where Winter and Sor had slept. They had started out with Sor's feet near Winter's head, but Sor had moved in the night.

The slender design made it perfect to paddle between the reeds, although it made balance a little tricky. The canvas covering was of a similar make to the cloth of the sails on the bigger boat, and Winter was grateful for having it. He was rubbing the fabric between his fingers when Sor woke.

Winter heard her huff and puff and groan. The boat rocked from side to side as she worked her way out from under the canvas. She smiled at him as she pulled herself up by his knees. She looked up into his eyes and then over his head.

'What's that?'

He turned around awkwardly and saw what she was pointing at.

'That's smoke. And coming from the direction of the pier.' The column was thick and black. It was blown on an angle by the gentle breeze out over where Winter knew the lake extended. *That's not good.*

He looked back at the monk and saw concern in her face.

'I'm sure the captain is fine.' He forced himself to smile. 'Why don't we go and have a look?'

Together, they removed the canvas covering and stowed it next to their baggage. Winter took the back seat and Sor the front. They carefully paddled between the reeds towards the open water. Winter counselled caution and they stopped and caught their breath when the reeds began to thin. He gently steered the boat to be parallel with the edge of the reeds, yet still hidden within them, so that they would be able to see what was going on safely.

Winter couldn't see Sor's face, but he heard her gasp. The pier was unharmed, but a hundred yards or so off the pier was the boat that they had travelled on. It was ablaze and half sunk. Winter couldn't quite tell from that distance, but it looked as though there were bodies hanging by the neck halfway up the mast.

Suddenly, from behind the blazing haze, came another vessel. This had its sails furled, but its oars were out and pulling quickly. Even from their distance, Winter could hear the thud-thud-thud of drums in time with the oars.

Fear gripped him. 'We must leave; now!'

Winter and Sor couldn't pivot the boat quickly due to the reeds, but had to guide it in a large arc toward the flaming boat. Winter prayed to the Gods as he paddled that the war vessel hadn't seen them. From the sound of her murmured words, Sor was doing likewise.

The gods must have been watching, for the oared vessel pulled away from the flames and then stopped to watch the burning boat sink. Winter and Sor seized the opportunity and soon found themselves deep within the reeds. They stopped paddling, and Winter made his way to where Sor sat.

She was sobbing, so Winter put his arms around her and she turned and clung to him. 'What have we done?'

'We could never have known that this would happen. We were just escaping from men who wanted to rape and kill us.'

Sor didn't respond.

'They will be hunting for us before midday. We are well concealed in these reeds, thank the gods, but we cannot see where we are going. As far as I can see that we have no choice but to follow the direction of the captain.'

Sor pulled back from Winter. He guessed she was considering returning to the monks.

'I have to keep moving forward. I have to find my father.' As he said this, he felt his resolve harden. 'It won't be safe for you to return home by yourself, I'm sorry.'

Sor cut him off. 'I vowed to look after you. I will not renege on my promise to the gods.'

'The best way to look after me would be by teaching me how to defend myself and fight.'

Sor's eyes narrowed. 'You know I cannot do that without you taking your vows to the gods.'

Winter got another pulse of inspiration. 'What if I promise to take my vows after I find my father?' He winked. 'I would vow to take my vows.'

Sor thought for a moment. 'Yes, I think that if you vow to the gods to take your vows once you've completed this journey to find your father, then I can begin your self-defence teaching.'

Winter felt his excitement bubble forth, and he hugged Sor as a reflex. 'Sor, I vow to the Night and Day Gods that once I've found my father, I will vow myself to their service.' He felt Sor relax under his hug.

'Then I will teach you. But first, we need to decide what to do now.'

Winter thought for a moment. 'We paddle near the shoreline and follow that until we reach this fabled marshland. We deal with that when we get there. One step at a time, I say.'

Sor nodded. Winter thought that she may have wanted to say something else, but he was more focused on the training that he would soon receive. He made his way back to his seat and together they started to paddle in the vague direction of the shoreline, leaving the column of smoke behind.

31

Druin woke after a restless sleep in the naval barracks at the docks of Roasline. He had sweated through the night and had slept little. The heat and sweat weren't a bother, he was used to that, but it was the thought of the day that lay ahead that had kept sleep from claiming him. His nerves had been put on edge two days ago when the Admiral had visited him in the barracks and spoken to him in private. That in itself was stressful enough for the young sailor; after all, the Admiral was a man to be respected and feared. But that was not all; the Admiral had promoted Druin to the rank of captain. This took Druin by complete surprise; he had never even shown the slightest interest to be in charge of a ship. Why would his admiral promote him? Since then, the prospect had bubbled away and instead of warming to the idea, Druin grew more and more nervous about it.

He got out of bed and looked at the uniform hanging on the door with its gold chain sewn in to the blue sash. *I feel sick.* What could he do? He had no other option but to start getting dressed; just like he had to accept the Admiral's promotion two days ago. He put the uniform on and placed a new, dark leather tricorn hat on his head. This was given to him by his uncle, the Alderman of Farmers, and it gave the new captain an inkling of confidence. He looked at his reflection in the window and felt like nothing more than a little boy playing dress-ups. He smiled weakly at himself. *I suppose I had better get this over with. I only hope my crew is nice.*

Druin made his way out of the barracks, preoccupied with what awaited him. When sailors were made into new captains, they were taken away from their crew and were placed on a different ship with a new crew. This was to ensure that the rank was followed and a chain of superiority was ensured.

Druin hoped that the crew were friendly and hardworking, but he doubted it. More often than not, a new captain had to prove their worth by shaping a difficult crew. At least he knew that the mission would be easy. He had been ordered by the admiral to sail down the coast away from the Outcasts on a simple patrol; watching for Outcast vessels that might try to land south east of Roasline. The likelihood of that happening was very slim and this gave Druin a small sense of ease.

He made his way from the barracks to the docks and couldn't help feeling uncomfortable when sailors stopped and saluted him as he went past. Then he saw his ship: *The Slippery Fish.*

There was nothing noteworthy about the single masted boat. She was small and old; a relic from generations before. She was not powerful enough to either be a weapon of war nor fast enough to be a scout. She was the sort of boat that would inspire no one, and Druin liked that. He wanted plain, simple and unnoticeable; it suited his personality. For the first time that day, he genuinely smiled.

He approached her and found his crew scramble on deck to line up at the top of the gangplank. This was a tense moment for the young man; he knew his crew would be scrutinising him as closely as he was going to scrutinise them. Druin quickly counted the first-mate and six other crewmen. He knew before embarking on his mission he would be joined by a dozen soldiers of the army. These were reinforcements should a fight develop with the Outcasts. This had become common practice since Admiral Tunley had taken charge, and the rank and file of the navy detested it. It was not uncommon for fights to break out between the sailors and the soldiers, and this was another thing that Druin worried about.

He made his way up the gangplank and when he reached the top, he waited for his men to salute.

The first-mate barked out the obligatory announcement. 'Captain on deck.'

The men stiffened up and saluted. Druin paced in front of them, eyeballing them all. *Oh shit, what am I going to say to them?* He stood before his crew and silence descended. The silence deepened for several moments, before Druin found the sense to say something.

'Good morning crew.' His voice came out in a squeak. He cleared his throat and tried again; this time stronger. 'Good morning crew.' Sweat beaded down his back. 'My name is Captain Druin.' He paused. 'Today we're going to take *The Fish* out and down the coast. You all look like hardy men who know how to sail well.' Sweat dripped down his forehead. 'First-mate, take charge to prepare this boat for departure.'

'Aye Aye, sir.'

Druin turned and made his way to his cabin to gather his thoughts and nerves.

The captain's cabin was small on *The Slippery Fish*. It had a hammock in one corner, a small window that looked out the back of the boat and a small desk with a map nailed onto it with a tallow candle on top of it. Druin sat down at the desk and put his head in his hands. He started to remember what he could of his crew; what he had taken in. All that he could muster up was that they were men dressed as sailors. He couldn't even remember what hair colour they all had. *I can never remember things when I'm nervous.* Druin's thoughts were interrupted by a firm knock on his door.

'Come in,' he called.

The first-mate entered. He was a man of average height with black hair that had been slicked back with some oily product. He looked at least a decade older than Druin and held himself with the confidence that came from years of successful voyages.

'Captain, *The Fish* will be ready shortly and the soldiers are boarding now.'

'Thank you... what's your name?'

'Gattic. Captain, may I ask a question?'

'Go ahead.'

'Which ship were you first-mate of before you came to us?'

The usual order of promotion was to become a first-mate for at least a year before being granted command of a ship. Druin acutely knew that he skipped this important learning step and moved straight to captainship. He didn't want his crew to know that though, as it would show his inexperience and that he had received special treatment in becoming a captain.

'I was on *The Crumpler* before coming here.'

Gattic's eyebrows rose. 'Really? I thought Rya was the first-mate on *The Crumpler*.'

'That will be all sailor. I'll be on deck shortly to take *The Fish* out to sea.'

Dismissed, Gattic saluted and left Druin to bury his head in his hands again.

After waiting as long as he thought he could, Druin lifted his head and looked about the cabin. His focus couldn't fix on anything and his mind refused to work. He opened the desk draw and found an old half empty bottle of rum. His gaze fixed on it. He knew that alcohol was banned in the navy, but he had heard rumours of captains being allowed their own private supply. Without really thinking about it, he popped the cork out and took a large gulp. He almost spat it across the room, it was that strong. He looked at the bottle and put it back in the draw.

The new captain finally decided that it would be time to have a look around his boat and then hopefully set sail. He stood and straightened his uniform and hat before making his way on deck. He found his crew idly sitting around or leaning on the gunwale. The soldiers, he could hear, were below deck in their quarters.

'Gattic, is she ready to sail?'

'Aye, Captain. Just waiting on your order.'

Druin turned his face to the southerly wind. 'Then you have it; take us out into the Rogaus.'

The crew looked at each other and slowly ambled to their feet. Druin felt his courage burn with the rum. 'Now, sailors! Or I'll show you the cat-o-tails.'

The crew all looked from him to Gattic and back again. Druin felt as though they were all about to laugh and sit back down. *Come on Druin, you can do this.*

'Don't just stand their staring at me like a bunch of ugly dogs. Get moving, you bastards.' He took a step forward. They all jumped into action and Druin breathed an internal sigh of relief. He knew that he had the authority to do what he wanted with his crew, but if they refused to obey him, how could he make them do his bidding?

Druin decided that now was perhaps not the best time to get to know his crew better. Instead, he went back to his cabin to try the rum once more.

Druin woke with his head spinning and the walls of his cabin swaying. He got to his feet and plopped straight back down into the chair. He tried again, this time knocking the empty rum bottle onto the floor as he stumbled his way to the door. *This rum is really strong, or something strange is going on.* He opened his door and immediately knew that it was a combination of the two.

Darkness had fallen and wind whipped across the ship. Rain lashed down onto the deck in sheets. The visibility was so poor that he couldn't even see the mast. He made his way a few paces onto the deck and then saw his first-mate.

'Gattic, come here! Where are we?'

The first-mate made his steady way to Druin from the tiller. 'Captain, we're a few miles east, down the coast from the mouth of the Liagar.'

'Where did this heinous storm come from?'

Gattic had to shout to be heard over the wind and rain. 'The south.'

'Well, find us some shelter; find us a cove.'

Gattic glared at his captain. 'What do you think I've been doing? Drinking rum?'

Druin snapped back. 'That's enough, sailor! Just find us shelter before we capsize.'

The ship pitched sharply and Druin fell to his knees. Gattic remained standing. 'I suggest you go back to your cabin; it's dangerous out here.' He then turned and made his slow way back to the wheel without waiting for a response.

Druin crawled to the side of the ship and pulled himself up. The ship dropped and he almost fell back down. *Perhaps I should return to my quarters.* The boat rocked again and he felt vomit coming. He leant over the edge and retched what little was in his stomach. *The Slippery Fish* dropped once more and Druin found himself spinning and falling as he went overboard. His head collided with the side of the ship and he didn't even feel the writhing water envelop his now lifeless body.

Admiral Tunley was woken by a violent banging on his front door. He lay on his back and listened intently as his servant went to answer it. He heard a man demand to see him and his servant's refusal. He then heard a thud and hurried footsteps coming up the stairs. He only just had time to roll out of bed, put a dressing gown over his naked body and conceal a long dagger in his pocket before the man reached his door.

The angry admiral stood there and waited in the dark room with the curtains pulled. Bursting into the room came the Alderman of Farmers with a swinging lantern. He pointed at Tunley. 'You dog! How could you?'

The admiral had been expecting a visit from the alderman ever since he heard of Druin's death at sea two days prior. He had not expected it to be in the middle of the night or accompanied by such ferocity. Tunley had miscalculated, as he had not thought that the cautious man could be so rash. *I need to calm him; I still need his vote.*

'My dear Alderman. You've entered my house and woken me from my sleep. Can you please tell me what you are yammering about?'

'Druin! He's dead. And you killed him.' The alderman took a step closer and pointed an accusing finger at the admiral.

Tunley opened his hands with the palms out in a sign of peace. 'I am sorry for the death of young Druin. I heard of it just this evening. The crew reports he was drunk and went overboard in a vicious storm.'

'Bullshit, you had him pushed over.'

The admiral spoke kindly. 'Why would I do that, Alderman? I had just promoted him as a captain on one of my ships. He had much promise and I had much invested in him. Surely you can see that there would be no reason for me to have him killed.'

'You're lying. I know it was you. I don't know why, but I know it was you.'

Tunley worried at the Alderman's lack of reason. 'I'm sorry that you feel that way. How can I make it up to you?'

'Ha, you can't bribe or threaten your way out of this one. I'm going to tell everyone who will listen how you blackmailed me. I'll tell them what kind of scum you really are. You have no more power over me and you no longer have my vote on the council.' The Alderman spat on the floor.

Tunley felt a sense of pleasure build within him. 'I'm sorry to hear that Alderman. Before you leave, there's something I want to show you. Come and look at my view and let me explain my position to you.' Tunley walked over to the window and drew back the curtain. 'Come on.' He casually waved the man over to him.

The alderman hesitated, but came in the end. He stood next to the Admiral who was fondling the curtain fastening cord in his hands.

'Can you see the river down there?'

The Alderman looked. 'Yes. What of it?'

'Good, because that will be the last thing you ever see.' Standing behind the Alderman, Tunley whipped the curtain cord around his neck and drew it tight. He kicked out the Alderman's knees and put his own knee into his back. The Alderman fell to the floor, clasping at his neck. He tried and tried to loosen the cord, but the sailor was far too strong. The Alderman's strength faded and Tunley bent down and whispered in his ear. 'Just so you know, I didn't kill Druin, but the weakling arse had no skill on a ship.'

He pulled the cord one final time and the Alderman collapsed dead.

Mmmm, that felt good. He looked down at the corpse and smiled. *And I know exactly what to do with you.*

Tunley went downstairs and found his servant starting to rouse from a state of unconsciousness. He looked bleary-eyed and was rubbing his head.

'Saddle my horse and bring it around to the back lane. The Alderman has had too much to drink and I'm going to take him home.' The servant stumbled off to obey his master.

Tunley went back upstairs and dressed himself, pulling a long coat on despite the warm night. With the man-servant out of the house, the Admiral dragged the Alderman down the stairs and to the back door. He sat him on the floor and waited for the horse to arrive. While waiting, he fumbled around in a storage cupboard and found a nice length of plain old rope.

It wasn't long before the servant arrived and Tunley ordered him to help position the *sleeping* Alderman on the horse in front of Tunley. It was uncomfortable and Tunley had to hold the corpse close, but in the darkness, no one would question the two men.

Tunley kicked the horse lightly and urged it into a gentle trot. He used the small laneways, that he knew would be deserted, and headed, not for the alderman's house, but rather to the Farmer's Guild Hall. The going was slow and twice the Alderman nearly fell off, but Tunley was determined. The downhill journey did not take very long, but it felt much longer to the Admiral.

He arrived and found the hall empty, as he had expected. A service laneway ran behind the big building and Tunley made his way down this. He dismounted and dragged the Alderman off his horse and up the two steps into the back of the hall. No one saw him do this and he hummed to himself as he worked.

The Guild Hall was large, with a wooden floor and exposed rafters. It was mainly used for meetings of the Farmer's Guild and sometimes used for trade negotiations between the three guilds: Farmer's, Merchant's and Producer's.

Chairs and tables lined the sides of the hall as if ready to watch a performance unfold in the hall's empty centre. Tunley dragged one of the chairs into the middle of the hall and then went back out to the horse and got the rope. He flung the rope high over a strong beam and tied a noose. He looped this around the Alderman's neck and, with great effort, pulled him high enough that he could have stood on the chair. Tunley then kicked the chair over as if the Alderman had done it himself. He stood back and admired his work.

'I reckon I could fit in a quick pint on my way home.' He mused to the room. 'I would share one with you, but, well, you're dead.' Tunley cackled loudly to himself.

The Admiral leapt out of bed and dressed. Today was going to be a good day for him. He went downstairs and asked his servant to fetch his horse again. He helped himself to a leg of chicken and a hunk of boned ham while he was waiting. He quickly drank a cup of wine and belched loudly, patting his ample stomach.

The horse arrived and he leapt on her back. He kicked her into action and trotted quickly down to the docks. Then he went to the barracks and collected a dozen surprised looking sailors. They didn't usually see their admiral down on the docks, but they knew that they best do everything he asked of them, and swiftly.

He marched them out of the barracks and down to the water's edge. He continued until he found *The Slippery Fish*. He led the men up the gangplank and found Gattic waiting at the top.

'Admiral on deck!' The first-mate shouted. The six crew quickly scrambled into formation.

The Admiral paced back and forth in front of the men several times before stopping in front of Gattic. He pulled him in close by the nape of his neck.

'You let Druin die. That cost me a vote on the council. You displease me.' He let go and took a step back. He raised his voice so that all could hear. 'This crew is guilty of mutiny and murder of a captain. This most heinous crime is punishable by death. Kill them all.'

Gattic had no time to think before Tunley drew his sword and drove it through his neck. The other crew scrambled and Tunley felt glee as he killed two more. The remaining four died at the hands of the Admiral's sailors who followed his orders grudgingly.

Tunley turned to his men. 'Well done. Strip them and burn the bodies.'

He left the boat pondering who will be the new Alderman of Farmers and how he might convince him to do Tunley's bidding. *What a lovely day this is.*

32

Avgar was excited. That evening he would be meeting the leaders of Psymryte, Nivera and the lands west of Bankton to the Woods of Sorrow. He hoped to make them not his allies, but his servants. They had all arrived at midday, but Avgar was not planning on meeting them until their scheduled greeting in his war room. During the afternoon, he had catered to their every wish, be it food, drink, gambling or women. He wanted them relaxed before he met them.

Evening came and Avgar made his way to the meeting room, alone with his thoughts. When he arrived, he looked around at the setup. The big table had been removed, so had the drab tapestries. Between the two fireplaces still hung the map of Fort Kykum and the lands about her. The crossed swords also remained on the wall. There was a small table to one side with five chairs around it; one for each of his three guests, Eyp and himself. Another table in the corner had cups for drinking wine and two jugs with different varieties: a rich tokay and a powerful red from Nivera.

Avgar faced the door and waited for Eyp to bring his guests into the room. While he waited, he thought of his time as Emperor of Balleny. It felt like an age ago. He had been so immature; to call one city and the farming lands around her an empire. That was nothing compared to what the Outcasts had; what he now ruled.

The door opened and Eyp entered, followed by Veltrene, the leader of Nivera. He was a tall, thin man with his shaved chin sticking out and nose held aloft. Eyp had told Avgar that Veltrene was an arrogant man who thought the sun shone out of his backside. *It will be a challenge to bend his knee.*

Behind him came Nigrath, the leader of Psymryte. Avgar already knew him as he had been in power when Avgar had lived in Psymryte. He was a bearded young man with wide shoulders and a deep voice. Avgar liked him, but knew him to be ruthless; you had to be to rule Psymryte. *If I'm strong enough, he will follow.*

Last of all came Quynt, the controller of the lands along the Liagar between Bankton and the Woods of Sorrow. He was thin with darting eyes and fidgeting hands. Eyp knew next to nothing about him other than the fact that he was feared by his subordinates and that he ruled massive, strategically important lands.

Avgar looked about at the men before him, supressed his nerves, and smiled to them. 'Welcome, welcome. Thank you all for coming all this way to meet with me, your new leader.' Avgar emphasised the last sentiment as he endeavoured to start strong. He wanted the men to know that he was in charge; they were his subjects and there would be no room for negotiation.

Avgar moved on before the men had time to respond. 'Eyp, fetch these men some wine.' Avgar did not miss the flicker of anger that briefly passed across Eyp's face. 'Veltrene, Nigrath, Quynt, come, sit, let's get things underway.' Avgar gestured to the table with his good hand.

Instead of complying, as Avgar had hoped, Veltrene spoke nasally. 'I'm happy standing.'

'Me too,' chimed in the other two leaders.

It's going to be like that, is it? Avgar decided it was time to use some of his unusual powers. While he was unable to read people's minds, he was able to sense their intentions. He turned from man to man and put his unstable magical feelers out. From Veltrene, he detected a sense of loathing and superiority. From Nigrath, a feeling of anger and frustration, and from Quynt, a sense of general amusement. He felt disappointed. *That was a risky waste of energy.* 'As you wish.'

Eyp was timely with the drinks and presented each man a chalice of the sweet tokay.

I must take control again. 'I would like to propose a toast to the coming together of great men under a new Empire of the Outcasts.' He raised his drink. 'To the new Empire.' The guests haltingly followed suit as Avgar took a big gulp.

Time to move this along, before they can think too much. 'Right, let's get straight to business. It was I who arranged the murder of Resvon by a trusted member of Roasline's army. Resvon was a fool to kneel and sue for peace when the Outcasts are so strong.' The men all nodded. 'But he seemed to have the support of the three of you, so he must have been doing something right.' Veltrene looked wary.

'While he was foolish, he had some sense. Resvon was wise to build up the navy and commence dialogue with Kathsum. While they were talking of peace, there were no attacks on our borders.

As a result, our army is strong, but not as strong as it needs to be. Gentlemen, I propose that we continue down a path of *false* peace to keep the bitch across the river occupied. Then, once our army and navy are strong enough, we pounce.' He drained his cup and waited for a response.

Quynt responded. 'You speak some sense.'

Avgar breathed an internal sigh of relief and nodded.

'But I have a question for you,' Qyunt continued. 'Rumours have been spoken about Resvon's death in Roasline. If you killed him, as you claim, why did you not kill Kathsum as well or even instead of Resvon?'

Avgar smiled, 'A good question.' As he spoke, he casually went and refilled his cup with the red wine from Nivera. 'If I had killed Kathsum, what would have happened?' He didn't wait for a response, but continued on, 'The scum from Roasline would have found a strong military leader, sealed their borders and attacked us with all of their strength.' He took a mouthful. 'I've already said that I don't think that our resources are ready to attack Roasline. And an attack from the full navy of Roasline, before the Outcasts were ready to follow me, would have been disastrous.' He took a gentle sip.

'To just kill Kathsum would have been even worse, for then our enemy would have held Resvon to bargain with. No, I think that this was the best course of action.'

The three men took a sip of their wines. The gruff voice from Psymryte spoke. 'I say we attack now. All our enemy is thinking about is peace; now is the perfect time to strike.'

The nasal Niveran spoke once more. 'Yes, Nigrath is right. We should attack now.' He drained his cup. 'I'm empty. Let me try that red you've got.'

Avgar didn't like his tone. 'Fill me up too.' He looked from man to man. 'Eyp, what do you think?'

Before Eyp could answer, the Niveran returned and cut him off. 'Of course, he's going to agree with you; he's your pet.'

Avgar saw Eyp was struggling to control his anger. Avgar drained his cup and put it down so that he could put a calming hand on Eyp. *This is not going as intended. Time to be firm.* 'It's irrelevant what he thinks and what you think. I'm the Leader of the Outcasts and the army will do what I command.'

'Ha, not the soldiers from Nivera. Avgar, you said that Resvon was a fool to seek peace and while I didn't agree that peace was the right way forward, he was a good man and I respected him. You, on the other hand, are a fool. But worse than being a fool, you're an outsider.' The Niveran squared his shoulders and Nigrath and Quynt stood behind him. 'You've been here a few months and you think you can lead us? I wouldn't even trust you to lead an army of mice. You will never command me and you will never command my men. And do you know why?'

Avgar felt the bristle of his sorcery tingling in his bones. He set himself for the risk of sapping all of his energy by performing a spell. *I'm going to kill you, Veltrene.*

'Because, Avgar, you're a dead fool.'

Avgar was not expecting that and spat out his retort. 'You're the only dead man here.'

The Niveran smiled. 'Can you feel the tingling in your toes? The numbness in your fingers? That's where it starts. Next, it will be your throat and then your heart.'

Avgar felt cold. 'What have you done?'

'That wine that only you've been drinking; that Niveran red, I poisoned it. You only have a few moments left to live.' Veltrene lifted his chalice and tipped the wine onto the floor.

Avgar could feel his fingers and toes burning. His throat started to tingle. He turned to Eyp and managed to squeeze out a single sentence before he lost his voice. 'Get me to the Healers.'

The three men laughed. 'You'll be dead before you make it out of the keep.' Nigrath looked to Eyp and spoke with his deep voice. 'Bring the corpse back when he dies and we'll give you command of Fort Kykum.'

Avgar wasn't paying attention to that though. He summoned his magical power and turned his mind inward. Eyp supported him and they staggered from the room. As he did this, he channelled his strength and fought the poison. Avgar knew it might be days before he reached the Healers, so he had to pace himself. The sorcerer magically found the poison within his bloodstream and slowed its progression. He forced it to leach out of his vessels and into his muscles. The poisoned man would have screamed with the burning pain, but his voice was no more; his voice box was paralysed. Instead, he tried in vain to close his mind to it and stop the poison seeping back into his bloodstream.

Somehow, they made it out of the keep and Avgar felt himself being shoved onto a cart. The bumpy ride to the docks was agonising, but he endured it. Avgar vaguely heard Eyp pay for a small fast boat and they set sail. The harbour gates were shut, but Eyp knew of a hidden door that could be opened from the inside for small scouting boats to leave when they needed. Avgar blindly gazed at the stars above as they headed through the door and made their way out into the swell of the Rogaus.

All across the Rogaus, Avgar drifted in and out of consciousness. He would fade, only to be woken by excruciating pain all throughout his supine body. He blocked his senses to the rocking of the boat and the spray on his face and focused on stopping the poison spreading further.

They made good progress across the Rogaus under a strong wind. Eyp navigated expertly by the stars and Avgar dreamt of that fateful day when he lost his hand and was ripped across the Moaks. Light showed on the horizon and on they sailed. The wind continued, rain came and fell sharply. Avgar became delirious and tried to shout out to the multitude of attackers that he imagined were knifing him. His voice remained unheard by Eyp. Shortly after dawn, his limbs stopped jerking and he lay still. He looked peaceful, as if asleep, but the battle raged vigorously within his body. He was oblivious to his surroundings as a nervous Eyp checked that he was still breathing time and time again.

The day wore on, but time meant nothing to Avgar, who was trapped in a revolving, never-ending furnace. Darkness eventually fell as the day ended and Eyp maintained their course for Headly.

Slender Harlorn stood on the end of his pier and watched the changing colour of the sea as dawn broke the horizon. He enjoyed the dance of the grey-blue-green shift under his gaze. Summer had definitely ended and the night had been cool. A fierce wind slapped him in the face, and Harlorn imagined he was sailing freely across the seas.

The Healers had not been receiving as many wounded this last month. Jacov had wrangled peace out of Resvon and Kathsum and although Resvon was dead, peace still lingered as a fragile reality. Harlorn was grateful for this and hoped that the new leader of the Outcasts would uphold the treaty.

Harlorn's mind wandered to the thought of what his life would be like in the years to come, should peace remain. *A pleasant thought indeed.* He looked out to the horizon and was glad to be who he was, doing what he did. Only then did he see a small, single masted boat flying across the water towards him. *That will be an Outcast vessel.*

He waited and watched as the boat, twice the size of a dingy, expertly rode the wind-swept waves without capsizing. It was not long before the boat was within throwing distance, but Harlorn waited until she was aside the pier and he could see the face of the sailor before making any further judgements.

'Greetings.' Harlorn helped with fastening the boat as Eyp replied to him in hurried words.

'This man has been poisoned. I don't know what by, but he should be dead by now.'

Harlorn helped Eyp lift Avgar onto the pier and two other Healers arrived with a stretcher. 'Yes, he does not look good.' He addressed the two Healers. 'Take him straight to the critical room; he is barely able to draw breath.'

Avgar was taken away and Harlorn looked to Eyp. 'I trust that you have the payment for him?'

Eyp looked taken aback. 'Payment? Are you that heartless?'

'I thought as much.' He pursed his lips and looked Eyp up and down. 'You look exhausted, but you're a strong man. You can rest with us for a day. We will then extract the payment out of you with work. After you have paid that debt, you will need to leave.'

'Leave? I can't leave him here alone.'

'Come on man, *if* he survives, he could hardly be anywhere safer.' Harlorn thought. 'But if you must be close, then you can stay on your boat. Anchored off the shore.' *I will not bend the rules; they are in place for good reason.* Eyp nodded, apparently too exhausted to argue. Harlon turned and led Eyp down the pier to the main town, where he would be able to rest and recover his strength.

Avgar slowly emerged from his state of unconsciousness. His eyelids were heavy and he felt a weird numb tingling in all of his muscles. His mouth was dry and his lips were cracked; they stung when he tried to lick his lips with his swollen tongue. He opened his eyes with an effort and tried to focus on the timber roof above him. He heard a movement to one side and with an effort, he turned his head.

'Welcome back to the land of the living.'

Avgar didn't recognise the voice. 'Urggghuu' He tried to talk, but only a faint gurgle came out. He tried to sit up, but found himself too weak.

The Healer, dressed in the usual white robe, came over and helped him rest against the bedhead. He put a small cup of water to Avgar's lips and Avgar drank a sip. He tried to speak again, but with the same result.

The Healer spoke calmly and with a gentle voice. 'My name is Lyafe and I'm the Healer Supreme. It sounds like you cannot talk, nod if that is true.'

Avgar nodded.

'Hhmm. Well, I will try to fill in some of the details that you may want to know. 'You are on Headly. You have been unconscious for six days and you are past the time of danger. Your man, Eyp, has visited from time to time to ensure that you're ok. He has also told us who you are. He was living on his boat offshore.'

Was living? Avgar thought about Lyafe's choice of words, but the Healer kept talking and Avgar refocused his attention on him.

'You can probably remember that you were poisoned. We don't know what with, but I am astounded that you are alive at all. We couldn't do much for you, but burn cleansing candles in your room and a touch of bloodletting. As the days went by, your body and spirit did the work and cleaned you of the poison. You seem to have a power that I've only seen once before. We will talk more about that once you heal some more.

'I'm hoping that your voice will return, and I expect it to, but it may take some time. Can you write?' Avgar shook his head.

'That's going to make things harder. I suppose you could have when you had your right hand, but it is always very hard to learn with the other hand.' Lyafe stood and made his way over to a cupboard. He returned shortly with a small pile of worn wooden cards. 'These are to help you communicate. Each card has a different meaning that all the Healers know. Black is for "no" and white is for "yes".' He held two cards the size of his palm up and gave them to Avgar.

Avgar took them and, with the numbness leaving his muscles, rubbed them between the fingers of his left hand.

'Does everything I've said make sense?' Avgar showed the white card.

Lyafe smiled. 'The other colours have different meanings. Yellow, if you want to urinate and can't get to the toilet, brown for defecating. Green tells us you want to know "why" and light blue if you have another question. Red is for if you're in pain. Dark blue is if you're thirsty and this purple card is for if you're hungry. They are all we have at the moment. Each card has the word on the back, so you can remember what is for what. Does that make sense?'

Again, Avgar held out the white card.

'Good. Now it is best that you try to have some more water and rest while I prepare some food for you. A week without food or water is longer than most could tolerate.'

Avgar lay down gingerly and closed his eyes. He could not remember the last time that he had been scared, but he was scared now. *My voice, I'm lost without my voice.*

Avgar woke the following morning, drenched from head to toe in sweat. A pungent odour reached his nostrils and he wrinkled his nose. Only as his senses fully returned, did he realise he had soiled himself.

A Healer walked calmly over to him with a basin of warm water. 'It seems you've had another accident.'

Avgar turned his head away in a mixture of shame, guilt, disgust and anger.

'There's no point ignoring the fact. You've lost control of your bowels. It sometimes happens when we're sick. Do you think you can stand up?'

Avgar nodded and stood slowly.

'Can you help me take off your gown?'

Avgar realised he was only wearing a simple gown, similar to that of the Healers. With help, he managed to remove this. He found himself almost vomiting when he lifted the soiled section past his nose. He had to steady himself by holding onto the Healer for support. Avgar looked into the man's eyes and saw a gentle pity there. Avgar felt ashamed and hung his head.

The Healer wiped clean Avgar's black, tattooed body from head to toe. Avgar noticed he left no crevice uncleaned. He then helped Avgar dress in a new gown and sat him on a different bed. The Healer changed the sheets of the soiled bed and then left Avgar to his thoughts.

This is horrible. A week ago, I was the Leader of the Outcasts, now I can't talk, I have no strength and I shit myself. This can't be happening to me, to me! Avgar couldn't believe his horrible twist of fate. *I must be able to talk.* He tried, but again only a gurgling noise came out.

Lyafe walked into the room carrying a steaming bowel of broth. 'Good morning Avgar, are you hungry? Of course you are.' He brought the food over on a small table and placed it in front of Avgar. 'Eat.'

Avgar looked at him and tentatively tasted the brown liquid. It was warm and tasty; like meat. Avgar finished the bowel hungrily before Lyafe spoke.

'I have been a Healer since I was a little boy. I have seen a lot of people live and a lot of people die. I have seen quick deaths and slow, drawn out deaths. The hardest death to watch is when someone gives up. It happens when they can find no reason to keep going and waste away.'

Avgar looked at Lyafe with confusion. *What is he talking about?*

'I've seen it more times than I can remember, and I don't want to see it again. You're a man who has clearly been through a lot and you cannot let this be the time that you give in and give up. You need to prepare yourself for the wave of despair that may sweep through you. Avgar, you haven't given up yet, you probably haven't even thought about it, but if you're not careful, you may fall down that trapdoor. I'm not going to let that happen.'

Despair? Give up? He doesn't know what he's talking about or who he's talking to.

'I'm going to visit you every day and talk to you. I'm going to fill your head with my voice so that you don't notice the absence of your own. I'll start right now. I imagine you want to know how you're faring and if you'll ever speak again.'

Avgar nodded, excited, yet fearful of the response.

'The answer is not a simple one. I personally believe that you will talk again, but I cannot promise it. The part of your throat where the voice comes from seems to be damaged, and in a normal person, that would be irreversible. But for you, I just don't know.'

Avgar sat up in excitement.

Lyafe looked over Avgar's head and about the room. 'The rumours that fly around on the mainland are that the Healers are magical and can even bring a dead man back to life. Let me assure you, we cannot. Yes, there is what laymen would call magic in this place, but not in the way that they imagine it.

'First, there is power in this land, so that nobody who is here may harm another without feeling that harm themselves. I have spoken to Jacov and I understand that you have witnessed that power in your meeting with him. That extends to everyone here, not just the Healers. This is how we can have both the Outcasts and their enemies in such close proximity.'

Lyafe looked keenly at Avgar who returned the gaze. 'Secondly, a power has been given to the Healers and only the Healers. That power allows us to mend and heal the sick. It is a mixture of knowledge on how the body works, as well as an unexplainable force that guides our hands and our actions. In our training, we learn to trust the gentle nudgings and instincts that enter our minds when we are treating someone. We don't fully understand how this influence comes about, but it is always correct and always heals.'

Avgar was astonished. *There must be others who control this power. The Healers are under their control.*

'You may be wondering why I am telling you this. We don't normally talk to our patients about our powers, but as I have previously said, you're different. What kept you alive for so long seems to me to be similar to the power of the Healers. I want to understand that better and I want to explore your healing possibilities. Your throat will be the first test of that,' Avgar massaged his throat tenderly, 'and I have an inkling that the healing will have to come from within you. Something I feel you are not too familiar with.'

Lyafe rested his hand on Avgar's leg. 'I don't want to give you too much hope, however, I've never seen anyone heal their voice box when it has been damaged such as yours.'

What? First you tell me I'm going to be able to speak again, and then you tell me that you've never seen anyone get their voice back from where I'm sitting? Agvar made an angry gurgle.

Lyafe seemed to miss Avgar's anger and smiled. 'Yes, that's good; you should keep trying to talk every so often.'

Avgar felt more anger, but could not figure out how to communicate this. He stood up and stomped his foot. Lyafe raised his eyebrows. Avgar felt dizziness coming and plonked back down on the bed.

'Best not to get too worked up, if you can avoid it.' Avgar felt the blood returning to his head and his vision stopped spinning.

A look of sadness crossed Lyafe's face. 'Now that you are starting to mend, I feel you should hear some sad news that I have to impart. Three nights ago, your man Eyp, died. He was on his boat, as he normally is at night, when Harlorn saw a great blaze burning. Harlorn and others rowed out to where Eyp's boat was anchored, but they were too late. The blaze had taken the boat and it was half sunk. In the morning they searched the wreckage, but could not find his body; the flames must have been very hot.'

Avgar felt like he had been slapped in the face. *What? No, not Eyp! How can this have happened?*

Lyafe seemed to know what Avgar was thinking. 'We don't know how this happened. Maybe he knocked over his lamp in the night.'

Really, is that what you think? Avgar raised his eyebrows. He fumbled through his cards and got out the light blue card to show he had another question. He held it up then made an action to indicate someone stabbing. *Could he have been killed?*

Lyafe watched Avgar repeat the action. 'Do you want to know if he could have been stabbed?' Avgar rocked his hand from side to side to indicate *not quite.*

'You want to know if he could have been murdered?'

Avgar nodded.

Lyafe thought for a moment. 'The protection only extends as far as the land, so Eyp wouldn't have been under that power, so I suppose he could have been murdered. But who would want to do that? Certainly not any of the Healers. And all of our patients are too sick to get out to his boat, and Harlorn would have seen them.' Lyafe's face flickered for a moment. 'I must leave you now Avgar. I'm sorry to be the barer of bad news, but I don't like withholding information.'

He knows something. He knows who has done this.

Lyafe stood. 'Before I go, I have something for you.' He brought a book out from underneath his robe. 'I assume you can read.' Avgar nodded, and the Healer continued. 'This is one of our many books of healing. It will teach you the basics about the blood and bones of the body. Something you might need to know in the months to come.' He put the book on the table and left the room.

Avgar glanced at the book briefly but was in no mood to read; so much was flying through his mind from all that Lyafe had told him. *Will I ever speak again? Who controls the Healer's power? Was Eyp murdered? And why do I need to know about blood and bones in the months to come?*

33

Marlvon and Islonda woke with the sun on their rocky outcrop. The morning was cool with little breeze. They packed up their few belongings and Marlvon strapped his sword to his side. Marlvon felt a mixture of excitement and trepidation to be on the move again. Islonda looked happy to be going to Bankton and had a grin broadly across her face.

They made their way down the steep hill to Nal and then walked in silence to where Marlvon had hidden the cart many weeks ago. It was here, well off the road, that Marlvon got the bag of makeup out to disguise the pair of them. He went to work on Islonda first and it was not long before she looked like an old woman in her fifties.

Marlvon explained to her it was usually better to make yourself look older than younger. 'An elderly person draws less attention, are less suspicious and less of a threat than a young one.'

Marlvon then had the much harder task of making his own disguise. Usually when he did this, he had a shiny mirror to perfect his makeup, but today the best he could do was to use the blade of his sword. He avoided doing too much work, opting for a subtle approach given his lack of mirror. He added crow's feet near his eyes and a touch of grey to his brows. He avoided distinguishing features, like scars, but enlarged his nose a fraction and softened his jawline. He looked to Islonda for an appraisal.

'You look liked you've aged a decade and put on ten pounds. You look the same and yet completely different at the same time.' Marlvon changed his posture and walked with a slight limp. He spoke slowly, with a soft voice to complete the disguise.

'Now, my dear, we have been married a lonnng time.' He drew out the word *long* for emphasis. 'Our new names are Mant and Lyre and we are corn farmers fifty miles up yonder road. We're coming to Bankton town to visit an old friend of mine from my childhood.'

'This is spooky, Marlvon.' Islonda's voice remained youthful.

'You'll need to change you voice a bit, my love. Best let me do most of the talking.'

Islonda tried to age her voice. 'Is this better?'

'Better, but not great. You sound too strained, my dear, like you're trying too hard. Relax it a bit.'

'Oh, Mant, you tease me so.'

Marlvon smiled. 'I think we are ready to go, but we should practice talking while we travel along this here road.'

'As you say, my love.'

Marlvon quickly prepared Nal and the carriage, concealing the bags of coins, gold and jewels with his sword underneath the seat. He was not satisfied, but it was the best he could do with the bare carriage.

Marlvon checked that the way was clear of travellers before he took Nal onto the road. The journey was uneventful and they made good time. Marlvon was hoping to get to Bankton before midday, find Islonda's mother, have a quick lunch and then be on their way to Fort Kykum.

It wasn't until they were a couple of miles out of Bankton that Marlvon sensed that something was wrong. They had not met anyone on the road, and there was an unnatural silence over the land.

They were soon to climb a gentle hill and then they would have a view down onto Bankton. Nal walked slowly up the hill and when they reached the top, Islonda let out a whimper of frightful surprise. Looking down, Marlvon saw Bankton had been burnt to the ground. The destruction was complete, with piles of black rubble spread where the town used to be; even the stone buildings had been torn down. Marlvon nudged Nal forward at a trot and took a sidewards glance at Islonda's face. Tears rolled onto her cheeks and she took sobbing gulps of air. Marlvon put an arm around her shoulders and held her tight. This was Islonda's home. She had spent all of her life here and now it was gone.

'Where has everyone gone?' Islonda managed to ask innocently with her youthful voice.

In response, Marlvon urged Nal forward and made for Islonda's old house. On the way there, he noticed remnants of burnt skeletons in the street. He did not want to point these out to Islonda and so pulled her against him for support.

When they arrived at Jault's forge, the building was the same as the rest of the town; burnt and destroyed. Islonda jumped down before Nal had stopped and Marlvon had to be quick to catch her up.

'We should have come sooner. Oh, Mother, where are you?'

Marlvon started to look more closely at the debris and regressed to his usual voice. 'This has not been done recently. Look, there are weeds and even some daisies pushing through the ashes.'

It was then that Islonda saw her first skeleton. She screeched and turned away. Marlvon came and held her. He looked at the skull and saw a weed growing through the eye socket. He let her cry into his shoulder for a long time before wiping her tears away.

'Islonda, come and look at this.' He led her by the hand to where Jault's workshop once stood. He moved some rubble and pointed.

'Look, your father's anvil. Standing as if it had never been touched. And here, the head of a hammer that he would have used for pounding metal into shape.'

Islonda looked at these and wiped her nose on her ragged sleeve. Marlvon saw her eyes smoulder and saw a purpose harden within her will. When she spoke, it was in a monotone with no emotion.

'We should leave this place; there is nothing here but death.' She turned and walked calmly back to Nal.

Marlvon paused for a moment to process her sudden change in character. *She will need to grieve for her parents at some stage. I'm going to need to be careful of her; I can't let her lose who she is.*

Marlvon made his way back to Nal, carrying the head of the hammer; he was not quite sure why, but felt that somehow it was important.

'Mant, you said that we needed to go to Kykum, then let us go now.'

Marlvon used the voice of Mant once more. 'As you say, my dear, but first we need to get you another dress and a load of goods.'

She looked at him enquiringly. 'Your dress is so worn that it's barely a dress at all, and we need a load of goods to give us a plausible reason to enter the Fort. It's all right though; I know exactly where to get both.'

Marlvon cracked the reins and Nal hopped forward in a brisk walk, heading towards the road that led from Bankton to Fort Kykum.

Marlvon and Islonda travelled all afternoon with nothing to eat. They took the back roads where they could, but had to take the main road towards Fort Kykum for the majority of the journey. Marlvon tried to talk to Islonda, but she only replied with short words and a firm voice. They neared Marlvon's olive farm and he directed Nal into a side lane.

Islonda looked confused. 'Where are we going?'

Marlvon was grateful that she was paying attention to their progress and he replied in a tone to encourage more conversation. '*You're* going to visit an old friend of mine. He lives a couple of miles down this lane and grows olives too. He presses them into oil and we share a healthy competition at the markets.' Marlvon yearned to be the simple olive farmer again.

'Why am I going to see him? Aren't you coming?'

'He knows me well and would recognise me even if I were covered in soot. I'm more of a hunted man than you are and I don't want to put him in danger too.'

Marlvon wished he could see his old friend and share a meal with him. 'Also, his house might be watched.'

'But, why am I seeing him?'

'I want to get a cart of firewood to take to Kykum. It will give us a valid reason for visiting the Fort, if questioned.' Marlvon paused for a moment. 'His wife passed away a few months back and I believe he will still have her clothes. You're about the same size as her and your disguised age is similar to hers. I'm sure he would sell you a dress if paid enough, especially if you mention that you're a friend of mine.'

Islonda sat silently for a few moments as they bounced along the bumpy lane. 'That sounds reasonable. I can also see if he has any food to sell us; I'm starving.'

Marlvon was pleased. *Good, she is thinking clearly.* 'Great idea. He may even invite you in for a meal.' Marlvon said. 'When we get close, I'll hide in a bush and give you enough money to be generous with him.'

Islonda nodded. 'What's his name?'

'Zad.'

They continued on for a short while before Marlvon pulled Nal to a halt. He rummaged for some coins and gave the reins to Islonda. He gave her a kiss on the cheek and wished her luck. She waved to him and urged Nal forward.

Marlvon ducked through a hedgerow and then, when out of Islonda's sight, ran hidden along next to the road. He wanted to observe his friend and how he reacted to see if he was compromised by Marlvon's pursuers. He sped ahead of Nal and stealthily hid himself within a bush not far from Zad's door. *I should be able to hear from here.* He sat and waited a few moments for Islonda to arrive.

The disguised old lady slowly got down from the carriage and walked to the front door of the farmhouse. She knocked firmly, but not urgently. Marlvon saw Zad open it a fraction and peek out into the fading light. On seeing Islonda, he opened the door more and looked at her suspiciously.

'Good evening, madam. How may I be of assistance?' He looked her up and down, noting her ragged clothes.

Islonda smiled at him. 'Good evening, sir. I'm a resident of what used to be called Bankton.' Marlvon saw her mock a sob. 'I've been wandering the countryside for days now. I'm hungry and in need of some clothes. A mutual friend said that you might be able to help me.' She hung her head in embarrassment.

Zad opened the door fully. 'My poor dear. Come in, come in.' Marlvon saw real concern on Zad's face. As they went inside, he heard Zad ask, 'A mutual friend, you say?'

Marlvon then realised that he wouldn't be able to hear what was being said from where he crouched outside. He stood with a bent back and made his way to the edge of the house. There were bushes of lavender along one wall and he made his way through this towards the back of the residence. Halfway around, he found a window open to let in the evening breeze. He smiled and hoisted himself through this; ever hopeful that no one was watching.

Marlvon found himself in a small sitting room with comfortable looking chairs and an empty fireplace. He snuck to the doorway and peaked through the slight opening. The hallway outside was empty and he crept out of the room and stopped to listen for voices. He heard Islonda's timid voice from what he guessed was the dining room. He followed his ears and wondered whether he should reveal himself or remain hidden. *I'll listen for a bit first.*

Zad spoke nervously. 'You shouldn't have come here; you're putting me in danger. Marlvon is a hunted man. If they saw you coming here and know that you're his friend, I'm done for. I want you to leave.'

Marlvon tensed and waited anxiously for Islonda's response. 'Please, I beg you. All I ask for is a meal, some clothes and a cart full of firewood.' *Begging won't work with him; he's too much of a miser.* Marlvon thought.

'Firewood? No, I will not help you. Now, please leave.'

Islonda changed tact. 'I will not leave until you give me enough food for a solid meal, some new clothes and help me load my cart with firewood. And if you don't, then I will find the nearest soldier and tell them you've been harbouring Marlvon on your property.'

Marlvon heard an intake of breath. 'No one would believe you.'

'Perhaps, but with what the reward is, they'd still tear this place apart on the off-chance of Marlvon being here.'

Zad growled, 'You're a thief and a blackmailer.'

'Not a thief; I will pay you well for your goods.'

Marlvon could almost hear the cogs in Zad's mind turning, trying to find the best solution to the woman before him. Before he came to a conclusion, he heard the sound of money clinking onto a table. *Smart girl, Islonda.*

'Very well, but we do this tonight, regardless of the darkness.' Zad did not sound happy at all.

'Good. To make things quicker, I will order my manservant to help with the loading.'

Zad grunted. 'Stay here. I'll get your dress and food.'

Marlvon realised Zad would soon enter the hallway where he was hiding. He spun around and raced back into the sitting room. From there, he slithered through the window and made his stealthy way back to Nal. When there, he hunched his shoulders and turned his face downward. In the dimming light, he hoped Zad wouldn't look too closely at a simple man servant. *I wish Islonda hadn't roped me in to this; it's too dangerous.*

Marlvon only had to wait a short while before Islonda appeared with Zad who led Nal by the bit to his woodshed. The three spoke little as they worked hard to load the cart with firewood, and it wasn't long before Marlvon and Islonda left Zad behind, his foul mood lifting lightly as they drove away into the night.

Ever cautious, Marlvon continued to maintain the role play as Mant. 'You did great, Lyre. A nice touch with the money on the table.'

'You heard that?'

'Yes, I was in the hallway, ready to help if he threatened you.'

'I was expecting him to be a bit nicer than he was.'

'He usually is. I think he was just scared.'

'Poor man.'

'Mmmm.'

'Where will we be sleeping tonight?'

'A few miles on, there is a lane that leads down to a creek. At this time of year, we should be able to cross a ford and make our way into a paddock that has an abandoned shed in it. We can hide ourselves and Nal in there for the night. We should get an early start tomorrow though; I want to arrive as early as we can to Kykum.'

'Mmmm, a shed. That sounds nice and comfy.' Islonda replied with light sarcasm.

'Yes, it is. Romantic too. There should also be plenty of field mice for company, as well.' 'Excellent.' She raised her voice a little. 'Crack on Old Nal, we've got a date to get to.' The two laughed as Nal tossed her head and stepped a bit quicker.

They made themselves as comfortable as they could in the abandoned shed and, as they said goodnight, Marlvon comforted Islonda, who wept for her dead parents. They both finally drifted off to sleep and the night passed with nothing out of the ordinary more than the few mice coming to say 'hello' to the pair.

They rose with the first light to the sound of a rooster crowing. After reapplying their disguises, they continued their journey to Fort Kykum with a grim sense of purpose.

They arrived at the gates mid-morning and, to Marlvon's delight, the sentries looked relaxed as they let the queue of people flow into the walled city. When it was Marlvon and Islonda's turn they paid the toll and answered the standard question of what their business was at the Fort.

'Bringing firewood to sell to the taverns down at the docks.' Came Marlvon's prepared answer.

They were admitted without a second thought. 'That was easy.' Islonda sounded surprised.

'Things often are to those who prepare well'

Marlvon directed Nal to the right and not up the central road to the keep. The streets were crowded and the going was slow. Islonda looked puzzled. 'Aren't the docks the other way?'

'Yes, but first I want to make a delivery. We're not actually going to sell the firewood to the taverns. The summer may be ending, but they won't be looking to stock up on wood for another few moon cycles. No, we're going to a marketplace to see a trustworthy man who will look after Nal for me. After that, we'll make our way to the dock taverns on foot.'

Marlvon finished explaining their plan and wrinkled his nose. 'We'll soon be going down Tanner Street. It will stink. Try to breathe through your mouth.'

The stink became more intense, and he urged Nal to push through the crowds quicker. He looked over at Islonda and she looked pale and uncomfortable. A moment later, she turned to the side and vomited into the street. She wiped her mouth, but kept her head hanging over the side of the cart. Marlvon put a comforting hand on her shoulder. 'We'll soon be through to fresher air, my love.'

After they passed the leather tanning pits, they drove down Blood Road, named after the abattoirs that were situated there. Channelled water was directed past both of these industries and their proximity to each other meant less transport was required for the hides after the beasts were slaughtered. Blood Road didn't smell all that much better than Tanner Street and Islonda found herself dry retching once her stomach was empty.

Marlvon felt guilty about taking this route, but it was too late now. A short while later, they arrived at the marketplace that Marlvon was heading for. He left Islonda on the cart looking seedy, while he bought her some herbs to crush and sniff. This helped and it wasn't long before she was back to her usual self, albeit a bit weaker.

Under Marlvon's instructions, Islonda found a man and offered their cart of wood if he cared for Old Nal. The man recognised the horse as Marlvon's and knowingly agreed to look after Nal until her rightful owner should return to claim her, or she died. He cautioned Nal would be made to work and Islonda agreed that it should be so.

By this stage, dusk was descending and Marlvon led Islonda on foot, while carrying the heavy hammer head, the last mile or so down to the docks. There were many people out, some rougher looking than others, so Marlvon saw no reason not to travel on the main thoroughfares.

They arrived at an inn called the *Wayward Sailor* as darkness fell. Marlvon arranged a private room for the two of them and paid in advance for ten nights. He did not expect to stay that long, but if anyone was looking for them, it may confuse the pursuers should Marlvon and Islonda leave early.

Marlvon ensured that both their disguises were intact, and then he and Islonda made their way down to the common room and ordered a meal. The fish soup Marlvon ordered was oily, but he ate it nonetheless. The bread and spiced pork stew that Islonda had looked and smelled delicious and Marlvon was envious of her. They ate their meal, each with a mug of ale, and chatted as an old married couple might. Marlvon was only half paying attention to Islonda as his ears were wandering the other guest's conversations.

'It seems, my dear, that the leaders of Psymryte, Nivera and that cunning man Quynt are at the Fort. If what I hear is correct, then the rumours say that Avgar has been killed.'

Islonda smiled brightly, out of character. 'Does that mean that we won't be hunted anymore? Does that mean that we don't have to go to Headly as planned?'

Marlvon frowned at her. 'Please don't mention that place again in public.' He took a drink of his ale. 'It's possible that the new leader, whoever that is, may not want me dead, but that is unlikely. The Outcasts have a rich history of killing any relatives of past leaders. But even if they didn't want me dead, they are hardly going to publicise that fact. There will still be many gold chases and bounty hunters out there who will still be looking for us. They probably just won't get their reward in exchange for our heads.' He took another drink. 'Also, from what I'm hearing, there is quite some debate as to whether Avgar is dead or still the Leader of the Outcasts.' He thought for a moment. 'I don't think that us staying is a risk worth taking.'

Islonda looked down at her hands, subdued and disappointed. 'I think I'm ready to turn in for the night.'

Marlvon spoke quietly so only Islonda could hear him. 'That's probably a good idea. I have some work to do in finding a ship and a captain. Lock the door and only let me in. I will knock twice, pause and then knock once more. Good night my dear.'

Islonda stood up and gave Marlvon a kiss goodnight on his forehead. 'Don't stay up too late.' She smiled and Marlvon watched as she left the room.

Marlvon and Islonda were staying in a reputable inn. Marlvon knew that he would have to go somewhere less reputable to get what he wanted. He stood and left the *Wayward Sailor* into the cooling night air. The thin slither of a waning moon was rising as he made his way downhill towards the water. He had not been to this part of the city in many years, but he knew exactly which tavern he was going to: *The Rusty Blade.*

When he arrived, he was not disappointed by what he found. The place was a hive of seedy activity, even this early in the night. There was low lighting to hide the goings on of tough men in hooded cloaks, prostitutes selling their bodies and rowdy fights and brawls that stopped as quickly as they started.

Marlvon made his way to the barman; the holder of so much power in this underworld of activity. The man had powerful looking shoulders and a thick neck. He wore a bushy moustache and was balding on the top of his head. He was cleaning a tankard with a dirty rag and chewed a clump of tobacco.

Marlvon ordered the house beer and asked for a clean glass. The barman raised an eyebrow, but complied. Marlvon paid four times what the beer was worth. As the barman looked at the coins, Marlvon spoke.

'I want to rent a boat.' He slid another coin across. 'Would there be anyone here who can help me?'

The barman smiled briefly and pointed to a man sitting in a corner. Marlvon did not fail to notice the two men wearing curved swords standing alert behind him.

'Thank you. I'm also looking for a captain who can sail a boat who has nothing to do with that man.' Marlvon slid four more coppers to the barman, who smiled knowingly.

'You won't find anyone here who fits that description.' The barman closed his lips tightly and raised his chin.

Marlvon cocked an eyebrow. He knew how the game was played; perhaps even better than the barman. To really get his attention, Marlvon passed a gold piece, worth more than one hundred coppers, to the strong man. The barman chuckled, picked up the coin and bit it to ensure its validity.

'Three streets over there is another inn, *The Outcast*. Order a jug of ale with a twist of lemon. Pay with a gold piece and the landlord with help you as much as he can.'

'Thank you for your troubles.' To the surprise of the barman, Marlvon handed him another gold coin.

Marlvon picked up his beer and made his way over to the seated boat renter. Marlvon thought the man was fat and ugly, but knew that he would be brutish and arrogant. He was not wrong.

As Marlvon got close, the two standing men placed their hands on the pommels of their swords. Marlvon ignored them and spoke clearly to the fat man. 'I have business for you. I want to rent a boat and I heard that you're the best man to come to.'

The seated man waved him closer, but did not invite him to sit. When he spoke, his voice was high pitched for a man of his size.

'What do you want?'

'A single-masted vessel that can be sailed with two men... and I want her to be fast.'

The fat man rocked his head from side to side. 'That's interesting; I have just finished speaking to another man who is interested in just that type of boat. He was willing to pay handsomely for her.'

'I'm more interested.' Marlvon flicked a gold coin onto the table in the knowledge that there was no other man.

'You may be. Suppose I do have such a boat, where would you be taking her?'

Marlvon smiled. 'For a tavern where no questions are asked, you ask too much of me.' He turned to leave as a bluff.

'Hold on, hold on. Let's be reasonable men. I just want to ensure that my boat, the *Wicked Princess*, will come back to me.'

'I understand. I plan to sail her up along the coast to Nivera. I would be gone no more than a moon cycle.'

'If you're willing to pay what she's worth, I can have her captained and ready to sail on the morrow.'

Marlvon smiled wryly. 'I already have a captain, good sir.' He paused and cocked his head as if sizing his opponent up. 'Will that be a problem?'

The boat renter puffed out his cheeks and then sucked them back in. 'You ask a lot. How do I know you won't just sail away, never to return?'

'You don't. But then, in your business you never can be sure that your goods will come back.' Marlvon paused again, as if considering. 'I'll tell you what, I'll leave you an assurance that I won't steal your ship.'

'It would need to be a substantial deposit,' mused the fat man.

Marlvon could see the seated man weighing up how much he could bleed from Marlvon without being utterly ridiculous. The two men stared at each other for a few tense moments.

'If you can leave me an assurance of one fifth of the boats worth, plus rent for *six* weeks, you can have her ready to sail in two days.'

'I will leave an assurance of one sixth of her worth and rent for five weeks *and* she will be ready tomorrow evening.' Marlvon didn't care how much he paid, but he had to keep up appearances to avoid suspicion.

'Five weeks' rent and one fifth and she'll be ready tomorrow evening. I like the number five.'

Marlvon fondled his money bag for the benefit of the renter. 'Very well. I will pay the rent now and the assurance when I board her tomorrow.'

The fat man smiled, thinking that he had got the better of Marlvon. 'Excellent.'

Marlvon knew he was paying a premium, but was glad to have secured a vessel so quickly. The two men haggled half-heartedly as they finalised what five weeks' rent would be. Before long, Marlvon was leaving the inn with his purse lighter and heading three blocks over to *The Outcast.*

As Marlvon walked into *The Outcast*, he had to duck as a wayward mug flew past his head in the smoke-filled air. He casually sidestepped around two brawling men as if nothing was out of the ordinary and made his way to the bar. *The Outcast* was a similar establishment to *The Rusty Blade* with less light and more shadowy corners. Marlvon noticed that although the night was just half done, there were several men slumped in chairs from too much drink.

He beckoned to the barman, who had wandered over and spoke disinterestedly. 'Wha do ya want?'

As casually as he could, Marlvon replied. 'I'll have a jug of ale with a twist of lemon.' The landlord's eyes narrowed. Marlvon produced a gold coin to pay.

'*The Knife* sent ya, did they?' He didn't wait for a reply, but poured a mug of beer from a barrel beneath the bar. 'What do you really want?' He placed the beer down and took the gold piece.

'I want a trustworthy captain who can keep his mouth shut and sail a single masted boat with one inexperienced crewman.'

'That'd be you, I take it.' He rubbed his whiskered chin. 'I can think of three men that fit that description. Two are in this room right now.' He placed both hands flat on the bar top.

Marlvon took the hint and gave him another coin. *This is becoming an expensive night.*

'The man slumped over the end of this bar to your right is one. The other is in the corner closest to the door with that busty wench sitting on his lap. If you want to talk to him, you'd best be quick.'

Marlvon turned to see a voluptuous woman kissing and fondling the so-called captain. While Marlvon had seen much prostitution in his time, he couldn't stand those who partook in the practice. He immediately wrote that sailor off and turned to the drunk on the bar. All he could see was a head resting on an outstretched arm with a worn and faded tricorn hat covering the man's face.

Marlvon turned back to the barman. 'Thank you for your service.' The barman nodded and turned to serve another customer.

Marlvon made his way over to the drunk and sat on a stool to his left. He sipped his beer and pondered how he should play this man. He nudged him gently to see if he would rouse. He groaned but didn't look up.

'Would you like a free beer sailor?'

That got the man's attention. He raised his head slowly and faced Marlvon with a bleary glance. Marlvon was taken aback; the drunk looked older than Marlvon had thought and had a vicious scar trailing from his hairline, over his glass eye and down to his mouth. When he spoke, it was in short, gruff words. 'Not beer, strong wine.' Marlvon nodded to the barman and ordered the wine.

'I hear you can sail a boat.'

The man grunted in a non-committal manner.

'I would like to hire you to captain a boat for me.'

'No. I'm happy here.'

Marlvon took a long drink of his own beer. He sized the man up and made some assumptions. 'You look like a hard nut; someone who's seen battle and won, but just. Your age tells me that your experience should warrant you to be a captain in the navy or even higher. Yet you're in this hole of a tavern drinking away the remainder of your now miserable life. I'd guess you loved sailing once. You probably relished the rough seas, the spray in your face, the men following your orders. But then something happened. Did you get scared of the fight? I doubt it. Did you lose your crew? Possibly. Whatever it was, you've decided to give up on life and become a quitter.' Marlvon saw the tell-tale signs of his opponent's hackles rising. 'And that's fine, but if you want to be a drunk for the rest of your life, you will need money; you don't strike me as the type of man to beg and you don't have much money saved or you wouldn't be drinking in this shit hole.'

The man squared his shoulders to Marlvon. 'You know nothing of my life.'

Marlvon put a comforting hand on his shoulder. 'And I'm happy to keep it that way, but at least hear me out.' Before the other man could speak, Marlvon continued. 'If you come with me and sober up, to hear my proposition on the morrow, then I will give you enough money to keep you in drink for a year. If you agree to my proposal when you're sober, I'll pay you enough to satisfy your thirst for ten years. And, as an added bonus, you may, just may, even remember what you loved about sailing.'

Marlvon watched the man before him sway on his seat a little and thought about his proposal.

'Sober up and listen to you tomorrow, for a year's worth of drink? No strings attached? You still pay if I walk away?'

Marlvon nodded. 'I still pay if you walk away. But you have to come with me. I don't want you changing your mind.'

The man nodded and spoke half to himself. 'Why not? I've got nothing else to do.'

Marlvon smiled and both men drained their drinks before leaving together and heading back to Marlvon's inn.

Dawn arrived and the strong southerly wind eased and shifted to a westerly. Marlvon let the drunken sailor continue to sleep on the floor while he and Islonda reapplied their disguise and went downstairs to eat some breakfast. They ate their cheap pottage as Marlvon recounted the events of the previous night.

Islonda listened in silence, surprised at the resourcefulness of her partner and the ease at which he had achieved what he wanted.

After they had eaten, Marlvon sent Islonda out to buy some bread for lunch and two second hand coats that would fend off the ocean spray. Marlvon himself went back upstairs and watched the sailor sleeping his drink off. The captain was not an attractive man, yet the scar added to his character in a roguish manner. It didn't make him look scary or vicious, just harder and weathered, like a rock that had been shaped by the ocean over centuries of abuse.

The man snored loudly while lying on his front and drooled onto the dusty floor. His right hand was outstretched and Marlvon noticed for the first time that the second and fourth fingers were missing. He supposed they had been lost in battle. The man's hair had clearly not been combed in weeks, and the unkempt style displayed his receding hairline and the grey streaks twisted about in the mouse-brown mess.

Islonda returned successfully by mid-morning and still the sailor slept, albeit with less snoring and drooling.

'Still sleeping, I see. I hope he's as good as you hope he is, Marlvon.'

'Please, keep calling me Mant for now. And, I hope he's good too. If he hasn't roused by lunch, I will wake him.'

Just before midday, the man on the floor woke. He groaned and licked his dry lips with a dry tongue. He opened his eye and croaked out a single word. 'Drink.'

Marlvon handed him a cup of water, much to the dissatisfaction of the sailor. He sat up gingerly and leaned against the wall. He held his hand to his head and closed his eyes again.

'Oh, no you don't. You've slept enough; it's time we had our chat.'

The man opened his eyes slowly and frowned. 'Oh. You. First, bring me a beer and some food and then we can talk.'

Marlvon threw him a chunk of bread. 'No beer, only water. You're almost sober and you'll remain sober until we're done with you.'

The man looked about the room and saw Islonda. 'You have a friend, I see. All right, let's get this over with.' He took another drink of water and his face registered disapproval at the lack of beer.

'As I mentioned last night, I have hired a boat and need someone to sail her. She is the *Wicked Princess*, have you heard of her?'

'No.'

'Well, she is supposed to be fast. As I also mentioned last night, if you agree to sail us, then I will pay you enough to keep you in drink for ten years.'

The man looked more awake at that comment. 'That's a lot of money. Where are we sailing?'

'That, I won't tell you until we are out in the Rogaus, but I assure you that it won't be too far or too dangerous. The journey should only keep you from the taverns for a few weeks.'

'That's a lot of money for a short voyage. Not to mention that there are many more legitimate ways to hire a captain.' He cocked his head to the side. 'You're running from someone and judging by your secrecy, it's the powers that be. Don't worry, I have no love for them either and I won't turn such a cash-cow as yourself over to the authorities. Speaking of that, how do I know you're good for your money?'

Marlvon tossed him a gold coin casually.

'Can I also know your names?'

Marlvon hesitated. 'My name is Mant and this is Lyre. I won't ask yours, for I have no need of it.'

'My name is no secret; I'm Ryde. It used to be Captain Ryde until I left the navy, but now it's just Ryde.'

Marlvon nodded. 'I take possession of the vessel this evening and would like to leave Fort Kykum before it is fully dark.'

'Night sailing. That's a risky business, especially being so close to a new moon.'

Marlvon marvelled that Ryde knew what stage of the moon cycle the celestial body was in. 'You look like a man who likes a bit of adventure. Will you sail with us?'

Ryde leaned his head against the wall. 'Why not? It might be a bit of fun having a sail at night, just like the old days.' He leaned forward and looked at Marlvon with his good eye. 'You say that you get this boat in the evening? The harbour gates shut at dark; we will have to leave as soon as we're able. Can you get provisions loaded in time?'

Marlvon hadn't realised that the ocean gates were shut at night, an oversight that he wouldn't have made five years ago. 'Leave that to me.'

Ryde leaned his head back again and closed his eye. 'Well, that's sorted then. I'll wait here with the lovely Lyre and you organise our departure.'

Marlvon pondered Ryde's words and the trustworthiness of the man. His instincts told him he could trust the man, and they were seldom wrong. 'Very well, but you only drink water until we part ways.'

'If that's your condition, so be it.'

Marlvon stood and gave Islonda his hunting knife for protection. 'I doubt you'll need this, but just in case.'

She nodded, and he left to organise the loading of the *Wicked Princess*.

Evening came and Marlvon, Islonda and Ryde boarded the *Wicked Princess*. Marlvon handed the fat boat renter his assurance and waved him farewell. Ryde untied the moorings, pulled the gangplank up, and ordered Marlvon around with a gruff voice.

The *Princess* was about twenty-five feet long and ten feet wide at her widest. The single mast had a square mainsail that hung perpendicular to the boat, as well as a triangular spinnaker that joined the mast to the bow. This could be moved depending on which direction the wind was blowing. There was no cabin on deck, with the sleeping quarters and storage below. As the vessel began moving forward, Ryde took the wheel in one hand and continued to order Marlvon around.

Marlvon was happy to be told what to do, now confident in Ryde, and felt a sense of relief as the *Princess* separated from the dock. Ryde took them out into the sheltered water and, with the end of summer's slow-setting sun, easily made it through the gates before they were shut.

By the time the sun disappeared behind the horizon and the light faded, Marlvon was happy that they had escaped the clutches of Fort Kykum. He yelled out a whoop of joy and hugged Islonda. Only then did he realise just how tense he had been since leaving their hideaway on the rock ledge.

He looked deeply into Islonda's eyes and saw Islonda's love there. The stirring of emotions made him throw caution to the wind. 'Let's bring back Islonda and Marlvon.'

'I thought you'd never ask.' They made their way to a water barrel and washed the thick makeup off their faces. Marlvon felt as if he was reborn a youthful man and kissed Islonda vigorously.

'Aha, there's more to you two than meets the eye, it seems.' The gruff voice and deep bellied laugh of Ryde reminded them that they were not alone.

He is no danger to us now... and truth will serve better than lies with him. Marlvon turned to the captain and smiled ruefully. 'That there is.'

Darkness descended and the stars come out with a tiny slither of a moon. Ryde looked to the sky. 'Where are we headed, Mant? You're still yet to tell me.'

Marlvon asked Islonda to prepare a modest meal and went to join Ryde at the wheel. 'We're going to Headly. And you can call me Marlvon; that's my real name. And my fiancé is Islonda. Can you sail to Headly?'

'Aye, I've done that journey many times before.' The sailor looked pensive for a few moments before mumbling to himself. 'Marlvon, that name rings a bell.'

Marlvon said nothing; it didn't really matter if Ryde figured out who he was at this point. Ryde looked closely at his face. 'You look familiar. Have we met before?'

'No.' Marlvon stared out into the night, ignoring Ryde's close inspection of him.

Then it clicked for Ryde. 'Ah, you're the fugitive that the new leader Avgar and his dog Eyp are after. They're willing to pay handsomely for you.' He rubbed his chin. 'You need not fear, Marlvon. I have no love for Avgar... and Eyp. They ruined my life.'

Marlvon looked at Ryde, whose eye had glazed over in a painful memory. 'We share something in common then.' Ryde looked sadly at Marlvon. 'Those two have made me an outcast, but worse than that, they've made Islonda an outcast, killed her family and burnt her town to the ground.' Saying the words for the first time drove home the significance of the events of the last few weeks. 'That is why we are fleeing to Headly; we cannot live safely anywhere else.'

'The impact on our lives that Eyp has had seems to run side by side. Perhaps it was fate that brought us together.' Ryde sounded sad. 'Eyp killed my sister.'

'That's awful.' Marlvon sighed deeply. 'You can be assured; he will get his comeuppance.'

Ryde didn't seem to be listening and continued talking absently, as if addressing the night. 'He held her hostage to force me to deliver a shipment to Roasline. On my eventual return, after imprisonment, I found out that he had been raping her as he pleased. That was his downfall, for he was captured when he went to visit her. The captor did a nice piece of work on him too, but the damage to Prie was done and she later jumped from a window to her death to escape the memory. Eyp was meant to be executed, but he somehow escaped and returned on the coattails of this Avgar.' Ryde spat. 'Eyp! Curse you and all those you stand with.'

Marlvon's mind was racing with serendipity and he couldn't contain himself. 'Ryde, I know all of this; I was the man who found Eyp with Prie. I was the one who turned him over to Resvon.'

Ryde looked clearly into Marlvon's eyes. Without a word, he lent forward and gave the man a solid hug. 'Thank you.' He pulled away. 'Without you, Prie's suffering would have been far worse.' He clasped Marlvon on the shoulder. 'I am forever in your debt.'

Marlvon felt a sense of pride that he had been able to help out Prie, regardless of the ultimate outcome. 'There is no debt, Ryde.'

Both men were all of a sudden brought to attention by an unexpected noise. Marlvon looked down to find Islonda vomiting over the side of the boat. The vessel was rolling quite severely in the ocean swell. He nodded to Ryde and made his way over to Islonda to help her out.

When he got to her side, she spoke thickly. 'I didn't realise that boats rocked so much. This is horrible.' She vomited again.

'I should have warned you, but it wouldn't have stopped the seasickness. All you can do is put your face to the wind and look at the horizon.' He sat down next to her and held her comfortly as Ryde resolutely steered the *Wicked Princess* into the night.

34

Three nights passed before Ryde, Islonda and Marlvon approached Headly from the southwest. The journey had been rough and poor Islonda had drunk little, and eaten less. They came into a berth in the early afternoon, just as the wind was easing in strength. Marlvon watched with interest as they approached a pier that jutted into a calm bay. At the end of the pier, Marlvon saw a path that led to several buildings that were nestled in the crevice of two rolling hills. Next to the path was a friendly creek that entered the bay to the right of the pier. The only other vessel in sight was a small boat anchored away from the pier and two rowing boats dragged onto the small section of sandy beach. To Marlvon, it looked rather picturesque, and he could easily imagine living there.

They approached the pier and were greeted by a Healer in white. Marlvon threw him a rope and he secured the *Wicked Princess*. Ryde jumped ashore and Marlvon helped the weak Islonda out of the boat. Marlvon let Ryde make the introductions as he had dealt with the Healers many times before.

'Harlorn, good to see you again.' Ryde spoke gruffly.

'What business do you bring me today? Yourself? You look rough around the edges.'

Ryde laughed his deep bellied laugh. 'No, Harlorn. This is Marlvon and Islonda.' He waved them forward.

Harlorn looked them up and down. 'Do you have payment?' Marlvon nodded. 'You, Marlvon, you don't appear to be sick or injured. You cannot stay.' Marlvon was taken aback at the brashness, but Harlorn continued before he could respond. 'Islonda, you look dehydrated and on the edge of malnutrition.' He stepped forward and placed his hands on her shoulders with outstretched arms. He closed his eyes in concentration.

Marlvon watched in puzzlement as Harlon's head rocked slowly from side to side. A gust of wind swept across the bay and buffeted the four people. Then Harlorn's eyes snapped open. 'Aha.' He looked Islonda in the eyes searchingly and spoke to her gently. 'My dear, you will be with us for a while. There are three reasons for your stay. First; your acute state. That should be resolved in a few days with the right food, drink and rest. Second; you're acutely grieving, although I doubt if you've admitted it even to yourself. We can help you deal with this grief, but it will take time.' He then looked at her closely. 'Third, you're with child. Still a long way to go; six or seven months, I'd say. Did you know?'

Marlvon was frozen in disbelief as Islonda shook her head and started to fall to her knees. Harlorn caught her and helped her straighten.

Marlvon found his voice. 'You must be mistaken. How can you even know that from putting your hands on her shoulders?'

He took Islonda in his arms and held her close, not caring to hear Harlorn's answers. 'Islonda, I will stay with you and care for you. We will get married soon; once you've regained your strength.' It was bad luck to have a child out of wedlock.

The stern voice of Harlon cut Marlvon off. 'You won't be staying with Islonda. Headly is only for the sick and the Healers, no one else can reside here.'

Marlvon felt this statement like a punch in the stomach. Luckily, Harlon continued. 'However, this is an unusual situation. We haven't had a pregnant woman here for many years, and you clearly care for her. You may stay in your boat off shore as long as Islonda is a patient here. There's already one Outcast doing it, so why not two?' He mumbled this last sentence to himself in dissatisfaction. Harlorn waved two more Healers over who carried a stretcher. 'Islonda, please lie down. The walk to the town is not a short one for someone as weak as yourself.'

She obeyed without question and was taken away after Marlvon gave her many goodbye kisses.

Harlon stood in front of Marlvon and Ryde, blocking their way off the pier. 'You may visit her daily if you wish.' His eyes narrowed. 'Now, do you have payment for her stay?'

Marlvon handed over the required price and then something in his suspicious mind clicked. 'You mentioned that there was another Outcast staying on his boat.' He spoke as casually as he could. 'Who may that be?'

Harlon responded absentmindedly as he counted the coins from Marlvon. 'Someone who calls himself Eyp.' He looked up at the two men. For the second time since stepping onto the pier, Marlvon was hit with surprise. He was quick enough to hide his feelings before Harlon looked at him. Ryde was not so practiced and Marlvon almost had to close the sailor's jaw for him.

Harlorn spoke in an indifferent tone. 'You seem to know Eyp. Well, that's none of my business, be it welcome news or not.' He turned to go and paused. 'Ryde, you would do well to remember that the protection of the Healers extends to all at Headly, not just the Healers.' Ryde nodded and Harlon made his way back to the watch-house at the base of the pier.

Marlvon turned to Ryde, took him by the arm, and led him back to their boat. 'I know what you're thinking, but first tell me of the Healer's protection. Then we will discuss Eyp.'

Ryde looked at Marlvon with a broad grin on his face. 'Fate has been kind to us, my friend.'

'Ryde, what's the protection he spoke of?'

'No one can harm another while at Headly without feeling the effects themselves. If I were to stab you right here, I would receive the wound and die. *And*, no harm would come to you.'

Marlvon thought about that. *Ryde will want to kill Eyp, no question about that. How can he do that without dying himself?*

'Ryde, we need to think this through clearly.' He furrowed his brow. 'Will the protection reach Eyp on his boat?'

Ryde looked greedily at the small floating boat. 'No idea.'

Marlvon thought some more. 'What would the Healers do if they found out that you had killed Eyp?'

'Don't care.'

'Would the protection still have an effect if he was killed indirectly? Say if you burnt his boat with him on it?'

Ryde looked calculatingly at Marlvon as they boarded their boat. 'Good question, but I don't know the answer.'

Marlvon could see that there was going to be no way to stop Ryde from seeking revenge, even if it meant he would die in the process. The man seemed to be blind to reason. He thought some more and came up with a plan as Ryde untied the *Wicked Princess*.

Before setting sail, Marlvon sat Ryde down and spoke slowly. 'Ryde, if you hear me out, I think we can give you the best chance of success with as little risk to yourself as possible.' Marlvon divulged his plan to Ryde, in slow, deliberate detail.

They set sail and Ryde steered the *Wicked Princess* directly further offshore than Eyp's boat; so, when the Healers looked out, they would see Eyp's vessel and the *Princess* behind her. He positioned their ship about a hundred yards further out to sea than Eyp's. Then they waited below deck for nightfall.

The night came and the two men ate a cold meal and prepared themselves for what lay ahead. They had watched sneakily at dusk when Eyp had returned to his boat with the help of one of the Healer's row boats. This he left tied to the side of his boat.

Marlvon and Ryde waited until the night had well progressed before enacting the next step of their plan. They stripped down to their undergarments and tied sharp knives to their legs. They filled two jars with spare lamp oil and tied these to a rope with the other end attached to their waists.

When ready, they eased themselves slowly into the cool water and began swimming slowly towards Eyp's boat. If anyone had looked from the shore with the eyes of an owl, the two swimmers would have been hidden behind the boat.

When they reached the vessel, they climbed quietly on board. They were concerned that the rocking from them clambering into the boat would alert Eyp, but they instantly saw Eyp sleeping soundly on his back under a thin blanket.

Marlvon felt disgust at seeing Eyp again and had to supress his emotions to get the job done. With lightning speed, the two attacked Eyp before he knew what was happening. Marlvon pinned down his arms, while Ryde looped a rope around his neck and then gagged him with a rag. The big man fought viciously and Ryde had to hit him on the head with an oar before he was subdued. Marlvon did not fail to notice that Eyp was not covered by the Healer's protection. Ryde, it seemed, did not register this.

They had him tied in the bottom of the boat before either of the two attackers spoke, and it was Marlvon who broke the silence. 'Remember me, Eyp? The last time you saw me, you lost your balls. What will you lose tonight, I wonder?'

Ryde stepped forward so that Eyp could make him out in the low light. 'Hello, Eyp.' The captured man's eyes widened in fear. 'Oh yes, it is old Ryde and I'm here to exact my revenge.' Without further comment, Ryde hit Eyp across the jaw. If they were on the land of Headly, Ryde would have been knocked clean over with a broken jaw, but they were not.

He looked at Marlvon. 'It looks as though the protection doesn't extend into the bay. Too bad for Eyp.'

'Ryde, I want this done quick and cleanly. I don't want a repeat escape like last time.'

Ryde conceded. 'All right, all right. Just a few quick cuts and then we'll finish him off.'

Ryde turned back to Eyp and quickly stabbed him in the eye with his knife. He held his blade ready for another attack, but Marlvon could see an internal battle going on within Ryde. He sighed audibly and turned to Marlvon. 'I'm ready now; I don't have the stomach for this kind of thing.'

Marlvon nodded. He rummaged around in the boat and found what he was looking for: something heavier than water, in this case a jewelled scabbard with a long sword inside. He tied this around Eyp's feet and, with the aid of Ryde, they sat the thrashing man on the edge of his boat.

Ryde had the last words to say to Eyp and he spat them out in mockery. 'Enjoy your swim.' They shoved the big man overboard and watched as he disappeared into the black water. Marlvon then poured their lamp oil on the deck of the boat and instructed Ryde to start swimming back. He brought forth his flint and sent a shower of sparks into the oil. The slow burning oil took immediately and Marlvon dived into the water and started the swim back to their boat. The two would be ready to act innocently if woken, should the Healers come looking for witnesses. As Marlvon swam, he felt the familiar self-loathing that came with violence and had to force the thoughts from his mind. Instead, he thought of Islonda and how soon he would be a father to her child.

Three days passed without suspicion being thrown the way of Marlvon and Ryde. Marlvon had been able to visit Islonda daily, and she was recovering remarkably well. Her cheeks were less hollow and she was laughing at Marlvon's poor jokes again.

It was one such time that he was visiting her and talking about how they would marry in the coming days, when five Healers entered the room.

'My name is Lyafe and I'm in charge of the Healers.' He pointed at Marlvon. 'You will say your goodbyes to Islonda now and leave Headly forever. You are not permitted to remain in the bay and you are not welcome ashore ever again.'

Marlvon was taken aback, but instantly knew what had triggered this eviction. 'Why? Have I done something wrong?'

'You know very well what you and Ryde have done. You have broken the law of life and killed another.'

Marlvon hung his head in shame. Then he had a thought. 'You can't make me leave. The protection will stop you hurting me.'

'Don't be stupid. We may not stab you or anything like that, but there are more of us and we can force you into the ocean where you will drown. Remember, you cannot retaliate without harming yourself. And if you tried to remain in the bay, we will make sure that your boat will sink.'

Marlvon detected true venom in Lyafe's voice and knew that he had lost. His thoughts turned to Islonda and his heart pained at the prospect of leaving her. He leant over and hugged her tightly to him. 'I love you so much. I will get word to you of where I am and send a boat for you once the baby is born.'

Islonda was crying freely. 'Let me come. I don't need to stay here; I'll be fine with you.'

Marlvon shook his head. 'There is nowhere safe for us now, and I do not want to put you or our baby at risk. You will stay, and in a few months, I'll see you again.'

Despite his heart's desire, Marlvon pulled apart from Islonda's clinging hug and said his farewells. The Healers escorted him to his boat and, together with Ryde, they set sail to nowhere in particular.

35

Burban had been working as the woman in charge of the kitchens in Fort Kykum for five years. She was efficient at what she did and led with an authoritative sternness. Those who worked under her knew her boundaries and knew not to cross them. If they were foolish to test her, they would find themselves punished or out of a job. She had little experience cooking, but knew how to handle people and get them to work for her. The staff admired her and respected her, but would never be friends with her. That was exactly how she liked it.

Those who were in charge of the running of the keep knew all of this and had learnt to rely on her unquestioningly. What they didn't know about Burban was that she was a clandestine agent who worked for Roasline. She had lived in the city of Fort Kykum for the past twenty years, in different clandestine roles, but it wasn't until she secured the job in the kitchens that she really showed her worth to the High Chancellor of Roasline.

The busy kitchens were the perfect place to gather information of the happenings at the Fort and she had an uncanny skill for instinctively being able to differentiate rumour from fact. This, combined with the ability to selectively hear the conversations she wanted from amongst the humdrum in the kitchen, served her well.

Getting the information was one thing, but the efficient Burban had also developed channels to pass her knowledge across the Liagar to Roasline. These methods were secure, even if they were much slower than Burban would have liked.

Ever since the coming of Avgar, Burban's channels had been working overtime with news of the new Leader. When he was dispatched, Nigrath, Qyunt and Veltrene began plotting and planning in earnest. But it wasn't until one steamy evening in the kitchens that Burban heard a rumour from a young serving boy that she realised that her time-consuming communication channels would not be fast enough.

Her usual ability to make quick decisions was waylaid, as she dithered whether to go herself or trust another in her stead. If *she* went, then she could ensure that the message would be delivered accurately and safely. If she sent another, then she could stay to gather more information. The choice was a hard one.

Burban looked about the kitchen, weighing up her options. She ignored the smells of leek soup, freshly baked bread and raw meat being beaten, and closed her eyes. A cacophony of noise edged into her thoughts and she finally made up her mind: she would beg leave for a week to care for her sick mother and then return to the kitchens once back from Roasline.

The thin woman sought her superior and begged leave from the tall man. He grudgingly granted it based on her five years of excellent service. Burban felt an excitement lift her usual calm demeanour as she realised the impact that her message would have on the fortunes of thousands of people, provided she could get to Roasline safely.

After being granted her leave, she made her way back to the busy kitchens. It wasn't long before she was able to leave and escape into the cool night air. She made her way home to change out of her work clothes and into a nondescript dark outfit. She donned comfortable soft leather boots and packed a small hamper of food. Before leaving, she pulled an olive-coloured scarf over her head to complete her outfit.

Burban left the walled city of Fort Kykum by the most direct route. She took wide streets to get to the main gate and only walked where there were crowds. Even at her age, she didn't trust the people of Kykum to leave her alone at night.

After leaving the city, she took the fork in the road that would have led to Bankton; the other road making its long way to Nivera. She walked with quick steps and long strides down the gentle slope of the road.

Clouds pushed across the sky and Burban found the darkness deepening. She walked for a good mile out of Kykum before turning off the road and making her way across farmed fields and small hills towards the Liagar. By midnight, she could hear the river flowing swiftly past reedy shores. She neared the edge and then slowed to a careful walk. In the dark, it was hard to see where she was going and the last thing she wanted was to fall down a steep incline into the powerful river.

Burban followed the river upstream and away from Fort Kykum. She knew she would sooner or later come across a boat of some sort. The farmers along the shoreline often went fishing in the river to supplement their sporadic income with a free meal.

It was about two miles further upstream that Burban found what she was looking for. The boat was tied to an old jetty and bobbed up and down in the current. The thinning cloud cover permitted a soft light, which allowed the slender lady to see well enough. She made her way to the boat at the end of the jetty and checked that there were oars inside. She smiled to herself and climbed into the boat. She took a moment to balance herself and then untied the simple knot. *These farmers are much more trusting than I am.*

She pushed off from the jetty and, with her back to the dark distant shoreline, started to row. Burban was not used to the arm work and it wasn't long before her shoulders ached. But she didn't rest and ensured that she remained calculatingly calm. She knew that if she took too long to cross the Liagar, she would be washed out to sea. No, that wouldn't do. If she rowed consistently, she knew she should be able to reach the further bank before that happened.

She progressed steadily across the expanse, but when she was a few hundred yards off her destination, a small naval patrol boat appeared out of nowhere. She looked at it warily, trying to discern what flags it was flying. The vessel, that was much larger than her own with four cannons protruding down each side, grew ominously in the darkness.

Burban stopped rowing and instead allowed the ship to come to her; rubbing her arms to get some strength back into them. As the boat came alongside her, she was hailed by who she assumed was their captain.

'You're going to be boarded. Do not try to flee or you will be fired upon.'

Burban thought that the threat was a bit over the top; her boat was a tiny two person dingy; there was nowhere that she could flee to. Regardless, she sat there and waited. A rope ladder was dropped into her boat and a burley looking sailor climbed down with a sword by his side. He jumped the last few rungs and twisted in mid-air. He landed and drew his sword without losing his balance. Burban was impressed with his skill, but she was less impressed when he pointed the sword tip to her neck. She raised her hands in a sign of surrender and smiled to herself as she saw he was wearing the blue sash of Roasline's navy.

The sailor told her to climb up the ladder and she did without question. She reached the top and was roughly shoved in the back. Her hands were tied behind her without hesitation and she was made to kneel in front of the ship's captain.

'My name is Captain Reeva.' He spoke cleanly while he looked down at Burban, a mild look of puzzlement on his face. 'What is a woman doing all alone in a boat in the middle of the Liagar?'

This was Burban's chance. She knew that the next few moments would decide her fate. She looked at Reeva directly. 'The stars are shining brightly tonight.' She spoke the first line of a code that only clandestine agents used. This code was taught to all the captains of the navy and army and required a very precise two-way conversation.

Reeva's eyes narrowed as he looked at Burban more intensely. 'They do, but not as brightly as the moon.'

'The stars always shine the brightest over Roasline.'

'And the moon casts her shadow over the Outcasts.'

'May the clouds not obscure the stars in the nights to come.'

'And may the moon shine brightly down upon Roasline.' Reeva looked at Burban's guards. 'Bring this prisoner to my cabin.'

Burban was hauled to her feet and an inkling of concern spread through her as she wondered why the captain had not released her.

A few moments, later she was alone with Reeva in his cabin. He walked around her without talking, and she felt him come close up behind her. She felt pressure on her wrists and a moment later, her hands were free from the restraints.

Reeva walked back around in front of her. 'We can't be too careful in front of my crew. All sorts of riffraff get accepted into the navy these days.' Reeva smiled warmly. 'Now, what is your name and how can I help you?'

'My name is Burban. It relieves me to find a captain well versed in the passcodes.' She smiled at him. 'I have information that the High Chancellor needs to hear. It is vital and time is short.'

Reeva rubbed his clean-shaven chin. 'My orders are to patrol the Liagar for another three days. Perhaps if you told me what the information is, then I can see if I'm happy to break my orders and ferry you to Roasline.'

Burban looked at him as sternly as if he were a child caught stealing. 'This information is for the High Chancellor and the Council only. If you will not help me, then I will get back in my boat and row the rest of the way.'

Burban watched as the captain looked her up and down as if assessing her character. He sighed and walked around his desk and faced her with his hands on the desktop. 'At least give me something. If I break my orders I could be stripped of my captaincy, or worse.'

'You won't. I will see that you are rewarded rather than punished.'

'How do I know that what you say is true; how can I trust you?'

Burban glared at him. 'The passcodes prove I am trustworthy.' She folded her arms across her chest. 'Don't you have superseding orders to help all clandestine agents if requested?' Burban hoped that this was still the protocol.

Reeva clenched his teeth. 'Under the old Admiral, yes, but under Admiral Tunley... it's hard to say. He's not a man who likes the sneaking and snooping that your kind do. He prefers things to be done boldly and openly. Or so he says.'

Burban considered her position for a moment before speaking. 'All I can say is that if the information doesn't reach the High Chancellor soon, then many citizens of Roasline will die. Now, Captain Reeva, how about you take that bottle of rum out of your drawer and share a drink with me while we journey back to Roasline?'

Reeva smiled wryly. 'I don't suppose I really have a choice, do I?'

The captain walked to the door and called out for his first mate to take them back to Roasline. Burban felt herself relax, only just realising that she was tense.

Reeva returned and did as Burban had instructed. They each had a small glass of straight rum, neither flinching at the harshness of the cheap, strong drink. Then, under mutual agreement, Burban's handcuffs were re-fastened and she was shown to a cell for the time it would take to reach Roasline.

When they arrived at their destination, Burban remained a pretend prisoner for the show of the crew and others who might see her. A bag was put over her head at Burban's request in an effort to remain unrecognisable. She bore this hardship easily and was taken to the dungeons underneath the citadel of Roasline. There she waited for a longer time that she would have liked.

When Burban eventually heard the clanging of keys, she stood to attention and awaited the High Chancellor. Her heart dropped to her stomach when instead of Kathsum, Admiral Tunley came to her cell.

The Admiral had an arrogant air about him and Burban found him ugly to look at. She tried to conceal her thoughts as he made his way to the bars of her cell and leaned casually against them. She felt Tunley's eyes examining her from head to foot and she felt dirty.

When he spoke, his voice was blunt and dominating. 'Who are you?'

'The stars are shining brightly tonight.' Burban tried the passcodes.

'Enough of that. Reeva reported that you know the passcodes. He also said that you had important information for the High Chancellor. But first, I asked who you are?'

'Burban.' She wanted to keep her answers short.

'Never heard of you. But then, that's probably not your real name anyway.' Tunley looked closely at her face. 'What information do you have for the High Chancellor?'

Burban straightened her back. 'That information is for the High Chancellor.'

'Burban, you have a choice before you. You can either tell me, a member of Roasline's Council, the information that you know, or I can walk away and you never leave this cell. You see, I have no idea if I can trust you or your information. For all I know, you could have tortured the passcodes out of someone to gain access to the High Chancellor.'

'If you tell the High Chancellor who I am, she will want to see me.'

'Again, just words, just shadows. I need proof.'

'You know I cannot give you proof.' Burban felt her heart sink. 'I am honourable and trustworthy. I risk my life every single day to pass information to the High Chancellor.' Burban felt a wave of frustration. 'Who do you think it was that told you about Avgar replacing Resvon, and that he claimed the kill as his own? Who passed the information that Avgar had been usurped by Quynt, Veltrene and Nigrath? It was me who told you these things. It was me who told you that Avgar's body hadn't been found and that he might be alive somewhere. I am your source of the most important information from the Outcasts. I am your channel to the leadership of the Outcasts. Don't you dare question my trustworthiness.'

Tunley grinned and Burban seethed as she realised he had complete control of the situation. She felt uncharacteristically flustered and forced herself to calm down by taking a few deep breaths.

Tunley's tone portrayed that he knew that he had the upper hand in the encounter. 'That may be, or it may not be. Either way, your choice still remains: to tell me what you know or rot in this cell.'

Burban closed her eyes for a moment and acknowledged that she had no other option but to tell the disgusting man what she knew and hoped he would use the information well. 'I will tell you, but you must promise to release me, so that I can return to Kykum to maintain my cover in the kitchens of the Fort.'

Tunley nodded. 'Go on.'

'The new leaders are planning a direct attack on Roasline.' Burban felt a mild sense of satisfaction to see that Tunley had not been expecting this. 'Each of the leaders will organise a simultaneous attack at the next full moon. Quynt will lead his men down the Liagar in small boats to land west of Roasline. Veltrene will lead a force from Nivera down the coast to land south east of Roasline and Nigrath will enter the Liagar from the Rogaus and hit Roasline directly from the river.' Burban paused as she thought about the implications of the three-pronged attack. 'Roasline will be surrounded. You must tell this to the High Chancellor immediately. There are only twenty-five days until the next full moon. Admiral, I beg you, for the sake of the people of Roasline, do this as soon as you can.'

'How can you be sure of this? What are your sources?'

'My sources can be trusted.' She didn't want to tell him that the bulk of the information had come from a twelve-year-old boy who had poured wine at the table of the leaders. 'I would not be here if the information was not solid.'

The Admiral's face was a blank mask that Burban was unable to read. When he spoke, it was in a monotone. 'I will consider all that you have said. Tonight, Reeva will come and take you back on his boat and see you safely across the Liagar.' He turned and Burban watched as the ugly man left her alone once more.

Burban breathed out her tension and sat down in the cell. She closed her eyes and let her mind wash to numbness in a half-sleep body-rest, hoping that Tunley believed her and was a man of his word.

❧

Admiral Tunley emerged from the dungeons after visiting the so called Burban. She had made some outlandish claims about the enemy's plans, but for some reason, he couldn't help but feel that she was telling the truth. He breathed in the dawn air deeply and smiled inwardly. *This is my time to shine; I will prove myself.*

The Admiral ordered a runner to go to the docks and summon any captains or ship masters that could be found to come to his office in the citadel. He sent a second messenger to call all the council members to an urgent meeting. After these had been dispatched, he made his way to the council chambers while working through his plan to defend the city, as well as how to manage the council members.

He arrived at the chambers and had plenty of time to pace back and forth until the other members slowly filed in. He spoke little more than a greeting to the Alderman of Merchants and the Alderwoman of Producers. The Farmer's Guild was yet to appoint a new Alderman. When the General arrived, Tunley pulled him aside and whispered hurriedly of the news and the action he would immediately take. The General listened intently. The Quaestor and the Head of Order entered together, engrossed in conversation, and Tunley greeted the High Chancellor respectfully when she arrived last of all. The Council seated themselves promptly and waited in silence for a moment before Tunley stood.

'I have called this urgent meeting of the council as I have received intelligence that Roasline will shortly be confronted by a significant threat.' Tunley looked about the room and saw a mixture of reactions on the faces looking up at him. He savoured the sweet moment of knowing more than everyone else in the room, especially the High Chancellor. 'The Outcasts will attack us outright at the next full moon; in twenty-five days' time.' He let the information sink in and noted that Kathsum was the quickest to recover from the shock.

'How can you be certain? Who is your source?'

Tunley also noticed she didn't dispute the possibility, but rather wanted to validate it.

'My sources are my own, but I give you my word that I speak the truth.' Tunley put his faith not in Burban, but in his instincts that she was right.

The Alderman of Merchants spoke hurriedly and with a quaver of fear in his voice. 'You're making this up. You just want more power. I don't believe you.' He folded his arms.

Tunley ignored this interruption and continued his report. 'They will attack in a complicated manoeuvre that I have already started to put measures in place to stop. I will work with the General and the Head of Order to prepare the defences as necessary.'

The High Chancellor cut in. 'I will join you.'

'So be it, but I will be in command until this threat is dealt with. It is important to have a clear line of authority and a military minded man in charge.' He nodded to the General, knowing he had the numbers if it came to a vote. 'The General has agreed that this is the best course of action. Now, if no one else has anything else to add, we will begin immediately in my office.' Tunley could see the dissatisfaction in Kathsum's face, and he smiled inwardly. *This is my time to lead, Kathsum, and it will be you who will be following the orders.* Without waiting for a response, he strode from the room and made his way to his office, where he would be in complete control.

Over the following weeks, Admiral Tunley was busy. He precisely positioned his fleet and the General's army on a detailed map and moved the pieces to and fro to help him devise the best possible battle strategy. As well as this, he oversaw the deployment of the army and the defences of the city.

Kathsum had been an annoyance on the first day of planning, but then the cunning Tunley had the idea to put her in charge of ensuring their plans and knowledge remained as secretive as possible. He knew that this would be extremely difficult and should they fail, he would use her as a scapegoat.

Despite being busy, to the excited Admiral the full moon seemed to take an age to arrive. Then, finally, dusk fell and Tunley knew that there was nothing he could do until the first news of battle came to him.

Summer had long finished and the mid-Autumn night was cold and windy. High scattered clouds raced across the sky from east to west, diffusing the full moon's brightness. The seas would be choppy and sailing conditions for the Outcasts challenging. Admiral Tunley knew this and rubbed his hands together at his good fortune.

Tunley had fluctuated where he should be on this fateful night and in the end had chosen to remain in his office, now his command centre, instead of going to the front line. At the command centre, he would be ready to respond to messages that came while remaining safe from harm. Not that he would admit that to anyone.

The night deepened, and after pacing for a while, the portly man sat down at his desk and poured himself a strong red wine to calm his taut nerves. He drank that quickly, then poured another and stood to look out of the open window. The city of Roasline lay before him and a silence rested over her that reflected the tense occasion.

The Admiral was considering whether to close the window or not, to keep out the wind, when he heard the first cannon boom. It sounded distant in the wind and came from up the Liagar. Tunley laughed as a dozen other cannons started their chorus.

The happy man spoke sternly to the night, ignoring those behind him. 'Let the bastards come. We will slaughter them like lambs.'

More cannons soon fired, but from the mouth of the Liagar, and then further south-east of Roasline. *Right, all three battles are underway. I do wish I was there, in the thick of it, but if I was lost, the navy and Roasline would have no hope.* He sighed and continued to watch out the window, waiting for the first messenger to arrive with news.

It was past midnight before a messenger arrived at the command centre. He was a young sailor with a dirty uniform, but held himself with pride. Tunley called him over, eager for his news.

'Admiral, sir, the enemy came down the Liagar just as night was falling. They were in small boats holding no more than twenty men each. As instructed, we had positioned the commandeered fishing boats to line the shore of the river to stop them landing. This worked perfectly. They were forced further downstream where they landed, just where you said they would.' The sailor swallowed nervously. 'They were forced to wade through thick mud before facing a climb up a hill. When they were half landed and making their way up the hill, our waiting ships sailed upstream and opened fire on the men still in their boats. Then the General's cannons fired down the hill into the massing soldiers.' His face blanched at the memory. 'Trapped, they had nowhere to go and many died in the muddy shallows. The General's cannons then stopped and a wave of our soldiers came down the hill in a tight formation. It was a glorious slaughter, Admiral. Those of the enemy who had made land didn't last long and many of those in the boats drowned.' Tunley saw his eyes twitch. 'There were, however, some who escaped back upstream and our ships couldn't reach them for the wreckage of boat and man was clogging up the river. Admiral, it was a perfect plan and well executed.'

Admiral Tunley felt his chest swell with pride and satisfaction. 'Thank you, sailor. Did we lose many men?'

'I was sent here before the count was done, but we lost no ship and few men, it seemed.'

Tunley nodded. 'Good, good. You are dismissed for the remainder of the night. In the morning, report to your commanding officer.'

'Aye aye, sir.' The sailor left appearing relieved with his head held high.

Tunley turned back to the river. *One down, two to go.*

The night passed and it wasn't until first light that the next messenger found Tunley resting in his desk chair. Everyone else in the room had found a place to sleep, but Tunley refused to give in; this night was far too important to sleep.

The messenger sailor that came was short and had the face of a rat. He had speckles of blood down his front, but was not wounded himself. When he entered, Tunley sat up straight and beckoned him over.

The Admiral's throat was dry and he croaked out his order. 'Report.'

'Sir, your instructions had been followed and the delta was clogged with our naval and merchant ships. The enemy's first wave came with great speed out of the night. They rammed us, but with their smaller vessels, we come out on top. Our other ships from the Rogaus closed in behind them to spring the trap. Alas, the spineless Outcasts were too quick and on seeing our comrades, fled back up the coast. Our ships gave chase, but the enemy sailed too swiftly and too close to Kykum for our armada to follow. They lost a dozen ships in their initial wave, and a further two more trying to escape. We lost five, with another three in dire need of repairs. The Outcasts were stopped well before reaching our shores.'

Tunley felt a mixture of success and failure at this news. *If only we could have trapped them all.* 'Thank you, sailor. You will report back that all ships in need of repair should be docked and repairs begun immediately. All other ships shall remain in the delta in readiness for a second assault.'

'Aye, sir.' The rat-faced sailor nodded and left.

Tunley stood to stretch his legs and watched the light spread across Roasline.

The large man couldn't fight the need for sleep any longer and slept in his chair, snoring loudly. Others in his office had risen and were breaking their fast in the late morning with freshly baked bread.

A third messenger arrived with bags under his eyes and stubble on his face. He had the unfortunate task of waking the Admiral and was greeted with a grunt and a curse.

Tunley composed himself quickly once he realised the reason for him being woken. He poured himself a cup of water and looked the man up and down.

'Well, out with it.' The gruff words hid his excitement at the anticipation of the news he was about to hear.

'Admiral, sir, the Outcasts came at us swiftly with their largest ships. They made a pass at us before sailing out of range. They made two more passes, each closer than the previous. The air was thick with the smoke of cannon powder before they managed to sink one of our ships. By then, six of our ships had circled around behind them in the darkness and we pressed from both sides. We sunk a handful of their slower boats before they ran for cover. Our fastest vessels pursued them and picked off three more of their damaged ships just before dawn. One of these was the command ship. While this was all taking place, two of their smaller ships broke away and made for land. I'd guess they landed about a hundred miles from Roasline. We sent fire signals to the army and it was not long before they signalled back that the Outcasts had been disposed of. We were victorious, Admiral.'

Tunley felt an overwhelming happiness sweep through him and he shook his fist in excitement. 'You bring good news, sailor.' He grinned. 'You are released from your duties for the remainder of the day. Go and get something from the kitchens to eat and drink. But before you do that, fetch the High Chancellor from her house and instruct her to come here.'

'Yes, sir.' The sailor smiled and went to complete the task given to him by the fearsome Admiral Tunley.

The cunning man paced the room with his chest puffed out as everyone in the room came and congratulated him. He brushed them aside, eagerly awaiting Kathsum's arrival.

Tunley didn't have to wait long before the High Chancellor burst into the room, grinning. Tunley thought to himself. *You really only see this as a victory for Roasline. Fool.*

'Admiral, I have heard the good news; we've won.'

'Yes, we have. It was a good plan, well executed.' Tunley replied.

Kathsum made her way over to him so that they could talk more privately. 'Well done Admiral. I may not be your biggest supporter, but I can recognise strong leadership with a swift and decisive action plan. Today, Roasline is in your debt.'

The attentive Admiral noticed a hint of sadness in the High Chancellor's voice and that almost made him happier than her previous sentiment. Before he could respond, Kathsum continued. 'Two days from now, we will hold a day of celebration throughout Roasline to celebrate our victory. You will be a prominent figure on that day.'

This is getting better with every sentence that she speaks. 'High Chancellor, I thank you for your kind words. If you would allow me to continue my strong leadership, I would encourage us to attack the Outcasts now. They will be weakened from their foolish foray into our territory and on the back foot. Now is the perfect time to strike.' The Admiral could see that Kathsum was hesitant, even before he had finished speaking.

'Now is not the time for this talk. We should think of peace, not more war. We have defended ourselves perfectly. Now is the time to negotiate generous peace terms with the Outcasts.'

Tunley felt frustration bubbling within him, but didn't want Kathsum to see that; she had already played into his hand by the forthcoming public acknowledgement of his involvement in the victory and he didn't want her to retract her unexpected support of him.

He smiled kindly at her. 'Perhaps we could discuss this further with the council on the morrow, High Chancellor.'

She smiled back. 'Yes. I think we can do that.' She straightened her ruffled dress. 'It has been a long night, Admiral. I am tired and in need of sleep. I will leave you to celebrate how you will, but please ensure that the city is secure before you do so.'

'You can trust me, High Chancellor.' They nodded to each other and Kathsum left the proud Admiral in his office, already hatching the next part of his plan.

36

Avgar sat in a wooden chair by his bed, trying to read the third book that Lyafe had given him. It was late in the afternoon and he was trying hard, but not having much success. He could see the words and pictures on the pages, but could make no sense of them. This inability to read had occurred several times over the last few days. At first, Avgar put it down to not having read a book since he was a young man, but when it persisted, he realised it must be something else.

The sick man gave up his attempt in frustration and put the book down. He closed his eyes and felt another sweating episode coming on. These too had been happening periodically since he woke seven days prior, although they seemed to be reducing in frequency. Lyafe explained the many reasons that these might be happening, but the one that Avgar knew to be true was the withdrawal of his herbal cocktail that he had been using to ease his sleeping.

He was acutely aware that on Headly he had no access to his hallucinogenic mixture or smoking herb. As Avgar's health slowly improved from the poisoning, and his sleeping habits began to return to normal, he longed for his herbs. On top of the sweats, he found himself getting frustrated and angry at inappropriate moments. This, coupled with the return of his nightmares, put him in a foul mood for most of the time. It was only when he was reading about the body, or Lyafe was talking to him, that he managed to be distracted enough to be content. So, he listened to Lyafe and encouraged him to stay as long as he could.

During the time that the Healer Supreme was absent, Avgar devoured the books about bones, blood, tendons and energy meridians. Then, when the reading block came, he stooped into a muddy mood; brooding on his loss of speech, his missing right hand, his nightmares and his inability to make it through the night without wetting himself.

He was in one such mood when Lyafe brought him a plate of bread and cheese for dinner. Avgar pretended not to notice the Healer Supreme as the food was placed on the table next to him. Avgar had a sense that Lyafe knew exactly what he was thinking and so the Healer came and stood directly in front of Avgar.

'I see you're in one of your moods again.'

Avgar stared at him with anger. *If only I could trade his life for my health.*

Lyafe pulled up a chair facing Avgar. 'Lucky for you, I do not have anything pressing to attend to, so we can have a little chat.'

Avgar instinctively wanted Lyafe to leave him to his brooding, but knew deep down that the Healer would drag him out of his depressed mood.

'I hear that you're still wetting your bed, but have gained control over your bowels. That is good progress and you should be happy. Regardless, I'm sure that you would like to start waking up dry.'

Avgar averted Lyafe's gaze and nodded his head.

'I muse that this is a hangover of your poisoning, but can't be certain of that. Whatever is the cause, I think that you have the power to change it. When you're going to sleep, Avgar, I want you to try and think of healing your bladder. That's where our urine is stored.'

To Avgar's surprise, Lyafe pulled a wobbly bag type object from his pocket and gave it to Avgar.

'This is a bladder,' the Healer stated as a matter of fact.

Avgar forgot the foul mood that he was meant to be in and raised his eyebrows at Lyafe.

The Healer laughed. 'It's not from a person, but from a pig. But the concept is the same. Our body fills up this bag and when it is full, we need to urinate. The urine comes out of this tube.'

Avgar inspected the pig's bladder closely.

'Your bladder appears to be releasing your urine when you don't want it to. So, from tonight, when you're going to sleep, picture this bladder and imagine the urine tube as closed. See if you can invoke that special power that kept you alive when you were poisoned to help. Do you think you can do that?'

Avgar nodded. *There's no harm in trying.*

'Good.' Lyafe sat back in his chair and picked up the book that Avgar had been trying to read. 'Making good progress, I see.' He flicked through the pages nostalgically. 'When you've finished this one, I have a most interesting one on different herbs and plants that can be used to aid healing.'

He put the book down. 'Marvellous, aren't they? Books. They contain so much information that can be read by anyone who knows how to. And they last… unlike the authors. This one was written before I was born, by a Healer who had a particular interest in the energy that flows through our meridians. He was able to pass his knowledge on to so many other Healers, even though he couldn't talk.'

Avgar looked at Lyafe with interest. *But I can't write either.*

'But you won't have that problem, because I have faith that you can heal your throat.'

Avgar felt Lyafe turn an intense gaze on to him. 'You do want to be able to speak again, don't you?'

Damn you, of course I do! He nodded earnestly.

Lyafe appeared to relax a bit. 'Show me your arm stump.'

Avgar obliged.

Lyafe mumbled under his breath. 'Interesting.' He pressed it gently and watched the white depression turn back to pink. 'This wound is not yet a year old and more likely only a few months old.' He looked up at Avgar. 'You seem to have adapted very well to using only your nondominant hand. Does this still cause you pain?'

Avgar nodded. *I have learnt to ignore it.*

'Hhhmmm, ok.' Lyafe let go of Avgar's arm and stood. 'Tomorrow morning, I will come here and we will try to go for a short walk outside. The sunlight and wind will help with your recovery. Goodbye for now.' Lyafe turned and left Avgar to eat his meal.

Only when the food was gone did Avgar realise his mood was lifted and that the prospect of going outside tickled an inclining of excitement within him.

Avgar ate his breakfast with a smile on his face. He had not wet himself overnight and soon Lyafe would be taking him outside. He finished eating his porridge and waited impatiently on the side of his bed.

He had to wait just long enough that he was wondering if Lyafe would come at all, when the Healer Supreme walked into the room holding a pair of simple sandals. 'Good morning, Avgar. I can see that you're eager to go; that is good.' He gave the sandals to Avgar to put on.

Avgar was thrilled to be leaving the room that he had spent longer than he would have liked in, but as he reached the door, he realised all too soon that he was still gravely unwell. His legs felt weak and his breath short. He tried to mask this as the pair made their way into the morning sun and along a paved road up a gentle hill. He looked at Lyafe and knew instantly that the Healer had noticed Avgar's weakness, but didn't offer to help.

Avgar soon had to stop to catch his breath and give his legs a break. Each time they started again, he felt his weakness and realised that it would not be long before he would need to stop once more. Each time he was forced to rest, his mood dropped a notch. He desperately wanted to know how much further they were going to walk, but even if he could speak, his pride would not have allowed him to ask.

Lyafe had remained uncharacteristically quiet until the fourth time that Avgar had to stop. When he spoke, it was with unjudging compassion. 'It's hard, isn't it? Your muscles are still recovering from the poison and I think it will take many weeks before they will be as strong as they used to be. As for now, we are in no hurry to get to our destination, and it will be worth the effort once we get there. It is only a little distance further, but there is a steep section just ahead. If you need, you can lean on me for that part.'

I will not do that. In response to the Healer, Avgar started walking again with renewed determination. They rounded a corner and Avgar could see what he guessed was their destination; a small hill clear of buildings and plants.

It took him three more stops to reach the hilltop, but he managed it without leaning on Lyafe. When they got there, the path led over the crest of the rise and ended on the side facing the ocean. Lyafe instructed Avgar to sit on the grass and he did so without question; his legs were exhausted and he was gasping for breath.

When Avgar had finally recomposed himself, he looked into the wind at the view before him. He was sitting on the left side of a gentle valley where the healing township of Headly was nestled. A river ran through the centre of it, which entered the ocean at a pleasant-looking beach. From where he sat, the sand appeared yellow and had small waves breaking on the shore that he could just hear. A pier jutted into the ocean a decent way and there were presently no boats moored to it.

Then he beheld the vastness of the Rogaus. Sparkling brilliant blue and stretching as far as his eyes could see, just to look at it made him smile. This was not the first time that he had seen the ocean in her fullness, but for some reason, at that moment, he sensed her vastness. He felt both important and insignificant in the one moment. He looked down at his arm stump and thought of his lost voice, and for the first time in his life, realised that he was just a mortal man; present only for a fleeting blink of an eye in all eternity.

Time seemed to warp for Avgar and he didn't know how long he sat there before Lyafe broke the silence. 'We are all guests on this great earth. It is a privilege to be here and each of us must decide what kind of guest we want to be.'

Avgar had always wanted to be a *guest* that led people, made a difference, and left a legacy behind. He had tried to do that his whole life. *What kind of legacy have I left? What kind of difference have I made?*

Lyafe continued to speak gently and was just audible over the constant wind. 'See those buildings down there, Avgar? Many of those are filled with men who have been wounded in war. Most will live, but many will be maimed for life. They will go home to their families and be unable to provide for them as young men should. And do you know what they were fighting over? Land, land for their leaders, not for themselves. What will they get out of war? Nothing but pain and suffering. Even those who remain unharmed will not profit; they won't be given any more land or silver or any other payment. No, they will experience the trauma of war and then go home to live out their lives in anguish.' Lyafe trailed off, clearly feeling passionately about this topic.

'You were a brief leader of the Outcasts. What would you have done if you were not poisoned? Would you have continued the peace that was brokered, or would you have thrown everyone back into the furnace of war?'

Avgar knew his response too well and was embarrassed that this simple truth had to be pointed out to him.

'So many have died needlessly from war.' Lyafe stood up and looked down at Avgar. 'In a few days' time, if you are ready, I will take you to see the wounded, so that you might realise what the true cost of war is. I will show you those who need treatment for their physical wounds as well as those who suffer internally for what they have been through. I am no fool, Avgar, I know that you have caused many deaths in your time.' Lyafe paused and looked out to the Rogaus. 'Perhaps you were sent here in penance for your past; perhaps you are here to start your life over.' He looked back down at Avgar. 'I am going to leave you here for the morning. You would be wise to think of your life, how you got here and what kind of a mark you want to leave on this earth.'

Avgar sat and watched as Lyafe left him alone on the hilltop. He turned back to the ocean and sighed to himself. *How did I get here? When I was a boy growing up, I wanted nothing more than to excel at everything that I did, and to please my parents. How did that little boy turn into this savage, ageing man?*

Avgar sat on the hilltop all morning and thought about his life, while periodically getting lost in the dazzling ocean view. He thought about his intentions in joining the army as a young man and then how he had broken away from the Sand People to eventually conquer Balleny south of the Moaks. He tried to remember why he had done that, was it out of greed, adventure, ambition or pure warmongering? He vaguely remembered that he wanted to improve the lives of those in Balleny and for many years he had. But then something changed. It wasn't an instant change, but a change that developed over years of being the Emperor. *I was blinded by my own importance, my own abilities.*

Then his thoughts would flip. *But I was a great leader; I got things done, less people suffered and people worshiped me. Lyafe doesn't know what he's talking about. Before long, I'll be able to speak and be strong and I will leave this place and bring vengeance to that snivelling weasel: Veltrene.*

But then he remembered his lost control over his magical powers and he grew bitter, scared, and sad. *If only I could regain my magical strength, then I would make my mark. But alas, how would I ever be able to do that?* Avgar then turned his mind to his nightmares and how, even at midday, night time was far too close.

As his thoughts roamed through his past, his present and his future, Avgar's gaze kept coming back to the sparkling ocean and the sense that he was nothing more than a small wave crashing on a vast beach. He was in this state of mind when Lyafe returned and took him, without conversation, back to his room for lunch.

A few more days passed and Avgar felt the strength returning to his legs and muscles. He had made it a morning ritual to climb to the hill and look out over the water. He did this regardless of the weather.

Avgar had noticed that some people needed to have the company of others to stay entertained. He had never been one of these people and he found this new solitary contemplation to be revitalising and nourishing.

Avgar's mood and outlook on life still fluctuated many times a day, but each time he went to his hilltop, he returned with a sense of growing strength. On the fifth day after being shown the lookout, he returned to his room to find Lyafe waiting for him.

'Avgar, the Healers have told me of your daily strolls and I'm glad of it. Self-reflection and contemplation are important to the balanced being. You appear to be healing well, with the exception of your throat, and it is time for me to show you the work we do here.'

Avgar nodded and was led by Lyafe out of the room and down a paved path to a nearby building. They entered and the first thing that Avgar noticed with the smell. He immediately recognised it to be that of blood. But there was something else and only on closer consideration of his olfactory senses, did he realise it was like meat that had gone off. He looked at Lyafe and wrinkled his nose.

'The smell always confronts newcomers; you will get used to it.'

Avgar wanted to know what caused it, but didn't have his coloured cards with him to help in the translation. Instead, he looked about the long room before him.

There were more than a dozen beds with men in them. Some of the men slept, others rolled around in discomfort, and several sat upright with pained expressions on their faces. Three Healers roamed the room talking to one patient, then looking at the wounds on another, then taking a full bed pan out from under another. The men themselves had bandages on various places; arms, legs, heads, and chests.

Avgar was taking in everything that he saw; he had never seen such a place before. When Lyafe spoke, it made Avgar jump a little.

'These men have all suffered injuries from war.' He pointed to a man close by. 'He has lost his legs from a cannon ball.' He pointed to another. 'Half of his face was removed by an axe; he's lucky to be alive. He also has diarrhoea from drinking unclean water.' Lyafe walked down the column of beds and stopped at a sleeping man. 'This man had a spear thrust into his lower leg and the wound was left to fester for a week before he was brought here. Tomorrow we will saw the leg off.' He looked at Avgar. 'I think it would be good if you could be here to see that.'

Avgar was not the squeamish sort, but he didn't like the sound of sawing through a leg in cold blood. Despite an impulsive rejection of the idea, he nodded in agreement.

Lyafe continued to explain why each man was there and what the Healers were doing to heal them. Avgar didn't know why, but he felt shame seeing all of the wounded. He tried to suppress this and focused on the role of the Healers which he found quite interesting.

After doing the rounds of the room, Lyafe explained that there were many other buildings the same as that one with men, and a few women, who needed healing as a result of war. He then led Avgar back to his own room to see out the remainder of the day alone. Avgar used this time to read more of the books that Lyafe had given him in an attempt to divert his thoughts away from the sawing through a man's leg that the morrow would bring. *It's funny, only a year ago, I would have felt no more than disinterest in the task that awaits me.*

It was early in the morning when Lyafe came to collect Avgar. The Healer looked a combination of grim and sad at the same time. 'It is always a great shame to have to remove someone's limb. It means that we have not succeeded as we should have and the patient pays the price for that. But we must use it as a learning example. That is why you are coming along to watch this morning.'

Avgar nodded and stood to follow. They walked out into the morning air and made their way to the building that they had visited yesterday. They entered the main hall and then made their way into a small side room. Avgar watched as Lyafe went around lighting candles and lamps to make the room as bright as possible. Once that was done, he took Avgar to a cupboard at the end of the room and opened the double doors. What Avgar saw was a collection of herbs, powders, elixirs and parts of animals. His eyes scanned the labels that read everything from dried pig's ears, flies' wings, wild mushroom, poppy syrup and many others. He quickly started a search for the herbs that he used to smoke and grind into a gloopy drink. Excitedly, he found his smoking herb with no issue, but before he could locate the other herbs, Lyafe closed the cupboard, having made his selection.

'The man is delirious and not aware of his world, but the Healers will still give him a concoction before the procedure. We mix poppy syrup, willow bark and rum with a slight sprinkling of a special type of dried mushroom. This combination sedates, helps with the pain and makes the patient feel as though they are far away. Our efforts are not complete though and when chopping a limb off, the patient more often than not ends up unconscious due to the pain.'

Avgar was only half listening, as he was toying with the prospect of getting his hands on the contents of the cupboard, specifically his smoking herb. *It will ease my dreams; that's all I want it for.*

Lyafe opened another cupboard which got Avgar's attention immediately. This one had a series of saws, knives and thick needles. 'Our tools.' Lyafe's only explanation was simple. Avgar looked closely and the blades looked clean and sharp.

Lyafe took Avgar's attention again. 'Here comes our man.' He turned to Avar. 'You will stand in the corner and watch, nothing more.' Avgar nodded and consciously chose the corner closest to the herb cupboard in case an opportunity arose.

The man was carried in on a stretcher, which was placed on a bench. He was half conscious and babbling unintelligibly. He was wearing a white robe, like the one that Avgar wore, which the Healers hoisted up around his waist.

Three Healers accompanied him; one closed the door after resting a jug of boiling wine at the foot of the stretcher, another forced the herbal concoction down the man's throat and the other Healer placed a basin of hot water on the bench. A blade was balanced to sit within the flames of a lamp.

Lyafe washed his hands in the hot water and prepared his tools while waiting for the medicine to take its effect. He spoke to the Healers of inconsequential matters which surprised Avgar somewhat in its casual nature.

The man's mumbling died down and one of the Healers forced a thick piece of leather between his teeth while remaining at his shoulders to hold him down. Lyafe first picked up a sharp scalpel while one of the Healers held down the man's upper leg with his body weight.

Lyafe turned and smiled wryly at Avgar, 'The cost of war and of our failure.' He looked back to the leg before him and positioned the blade just below the knee. Lyafe cut quickly and precisely through the man's skin. The man grunted and squirmed with the pain.

Lyafe soon handed the scalpel to a Healer and reached for a long knife. He skilfully cut through the muscle of the leg and passed the blade aside.

Finally, he picked up a saw with shallow teeth and a wooden handle. 'This is called a bone saw.' He positioned the saw above the man's leg and began to cut.

Avgar's eye widened as Lyafe put his full strength into sawing through the bone. The man screamed out for a moment and then fell quiet in a state of unconsciousness. Avgar found himself both intrigued and disgusted at the same time; he wanted nothing more than to look away, but he just couldn't drag his eyes from the procedure. Before he knew it, Lyafe was through the leg and pouring the boiling wine over the wound while cauterising it with the heated blade. The smell of burning flesh filled Avgar's nostrils as he watched Lyafe sew up the amputation with a flap of skin that he had left on the underside of the leg. Avgar was a bit surprised by the amount of blood, which made the room stink.

When Lyafe had done his part, he washed his hands and arms in the basin of water and turned to Avgar. 'There is nothing gentle about what we Healers do; you would do well to remember that.' After what he had just seen, Avgar knew he would never forget Lyafe's sentiment.

The wound was bandaged up, and the man carried back out to his bed on the stretcher. Lyafe picked up the lower leg that had fallen to the floor and handed it to Avgar. 'You should study this. Examine it, cut it, sew it up, do what you will, just be careful that the festering wound doesn't come into contact with your blood.'

Avgar didn't know how to feel; Lyafe spoke in such a matter-of-fact way that he could have been talking about a piece of woodwork.

Avgar took the leg out of obligation and immediately noticed the smell from the wound. His nose wrinkled and Lyafe smiled. 'A good observation, Avgar. Right, I'm going to find something to eat. You can make your own way back to your room.' Lyafe didn't wait for a response, but left immediately. Avgar paused for a few moments before shaking his head in amazement and returned to his room to examine his new leg.

37

Four days had passed since Winter and Sor had watched as the boat that they had sailed on across Green Lake had been consumed in flames. The days since had been frustratingly long. Sor sat at the front of their skinny boat and Winter sat at the back. Tempers had been short and the silences deep as the two made their slow progress along the shoreline through the high reeds towards the Sempa's origin. Winter bitterly watched as Sor seemed to handle the lonely silences with calmness and prayer. This irked the half monk, who struggled with his own thoughts, stroke after stroke, as they paddled along.

There had only been two sources of amusement for Winter since entering the reeds. The first time that Sor had tasted uncooked eel produced a facial expression that had Winter rocking back and forth, unable to contain his laughter. Sor had paid him back when it was his turn to try the slippery flesh. From that point on, neither had laughed when it was meal time and sometimes they even wept at the necessity of eating.

The only other time Winter had laughed was also at Sor's expense. She had been squatting over the edge of the boat to relieve herself, when she lost her balance and splashed into the muddy water. She had floundered for a moment before realising that the water was only waist deep. She quickly climbed back into the boat and shot Winter a look that stopped his laughter immediately.

Aside from those brief moments, Winter's thoughts cycled between frustration at their apparent lack of progress, fear at being discovered by Olswerth's men, excitement at the training that he had started to receive in the evenings from Sor and uncertainty about what lay ahead of them. As another day drew to an end, his mood improved as they put the paddles away and resumed his self-defence training.

The lesson that night was to be the same as the previous three, with balance being central to a good defence. Sor made Winter stand with one leg on each side of the boat as she gently rocked it from side to side. Winter could handle this gentle, predictable movement, but as soon as Sor made a movement unexpectedly, he came unstuck. Despite this, he was improving enough for Sor to comment on it.

'Winter, you're getting the hang of this. I think in a week's time you will be able to progress to me throwing things for you to catch while you balance.'

Winter beamed at the praise and keenly looked forward to any progress in his training. While most pupils would have been acutely discouraged at the slow progress, Winter had grown up under the tuition of Avgar and had learnt that any skill worth having required time, patience and repetition; lots of repetition.

"Thank you Sor. Can we keep going some more tonight?'

Winter watched Sor's smile fade. 'Alas, the light is fading quickly and we still need to catch our dinner.'

Winter felt his stomach churn at the thought of it. 'Perhaps we can catch a fish tonight; I'm so sick of eel that I want to vomit at the thought.'

Sor looked at him kindly. 'I know. Let's pray to the gods for a quick catch.'

Despite their prayers, they only managed to net a small eel, which they ate in bitter silence.

After finishing their meal, they prepared themselves for sleep in the darkness. They had taken to sleeping side by side, at Sor's request for comfort from Winter. Although he didn't admit it, the sleeping Sor lying against Winter's body helped him relax into sleep as well.

At some stage in the night, Winter woke with a frightening start that shook the boat violently. He had dreamt a dream as vivid as life, of pain and anguish. It took Sor a long while to calm him down and only managed to do so by holding him close and rocking him back and forth like a child. She whispered calming words in his ear and sang soothing lullabies. Winter slowly returned to Sor in gasping breaths and tear-streaked cheeks.

'Winter, you're safe now. It was only a night terror. You're here with me, Sor, no one else. You're safe with me.'

Winter's mind slowly cleared and he looked up at Sor's concerned face staring down at him. 'I saw him, I mean, I was him.'

Sor's voice was gentle and supportive. 'Who did you see?'

'My father. I *was* him and I was poisoned. People were laughing at me and I was in immense pain. But worse than the pain was that I couldn't breathe. I tried and tried, but my throat closed over. Then I was gone and I was Avgar no more. It was brief, very brief, but so real.'

'You are back here with me now, Winter.' Sor paused for a moment. 'Do you think he is all right, your father?'

'I don't know. I don't feel like we died, but then we weren't far off it.'

'Perhaps it was only a dream, albeit a bad one.'

'No, it felt more than that. I'm sure he was trying to communicate with me.'

Winter observed Sor hatching an idea. 'Was there any information in the *communication* that would help us know where he is? Anything would be helpful.

After all, we're blindly going to Psymryte on a dream you had months ago.'

Winter thought. Sor was right; they were travelling with no solid reason for aiming for Psymryte. 'No, it all occurred in a closed room with no windows. It could have been anywhere. Still, if he has been poisoned, then he is likely to be making a name for himself and easier to find. If he's still alive, that is.'

Sor hugged Winter closely in what Winter felt was a tighter embrace than was wise given what he suspected of her feelings for him. He gently pushed back. 'We should try to get some more sleep; dawn can't be far off and we have another *exciting* day of paddling tomorrow.'

'If you dream again, know that I am here for you.'

Winter nodded and settled down to search for slumber. Sor followed and it wasn't long before Winter could hear her breathing slowly and steadily. Sor went to sleep easily, but for Winter it took a long while to find peace enough in his mind to ease him back to sleep.

Dawn came with heavy clouds and an eerie silence about them. Winter grumbled complaints of a sore back and ribs to the half listening Sor, who in turn grumbled about a hungry stomach, but no appetite for raw eel or fish. Winter agreed and they settled for a drink of the unpleasant water before taking up their paddling positions.

The morning wore away into tedium and the eerie silenced deepened as the clouds became heavier still. Winter felt as though he could only talk in whispers for fear of breaking the silence. 'I'm guessing we're going to be getting rather wet before too long. Maybe we can catch some of the rain to drink.'

The only reply he got back was a mumbled 'Mmmm'.

They continued to paddle on and Winter looked about in interest. 'Sor, I think the reeds are starting to thin out. The bank to our left is clearer and my paddle is not being met with as much resistance.'

Sor stopped paddling and raised her head. 'You're right. We had best move further from the bank; if the reeds are thinning, that could mean that we are finally nearing the end of these marshes.'

'That's a pleasant thought.' He pushed with more force to change the boat's direction, full of excitement to be nearing the end of this drudgery. As he did so, he saw something whizz past out of the corner of his eye. 'What was that?'

'What are you talking about?'

He pointed. 'There it goes again. Something is moving away to the right there. Something pink.' Winter strained his eyes to search amongst the thinning reeds. 'Over there.' He pointed to show Sor where he was looking.

Sor drew in an excited breath. 'I've heard tales tell of these... I forget what they are called, but they are a type of bird.'

They paddled closer to get a better look. Winter was amazed at what he now saw were at least a dozen bright pink birds with spindly long legs and snakelike necks. Their heads were mostly underwater eating goodness knows what, and this brought an involuntary smile to Winter's face. 'They're beautiful, aren't they Sor?'

'They certainly are.'

Winter wanted to get closer and paddled once more. Alas, as the boat neared the closest bird, they all opened their wings and took to the sky, several making a honking sound as they went.

'That was marvellous. I never knew such creatures even existed.'

'I think that this is a good time for a lunch break.' Sor rubber her stomach.

Winter's smile turned into a scowl at Sor's suggestion. 'I suppose so.'

They were lucky enough to catch a fish this time, using the remains of the eel from their previous meal as bait. The flesh tasted like mud, but they both forced the food into their mouths and were glad that it was not eel.

Winter suggested they start off again to put lunch behind them and make some progress before the rain that had plagued them, returned.

Sor had just agreed when the first drops fell, but still the two pushed on. 'Let's keep a vigilant watch on that bank.' Sor nodded in reply.

The reeds brushed past for a short while longer and then came to an abrupt stop. The monks ceased paddling without a word and Winter scanned the bank through the gentle rain for any watchmen.

His heart sped up when he saw what he was hoping he wouldn't. He made his way up the boat to Sor and whispered in her ear while pointing down the bank about a half mile. 'There, can you see them? I can see two on horseback and a further two doing something with sticks, maybe trying to light a fire. And there, they have a boat drawn up onto the bank.'

Sor's reply came in fearful tones. 'What can we do? How can we get past them?'

Winter looked the other way and saw the other riverbank. *It's probably about a half mile wide; easy for them to see across.* It was then that he noticed they had been drifting towards the open water without paddling. He spoke hurriedly. 'Sor, first we need to back paddle or we will be in the open in no time.'

He climbed back to his seat and they started to paddle backwards. Winter noticed Sor's paddling was erratic and hurried. When they were back enough and out of sight, Winter turned the boat perpendicular to the flow of the river and the boat gently pressed against reeds; stopping their progress.

'I didn't even notice until now that the river was flowing. This is a good sign, for it means that it will be easier paddling soon.'

'*If* we can get past those watchmen.'

'Why don't we have a rest, take some water and pray to the gods for a solution?'

The suggestion of praying seemed to ease Sor's tension and she agreed.

Winter had the urge to talk through their plan. They met in the middle of the boat and sat facing each other. They had drawn the canvas over the boat, but sat in the rain to avoid having to lie down.

'Sor, I want to talk through our choices.' He started hesitantly, but became surer of himself with each sentence. 'The way I see it, we have a few options: wait until nightfall, hoping that this cloud cover holds, then paddle as close to the east bank as possible, alternatively we can find somewhere to land on the bank and carry our boat inland. The other options are to land on the west bank, paddle now, or give up and go back. I will not entertain the last three.' Winter looked into Sor's eyes. 'Have you thought of any other ways around this?'

Winter could tell that she had not. 'No. I think waiting till nightfall is the best course for us; the east bank looked like thick mud stretching many hundreds of feet back from the river and I don't fancy wading through that.'

Winter smiled. 'Then we will wait until nightfall.' He then thought practically. 'We should get some rest for the remainder of the day; it might be a long night.'

Winter ensured that the boat was secure and not going to float downstream, then pulled the canvas to cover them.

They lay side by side in the middle of the boat and it wasn't long before their rain-soaked bodies made the air humid. Winter had just closed his eyes, when he felt Sor's arm over his chest. He opened his eyes and, in the dim light, saw that she was looking fixatedly at him.

'We should get some sleep, Sor.'

She didn't respond immediately, but he saw something in her eyes that made him hesitate. It wasn't fear, but raw nervousness. 'Winter, this could be our last day alive. Tonight, we may be captured or killed and I don't want that to happen without me telling you something.'

Winter heard the pause and knew what Sor was about to do before she did it. He couldn't stop her and a fraction of a moment later, Sor's lips closed onto his own. An immediate sense of sadness swept through his heart, and he softly pushed her back.

'Sor…'

'You don't like me, do you?'

Winter rolled onto his side to face her and put a caring hand on her shoulder. 'Sor, I do like you. Actually, I love you… but as a friend; as a sister.'

Sor breathed out loudly. 'I'm such a fool.'

'No, you're not. Come; let's get a bit of air.'

Sor followed Winter up the boat to one end and they opened the canvas and sat facing each other in the rain. Winter spoke first. 'Sor, I think I've known how you've felt for a few days now. I should have said something. I'm sorry.'

'You've known?' She looked downcast.

'I think so, but I wasn't really sure and I didn't know what to say.'

They sat in silence, neither looking directly at the other. Then Winter was intrigued by a thought. 'Sor, what are the monks' views on couplings? It seems like something that they would have rules about.'

The corner of Sor's mouth twitched with a momentary smile. 'They are permitted, even encouraged, between monks, but banned between monks and non-monks. Something as strong as love is clearly an action of the gods and should not be denied within our order.' She paused and looked sad. 'I thought I knew you and had hoped that you might feel as I do.' She looked him in the eyes. 'Do you think we could try to act as a couple for a few days? Maybe… is there a chance you'll change your mind?'

Winter detected hope and longing in her voice and felt sad once more. *You don't know the half of me.* 'You *do* know me, Sor, better than anyone alive, but I'm sorry, no, I don't think that we can pretend to be a couple.'

Tears welled in Sor's eyes. 'I've prayed to the gods that you would love me…'

Winter lent over and hugged her tightly. He bit his lip as he decided that he should tell her one of his secrets. He released her and held her by the shoulders at arm's length, feeling nervous, he started to speak. 'Sor, I want to tell you something that no one else knows, not even my siblings who are no more, and certainly not my father.' Winter paused and took a deep breath; steeling himself for her reaction. 'Sor, the reason that I don't love you the way that you want me to is because I can't love any woman that way. I'm drawn to men, not women.' Winter held his breath, waiting for her response.

Sor's brows furrowed. 'You mean you prefer the company of men over women?'

'Yes.' Winter still held his breath

Sor smiled wryly. 'Trust my luck to love a man who doesn't love women.'

Winter was surprised. 'You're not repulsed by me?'

'No, why should I be?'

'Well, most people see it as not being natural. Where I come from, if a man is caught with another man, they will both be stoned to death.'

'That's horrible.' Winter registered sympathy on Sor's face. 'There are monks, just as you are, who function in our society as anyone else would. The only difference is that their couplings won't lead to children, unless they adopt an orphan. We see love as the will of the Gods and who are we to judge the gods? I'm just disappointed that you're one of those men, for purely selfish reasons.'

Winter felt enormous relief at Sor's reaction. Never would he have thought that he could be openly accepted as loving men, anywhere in the world. He suddenly had a strong desire to return to the monks and live a happy, quiet life. He then noticed Sor staring at him and he raised an eyebrow in question.

'How long have you known?' She asked.

'Probably as long as you've known that you like boys. When I turned from a boy into a man, I tried to deny it and my father made my brothers and I lie with women. That was a horrible ordeal and the only way that I could get my body to respond was to imagine the women were men. But once that hurdle was over, Avgar accepted that I didn't want the distraction of women and wanted to focus my energies on my duties.'

Sor looked curious, but embarrassed.

'I'm sorry, Sister, if I have spoken too plainly; too intimately.'

'Not at all… I just wanted to ask…'

Winter raised his other eyebrow. 'Yes?'

'No, it's too personal; never mind.'

'Sor, now is the time to ask questions that you might have; we may not survive much longer.'

'Very well then, I wanted to ask if you have ever lain with a man.'

Winter thought back many years and smiled. 'Yes, but not as many as I would have liked. It was always in secret and could be no more than a physical encounter. I could not afford to fall in love with another man for fear of being caught.'

'That's sad, Winter. I'm sorry that you have had to live in fear.'

'It is what it is.' Winter wanted to turn the conversation back to Sor. 'It's my turn to ask the questions.' He smiled cheekily. 'Have you ever been close to anyone?'

Sor smiled, and Winter knew the answer before she spoke. 'Twice, although I don't really want to talk about them.'

'As you wish.' Winter stopped smiling and looked at Sor seriously. 'Are we going to be ok? I mean, can you love me like a brother?'

Sor smiled sadly. 'Probably, although not today. Perhaps, if we get through the night, I will try to look at you differently.'

'I think that's a good starting point. Now, can we get some rest before dark?'

'We should at least try to, although it's going to be uncomfortable given how wet we both are.'

'Let's try at least.'

Winter roused Sor as dusk was settling in. They took their positions in the boat and carefully paddled as close as they could to the mud flats that were the east bank of the Sempa. As they sat and waited for complete darkness, the rain progressed to a constant heavy fall. *Hopefully, I'll be dry at some stage in the future,* thought Winter.

With the heavy clouds and unceasing rain, when darkness came, it came completely. That was until the watchmen of Olswerth decided to start a fire. Winter didn't know how they managed to start a flame in the weather conditions but it made him happy, for it allowed them to know where the watchmen were and the west bank was.

His smile soon faded when he saw a lamp being carried to the edge of the river where he guessed it boarded a boat. Winter and Sor positioned themselves as close as they dared and waited patiently. *The captain said Olswerth would guard the river.*

The two monks looked on with concern as the lamp bobbed its way across the river and then back again. It repeated this motion twice more before Winter felt sure that they could time their passage to avoid the watchmen.

Shortly after the lamp began its return journey, Winter and Sor started paddling in an earnest silence. Despite the rain, Winter felt his sweat trickle down his forehead as he placed the paddle in the water and pulled it time and time again.

They were level with the lamp when it started to make its way back towards them. Winter wanted to yell for Sor to paddle harder, but he dared not speak. He also prayed that the light from the lamp wouldn't reflect off their boat, paddles or bodies, but he had no choice but to keep going.

They eventually edged away from the lamp and they both eased off their efforts when the lamp-boat reached the east bank and began its path back to the west shore. They only had a moment's reprise though, as they rounded a bend in the river and Winter saw another watch fire and lamp on a boat. Worse still, he looked down a straight section of the Sempa and counted five more watch fires at what he guessed were mile intervals. *Oh God of Night, help us pass this gauntlet of fire.*

Winter couldn't see it in the night, but small tributaries started to enter the Sempa and the speed of the water increased. He quickly realised that the paddling should be easier, but if they needed to pause between watch-boats, they might struggle to hold back their progress.

The monks approached the second boat as they had the first and made it past with little difficulty. The third boat proved more challenging, as they had to slow their progress just the right amount to get the timing right. Once past this boat they then had to put in some real effort to gain enough speed to make it past the fourth. They could have slowed to wait for it to do a full cycle, but Winter found slowing harder than paddling quicker.

With two more boats to get past, Winter wanted nothing more than to rest and he was sure that Sor felt the same. He thought about beaching themselves in the muddy bank for a break, but dismissed the idea: the rain had eased and they needed all the cover they could get while it lasted.

The monks approached the fifth boat with caution, pausing momentarily to get their timing right, but once they did, they shot past it without being seen.

Winter could smell their escape, but chided himself for getting too excited before the job was done. Halfway between the fifth and final boat, the muddy east bank changed into a more solid and very steep rise. Winter noticed the river narrow and the water speed hasten. The lamp-boat had less distance to travel between shores and their window of opportunity was less than with previous watch-boats. *This is going to be tight.*

Winter and Sor had to retard their progress once more with backward paddling and wait for just the right moment. Winter hoped with his entire being that once the lamp started westward, the watchmen would not be looking behind them.

Winter had no other choice, but had to risk trying the pass earlier than he would have liked. The lamp-boat paused at the east bank and slowly moved westward. The time was ripe and they dug their paddles into the water and pulled strongly. Their muscles ached and their hearts yearned for freedom. They came level with the lamp-boat and then Winter's paddle struck something in the water. It could have been a submerged log or it could have been the bottom of the river, it didn't matter which. Winter felt that the scraping noise would have been loud enough to wake the dead, and he prayed and prayed that the watchmen's hearing was deadened by the rain on their likely hooded heads.

Winter watched the lamp keenly while continuing to paddle, not daring to stop, even for a moment. *Did the lamp just change direction or speed up?* He couldn't tell. But with each stroke that he took, he became more confident that the enemy had not heard them. Then, before much longer, the watch fires were behind them and they were paddling easily down the river.

Winter finally dared to speak to Sor after what felt like half of the night had passed. 'We should keep paddling for a while yet; I want to put many miles between us and them.'

Sor agreed and they continued to make their way down the Sempa until the first hints of light appeared. The rain eased further and they found a clump of bushes on the east bank that they drew their boat up into; confident that they had escaped Olswerth's men.

Winter and Sor journeyed down the Sempa River for many days. The hot and humid late summer conditions changed to milder days, past the middle of autumn. They travelled swiftly and stopped briefly at several villages along the way. To the east, they passed a shadow in the distance that was the Woods of Sorrow and to the west the Lingos Hills and then the Tilted Plains.

Winter continued his training under Sor's tuition and his balance had developed well. They shifted their focus to Winter's defence of his body and awareness of his surroundings. Winter was keen to progress to counterattacks and advanced techniques, but Sor refused to teach these at his level. All the paddling had made their arms and shoulders strong and lean and to complement this, Winter insisted they use their legs by jogging each night to prevent them wasting away.

With the passing weeks, Winter had noticed Sor's mood towards him change subtly until he was hopeful that she thought of him as a brother and not as a prospective lover. This allowed the two to work more efficiently and have many fun times.

Knowing where they were headed, Winter suggested they both grow their hair and him, his beard. He spotted Sor smiling whenever she looked at his pale complexion, often sunburned, with his blazing orange hair. He also observed her running her hand through her hair many times a day; after all, it had been years since she had last had a head of hair.

Their clothes became stained and what was once grey became a dirt-brown hue. Neither of them minded this, as it disguised their monk origins and portrayed them more as travellers.

Sor finally became accustomed to sleeping at night and being awake during the day, and she dreaded the time when she would have to revert to day sleeping.

One afternoon, when the sun was high in the sky, Winter spotted a sort of smoky haze to the north and west. He pointed this out to Sor, and they both guessed that this was the infamous Psymryte. They stopped early that night in preparedness for their day on the morrow. They ate a frugal meal of salted fish and raisins that they had picked up from a small fishing village before settling in for sleep on the riverbank.

Dawn broke and they were in the boat again and paddling in sync. The city grew closer and it wasn't long before they decided to draw up their boat and travel the rest of the way on foot. They shouldered their packs and set off, farewelling their well-loved boat.

'Winter, what is our plan when we get to Psymryte?'

They had talked about this often, and Winter knew that Sor just wanted to go over it once more. 'Psymryte is a cesspit, so we will try to find the nicer part of the city. Then we will start to make gentle enquiries at taverns. First, we will listen to others and then, when we hear something of value, we will ask questions. We should stick together at all times and keep a wary eye out. As you know, we have very little money, so we will need to find somewhere cheap to sleep. Does that sound about right?'

'You forgot to mention that we are not to get drunk.'

'Ha, that is a risk I'm not willing to take.'

The monks reached the city outskirts and were not surprised to find rundown hovels with many people living under the same roof. The men watched them suspiciously as they passed, and it wasn't long before neither Winter nor Sor felt safe.

The further they walked, the more crowded the houses became and the more suspicious the occupants. Winter advised Sor to keep her hood drawn and her head down.

By mid-afternoon, they were in the city proper and were confronted with more ugliness than they thought possible. Homeless men, women, and children lay on the side of the road covered in a mixture of mud and human refuse. Cheap prostitutes preened on every corner, offering themselves for less than the cost of a stale chunk of bread. Tough men sat nearby on wooden boxes, playing with knives and other weapons. Mangy dogs roamed, eating what they could and trying not to be eaten themselves. Fires burned here and there and more than one person was seen to be cooking a rat at these communal fires. There was no doubt about it; Winter and Sor had arrived in Psymryte.

Amidst all of this filth, Winter felt an immense sadness for the thousands of people who lived here. This was mixed with great fear at what might happen to them should they look at someone the wrong way, so he kept his head down and kept moving.

The monks wound their way to the docks and found an inn where they could spend the night at a low cost. They ate the remainder of the food that they had brought and neither wanted to leave the relative safety of their room in the evening or at night.

Winter insisted that they push the flee-ridden bed against the door and sleep on the dirt floor in shifts. At least this way they would not be taken unawares in the night.

The night passed with no harm to Winter or Sor. They had been woken many times though, by all manner of noises occurring outside their door. They left the tavern early and began their search of the *nicest* part of the city. As it turned out, the most liveable section was where they had spent the night; down by the docks.

They passed their morning by wandering around a makeshift market trying to catch snippets of conversation. This bore no fruit and so in the afternoon, they found a new inn to sit in and eavesdrop on others. To remain in the inn, they had to purchase a drink of some kind and so chose the weakest beer available. This was horrible to drink and both of their cups sat on the table untouched for a long time.

They listened to other patrons, but again learnt nothing of use. Night was approaching and they were getting ready to return to their inn. Sor excused herself to use the privy, and Winter pondered how fruitless this trip had been so far. He stood in preparation for Sor's return when the barman came over and stood facing Winter with his hands on his hips.

The man was taller than Winter and several years older, but not as broad. He continued to stand there, staring at Winter, waiting the monk to speak.

'Hello, how can I help you?'

The man was brisk in his reply. 'Who are you? What are you doing here?' He didn't wait for Winter to reply. 'You come into my establishment, buy my cheapest drink and then sit there all afternoon without touching it. There's something queer about you two.'

Before Winter could utter a response, the man hit him viciously in the jaw and knocked him flying across the table. Winter saw stars as he clambered onto all fours. A moment later, a heavy boot smashed into his ribs and he felt them snap once more. He rolled over on the floor, coughing up blood and trying to get his breath back. The man kicked him again and again in the stomach and groin. Winter was in so much pain that he had gone numb to the world.

The barman knelt down next to Winter's half-conscious head. 'I'm going to take your woman, chain her to my bar and let any man here have a go for a copper.' He brought his fist up and rammed it down full into Winter's face.

Stars appeared before Winter's eyes once more and he vaguely registered Sor leaping at the barman and smashing his windpipe with her foot. The disgusting man fell heavily onto Winter's head and the last thing that Winter registered was the stink of sweat mixed with piss.

38

It had been a few days since Avgar had received the amputated leg to study. He had first examined where it had been sawn off, looking closely at the bone, blood vessels, and muscle tissue. Thereafter, he had requested a sharp knife and had cut into the flesh at different points. He marvelled at the strength of the skin, the range of the ankle joint, and the discolouration of the festering wound. The smell from the wound didn't improve, and after a couple of days, Avgar had played with the leg for long enough. He gave it to a Healer to dispose of and turned back to his books.

That night, Avgar's nightmare was worse than usual and he found himself sleeping little. He rose and skipped breakfast; eager to get to the lookout. When he got there, a woman that he did not recognise was already there. Avgar was not in the mood for a conversation and so returned to his empty room in a foul mood.

Avgar picked up a new book that Lyafe had left him about herbs and other remedies used to heal and soothe. He found himself unable to make sense of the words, especially the complicated names of the plants, and slammed the book down in frustration. *I just want to be my old self. I want to talk and feel strong.* He would have wept out of self-pity, but he found himself loathing his situation instead.

Wanting to vent his rage, Avgar paced around his room. His eyes settled on his chair and without thinking about it, he flung the chair across the room with his single hand. The throw off-balanced him and he fell down in a bundled heap. He sat on the cold floor in extreme discomfort and welcomed the sharp pain throughout his body.

He finally unravelled himself and it was then that a sudden thought struck him. *I need my smoking herb.* He stood up straight and, before leaving, brought his chair back to where it belonged, not noticing that it was undamaged.

Avgar knew that there would be Healers where he was going and so he put on a relaxed persona of someone going about their rightful duty before he left his room.

He entered the long sick room and nodded a greeting to a Healer who looked up at him. The Healer smiled back. Avgar then made his way to the room where the amputation had taken place and found it empty. He went to the cupboard with the herbs in it and opened it in excitement.

There it was: a jar stuffed full of the brown-green buds. A smile raced across his face, and he grabbed the jar down. Unstoppering the lid, he breathed in the distinctive sweet smell.

Avgar quickly looked over his shoulder in a sudden thought that he was being watched, but found no one there. He reached into the jar and withdrew a small handful. *I don't want to take too much or they'll wonder where it's gone.* He scrunched the herb up tightly and put the wad under his armpit to hide it. Replacing the jar, he closed the cupboard and quickly made his way to the doorway of the small room. Avgar then realised that he didn't have his smoking pipe and so started rummaging through the other cupboards, trying to find one. He soon became anxious that he would be interrupted and felt his anger rising. He thought about using his magic to locate a pipe, but dismissed the idea out of fear.

What really was a quick search felt like an age to Avgar, but in the end, he found a small pipe that would serve his purpose. He tucked this under his arm as well and escaped through the door in a flash.

The nervous man entered the main room and headed straight for the exit. Just as he was leaving the building, a Healer was coming in and stopped to speak to him. 'It's good to see you in here, Avgar. Did you enjoy the leg removal?'

Avgar thought that this was an odd question, as if an amputation was a spectator sport, but nodded regardless; eager to be on his way.

The Healer looked closely at him. 'Are you alright, man? You're all sweaty.' Without waiting for a response, the Healer put his hand on Avgar's forehead. Avgar instinctively batted it away and brushed the man aside. Avgar felt the impact himself and was reminded of the Healer's protection on Headly.

'I'm only trying to help,' said the annoyed Healer.

Avgar ignored him and made his way back to the security of his own room. When he got there, he ensured he was alone and withdrew his now sweaty stash and examined it. He smiled to himself in the full knowledge of the relief that he would soon be feeling.

The craving man hid the majority of the herb under his mattress and packed a small amount into his new pipe. *I won't smoke it in here; those nosey Healers will smell it a mile off.*

Avgar took a scented candle outside and around the corner of his building and hid behind a small shrub. He lit his pipe from the candle and breathed deeply. He held his breath for as long as he could before breathing out the smoke in a stream. After that single puff, he could feel his muscles relaxing and his mind easing.

It wasn't long before he had finished his pipe and felt a wave of relaxing sleep come towards him. He meandered back into the room, returned the candle, and hid his pipe with the herb. He lay down on his bed and before he knew what was happening fell asleep where, against his wishes, he once again relived a warped version of his nightmare.

It only took a few days for Avgar to use up the small wad of herb that he had first stolen. He had also amended his routine so that instead of visiting the hilltop in the morning, he made his way up the hill in the evening and watched the sun set over the Rogaus while smoking his pipe. This, he did, to ensure that he was not sober when he wanted to sleep.

Yet Avgar found not the peace that he was hoping for, but rather a sense of guilt and self-loathing. At least until the effects of the herb took hold, and then he was lost to a relaxed calmness.

The addicted man found the guilt worse than the self-loathing, but neither was strong enough to stop him from smoking his herb. They also did not prevent him from returning to the Healer's supply and taking a larger pile of the stuff.

After a couple of weeks of this new routine, Lyafe found Avgar on the hilltop. He was lying down and gazing at the stars above, not thinking about anything in particular. His pipe lay by his side, having finished his evening smoke.

Avgar's vision of the stars became obscured by Lyafe looking down at him. This made him sit up and look around at the Healer Supreme.

'You seem relaxed, Avgar.'

Avgar moved his position to conceal his pipe beneath him while nodding at the same time. He had to stop himself from nodding too many times, as he didn't want to appear out of the ordinary.

Five nods should be about right.

Lyafe came and sat next to him and they looked out over the starlit sea together.

'The Healers tell me that a change has come over you in the past couple of weeks. They say that you are more relaxed, sleeping better and eating well; especially after your visits up here.'

Fear struck Avgar. *Does he know? What will he do? Will he take my herb away?* He shrugged his shoulders in response.

'That is both good and bad. I'm glad that you seem to be coming to terms with your position, although I'm disappointed. You see, when someone accepts their injury, they lose the desire to heal. So, I will ask you this question and I want you to think about it before you answer. Do you really want to get your voice back?'

Of course, I want to get my voice back! Avgar nodded vigorously.

Lyafe spoke sternly, as if talking to a young man. 'I'll be honest with you Avgar, it looks to me, and the other Healers, that you don't. You seem to be getting too comfortable here. So, I will give you an ultimatum: you have seven days to prove to me that you really want to heal your voice. If you fail, then you will be on a boat back to the Outcasts. If you indeed prove your intention to heal, then I will provide you with guidance for something much harder than getting your voice back.' Lyafe stood and did not wait for Avgar to reply, but left the hilltop with quick steps.

Avgar felt the tug of confliction. *Yes, I want my voice back, but I am so comfortable and using my magic to heal could be so risky. But what about this other thing he wants to tell me? What could that be?*

A full day passed before Avgar finally made up his mind. The fear of returning to the Outcasts with no voice and weak muscles was too great, so he turned his attention to healing his voice.

Despite this resolution, he continued his daily smoking habit; not wanting the full force of his nightmare to return.

He often spent the first part of the morning scanning the texts in an effort to find something that would help his plight. In particular, he searched for drawings and explanations of the structures of the neck. These were few and he really only managed to glean that the power of the voice came from a structure that showed as a hard lump in his throat. This works together with the tongue to refine the sounds. Avgar also discovered that as breath passes through this structure, cords open and close to make different sounds. He surmised that, as his tongue and breath were working, it was these cords that weren't functioning.

After discovering this information, Avgar made his way up to his hill on the third day since Lyafe's ultimatum and sat down cross-legged. He closed his eyes and listened to the rumbling waves before turning his mind inward.

In a deep, meditative state, Avgar delved within his body. He sought his magical powers and released what he hoped would be a small amount to aid him. Using this, he was able to visualise his body parts in his mind's eye. He located his neck and travelled down the inside of his throat to find the voice cords. He saw them as white, taught bands that were covered in many dark grey nodules.

He tried to get a closer look, but was whipped out of his trance, gasping for breath and sweating from head to toe. He lay down on his back and breathed deeply, trying desperately to ride a wave of impending death. Slowly, the wave subsided. *That was a lot closer to death than I would have liked.*

He remembered the warning that he had received on the beach after travelling over the Moaks: without his crystal in his being, he would have little control over the amount of magical power that was used once accessed. This could result in his death.

But I am not dead yet. He sat up. *What were those bumps? They weren't in any of the pictures or descriptions in the books. If only I could ask Lyafe; oh, the irony.*

Avgar stood slowly and felt real weakness through his legs. *I'm not trying that again today.* He slowly made his way back to his room to eat some lunch and regain his strength, contemplating how he could communicate with Lyafe about the grey lumps.

Over the following few days, Avgar continued to use his magic to look into his throat. Now that he knew what to look for, he found it less draining, but still exhausting. He tried to speak often, but could still manage no more than a guttural noise.

On the sixth day, he had the idea to try to speak while looking into his voice cords. They vibrated erratically for a moment before the experimenting man blacked out from the effort. He spent the rest of that day in bed and only managed to stumble outside for a quick smoke before he went to sleep that night.

On the seventh day, Lyafe strode into the room with the rising of the sun. 'Good morning Avgar, how are you today?'

Avgar grunted and sat up in bed.

'It doesn't look like you can talk yet.' Lyafe frowned and then quickly smiled again. 'But the Healers tell me you've been making a real effort. I'm pleased; to send you back to the mainland would have been disappointing.'

Avgar rubbed sleep out of his eyes and looked at the Healer Supreme with a questioning look. He dearly wanted to hear what Lyafe had in store for him, but wasn't sure how to bring the topic up.

Instead, Lyafe sat on the chair facing him and reached out to touch Avgar's neck. Avgar flinched at first, but then let the Healer feel around his voice box. Lyafe looked inside Avgar's mouth, but mumbled that it was too dark to see in there. He then sat back and looked as if he was thinking hard. He glanced at the book on the bedside table, open to a diagram of the throat.

Then a sudden thought struck Avgar. He picked up the book and his eyes read through the words in haste. He found what he was looking for and then pointed to himself. Immediately afterwards, he pointed to the word *throat* in the book. He then found another word: *has* and finally found *bumps*. He looked up at Lyafe pleadingly.

Lyafe smiled at him broadly. 'Of course, you can't write, but you can point to words in the books to communicate.'

Avgar nodded.

'Your throat has bumps?'

Avgar nodded again.

'Where?'

Avgar pointed down his throat and then on the diagram where the voice cords were. Lyafe nodded in amazement. 'But how can you know that?' He looked at him sternly.

I just do.

'Of course, your internal powers. Bumps you say… are they big or small?'

Avgar indicated *small* with his fingers.

'I must confess; I'm out of my depth here. I've never seen or heard of bumps on the vocal cords.' He thought for a moment. 'They clearly shouldn't be there. If only there was a potion that could shrink or remove them, we could give that a try. I will think on it over the coming days.' He smiled at Avgar again and leant back.

'I promised that if you put in a real effort to heal, then I would give you something new to consider. And this turn of events gives me confidence that you will be able to complete your new task.' He looked Avgar directly in the eyes. 'I believe that with a focused mind and your uncanny powers, you will be able to grow your hand back.'

Avgar swore he had misheard. *Grow… my … hand back?* He looked at Lyafe with his mouth agape.

'You have been studying what makes up the body, including the arm and hand, and with more study, you will learn what exactly goes where. Then, you have to focus on building what already remains at your stump. You could perhaps try and use the stump flesh as a starting point and work from there.' Lyafe looked gleeful at the prospect.

Avgar looked at his stump in disbelief. *If I could get my hand back and my voice back, then all I'm missing is my full powers.'* Elation crashed through his body as he thought of the possibilities.

Lyafe rose.

Where are you going? Tell me more. I need to know more! Avgar tried to talk, and a vicious gurgle came out.

'I'm not saying that it will be easy or pain free. Oh, no, in fact, I expect it will hurt quite a bit. But then, I expect it will be worth the pain.' Lyafe pulled a book out from the folds of his robe. 'This book will tell you all that the Healers know about the arms and legs and what they're made of. Study it closely; the better you know the structures, the more likely you will get a functioning arm at the end of it.'

Lyafe half turned to leave. 'I think that is enough for today.' Avgar thought that the Healer looked gleeful. 'This really is the most exciting prospect. If you can do this, then the possibilities will be endless.' With an amazed shake of his head, he left Avgar alone once more.

He always leaves abruptly, just when I have more questions. Avgar sighed and looked closely at his stump. *Could you really grow back? I've missed you so much;*

life will be so much easier with you again. He glanced over at the book and hungrily took it in his left hand to begin digesting its contents.

Avgar threw himself at the task before him. Every waking moment he spent reading the texts or thinking about how he might grow his arm back. After a few days, he decided to visit his hill and use his magic to probe inside his arm stump.

He made his way there with the rising of the sun and settled on the ground. He had learnt that it was safer to lie down than sit when using magic in case he lost consciousness. He lay down and closed his eyes and regulated his breathing. He held his stump in his left hand and gently reached for his magic.

Avgar felt his magic flow and was immediately taken to just below the surface of the stump's skin. He sensed a conglomerate of blood vessels, scar tissue, fat and muscle. He probed in further with a burst of magical energy and found two arm bones that ended abruptly. In the back of his mind, he could feel his breathing and heart rate quicken. Then, uncalled for, a flare of magic flashed through his body.

His mind went blank for a moment and then he saw his body falling away below him; lying prone on the hilltop. His vision moved and he flew over the Rogaus and saw the sun set, then rise several times. Avgar watched the moon wax and then wane. The ocean turned to land and on he flew faster than any bird, the sun setting and rising as quickly as he was blinking.

His vision slowed at a snaking river and he saw a boat with two people paddling downstream. He flew with them as they made their way down the river in a matter of moments to a city that was unmistakably Psymryte.

Avgar's vision descended and he recognised the man to be his son: Winter. Avgar felt no emotions as Winter wound his way through the streets and into an inn that he recognised. The night passed and then Avgar watched Winter weave his way through more streets and eventually into another inn. This time Avgar's vision went with him and he watched his son wile away the rest of the afternoon. Then Winter stood, and not hearing what was being said, Avgar watched his son being beaten to a bloody mess.

Avgar's vision retracted and he stole a glimpse at the half-waxed moon before he flew back to his body in an instant.

Avgar's mind reconnected with his body and he convulsed violently. His limbs flailed madly and his torso writhed about in the grass. Avgar lost consciousness before the seizing stopped, but when it did, he lay there as still as a corpse.

The morning passed into afternoon and the sun beat down on Avgar. A crow landed next to the still man and pecked his cheek, looking for warm meat. With the sharp nip, Avgar woke and sat bolt upright, making the bird fly hastily away. He gasped for breath, bent forward and vomited. *Winter, oh Winter. You've come so far only to be beaten like a slave. And where is Dusk? Why is she not with you?* He lay back down and caught his breath more calmly. *But wait, that has not happened yet. At least, I don't think it has. Lyafe. I must tell Lyafe, he can send help. He must send help.*

Avgar tried to stand but found his strength failed him. Determined to get to Lyafe, he began crawling his way painfully over the hill and down to his room, ever cursing the long distance.

He needed many pauses along the way, but the weak man eventually got to his room. He found this empty and so he began to make his way towards the closest building, still crawling. Halfway there, he met a Healer who immediately came to his aid.

'My dear man, you need rest. Come, let me help you return to your room.'

Avgar grabbed the Healer with his good hand and forced the man to look at him. He mouthed the name *Lyafe*, but the Healer didn't understand.

If only I could bloody well talk.

Avgar tried talking, tried yelling, but all that came out was a growl like a dying pig.

The Healer looked at him with nothing but concern in his eyes. 'Let me help you back to your room and then we can work out what you're trying to say.'

Avgar had no choice, nor the energy to fight, and so let himself be helped into his room and onto his bed. Once there, he immediately opened the closest book to a random page and started pointing at the letters to spell *Lyafe now*. The Healer understood and hurried away in a fluster.

Avgar lay back on his bed and tried to remember everything he could about his fleeting vision. *How am I going to explain this to Lyafe?* After a few long moments, he sat up and started fingering through the book in front of him. *I'll have to spell it out with words.*

It wasn't long before Lyafe arrived with the other Healer in tow. 'Avgar, I understand you want to tell me something urgently?'

Avgar nodded and then started pointing at the words in the book.

'Hang on a moment. I'll get a quill and paper to write what you're trying to say.'

Lyafe returned a moment later and began writing every word that Avgar was pointing at. When Avgar couldn't find the word he wanted, he pointed to individual letters. The process was painstaking and Avgar found himself getting frustrated with how long it was taking; the words in the book just didn't seem to match what he wanted to say.

Eventually, as darkness fell, Avgar had finished his message to Lyafe. The Healer Supreme sat back and read what he'd written.

Had vision with powers. Saw future. Son beaten. Needs Healer help. In Psymryte at The Jilted Lover inn on next waxing moon. I must go with Healer. Urgent.

Lyafe looked up with amazement all over his face. 'You saw the future?'

Avgar nodded.

'Have you done this before?'

Avgar shook his head.

'How can you be certain that it will come to pass?'

Avgar flushed with anger and pointed to two words brutally. *I am!*

Lyafe sat back and looked as though he was thinking about the situation. 'You're a very gifted man, Avgar.' He paused and bit his lip. 'I'll tell you what I'll do: the moon is just waxing now, which means that there's more than enough time for a voyage to Psymryte before she waxes again. I will send a Healer there in a few days' time; you will stay here. You have your own work to do. If the Healer finds this son of yours, and he is injured they will bring him back here.'

Avgar felt a wave of relief wash through him and he smiled.

'Keep in mind, this is highly peculiar and I would not normally do this. Indeed, the only reason that I am is because you're a truly unique specimen and your powers hold so much potential.'

Lyafe stood and Avgar lay back on the bed, feeling utterly exhausted. 'And one more thing, Avgar, I'm placing a condition on me doing this.'

Avgar raised his eyebrows. *Anything*, he thought, exhausted.

'That you stop smoking your herb, effective immediately.'

Avgar felt dumbstruck. *He knows! Why didn't he say anything?* Avgar weighed up his son's life with the peace that the herb brought him. *But my herb is special. I need my herb. But Winter is my son. My only son left.* He struggled to do it, but eventually he nodded in agreement.

Lyafe bent down and removed Avgar's supply from under his mattress. 'I'm not blind, Avgar. And I have a keen sense of smell.'

Avgar closed his eyes and felt sleep overwhelm him almost before Lyafe had left his room. With the deepening of sober sleep, the old painful reliving began to play out once more. *I want my herb…*

39

Kathsum made her slow way from the Citadel of Roasline to her house, well past the middle of the night. Two guards flanked her, and she found the walk in the cool autumn night to be sobering. Usually, the High Chancellor was tucked up in bed by this time of night, but she had been celebrating their victory over the Outcasts seven nights previous.

The turnout at the public event exceeded her predictions, and the crowd remained pleasantly civil. Kathsum had spoken proudly of her people and the formalities had been over by sunset. She had even been magnanimous enough to praise Admiral Tunley and invited him to say a few words to the gathered crowd. She had been surprised with his eloquent speech and generous praising of the rank and file of the navy and army. She noted he was received with applause, although she was pleased to note that it wasn't as much applause as she received.

Kathsum arrived safely at her house just as her feet were beginning to tire. She instructed the two guards to wait outside her door, knowing full well that they would refuse to be dismissed from their duty. She entered her hallway and removed a lilac wrap from around her shoulders, hanging it by the door. One of her maids bustled down the hallway to greet her.

'Welcome home, Ma'am. There is a messenger waiting for your arrival in the sitting room. I told him you would be out late, but he insisted he wait. Very important, he said his message was, and only for you.'

'Thank you.' Kathsum was intrigued; if the message was so important, why didn't he bring it to her at the citadel?

She left the maid in the hallway and made her way to the sitting room. Before entering, she straightened her dress and composed herself to appear more sober than she felt. She entered the room and found the young man slumped, half dozing on her window seat.

Kathsum cleared her throat and the man sat up straight. When he spoke, it was with a lower-class accent, although that didn't bother the High Chancellor one bit. 'Ma'am, High Chancellor, I have an urgent message for you.'

'So, I hear.'

The man hesitated. Kathsum stared at him with piercing deep blue eyes. 'Well, you'd better get on with it then.'

'Yes Ma'am. It's a letter for you.' He picked up a roll of parchment that had been on the seat next to him. 'I was told to say that this has come from someone called Burban.' He reached out and handed her the letter. *Burban! This will be important, but I'll not open it with this scallywag here.*

'Thank you. If there's nothing else, you may go.' She handed him a small coin, as was the customary payment for messengers. The young man bowed and then left Kathsum alone in the room.

The High Chancellor rubbed the paper between her fingers and examined the wax seal. The emblem was that of a clenched fist. *I don't recognise this.* She frowned and then broke the seal with trepidation. She unrolled the letter and read the slanted writing slowly.

Dear High Chancellor of Roasline,

It is with great urgency and hope that I write to you. My name is Nigrath and I am one of the two leaders of the Outcasts left since our embarrassing recent defeat. I am writing without the knowledge of my counterpart in the hope that you and I may be able to agree on terms of peace. I realise now that the best course of action for the people north of the Liagar is to reach a peaceful solution.

I have recently met with a representative from the Healers of Headly and they are willing to honour the arrangement that you had with Resvon. That is to say, they will provide protection for only yourself and myself should we wish to meet. I have agreed with them that you and I will meet on the coming new moon.

It may be presumptuous of me to assume that you will come, but I have made arrangements to be at your private pier with a Healer on the night of the new moon. I will be in a small boat and we can journey into the river to discuss how we might reach a successful peace deal between our two peoples.

I look forward to meeting you soon,

Nigrath.

Kathsum was flabbergasted. *Could this really be true? Am I to believe this letter? It is everything that I've dreamt of, and only a handful of nights away. But what if it's a trap? How can I trust what is written? It's true, the boy said it came from Burban, and I know I can trust her, but can I trust him?*

Kathsum felt her head sway. *Too much rich food and wine tonight. I'm in no state to make these kinds of decisions. I'll see how it looks in the light of a new day. Perhaps, this time I'll ask the opinion of the Council. I wish Guflinkov was here. He would know what to do in an instant and I trust him more than the entire council twice over. But he's not, and so I must face this on my own… again.*

The next day, Kathsum made her way by foot to the citadel. The walk was refreshing and allowed her to expend some of her nervous energy. When she arrived, she went directly to the council chambers and waited impatiently for the other members to arrive.

They eventually filtered into the room and sat at their usual positions around the rectangle table. Kathsum noticed bags under several eyes and tired looks on most of the faces. The conversation soon died down and all eyes turned to the High Chancellor.

'Thank you all for coming. Last night when I returned home from the celebrations, I was greeted by a messenger. He claimed to have been sent by Burban, a trustworthy agent of Roasline. He had few words for me, but gave me this letter.' Kathsum held out the well-read page. 'The seal was intact and was of a clenched fist. Before I tell you my thoughts, I will read the letter in full.'

She cleared her throat and took a drink of water to moisten her dry mouth. The High Chancellor then read the entirety of the letter to the council and waited for their responses.

Those around the table looked stunned at first, and then Kathsum could see six minds working to process the information, just as she had the night before.

Kathsum was pleased to see that the first to recover was the Alderwoman of Producers. 'This is fantastic news; peace, at a time when it was least expected.'

She was rudely cut off by the Head of Order. 'Humph, sounds like a trap to me.'

Tunley spoke next with an air of condescension. 'Yes, yes, we can all work out that it might be a trap. What we need to decide is whether the risk is worth the outcome. In my opinion, I don't think it is worth the risk to our High Chancellor.'

Kathsum tried to analyse Tunley's response; he was the most cunning, and she needed to know what angle he might be playing. *Does he want to goad me into going by saying I shouldn't? Maybe. He certainly doesn't want peace; the more we war, the better it is for him.*

The hungover General finally understood the situation and broke Kathsum's thinking. 'This seems very similar to how Resvon met with you. Would this Nigrath even know about those meetings?'

'Probably. It is likely that Resvon told his other leaders once the peace was achieved. After all, I told the council, didn't I?'

The astute Alderwoman spoke next. 'Although, Resvon met you at the full moon, where it's a lot brighter. Nigrath wants to meet at the new moon; why?'

The Quaestor spoke for the first time with his thin voice. 'It sounds like this meeting is urgent; the next full moon is weeks away.' He looked at Kathsum. 'It would be better for our bursary if peace was reached. I say you risk it.'

The Alderman of Merchants spoke next, 'It seems fishy to me. Is there any way we can test the validity of the letter?'

Kathsum thought. 'I've been wondering that myself all morning. The only way I can come up with is by testing the Healer's protection. But that might seem rude and get the negotiations off to a bad start.'

Silence followed this comment with a few nods around the table. Tunley spoke again. 'If you're going to be close enough to test the protection, then Nigrath could easily kill you if it is a ruse.'

More silence filled the room. Kathsum pondered the dilemma. *I want peace so much, but is that blinding me?*

'If I don't take the risk, then we could be at war for another decade. If I do take the risk and it proves false, then I will be captured or killed. That's the decision we have to make.' Kathsum let that prospect sit in the air for a moment. 'I will put it to a vote; if nothing else, I am a servant of the people of Roasline. My life is theirs.' She paused. 'If you're in favour of me pursuing this course of action, raise your hand.'

There was much dithering, but eventually Kathsum was able to count the hands. The Quaestor, the Alderwoman and the Alderman all raised their hands. That left Tunley, the General and the Head of Order to vote against the motion. 'Three apiece, so the decision falls to me.' She smiled wryly. *I don't usually struggle to make a decision. There simply isn't enough information.* She sighed out loud. *I think I will have to go with my heart.* 'So be it. I will follow this course to its conclusion.' She looked directly at Tunley. 'But I want your fastest boats and best fighting sailors to be close at hand. While they may not be able to save me if I'm attacked, they should be able to capture this Nigrath.'

Tunley nodded. 'As you wish, but I still think you're making a grave mistake.'

'As High Chancellor, it is my mistake to make.' She looked around the table at each member of the council. 'Over the coming days, we will prepare for both eventualities, but talk to no one of this plan. Secrecy is all important. Now, you all look like you could do with some sleep, go and rest. I want you working hard tomorrow morning.'

The council members all stood and nodded politely to Kathsum as they left the chamber. The High Chancellor could tell that they didn't quite know how to feel. She herself didn't either.

The day finally ended, bringing the night that would see the new moon. Kathsum was anxious, excited and weary all at the same time. She had slept little since she had decided to meet Nigrath; being busy with preparations for both eventualities. As night closed in, she climbed into a nondescript carriage that would take her to the docks. It was driven by two highly trained guards and another two rode on the back.

She bumped her way down the cobbled streets, wondering how long she would have to wait at the pier to meet Nigrath. The letter had said nothing about the time of a meeting and, unlike a full moon, a new moon was not visible to present a natural meeting time. For all she knew, she could be waiting most of the night at the docks. She dearly hoped that this would not be the case.

She arrived at the High Chancellor's pier and a guard opened her carriage door. She looked about, but could not a see boat. What she did see was Admiral Tunley walking towards her from the water's edge.

'High Chancellor, all of my men are in place on the river. All has been quiet so far. Remember, we will be keeping a close eye on you.'

'But not so close that it will frighten Nigrath off?'

'No, as we agreed.'

Kathsum felt a moment of softness. 'Thank you, Tunley; you have been most accommodating with this.'

'I am just following orders.' He smiled, which Kathsum did not think improved his appearance.

'There's no need for you to be here, Admiral. You may go.' Kathsum didn't fancy spending more time with the unpleasant man.

Tunley nodded and left Kathsum with her guards. She made her way to the pier and stood looking out into the darkness.

The night lengthened and Kathsum had long sat down with her legs dangling over the pier's edge. A thin layer of cloud had pushed across the sky and this shielded the little light that was given off by the stars. Kathsum fondled her garnet, gold and moonstone necklace and tried not to think about what was to come. Instead, she thought of her childhood, growing up in Roasline and how simple life had been.

She continued to gaze out across the black Liagar and then slowly she saw a gentle light coming towards her. She quickly got to her feet and straightened her dress. The lamp light grew larger and Kathsum felt her legs twitch with nerves. Her stomach felt squirmy and her head slightly dizzy. She had to remind herself to breathe calmly and she soon settled herself.

Nigrath's boat eventually came close enough for Kathsum to see that it was a single-masted vessel steered by a seated man. At the stern of the boat stood a Healer all in white with a shaved head. As the boat touched the pier, he stepped ashore and greeted Kathsum with a slight bow.

'High Chancellor, my name is Swarth and it is a great honour that I can assist with facilitating this peace treaty.' He waved a hand at the boat. 'Nigrath awaits your presence, but has said that he will not step ashore or speak until we are in more neutral waters. If you do not agree to these terms, then he will depart immediately.'

Everyone has their little quirks and securities. 'Very well.' *I still don't know if this is a trap.*

Swarth spoke again with an air of superiority and indignation. 'I suppose you would like to test the Healer's protection?'

This is a diplomatic test of trust. She spoke loud enough for Nigrath to hear her. 'Thank you, but I will not.'

The Healer nodded in acknowledgement and directed her to sit in the stern between himself and Nigrath. Kathsum did so and realised for the first time that Nigrath was wearing a hood. She tried to peer into its depths, but the night was just too dark. With his broad shoulders and hood blocking the lamp's light, there was no chance of making out any of his features. *He looks like a powerful man, but more than that, I cannot say.*

The boat pulled away and sailed out into the Liagar. Kathsum watched the shoreline recede and then the lights of Roasline grow smaller. They sailed until the current was swift; Kathsum could even feel the pull of it on the boat's hull.

'I'm going to drop anchor now; I think we're far enough out to be in neutral waters.'

The High Chancellor heard the anchor being thrown overboard and then felt a slight jolt as it dug into the riverbed. She sat up straight and looked keenly at Nigrath, uncertain if she should speak first. Then, all of a sudden, she felt Swarth tower up behind her. He reached over her and shoved a firm ball of cloth the size of her fist into her mouth. She tried to scream, but the ball stopped the noise. She yanked and tried to rip it out, but it had been secured in place by a cord around her head. She scratched frantically at this, but steel-like arms gripped her. She writhed like an eel, trying vainly to break free.

Then Nigrath spoke slowly and firmly. 'Kathsum!' The High Chancellor froze. *No… it cannot be…* Nigrath raised his arms and slowly lowered his hood. There staring wickedly at Kathsum were the hateful eyes of Admiral Tunley.

Kathsum felt her body go limp as all of the fight left her.

'Kathsum, oh Kathsum, how nice it is to see you again.'

The High Chancellor barely noticed as Swarth bound her arms and slipped a noose about her neck, holding the cord's end.

Tunley continued talking. Even in the darkness Kathsum could see the joy across his face. 'I think it's time that you and I had a little chat. I suppose I really should thank you. You held me up as a beacon against the evil Outcasts. You made the initiation of my plans a reality. Without you, I would still be unknown to the masses. Now, once you're disposed of, I will be elected the new High

Chancellor, and then the reign of Tunley will truly begin.'

Kathsum felt horror-struck. *What have I done? Tunley as High Chancellor will ruin Roasline. No, it will never happen; I must trust the wisdom of the people of Roasline.*

Tunley looked at her hungrily. 'I suppose you might be wondering why I voted against you coming on this evening's jaunt? It's simple really: you despise me and are more likely to do the opposite of what I suggest than to follow my advice.'

You're wrong, arrogant man. I'm more likely to ignore you outright. Kathsum wished she could talk, but knew that Tunley would not be foolish enough to lower her gag, lest she yell for help from the nearby boats. *They cannot all be in on his plan.*

'When I was plotting this evening, there were many parts that I was looking forward to and I think seeing your face when you recognised me was almost on the top of my list. I had also looked forward to raping you.' He paused and Kathsum blanched at the thought. *Oh no, please no. Kill me instead.*

'But now I see you keenly and I realise that you're almost an old woman, far too old for my tastes.'

Kathsum felt relief wash through her, but tried not to show him in case he saw it and changed his mind.

Tunley looked up at Swarth, smiling. 'Would you like to have a go at the High Chancellor? Once in a lifetime opportunity.'

Kathsum felt her head sway with horror as she heard the fake Healer chuckle with pleasure. He stepped around in front of her and Tunley came and stood right behind him.

'I'm not going to say no to that offer.' Swarth lifted up his robe and Kathsum started to weep.

She began thrashing about as he held her down with strong arms. Swarth went to lift up her dress, but paused with an odd expression on his face. The next moment, he spat blood out of his mouth and he fell on top of Kathsum. She lay there frightened, not knowing what was going on.

Tunley heaved Swarth's body off her and sat her up straight. He wiped a long bloody knife on her dress and smiled at her. 'He was the only other person who knew of my plan.'

This man is deranged. She looked down at the corpse before her feet and shuddered.

'Just you and me now, High Chancellor, and soon, it will just be me.'

Kathsum knew her end was coming soon, but she surprised herself to realise just how calm she felt.

'What's that?' Tunley cupped his ear in a mock listening action. 'You want to know how I'm going to escape? Oh, well, I can certainly tell you that before I kill you.' Tunley puffed out his chest. 'I have another boat anchored sightly downstream from here. I will swim on the current to it and then sail through my well positioned sailors back to shore.'

The arrogant scheming bastard, he ought to be killed.

'The lamp on this boat should splutter out shortly before dawn and then the hunt will be on; first for your boat and then for the escape vessel of *Nigrath*.

'With your murder, the people of Roasline will call for an all-out attack on the Outcasts and who better to be elected as the High Chancellor to lead such an attack than myself.'

No! Not war, not more suffering. Kathsum could see the simplicity of Tunley's plan would lead to success. Tears for the fate of the people of Roasline rolled freely down her cheeks.

'You fear your death. I think that's just about the cherry on top of my cake tonight.' He grinned at her for the last time. 'Now Kathsum, it is time for you to die. It will be quick, but not painless.'

He knelt down before her so they were eye to eye. But the High Chancellor wasn't looking at Tunley with her eyes; she was lost in the forced thoughts of her parents, her loved ones, her friends, Guflinkov, and thoughts of happiness. She barely felt the blade enter her chest and pierce her heart as a peaceful darkness took her, and all that she had strived for, away.

40

Admiral Tunley was woken by a hurried rapping on his bedroom door. He rolled out of bed and tried to make sense of the noise. His brain eventually clicked into action and he straightened up with a smile on his face; it had not been long since he had driven a knife through the High Chancellor's heart. He grabbed a dressing gown to cover his nakedness before calling to the door gruffly.

'What do you want?'

His servant's muffled voice replied. 'Sir, there is a man here who insists on speaking with you urgently.'

Tunley noticed the frustration in his servant's voice. 'He may enter.'

The door flung open and a captain from the navy, that the admiral only half recognised, came in with a rush. His face was drained white, but his cheeks were rosy red from exasperation.

'Admiral, Sir, you are required down at the docks immediately. It's the High Chancellor.' The captain looked around furtively to ensure that the servant had gone. He lowered his voice so that only Tunley would hear. 'The High Chancellor; she has been killed.'

Tunley was prepared for this news and made an effort to show shock and anger at the information. 'What? Surely not. Shit!' Then he spoke half under his breath but making sure the captain could still hear him. 'She was too trusting of that Nigrath.' He looked directly at the man before him. 'Tell my servant to ready my swiftest horse. I will dress and come down immediately. You go back to the docks and ensure that no one touches her; I want to inspect the body myself. Set up a perimeter to ensure that the public don't get wind of this as well; we need to manage this carefully and secretly. We don't want to cause panic.'

'Aye, sir.' The captain saluted and closed the door on his way out.

Tunley stretched his arms above his head and breathed deeply. He made his way over to the window and opened the curtains to reveal the grey monotones of the day's first light. He smiled and relieved himself in a chamber pot on the floor while still looking out the window. *Well, that was an exciting start to the day.*

Tunley dressed and made his way downstairs to the kitchen. He grabbed a cold leg of roast chicken and went outside to find his horse saddled and waiting for him. He climbed up, threw the chicken bone into the gutter and dug his heels into the stallion.

The trip to the docks was quick, but the sun had still risen by the time he arrived. He was pleased to see that the perimeter was in place, and even more pleased to see that Kathsum was still in the boat.

The Admiral dismounted and climbed into the boat to go through the motions of checking her over. She was cold to the touch and her body had started to stiffen, as all corpses do. Tunley smiled inwardly, but put on a sad and concerned face as he stepped out of the boat.

He spoke to the captain in charge, the same who had visited him earlier that morning. 'She's been killed with a single stab wound to the heart. I'd say it was done with a sharp blade no longer than a foot. The other man appears to be dressed like a Healer, but clearly did not have the Healer's protection. Nigrath probably hired him to pose as a Healer for the High Chancellor.' He paused and drew a deep breath. 'This is a sad day, Captain.' The captain nodded and looked wary.

Tunley knew he had a reputation of being quick to anger and quick to punish when things didn't go his way and this could be no exception. 'Captain, who found her?'

'I did, sir. About midnight we heard voices talking from her boat as she moved into the Liagar. We could not make out the words and assumed that things were going well as they seemed not loud or angry. Then silence settled over the river. We waited in case this was part of the negotiations. Then, I started to worry and drew my boat closer to where I thought the High Chancellor was. It was dark, very dark, and it took some time before we could pinpoint the dull lamp of her boat. We could not see anyone sitting or standing and then made haste to her vessel. It wasn't until we were alongside her that we realised the tragedy. We immediately lit lanterns and called for our comrades and we began searching the river for the escaped Nigrath. Alas, we found nought and failed in our duty.' The captain hung his head.

Tunley would normally have killed him then and there, but for his own reasons, chose to be merciful. 'You have failed miserably, captain. Your failure has not only killed our leader, but it has given our enemy a perfect opportunity to strike at us. If we didn't need all of the men we could get, I would have you executed. However, with another attack now imminent, we need sailors, therefore, you and your men, and those others who were nearby, are hereby demoted to the lowest rank we have in the navy: novice seamen.' He looked the man up and down with disdain on his face and then growled out his next order. 'Now, organise the body to be taken to the council chambers up at the citadel. Have her covered for transport and make sure it's done in secret. You will also send for the other council members to meet at the citadel immediately. Do this without incident or I will reconsider that value of your life.' Tunley turned and made his way back to his steed before the novice seaman had time to realise what had just happened.

The Admiral mounted and sat upon his horse and looked out over the water before turning to the man he had just demoted. 'All available captains and ship masters are to meet at my headquarters at noon. See that it happens.' He turned his horse and spurred him into action; racing away from the docks and up to the citadel.

Tunley found himself in the council chambers with Kathsum's corpse lying on the table. He paced back and forth, waiting for the council members to arrive. He knew they would not be long and he was looking forward to keeping things moving.

The Admiral had been in close proximity with many bodies before, but there was something about the way that Kathsum lay there that unsettled him. He felt as if she was smiling at him, and he tried hard to banish the notion from his mind. He tried turning his back on her, but couldn't maintain that for long. He tried moving her mouth into a frown, but her face muscles wanted to remain in a half-smile. He slapped her as his frustration and his unease grew, but all that did was leave him with a sore hand. In the end, he returned to pacing back and forth; scowling at her as he passed.

Before long, he heard voices approaching and he steadied himself for the councillors. They entered the chamber and stopped talking immediately. The Alderwoman of Producers, Jaid, covered her mouth in shock and rushed to Kathsum's side. The others just stood and stared stupidly, leaving Tunley to break the silence.

He mustered his cunning and poured sadness into his voice. 'The High Chancellor has been murdered by Nigrath. Her trusting nature has led to her death.' He hung his head.

The Alderman of Merchants spoke angrily to Tunley. 'This is your fault! You were supposed to be protecting her; you are to blame.'

'Alderman, I understand that you're angry, but please be under no illusions: Nigrath took advantage of Kathsum's desire for peace. My men, who were protecting her, failed their duty and have been punished accordingly. This is a sad day.' He hung his head in sadness again and gave the others a few moments of silence.

Tunley spoke again with a voice of kind firmness. 'This tragedy has put us in a vulnerable position. Thinking as a military man, Roasline is at great risk of an attack. We need to unite under one leader and present a strong defence of our city.' He looked around warily at the other council members, trying to gauge their responses.

Jaid scoffed and spoke strongly while tears rolled down her cheeks. 'I suppose you think that we should unite behind you. How convenient.'

'We need to unite behind a military leader until a new High Chancellor can be elected. Whether that is myself, the General or the Head of Order, this council will decide, but of course I think it should be me. I control the navy, the first line of our defence. I planned the last defence of Roasline and if you remember, Jaid, that was a success.' Tunley said this strongly, but ensured that he kept all venom out of his voice; he needed to seem reasonable.

The General spoke plainly. 'I do not want to lead everyone; I know little of governing past ordering the army. I would support Tunley to lead until the public gets a chance to vote.'

The Quaestor's weasel voice entered the conversation. 'Whoever is put in charge won't be there for very long; our laws state that if a High Chancellor dies, an election needs to be held within fourteen days of their death.'

Silence passed around the room until Tunley broke it with a quiet voice. 'That is plenty of time for Nigrath to attack.'

Jaid spoke again with her voice thick with emotion. 'Listen to us, we're discussing who will rule before Kathsum is even in the ground. This woman, who gave so much of her life to the betterment of Roasline, who in the end gave her life for the mere hope that peace could be reached. She's not even out of her bloodstained dress.'

Silence full of sadness filled the room and Tunley needed to reassure the council members that he was not callous. He thought furiously and found what he thought would be a solution.

'Jaid, I know Kathsum was dear to you. I think it would be fitting for you to arrange her funeral and celebration of her life.'

The Alderwoman nodded her agreement.

'I would also like to propose that I lead the military defence of Roasline until the election.' He hastened to add an assurance. 'I will not have powers that extend outside of the defence of our people. Alderman of Merchants, can you organise the upcoming election; working with the Head of Order for the security aspects of the day?'

The Alderman nodded.

'I wish that the Farmer's Guild had elected a new Alderman to assist, but we must do without. General, you can work with me to arrange your troops. Quaestor, you will be needed by all of us, so please make yourself available.' Tunley looked around the room. 'Does everyone agree with that plan?' He held his breath and waited and was relieved to see everyone nod their assent.

'Good, then let's get to work and get the sad word out to the public about

Kathsum.'

They started to file out of the room, but Jaid caught Tunley by the elbow. 'Are you going to run for the High Chancellor?'

He tried to read her tear-stained face, but could not. His heart yelled *yes* but he measured his response. 'I have not thought about that yet; Kathsum only just died and there is a lot of work to do and a lot to think about.'

She released him and he saw her eyes narrow fleetingly.

She knows I will. The real question is; will she?

The Alderwoman nodded and they all went their separate ways.

The funeral for Kathsum was held four days after her murder. A day of mourning was declared and no trade was to occur on that day. Black was worn by all and candles were burnt in windows that lined the streets.

A service was held at the citadel and an open celebration of Kathsum's life was held in the courtyard. This was a sombre affair, but the turnout was significant; Kathsum had been well liked by the people.

Kathsum was without family and so Jaid read a eulogy that was full of Kathsum's achievements without being overpowering with emotions. Little money had been available to spend on food and drink for the masses as the cold Quaestor kept a tight string around any *unnecessary* spending; the defence of the city simply took priority.

All of the council members were present at the wake and Tunley forced himself to mingle with the citizens of Roasline, or at least those he thought might turn out to vote.

He was yet to declare himself as a candidate and was planning on doing so the following day. In readiness, he had paid men to talk glowingly of him and his recent defence of Roasline at all of the inns and taverns. This was not a cheap exercise, but he had funnelled some of the money directed to repairing a ship to his own purse. He also planned on paying men to vote for him, but he couldn't guarantee that in the end they would actually vote his way. So, he limited that practice to a couple of hundred hungry looking poor people.

By the day of the funeral, Tunley was sure that Jaid would be running for High Chancellor and there would no doubt be others to come out of the woodwork. The process was that those who wished to run did not need to declare themselves until the eve of the election. Traditionally, the majority of the electioneering occurred in the citadel courtyard as the citizens were about to cast their votes.

It was not compulsory to vote in Roasline and usually it was the wealthier citizens who elected the High Chancellor. Tunley himself had voted in the past and last time he certainly didn't vote for Kathsum.

Tunley knew that on election day, the citadel's courtyard, where Resvon had been murdered, would be secured with one entrance only. When a citizen entered the courtyard, they would be given a wooden coin carved uniquely for this election. They would then have a chance to listen to the candidates spruik themselves, or as more commonly occurred, someone else spruiking the candidates. The voter would then cast their wooden coin in a barrel that sat by each candidate. These barrels were sealed, but for a slit only large enough for a coin to fit through. Once the citizen had voted, they were required to remain in the courtyard until the voting closed. This prevented people going around and voting more than once.

Entertainers and musicians would be hired to keep the growing crowd happy and simple food would be available to purchase. If the number of voters grew too great for the space in front of the citadel, a secondary area would be set up to take the overflow.

The voting would open with the rising of the sun and close when the sun dipped below the horizon. Few people voted in the morning as a result of being unable to leave the compound, but the voting action really heated up as the sun neared the horizon at sunset. The barrels would then be split open and the contents weighed. Those in close contention for weighing the most would be counted in front of all those who had voted. The new High Chancellor would then be announced and they would begin their reign immediately. Tunley was looking forward to this moment very much.

The days rolled slowly along towards the election and Tunley spent much time with people that he neither liked nor cared about, in the hope of securing their vote. He forced himself to be pleasant, but firm like a rock that would be needed in the uncertainty that lay ahead.

Finally, the day of the election was upon the Admiral. He felt nerves unlike any he had felt since he was a teenager courting his first girl. He dressed himself smartly in his Admiral's uniform and made his way to the citadel in the pre-dawn darkness. He was permitted to enter the compound and was handed a wooden coin to cast his vote. He found this amusing, but voted for himself nonetheless.

First light came to the sky and Tunley looked about at the other candidates. They were all there milling around their stands awkwardly. Tunley noted Jaid was at the far end from where he was stationed and thought that it was wise of the organising Alderman to separate the two. In between, were five other candidates: a tall man who was also vying to be the Alderman of the Farmers, Karn who was the son of the wealthiest citizen in Roasline and was building his reputation, and three others who, in Tunley's opinion, might as well not have been there.

The Admiral didn't have to wait long before the sun peeped over the horizon and he heard a clang as the gates opened. He watched the entrance carefully, but was not surprised to see only one or two people enter.

The few early morning voters made their way around to all the candidates and listened to what each had to say. They then cast their votes under the watchful eyes of the candidates. Three went to Jaid and one to Tunley. The Admiral felt his stomach turn but smiled and talked to new voters who had just arrived. The morning wore on and the crowd in the voting compound grew. Tunley had long ago lost count of his, or anyone else's, votes and he decided it was time for his hired voice to get to work.

The man, dressed as a captain in the navy, stood upon the provided stand and filled his large chest with a deep breath. He then began calling out to the crowd all of Tunley's strengths. He smattered these with quick jokes about the opponent's weaknesses and Tunley was reminded of the well-worn sellers at markets. He smiled and already thought his investment was worthwhile. He looked over at the other candidates and they too had similar *voices*, although Tunley thought they were not as impressive as his.

With his spokesman in full flight, Tunley was able to mingle and speak directly with undecided voters. It didn't take long before he was pleased to note that everyone seemed to know who he was and what he stood for; strong defence and retribution for Kathsum's deceitful murder.

The day wore on and Tunley had almost lost his voice by mid-afternoon; he had never talked so much in his life and was thoroughly looking forward to sunset.

The arena was full to the brim and people were being siphoned off to the secondary holding courtyard. Tunley noted that this was happening a lot earlier than usual; indeed, sometimes the compound didn't even get full on election day. His arrogance put this down to the fact that he was running for High Chancellor.

The sun was soon mere inches away from vanishing and there was an excited frenzy of votes being cast. Tunley was wringing his hands in anticipation when the sun disappeared and a gong sounded across the area. Officials put stoppers in the slots of each of the candidate's barrels and cheers went up from the crowd. The Head of Order announced that the voting was closed and the contents of the barrels were to be weighed.

Each barrel was rolled on its side up a ramp and onto a platform where everyone could see the process unfold. Tunley followed his barrel with excitement and pride. He stood on the platform and looked out at the sea of people before him. *Soon I will rule you all!*

The Head of Order chose Jaid's barrel to be weighed first, which meant that Tunley would be last. The Alderwoman followed her barrel to the giant scales, which had a pan dangling on each side of a crossbar. The pans were like those used by gold prospectors who sifted for gold pebbles way up in the mountains, but many times larger.

A thick man with a sharp axe stood by as Jaid's barrel was hoisted over one of the pans. The man swung the axe into the barrel, which split the timber, resulting in a cascade of wooden tokens like a waterfall into the pan below. Immediately, the pan dropped several feet and a loud cheer went up from Jaid's supporters.

The second candidate's barrel belonged to Karn. This was hoisted over the other pan and again the man with the axe struck the barrel. As the many wooden coins fell into the pan, Tunley marvelled at the construction of the barrels: they were easily broken without letting their timber fall onto the pan, but remained dangling from the hoist. Karn had got many votes and for a moment Jaid had a look of concern on her face, but when the last token fell, the scales were heavily in Jaid's favour. *She is the one to beat; she sure has a lot of votes.* Karn's tokens were tipped off the pan by the axeman and the next barrel rolled into place.

Tunley would have laughed at the next four weighings if he wasn't so nervous. The four candidates combined wouldn't have had enough votes to beat Karn, let alone Jaid. *No wonder the Farmer's Guild can't decide on a new Alderman with candidates as unpopular as that.*

Then it was Tunley's turn. He clenched his teeth as his barrel was rolled over to the scales. Silence fell over the thousands of people watching and he dared a quick look at Jaid. Her face smiled, but her eyes looked worried. Tunley hoped he looked more confident.

The large barrel was hoisted into place. The full moon poked her face from behind a cloud and the axe swung into his barrel. A loud crack echoed across the watching faces. This was followed by the almost water-like sound of thousands of wooden coins spilling onto the metal pan. *There's a lot. But is there enough?* The scales moved. Jaid's pan rose slowly and Tunley's dipped. *Keep going, keep going.* Tunley pleaded. Jaid's rose some more, Tunley's sunk some more. Then they both stopped.

From where Tunley stood, he was sure that his was lower, but not by much. Murmurs rippled through the crowd, and then the Head of Order stood up and shouted. 'They must be counted.'

Four impartial judges came forward and two approached each pan. Tunley knew that the counting would take a long time and so signalled for someone to fetch him a chair and a drink. Jaid did the same and while the other candidates left the platform defeated, Jaid and Tunley sat mere feet apart watching the counting process avidly.

Tunley found himself transfixed by the counting and was grateful for his mind to be occupied. As each coin was counted, it was put in a new barrel. When one hundred coins were reached, a mark was put on a piece of slate for the entire crowd to see. When one thousand coins were reached, a star was drawn.

Darkness had fully descended and the Alderman of Farmers arranged for bright torches to be brought to the platform so that the attentive crowd could watch the proceedings. The night deepened further and a cold wind sprung up, chilling the large Admiral's sweaty body.

Each of the candidates were sitting on 65,000 votes and the piles were defiantly dwindling. Tunley found himself unable to sit anymore and stood instead. He snuck a glance at Jaid and she was sitting with her hands folded in her lap, looking tense. *I'd better beat that bitch; I've put everything into this.*

Then all of a sudden, Jaid's counters stopped at 66,734. Tunley quickly looked at his own figure, which was at 66,100 but he still had a small pile of coins to be counted. He tried in vain to estimate how many were left, but the quick hands of the counters kept obscuring his vision.

His number crept up past 66,500 and his hopes began to rise. His votes kept being counted and then he passed 66,734 and he still had coins remaining. He yelled in unison with those who had voted with him and he punched the air. The counters kept counting, but Tunley didn't care; he was the new High Chancellor of Roasline.

The High Chancellor stood up and his people fell immediately silent. He took a sip of wine and cleared his throat; all thought of his lost voice vanquished.

'You have done a great thing today. You have strengthened Roasline and your homes in a time when she was weak.' Cheers raced through the crowd and Tunley felt his power pulse through his entire body. 'Those scum across the Liagar will pay for their insult. They will learn the hard way that the people of Roasline are determined… fierce… deadly. They will rue the day they set foot in their boats to attack us. Because we are strong and we are united behind a great leader. We will not lie down meekly and let them attack us anymore. We will fight back. And WE WILL WIN!' Tunley found himself shouting passionately.

Yells of approval flooded the night air. Tunley chanced a glance at Jaid, who had her head buried in her hands and was weeping. He scoffed to himself.

'People of Roasline, enjoy tonight, for tomorrow we start work righting the wrongs that the Outcasts have done to us.' He paused and raised his right hand. 'Thank you all!'

Tunley stood waving to his people before him for several moments then chose to leave before the applause died down.

I've done it! I am the High Chancellor of Roasline and my people love me. Tunley, now it's time for the real fun to begin. And the High Chancellor laughed, not to himself, but to the night and the moon above, imagining what delights lay before him.

PART 3

41

Avgar lay on his bed with his eyes closed, clutching his stumped arm. The end was red, raw and oozing small amounts of blood and some other clear liquid. He breathed through clenched teeth and tried to block the pain from his mind. Despite the discomfort, he was deeply happy with his progress.

Over the last cycle of the moon, he had focused obsessively on regrowing his hand. His progress had been slow and full of pain, but there was no denying that there was more of a wrist than there had previously been. Indeed, he had a clear indicator that there was growth by the inch or so of pale new skin contrasting with the black tattooed old skin.

Avgar had accomplished this by delving into his magic each morning and trying to reconstruct his arm, layer by layer. Before extending the flesh though, he had needed to remove the stump's scar tissue so that more bone, muscle and fibre could be added. This had been a particularly painful experience.

The concentration, detail and energy needed meant that he only had the strength to do this in the morning before needing the afternoon to recover. Several times, he had lost consciousness due to his inability to control his magic, but this did not dissuade him from continuing on. Almost in rebellion of this, Avgar was becoming reckless in his eagerness to get his hand back. This *rebellion* had resulted in swifter progress, but more risk.

Avgar had been so excited with his success that he had neglected to focus on healing his voice cords. As he lay on his bed that afternoon, holding his stump, he realised this and vowed to spend the next morning trying to remove one of the grey lumps in the throat. With his eyes now closed, he pictured what he would need to do, but dared not to dip into his magic at that point for fear of passing his limits once more.

His contemplations were abruptly interrupted by a Healer placing a tray of food beside his bed. 'Are you awake, Avgar?'

He opened his eyes and looked up at a Healer that he did not recognise.

'Good. Some news has just reached the Healers and Lyafe has instructed me to pass it on to you.'

Avgar sat up, all thought of his voice momentarily forgotten.

'The High Chancellor of Roasline, Kathsum, has been murdered. There are many rumours wafting around as to who the murderer was, but nothing is certain at this point. Roasline seems to be blaming Nigrath, one of the Outcast leaders, but this has not been confirmed. The High Chancellor was killed a few days ago and her replacement should be appointed shortly.'

This news interested Avgar immensely and rekindled in him a desire to seek power and to rule. His mind started racing about what this would mean for the region, but he didn't know enough about the major players in Roasline to postulate who the new High Chancellor would be. Either way, this would be a once in a lifetime opportunity for the Outcasts; surely, they must attack Roasline.

Avgar looked up and found that the Healer was surveying his response. Avgar nodded to indicate that he understood the news.

'And this, so soon after the Outcasts' failed attack of Roasline; man's lust for blood is despairing.'

What?! Failed attack! What are you talking about? This was the first that Avgar had heard of the three-pronged attack on Roasline and couldn't believe his ears. *Those fools; I told them that the Outcasts were not ready to defeat Roasline. If only they had waited until now.* He grabbed his book and hastily pointed to words spelling out: *tell me more.*

'What's there to tell? The Outcasts attacked Roasline, and rumour has it, were spectacularly defeated. Exact details we never received and only a few wounded come our way talking of cannons in the night.'

Avgar looked pleadingly at the Healer, but the man shrugged his shoulders, clearly not interested.

'That's all I know. Now, I best be off. I have duties elsewhere.'

Avgar lay back on the bed and thought about how different the prospects for the region were since he was poisoned a couple of moon cycles ago. *The Outcasts are ripe for the taking, but with Kathsum gone, Roasline will equally be vulnerable. If only I had a fleet of ships with an army in it at my disposal… I could take both Roasline and the Outcasts and be leader of so, so many people.*

Avgar felt surprisingly nervous about attempting to heal his throat, which he dismissed as excitement at the prospect of getting his voice back. His confidence had been boosted since his success with his arm and the uncertainty that he had originally felt was replaced with an imagined self-assuredness. This seemed to abandon him now. He predicted that once started there would be great pain, but knew that in the end, his voice would be worth it.

The sorcerer lay back on his bed and cleared his mind in preparation. He breathed calmly in through his nose and out through his mouth and closed his eyes. Avgar reached for his powers and released what he hoped would be a small amount of energy. He used this to search inwardly until he found his vocal cords. They looked as lumpy as they had a month ago. This comforted him, as it meant that they were not getting any worse.

Avgar searched around until he found a small nodule sitting by itself on the upper vocal band. He prepared himself for the pain that was about to ensue and imagined a hair-thin knife slicing along the length of the fibrous cord and underneath the lump. The knife bit into the nodule and blood and yellow pus erupted out. This hit the inside of Avgar's throat and made him cough violently. As his throat contracted, Avgar felt an unbidden burst of magical energy flow through him and he lost control of the hair-knife. This savagely sliced through the entire vocal cord, severing it cleanly in two.

Avgar yelled out a cry of pain and was instantly brought out of his magical trance. He sat bolt upright coughing and spluttering blood all over himself.

A Healer promptly came, but could do little but watch the poor man coughing up his blood.

Avgar knew instinctively that the damage was severe, but forced himself to calm his breathing and supress his coughing.

I have to know what the damage is. Avgar hastily waved the Healer away and lay back on the bed. He forced his eyes closed and dipped into his magic once more. He instantly transported his vision to the inside of his throat and sought out his vocal cords once more. He found one to be exactly as it had been moments before, but the other cord dangled loosely against the wall of his throat. The despairing man wanted to attempt to fix it there and then, but dared not tempt fate by calling on more magic. Instead, he withdrew and returned to reality.

Avgar felt weak from the exertion, but urgently needed to leave the room in order to process what had just happened. He gathered himself together and walked into the sunlight slowly. He determinedly made his way to the hilltop, where he hoped the wind on his face would calm his anxious mind.

Several days passed and Avgar probed his throat time and time again; each time trying to heal his voice cords, but failing. He grew frustrated and bitter and grudgingly abandoned his efforts in favour of healing his arm. His success there was obvious, but bitter-sweet as it reminded him of his failure with his throat.

Several more slow and boring days passed and Avgar consumed himself in his growing hand. He had succeeded in completing the main body of the hand and had started to work on the thumb.

He was sitting on the side of his bed and massaging his aching first knuckle when two Healers came into his small room carrying fresh linen. Avgar looked enquiringly at them, but they ignored him and made the bed next to his. They refused to answer Avgar's looks and left him grumpy and unhappy.

For lunch, Avgar ate a thin meat broth with stale bread and stared contemplatively at the freshly made bed. The afternoon passed and real boredom gripped Avgar. During these times, he lost interest in the healing books and his mind wandered to his past. His life had truly been one mistake followed by another.

The light faded into evening and he lay on his side staring blankly at the wall, which had nothing of interest for him. He felt a hunger rumble in his stomach and wondered half-heartedly when his evening meal would come.

Approaching footsteps broke into his slow thoughts, and he turned his head to look at the door. Then, into the room burst a young lady with two Healers carrying a stretcher. A heavily bandaged man lay on the stretcher unconscious to the world. Lyafe followed the party with an air of excited authority about him.

'Set him on the bed.' He turned to Avgar. 'You now have a roommate, Avgar.'

Avgar sat up and looked interestedly at the still form of the man. His hair was short and orange and he had thick ointments covering multiple face wounds. His neck and chest had bandages wrapped tightly about them and Avgar knew that the man would be in pain when he woke.

Avgar made his way over to the patient as the two stretcher bearers left. Avgar felt the eyes of Lyafe watching him and he wondered if he should attempt to use his magic to heal the man.

Avgar looked down at the man and recognition struck him. *Winter!* He quickly looked from Lyafe to the girl who had accompanied the stretcher.

Lyafe spoke in answer to Avgar's glance. 'That's right, Avgar, this is your son, Winter.'

The girl made a start and stepped back a pace.

'And this is Sor, a monk from far away. Do not fear, Winter will be fine. He has a few deep cuts and severely broken ribs, but he's past the danger point.' A twinkle sparked in Lyafe's eyes. 'It seems that your vision was accurate. You are a marvel to behold.' The Healer Supreme nodded and left the room.

Avgar looked down at Winter with a mixture of feelings. Here was likely the last of his offspring lying before him in a bloody state. Avgar felt joy that Winter was alive and safe, disgust at the weakness of his son for having been beaten by a simpleton in an inn, and finally pride at how far his son had come to get to Headly. He smiled inwardly, but scowled externally.

After several long moments of staring at Winter, Avgar turned to Sor with a look of interest. He wanted to ask what *monks* were, who she was and why she was with Winter, but instead settled for appraising her physically. She had a wiry look about her that verged on malnourishment, but she held her head firm. He looked into her eyes and she stared back with what Avgar thought to be hatred. *How could she hate me? She doesn't even know me.* He watched as Sor broke his gaze and moved around the bed to be at Winter's head. She pulled up a chair and sat down with her arms and legs crossed. Avgar shrugged before moving back to his own bed where he sat on the edge and thought of his son.

Winter. He had always been the weakest of my children. Never one to confront his deficiencies. And yet, he survived when the others appeared to have perished. He probably ran away from the battle before Balleny; if he was courageous, he would have fallen in battle... but then he would not be here now. His thoughts circled around in this vein for a short while before he looked over to Sor. *Who are you, girl? What are you doing with Winter? Why are you here?*

They sat in silence for a while, with Avgar keeping an eye on Sor. She closed her eyes and he wondered if she was sleeping. He took this opportunity to study and ponder her more closely. From his bed, he was looking at her long dirty fingers when he felt her gaze upon him.

'I've been trained not to feel anger or to hate; but to realise that everyone has different pressures placed on them; different experiences that influence who they are and the choices they make. And yet, despite that way of viewing the world being ingrained in me since I was a child, I cannot help but feel an overwhelming sense of loathing towards you.' Sor's gaze bore into Avgar and he felt it like a slap of cold air on his face. 'What you did to Winter, when he was only a boy, is inexcusable. There can be no pressures on you that can justify the way that you treated your own flesh and blood. You are the epitome of evil.'

Avgar felt the hatred in her voice and doubted not that she told the truth. In response to this onslaught, Avgar did nothing. He sat there and stared straight back at her; keeping his expressions purposefully blank. *How dare she throw such accusations at me! She can hardly know what I've done and the reasons behind it. Stupid bitch.* He curled his face into a sneer.

'Is that the best response you can muster?' She cocked her head. 'After all you've done to Winter, he still chose to seek you out and when he's finally here, close to death, all you can do is stare at me. You're pathetic.'

Feeling his hackles rise, Avgar stood up threateningly and took two steps towards Sor. He growled at her in anger and immediately felt a searing pain rip through his throat. He shut his eyes tightly and was all consumed by the pain. After a few short moments that felt much longer to him, the pain eased and Avgar could think once more.

When he opened his eyes, he saw a fleeting look of pity pass across Sor's face and he immediately knew that she was more of a carer than a hater. He felt the anger drain out of him and he sat wearily back on his bed. Reason presented itself to him. *She is just angry because her friend is hurt.*

He smiled and tried to convey his feelings in his expression. She did not respond. Avgar wanted to distract Sor from her hateful thoughts and so pointed to his throat and shook his head. Sor looked puzzled and so Avgar found the words he needed in a book and indicated: *I no speak.*

She reluctantly read what he was pointing at and nodded curtly. 'You're lucky I can read.' He nodded and watched her to see what she would do next. Sadness crept into her eyes and she looked back down at Winter.

'He has gone through a lot for you.'

Avgar nodded and hoped that she would continue.

'Remember that in the coming days.' He nodded again. 'And if you treat him ill, then you will have me to answer to.' She stated it firmly but evenly, as though it was a fact and not a threat. Avgar nodded his acknowledgement once more before they settled into a mutual, long silence.

Winter didn't wake until late into the following day. Avgar had passed the day lying on his bed thinking about Winter as a child and young man. Despite Sor's personal attack on his treatment of his son, Avgar managed to justify to himself his actions towards Winter that could have been considered *questionable*. After all, he had been a ruler and needed to raise his son to be powerful.

Throughout the day, Avgar had periodically looked over to Sor, who appeared to have been in a deep sleep, even though she was sitting up.

When Winter did eventually wake, he groaned and tried to roll onto his side. Sor leapt to him and gently held him back while whispering words that Avgar could not hear. Avgar himself, made his cautious way over to Winter's bed and was surprised to feel a level of nervousness in his stomach.

Winter opened his eyes wide to Sor's whisperings and then sought out Avgar. The standing man tried to read Winter's expression, but could not. He made his slow way to Winter's side and then stood there looking down into his face. *You look so much older than when I saw you last. You look much more like a man now.*

'Father.' Winter managed to croak out the statement.

Avgar nodded and knelt down beside his son.

Winter moistened his mouth with his tongue and then spoke more clearly but with shallow breathing. 'You should be proud of me; I crossed the Moaks.'

Avgar smiled. *And then got beaten up by an untrained commoner in an inn.*

Winter closed his eyes, but continued to speak. 'I saw you in a dream, many months ago, and then you were a goat. I followed you into the Moaks and then Dusk fell. They're all dead now; your children.' Tears rolled down Winter's cheeks and Avgar felt a level of disgust at the weakness. 'I followed the goat higher and higher into the Moaks and then the cold took me. I woke up with the monks.' He looked fondly at Sor. 'They brought me back to full strength and opened my eyes to the Gods. The Gods of Night and Day gave me a new purpose until you entered my dreams once more. I then sought you out and Sor and I have travelled many miles to get to you.' Winter looked piercingly at his father. 'And now that I have found you, I can begin *your* healing.'

Avgar felt confused. *Have these monks given him healing powers? Maybe he could heal my voice!* Avgar felt excited at the prospect and looked closely at Winter. The colour that had been in his face after waking had drained and Winter looked pale and wan.

Sor noticed this too and spoke kindly to Winter. 'It is time now for you to rest. You can begin your mission tomorrow; there is no hurry, your father is not going anywhere.'

Winter nodded then looked confused. 'Why don't you speak, Father?'

Avgar closed his eyes in resignation, but Sor answered for him with a tone of disbelief. 'He claims he cannot speak.' She shot Avgar a fleeting glance. 'Now, you need to rest. You can get more information when you've healed a bit.'

Winter nodded again and settled down to sleep once more. Even though night was descending, Avgar wanted nothing more than to be alone. He grabbed a cloak to keep off the chill and left the room without looking at either Winter or Sor.

Eight days had passed since Winter had arrived at Headly. Avgar had stubbornly continued to regrow his hand in the mornings and had listened to Winter talk in the afternoon. His son had spoken at length of his journey as well as briefly touching on the teachings of the monks. Sor had come and gone throughout the days, opting to spend time assisting the Healers in their duties. Winter had almost fully healed with the aid of the Healer's knowledge and skill, but he still chose to spend the days with his father.

Avgar had found the concept of gods interesting, but could not bring himself to believe that such things existed, preferring to put his faith in the natural world and man's abilities. He wanted the credit for all that he had done and didn't like the thought that someone else may have helped him on his way.

Avgar had also shown Winter around Headly and had spent much time on his hilltop overlooking the Rogaus. The wind was blowing in his face as father and son watched the whitecaps of the ocean swell ever changing. They had been standing in silence for a long time before Avgar noticed Winter was fidgeting with his hands. *Come on boy, out with it.*

'I made a promise to Sor that I'm not sure that I want to keep.'

Avgar looked away from the ocean and faced his son.

'I promised her that once I found you, I would take my vows as a monk and commit my life to their service. But now that I've found you, I want to spend my time with you. I want to teach you what I have learnt about a peaceful, selfless life and how to find happiness in that.'

Avgar scoffed.

'I know all you can think of is hurting others on your way to power, but that is because you have not thought deeply enough about other options.'

That's a bit harsh; I don't just think about that. Avgar felt irritated.

'And I know I should not want anything to do with you after the way you treated me, but I have found peace within myself for your brutality.'

Avgar felt Winter's gaze pass to his stumpy arm.

'Since coming to this place and seeing you so impaired in both arm, and speech, I have come to realise that you are mortal and now just an old man. And in that mortality, you have flaws and fallacies and I now pity you.'

Avgar saw that there was genuine pity in Winter's eye and felt a wave of embarrassment, anger, and fear at his own fragility.

'I no longer hold you up on a pedestal to idolise. I no longer fear you, and I will no longer do your bidding. The power you held over me for so many years is gone and I feel free from your hold.' Winter paused and bit his lip. 'In that freedom, I choose to heal, not your body, but your spirit.' Avgar watched Winter flush red in the face.

You don't know what you're talking about, you stupid boy. Avgar felt his anger quickly rise above all other emotions. He wished he could yell back at the fool before him and put him in his place. Instead, he yelled inside his own head. *I have lived longer than you have. I know how the world works. You can't spend a few months with these monks and claim to know all about a peaceful world.*

Peace is built on dead bodies. He took an aggressive step towards Winter, who held his ground and even smiled knowingly, as if goading his father.

That was the last step: Avgar struck out with his left hand and hit Winter in the jaw. Avgar instantly felt a shattering pain in his own jaw and found himself on the ground. *Curse the Healer's protection.*

He rose to his feet and glared at his son, then turned his back on Winter and marched back towards Headly with his jaw still throbbing.

Avgar tried to avoid Winter over the next two days. This proved particularly challenging, as they shared the same quarters. When they were together, Avgar noticed Winter resisted lecturing him on a peaceful existence, but instead seemed to complain about Sor's persistent nagging of him to take his vows to become a monk.

Avgar got so frustrated that he vigorously pointed out the words, *just make a decision and stop your whining.*

Winter had smiled at that and said, 'A-ha, so you have been listening to me.'

Avgar had rolled his eyes and turned away from his son in annoyance.

While Winter might have been like a flea on his back, Avgar was very pleased to see his own hand regenerating. Each of his fingers were now at the first knuckle and he knew it wouldn't be long before his hand was complete once more.

Then he thought of his voice and bitterness swelled within him. Every time he had ventured into his throat since that fateful day, had ended in the same result: no progress and a highly irritable man.

He often ran through the events in his mind and tried to make sense of what had happened. Why hadn't he thought to suppress his cough reflex before starting to cut the nodule? Why had a surge of power swept through him at that exact moment? What had he done to deserve this? Why couldn't he heal it now?

His sleep had become even more disturbed than it already was. In addition to him reliving his horrible defeat every single night, he now also had recurring dreams where he was trying to save the life of someone that he couldn't quite see. He knew that all he had to do was to tell them to watch out for the wolf and they would be saved. Except, that he couldn't speak and the unknown person kept getting mauled by the huge beast. He dared not attempt to interpret the dream, but instead tried in vain to forget it as soon as he woke up.

The next eleven days passed much the same, with the exception of Avgar slowly allowing Winter to talk to him more. His son perplexed him; seeming to be both strong of mind and yet unable to make certain choices. He was still yet to accept or deny Sor's request and Avgar could see the young woman's frustration building.

Avgar also noted the way that Sor looked at Winter and thought he saw there the shadow of love. He smiled to himself and hoped that the two would make a couple. He surprised even himself at wanting Winter to have a loving partner, as he usually cared little for such things. In the same thought process, he realised that he must have given up on Winter ever being the man that he wanted him to be. *He will never be like me.* Avgar then was struck by a melancholy thought. *That is probably a good thing.* Avgar had then looked over at Winter eating his breakfast and sighed. *I am not a good person.*

Winter caught his eye. 'Are you all right, Father? You look a bit odd.'

Avgar nodded and left the room; wanting to be alone. He made his slow way to his hill and massaged his almost-completed hand as he went. His thoughts delved deeply into who he was and his feet carried him where he wanted to go without having to think about it. He reached the top of the hill and looked up from the long waving grass at his feet to see the Rogaus.

What Avgar then saw made him take a step back. He turned on the spot and ran as quickly as he could to his room. He had to tell someone, anyone. Oh, the irony; the one person to see the armada of ships heading his way was the one person who could not yell it to the town of Headly.

He burst into the room and saw Winter arguing with Sor. Ignoring this, he grabbed his son by the shoulder and dragged him to the window.

Winter gasped in shock. 'Oh shit!'

Sor raced over and she too was shocked to see what was there. Avgar was surprised even further when it was Winter who recovered the quickest.

'I don't care what protection we have on Headly; that is not going to end well for us. We need to get away from here as quickly as we can.' He turned to Avgar. 'Is there any hiding place that you know of that we could go to?'

Avgar's thoughts seemed shrouded in a fog and before he could shake his head, Sor spoke. 'I know of a place. There is a cave where the stream that runs through Headly comes from.'

'No, that is too obvious. They will search there.'

'No, they won't. At the back of the cave there is a fissure in the wall. The three of us should be able to squeeze through. Once through, there is a small chamber we can hide in. It is not big, but we will fit.'

'Wait, what about everyone else in Headly? We at least need to tell the Healer's what is coming.'

Sor agreed immediately. 'I'll go and find someone. You two prepare yourselves to leave.'

Winter nodded. 'We'll bring what food and clothing we can find. Be quick… please.' Avgar heard the fear barely hiding in Winter's voice.

Avgar and Winter busied themselves by collecting coats and what little food they could find in the room. Before they knew it, Sor returned puffing.

'I found the Healer Supreme. He knew the ships were on their way before I told him, but he did not seem concerned. In fact, he seemed thoroughly intrigued by their approach. He would not heed my warning, but was himself going down to the docks to meet the vessels.' She looked about the room. 'Are you two ready to go?'

Avgar nodded and Winter said, 'Yes'.

They hastily left the room, where Avgar had spent many months, and the seasoned campaigner couldn't help but feel a subtle sadness about it. He knew that while they were only going to hide now, one way or another, things would change with the arrival of the ships.

Avgar assumed that a battle would take place, but he didn't know what type of battle it would be, given that one cannot harm another while on Headly. Yet there was no doubt that the ships were coming. Their speed, direction and the fact that they weren't flying any colours informed Avgar of their ill intent. He quickly realised that, although the ships may not have been displaying their allegiance, Avgar knew they could not belong to the Outcasts by their sheer size and number. So, unless a new power had entered the territory, he mused that they must be from Roasline and under the direction of the newly appointed High Chancellor.

Sor led them around a sharp corner and they almost ran into a Healer with a pregnant woman by his side. They appeared to be chatting casually about the unexpected approach of the ships.

Sor pleaded with the lady to join them, and although she seemed less sure than the Healer, she refused and went with the Healer down the hill.

Winter looked enquiringly at Sor. 'Who was that?'

'Her name's Islonda. I've only met her a couple of times, but she seemed nice enough and sensible. I'm surprised she didn't come with us; that's a shame. Regardless, let's keep moving.'

Avgar followed the monk as they passed a few buildings used as storehouses. They soon left them behind and made their way up a narrowing valley. Sharp hills soon rose on either side and they found themselves walking next to a rocky river. The water was clear and bubbled merrily to itself as it cascaded down the slope behind them. Avgar looked back the way that they had come. They had climbed higher than he would have thought and the village of Headly seemed distant.

They kept walking as the sun moved across the sky and when Avgar turned. he saw that the first ships had reached Headly's pier. He was glad to see that they had docked and hadn't just opened fire with their cannons from afar. *Perhaps they aren't here to cause trouble.*

The trio walked only a short while longer when Sor stopped them. The river disappeared into a low cave and the three had to bend over to enter it. Avgar was the last to enter and had only walked a few steps into the cave when he bumped into Winter's backside.

Sor spoke and her voice bounced around the enclosed space. 'There is a small crack through here. Once you've squeezed through, there will be an opening where one person can stand. There will then be a tunnel that we will crawl through for a couple of yards. Once through, we will be able to stand or sit. There will be a little light in the chamber that comes from cracks in the rock above, but near total darkness in the tunnel.'

Winter asked the question that was also on Avgar's mind. 'How and why did you find this place?'

Sor seemed to hesitate before replying. 'Lyafe showed me… he said it was called the Cave of the Gods and has been here for longer than records have been kept. He thought I would be interested.'

That's odd. Something else is at play here, thought Avgar.

Winter seemed less sceptical than Avgar. 'That's good enough for me. Let's get going.'

When it was Avgar's turn to go through the crevice, he felt as if the walls were moving ever closer together. He had to squeeze his big frame through the smoothly jagged rocks and was not at all comfortable when he had to pause to allow Winter to move into the tunnel. While moving through the near total darkness of the crevice had been crushing, making his way through the tunnel felt oppressive. He hit his head many times and felt as if the rocks above would fall down on top of him at any moment.

He thankfully reached the end of the tunnel unscathed and only then realised that he had been holding his breath.

The air in the small chamber was dry and earthy. He looked up and saw light sneaking through tiny holes and cracks that must have penetrated many feet of rock above them. The chamber would be big enough for them to lie side by side, but not much bigger.

On two of the walls, Avgar could just make out writings carved into the stone. These were not a language he understood, but he did recognise prominent pictures of both the moon and the sun. He wanted to ask what this place was, but couldn't figure out how to communicate without his books. In a huff, he sat down and lent against the wall. *I just want my voice back; I hate this.*

Winter broke into Avgar's brooding. 'When it's dark, I'll sneak out and try to find out what's going on.'

'That's a good idea, Winter. In the meantime, we should rest and not talk louder than a whisper.' *What else can we do?* thought Avgar sarcastically.

Over the rest of the day, there were periods of resting silence and periods of whispered talk. Winter and Sor prayed several times and Avgar found this concept interesting to watch, but would not partake. Winter seemed to realise that he had his father as a trapped audience and so spoke of all the good that needed to be done in the world and how helping others would benefit Avgar's spirit.

Avgar tried to ignore Winter, but found this difficult and so listened without engaging. As darkness fell, Avgar found that he was in a surprisingly pleasant mood, although had the urge to hide this from his son.

Winter waited until it was pitch black in the cave before feeling his way out to investigate Headly.

With Winter gone, the night ticked slowly away, and Sor said little to Avgar. He felt her presence in the cave, as well as her continued dislike for him. Putting this from his mind, he closed his eyes and thought about his hand and how close he was to completing its healing. His thumb was finished, and his four fingers only had the length of the nails to go. If he had a quill and parchment, he would have been able to write, albeit clumsily, but he still yearned for the finished job. He thought about working on it in the cave, but dismissed the idea to reserve his strength should it be needed.

Footfalls and scraping noises eventually found their way into the cave and Avgar felt like a trapped animal. Moments later, someone came into the chamber, but Avgar couldn't see who it was.

'Winter?' Sor asked tentatively.

'It's me.' Winter replied breathlessly. 'You have to come with me, now. It's burning, Headly is burning.'

Avgar stood, but was careful not to hit his head on the rocky ceiling. They all felt their way around the chamber and each other and eventually made their way out through the tunnel, then the crevice and into the night.

Avgar smelt the smoke on the air before he saw the glow of the burning town and wondered why it had taken Winter so long to return. Without needing to talk, they all started towards the town by the light of the waxing moon. The walking was a lot harder than during the day, but they steadily made their way to the first burning building.

Smoke blew in Avgar's face and his nostrils flared at the acrid smell. He kept his head down as they continued further into the town. He tried to look past the buildings and out to the water and could just make out the absence of ships. *So, they've burnt the village and left. But why?*

Winter spoke through occasional coughs. 'I have found only one survivor. He's down by the water's edge and unable to walk. This way.' Winter led on.

Avgar and Sor followed, passing the burning room where Avgar had spent many months healing. They soon reached the beach and fresh salty air splashed across their faces with an onshore wind that felt cuttingly cold after the heat of the burning buildings. They soon found the man who was lying on the pebbled shore as if asleep.

Winter spoke. 'Ustek, I'm back with the people I told you of.'

Ustek looked up and smiled a grim smile. The man had grey grizzled hair that fell about a weather-worn face. He wore the gown of a patient of the Healers which was covered in dirt and ash all down the front, as if he had dragged himself along the ground. Avgar saw his legs were naked and looked to be burnt in several places.

He noticed Avgar looking at his legs and pre-empted his query. 'I can't walk; my legs were badly broken. I was almost going to be able to walk again, then this happened.' He gestured to the burning Headly.

Sor knelt down beside him and spoke kindly. 'What happened here?'

Ustek looked at her closely, as if wondering how she could not have known. 'Well… I watched the ships come, through my window. They docked and Lyafe went to speak with them on the pier. He did not get much of a say before he was surrounded by men who looped a rope about him and put a bag over his head. He was then carried onto one of the ships. The way they handled him,' Ustek shook his head, 'there was no way that he could break free.

'Within moments, there were hundreds of men pouring off the ship and dozens of small boats rowing to shore from the other vessels. The Healers had no chance. They were rounded up and carried away in much the same way that Lyafe was.

'As for us who were here to mend, well, those from Roasline who were almost healed and could walk were taken aboard the ships and those of the Outcasts, and us lame men, were locked inside the buildings. Once the Healers were gone, the buildings were set alight. Then the soldiers fled.' Ustek cleared his throat. 'Everyone left behind died, as far as I know. I only managed to escape through a wall that had fallen down from the fire. It required all of my willpower and was excruciating to run through the flames. Once on the outside, the rest of the building collapsed.

My legs gave out and I dragged myself down here, where Winter found me.'

'Where were the soldiers from?' Winter asked.

'Haven't you been listening? They saved the Roasline men, so they must have been from there.'

'Where are you from?' Sor enquired.

Ustek eyed Sor suspiciously. 'What does it matter?'

Winter cut Sor off. 'It doesn't matter at all.'

Avgar saw the monk give Winter an odd expression before speaking. 'No, it doesn't matter.' She sighed before speaking decisively. 'We should all get some rest until daybreak. Then we can take stock of the damage and plan what to do next. With so much burning wood, I'll get a fire organised down here to keep us warm.'

The remainder of the night passed uneventfully and Avgar even managed to get some sleep; after his usual nightmare at the beginning of his slumber.

With the morning came rainclouds; thick, bleak clouds that drizzled, not heavily, but constantly. The rain was cold and it wasn't long before Avgar was wet through and less than impressed.

Winter, Sor and Avgar searched the ruined town for the entire morning trying to find survivors, but found none. The buildings were long past being of any use, but Winter and Sor managed to erect a small shelter from the rubble to keep the rain off their heads.

By midday, the four of them huddled under the shelter, wishing that the rain would stop. They shared what food they had between them, which made Avgar acutely aware of the struggles they would soon face.

Winter spoke tentatively into the miserable silence and roused them all from their independent thoughts. 'We should come up with a plan on what to do next.'

Avgar nodded and smiled, while Sor replied cautiously. 'I've been thinking about that too. As far as I can see, there is little point in us staying in Headly. I think that we should go back to the mainland.' She looked accusatorily at Winter. 'And then, Winter and I should go back to the monks. Ustek, you can go where you please, as can you, Avgar.'

'Wait a moment there, Sor. I still haven't taken my vows…'

'I know.'

'And I'm not sure if I want to spend my life in the service to the Gods.'

Sor retorted quickly with a rising voice. 'You promised me that if I trained you, then you would take the vows when we found your father. We have done that. Does your promise to me mean nothing?'

'No… no. It's just—'

Ustek cut over Winter. 'Stop bickering like children. This is all irrelevant without a way to get back to the mainland. So, unless you can pull a boat out of your holy arses, we had better build a better shelter and find some food.'

Avgar nodded in agreement and was surprised to see Sor smiling. 'As it happens, I think I know where a sail boat can be found.' She pointed towards Avgar's hill. 'There is a small cove on the other side of that hill and three days ago, there was a boat drawn high up onto the shore. Much like the fishing boats that the Healers use.'

Winter spoke with concern. 'Do you know how to sail, Sor? Or you, Avgar? Or Ustek?'

Sor frowned and shook her head with lowered shoulders. Avgar shook his head too, but Ustek hacked up some phlegm and spat. 'Yea, I know how to sail. But the Rogaus is big and vicious and I won't sail with you lot unless I get your promise to do exactly as I say.' With this comment, he looked slyly at Winter. 'That's if we decide this is the best option for us.'

'What other options are there?' asked Sor. 'Stay here and build a town for the four of us? Wander inland or down the coast looking for who-knows-what?'

Ustek eyed her thoughtfully. 'It may be as you say, but being alive here is better than being dead at the bottom of the Rogaus.' He rubbed his whiskered chin. 'Pfft, what do I care? I'm old and not far from the end. Perhaps I'll have one more adventure. All right then; I'll go with you, if you're up for it.'

Sor immediately agreed, but Winter agreed more hesitantly. Avgar thought for a moment and realised the truth in Sor's words; there was nothing for them in Headly. He nodded his consent to the plan.

'That all sounds like sunshine and roses, but how are you going to get me over that hill to the boat?' Ustek grumbled.

'Winter and Avgar will carry you on a stretcher.' Sor smiled ruefully.

Avgar chuckled, but Winter retorted like a child. 'Only if you help too, Sor.'

'Oh, stop being difficult, Winter.'

Just as Winter opened his mouth to argue, Ustek spoke gruffly. 'It would be stupid to sail today anyway. The wind's no stronger than a sparrow's fart and by the time we get to the boat, night won't be far off. You, Winter, should go look over yonder hill to see if the boat's still there. Sor and this silent one,' he pointed to Avgar, 'will need to make a stretcher and gather whatever food they can find. You'll also need to bottle as much fresh water as you can. Drinking the salty Rogaus will make you sick.'

Avgar was comforted to realise that this man had some sense of survival about him, yet didn't much like the idea of trawling through rubble in the rain to find supplies. Then a thought struck him. *I wonder if any of my herb has survived.* He felt a tingle of excitement lift his mood. He stood to indicate his agreement with the plan.

The afternoon passed with little change to the weather. Avgar searched where the herb should be and miraculously found it still dry within its glass bottle. He wrapped the herb in a piece of leather he found, so that he could conceal it more easily, and used the glass bottle to collect water for their journey. A flint was harder to find though and this caused him great frustration.

As Avgar searched through the debris, he couldn't help but feel as though Ustek was watching him. He didn't really care, as he knew that there was nothing that the wizened old man could do to him, but it unsettled his mood and made him somewhat paranoid.

Trapped in his thoughts, Avgar brooded on not being able to talk and the impact this had on his ability to lead the other three. He had no option but to remain a follower, and this did not sit well with the experienced leader. He longed to tell people what to do and he then realised that it had been several months since he had been able to. *I'm sure that Winter would say that this experience has been good for me; healthy for my being. Humph.* These negative thoughts continued to swirl around Avgar's mind throughout the afternoon.

Winter returned and reported that the boat was still there. What's more, he had also seen a half derelict shack a mile past the boat. That discovery settled it; they got themselves ready and Winter and Avgar bore a makeshift stretcher with Ustek on it.

The going was tough, with the uphill climb being particularly challenging. Avgar acutely missed the tips of his fingers and the stretcher kept slipping out of his grip. Every time this happened, Ustek grunted in annoyance, but did not go so far as to chastise him for it. As they tired, Sor lent a hand so the three of them rotated through having a rest.

They reached the top of the hill and rested for a few moments to rub their weary arms and shoulders. Avgar realised that this would be the last time that he would look out at the view and a sense of sadness passed through him. He was a changed man since coming to the Healers and he put part of that down to spending countless days looking over the ocean in contemplation.

In order to beat the descending darkness, they continued their journey before Avgar was really ready to leave. As they walked, Avgar took his mind off the pain in his shoulders by admiring the coast stretched out before him.

At the bottom of the hill sat a pleasant, pebbled cove. This curved away to another hill with yellow cliffs plunging sheer into the ocean. Several yards up from the cove's beach, short trees grew with tough looking bark and wiry frames. On the farther hill no trees grew, except a lone twisted gnarly old pine. Even from this distance, it looked like it was shaped by the harsh winds that would blow fiercely onshore. To Avgar, this tree reminded him a little bit of Ustek and he smiled at the comparison.

The four made their way down to the cove with little trouble and continued past the boat to the shack. Once they had deposited their luggage, they returned to the boat and inspected it for sails and seaworthiness. Ustek was satisfied that she would sail without sinking, but would provide little shelter for them on the open sea. The boat itself was a small vessel with two sails hanging off a single mast. She was not big enough for a cabin and certainly not designed to travel long journeys, but as Ustek said; 'she'll do.'

Avgar looked at the sky and squinted his eyes in the light misting rain. The wind had picked up and was now a mild breeze. It was a cool morning, but not cold, and Avgar was glad to see that the ocean wasn't too rough.

Ustek evaluated the weather for the benefit of the group. 'The wind will be enough to sail, but she won't take us quickly.' He flicked dirt out from under his fingernail. 'But there's a fair chance it will get stronger as the day goes on.'

They all had a small bite to eat, drank some water and made their way to the boat. The three able bodies struggled to get the vessel into the water, but they managed it and were thankful for the high tide.

Winter carried Ustek to the water's edge and passed him to his father, Avgar hauled him into the boat, before they all leapt in. Ustek immediately started barking orders and before long, they had made their way out of the cove and were heading in the direction of the mainland. Avgar smiled. *It feels good to be doing something again.*

42

High Chancellor Tunley woke with a thunderclap headache. He rolled over in his bed and pulled the covers about his head. He shivered as though with cold, but winter was only just beginning and it never really got *that* cold in Roasline anyway. He held his hands to the sides of his head in an attempt to squish the pain away. It did not work and when his hands came into contact with his head they felt sticky, as though they were caked in mud. He was only puzzled for a moment before his memories of the previous night came crashing back to him.

Tunley had drunk heavily of the best wine to be had in Roasline. After dismissing his friends, or rather sycophants, he felt a burning desire in his loins. He sought his usual whore, but she was unavailable due to being struck down with a crippling fever and a red-brown rash. Tunley ended up settling on a fiery-looking woman half his age. He had taken her to his house; which he knew would be a great honour for her, and he was excited to try something new. However, when she touched him, he did not respond as a man should. She tried and tried, but failed. The High Chancellor had grown angry. She then had the audacity to suggest that he must have had too much to drink, which can sometimes cause this *little* problem.

Tunley had raged at her, spitting insults at her worthless being. She had then shrugged and went to gather her clothes; clearly used to such treatment. That was when Tunley's anger had peaked. Before she had taken three steps to the door, he had grabbed a knife, lunged at her, and slit her throat. Her body had fallen half naked to the floor and only then did the High Chancellor feel himself aroused.

The heavy man burrowed out from under the covers and peeked over the edge of his bed. There, lying twisted and deranged on the floor, was the woman. Blood was everywhere and it filled his nostrils. He wanted to be sick, but forced the impulse back down. *Stupid whore; what a mess she's made of my room.*

The High Chancellor's head still throbbed, but he forced himself from the bed and over to the washbasin. He splashed water on his face and cleaned the blood from his hands and arms. He wrapped a mohair gown about himself to ward of the cold and pulled open his door, calling to his man servant.

'The woman tried to knife me in my sleep. Clean up this mess before lunchtime.' Tunley barked the order and watched as the man's face turn pale when he saw the bloody corpse. *He is no soldier.* 'Then take the rest of the day off.'

Tunley grabbed some warm clothes and left the man to organise the clean-up of his room. He made his way to the kitchen with a strong need for fried bacon and a mug of ale.

He had only just finished his meal when there was a smart rap at his door. This was followed by the entry of a sailor without invitation.

'What the bloody shit do you think you're doing, Captain?' Tunley was aggressive in his greeting.

The man took a step back, but did not shrink from his duty. 'You ordered me to notify you as soon as the Healers had arrived in Roasline. They are here aboard our ships, High Chancellor.'

Tunley quickly remembered giving that order and his aggression was replaced by elation. He stood and grasped the man's shoulder. 'Good man. Have their leader locked in the dungeons of the citadel and bring a handful of the Healers to the naval barracks' courtyard. Make sure they're restrained.'

'Aye, sir.' The captain saluted and left.

Tunley smacked his hand down on the tabletop in glee. 'Yes! This is going to be fun.'

High Chancellor Tunley made his way to the Roasline dungeons at midday. The day had turned into a mild winter's day with a gentle sun and a playful breeze, but when he descended below ground, he felt damp and cool and wrapped his high collared cloak about him.

The warden, a heavy-set man, directed Tunley to where the Healer Supreme was being held. Tunley dismissed the guard before sliding the bolt back on the weighty door. It screeched as he swung it open and he boldly walked into the small cell.

Standing in the centre of the room was a plainly dressed man with a sad expression on his face. He looked a similar age to the High Chancellor and he had interest in his eyes. The High Chancellor looked him up and down, assessing the best way to get what he wanted.

The man before him broke the silence first, which caused Tunley to frown. 'My name is Lyafe and I am the Healer Supreme.' He paused for only a moment. 'High Chancellor, you have broken a fundamental rule of the treaty between the people of Roasline and the Healers. It is with regret that I must inform you that the Healers will no longer assist the peoples of Roasline and the lands that fall under your rule.'

Tunley smiled knowingly. 'I am the High Chancellor Tunley and you are wrong in your conclusion, for you will assist us greatly.'

Tunley expected Lyafe to retort, but the Healer stood in silence surveying the High Chancellor. Tunley didn't quite know what to make of this.

'What you see, Healer, does it frighten you?'

'Ha, not in the slightest. It takes more than a sick man to frighten me.'

A sick man? What is he talking about? He's just trying to play with my head. Tunley brushed this thought aside. 'You say that you won't help us and I say that you will. Do you want to know what I need your help with?'

'Not really. Tell me, that rash on your hands, is it anywhere else on your body?'

Tunley looked at his hands before he realised what he was doing.

'And you feel cold, yes? Even though you're wearing heavy clothes. And your muscles, do they ache also?'

'Enough of your mind games, Healer.' Tunley stepped threateningly close to Lyafe, but the Healer only smiled.

The Healer Supreme spoke quietly and with confidence. 'The only help I can offer you is to ease your sickness.'

Tunley spoke equally quietly, but with hunger in his voice. 'You're wrong. You're going to give me the Healer's protection.'

Lyafe took a step back and frowned. Tunley was pleased to see that Lyafe was not expecting this request. 'Certainly not. That's reserved for Healers only.'

'You're wrong again, Lyafe. The High Chancellor before me was granted your protection, albeit for a short time only.'

Lyafe rubbed his stubbled chin. 'If you say so.'

'Oh, I do. And I know it was successful.'

Lyafe conceded. 'But that was not done by me. I have not the power to grant you our protection, even if I wanted to.'

'You're a terrible liar, Healer. I have sources, Healer sources, that the power to grant the Healer's protection lies solely with the Healer Supreme.' Tunley smiled wickedly. 'With you.' He poked a finger at the Healer.

'If you say so, High Chancellor.'

The repeated comment frustrated Tunley, but Lyafe continued with passion in his voice. 'I can think of no reason to grant you such protection and many reasons not to.'

'Lyafe, you injure me.' Tunley paused to enjoy the helpless Healer Supreme. 'Before the day is out, you will have your reason and, moreover, you will willingly grant me the Healer's protection.'

Lyafe appeared to sense danger and kept his mouth shut. Tunley stood with his face but an inch from Lyafe's and punctuated each word with a pause. 'You will do every little thing that I ask you to do.' He then stepped back.

'Guards, bring this man to the naval barracks courtyard; he requires some education.' Tunley left Lyafe to be bound and dragged from the cell unceremoniously.

Tunley arrived at the naval barracks ahead of Lyafe and quickly confirmed that five Healers were being brought from the ships to the courtyard where he was to meet with Lyafe. Once satisfied, the High Chancellor made his way to the empty training ground and paced impatiently while he waited. He rubbed his hands together in excited anticipation and kept turning to see if Lyafe or the other Healers were arriving.

The courtyard was nothing special, just an expanse of open packed dirt where training sailors could complete drills. Unusually, there were hanging gallows set up as well as an empty horse trough and an assortment of other odd apparatuses.

Tunley was inspecting these when Lyafe was marched into the courtyard with his hands bound. Tunley smiled broadly when he saw just behind Lyafe the five Healers that he had requested also arriving.

'Lyafe, welcome, welcome.' Tunley greeted the Healer Supreme with glee. He then looked to the sailors escorting the other Healers. 'Put them over there, near the gallows.'

Tunley turned back to Lyafe. 'I'm a generous man, so I'll give you one more chance before we get our hands dirty; grant me the Healer's protection… please.'

Lyafe shook his head, while he's eyes watched the other Healers apprehensively.

'Then let us have some fun. You see, I've been doing some thinking about the Healer's protection and I believe that I have found some limitations; loop holes, if you will.' Lyafe's eyes snapped to glare at Tunley. 'I thought that with our abundance of captured Healers, we could test my theories.' The High Chancellor began pacing in front of Lyafe in elation. 'The way I see it, the protection only protects against direct attacks. If I hit you or stab you, I feel the effects of that attack. But what about indirect attacks or actions. Say, what would happen if I pushed a Healer off a cliff… or hung him on the gallows… or shot him with an arrow… or put him in a horse trough and covered him in water. Would I feel those effects? How powerful is this magical protection that everyone seems to revere and fear?' Tunley looked at Lyafe, whose face had gone pale.

'Yes, you would feel the effects and die.' The Healer replied his voice clipped.

'You see, I'm not sure that I believe you. I think you're bluffing.' Tunley threw his hands up in the air as a question. 'Let's give it a test. Unless, you want to grant me the protection now?'

Lyafe shook his head.

'Why don't we start with the gallows? Come and stand next to me, Lyafe.' They made their way over to the gallows and Tunley directed a sailor to string a Healer up, ready for execution.

Before Tunley could proceed, Lyafe spoke. 'If you really don't believe me, you should be the one to pull the lever.'

'Ha, you're a funny man. If you think I got to be High Chancellor by taking needless risks, you're a fool.' Tunley clapped Lyafe on the back harder than he intended and felt the blow himself.

He straightened up and looked to the gallows. 'Sailor, pull the lever.'

The sailor looked frightened, but pulled the lever regardless. The floor of the gallows swung open and the Healer dropped to the end of his rope. His body thrashed and jerked for a few moments and then stopped moving. Tunley grinned broadly. 'Sailor, how to do feel?'

The sailor replied shakily. 'Fine, sir.'

Tunley let out a whoop and glared at Lyafe. 'Your type are not invincible, it seems. Remember that it was your refusal to help me that killed him.'

'No, it was you that killed him, not me.'

Tunley growled. 'Of course, it was me who killed him, but it was also your inaction that killed him. Right, what's next?'

Lyafe remained tight-lipped, but frightened.

'I think the horse trough.' Tunley directed a Healer to be placed into the dry horse trough and tied to the bottom. He then ordered bucket after bucket of water to be poured into the trough. Lyafe squirmed uneasily as the water level slowly rose.

'Come a bit closer, Healer Supreme. Let's watch as the water goes into the man's lungs.' Tunley pulled the Healer over to the trough side. The water had reached the sides of the man's mouth and he was trying to thrash his way out of the bindings.

'It looks like he doesn't want to die. You know, you can save him if you want. All you have to do is give me the protection of the Healers.'

Lyafe appeared to be crumbling on the verge of tears.

'Equally, I'm happy to kill this man and move onto the next, if you want. The choice is yours.'

The Healer Supreme looked like a tired, defeated man. He sighed deeply. 'All right. I'll grant you the protection you seek.'

Tunley smiled. 'There, that wasn't so hard. Once you've granted me the protection and I've tested it, I will order the water buckets to stop.'

Lyafe seemed to be mumbling under his breath, deep in concentration. A moment later, he stopped and looked at Tunley spitefully. 'It is done.'

'Excellent, excellent.' Tunley called a sailor over to him. 'I order you to slap me hard on the back. It's all right, you won't be punished for doing this.'

The man looked frightened out of his wits and hesitated. Tunley saw Lyafe glance over as the water in the trough continued to fill.

'Sailor, if you don't do this, I will have you flogged.'

The sailor drew back his arm and smacked the High Chancellor on the back. Tunley felt nothing more than a gentle brush, whereas the sailor groaned in pain and coughed to catch his breath.

Tunley swelled his chest in delight. 'Excellent, excellent!' He turned to Lyafe. 'Now, I want you to grant the same protection to all of my soldiers.'

Lyafe's face dropped further. He pleaded with Tunley. 'Get that man out of the horse trough and we can talk more.' There was definitely panic in his voice. 'I mean, think about it, High Chancellor. Do you really want that many men with the Healer's protection? Wouldn't that be a threat to you?'

Yes, I hadn't thought of that. Tunley snarled at his sailors, 'Get that man out of the trough.' He looked back down at the shaking Healer Supreme. 'You're right. I will need to pick those who will be of no danger to me.'

Tunley watched as Lyafe bit his lip. 'I won't grant our protection to masses of your soldiers; you would decimate the Outcasts. I simply won't do it.'

'Of course I'll decimate the Outcasts; that's the point.' The High Chancellor looked to his sailors. 'Drown the Healer.'

'No!' Lyafe made towards the horse trough. Tunley stepped in front of him.

'Then help me protect my soldiers.' He paused for a moment. 'Blank refusals will only result in more deaths.'

Lyafe looked past the High Chancellor and Tunley felt him squirm as the Healer in the trough coughed and spluttered before lying still; his life taken from him.

'Right, time to test out my theory with the bow and arrow.' Tunley ordered the next Healer to be targeted. 'Lyafe, what say you?'

Lyafe remained silent with pursed lips and tears in his eyes. Tunley was mildly impressed. *His will is stronger than I thought. I'll have to step up the show.*

'Fire.' A twang rang out through the early winter air, which was quickly followed by a thud. Tunley was partially delighted to see that the next Healer was dead with an arrow through his heart, while being somewhat disappointed in the knowledge that *he* wouldn't be protected from an arrow attack. His sailor was rubbing his chest. 'What do you feel seaman?'

'A pinching pain, right here, in my chest.'

'You'll be fine.' *But that's interesting… the magic could tell who shot the arrow… but was not strong enough to stop it.*

He turned back to Lyafe. 'What's it to be, Healer? More deaths or your cooperation?'

'I will not arm your soldiers with this weapon.' He looked closely at Tunley. 'And if you keep killing us, there will be no one to heal your wounded.'

'True, but lives are cheap.' He thought for a moment. 'You make a good point.' *I know how to get him.*

Tunley turned to his sailors. 'You, you, and you, go out into the market and round up some women and children, babies, if you can. Bring them back here. Promise them food to get their cooperation.'

'Aye, sir.'

The three seamen jogged out of the courtyard and Tunley turned back to Lyafe and spoke gruffly. 'Let's see how strong your resolve is when the arrows are pointed at children.'

'No! You can't!'

'I'm High Chancellor, I can do whatever I want.' He turned to face the entrance. 'I hope you have a strong stomach.' Tunley said no more. He could tell that Lyafe was holding something back and he could feel his resolve snapping one string at a time. It wouldn't be long before the Healer would completely snap. *I just have to be patient... and ruthless.* He smiled to himself.

Tense moments passed and the two men stood side by side in the courtyard. A cool wind whipped around the open space and Tunley felt it keenly. Before the sailors returned, Lyafe finally gave in.

'Tunley, let these people live, please.'

Tunley remained silent, knowing that Lyafe would continue.

'I can't grant our protection to your men because I can't just give a blanket protection to anyone. I... I have to have seen that person, know their name and be able to bring a picture of them to my mind. I then have to say certain words and think certain things to grant the protection. It is not a simple process. I can't protect your army, even if you kill every man, woman and child in Roasline. I simply can't.'

Tunley felt taken aback. *Why did I think it would be a simple process to grant the protection? What a stupid assumption I've made.* What he said was quite different from what he thought. 'You're lying to me. We will test your truth when the children arrive.'

The Healer got down on his knees. 'Please, High Chancellor, I'm telling you the truth. Let me help you still. Choose some men, well-trusted men, and bring them to me. I will get to know them and grant them the protection. Just please don't kill innocent people.'

That seems like a reasonable prospect.

'Stand up, man.' He lifted Lyafe up by the arms. 'I will bring my trusted captains and a random selection of troops to you. That way the enemy won't know who has the protection and who doesn't.' Tunley felt satisfied with the outcome and was beginning to tire of Lyafe. 'Before you return to your cell, know this. Every day, at a random time of day, I will test the protection that you have placed on me, for I know that you can remove it. If I find that it is not in place, I will order you to witness the torture and slaughter of one hundred children… every day.'

Lyafe looked as if he was going to vomit. 'It will stay in place.'

'Yes, it will.' He looked Lyafe up and down. 'You need to rest; you have a big task ahead of you.'

The High Chancellor signalled to the sailors to return Lyafe to his cell.

The following day, the High Chancellor sent well over a hundred men to Lyafe. He instructed them to look at the Healer Supreme, say their name and then wait until he said they could leave. They did this one man at a time and Tunley made sure not to tell them they were getting the Healer's protection.

The High Chancellor's suspicious mind suspected that Lyafe might deceive him and so had each man's protection subtly tested. He also threatened Lyafe that he would test the men at random times and, if he found the protection lacking, there would be grave consequences. Lyafe had cowed and Tunley felt confident that the threat would prevent the Healer from removing the protection.

As well as organising these men's protection, the High Chancellor set about the final preparations for his invasion of the Outcasts. He spent time with the General and the new Admiral, Nach, a young man with stunted expertise, but sound loyalty to the High Chancellor. The three agreed on a simple battle plan, not dissimilar to that which was used by the Outcasts. They would transport vast numbers of troops across the Liagar while simultaneously sending the bulk of the fleet around to land troops north-east of Fort Kykum. These ships would then retrace their voyage and open fire with cannons on The Fort as the ground troops attacked.

The structure of Fort Kykum meant it would be a challenge to capture, but Tunley knew he had the superior firepower and manpower. His will was strong and he would be victorious regardless of the cost of life. Once the Fort was taken, the surrounding lands would be easy to sweep across; no real resistance would be met until they reached Nivera, many, many miles away. Yes, there would be battles and skirmishes in between, but with the Outcasts' army decimated, there would be little real threat to his attack.

The High Chancellor could smell his victory before he had even set sail. He imagined the spoils of war; the treasure, the land, the women and the violence and he longed to get his plan underway.

Tunley knew that in his absence he would have to leave a trustworthy man in his place and appointed the Head of Order to be in charge of Roasline. He had long disbanded the Aldermen and Alderwoman from the council meetings, citing that Roasline was in a *state of emergency* and that the need for non-military leaders was negligible. Jaid had protested strongly in this and he had hoped that she would overstep her mark and give him an excuse to lock her up. But she was restrained and so he would not be able to have his way and imprison her.

The night that he had dismissed the Alderwoman, he had selected a prostitute who looked as similar to Jaid as he could find. He violated her before leaving her corpse close to where Jaid lived to send the Alderwoman a message. After that, she had left Roasline to stay with a cousin on a distant farm. Tunley was both satisfied and disappointed at this and became more and more restless while waiting to begin his invasion.

He had set the date of embarkation at two days' time and he now regretted not setting it earlier. But it was done, and so he was left to entertain himself in whatever way he could. He did this by drinking steadily and exerting his power freely.

Eventually, Tunley's army was ready to set sail as day turned into dusk. Excitement ran through Tunley as the sails filled with wind and he stood on the bow of the finest ship in the navy and watched the water begin to part before him. As the ship picked up speed, his thoughts strayed to his own prowess. *I am power incarnate.*

The attack of the Outcasts had begun.

43

The second day dawned since Avgar, Winter, Sor and Ustek had set sail from Headly. The day gradually got brighter with a diffuse dull light spreading as far as the eye could see. The cloud cover was heavy, such that Avgar could not tell where the sun was in the sky. This gave him an unsettled feeling for he couldn't be sure which direction they were heading in.

The sight of land had evaporated the day before and either the wind had changed direction overnight or they had. Originally, they had set out in a southerly direction with the wind blowing from the west, but now the wind seemed to be blowing from the north, speeding them on their way.

Avgar looked about the small boat to see Winter and Sor still sleeping soundly at the bow. It looked as though their sleep was not disturbed by the toing, froing, upping and downing of the boat through the ocean swell. Avgar then looked to the stern and found Ustek sitting up and looking intently at something in his hand. Avgar moved to see what it was and Ustek silkily concealed it beneath his leg. *I wonder what that was… I'll have to find out.*

The seaman smiled kindly at Avgar. 'How was your sleep? You're a bit of a snorer, you know.' Avgar was distracted by the accusation. He waved his hand to indicate that his sleep had been rocky.

'Still not talking I see. Humph, that's going to make things a bit boring.' Ustek motioned for Avgar to join him at the stern.

'I'm not usually a big talker myself, but you look a bit fresh in a boat, so let me talk a whiles.' As Ustek spoke his grey hair flipped about his face in the wind. Avgar noticed that he didn't seem to care, but the constant movement distracted the silent man from the conversation.

Avgar had to refocus his mind to listen to what the wizened man was saying. 'We've got the wind behind us, so we'll make good time. At this time of year, she'll usually blow like this for a few days; keep us skipping along. Now, I'm no weather predictor, but I'm hoping these low clouds hold their rain for a few more days too, but it's hard to tell. Either way, our food won't last for us to reach where we're going, so there's going to be some hard decisions and high tension. You can't talk, so the trouble will come from those two down there.' He pointed at Winter and Sor.

Avgar supposed he was right, but didn't really want to think about the inevitable arguments. *When people get hungry, they argue and those two seem to have a knack for it even with full stomachs.* He sighed.

'My thoughts exactly.' Ustek looked Avgar up and down slowly and Avgar began to feel uncomfortable.

When Ustek next spoke, it was quietly and with meaning. 'There were strange rumours on Headly about a man who had one hand and couldn't talk.' He looked at Avgar's right hand and Avgar felt his fingertips prickle. 'Rumours that he had special powers… magical powers.' Ustek inflected the last word making the statement into a half question.

Avgar remained still and stony faced; not wanting to confirm or deny this.

'You know, some people get scared of such powers… others… seek them out.' Ustek looked very serious. 'This man would be a dangerous man to travel with. He would either be dangerous himself or attract danger from those who seek him.' Avgar felt a chill down his back, but couldn't quite tell why. 'If such a man was captured, he could fetch a large reward…' Ustek trailed off.

Avgar didn't know what to make of this. Ustek had certainly been watching him closely, but what could the lame old man do. Without wishing to, Avgar displayed his feelings on his face. Ustek made a sudden movement and Avgar flinched back as a reflex.

Ustek slapped his own knee and roared with laughter. 'You didn't think that I was going to attack you, did you? Ha! Then what would I do?' He laughed again and Avgar felt embarrassed. 'You're fun, you are. I think I like you.'

Avgar turned away from the old man and watched as Winter and Sor began to move about, having been woken from Ustek's laughter.

Winter looked bleary eyed and a bit confused, but Sor woke up alert and ready for action. The only problem was that there was no action to be had on the boat. She seemed to realise this and settled down to her morning prayers. Out of the corner of his eye, Avgar watched Winter look at Sor, then frown and sigh and then do as she was doing. *His heart is not into this monk business.*

Winter's prayers were short, after which he started rummaging around for the food. Avgar watched him closely and he could sense that Ustek was too. Winter produced a wrinkled apple and started eating it without so much as a glance at anyone else.

Sor finished her prayers and looked around the small boat. 'Well, what's the plan for today? Oh, I know, let's sit in this tiny boat for the entire day.' Her sarcasm clearly displayed her dissatisfaction at the day's outlook.

'If you want to go for a swim, that can be arranged?' Ustek played back. 'Perhaps we can find a shark to keep you company.' He smiled ruefully.

'What's a shark?' Winter asked.

Ustek gave him a stare of annoyance. He mumbled something under his breath that Avgar couldn't quite catch and then spoke to Winter. 'A shark is a big fish with sharp teeth. Very strong and hard to catch, but good eating if you do. Unless they eat you first, of course.'

'Why would Sor want to swim with a shark?' Winter ignorantly asked.

Nobody answered him.

The morning wore away, then turned into afternoon and Avgar felt restless and grumpy. He had seen Ustek look at the small contraption when he thought no one was watching a few times, before hiding it swiftly again. The four would soon be eating their evening *meal* and Avgar was feeling the effects of hunger.

Ustek had just put the device away again and Avgar decided he wanted to know what it was. He made his way to Ustek and stood before him while maintaining his balance. Ustek looked at him questioningly. Avgar made a sudden movement to grab the thing from under Ustek's leg. The older man was quicker and pulled it away from Avgar's grasp.

'Now, now, let's all play nice.'

Avgar pointed at the object in Ustek's hand and then pointed to his eyes; indicating that he wanted to see it.

Ustek looked at Avgar, calculated the man, before shrugging his shoulders and pointing to the seat in front of him. 'Sit down and I'll show you.'

Avgar sat down promptly. Ustek withdrew the device and held it in his palm. Avgar took it and inspected it closely. The object was a small wooden box with seven sides and intricate carvings of waves crashing against rocks. He saw a hinge and unclasped a latch to open a lid. Inside were more of the carvings as well as the letters N E S W. A small bit of metal pointed to these letters and moved as Avgar moved the device. He soon realised that no matter which direction he held the device, the pointer pointed to his right. It was a curious object and nothing like anything that he had seen before.

Still looking at the device, Ustek explained. 'It is called a compass. The hand will always point towards East. So, you can see that we are travelling south. This is how I know we are going in the right direction.' Ustek licked his lips and Avgar felt his eyes flicker between the compass and Avgar's face.

This is amazing. With this you could travel accurately and quickly and never get lost. Where would you get such a thing?

Avgar handed it back to Ustek and tried to mouth *where from?* but was not very successful. He also tried spelling the words out with his hands, but Ustek couldn't understand. He then had a thought and pulled a knife out. Ustek looked cautious, but Avgar merely scratched his question into the side of the boat.

'It is a very rare piece of equipment, this compass is. I only know of one place to get them made and where that is, I'm not willing to share.'

Avgar looked angry. *Stupid old man keeping secrets.*

'There's no point getting angry, I was sworn not to tell anyone. I shouldn't have even shown it to you to begin with.'

Avgar waved Ustek away; having had enough of the man for one day. He picked up his small ration of food for the night and made his way to a more comfortable position, alone. Night darkness descended and after eating his food, Avgar focused on growing his hand once more before he would allow himself to sleep. *It's not like I need a lot of energy to sit all day in this boat. I might as well do something useful.*

Dawn broke and for a moment the sun poked through the horizon between the earth and the heavy cloud cover. This brightness woke Avgar, who squinted over the bow of the boat and into the sun's full brightness. By the time he roused himself enough to sit, the sun was gone and another dreary day of threatening clouds with a strong tail wind loomed.

He looked about and saw Winter and Sor both sleeping. Ustek was awake again and Avgar wondered if he ever slept. As he looked at the old man, he rubbed his bristly chin and a thought struck him. *We're travelling east!* He looked at Ustek again, this time to see if he might already know this. Avgar made his wobbly way over to Ustek and motioned for the compass.

Avgar thought Ustek looked a little fearful, or was that just Avgar projecting his own thoughts? The old man handed him the compass and Avgar opened the lid. The arrow still pointed over the left of the boat, to Avgar's right, and then Avgar's mind clicked into understanding. *The compass points north, not east! Ustek is taking us east, not to the mainland.*

Avgar jumped to his feet and tried to convey his thoughts in his expression and actions. Ustek responded as if he had no idea what Avgar was on about. 'I'm sorry. I don't know what you're trying to say. I think you should calm down before you do some damage… or fall over the side of the boat.'

Was that a threat?

Ustek let go of a rope that he was holding and the sail swung outwards. The boat pitched and Avgar lost his balance for a moment. He promptly sat down to hold on to the safety of the side of the boat. *What is he playing at?*

Ustek's move had woken Winter, who blearily called out. 'What's going on? What was that bump?'

Ustek responded. 'Avgar was getting a bit excited and fell over.'

I need to get Winter to understand what is happening. Avgar made his way over to his son and tried to gesticulate where the sun was and which direction they were travelling in. Winter watched closely, but after a short while, shook his head.

'I'm sorry, father, I don't know what you're trying to tell me. Something about the sky… is it the clouds… do you think it's going to rain?'

Avgar shook his head in frustration. *Stupid boy.* He waved Winter away and sat down by himself. He stared out into the ocean and felt her full vastness. *The water always looked so calm from my lookout on Headly. But now that I'm on the Rogaus, there is nothing calm about it.*

The wind had continued to pick up even more and the small boat climbed tall white-tipped waves before speeding down the other side. *We're so alone here; so vulnerable. What were we thinking taking on the Rogaus?* Avgar felt fear spread through him. *What's stopping us from capsizing?* He looked at Ustek. *That man is our only protection, but he is deceiving us; taking us to who knows where. What a mess we're in!*

The day wore away and Avgar tried several more times to make Winter and Sor understand what was happening. Each time he did, Ustek made a subtle move that sent the boat rocking. Avgar understood the meaning and stopped trying by early afternoon.

The clouds descended further and the wind continued to blow strongly. It was mid-afternoon when the first raindrops fell. They were big and fat and hit with force.

The four *sailors* huddled under what clothes and blankets they had in an attempt to keep as dry as possible. It was only moments before they were saturated. They all looked miserable and fearful, except Ustek who seemed to be enjoying himself. Avgar noted this and his trust in the man slipped further. *He's got a death wish, he does.*

As dusk fell, the waves became enormous and the rain turned into a vicious downpour. Control of the small boat was lost completely and they were tossed to and fro at the whim of the storm.

Avgar was drenched and numb with cold, but still jumped a mile when a fork of lightning split the sky over their bow. The following thunder was so boomingly loud that it felt like a shockwave in itself. Once Avgar recovered from the force, he was greeted once more with the constant noise of the wind and rain.

Time seemed to warp, and the present enveloped all of Avgar's senses. He felt as though he had been battling the storm alone for an age. Then, a massive wave loomed up in behind them. It seemed to sit on top of another wave and consume all of Avgar's vision. He knew that the little boat had no chance and swung into action by diving from the vessel, lest he be struck by her mast or taken down with her.

He hit the water and felt an unexpected sense of warmth as he was submerged. A moment later, he bobbed to the surface and found himself rising up the enormous wave. As he crested its peak, lightning struck again and lit the scene before him. His vision was short and all his attention was focused on the frothing, angry ocean that he was a tiny speck in. He knew not where the boat had gone or where the others were, but found he cared little; acknowledging that his end was now near.

Avgar felt a strong sense of fear pulsing through his body, but he managed to supress this for a moment and smiled inwardly. *At least I'll be beaten by a force well above my own power.* An instant later, he was swept down the back of the wave. He would have found this to be an exhilarating experience if he knew he would be safe. But he did not, and so balked at the sensation of his stomach being left behind him.

In the blink of an eye, he was at the bottom of the wave and thrust underwater unceremoniously. He sucked in a lungful of air before this, but was thrashed about. His lungs began to throb and he thought that this was it; he had taken his last breath of air. But then he popped out onto the surface again and sucked in a mixture of air and salty water. This caused him to cough and splutter, and he started to wish for peace.

Another wave approached him and he was flung over her; bobbing like a cork. Again, he was thrust under and churned around, and again he surfaced.

So far, the waves had all been white tipped, but unbroken. This had been his only saviour. The ocean then sloshed and turned Avgar around and he saw, rumbling towards him, a monster wave at breaking point. He instinctively knew that if it broke before it reached him, he would be slammed underwater for a very long time. He earnestly started thrashing towards it in the vain hope that he would reach it before it broke. He gasped for breath and doggedly slopped one heavy arm in front of the other; inching towards the beast. He started to rise up her front, but saw the tip above him start to curl. He was halfway up the wave when it started to really break. Avgar breathed in a massive lungful of air and attempted to dive through her width. He sought his magic to propel him forward. Then the wave crashed down behind him. He bobbed to the surface but was instantly sucked backwards and down into the churning water. He continued to hold his breath, but lost track of which way was up and which way was down. His lungs began to burn and he tried to concentrate his magic to pulling himself to the surface. He felt himself begin to rise, but also felt the effects of the use of his power, and his mind started to go dark. He tried to refocus once more, but was unable. The churning water pressed him closely and he thought he heard it say: 'you're mine now.' Then darkness of the mind took him and he knew not what would befall his body.

A peaceful dawn broke over a calm ocean beach. The warm sun breached the dissipating clouds to touch gently down upon the yellow sand. This sand was wet with the outgoing tide and littered with driftwood and other debris; a result of the ferocious storm. Amongst this debris, the body of Avgar lay face down. His feet were still in the water and his head was turned half to the side. A sea albatross gracefully flew overhead and let out a loud call to anyone who would listen. This noise echoed through Avgar's head and brought him sluggishly back from a dark, black place.

Avgar felt pain seep through his entire body, but felt it most of all in his neck that was bent uncomfortably; forcing his head to the right. He brutishly tried to realise that he was still alive, but was confronted with a body that didn't want to respond to his wishes.

The albatross called again; rousing Avgar further. Then Avgar heard an odd crunching sound approaching from his left. He forced his eyes open and immediately had to squint from the brilliant sunshine. His next aim was to push himself up onto all fours so that he could move his neck and discover where he was and what was causing the noise. He dragged his hands to be by his shoulders and pushed with just enough force to lift his chest and head off the sand. He raised his head and turned to his left. Wet sand fell from his cheek in chunks and he perceived he must look a real mess.

The crunching stopped and Avgar saw, standing before him, an old man. The man had the sun on his face and smiled broadly. There could be no mistaking that it was Ustek grinning down at him, but Avgar couldn't imagine how the lame old man had survived the storm, let alone now stand so strongly.

The prone man put in a surge of effort and heaved himself onto his knees. He then clumsily twisted and sat down on his backside, exhausted. He looked up at Ustek with questions in his eyes.

The old man looked down in sympathy and crouched before him. 'It is good to see that you have survived, Avgar; we feared for you greatly. It was foolish to abandon our boat that turned out to be more stable than you gave her credit for. But that is done now.'

Avgar looked at Ustek's legs, which seemed to be working perfectly well.

'Ah, yes, well, I haven't been completely truthful with you Avgar, but now I feel that the truth is warranted. The name and persona of Ustek was only a ruse; a made-up person. My real name is Guflinkov and I am perfectly well and healthy.' He handed Avgar a full waterskin. 'Drink this. It will give you some strength.'

Avgar took a mouthful and was blown by the kick of the drink.

'It is a concoction of my own design. I call it a honey whisky, but that doesn't seem to do it justice.'

Avgar wanted desperately to ask what in the world was going on, but he couldn't find a way to communicate his query. His thoughts were interrupted by Guflinkov reaching out to help him to his feet.

'Winter and Sor are safe and sound. If you can walk, we will make our way there now.'

Avgar nodded and suppressed the pain of standing. He looked up and down the beach, then to where the sand met the tree line. There was a variety of tall coconut palms along the border and other thin trees further back. Vines hung aplenty in a mess and tangle. Jutting up behind the trees was a tall mountainside, which was a mixture of dark rocks, dirt and greenery. Avgar hoped he wouldn't have to climb this. He looked further along the beach and saw the same mountainous coastline for a mile or so before it bent around a curve. He could see no one else on the beach and wondered where everyone was.

Guflinkov made to set off along the sand and, without asking, put Avgar's arm around his shoulders to support him. Avgar was grateful, but detested the need to rely on the man many years his senior.

They started to move slowly along the sand when Avgar saw movement amongst the storm's debris. Looking closer, he saw the oddest creature that he had ever seen. It was about two feet tall and had a dull green hide with a reddish stripe dotted down its back. It looked a bit like a lizard, but it ran on its hind legs and had sharp looking teeth. Its tail looked whip-like and when the creature moved, it was with astonishing speed. Avgar looked closer and saw a dozen or so scattered down the beach. As the two men approached one such animal, its head snapped in their direction. It opened its mouth and hissed at them before scampering away.

Avgar looked at Guflinkov in question.

'They are funny little things, aren't they? Harmless by themselves, but I've seen a pack of them take down a wild boar. Sharp teeth, you see. We call them snaplings. They won't harm us today; you can trust me.'

Guflinkov was talking as though Avgar were scared of the creatures. The old sorcerer was more interested than scared, but he took note that in a pack, these snaplings could be a threat.

It suddenly occurred to Avgar that he didn't even know where they were. Were they near Roasline or closer to the Outcast territory? He looked to Guflinkov and tried to mouth *where*, but the old man failed to understand him.

Avgar tried to calculate where they could be, but was hopelessly out of his depth. The storm had thrown all possibility of navigation out and he only had a very rudimentary understanding of ocean travel times in a boat. He remembered that Ustek, or Guflinkov, had not been steering them in the direction that they were meant to be going, so he surmised that they were not near the Outcasts. Further than that would only be guesswork; for all he knew, they could be back on the same shore as Headly, but further down the coast.

He soon gave up his calculations when Guflinkov led him up the slope of the beach and towards the tree line. The sand underfoot turned soft and Avgar found the going harder in his exhausted state. They were headed for a small opening that appeared within the trees and issued a trickling creek.

The two made their way to the edge of the trees and paused for Avgar to catch his breath. His eyes followed the playful creek into the shade, and he saw a slender path running beside it. They followed this path and were soon thrust into the cool darkness.

The path and stream wound up a gentle hill through the jungle. It jutted to the right, where it was blocked by a near vertical slope. It made its way along this for a while before the cliff ended. The path turned abruptly left and went into a sharp valley between two hill-cliffs. Shortly after the path entered this valley, Avgar and Guflinkov were confronted with a thick stone wall.

The creek bubbled out from a small caged opening at the base of the wall that looked too small for a man to fit through. The path itself led up to a solid oak door no bigger than a regular door in a house. He thought this odd, but still followed Guflinkov's lead to stand before it.

The old man knocked three times, causing a booming echo from beyond the wall. Moments later, Avgar heard a series of clicking noises as the door was unlocked. The two had to step backwards as the door swung soundlessly outwards. It was then that Avgar could see the true thickness of the wall as the doorway was the start of a twenty-foot tunnel. He followed Guflinkov into the darkness and could feel the immense weight of the rock above him. He started to feel trapped, even though the tunnel was only short. Avgar's discomfort meant that he didn't notice that no one had been present to unlock to door for them.

When Avgar reached the archway opening into the light, he felt a slight resistance to his passage, as though he were walking through a thin cobweb, but could see nothing physical. When he came into the light more fully, he was amazed by what he saw. The valley opened out into a basin that he guessed was a couple of miles from end to end. This basin was surrounded by mountainous peaks, making it private and secure. Paths ran hither and thither made of the same grey rock that the wall was, and there were buildings of various sizes nestled amongst clumps of trees. The effect was that of a patchy forest at one with the people who lived there. Birds of magnificent colour flew about playfully and although the mountains shielded the direct morning sunlight, the basin was beautifully lit.

Guflinkov had started to walk down a path that ran from the gate to something that looked vaguely like a town square. Avgar hurried to keep up, all thought of soreness and exhaustion forgotten. They walked for a short while and Avgar was amazed to see not only birds, but other animals wandering comfortably about the township. He saw small deer, more snaplings from the beach, goats, furry little creatures with long snouts, pigs and several dozy looking dogs. He had never seen such a thing in his life and he was so consumed by the animals that he barely noticed that there were no people out on the paths.

They soon reached an open grassed oval that was Avgar's assumption of the town square to find an elderly lady standing there alone. When they reached her, she waved a hand and beckoned them to follow her. Avgar could clearly see where she was taking them; to a hall type structure at the far end of the open space.

The building was made of stone walls with solid wood beams supporting a high gabled thatched roof. The doorway was wide and open and seemed to draw Avgar inwards. He followed the lady inside, intrigued by what he might find. Once inside, the doors swung shut behind him with a thud and only then did he realise Guflinkov had left his side. A tremor of fear rippled through him of the unknown. He quickly looked about the room before walking any further. There were blazing torches along each wall, giving off a soft orange glow, and filtered light came through windows in the roof. If Avgar had not been on edge, he would have been interested in the strange design that he had never seen before.

At the far end of the hall to where he stood, the woman was seating herself comfortably on a chair that was not quite a throne. Avgar looked above her, then stepped back in surprise. Attached on the back wall were two enormous skulls. These looked to be from an animal that Avgar had never seen and, at that moment, decided that he never wanted to see. They were many times bigger than a buffalo skull and had a jaw full of sharp teeth. The eye sockets themselves were as big as Avgar's head and the snout jutted out as if sniffing out its prey. Avgar shuddered, then looked at the lady again.

The flickering of the torchlight caught her face differently than the daylight had and, in a flash, he knew he had seen this lady before. He racked his brain, but could not drag the detail of his memory to the fore. He moved closer in an effort to jog his memory and found himself standing before her, still having no idea where he had met her.

She smiled at him and he instantly felt his fear vanish. A wave of relaxation spread through him and he could not have explained this change, even if he had tried.

When the lady spoke, her voice was gentle, but authoritative. 'Welcome to Myrth Isle, stranger. They're fearsome creatures, aren't they?' She pointed to the skulls behind her. 'They are a reminder that humans were not always as dominant as they are now; the world is always in flux; what is normal today, may not be tomorrow.'

Avgar frowned at her and wondered who she was.

She smiled slightly then spoke again 'Who I am does not matter, Avgar. The question you should be asking is, who are you?'

Avgar blanched. *Can she read my thoughts?*

'Yes, I can.' She paused and turned the corner of her mouth up. 'Is this not what you have been wanting? To communicate with people again?'

Avgar tried to control his thoughts in an effort to stop her delving too deep within his mind. *I suppose… but I wanted to choose what I said.* Avgar wanted to run from the room and away from the woman. He tried desperately, but could not seem to move his legs. His breathing quickened, and he could feel his heart pounding violently.

The lady's voice then sounded in his head and her lips remained closed. *Calm, Avgar, calm. I will not ravage your mind for your innermost thoughts, for that is against our laws. Do not fear, you will soon learn to control which thoughts you have on display. It will be as if you were speaking out loud.*

Avgar did start to feel calmer and he was glad of her reassurance, but something she had said clicked a memory within him. *Against our laws.* The way it was said evoked a flash of vision into his mind and he was once more on the beach near Psymryte, having the control of his magical powers ripped from him. This woman was one of those who had stolen a part of him and cursed him with the nightmares.

Avgar clenched his jaw in tension, but the woman spoke first. 'Well done. You have remembered me. You should also remember the power that we wield and do not attempt violence towards us.'

Avgar felt a real mixture of feelings; anger, wonder, rage, intrigue, fear, and excitement. A million questions swam through his mind and a wind of angry rage tore through his muscles. He was conflicted and could do nothing out of his indecision.

The woman laughed. 'You are a changed man, Avgar; disability has served you well.' She stood and made her way down to him. 'You are weary and sore; you will rest now and, on the morrow, you will be reunited with Winter and Sor. There are other outsiders here who have crossed your path and you will do well to meet with them too. But all of that can wait.'

She rested a hand on his shoulder and looked towards the door. 'Guflinkov will show you to your quarters.'

Avgar turned and saw the old man standing in the open doorway. He looked back at the woman to ask her what her name was, but she was no longer there. He felt an intense sensation of inevitability and meekly followed Guflinkov out of the hall.

They made their way past several dwellings and eventually arrived at a small bungalow with pretty wild flowers out the front. Avgar barely noticed the furnishings as he was led to a bed, where he collapsed into a strong slumber.

44

It did not take long for High Chancellor Tunley's armada to sail from Roasline out into the Rogaus and around the point where Fort Kykum was nestled. This trip was done seamlessly and without incident. The weather had favoured the fleet and the sea had been calm.

Tunley himself was glad to be back on a ship with the wind in his hair and a gentle rocking under his feet. He roamed the deck in anticipation of the battle to come and was pleased to see that the crew remained excited and well organised too.

The night deepened and his excited anticipation grew stronger. He stopped pacing and peered over the bow; eagerly searching for their destination. It was past midnight when they arrived north west of Fort Kykum. The beach was unsuited to the ship's landing, so small boats full of troops were lowered into the water and rowed ashore. The boats then returned to the ships to carry more men to the land. This process took longer than the High Chancellor would have liked, but he smiled as he was reminded of the size of his army. He felt glee as he watched the last soldier leap ashore and the boats return to their ships.

The first grey hints of dawn were softening the night sky by the time Tunley and his fleet started their journey back to the Fort. His ship took the lead again and Tunley struggled to contain his hunger for battle as they sailed into the wind.

The plan had been to attack Fort Kykum at midday; allowing each of the attacking forces to get into position. Tunley knew that there would be no element of surprise and that all of his armies would have been spotted by the Outcast lookouts. In his mind he dismissed this idea, for half a day would not be long enough for the Fort to prepare adequately.

By mid-morning, Tunley and his fleet were in position offshore from Fort Kykum. They ordered themselves out of reach of the Fort's cannons, but close enough that when the time came, they only had to sail a short distance before they could begin their assault.

Tunley grew restless and irritable and the captain of the ship intelligently left him well alone. From his position on the bow, he kept looking skyward, hoping that the sun had moved into position. Lucky for him there were only scattered clouds, meaning that it would be relatively clear when the sun was at her zenith. He brushed off the realisation that a coordinated attack would have been impossible if there had been complete cloud cover.

The sun continued to move slowly and eventually Tunley had waited as long as his patience would allow. He ordered the attack to begin. The sails of his fleet unfurled with a satisfying woomph and a moment later the ships started to move.

They came at the fort head on in order to reduce the target size for the Fort's cannons. Once the fort was within their range, the plan was to swing around and concentrate their fire on the water gate to the docks. They would then sail away out of reach and repeat the formation.

It was not long before Tunley heard the first boom of the fort's cannons and he watched the slow arch of the cannon ball splash down some hundred yards off his prow. This was followed by a series of booms and the midday air was soon full of the noise.

Tunley found himself both excited and fearful. He could do nothing to defend himself, but was thrilled to be on the attack. The cannonballs continued to fall around his ship in dramatic splashes.

Before Tunley was close enough to start their attacking manoeuvre, the ship behind his received a direct hit to her main mast. Splinters flew everywhere mixed with screams of the wounded. Tunley blocked these out and looked to the fort once more. *They can sort themselves out.*

The fort loomed closer and Tunley noticed that she looked enormous and hard. Miraculously, the cannonballs kept missing his boat and then, all of a sudden, he was at the point of attack. The captain gave the order and Tunley felt the strain on the hull as the ship was whipped sharply around. As they slowed with the turn, Tunley knew that their biggest danger was now. Moments later, he grinned broadly as the cannons below deck opened fire on the gate. The first ball hit directly and bounced back into the water, leaving a small dent. Tunley frowned, but was then captivated as the gate opened slowly. From between the gates came the ships of the Outcasts. They were much smaller than his, but looked speedy. *Here comes our prey.* Tunley rubbed his hands together.

The High Chancellor's ship then turned again and left the gate behind. Tunley hurried to the stern and watched as Roasline's ships that followed his continued to barrage the gate and incidentally hit the outcoming ships. Tunley let out a whoop of joy.

They could not have chosen a worse time to send their boats out. Their commanders are morons. Tunley watched as the first of the Outcast ships began to sink and blocked the exit of their followers. Further to this, the ships sank right at the entrance of the gates, so even if the Outcasts wanted to, they would not be able to shut the gate again. It was true that Roasline's fleet couldn't entre, but Tunley had already started to tackle that problem in his mind.

The High Chancellor's ship was soon out of range of the Fort's cannons and she turned to sail parallel to the fort. His other ships followed suit and he surveyed the damage. Four of his ships were sinking or had been rendered useless and several more had been mildly crippled, but still sailable. His desire was to have another run at the gate, but reason told him there was no point. Even if they smashed the gate down, the Outcast ships were blocking their way into the city.

He briskly called the captain over to him and pointed to the blocked gate. 'How do you propose we get through that mess?'

The captain rubbed his clean-shaven chin. 'We could send in a rammer, sir, and try to clear it away… but that would probably just get stuck too.' He thought some more. 'We could smash those gates off their hinges with our cannons and sail around the wreckage… it would be tight though, sir.'

Tunley had already thought of these options and dismissed them as having a low chance of success. His last ship was just leaving the range of the fort's cannons and Tunley watched as a final cannon ball was fired into the air and splashed down a hundred odd feet short of the vessel. That last vision of the cannon ball gave the High Chancellor an idea.

'Captain, how much spare cannon powder do you hold?'

'A good many barrels, sir.'

'And the other ships? What about them?'

'Some more, some less. Depends on the captain.'

Tunley was annoyed; when he was Admiral, he would have known how many barrels each of his ships had, but as High Chancellor, he had stopped paying close attention to these minor details.

'Right.' He pursed his lips. 'Have all the Captains summoned to me immediately.'

The captain saluted and left at a brisk march.

It was midway through the afternoon when all the captains were standing before Tunley on the deck of *Destroyer*. They looked nervous at being summoned by the High Chancellor and Tunley soaked in the atmosphere that was created.

'Captains, we have both succeeded and failed in our duty. The pitiful Outcast navy is crippled, but our entry to the Fort is blocked. The enemy's defensive cannons mean we can't continue bombarding the gate by sailing in circles. We need to make a decisive direct attack; we need to obliterate the mess that is their pitiful boats.' Tunley spat on the deck as he felt himself starting to get worked up. 'We're going to make a sacrifice that will bring about our victory. This ship, *Destroyer*, that we are standing on, this is what we are going to sacrifice.'

Destroyer's captain stepped forward. 'No!' He checked himself. 'I mean, sir, there has to be another way… surely.'

Tunley felt a rare moment of sympathy towards the captain, who was about to lose his pride and joy. 'I am sorry, Captain, but there is not. This ship is in full working order and is the sturdiest of the fleet. She may not be the speediest, but her design means that she will be the hardest for the fort cannons to sink.'

He turned back to the rest of the captains. 'You're going to bring all the cannon powder you can reasonably spare and stuff it in *Destroyer's* belly. We will then light a fuse and she will be sailed straight at the blockage in the gate. Once there, she will blow the Outcasts to smithereens. In the confusion, we will sail right into the Fort and impregnate her from within.'

Tunley watched as the captains looked about at each other excitedly. 'You all have until nightfall to transfer your powder over. You're all dismissed.'

The captains saluted and hurried back to the gunwale to board small rowing boats to return to their own vessels.

Destroyer's captain came hesitantly over to Tunley. Tunley spoke first. 'Ah, Captain. You can start sending your men to the other ships, leaving enough here to bring aboard the powder. I will remain here until all is set. And… you will be the brave man to sail your ship to her end.'

The captain's face blanched. 'Surely someone else could do that task.'

'I need someone I can trust… and besides, you can jump ship well before you hit. We can pick you up on our way through.'

Colour returned to the man's face. 'Aye, sir.'

'Go now and organise your men.'

He saluted and left Tunley alone.

Tunley watched the afternoon sweep by in a scurry of activity as he saw barrel after barrel brought aboard *Destroyer*. He supervised the laying of the fuse himself and made sure that it would be long enough to last until the ship reached her destination.

Evening arrived at last and *Destroyer* was empty except for Tunley and the Captain. They both stood at the wheel and looked at the fort. Tunley felt thrilled, but nervous. He subconsciously rubbed his thigh where a splinted piece of his old ship had pierced his leg many long months ago, when he was a simple captain. He thought briefly of it and smiled at his own advancement since that day. *Soon I will rule the Outcasts and then my dominion will be complete.*

He nodded, signalling the captain beside him. 'Captain, it is time.'

The man nodded and set about finalising the ship to sail. While he was doing this, Tunley went below deck and lit the fuse. It sparkled into life and he laughed with glee. He made his way back to the deck and saw that the ship had started her final journey. He made his way to the captain at the wheel once more.

'You had better leave, High Chancellor, before we pick up too much speed for you to disembark.'

Tunley nodded and then, as quickly as he could, whipped out a set of cuffs and locked the captain's wrist to the wheel.

The captain looked dismayed. 'I had no choice, sailor… And don't think about steering off course; the fuse it lit and the ship will blow whether you're at the gates or in the open water. It's time for you to make your noble sacrifice. I will care for your family; do not fear for them.'

The man seemed to stiffen in resignation of his fate. Tunley clasped him on the shoulder before fleeing to the side of the ship. He scrambled down a rope ladder and into a small boat where a pair of rowers were waiting for him. *Destroyer* had already gained speed and the transition to the boat was challenging with the small vessel bobbing up and down vigorously. Tunley leapt off the ladder and ordered the sailors to detach the boat and row to the nearest ship.

As his fleet started to move into an attack formation, Tunley clambered aboard his chosen ship and watched from the bow as *Destroyer* made her way ever closer to the gates. He was pleased to see that she was still on course and even more pleased to see that the fort's booming cannons couldn't seem to hit her.

Destroyer sailed closer and closer to her destination. Tunley's heart pounded in his chest and his ears blocked out all noise in concentration and hope. The floating bomb was suddenly stuck by a cannon ball on the port stern which took a chunk out of the woodwork, but didn't seem to slow her. Again, she was hit. This time her front sail was ripped from the mast and dragged lifelessly into the water. She was then hit thrice, this time to her bow. Splinters flew into the air and Tunley gripped the gunwale like a hawk. He willed *Destroyer* to keep moving forward. She was getting closer and closer, but that only meant she was an easier target. *What if she fails?* Tunley's knuckles whitened.

A fourth ball struck and *Destroyer* slowed considerably, but she still kept moving. Then it happened; clunk, she smashed into the gate blockage and sat there still afloat. *What if water reaches the powder? What if the fuse goes out? Hurry up and blow!* Tunley grew agitated. He tapped his fingers on the woodwork and started cursing out loud. *How long was the fuse for? Surely, she should have blown by now…* He slammed his fist down hard, but did not feel the pain.

Tunley wiped sweat from his brow and then he saw what he had been waiting for. For Tunley, it was like he was watching in slow motion. *Destroyer* seemed to lift out of the water and hover for a moment, suspended. Then her belly ripped open and an almighty flash of brilliant light tore through the darkening night.

Destroyer vanished in the light show and thick smoke billowed forth. Until then, the explosion had been all watched in silence, but all of a sudden, Tunley was thrown back by both the sheer noise combined with the shockwave. He took a step back and yelped in delight. His heart raced and he felt exhilarated by the living destruction before him.

Debris flew hundreds of feet in the air, then came raining down in a shower of smoulder. Destroyer was completely gone, as were the ships that had blocked the entrance. The blast had been so successful that even the gates had been torn from their hinges. Tunley saw the opening he wanted and turned to the captain.

'Signal the advance with full sails. Let's take the Fort!'

A moment later, the fleet was on the move and gathering speed; their way lit by burning debris strewn about the water.

By the time they reached the fort, night had fully arrived. The slightly waning moon gave the attackers enough light to sail by, but would also make them easy targets for the cannons. However, Tunley soon realised that the cannons had ceased firing. He could not have been happier and congratulated his strategic prowess.

The fleet was moving quickly, but Tunley had enough sense to curb their speed before entering the port. After all, he didn't know what he might find past the clearing smoke. He glided through the gate entrance and found himself in a small bay with calm water. There were several docks and plenty of room for his fleet to stop and drop anchor.

The High Chancellor's plan was for the ships still holding soldiers in their bellies to land at the docks and invade the city immediately. The other ships were to give covering cannon fire, by targeting any resistance that might arise. As Tunley entered the port, he realised this plan was superfluous; there would be no resistance. The remaining few Outcast vessels in the bay flew white flags of surrender. Tunley then looked to the town and saw more white flags, bed sheets and clothes hanging from many windows, including from the Keep.

Tunley had mixed feelings of joy and disappointment. He was glad to have the victory, but he had been looking forward to the slaughter and other wild activities that came with conquering a city. Then he had a suspicious thought. *What if this is a trap?*

He called the captain over and pointed to the Outcast's ships. 'I want those ships boarded and captured as soon as possible. I also want the town invaded as planned. Everyone needs to be ready; this could be an ambush.' The captain saluted and went about organising the attack.

Tunley wanted to join in the land attack, but refrained out of paranoia of an ambush. Instead, he planned to watch from the deck of his ship as his soldiers landed and formed ranks on the docks. The night darkness made it hard for him to see what was happening, but the torches of his troops allowed him to just see enemy soldiers walk out of the buildings with their hands in the air and no swords on their hips. *Excellent, perhaps this is not an ambush.* His excitement soon got the better of him and Tunley ordered for a boat to row him ashore.

The High Chancellor of Roasline's invasion of Fort Kykum met absolutely no resistance all the way from the dock to the Keep. On that journey, he saw women weep and men standing with slumped shoulders. He mocked them in his mind, but walked proudly with his coat wrapped tightly about him for warmth.

He entered the Keep and was directed by his soldiers who went before him to a room high up. He found himself short of breath as he climbed the stairs and when he entered the room, he found two bodies hanging on the end of ropes from the rafters. A cowering Outcast servant was crying in the corner, but was compliant enough to tell Tunley that the two men were the bearded Nigrath, leader of Psymryte and the rat-like Quynt, commander of the land bordering the Liagar.

On hearing this, Tunley pumped his fist and roared in glee; High Chancellor Tunley had defeated the Outcast stronghold of Fort Kykum.

45

'Father, come and sit.' Winter stood from his wing-baked chair and greeted his father. 'I've heard that the storm treated you harshly.' Sor remained seated as Avgar entered the sitting room of their hut feeling sore, stiff and strains all through his body from being thrown about in the ocean.

Avgar made his way to the spare chair and eased himself into it. He wanted to ask a thousand questions about where they were and the people of Myrth Isle as his knowledge of the place before arriving had been no more than an uninhabited inhospitable island in the middle of a rough sea. Unfortunately he was restricted to letting Winter and Sor lead the conversation.

'Sor and I arrived with Ustek early yestermorning and were brought directly here to sleep. We learnt that the old man can actually walk and was only pretending to be lame.' Winter looked thoroughly amazed. 'When we woke, Ustek was gone and we found food laid out for us. A messenger came and told us to remain indoors for the day. Although we hadn't done much on the boat, we both felt weary and so didn't argue with the instructions. When we woke this morning, your door was closed so we ate breakfast while we waited. Now you've appeared.' Winter recounted this pleasantly with no inquisitive aspect at all.

Avgar thought his son seemed a little too calm and relaxed considering he was in an unknown land in an unfamiliar house eating food that just seemed to appear. He looked over to Sor and raised his eyebrows. *Maybe she is a bit more suspicious.*

'It is as Winter recounts.' She responded curtly. 'Although, I was just saying to Winter that I think we should explore our surrounds; see what's outside. It would be good to find someone to tell us where we are and where Ustek has gone.'

Avgar realised they didn't even know that they were on Myrth Isle or that Ustek was concealing his true identity. He wanted to scream it to them and again silently cursed his lost voice. Instead, he stood to indicate that he was ready to explore. Sor got the idea and stood as well. Winter was slower to come, but eased himself out of his chair nonetheless.

Avgar walked to the door and waited for the other two. Sor left the room for a moment and returned with a chunk of bread and an apple which she handed to Avgar. He smiled at her and was reminded that he was actually rather hungry. *She is thoughtful at heart, even though she doesn't like me.*

They left the cabin and immediately stood onto a worn path that led both left and right. Avgar took the right without hesitation while taking a bite out of the apple. Winter and Sor followed without question.

Avgar led the three of them back to the hall where he had met the woman the day before, but found it empty. They looked around it, inside and out, paying particular attention to the giant skulls that sat behind the dais. Avgar continued to find these both terrifying and intriguing at the same time.

It was midmorning when they left the hall and they then meandered their way through the village. Avgar had never seen a town in such a symbiotic merging with nature. Animals roamed, skittered and lumbered about while shrubs and trees grew adjacent to dwellings. Avgar even saw a few houses where tall trees grew right through the middle of the house. He couldn't seem to work out if the house was built around the tree or the tree grew through the house after it was built. Either way, he thought they looked magnificent.

Several creeks meandered through the village and their babbling could be heard from anywhere the three went.

Time passed and they met few locals. Those they did meet were polite when spoken to, but excused themselves from answering any real questions.

As midday approached a young man no more than fifteen years of age approached them with a wicker basket. 'Good day to you all. I have been instructed to bring you lunch of fresh fruit, goat's cheese and bread. I hope it will suffice.'

Sor took the basket. 'Thank you, it will do nicely. Would you care to join us? We have met several of the townsfolk, yet they don't really want to talk to us.'

The boy took a subtle step backwards. 'I would very much like to stay, but alas, I have many other duties to attend to.'

He's lying, Avgar thought.

'Oh, well thank you for the food,' replied Sor.

'When you're finished, you can leave the basket on the ground and someone will collect it.' He turned and left without futher room for conversation.

Something unusual is going on here.

After eating, the three set out with the aim of circumnavigating the village. They started at the gate where Avgar had entered, which was shut tightly. Avgar felt further misgivings at the intentions of the locals when seeing this, but supressed his unease as the three started their walk around the wall.

Despite what Avgar initially thought, the wall only ran a few hundred yards before merging seamlessly into the bedrock of the mountains. Avgar was impressed at the craftmanship to make the wall look as though it had been carved out of the mountains instead of being constructed and joined. He then remembered the awesome power of these people and wondered if the wall had indeed been carved from the mountain. Either way, he was awed at the structure.

Much of the mountain slope was sheer or cliff-like, but there were a few sections where someone could scale the side if they had strength, patience and a strong nerve. Avgar certainly didn't fancy that prospect.

The three found another gate at the opposite end of the town to the one where they had started; this was equally locked shut and did not hold their interest for long. They continued to walk until they were back where they had started and then returned home as darkness was descending.

Slow cooked goat with carrots and a white starchy root vegetable awaited them. Avgar realised that it was warm when they arrived. *If we had come back earlier, we would have met whoever left this for us.* It all tasted delicious and made Avgar dozy. He started to nod off to sleep in an armchair when a gentle rat-tat came from the door.

Winter opened the door and Guflinkov entered. 'Good evening. Your presence has been requested tomorrow morning in the central hall. You've been asked to come as soon as you're finished breakfast.'

'All three of us?' Winter asked.

Guflinkov raised an eyebrow at Winter. 'Yes.'

'What's all this about?' Sor asked the question that Avgar had been pondering.

'That is not for me to say.' Guflinkov replied briskly.

Avgar smiled. *He doesn't know.*

'Can you tell us nothing?' Sor sounded tense.

Guflinkov hesitated. 'I can tell you that you are safe here, in this village. Now sleep well, young ones.'

Avgar chuckled. *I know he's old, but I'm not young.* Avgar found the whole situation amusing. He knew that tomorrow he would find out a great many things, but for the time being he could not.

Guflinkov left politely and Winter and Sor immediately started discussing what could be happening on the morrow. They sounded a mixture of nervous, excited and scared. In the end, Avgar decided that he'd had enough of the two for the day and went to his room to seek the solitude that he was missing from Headly. *Ah, peace at last.*

Avgar ignored Winter and Sor as the two chattered on their way to the town's hall. His mind flittered through the options of what would await them when they got there. He hoped he would meet more of the Myrthians, but found himself nervous at that thought. *I hope they're more forthcoming than yesterday. Of course they will be; we wouldn't be called to a meeting if they had nothing to say. But what if that woman is there who can read my mind? I don't want her in my head again. And what about her other powers? Is she going to punish me further?* Sweat trickled down his neck.

They arrived at the hall and Avgar led the way through the open door. His eyes darted around as they adjusted to the dimmer inside light and soon saw two men standing near the throne, involved in what appeared to be a casual conversation.

Failing to see anything else of note in the room, Avgar cautiously made his way towards them. As he got closer, he surveyed the men. They were both dressed in comfortable looking wool garments similar to those Avgar had been provided with. The first thing to catch Avgar's eye was a scar on one of the men's faces. It ran from his receding grey hairline down across his eye, which appeared to be made of glass, and to the corner of his mouth. He wore it well and it enhanced his appearance of toughness. The other man was much younger and looked frustratingly familiar to Avgar. He racked his mind, but could not remember where he had met the man. Avgar decided that these two were not local to the island and felt a moment of disappointment.

This was broken by his realisation that he couldn't speak and so was not the ideal person to lead the introductions. He turned to Winter and Sor and instantly decided that Sor would be more suitable to lead their party. He beckoned her over and motioned for her to take the lead.

Sor stepped forward and walked to within a few yards of the two men. While this had been happening, the men had stopped talking and stood waiting for the three newcomers to reach them. Avgar read their firm body language as cautiously defensive and was not surprised when they closed their lips tightly and waited for Sor to speak first.

'Good morning, I am Sor, a monk of the Night God. I have travelled far to be here. With me I have Winter of the Day and Night Gods and Avgar. We have been invited to come here this morning, I assume, to meet you.'

Avgar was impressed by Sor's introduction. It told the men little past their names. The talk of Gods would either confuse the men, if they didn't know the word, or pacify them if they knew the monks to be peaceful. The men seemed to relax a touch and Avgar was glad when the younger man spoke next.

'I am Marlvon and this is Ryde. We equally have been requested to come here this morning.'

Avgar felt his face flush as the eyes of Marlvon flashed in recognition. *This is Resvon's nephew! I ordered his execution. He survived the man-hunt; he must really be a tough nut. I could be in trouble here.*

Sor missed the venomous look that Marlvon had given Avgar and continued talking pleasantly. 'Well, I guess we can assume that we were brought here to meet each other.'

She was cut off as Marlvon sprung at Avgar. The old sorcerer instinctively reached for his powers to defend himself. This was not needed as, to his surprise, Sor twisted on the spot and snapped a kick towards the lunging Marlvon. The man was caught completely by surprise and went sprawling on the floor from the impact to his head.

Sor moved to stand between Marlvon and Avgar and took up a stance of defence. When she spoke, her voice was firm but not loud. 'I doubt very much that we have been brought here to fight.' She looked from Avgar to Marlvon. 'Clearly, there is some history here. You must put this behind you so we can figure out why we are here.'

Avgar was taken aback and impressed at this new side of Sor.

Marlvon stood and glared at Sor. He matched his voice to Sor's while pointing at Avgar. 'He ordered my assassination. He's the reason I lost my home and my way of life. He's the reason why I don't have my soon-to-be wife by my side, why her father is dead and her home town burnt to the ground.' He spat on the floor at Sor's feet.

Avgar felt a wave of guilt and concern. *At least he doesn't know that I arranged the assassination of his uncle.*

Avgar then watched as Marlvon advanced on him, only to be intercepted by Sor. He barraged her with a series of punches and kicks. He was fast and Avgar was amazed to see that Sor could deflect all his blows. Before long, however, the monk started to retreat under the onslaught. *She's good, really good… but he's better.*

Then Marlvon broke through and struck Sor in the diaphragm with a fist. She folded over and gasped for breath. She was at Marlvon's mercy. Avgar could see the resignation in her posture. All it would take would be a swift attack and Sor, the monk, would be dead. But Marlvon did not press his advantage. Instead, he shoved her aside and advanced towards Avgar.

While Avgar was an accomplished fighter, he was leagues behind Marlvon's skill, and he knew it. He reached down for his magic to defend himself, but was disrupted again as Winter jumped to the fore. His son clenched his fists and took a stance between Marlvon and Avgar. The father wanted to yell at Winter to move, knowing that he was no match for Marlvon, but of course could not speak.

Winter attacked, but Marlvon darted aside and landed a well-placed kick to Winter's head. Avgar watched in anguish as his last remaining offspring collapsed on the floor, motionless. *Please, let him not be dead.*

Avgar refocused on Marlvon and his magic. The young man looked calm, full of energy, and in control. Marlvon attacked swiftly. Avgar ducked the first kick and blocked the follow-up punch. He sidestepped Marlvon's right foot and then felt an almighty crack to the head. As Marlvon's left fist connected with Avgar's skull, a burst of energy released from the sorcerer. A flash of light erupted and both men were thrown apart. Avgar felt the impact of the magical blow, and felt his energy drain. He'd overused his magic. Despite the aches to his body, he dug into his willpower and urged himself to stand once more. He got to his knees and saw that Marlvon was already standing and advancing on him. *This is the end.*

Marlvon reached Avgar and a thunderous yell ripped through the hall. 'Stop this nonsense!'

Both men stopped as if frozen and looked about for the man who had spoken. Avgar breathed a great sigh of relief as he saw Guflinkov furiously pacing towards them.

Marlvon stepped towards Guflinkov and gesticulated his anger. 'Do you know who this man—'

He was cut off by the sharp Guflinkov. 'How dare you behave like this? You are guests on this island, and the five of you are of great importance. Children, you're like children!'

Avgar was surprised to see such fury, it flashed like a thunderous summer storm in the old man's eyes. Marlvon again yelled at Guflinkov. 'Do you—'

Again, he was cut off. 'Of course I know who this man is. Do you think I'm a fool?' Guflinkov reached Marlvon and put a hand on his shoulder. 'Now calm, young man, calm yourself. All will be explained.' He turned to Ryde. 'Captain, check that Winter is alive. If he is not, there will be grave consequences.'

Avgar finally stood and watched anxiously as Ryde walked towards his son. Sor gingerly made her way to Avgar's side, still gasping for breath and clearly in pain.

Ryde bent down and felt for signs of life. He looked up at Guflinkov. 'He still breathes.'

Avgar felt relief sweep through his body and was then able to find the energy to walk over to his son. He bent down and rolled Winter onto his back. He looked peacefully asleep and felt warm to the touch. Avgar sat down next to him and breathed deeply. *The magic spell drained me more than it should have.* He looked up at Guflinkov, who had started speaking again, this time in control of his emotions.

'There are severe grievances between the five of you. Some known, some unknown. These are all of little importance, but cannot be ignored. They will not be addressed now, but may be in due course. Too much is at stake to waste time squabbling amongst ourselves over things that have happened, but cannot be changed. Instead, we need to be looking to the days and weeks ahead. It is with that purpose that you have been invited here this morning. The locals of Myrth Isle would like to meet with you to discuss serious matters.'

Avgar was curious about what was to come.

'You will be taken to a meeting place that only select inhabitants of Myrth Isle know about. To get there, your vision will be temporarily removed from you.'

An instant later, Avgar lost sight of the grand hall and was thrown into absolute darkness. Cries of surprise and fear came from the others, and Avgar guessed that they too had lost their sight.

'Stay calm and you will be guided to where you need to go.' Guflinkov reassured the outlanders.

Avgar felt gentle hands grip him and turn him around on the spot several times. He didn't much like the sensation and lost his balance. He fell hard onto his right knee and jarred it. He was firmly hoisted to his feet and nudged to start walking. His knee pained him with each step and he had to limp along like an old man. *Perhaps that's what I am now.*

The floor sloped downward, gently at first and then steeper. Walking hurt Avgar's knee further, but he was glad that there were no steps.

Avgar had no perception of time, but it felt as though he had been walking far longer than he would have liked. There had been no sound while they walked except their echoing footsteps and the occasional grumble from Ryde. The floor flattened out and Avgar sensed the air changing. What had previously felt closed and stuffy felt fresher with a gentle breeze ruffling his hair.

Avgar sniffed and detected smoke from a wood fire, as well as what he guessed was the smell of candles burning. The smell was accompanied by the crackle of a fire and the sound of shuffling feet and chairs scraping the floor. From this, he surmised that there were quite a few others in the room ahead of them.

As his vision was returned to him, he glanced around the room. He found himself standing in a huge room with a high ceiling. The floor, walls and roof were made of the same stone as the gate of the village and once more the construction looked as though it had been carved out of the rock. No flagstones had been laid and there were no lines or cracks on the entirety of the surface of the floor or walls. While he marvelled at that feat, he was mesmerised by the four pillars that were adorned with carvings of snakes and monsters with sharp teeth. These pillars held many burning candles and torches to light the room well.

In the middle of the four pillars was a round table that joined the floor seamlessly and was itself carved of the rock too. Around this table sat a dozen men and women, all looking keenly at the new arrivals. Avgar turned behind himself to look for the others. Sor, Marlvon and Ryde were staring at the room in awe and Winter was just rousing and was on all fours. Avgar felt a sensation of relief to see his son conscious and turned back to the table before him, noticing the crackling fireplaces lining the walls as he turned his head.

Guflinkov sat at the table and beckoned the new arrivals to join him in the five spare seats. Avgar led the way and sat in a cushioned wooden chair. He looked at the figures around the table and at once recognised the woman that he had met in the hall in the village two days before. Avgar thought her to be the leader and was reminded of her power when her voice echoed in his head. *We have no leaders here Avgar; all those before you are equal.*

Avgar felt a tingle of fear and tried to supress his thoughts. She turned her gaze to the others and spoke aloud. 'Welcome to Myrth Isle. I am Phlyte. You have journeyed here on different paths, at your own pace and timing. We are not going to hurt you, interrogate you or use you against your will. But… through these discussions, ponder this. Was it coincidence, accident, happenchance, providence, design or purpose that brought the five of you to be here in this room, on Myrth Isle, today? Perhaps each of you will think differently on this.'

Avgar found himself thoroughly intrigued and wanted her to keep talking.

'Whatever the case, you are all here with us and that may be used to the benefit of all the lands… or not.' She paused and smiled a kind smile. 'But first, I will tell you about who we are and what is going on in the world. Listen hard, for you are the first outsiders that we have allowed into our sanctum for many decades. You would do well to remember that and let it highlight our concern at the current situation.'

Avgar felt as though he was drinking a strong draught, and he loved it.

'We are an order of people different from those on the mainland. We have been allowed to develop our ways, customs, and laws in privacy on Myrth Isle. We are gentle beings by nature and curious, very curious. We are curious of the natural world, the world of people and the world within each being.'

Avgar leant forward and rested his elbows on the table while Phlyte continued. 'Ancient stories tell of how our ancestors arrived on Myrth Isle long before the city of Roasline was begun and just after the people of Headly had settled. Our forefathers soon developed a friendship with the Healers of Headly. These gentle people we have watched over since those early days; almost as our ward. To aid in this, a protection we placed on them and guided their healing hands with our powers. Of our particular involvement, they are ignorant, but perform wonderful work with their gift.' Sadness tinged her voice.

'Over the centuries, we have also watched the mainland culture develop and change. For many, many years, this was a marvellous thing to behold. Yes, there were challenges for the people, and even some short-lived wars.' The woman smiled to herself as if reminiscing of years gone by. 'And then the colony of the Outcasts was established. We did not predict that this would be the precursor to much pain and anguish.' She sighed.

'We could have intervened then, but you must understand that our laws have always forbidden direct involvement and we had no way to foretell what would eventuate. We were caught off guard and before we knew what was happening, we failed in our watch and the current war began. Again, we did nothing, this time out of our misunderstanding of how long the dispute would prevail.

'While I said that we did nothing, that is not entirely correct. We joined an Alliance with peoples from distant lands. As part of this Alliance, we were given the responsibility for Roasline, the Outcasts and Headly. We perhaps hoped for peace a little too much and failed to act with enough purpose. The Alliance was disappointed with us and we were disappointed with ourselves and our laws.

'Our law states that we are not to interfere directly, but as a people, we also desire peace in the world above all else.'

Avgar thought, *why couldn't you change your laws?* He was ignored.

'In the past decade, we have walked a fine line between obeying our laws and working towards peace. And we came so close to success; Kathsum and Resvon… but alas, it was not to be.'

Avgar felt a massive wave of guilt and shame as the woman's eyes bored into him. He then heard her voice in his head and stirred uncomfortably. *You are here to right that particular wrong.*

She continued aloud to the room. 'This brings us to the current problem. Since Resvon and then Kathsum were murdered, the brutal Tunley has come to power. He is a loathsome man of violence with evil ways. He has taken Roasline and most recently Fort Kykum. This, perhaps, is not enough of an indiscretion for us to intervene outright, but his other crime has our blood boiling and urges us to act.' She shifted in her seat and banged a clenched fist onto the tabletop in supressed passion.

Her voice rose in anger and Avgar could feel her wrath. 'Tunley has attacked the Healers of Headly and is forcing Lyafe and his people to his will. He has used his vile mind to discover a loophole in the Healer's protection and he is exploiting this to his own gains.' She rubbed her hands together and took a breath to calm herself. 'Many of us want to strike him down with our powers. It would not be difficult for us to do, but we hesitate.'

Avgar couldn't believe his ears. If they had the power to bring about peace; what they truly wanted, then why wouldn't they?

'If we end his life, then how does that make us any better than Tunley himself?'

Avgar scoffed. *That is a weak argument and you know it.*

'Beyond this, our laws must be obeyed. If we break these wars, there will be grave consequences for ourselves and the lands about. A breach of this nature would end our existence and cause the oceans to boil.'

Avgar felt stunned at the information while the other outsiders stirred in their chairs. *But how?* Avgar pondered.

'Our ancestors, in their wisdom, valued a policy of non-interference above all else. They used their magic to place safeguards around our people interfering directly in the lives of those on the mainland. Alas, we have tried to remove this law, but have not been able to.'

Avgar thought of himself. *But you brought me across the Moaks and stole my power? That was interfering!* He felt angry.

She smiled. 'This law applies only to those living on the mainland this side of the Moaks. Alas, we cannot touch Tunley… directly.'

And that is where we come in, no doubt.

'That is where the five of you come in. We are hoping that you will work with us to tear down Tunley and all that he stands for.'

Avgar sat back and let this proposition sink in. He was a changed man since spending time in Headly. Before his solitude, he would have raced into a decision, now he thought about it carefully. He had many questions to ask, but the one that stuck out was, *How?*

'Tunley has amassed a force at Fort Kykum, which he has taken more easily than he should have. He has also channelled the Healers to his purpose. He is arrogant and greedy.

'Our best guess is that he will press his advantage over the Outcasts. We believe he will sail his forces north and attack Nivera. That is a great and beautiful city, but not easily defended. It will not be long before Tunley will control vast swaths of land.

'After his possession of Nivera, his only significant hurdle will be the cesspit of Psymryte. After that falls, and it likely will, he will be the most powerful man in history. And what he does then… well, if his treatment of the peaceful Healers is anything to go by… tens, if not hundreds, of thousands will suffer. Would any of you condemn innocents to that fate?'

Avgar pondered this. *There are many ifs in this scenario…*

Phlyte looked grim. 'If you're willing, we want you, or most of you, to kill Tunley.'

And there it is; the blunt reality of our purpose.

'While an army may not defeat this man, a small skilled force may end him.'

The soft voice of Sor interrupted Phlyte. 'You plan for *most* of us to kill him. What if we refuse and what of the others?'

Phlyte smiled. 'You miss nothing, monk. I believe that your training as a monk will prevent you setting a course of murder and we do not wish you to go against your Gods. You can still provide a valuable service to the betterment of all. We request that you travel with Guflinkov on a journey of great importance.

We want you to go to Lord Olswerth and garner his support for opposing Tunley. After you have secured this, we want you to return to your home and speak with Lunar and Solar and see if they are willing to fight with Olswerth to prevent the scourge of Tunley from covering all the lands.'

Sor replied firmly. 'The monks will not fight, except to defend themselves.'

'Do the Gods not teach to preserve good and dispel evil? Would the Night God and the Day God not prefer the staining of a few souls for the protection of countless innocent lives? Carry our message to Lunar and Solar, please, and let the leaders of the monks decide for themselves and their people.'

Avgar could see that Sor was riled at being dismissed like a child, but Phlyte continued. 'Is it not worth an attempt? Should we not try to get all of the help that we can to defeat someone who bastardises the purity of the Healers to kill and rule over others?'

Sor sat back in resignation.

'Sor, kind monk, if you're willing, we would have you leave tomorrow. Time is of the essence and reaching Olswerth and the monks will take a great deal of time.' She smiled kindly. 'If all goes smoothly, the monks won't need to be used at all; Tunley will be dead at the hands of the others in this room.'

Avgar watched Sor closely as she looked about the room. Uncertainty creased her face until her eyes settled on Winter. 'What of Winter? He is nigh on being a monk, should he not come with me?'

Sadness passed over Winter's face, but it was Phlyte who spoke. 'It is true that once Winter was heading down that path, but his mind is now set and he will never be a monk.'

Sor glared at the old woman. 'Let him speak for himself.' She snapped her head to Winter with tears welling in her eyes. 'Is this true, brother?'

Winter hung his head and avoided Sor's gaze. 'I'm sorry, Sister Sor, but it is. Since finding my father, I… I have found a greater purpose to undertake.'

Sor mumbled under her breath. 'There is no greater purpose than serving the Gods.' She spoke to Winter more loudly and Avgar felt awkward at being present for this conversation. 'You promised me… and I believed you. I trusted you.' Tears rolled down her cheeks. 'I loved you.' She hung her head and an uncomfortable silence filled the room.

After several long moments, Sor lifted her head, wiped her eyes, and spoke firmly to Phlyte. 'Guflinkov and I will leave tomorrow, at dawn.'

The old lady breathed a sigh of relief. 'Good. Then I suggest that you and Guflinkov leave here now in order to prepare.' She stopped talking and waited.

Guflinkov stood and gestured for Sor to do likewise. The old man spoke kindly. 'The less people that know of their plan, the better.' He looked at Phlyte.

'I wish you well in your endeavours, as always. I hope that the next time we meet, it will be over a peaceful land.'

'Indeed. May the wind speed you on your way and the world grant you easy passage.'

Guflinkov nodded and led Sor to the back of the chamber. He blindfolded her, then guided her out of the room and up the ramp.

Avgar looked back at Phlyte and the others at the table.

Marlvon spoke next with a resigned tone. 'What would you have us do?'

Phlyte looked mildly annoyed; Avgar was not sure why. 'We want you to go to the mainland, specifically Fort Kykum and kill Tunley using your unique skills.'

Ryde spoke gruffly. 'Is that all? Yes? Excellent. Let's go lads; should be easy.'

Phlyte scolded the old sailor. 'To take on this task lightly would be foolish. Tunley is not a man to be underestimated.'

'What if we say no?' Winter asked.

'Have you not been listening to me? Tunley will succeed and the world will be thrown into decades of suffering.'

Marlvon spoke again. 'We really don't have a choice, do we?'

'Everyone has a choice in everything they do,' she looked keenly at Marlvon, 'the peace that you have desired your entire life may be found on the other side of one more bloody encounter. If that is not reason enough for you to agree, then know this: all those who were at Headly were killed or captured by Tunley.' Phlyte let that hang in the air as Marlvon's face blanched.

His voice then came as a pained whisper. 'You're only telling me this now? You held this information from me until now?' His voice rose in urgent anger as he stood shaking. 'You answer me this one question and you answer truthfully. Was Islonda captured... or killed?'

Phyte looked sad. 'In truth, we don't know.'

'Can you not use any of your *awesome* powers to find out?'

Phlyte looked about the table at the other residents of Myrth Isle. She then looked back at Marlvon. 'Our powers are not as simple as that, but if you agree to our plan, then by tomorrow, we will have an answer for you.'

Marlvon snarled. 'You would withhold that information just to get me to go along with your plan? You disgust me.' He threw his hands up in the air. 'Of course I'll seek out Tunley; he either has my pregnant love prisoner, or he has killed her. Either way, he will not be safe from my wrath, however powerful he may be!' Marlvon sat down and buried his face in his hands.

Ryde spoke next and spoke simply. 'I will go wherever you go, Marlvon. We will hunt this bastard together.'

Winter looked at Avgar with fear poorly hidden on his face. 'I will go wherever you go, Father.'

Avgar nodded, then looked at Phlyte cunningly. He concentrated to project his thoughts to everyone in the room. *If I am to do this, I will need my full powers back; the ones that you stole many months ago.*

Phlyte's response was not immediate, and Avgar guessed the Myrthians were discussing the matter in their minds. When she responded, she spoke carefully. 'I know you desire this greatly, however we cannot give you your powers back.'

Avgar was somewhat surprised at this response; he knew how much Phlyte wanted the demise of Tunley and he thought that his request would have been within reason. He wanted to push harder; but had to concentrate so that only the thoughts he wanted were broadcast. *Very well, I will take no further part in your plan.* He crossed his arms and sat back.

Phlyte scrutinised him carefully for several moments. 'We cannot grant you the full power and control that you had when you ruled Mirny. This you largely gained from your crystal and that has been removed forever.' She spoke slowly and carefully. 'What we can do, is remove your nightmares… and we can put a protection in place so that if you are nearing death, from overuse of your magic, you will be alerted. With this in place, you will be safe, but not be able to fully control the flow of your powers. You will still be susceptible to drawing too much or too little power when you reach for your magic.' She lowered her gaze. 'I'm sorry, but that is the best that we can do.'

Avgar tried to weigh up the truth of her words. In the end, he decided that she was telling the truth. *If that is the best you can offer, then I will take it and destroy this Tunley with my hands tied.* Avgar felt fired up to begin the task and then checked himself. *Look at me; I'm choosing the path that will be better for all, despite the potential cost to me.* He scoffed. *Winter will be pleased.*

Phlyte rubbed her hands together and the Myrthians at the table looked more relaxed. 'You will not leave immediately; there are preparations that need to be made, information about Islonda to be gathered and spells to be reworked on you, Avgar.' She looked at the four outsiders. 'This meeting is at an end. I will speak with each of you on the morrow with more details. You would be wise to prepare yourselves to leave at the shortest notice.'

Avgar followed suit as everyone stood. His sight was removed once more and he felt himself being led to the back of the hall. When he stepped on the first part of the ramp, he had an acute sensation of falling and felt his stomach in his throat. He put out his hands in instinct and immediately felt something soft. His mind whirled with confusion and he scraped at his surrounds. His vision suddenly returned.

He cursed in shock as he looked about his small bedroom and found himself all alone. How he got there puzzled his brain and he sat down on the soft mattress and felt exceedingly tired. *I am awed by their power.* Before he knew what was happening, Avgar was lying on his back and falling fast asleep. He didn't even realise that it was the first time since crossing the Moaks that he didn't relive his nightmare before finding a peaceful sleep.

46

A gentle breeze played across the short grass and Marlvon welcomed the cold air. He removed his shoes and stepped onto the grass, feeling the moist dew between his toes.

Marlvon stood in the middle of the clearing and tried to clear his mind. He held his fists in front of him loosely clenched at waist height. He exhaled and then began a pattern of stances, blocks, kicks, punches and other attacks. Marlvon had chosen this pattern to start with as it consisted of slow, fluid movements. He had practised this particular pattern countless times and his body flowed through the moves like the breeze through the grass. His body tensed and relaxed at the appropriate moments and before long, Marlvon was lost in the process; forgetting his troubles.

He repeated this pattern five times, ensuring that each time was more precise than the previous one. Afterwards, he wiped a few beads of sweat from his brow and then stood in a stance that was like riding a horse. While he was holding the position, his mind wandered once more to the day before. The real concern that was troubling him was not Avgar or the innocent Outcasts, but rather Islonda and his child she carried. He exhaled as he thought of her and held an image of his love in his mind; wishing he knew if she was alive or dead. He vehemently hoped that she was safe and not suffering.

Marlvon's demeanour changed to one of sadness and he longed to see her, hold her and kiss her. When he was reunited with her, he would vow to never leave her side again. His dour mood was interrupted by his legs aching. He stood and shook out his muscles.

Marlvon felt a wave of anger towards Islonda's fate rise before him and prepared himself for a more intense pattern. This one was fast and forceful. His fists and feet struck imaginary foes, he swivelled on the spot, dodged sweeping swords and disarmed his opponents before breaking their limbs and disabling them. He intimately knew the purpose behind each of the moves in his patterns and executed them with the same skill, ferocity and power that he would have if he were fighting real opponents. He completed his movements with an accurate punch to the diaphragm, at which point he cried out with the effort. He stood and then breathed deeply while he sweated profusely.

Marlvon looked to the sky and could just see the beginnings of a grey day. He then looked down across the clearing and was surprised to see the monk Sor walking across the grass towards him.

She hailed him before he could speak. 'Good morning, Marlvon. I'm surprised to see you awake so early.'

His reply was not unfriendly. 'And I'm surprised to see you at all; I thought you would have left by now.'

She smiled. 'The plan was to leave at dawn; which is not yet here.' She stopped talking until she came face to face with Marlvon. 'Before I left, I wanted to apologise for fighting you yesterday. I am not going to make excuses, but rather will just apologise unreservedly. So, I'm sorry.'

Marlvon was puzzled. 'There's no need to apologise. We both did what we thought was the right thing.' He pondered Sor for a moment. *She's very unusual.* 'Avgar has brought me a lot of sorrow… It's going to be hard to work with him. I can't decide if I want to kill him or use him to the end of his abilities.'

Sor rested a hand on his shoulder. 'I understand.'

Marlvon instinctively knew that she did. 'I am not a violent man by nature, but what he has done to me… it should not go unpunished.'

'That is a fair statement.' She thought for a moment. 'Perhaps, he has already received some of that punishment. Perhaps, it is for the Gods to punish him and not your purpose to do so.'

'I'm sorry Sor, but I do not follow your gods.' He rolled his shoulders, considering her words. 'What do you mean he has already undergone punishment?'

Sor narrowed her eyes. 'I have no love for the man myself. He has a cruel history and has committed many unforgivable sins to many people, including his son, Winter.' Sor let Marlvon think on that point for a moment. 'I have not known him long, but I can see that his soul suffers and he is conflicted. I believe that once, he was probably an ambitious, well-meaning young man. It is so often seen in the world; ambition and power ruin the good in people.' She looked thoughtful for a few more moments. 'Having spent time with Avgar, I believe that in the twilight of his years, he is returning to being a good man. He clearly cares for Winter, even though he tries to hide it.' She smiled wryly at Marlvon. 'Of course, given his complete lack of speech, he is a lot harder to read than most, so I could be completely wrong.'

Marlvon interrupted gently. 'How did he lose his speech?'

'I don't know exactly. The Healers on Headly would only tell me it was something to do with his magic. Now, you may not agree with me, but as a monk, I see the gods' hand in this. Perhaps this is part of his punishment for past sins.' She pursed her lips and looked past Marlvon. 'Do you know that he also lost his hand before he came over the Moaks many months ago? Imagine that, losing your right hand. I can't imagine how hard that must have been for him. But these are both insignificant next to his greatest loss.' She looked at her toes. 'Although, he may not recognise the significance of it yet.' She looked back at Marlvon. 'Winter is the only child of Avgar left alive. He has lost four children. All as a result of his warring. As he ages, I believe Avgar will mourn acutely for these lost children and be filled with guilt.' Sor looked sad. 'There are much worse punishments than death in this world; the worst are often self-inflicted.' She stopped talking and looked very thoughtful. 'There is a part of me that feels sorry for Avgar.'

'Why are you telling me all of this?'

Sor's brow furrowed. 'I don't know exactly. I first came here to apologise for fighting you, but then I was directed to talking about Avgar. Perhaps I want you to be successful in whatever it is you're doing and I if I can prevent bloodshed, then I should.'

'Fair enough.' Marlvon looked to the sky, which was lightening as the sun rose higher and the day arrived in true. It was going to be an overcast day with high clouds. 'Before you go, would you like to spar with me? I've had no one skilled enough to practice with for quite some time and I think you might be up to the task.'

Sor smiled broadly. 'I'd like that very much.' She took off her shoes. 'It's ironic how us fighting together this morning will bring us closer together.'

The two stood facing each other. They bowed and then took up stances of attack. Marlvon pompously thought that he could defeat Sor, but quickly re-evaluated this when she quickly smacked him lightly across the jaw.

'Come now, Marlvon, keep your guard up.' She retorted with a grin.

Marlvon focused a lot harder from then on and the two danced around each other, exchanging blows, blocks and snide remarks. They continued until both were bruised, but not exhausted, and then Sor called a stop to the exercise.

'I must stop. The sun has risen and I must be off; Guflinkov will wonder where I am.'

'As you wish.' Marlvon bowed to Sor. 'May we meet again, once this is all over, and continue our developing friendship.'

'Thank you, I'd like that.' Sor put her shoes on and they said their farewells. Marlvon watched her depart with a completely different opinion of Sor from when he had met her yesterday.

Marlvon suddenly felt a rumbling in his stomach and realised that he was ravenous. He gathered himself and turned for home. He had only walked a few steps when he saw Phlyte coming towards him. His heart stopped as he realised from her grim facial expression that perhaps he was about to learn Islonda's fate.

Marlvon stood still as Phlyte approached. She eventually stood in front of him and the anxious man had to forcefully stop his hands from shaking.

'Good morning, Marlvon. I hope you rested well last night.' She did not wait for a response before continuing. 'There's no easy way to say this, so I will be direct. Islonda is dead. She was imprisoned at Fort Kykum, where she caught a fever. Being pregnant, she was too weak to fight the illness and died. There can be no doubt that Tunley has caused your love's death.' She let that hang in the air for a few moments.

Marlvon took on the news slowly and felt an overwhelming wave of exhaustion and grief smack into him. Stinging tears rolled out of his eyes and down his cheeks. Phlyte appeared to blur with the rest of the world. He wiped his eyes and tried to look at her more closely. 'Did she suffer? Was she in pain?'

Phlyte looked uncomfortable. 'We don't know.' Marlvon's instincts twitched and he felt as though Phlyte wasn't telling him something. He tried to look deep into her eyes and found them to be transparent. The young man became confused; a myriad of thoughts swirled through his mind.

Marlvon noticed that Phlyte was studying him He tried to clear his mind and found a driving emotion bubble to the surface; hatred, hatred of Tunley and his dictatorship.

Phlyte spoke kindly. 'I'm truly sorry for your loss. And, if you work with us, we can stop this happening to thousands more. Fight with us to end this tyrant.'

Marlvon looked hard at Phlyte. 'There is nowhere that Tunley can hide, that I will not find him and tear him apart.' While Marlvon said the words and his resolve hardened like a diamond, deep down, there was something there, something supressed for the time being. In that moment, Marlvon's essence vowed that in this conquest of death, he would not lose who he was; he would not become evil.

The two stood facing each other for several silent moments, lost in their own thoughts. It was Phlyte who broke the silence.

'We have heard reports that Tunley is preparing to travel to Nivera. We would like you to get there ahead of him and prepare for his demise. You should rest now and prepare your mind and body. If there is anything that you need, be it weapon, armour or item, please ask. We will station a man at your lodgings who will assist you.'

Marlvon nodded. 'As you wish.' He was tempted by the numbness that beckoned him to dull the pain, but he knew he needed to stay sharp to exact his revenge. He walked past Phlyte and brushed his shoulder against hers. The young man was too much within himself to even notice that there was no contact and his shoulder passed straight through Phlyte's being.

Marlvon made his slow way home and found Ryde chowing down on his breakfast. In no mood to talk, Marlvon tore off a chunk of bread and retreated into his bedroom. Once there, he sat on his bed and chewed through the day-old loaf. He was not at all hungry, but knew that it was in his interest to eat. As he did so, he thought of all that Phlyte had said. The weight of his loss crashed onto him and he wept openly. Although he had not seen Islonda for several weeks, he managed to bring a sharp image of her to his mind. He cherished this and hugged himself tightly.

In a moment of logical thought, Marlvon made himself a pact; he would grieve for Islonda for the morning, after which he would focus on killing Tunley. Once that task was achieved, he vowed he would visit his secret lookout and mourn her appropriately. He would then find peace in a secluded part of the world and distance himself from all violence. With these thoughts in his mind, he lay down and rested in the memory of Islonda.

Afternoon came with a sense of purpose and resolve to Marlvon. He sorted through his belongings and decided which he should take and which he should leave behind. He still had his longsword, his hunting knife, considerable gold and minimal clothes. When he picked up a tunic, something heavy rolled out and clunked onto the floor. He looked down and saw Jault's blacksmith hammer. A wave of memory flowed through him of when he and Islonda had found her father's house and forge burnt to the ground under the direction from Avgar.

Marlvon picked up the hammerhead and looked at the steel. To his untrained eye, it looked strong and of good quality; *I wonder if this could be made into a sword… that would be a fitting weapon to kill Islonda's murderer with.* Jault's work had always been of fine quality.

He stood and went to the doorway of the house, where he found Phlyte's man resting against the wall.

'Tell me, are the smithies on Myrth skilled?'

The man straightened. 'They are better than any on the mainland. Do you need a new weapon, or armour? We have many in our armoury that should serve your purpose well.'

'Thank you, but I have a very specific request… can you direct me to the swordsmith please?'

'Phlyte might have asked me to wait here and fetch anything that you might need, but the forges are hidden from outsiders. I'd be more than happy to take you to the well-stocked armoury though.'

Marlvon couldn't be bothered with this. 'I would like to see Phlyte as soon as she can be spared from her many duties.'

'Very well.' The man walked off a little too slowly for Marlvon's liking.

Marlvon returned inside to find some more food. He also found Ryde and told him all that had happened that day while he ate a tart apple. Before long, there was a knock on the door and Phlyte entered. She wore a flowing white gown and looked mildly intrigued.

'I hear you want to see our forges. We have a fine stockpile of arms and armour. Perhaps something from there will suffice.'

Marlvon forced himself to remain polite. 'Alas, I am afraid that it will not. I have a hammerhead that once belonged to Islonda's father. I would like it melted down and made into a sword. That is, if your smithies are of a high enough quality.' He held out the hammerhead and Phlyte looked at it. 'Or perhaps, if this is too hard, I will find that Tunley is just too hard to kill. After all, I get little benefit from his death.'

Marlvon watched the resignation on Phlyte's face that she would have to acquiesce his request.

'That would be a fitting weapon indeed. Come with me and we will speak to someone skilled in the art of sword making.'

Marlvon followed her out of the house and towards the town centre. They passed the hall and kept walking until they reached the outskirts of the village. All the houses soon fell behind them and all that was in front was the steep cliffs of the ring of mountains.

The two made their way to a boulder that was camouflaged by the cliff face. Once there, Phlyte mumbled a few words that Marlvon couldn't quite hear and waved her arm in a flowing pattern. The rock shifted and creaked and moved to the side to reveal a doorway to a black tunnel. Marlvon was awestruck and stepped back in reflex.

Phlyte had no trepidations and walked through with no hesitation. Marlvon swallowed and followed. Once in the tunnel, the light started to fade. Marlvon looked behind him and the boulder was rolling back into place. There was a moment of complete darkness before a warm, red glow spread along the floor. This brightened the tunnel to allow Marlvon to see clearly. The young man squatted down to touch the floor and found it felt like hard bedrock. He was perplexed by this phenomenon and looked at Phlyte, who was watching him closely.

'We have many powers of which you are not aware. Consider yourself lucky; an outsider has never trodden this path. Now come.' She turned and started walking along the tunnel.

Marlvon stood and followed, finding it disconcerting to walk on the glowing floor. The tunnel ran straight for a hundred yards or so and then curved slightly to the left. When Marlvon rounded the bend, he saw a fierce orange glow coming from a chamber ahead. With the glow, Marlvon felt a wave of heat.

Marlvon entered the chamber and found himself to be standing on a rocky outcrop overlooking a deep crevice. The roof was a dozen feet above where he stood, and the opposite wall was half that far away. Phlyte stood back as Marlvon peered down the crevice and saw the source of the light and heat. A river of molten rock oozed its way along from right to left. His eyes dried quickly and he had to pull back at the intensity of the heat. *My goodness. I never knew something like this existed.*

He stepped back from the edge and asked in an awed voice, 'What is it?'

'It is rock. Rock that is so hot that is flows like water. Come, we will speak to Fec about your hammer.'

Phlyte led Marlvon along a walkway that ran by the crevice to a small room set back from the edge. In the room Marlvon met a man wearing only short breeches. He had broad shoulders and had a muscular hairy chest. His head was bald and his jutting chin was black with stubble and grime. He smiled questioningly to Marlvon and held out a calloused hand in greeting. 'My name is Fec. How may I be of service?'

Phlyte answered. 'Marlvon here would like a new blade… made from mainland steel.'

Fec frowned. 'Show me this metal.'

Marlvon handed the hammerhead over to Fec, feeling somehow childish. 'This is of great personal value to me.' He watched as Fec inspected the metal. 'Are you able to make it into a sword?'

'Aye, I'll be able to. I might have to blend it with our own steel to make it the right size… and quality.' Marlvon saw Fec quickly look at Phlyte, who nodded her consent. 'Have you thought about what design you would like?'

Marlvon felt a rush of excitement. It had been a long time since he had received the pleasure of choosing the style of a newly forged sword. 'I have indeed. I would like a rapier with a basket hilted cross guard.'

Fec looked Marlvon up and down, grabbed his arm and held it out straight. 'I can make one for your size. I'll have it delivered to you in ten days.'

Marlvon felt his heart sink. 'Ten days is too long.'

Phlyte stepped closer to Fec and whispered. Marlvon knew she didn't want him to hear, but he managed to just catch what she was saying.

'Have this blade ready by tomorrow. See that it is done using *all* of your talent.'

Fec looked at Phlyte sharply. 'Are you sure? He is an outsider.'

'I am sure. See that you imbibe it with strength and speed.'

He squinted at her, then nodded. 'As you wish.'

Fec turned to Marlvon. 'You're a lucky man. The blade will be ready by tomorrow.' He stood up straight. 'I will make sure that it will be of such a quality that it could rival Moon Song; the only other blade given to an outsider.'

Marlvon didn't know of Moon Song, but the actions of Phlyte and Fec filled him with a shiver of anticipation. He also knew that there would be no way that a sword could be crafted in such a short time… without the use of magic.

'I am honoured, Fec.'

'I best get to it then.' He bid them farewell, then walked to the back of the nook where he opened a trapdoor and disappeared down a ladder through the floor.

Phlyte explained. 'The forges are below us. The molten rock is channelled through rivulets to our advantage.'

Marlvon was intrigued and would have liked to watch Fec work, but found Phlyte directing him back the way that they had come. He heeded her guidance back down the tunnel and out into the daylight and the cool, fresh air.

The next day, Marlvon prepared for departure with Ryde, then the pair sat together and spoke of how the world had changed since they were children. Marlvon was many years Ryde's junior and marvelled at the adventures Ryde had experienced, most of them on the wild Rogaus.

Marlvon was beginning to think of lunch when a firm knock sounded on his door. He stood and made his way over, hoping that it would be food. When he opened the door, he found Fec standing there, cradling a long package in his arms. Marlvon felt instant excitement and hurriedly invited him in.

The muscular man entered and held up the wrapped parcel. 'Here is your sword.' He removed the cloth wrappings to reveal a rapier encased in a simple leather scabbard. He handed the sword to Marlvon with both hands.

Marlvon took the sword and withdrew it from its housing. He immediately recognised the superb craftmanship. As he inspected it, Fec described his new weapon.

'Steel from your hammer has been worked into the blade and hilt. The length is forty-one inches and the width one inch at the widest. She weighs three pounds, a touch heavier than normal on account of your mainland metal. The handle is wrapped with unique snapling leather; durable and it won't slip when wet with sweat. The basket is entirely made of Myrth steel and will not bend or break under any punishment. At the bequest of Phlyte, I have imbedded a chatoyant stone in the pommel as a gift from the Myrthians. This aids in the balance and will help you see your opponent's movements clearer.'

Marlvon had never heard of a chatoyant stone, but the yellow gold-brown gem reminded him of the eye of a fearsome creature. As such, he supposed Fec to be speaking poetically.

He looked at the artist. 'I am eternally grateful for your work. Thank you, Fec.' He looked at the rapier again. 'This is a fine blade; how did you manage it in less than a full day?'

Fec shifted on the spot. 'I used all the skill at my disposal.'

Marlvon's eyes narrowed. 'You used magic, didn't you?'

Fec appeared to be weighing up his response. 'I'm glad that you're happy with the blade. Treat her well and she will treat you well.'

Marlvon chose not to push the matter. 'I thank you again.'

Fec nodded and left Marlvon to his new weapon. Ryde came over and Marlvon showed him the sword.

'You've got a good one there, Marlvon, you lucky bastard. Although, I prefer the strength of a longsword myself.'

Marlvon had thought hard about his choice of sword. 'I too like a good longsword, but this double-edged rapier will provide me with agility and speed.' He smiled ruefully. 'Why don't we test her out? Shall we spar?'

Ryde dropped his shoulders and looked resigned. 'I suppose. The bruises you gave me last time we sparred are almost gone.'

'Ha. I'll go easy on you this time.'

The two made their way out to the ground, where Marlvon had sparred with Sor. He weighed the sword in his hand and took up a stance of preparedness. Ryde did likewise with a longsword that he had been given by the Myrthians yesterday. They eyed each other in their side-on stances for a few moments. Then Ryde leapt at Marlvon. The skilled warrior easily leapt to the side and deflected the longsword. The new rapier felt strong at the contact and Marlvon smiled in satisfaction.

The young man then swung his sword in an elliptical arc and knocked Ryde's tricorn hat off his head. 'Come on old man, you can do better than that.'

Ryde grunted and spun around to advance again. Marlvon parried the blow and then another. He found these simple moves like a reflex and felt as though the sword was part of his being. He set to attack and smacked Ryde with the flat side on his shoulder.

'She moves well.'

'And hurts like buggary. How much longer do you want to beat me up for?'

Marlvon took Ryde's point and stood back. 'I suppose I'll get enough practice in the coming days, but thank you for breaking in her first blows.'

'My pleasure.' Ryde responded sarcastically.

Marlvon inspected the blade before sheathing her. 'I'll have to give her a name.' He fondled the gem in the end of the hilt and thought of the steel's shadowy grey lustre. *Peacemaker? She will bring about peace. But that doesn't seem to do her justice.* He sighed. 'Let us go, I'm hungry.'

They made their way back to the house and found Phlyte waiting there for them.

'Gentlemen.' Phlyte ignored Ryde's scoff. 'At dusk today, you will leave for the mainland.'

Marlvon felt a sense of purpose pulse through him and he stepped closer to Phlyte. As he did so, a flicker in the light made her appearance waver. He ignored it and asked a question.

'Where on the mainland will we be going?'

'To Nivera. We believe Tunley is ready to leave Fort Kykum and you must get to Nivera before he does.'

Ryde spoke next. 'How will we be getting there?'

Phlyte raised an eyebrow. 'The usual way; by boat.'

'It's just that I had heard rumours that the Myrthians could fly in baskets under huge bubbles…' Ryde finished lamely.

'Childhood fantasies, nothing more.'

'Who will be captaining us?'

She looked at Ryde firmly. 'You will. You're an experienced sailor and can handle the crossing easily.'

Ryde rubbed his chin and smiled. 'That's true enough.'

'Then it is settled. We'll meet at the south gate before dusk and I'll show you to your boat.' She made her way to the door and walked through it without so much as a second glance.

Marlvon thought of one more question and raced out of the door after her. He opened the door and saw her walking away to the right. He was about to call her name when, right before his eyes, she disappeared into thin air. His jaw dropped and he stared at the spot where she had just been standing. *Is there no end to the power of these people?*

Phlyte, Avgar and Winter were already waiting for them as Ryde and Marlvon met them by the gate. The sun had dipped behind the hills and the clouds above were blushing pink. Marlvon felt an urge of hatred towards Avgar, and dropped his hand to the pommel of his new sword. He supressed his violent urges as he thought of Sor. *Those thoughts and emotions will not help our mission.*

In contradiction to his feelings, he greeted everyone warmly. 'Good evening all. I hope you are ready to undertake this most noble adventure.' He felt as though Phlyte saw through his ruse, but he didn't really care.

He wanted to ask her about her powers and how she disappeared, but did not want to do so in front of the others. His thoughts were interrupted, as Winter started babbling about how cold he was. *This is going to be a long journey.*

Phlyte cut off the conversation. 'Right, we're all here. Now, let us go.'

She briskly walked away from the men and into the open tunnel that led under the mountains. Marlvon and Avgar both had the idea to be second in line, but Marlvon decided to let Avgar have this small victory. He followed the ageing man through the torch-lit tunnel and out of the open gate at the other end.

For the first time in weeks, Marlvon found himself on the outside of the ring of mountains. The air seemed fresher and a crisp wind blew in his hair. He raised his hands above his head and breathed deeply.

Phlyte led them to the water's edge and as Marlvon looked at her more closely, she seemed pale of face in the setting rays of the sun. He wondered at this, but was quickly distracted by the vessel that was lying half on the sand, half in the water. She was a two-masted boat with a cabin and obvious room below deck. She looked clean, strong and fast to Marlvon's untrained eyes. He deferred to Ryde for an assessment.

Ryde spoke gruffly, half to himself, half to the others. 'She sure is a fine-looking beast. I've no doubt she's fast and agile; responsive to my caress.' He broke off then spoke more loudly to Phlyte. 'What have you done with *The Wicked Princess?*'

'Sor and Guflinkov took her. I thought a ship with more *prominence* would be more fitting for this undertaking. We have named her *Hope*.'

Ryde smiled and ran his hand through his long grey hair that poked from beneath his hat. 'How do you plan to get her in the water? We sure can't push the weight of her and the tide won't be high enough for a long while yet.'

Phlyte smiled and pointed to a rope ladder that was dangling down the side of the ship. 'First, you all climb up there. You will find supplies of food on board for many days.'

Without argument, and with a real sense of adventure, the four men climbed aboard the ship. With the exception of Ryde, they all found this process awkward as the boat was at on odd angle due to her resting on the ground.

Once aboard, they eagerly looked over the rail to Phlyte. She closed her eyes and raised her hands with her palms out towards the boat. She clenched her jaw and dug her heels into the sand as if she were going to push the boat herself. A visible ripple pulsed through the air and blew Marlvon's hair backward. Then, slowly at first, the boat eased into the ocean.

Winter let out a gasp of amazement, Ryde gripped the gunwale, Marlvon smiled with excitement and Avgar grinned.

Moments later the ship was fully afloat and bobbing in the gentle waves. She then turned of her own accord until she was pointing directly away from Myrth Isle.

The clear voice of Phlyte rang in Marlvon's head. 'Fare thee well. Stay safe, hunt well and avenge Islonda. May we meet once more in a time of peace.'

Marlvon nodded to Phlyte, then turned to Ryde. 'Captain Ryde, you have the command of this vessel; direct us as you need.'

'Aye, that I will.' He paused then smiled. 'But truth be told, this fine ship will almost sail herself. Unfurl the sails and I'll set the wheel and then she'll take us as straight as an arrow.'

'Then take us to Nivera so we may get this filthy business over with.'

The course was shortly set and they were soon skipping along at a rapid rate of knots. Marlvon smiled to himself, he would soon have his revenge.

47

Driving rain filled the air, which was pushed in all directions by a squally wind. A lone seagull fought bravely against nature's onslaught, but found herself tiring with the effort. She was briefly thrown onto her back and became confused between the dense, low clouds that should have been overhead and the rolling sea that was meant to be below. She tucked her wings into her body and shot the way that gravity took her. Mere yards from the heaving water, she spread her wings wide and felt an immense strain on her shoulders as she arrested her descent. She then flapped vigorously to control her flight and looked around in the distant hope that she might see land. The bird saw none, and her hopes faded. Her strength was leaving her and she began to fear for the worst. She considered landing in the ocean, but was fearful of the crashing waves. Again, she cast her beady eyes around in all directions in the vain hope that something would save her.

Then she saw it; a dark blur through the rain. She didn't yet know what it might be, but had little choice other than to gather her remaining strength and fly towards it. Her tired wings fought against the wind, but slowly the blur in front of her gained definition. Then, before much longer, she recognised what it was and found a new wave of strength to spur her on. She clasped her beak firmly and flew as best she could towards what was not one, but many, ships.

The gull's wings burned and her feet felt chilled through. She laboriously made it to the first vessel. With her last remaining strength, she climbed her way to the top of the crow's nest and landed with a sense of exhaustion and relief. She bunkered down into the corner of the basket, looked across at the soaked man doing exactly the same as her, and closed her eyes to sleep.

A hundred odd feet below, High Chancellor Tunley stood and looked out over the hill sized swell. The galleon sped down the face of a wave before crashing at the bottom in a forceful spray of salty water. Moments later, it was rising up the next wave. The noise was enormous and the exhilaration within Tunley matched it.

The High Chancellor's fleet had left Fort Kykum fifteen days prior and the sailing had been smooth with a favourable wind towards Nivera. Then, that morning, without any warning at all, the weather had turned. The sea whipped up into a frenzy of rolling waves and the wind was cold, bitter, and strong.

It was the worst type of wind to sail in, as it blew in no single direction. A tail wind, Tunley would have loved, a head wind or cross wind could be worked with, but a squally wind rendered the fleet useless. Had they been close to land, he would have found a sheltered cove and dropped anchor. As it was, there was no land in sight and they were too deep for their anchors to be used. The only small blessing was that the waves seemed to roll unusually in a single direction. To be safe, they only had to keep the ships pointing into the waves. Tunley knew all of this and drank in the ferocious force of nature.

The ship, *Ocean's Fury,* crested another roller and Tunley marvelled at the hill after hill of waves that were in front of them. He let out a whoop and wrapped his full-length leather cloak around him in preparation for the next splash of water over the bow. It did not disappoint him and it drenched him from head to toe. Tunley shook his long lank hair out of his face and laughed inwardly. A shiver ran through his body and he finally felt cold. *Time to go inside and get warm.* A wicked smile crossed his face. *And I know just how to do that.*

Tunley made his slow way over the slippery, moving deck to the captain's room which he had commandeered as his own. He locked the door behind him, flung his sopping clothes on the floor and strode over to a chest completely naked. He flung back the lid and pulled out a half empty bottle of whisky. He took a sharp swig and wiped a drip from his lips. He looked at the bottle and mused that he had never understood the common sailor's fascination with the lesser spirit of rum.

He took another slurp and turned to his bed. Lying under the mounded covers was not one, but two, women. He ripped off the blankets and they both roused from their half sleep.

'High Chancellor, what's happing? My head is going up and down.'

'Ha! It is nothing more than a spot of bad weather. Nothing for you to worry about.' He threw the corked bottle of grog onto the bed. 'Drink up. It will ease the rocking… after all, I don't want vomit all over me.'

The women eyed the bottle then took it to share between them. Tunley watched as they gulped down the amber liquid and felt himself warming. His sinful eyes wandered over their displayed bodies and he felt his heart rate quicken. *They are different, these two. Sure, I'm paying them, but they seem more willing than the usual whores.*

Tunley thought back to when he had been presented with his options. These two came recommended as the best in all of Fort Kykum. At first the High Chancellor was sceptical; their skin was of a different colour to his, but he soon began to see this as exotic. After his first try of the women, any doubts he had were wiped clean and he immediately contracted them to be for his personal use only.

He continued to look at them and thought of the old superstition that to bring women on board a ship was bad luck. *Horseshit; I make my own luck.*

'High Chancellor, what are you waiting for? You look cold and we are so warm. Come and let us warm you.'

He smiled like a boy in a sweets shop and climbed onto the bed and immediately wished that he had come in from the cold sooner.

The wind, waves, and rain continued for the rest of the day and night. Tunley kept to his room and his private entertainment. When he woke in the morning, he noticed a certain stillness in the ship. He quickly dressed and headed onto the deck. When he got there, an eery silence sat over the vessel and ocean. He made his way to the gunwale and peered about in amazement.

The Rogaus was completely flat with not even a sigh of wind blowing. There were high clouds far up above, which the dawn light filtered consistently through. The High Chancellor looked back to the water and marvelled at the sight. The surface looked like a polished sheet of silver that stretched as far as the eye could see. He peered around at his fleet and quickly calculated that three boats were missing; likely to have sunk in the storm. *Ineptitude will ruin us.*

The captain of *Ocean's Fury* came and stood beside Tunley. He looked spooked and spoke in a hushed voice. 'Have you ever seen anything like this? And after the fearsome night we had.'

Tunley ignored the sailor's lack of courtesy. 'I have not. It is, though, better than the squally wind of yesterday.'

'Aye, but it sends a shiver down the spine, sir.'

'Hhmmm.' Tunley looked at the captain's pale face. 'Order the oars out and signal to the other ships to do likewise. Not all our ships can row, but those that can should continue onto Nivera. We don't know how long this stillness will last.' *And I want Nivera to be mine.*

'Aye aye, sir.' The captain scurried away to do as he was bidden.

At least the water will be easy to row in.

It was not long before roughly half the fleet were on the move once more. They were unsure how far off course the storm had blown them, so the mixture of galleons and war-sloops rowed south-west in an attempt to find land.

They spied it later that day and Tunley was thrilled to see that they had not been set off course by nearly as much as he had feared.

He ordered the ships to sail just within eyesight of the land and they continued on their journey to Nivera under a fresh wind.

❧

Three days later, Tunley stared through his looking glass at the beautiful city of Nivera. He had been eager to clap eyes on her, and was not disappointed to see the fabled artisan city.

Nivera was set directly against the Rogaus and a few miles from the delta of the Sempa River. A great white wall surrounded Nivera at least a mile from the nearest homes. This had clearly been planned to allow for more dwellings to be constructed within safety. Between the wall and the city, vast fields of flowers grew. Tunley didn't know what type they were, but there were various shades of orange, purple, red, yellow, and magenta. The colours were designed in a pattern of curved beauty, with paths meandering throughout the flowerbeds. Tunley marvelled at this and thought of how much time had been wasted maintaining this creation. He then looked to the city itself and saw the sun dance playfully across many gold, silver and red domed buildings. Even at his distance, Tunley could tell that the streets were wide and luxurious with coloured stones of green, purple and white.

The High Chancellor of Roasline adjusted his eye piece to look closer and saw that the buildings themselves were made of a combination of stone and wood; expertly designed to blend together. Some of the roofs were tiled in deep reds and others were thatched. Each house had eaves with playful creatures sculpted into the design. Tunley was forced to admit that Nivera was a beautiful city indeed.

The waring man then turned his attention to the defences of the city and was surprised at the lack of fortifications. He smiled at the few turrets that sat on the wall and was happy that he would have an easy victory.

Tunley had initially planned to wait for the remainder of his fleet to arrive, but seeing the city before him drove his hungry desire to take her and he decided to attack that evening. He greedily hoped to have the city in his hands by the time the rest of his ships arrived. He would then begin preparations for the much more challenging task of taking the cesspit of Psymryte. Once he had taken Nivera, he would have plenty of time to fill while he waited for his troops to arrive on foot from Fort Kykum. Only once his full force was mustered would he consider attacking Psymryte.

The captain of *Ocean's Fury* was summoned and before long the fleet began to move slowly towards Nivera with cannons bristling. The evening was cool and cloudless and Tunley wrapped a warm cloak about himself as he stood at the bow of his ship.

They soon came within firing range of the cannons sitting atop Nivera's wall. The distant *kaboom, boom!* reached Tunley's ears and he watched two cannon balls fly through the air and splash down many yards from his ship. He never liked being within the firing range of the enemy without being able to retaliate. He shifted from foot to foot as more cannon balls were shot his way. It felt like a long while before Roasline's fleet were able to retaliate with shots of their own.

The wall of Nivera sat a hundred yards back from the sandy beach and was situated on a small rise. This meant that the ships had to be all the closer before their inferior cannons could hit their target. Eventually, Tunley's cannons found their marks and shards of rock shattered from the wall. His ships knew to concentrate their fire on the turrets and it wasn't long before the first one was rendered inert.

While that eased the barrage on the fleet, the air was still heavy with balls. The fleet turned their attention to the next turret and had to sail parallel to the coastline to bring it within range. They soon had it within their capabilities and shortly after it was destroyed.

Tunley banged his fist on the railing in excitement and glee at their first two victories. He looked up and down the wall and saw that there was only one cannon turret remaining that faced the Rogaus. It seemed to house three cannons that were firing rapidly. His ships approached this as fast as they could and opened fire. *Ocean's Fury* soon gained a direct hit on the turret and then stillness filled the air.

Tunley looked about his fleet behind him and lost some of his joy; eight ships were sinking quickly and a further five were damaged but still afloat. *It matters little, I've removed any threat to us.* He then looked back at Nivera to plan his next move. He stared at the barely damaged wall and tried to find its weakest section. He signalled to the captain that the fleet should punch through midway between two of the turrets.

The ships ordered themselves and as dusk turned into night, they advanced towards the wall. Tunley couldn't wait to get closer and it wasn't long before he heard his cannons firing freely. He wanted his fleet to be nice and close to ensure his balls hit the wall with maximum force.

The High Chancellor struggled to see in the moonlight and then, amidst the booms of his cannons, he heard a strange *woomph* noise came from Nivera. An instant later, he thought he saw a huge chunk of rock hurtling through the air towards his fleet. He watched the slow arc of the projectile reach its zenith and then begin to rapidly descend. Complete silence filled the air as Tunley realised that all of the sailors on deck had stopped what they were doing to watch this new development. A moment later, the shadowy rock struck the ship the furthest from Nivera and smashed a hole right through the centre of her. Water shot up and screams of pain and fear ripped through the air. *Shit!*

Woomph, woomph, woomph! Three more rocks were flung into the air. No one in the fleet stayed silent to watch anymore. They scrambled and panicked to get the ships moving as quickly as they could in a disordered retreat.

Tunley felt a rare wave of fear pass through him and he willed his fleet to outdistance the flying rocks. *What is this new device? It shoots like a catapult, but the range and the arc… it is impossible.* Tunley watched the rocks splash harmlessly off target and breathed a sigh of relief. *At least they're not as accurate as cannons.* He ran his hand through his hair. *How can we shoot them if we can't even see where they're slinging from?* He spat on the deck and resigned himself that he may not achieve an easy victory after all.

Tunley thought long and hard on the matter and decided that the rock-slinging machines of war were from a bygone era. He remembered childhood stories of devices that could fling their payload both high and far. He struggled to remember their name, but in the end knew to call them *trebuchets*. These contraptions were less accurate than cannons and had a much shorter range. Tunley quickly decided that in the morning, his fleet would stay out of their range and bombard the wall with all the balls that they had. He refused to be defeated by weapons of the past. He would then land his men, who would swarm through the wall's opening and take Nivera.

By the time the morning rolled around, Tunley had changed his mind. He now decided to play the smart way and await the rest of his fleet to arrive at Nivera. He filled this time by sending scouting parties up the Sempa River as well as onto land well out of reach of Nivera's range. Those who journeyed up the Sempa found the voyage difficult as the delta was shallow with fast, ever changing currents. On top of that, the wall surrounding Nivera seemed more fortified on the Sempa side than the side facing the Rogaus. Tunley deemed the Sempa to be a poor route of attack.

The men who had gone ashore dared not travel far inland for fear of being ambushed. They did, however, find farms abandoned and townships deserted. With this news, Tunley began to devise a backup plan.

Two days passed before the rest of his fleet arrived and the heavy man had grown impatient. The girls he brought could only provide so much entertainment and he had turned to the bottle to pass the time. To aggravate his boredom, his old leg wound pained him and he couldn't help shake the feeling of being cold. His rash was still present and he struggled with dark thoughts of torture, murder, and suicide.

When his fleet finally arrived, Tunley breathed the air afresh and set about putting his scheme into action. He met with the captains and told them of his plan for the following dawn.

The ships with the longest-range cannons gathered together away from the smaller, faster vessels. The assault began with a brisk southerly wind propelling the heavy ships forward. They aimed directly for Nivera while the smaller ships sailed off to land south-east of the artisan city. Tunley remained with the big ships and where the naval action would be.

The High Chancellor stood next to the Captain at the tiller and looked hungrily at Nivera. Soon they would be within firing range and he rubbed his hands together in anticipation.

Boom, boom, boom! Three rapid shots were fired from the wall of Nivera. Tunley's mouth dropped as three cannon balls flew aggressively into his fleet and sank his foremost ship.

'The whores! They've moved more cannons into place!' Tunley spat. *Why had I not predicted that?*

'Sir, what should we do?' The Captain's voice sounded concerned.

Boom! Boom! Two more shots arced towards the ships. Tunley tried to think, but his thoughts came slowly and thick. *How many ships can they destroy before we are in firing range?* 'I… um…' *Why did I wait for my fleet?*

Boom! Boom! Boom! Boom! Boom!

'How many cannons do you make out, Captain?'

The captain looked at him with mouth agape. Tunley slapped him across the jaw. 'How many?' *Why am I doing this? It serves no purpose.*

'Um… five that can hit us now. As we get closer…. who knows?'

And there it is. That's the point. We don't know how many cannons they've been able to reposition along the parapet: it could be five in total; it could be twenty. I just have to decide one thing: is it worth the gamble? Tunley's mind suddenly switched to thoughts of self-preservation.

'Signal the retreat, Captain.' *If I was not in the midst of this, I would order them to push on and pay the ultimate price for our victory.*

'Aye aye, sir.' The captain looked happy.

A series of signal flags shot up a rope and the fleet began to turn as one. Nivera's cannons continued to boom away, and Tunley flinched every time one did. Eventually, they stopped and Tunley relaxed. He made his way aft and looked back at Nivera as she grew further away. A moment later he turned and yelled to the captain.

'Signal for us to land with the remainder of the fleet.' *We will regroup and try an approach on land.*

Tunley realised that his safety was fully assured for the time being. He spat over the edge into the ship's wake as waves of disgust at his own cowardice seeped through him. He skulked back to his cabin, avoiding others, and locked the door behind him. Fumbling around for his drink, he drained a bottle. *I need to bring my confidence and ferocity back.* He turned and saw the two women still in his bed. His mind quickly turned to evil acts of blood and lust and he made his way over to them with a hideous smile etched into his face.

It took all night for the fleet to be emptied of her troops. Only a skeleton crew remained on board to defend the vessels if needed and, under Tunley's direction, they positioned themselves in a semi-circle with cannons facing outwards and the landing bay behind them. Tunley didn't expect an attack from the sea as he finally realised that Nivera had not sent any ships to defend her. He mused that they must have realised that it would have been futile to send ships against him.

Tunley himself remained on *Ocean's Fury* through the night in an attempt to get a good night's sleep. When he woke at dawn, he ordered a bowl of warm water to be brought to his cabin and proceeded to wash the blood from the previous day's activities off his body. As he did this, he looked over at the two mangled corpses bundled in the corner and not a hint of regret entered his mind.

When he was ready, he tied his long hair back and was rowed to shore alone. Once he landed on the rocky sand, he made his way to the tent where the captains were meeting. He passed many campfires and took food from each of them to satiate his hunger.

Tunley entered the captain's tent and everyone stopped talking immediately. He felt their stares of uncertainty and fear and he realised that they had no idea what he was going to do. He used this to his advantage and smiled wickedly. He then jumped at the closest captain and yelled, 'Boo!' The poor man jumped a foot in the air and Tunley laughed out loud. He found his joke so funny that he failed to notice that everyone in the tent was pretending to laugh with him.

'Captains and Ship Masters. We should be proud of ourselves. We're the first men from Roasline to set foot so far into the heartland of the Outcasts. We… are… great!' Tunley paused between each shouted word.

'I suppose you're all wondering what my plan is to deal with that shitful city of Nivera. You're probably all thinking that you belong on the sea and not on the dry land. At least, I hope that's what you're thinking, otherwise you shouldn't be a captain in my navy.' He looked sternly about the tent.

'I'll tell you what we're going to do: we're going to lay siege to Nivera and find a way through that hateful wall.' He smiled to himself at a funny thought, 'We will find the key to her chastity belt!' His smile turned into a full bellied raucous laugh.

Tunley wiped a bead of sweat off his brow with his sleeve. 'But first, we're going to circle her, cut off her food supply, take what, and who, we want from the farms and towns here abouts and then smash our way into her.'

Tunley looked about the tent and the captains seemed to be reasonably pleased with his plan. 'I am in this with you and we *will* be victorious.' *Even if we have to wait for the General's slow troops to arrive,* he concluded to himself.

48

Sor and Guflinkov found easy passage across the Rogaus. The weather played nice and the *Wicked Princess* was a fast vessel. Eleven days after leaving Myrth Isle, they arrived just outside Nivera, in the same cove where Tunley would land in ten days' time.

Sor had discovered Guflinkov to be a pleasant travel companion, despite being aloof at times. He told her stories of past days and Sor tried to pick which stories he told were true, which were embellished and which were made up entirely. Despite her attempts, Guflinkov would not let on and advised Sor that the purpose of his stories was to teach and make her think. Then the old man would smile ruefully and add, 'And sometimes they're just for fun.'

Sor was grateful to find that Guflinkov respected her beliefs and she was even surprised to learn that he knew a great deal about the monks and their way of life. He seemed inquisitive to learn more about the Gods and in turn taught her about the people of Roasline. During these conversations, Sor became suspicious that Guflinkov was keeping her mind busy, which prevented her from thinking about her confused feelings for Winter. She dismissed these thoughts as foolish. *How could he possibly know what I'm thinking?*

Aside from Guflinkov, Sor also travelled with two of the Myrthians. These two spoke little and kept to themselves. Their main purpose was to get the monk and the old man to the mainland in safety and then return with the *Wicked Princess* to Myrth Isle.

Once they arrived in the cove, Guflinkov and Sor were rowed ashore. They watched the *Princess* turn and depart before gathering their few possessions, which included more than enough gold for their journey. The Myrthians had made packs from sticks, leather and canvas that could be carried on one's back. Sor hoisted hers onto her back and watched Guflinkov do the same. *This will take a while to get used to.*

'Shall we visit Nivera?' Sor asked lightly.

'Aye, that we shall. I think, Sor, that you will be pleasantly surprised, for she is a beautiful city.'

The two set off towards Nivera as the sun reached her zenith. Sor started slowly and her legs seemed to sway, as if she were still on the boat. Guflinkov smiled and merely commented that she had *sea legs*.

They soon came across a narrow road and followed its cart-wheeled divots. A few farmers trundled along behind them and Sor and Guflinkov travelled the last mile up a gentle slope to Nivera. They reached the gate in a great wall and were stopped by the pikes of two soldiers who were wearing rusty chainmail and leather coifs.

'Hello, hello, what have we here?' The soldier on the right grinned a toothless grin. 'Don't she look funny with no 'air?' Sor had shaved her head once more before leaving Myrth Isle. Short stubble had grown while sailing the Rogaus, which she intended to remove when the chance arose.

The other soldier rolled his eyes, clearly tired of his fellow guard. He looked at Guflinkov and ignored Sor. 'What business brings you to Nivera, old man?'

Guflinkov spoke slowly, his voice sounding much older than Sor had heard him use before. 'I'm on a great pilgrimage with a monk of the Night God. We started our journey in the delightful city of Fort Kykum. We then passed through many towns, both big and small, on our way to the Woods of Sorrow. There is a particular tree in that vast woodland that houses an interesting variety of fungus. This fungus only grows on the south side of the tree and starts its life as a pale beige colour. As it matures, the hue moves to more of a grey-white. If it's picked at this particular maturity, it tastes fresh and bouncy.'

Sor watched as the guard's eyes glazed over with boredom. She smiled inwardly. Guflinkov continued to ramble about a made-up journey, listing many plants and animals that they had seen along the way. It wasn't long before a queue of farmers gathered behind them and started to protest at the delay.

The guard with no teeth snapped out of his daze and spoke dozily. 'Righto, righto, through you go.'

Sor followed Guflinkov through the gate and widened her eyes at the sight before her. Fields and fields of colourful flowers circled the city. She had never seen anything so delightfully amazing in her entire life. Their scent then reached her nostrils and she breathed it in deeply and closed her eyes. 'It's wonderful.'

'Yes, it is.' Guflinkov smiled; clearly delighted to see Sor's response. 'The inhabitants of Roasline deem the Outcasts to be dirty, savage half-wits. Ha! There is nothing so beautiful as this in all the lands south of the Liagar. But come, my stomach longs for a decent meal and we need to find lodgings for the night.'

Sor and Guflinkov wound their way through the paths of flowers and into the city of Nivera. Sor was delighted to see that, as she walked through the city, the theme of the flowers prevailed. Many houses had boxes on their windowsills filled with colourful blooms and etchings of blossoms carved into their walls and doors. The streets themselves were wide and exceptionally clean and Sor felt more like she was walking through a town and not a city, for the people seemed cheerful and openly greeted passers-by.

Guflinkov knew where he was going as if he lived in Nivera and Sor marvelled at his memory; Guflinkov had told her he not been to Nivera in two decades. They bought freshly baked meat pies from a pie bakery and Sor savoured the hearty meat and rosemary flavouring as they continued to walk.

It was mid-afternoon by the time they entered a place of lodging. The inn was a two-storey establishment which sold drink, but no food. The room they rented was simple but comfortable and met their needs.

Instead of settling into their room or relaxing in the common room, Guflinkov reminded Sor that time was important and insisted they attempt to organise their transport for the next day. As they made their way to a stable, Guflinkov explained that it would be best to visit not one, but two stables.

'We need four fast, strong horses, you see. Each stable will usually have a couple of such beasts, but no more. The demand just isn't there for expensive horses. And so, we will go to two stables.'

True to Guflinkov's word, the first establishment had a range of horses, mules and donkeys for sale, but few animals of the quality that they were after.

Guflinkov haggled with the owner over a good price and eventually came away with two fine gelding horses with all of the saddlery that would be required for the journey. They agreed to leave their mounts at the stable until the morrow.

The next stable was not dissimilar to the first one, except that the owner tried to sell them a lame horse. Guflinkov threatened to walk away from any deal and the man gave in and sold them two mares with strong haunches. Guflinkov and Sor had little trouble paying for their transport, as the Myrthians had given them a small fortune to prevent finances from being a barrier. Once all was organised, the two retired to their lodgings for the night.

Guflinkov and Sor woke before dawn and made their way through the sleeping Nivera to collect their horses. Once all was ready, they left the beautiful city via the Sempa gate. Sor was sad that she couldn't spend more time in Nivera to discover all of her wonders and beauty. *Alas, as always, I am bound by what I must do, not that which I want to do.* And so, they clip-clopped along the hard road, with Sor carrying a heavy heart.

From Nivera, the road ran on the west side of the Sempa River for many hundreds of miles. The two travelled quickly and with little incident. They avoided towns, except to buy food from, and travelled from dawn to dusk. They followed the road when it suited them and cut many miles off their journey by going off-road from time to time. The miles passed by in a blur, and the main sensation that Sor felt was bruising from being in the saddle all day, every day.

After twenty days of solid riding, they reached a ferry and crossed over the Sempa. By this stage, they had left the Woods of Sorrow in the distance and found themselves well south of the Lingos Hills. The Moaks loomed tall before them and Sor began to feel a mixture of excitement and trepidation. She was eager to see fellow monks again, but knew that she had to navigate a meeting with Lord Olswerth first.

As they neared the mighty Moaks, Sor noticed the temperature begin to cool. She often had to pull a coat around her shoulders when the sun hid behind a cloud and she was reminded of the chill winters of her town.

Sor and Guflinkov had ridden for twenty-two days when they passed into Olswerth's dominion. They set up camp a few miles inside his border, in a shallow dale with trees dotted here and there for shelter. The sun was just about go to bed for the night when Sor heard the distinctive sound of hooves approaching.

'Guflinkov, can you hear that? It sounds like a lot of horses.'

'Hhmmm, yes.' The old man frowned, then pointed west. 'They'll come over that rise in a moment.'

Sure enough, a short while later, Sor watched a company of twenty odd horses canter over a small grassed rise. They came directly towards the pair and Sor regretted lighting a fire to ward off the chill.

When the men got closer, Sor could see that they were fitted out as if for battle. She moved to be close to Guflinkov and they waited for the arrival of the company.

The men pulled up their steeds no closer than ten yards from Sor and Guflinkov's camp. They aligned themselves in three rows with the fore row drawing sharp swords. A single rider urged his angry looking stallion forward and spoke in a commanding tone. 'Who are you and what are you doing away from your homes?'

Guflinkov smiled gently. 'I am Ustek and this is Sister Sor, a monk of the Night God. We've journeyed far with a message for Lord Olswerth.'

The man shifted in his saddle. 'You can tell the message to me and I shall pass it on to him.'

'Alas, if it were that simple I would do so happily. However, I am under strict instructions to hand the message to him directly.'

'How can I know what you say is the truth?'

Guflinkov smiled and shrugged his shoulders. He held his palms out to show that he was holding nothing. 'You can't. But then, what risk is there in putting me in a room with him? I'm more than happy to hand you, or anyone else, the message in his presence.' He looked thoughtful.

'You can even keep a sword on my neck if you think an old man is that much of a risk.'

'I could just kill you here and take the message for myself.'

'That's right; you could take the written message, but the scroll is scribed in code and would make little sense to you or anyone else without the cypher.'

'What do you mean, old man?'

'I mean, that the words on the page tell a story of no importance. It is only when you know the correct way to read it, that it makes strategic military sense.'

Sor gazed between Guflinkov and the man in the saddle. *This is the first I've heard about a scroll... or a code.*

The soldier sat up straight on his horse. 'As it turns out, old man, you're in luck. Our liege-lord will be riding this way on the morrow. We have been sent out before him to scout out the land and pave the way for his arrival.'

'Well, that's all very convenient, isn't it?'

'I will leave two men here to protect you through the night.' Sor had little doubt that he actually meant *guard* and not *protect*. 'You would do well to stay by your fire.'

'I am in agreeance with this plan.'

The man turned and pointed to two men in his command. 'See the message that Ustek has reaches Lord Olswerth in the morning.'

'Yes, sir,' came the immediate reply.

The leader stood up in his stirrups and waved the rest of his men forward and away. They trotted off before speeding up to a canter.

Guflinkov turned to Sor as the two men dismounted and picketed their mounts. 'They won't get much further tonight, unless they want to fall in the dark, but I'm glad to have them gone.'

Sor nodded. 'Yes, he was rather a prickly sort of man.'

'Let us eat and rest for the night; who knows what tomorrow might bring.'

Sor bit her lip and looked at the two soldiers who were settling themselves by the fire and getting their own food out. *Clearly, they don't think we're a threat.* As she had that thought, she was reminded that she actually could be a threat to their mission.

Sor whispered under her breath. '*Ustek*, there's something that I should probably tell you before we get entangled in Olswerth's webs.'

Guflinkov raised an eyebrow and responded in equally hushed tones. 'I know well his aptitude for brutality, if that's what you're referring to.'

She shook her head. 'Can you please help me see to our horses?'

The old man raised both eyebrows. 'Certainly. I think I did see one of them limping earlier.'

Sor led Guflinkov over to the horses and spoke in a quiet voice to avoid the soldiers hearing. 'Last time I was in Olswerth's domain, I was a wanted woman. There were soldiers searching for me and Winter.'

Guflinkov sounded surprised. 'Oh, and why was that?'

Sor continued sheepishly. 'Before we crossed the Green Lake, we were ambushed by ruffians in the woodlands. I defended us and broke the toes of our attackers. Unbeknownst to me, Olswerth's nephew happened to be one of those attackers. It was dark when the attack took place, but if Olswerth's nephew recognises me now, then my life will be forfeit and our mission will likely fail.'

When Guflinkov spoke, he had a coarse note to his voice. 'You're only telling me this now?'

'I'm sorry, Guflinkov, I had put it from my mind and only just recalled it.'

The old man rubbed his chin. 'We have two options; take our chances together or use tonight to enable you to escape and go straight to the monks. Both options have risks; both options could render our mission a failure.' Guflinkov did not sound happy and Sor felt a mixture of guilt and fear.

The monk closed her eyes and prayed quickly to the Night God to help her decide. 'I am not one to run away from my actions or shirk my duties. I will stay with you and if I am found out, then I will pay the price for what I did.' As Sor spoke, she solidified her opinion that this was the best course for her.

Guflinkov scoffed. 'That's all very noble of you, but this is bigger than just you. The real question we need to answer is: which action will be a greater risk to the Outcast people?' He scratched his chin in contemplation. 'But I agree, it will be best for you to stay. If you run, then there will definitely be questions to answer, and I may not even get to see Olswerth. No, you will stay and we will run the risk of you being discovered.'

The plan sounded reasonable to Sor and Guflinkov continued, 'You will say that you have been in Nivera for two years and that we met on the road travelling in the same direction. What you were doing in Nivera is a fabrication that you will have to come up with. You will need to make it believable and immune to probing questions.'

'What do you mean by that?' Sor whispered.

Guflinkov thought. 'Here's an example: if you say that you have been learning how to tend the great flower fields of Nivera, then Olswerth might ask if you can advise him on the growing of his own flowers. He might ask when particular flowers bloom and which varieties need pruning. If you don't know the answers, he will know you to be lying.'

'But surely, he wouldn't know the answers himself.'

'That is not the point. He will be able to tell by your response if you're making the answer up. It is a tricky business fabricating a past.'

Sor understood and nodded.

'You will have until morning to decide upon your story. Now, we should get back; before our guards become suspicious.'

The two travellers returned to the fire and sat in silence eating a frugal meal. They spoke little to the armed men and excused themselves early in order to rest well. Sor had much thinking to do and was troubled by her task. She was never very good at lying and she struggled vainly to come up with a sound story of her doings for the last two years. *What if he asks about people I've met, or streets that I should know? Oh, this is horrible.* She went to sleep with absolutely no idea as to how she might survive an interrogation on the morrow.

Sor woke from her poor night's sleep and ached all over. She hobbled into a nearby bush to relieve herself and returned to see one of her guards watching her closely. Her skin itched like ants were crawling over her.

She stood and rubbed her arms to warm up while watching her breath steam out of her mouth. She looked over at Guflinkov, who was sitting up, dressed and ready to go for the day. She completed her morning prayers, pulled on her soft boots, and packed her meagre possessions away.

Guflinkov handed her a wedge of cheese and a chunk of salted meat, which she ate half-heartedly. This she followed with a mouthful of water from her waterskin.

'Are you ready for today, Sor?'

Sor knew exactly what Guflinkov meant and felt ashamed that she had not tried harder to develop a back-story. She answered shortly. 'No.' The best story that she had come up with was that she had been staying with fellow monks and learning of the ways of the outside world.

Sor's thoughts were interrupted by the creepy soldier who came and stood over her. 'Time to get up, both of you. Leave your bags and horses behind and come with us.'

Sor and Guflinkov stood and did as the armed man said. The four of them left their camp behind and walked a short way to the top of a gentle hill where a packed dirt road passed over.

When they arrived, the soldiers stood on either side of Sor and Guflinkov and looked west over rolling hills. Sor couldn't help but notice how silent the pair had been since meeting them and found it disconcerting.

The morning was still young and cold when the monk saw what she had been waiting for; a line of horses trotting at a fair pace in their general direction.

She watched in silence as it drew closer and she was surprised to see how many horses there were. She counted their number while she waited and lost count somewhere around the two-hundred mark. There were still many horses behind those, and she estimated there to be at least three-hundred beasts.

Near the front of the cavalry, but not in the lead, rode a man in long crimson robes. As he drew nearer, Sor could see a simple crown on his head and the flash of plate armour beneath his garb. The leading horse bore a crimson and green flag with an image of a pouncing mountain cat in black. Sor supposed this to be the emblem of Lord Olswerth and tensed at the thought of the imminent meeting.

The train of horses drew nigh before slowing to a walk. Sor and Guflinkov stood on the side of the road and their guards hailed the flagbearer. The army stopped at a signal from Olswerth, who came up beside Sor and Guflinkov. Sor looked at him closely, but not intrusively. She guessed he was a man in his forties, past his prime, but still a force to be reckoned with. As he sat in his saddle, he reminded Sor of a gnarly, tough tree root. He had a hooked nose and beady little eyes rather close together. His face was shaved clean and he wore a scowl as if it was his natural disposition. He looked keenly at the soldiers who had stopped him, and then at Sor and Guflinkov.

'What is the meaning of this?' His voice was as gnarly as his body and sounded strong and sharp; used to giving orders and having them obeyed.

His soldiers bowed to him. 'Sir, we found these two entering your lands. The old one claims to have an important message for you.' His voice quavered slightly as he addressed his lord.

Olswerth moved his war-horse closer to Guflinkov. 'What say you, old man?'

Guflinkov stood firm and showed no sign of fear. 'My Lord Olswerth, I have a message for you of the utmost importance. It would be best for your ears to hear this message in private.'

Olswerth leaped off his horse more nimbly than a man of his age should have been able to. 'You presume to tell me what is best for my ears?'

Guflinkov spoke quietly and calmly. 'The message I contain is not for your rank and file to hear. Could we not speak more privately?'

Sor watched Olswerth bristle. 'I have no idea who you are.'

'I am Ustek and a simple messenger.'

Olswerth looked him up and down. 'If you're a simple messenger, then you would have your message written down.' He snapped his head and looked at Sor. 'And who is that?' He pointed a gloved finger at the monk.

'That is Sister Sor of the Night God.' Guflinkov quickly moved on. 'My lord, I do indeed have the message written.'

'A-ha. Then hand it over now.'

'As you wish, but it will offer you little knowledge.' Guflinkov withdrew a scroll from his sleeve and handed it to Olswerth.

The wiry man inspected the wax seal with a look of confusion, before breaking it apart. He unrolled the parchment and read the message.

He looked up at Guflinkov. 'What is this dribble? You're wasting my time!' He threw the note on the ground. Sor picked it up gently and read it surreptitiously.

> *Terror reigns unchecked; scheming Tunley.*
> *Burning, assaulting, attacking; he's skilful.*
> *Campaigning, joyfully, all dwindling battlements, ultimately colonising*
> *everywhere.*
> *Slyly delicious skeletons, galloping away; compassionately, deliberately*
> *collaborating to fell the slayer.*

She agreed it sounded like gibberish, but then she remembered something that Guflinkov had said the day before.

Guflinkov spoke carefully to Olswerth. 'My lord, there is a message within the message. Allow me to tell you the code to read the true message in private.'

Olswerth snatched the paper from Sor. He eyed them suspiciously, then looked at the note once more. To Sor, it looked as if Olswerth was weighing up his intrigue at finding a coded message with his hatred of letting someone else dictate events. Eventually, he signalled to his guardsmen to keep their distance and he pointed at Sor. 'If this man does anything out of the ordinary, kill her.'

Olswerth stepped off the road with Guflinkov. They went far enough to satisfy Olswerth, but not too far that Sor could not hear what was being said, albeit only just. She smiled and suspected that Guflinkov had planned this perfectly.

'Well, what's the code?'

'You take the first letter of every word in the first line, the second letter of every word in the second line, the third in the third line and the fourth in the fourth line. Put the letters you get together to read the new message.'

Guflinkov gave Olswerth time to work out the true meaning of the scroll. Sor watched him closely. Olswerth frowned at first, but then a look of utter surprise spread over his features. This was quickly followed by anger, then hunger, and finally confusion.

'What is the meaning of this?' His voice sounded shaky, almost scared. 'TRUST USTEK MY LITTLE LILLY PILLY.'

'I am Ustek. If you trust me, then I will tell you much.'

'How... how did you... is she... she can't be... that's what she used to call me... my mother.' His face grew stern. 'What trick are you playing at?'

Guflinkov spoke kindly to Olswerth. 'No trick. Ask your men to rest and set up a pavilion for us and I will tell you more.'

Olswerth nodded, conceding defeat. He turned to his men and barked out a few quick orders. Sor watched as the soldiers seamlessly dismounted and set up a tent for Olswerth. In no time, at all she found herself sitting in the tent with Olswerth, Guflinkov and an empty chair.

Olswerth ordered a servant to bring him a goblet of wine. He offered some to Guflinkov, who refused, but did not offer any to Sor. He took a big gulp, then stared at Guflinkov.

'Ustek, tell me all that you know of my mother.'

'Very well.' Guflinkov placed his crossed hands in his lap. 'You would have been a boy of ten when you last saw your parents. They left you to go on a journey down the Sempa. They should have returned within a moon cycle, but they did not. You probably don't remember it, but I was one of their party of fifteen. We travelled for ten days before we were set upon by bandits. They came at us in the night. Your father fought well, but was slain by an arrow. Your mother, myself, and two other women were captured. To this day, I know not why they killed all of the men except me. They kept us prisoner for many days, beating me and abusing the women. Then they left us alone for a few days before taking us to be traded as slaves.

'At the slave market we were ready to be auctioned when a very young man by the name of Resvon rode in with two hundred soldiers. They slew the traders and set the slaves free. In the confusion of battle, your mother lost a hand and was stepped on by a horse. Everyone thought she would die, but I insisted she should be taken to the Healers. Resvon had little interest in us and so I got her there by my own means.

'It took a long time for your mother to heal. She was a strong woman, but the loss of her husband had affected her deeply. She pined for you in those days of convalescence. But, by the time that she was fully healed, I had convinced her to journey with me before returning home to her *little Lilly Pilly* as she had often called you.

'We sailed to Myrth Ilse, where she met with a collection of people who strive for nothing else but peace. I wanted to recruit her to our cause, but she was too devoted to you.' Guflinkov shrugged. 'The whole reason that I was with your father in the first place was to bring him into the group of those who sought peace. He would have joined too, I believe, if he had not been struck by the arrow. Your mother, though, she was a different person.' Guflinkov cast his eyes down in sadness. 'Again, we sailed together, but this time we parted ways at Psymryte. She had an escort of two men-at-arms, but alas was met by more cutthroats. This time she did not survive.' Guflinkov let that sit in the air and Olswerth cleared his throat.

He's touched by this, thought Sor.

'I used the knowledge of your mother's little name for you to gain your trust. Your mother trusted me and would have approved.'

Olswerth nodded and his hard disposition softened. 'She was such a stern woman, unless the two of us were alone. Then, she was all games and kindness.' His distant eyes smiled. 'Thank you, for telling me this. I had often wondered what had become of my parents.' He paused for a moment of thought. 'Although I can't shake the feeling that had you not been involved, my mother would still be alive.' The accusation was not said with spite, but as a fact.

'Perhaps, but one can never tell what life will throw at them. Without me, she might have died when she lost her hand.' Guflinkov paused and looked as if he was recalling the long-lost past. 'It is futile to guess at different outcomes of different courses of action. We can only make our decisions based on the knowledge that we have at the time that we make the decision.'

'Indeed.' Olswerth's reply was gruffly mumbled.

'If it pleases you, my lord, I would now tell you the information that I have journeyed many leagues to share with you.'

'You may, but first let me call for my nephew. I did not want him to hear about my mother, but he should hear that which you have to tell.'

'So be it.'

Sor felt a shiver of fear trickle down her spine. She resisted the urge to fidget in her seat and sat on her hands to prevent all suspicious movements.

While they waited, Olswerth explained that Saidwerth was his older sister's bastard son. 'He has worked his way up the ranks of my army on his own steam; not an insignificant task to achieve. He will make General if he can keep his head in the right place and bides his time.' Olswerth smiled to himself, seemingly at ease in the company of Guflinkov and Sor; a change which Sor noticed. *He is a fickle man.*

Footsteps approached and Sor prayed to both the Day and Night Gods. Her vision swirled before her at the prospect of being found out and had to focus on what Olswerth was saying to straighten her mind. 'Saidwerth is the exact opposite to my sister's other son, the true born one.' He scoffed. 'That one is a brute and does as he pleases. Frankly, he's a disgrace to the family. If he was the bastard nephew, he would be long gone from my lands.'

Saidwerth entered the tent as Olswerth kept talking with a smile on his face. 'The brute was bested by a woman a few months ago. She broke his toes and he couldn't walk for many a day. Served him right, I say, for ambushing travellers in a dishonest manner.' Olswerth changed his tone to one of venom. 'But… he is of my blood, so if I ever catch the bitch who defeated him, she'll wish she was never born.'

Saidwerth entered the tent fully and bowed to Olswerth. 'You wanted to see me, my Lord.' Olswerth's nephew was young, tall, and muscular. He had a wiry black moustache that covered his upper lip and curled down at the ends around his mouth. He wore full armour and had a hand and a half sword sheathed by his side. Sor breathed a massive sigh of relief; this was not the nephew who had attacked her and Winter. She thanked the Gods and refocused on the proceedings.

'Indeed, I did. This man, Ustek, has news of great importance that he is about to share with us. Sit and let him begin.'

Saidwerth sat and Olswerth gestured for Guflinkov to begin. Sor knew part of the story that Guflinkov told, but learned many things that surprised her. Guflinkov told of the peace treaty between Kathsum and Resvon and how the hopes of many were shattered when first Resvon and then Kathsum were murdered. He told of Tunley's rise through the naval ranks to the position of High Chancellor and Tunley's successful defence of Roasline and counter-attack of Fort Kykum and his harnessing of the Healer's powers through intimidation and brute force. After all was told, Guflinkov made an anguished plea to Olswerth to ride to the aid of Nivera, which would surely fall to Tunley's might.

At first, Olswerth was sceptical and Saidwerth sat in thoughtful silence until Guflinkov finished. He then turned to his uncle and eloquently pointed out that if Nivera fell, it would not be long before Psymryte fell under Tunley's domain and then it would only be a brief moment before Tunley's forces were on their very doorstep.

'Lord, we must take the battle to this Tunley; we just have to.'

Olswerth rubbed his chin, then stood and began pacing. 'Would it not be too late for us to arrive at Nivera? Perhaps we should bolster our own or even Psymryte's defences.'

Saidwerth took a sharp intake of breath. 'Those scum would just as likely eat our horses as let us align with them.'

'I fear there is truth in your words.' He slammed one fist into his palm. 'Curse this Tunley for breaking the semblance of peace that we have.' He stopped pacing and stared at Guflinkov. 'You're sure he means to attack Nivera?'

Guflinkov stared straight back with a face of steel. 'I would bet my life on it.'

Olswerth spat. 'So be it. We will ride to the aid of Nivera. I have some three hundred and fifty horses with me today. We can leave immediately. I can muster another nine-hundred to be two days behind us.' He rubbed his chin again. 'I have infantry too, but they would take far too long to reach Nivera. No, I will leave them to defend my realm, should it go ill in Nivera.' He looked at Saidwerth. 'Make it happen, Captain.'

Saidwerth stood with a spark in his eyes. 'Yes, sir.'

Olswerth turned his attention to Guflinkov and Sor. 'What will the two of you do?'

'I will accompany you. I have a detailed knowledge of Nivera and so can be of assistance in battle. Sister Sor will continue on to the Monks to rouse those sleeping worshippers.'

Sor was taken aback; she did not realise that she would be parting ways with Guflinkov. She liked it not, but couldn't deny that there was sense in his plan.

'It will be good to have your knowledge with us. Before you prepare for departure, is there anything else that you should tell me?'

Sor could see Guflinkov thinking before he answered. 'Not information, but a request. It would aid the cause against Tunley if Sister Sor could be guaranteed safe passage through your domain.'

Olswerth eyed first Guflinkov and then Sor suspiciously. He then shrugged. 'Very well, I will spare one man to escort her via the quickest roads to the far border of my land.'

'Thank you, my lord. We all have much to prepare; we shall not take up any more of your time.' Guflinkov and Sor stood, bowed and left the tent. As soon as they were out of earshot, Sor turned on Guflinkov.

'I don't need an escort! I can look after myself.'

Guflinkov turned to face her and grabbed her arm, his fingers digging into her flesh. When he spoke, his voice was sterner than Sor expected. 'The best way to defeat Tunley is for you to get to the monks as quickly as possible. Olswerth's help can cut at least two days off your journey, not to mention preventing you being waylaid or killed.' He released his grip. 'I know you can look after yourself against one, two and maybe three opponents, but what if you're set on by more than that? Hmm? This is far bigger than you and whether you want to have an escort for a few days.' Guflinkov's voice softened. 'There is much of this that I don't like. Begging the likes of Olswerth for one. I mean, sure he came across as civil in our meeting, except that he completely ignored you, probably because you're a woman, but deep down he is a sadistic beast of a man who will do anything to protect his blood and grasp on power. If he knew you were the one who broke the toes of his flesh and blood, be assured, he would take great pleasure in ripping you apart. No Sor, you can deal with an escort for a few days for the betterment of humanity.'

Sor felt embarrassed by being chastised in such a comprehensive manner. Her knowledge that Guflinkov spoke the truth reduced her to feeling like a young girl being told off by a senior monk for being selfish and not thinking of others. There was little she could do but utter an apology and strengthen her grasp on what was important.

'I'm sorry for speaking harshly, Sister Sor, but I would sooner be travelling with you to the monks than with this scum of a man. I am not happy with my current lot in life either. Especially considering the story about Olswerth's mother is not entirely true.' Guflinkov looked downcast. 'She never made it off Headly, but died calling for her little Lilly Pilly. But that is in the past and I have rolled the dice with Olswerth. A gamble that I needed to take.'

Sor was surprised to hear this and smiled weakly. She didn't know what to say in response to Guflinkov's confession and so addressed her own faults instead. 'I know. I was foolish and selfish. It really has been a pleasure travelling with you from Myrth.'

Guflinkov nodded. 'That it has been. But for now, we must part ways. You have a shorter journey than I, but a longer one to Nivera. You should ready your horses and leave immediately.' 'Will you at least come back to our camp to prepare as well?'

'Nay, I have other tasks that I must see to before I have the luxury of packing. And so, I must say farewell… for now.'

Sor felt a pang of sadness and gave Guflinkov a hug. 'May the Gods watch over you and aid you in your endeavours.'

Guflinkov smiled. 'And you.'

The old man patted Sor on the shoulder before turning and walking away towards the bulk of Olswerth's forces. Sor sighed and turned her back on Guflinkov. She made her determined way back to her camp and quickly saddled her horses in preparation of departure. Just as she was ready to leave, a man trotted up to her and announced that he would escort her through Olswerth's territory quickly and safely.

'Thank you. I hope your steed is strong and fast, for we have little time to waste.' She climbed onto her mount and kicked her heels into her horse. He reared slightly and set off at a substantial pace; Olswerth's man was quick to follow.

49

Avgar stood at the rail of *Hope* and grasped the side with both hands. The ship skipped along the water with a bubbling joy under the influence of a strong tail wind. They were two days into their journey and he was reflecting how different this one was compared to his last ocean voyage. He stretched the fingers of his right hand and tapped the wood to a tune from his boyhood. He revelled in the sheer fact that he now had a right hand and felt at peace.

The ageing man had found *Hope* was large enough to permit him some time alone. He had used this time to think about all that had happened in the preceding months to bring him to this spot. He had faced so many unexpected happenings, from losing his hand and magical control, to gaining dominance over the Outcasts, to being a hair's breadth from death, to learning of the Healer's powers and finally those of the Myrthians. He had been surprised too many times to count, not the least of all being Phlyte's lack of vengeance for his murder of Resvon and, therefore, shattering the prospect of peace between Roasline and the Outcasts. He guessed part of the reason to be his usefulness in bringing Tunley down, but he mused that her greater reasoning was that the past is past and that the Avgar of now was not the same Avgar that she had met many moon cycles ago.

Phlyte had come to meet with Avgar the day following the great meeting. He had found her kind, but direct with him as they sat in the sunshine after his midday meal. As Avgar stood on the ship, he recalled their meeting in vivid detail.

Avgar had sat facing Phlyte, who was wearing a crisp cream gown with a low neckline. She smiled at him with knowledge as they exchanged pleasantries in their minds.

I enjoy the sunshine filtering through the trees and the caress of it on my old back. Her voice sounded in his head as if she had spoken aloud.

I did not care much for such pleasantries until I was forced to spend day after day with little to do but heal on Headly.

It is amazing how when one is inches from death, they are reborn as a different person.

A silence dropped between them as their thoughts turned inward.

It was Avgar who continued the communication. *Phlyte, you have not come here to talk about the sun warming your back. I am sure that you are busy… and I am anxious to regain a semblance of control over my magic. Are you able to make the modifications?*

I am. She paused for a moment. *Do you remember what it was like to drink your crystal powder?*

I will never forget that feeling. The intense pain started at my throat and ripped through my entire body until I thought I would be torn asunder. But then it passed and a feeling of intoxicating power filled my being. Avgar remembered it well, with a sense of both fear and awe. *Will this change be like that?*

It will and it won't. Pain will briefly fill your body, but there will be no sense of power afterward; there will be a different sensation.

Avgar nodded. *Even though pain is an old friend of mine, I prefer it when he is not around. Can we get this over with?*

As you wish. Put your hands on the table, palms up, and close your eyes.

Avgar did as he was asked, feeling trepidation at what was to come. Several moments passed before Avgar noticed a warm sensation on his palms; as if he was holding a nice cup of tea. The warmth ripped into a scorching heat that instantly spread through Avgar's body. He grunted, as a reflex, to the horrid sensation that he would burst into flames. To distract himself, he tried counting in his head. *One… two… three…* As he made it to fifty, the painful heat subsided and a coolness oozed through him from head to toe. He breathed in deeply and opened his eyes. For a moment, the world was shaded in indigo, but he blinked twice and his vision returned to normal.

'It is done.' Phlyte spoke aloud.

Avgar nodded, feeling relieved.

'Yesterday, I explained that I am not restoring the control of your powers; that is not possible without a new crystal. What I have just done is put a warning point on your energy levels. Think of it as a canary in a mine. When you are nearing the end of your limits, you will know that you are doing so. When this occurs, you should stop using your magic if you can. If you continue, you will die. This warning is no more than that: a warning. It does not prevent you killing yourself should you overreach your abilities and it does not allow you to control the amount of energy that you are using. The lack of this control makes using your magic perilous, so beware; use magic sparingly.'

Agvar felt a wave of acute grief as he remembered days when he had been in complete control of his powers.

Phlyte looked at him sternly and spoke inside Avgar's head. *I know you feel the loss of your full magic, but this is the price you pay for your heinous crimes.*

With an effort, Avgar pushed these thoughts aside. *I know.*

The two sat staring at each other for a few long moments before Avgar broke the silence. *I appreciate being able to speak to you; it removes so much frustration.* Avgar bit his lip, feeling nervous at what he was about to ask. *But do you think there is any chance that you can heal my throat? It would improve our odds against Tunley if I could speak.*

Phlyte raised an eyebrow and smiled. *I am surprised that you have not asked this earlier. I understand it was damaged by the poison you drank after taking over Fort Kykum?*

Avgar did not fail to notice the subtle implication.

I will see what I can do; if it is no more than the poison's wound, there will be every chance that I can fix it.

Avgar felt elation; to be able to talk would be a gift beyond his highest hopes.

You will need to sit still and try not to swallow. You may feel strange sensations, but complete stillness is essential.

Avgar smiled. *Thank you.* He then closed his eyes and calmed his body. He delved into his power and used it to paralyse his throat. After doing this, he projected his thought to Phlyte. *I am ready.*

Avgar was immediately glad that he had paralysed his throat, for he was confronted with a hugely uncomfortable sensation of having non-existent fingers poked down his windpipe. He wanted to gag, but he could not. Then he was greeted by a sharp pain right where his voice cords were located. Blood trickled into his lungs and he fought vigorously to suppress his coughing reflex. Then, all of a sudden, he felt a sharp pressure on his brain and his own voice yelled in his head for him to stop using his magic. He listened to the warning and cut off the flow of magic. He immediately coughed violently and gaged; his lungs and stomach heaving. A wave of weariness spread through him and he grabbed at the table to steady himself.

Avgar slowly regained control of his body and opened his weeping eyes to see Phlyte with a downcast face.

You did well, Avgar.

But… it sounds like there is a 'but' in there. He tried to talk, but could not. *What happened? What went wrong? Do you need more time to finish the job?*

The nodules that the poison caused; I have removed. There is, however, a greater concern. One of your voice bands has been severed. I tried to join it back together, but it seems to have been severed with powerful magic. This, I cannot fix.

Avgar felt hopeless. His elation at the thought of being able to talk had not only evaporated, but had left him dry, cracked, and broken. *There has to be more that you can do. There just has to.*

Avgar missed the pity in Phlyte's voice when she spoke. 'I am sorry, but I cannot fix your voice.'

Avgar wanted to cry, but forced himself not to.

'I can, however, give you the ability to project your thoughts to those accompanying you on this expedition.'

Avgar felt a twinkle of excitement through his grief.

Phlyte hurried on. 'They will not be able to project their thoughts to you, but they can still speak normally to you.' She smiled.

Do it… please.

'Very well. This time you will not feel any pain.' Phlyte closed her eyes and her brow furrowed. Avgar felt an odd sensation deep within his head, like someone was tickling his brain. To accompany this, he heard a grating sound like a whetstone being run down a blade. Phlyte opened her eyes. 'It is done.'

Thank you, Phlyte.

She nodded in acceptance. 'A word of warning to you, Avgar. When you first make contact with your accomplices, they may fear you. Tread carefully.'

I will.

'Good.' Phlyte looked distracted for a moment and then stood. 'I must go now; I am needed elsewhere. If you haven't already done so, prepare your body and mind to depart at the shortest notice.'

The day of his first meeting with Phlyte flashed through his mind. He recalled being sprawled on the sand of a far-away beach surrounded by strangers. His anger at Phlyte and the Myrthians had certainly subsided and he marvelled that he was now able to work with someone who had shattered his life.

Phlyte turned to leave, and Avgar had a querying thought. *Phlyte, before you go, I have a question for you. When we first met, on the beach, you and the Myrthians appeared before me out of thin air. Could you not do the same for Lord Olswerth and the monks? Why did you need to send Sor on a slow journey?*

Phlyte looked at him with a smile. 'Good, good; you are thinking well. To bring you over the Moaks required an immense amount of energy. We could only manage it with many of us combining our strength to manipulate the wind. By comparison, to appear before you was child's play. You are right; we could appear before Lord Olswerth, but we would be transparent due to how far away Olswerth is from Myrth. To project ourselves over such a large distance would test our abilities, but I believe we could achieve it.' Phlyte looked thoughtful. 'Let me ask you this: how would Lord Olswerth, someone unfamiliar with magic, react if I was to appear before him only half visible?'

Avgar immediately saw the conundrum.

He would think that he was going mad and likely lock himself away in his lands.

'Or worse… he might think me to be a spectre of the afterlife and rile against all that I wanted to achieve.'

And what of the monks?

'They would either follow us without hesitation or damn us as an enemy of the Gods. We weighed these options carefully and we deemed the risk to be too great.'

Tunley… you could appear before him and drive him insane.

Phlyte let out a mirthless chuckle. 'He is dangerous enough without believing that he is seeing ghosts. Who knows what damage he would inflict if that were to happen.'

Avgar accepted Phlyte's reasoning. *The world is never simple, is it?*

'Sometimes it is, but rarely so.' She smiled kindly. 'Farewell for now, Avgar. You shall see me once more prior to your departure.'

Farewell and thank you for all that you have done for me today.

'You're welcome. I am glad that we can both look past the wrongs of the past to work together in bringing peace to the lands.'

Avgar was transported out of his memory and back to the present with that final sentiment; the importance of working together.

The sun was beginning to set and Avgar made his way to the tiller where Ryde was standing with his legs steadily apart.

Avgar projected his thoughts to Ryde using a gentle voice. *How are we progressing, Captain?*

'Shiver-me-timbers, Avgar. I'm still not used to hearing your voice inside my head. It's eerie, you know, hearing you without seeing your mouth move.' He shrugged his shoulders as if shaking off a chill. 'We're skipping along at a merry old pace. If this friendly wind continues, we'll reach land in about ten days' time.'

Avgar looked at Ryde appraisingly, but kept his thoughts to himself. *He's an honest man, Ryde, and true to himself. And tough too, like an old stump; I'm glad he's on our side.*

Avgar nodded and thought to Ryde once more. *Will we be continuing through the night again?*

'Aye. The sky is clear and the sea calm enough. I'll navigate by the stars and moon; should be easy on a night like this.' Ryde took a swig of his waterskin that Avgar wrongly guessed held more than water.

Avgar smiled and excused himself. He thought to get a drink of his own and then seek out Marlvon.

After sourcing some wine, he found the young man on the foredeck wearing leather breeches and sporting a bare chest. The evening was cooling fast, but

Marlvon was sweating freely as he swung his new sword in a series of slashes, jabs and imagined parries. Avgar had watched the man practising several times over the past two days and found himself to be jealous of Marlvon's obvious skill and youth. On these occasions, it had reminded Avgar of his own life when he had lived in the hills south of the Moaks.

Avgar pushed those memories away and waited until Marlvon was finished his current routine. It was not long before Marlvon noticed Avgar and brought his practice to an end. Avgar watched as Marlvon covered his lean but muscular torso with a lightweight shirt. He stood and faced Avgar with his hand on the hilt of his sheathed sword.

'What do you want?' There was no friendliness in Marlvon's voice.

You're a skilled fighter, Marlvon. You must have committed a considerable amount of time, energy, and effort into your training. Avgar did not say this to flatter the man, but merely to show his admiration. *We're not too dissimilar, you and I… at least in some aspects.*

'I'm nothing like you.' Marlvon retorted coldly.

Perhaps. Avgar conceded. *But you remind me of myself when I was a young man. I was the best fighter and tactician that my people had ever seen. I was fast, committed and a force to be reckoned with. I took what I wanted, but then when I had it, it was never enough.*

Avgar smiled at his rare honesty to both Marlvon and himself. *I sought power, thinking that I could lead others to a better life. Over time, that power ruined me.* Avgar looked over the ocean without seeing it. *I don't know why I'm telling you this. I suppose I'm just reminding myself that good intentions can easily be deviated.* He looked back at the silent Marlvon. *What I did to Islonda's family and her town, there is no excuse for that. I did it out of self-preservation; for my own gain. I saw you as a threat to my reign of the Outcasts, when I should have been looking to those already in power. Ha, my reign of the Outcasts; that was a feeble attempt that was.*

Avgar noticed Marlvon's face soften, but the younger man remined silent. *I know little of you, Marlvon, but from what I have observed over the past days, my guess is that you're honourable and true to your word.* Avgar smiled. *I am thinking of my own skin again, but I was wondering what your intentions are after Tunley is removed.* Avgar locked his eyes keenly on Marlvon.

Marlvon spoke in a level monotone. 'You want to know if I'm going to seek revenge on you?' He wiped beading sweat from his brow. 'Islonda is dead and gone. I have nothing left to care for. So yes, after I have killed Tunley, you will pay for your crimes.'

Avgar was not surprised with this response, but he did not want to hear it nonetheless. The old man calmed himself by breathing slowly. His odd sense of honesty continued when he projected his thoughts to Marlvon. *It is as I deserve.* He bowed his head.

'You seem to me to be a more reasonable man than the tyrant that the rumours made you out to be.' Marlvon made this statement sound more like a question.

Since losing my voice and hand... and spending many weeks on Headly, I have changed my outlook on the world.

'That may be so, but it does not excuse the crimes of your past.'

No, I suppose it doesn't. Avgar looked over Marlvon's body. *I don't believe that I'm the only one on this boat with crimes in his past. Should you be punished for yours?*

Marlvon's face flushed. 'You think I like violence? You think I'm proud of my past?' He spat on the deck. 'No, I hate my past. I hate having to use violence; it makes me sick. I revolt myself whenever I need to inflict harm on others.'

Avgar could hear the pain behind Marlvon's voice and he felt sorry for the man. *Why don't you stop then? Why don't you abandon this course and live a peaceful life?*

Marlvon turned away. 'For all the reasons that Phlyte gave. My pain at killing Tunley is insignificant compared to what he will inflict on the world if he's allowed to continue. And Islonda, my beautiful Islonda, she needs to be avenged.'

Avgar felt sadness for the conflicted man and wondered what he would do if he was in Marlvon's position. A thought then struck Avgar. *How do you know that Islonda is dead?*

'Phlyte told me of her death in a prison in Fort Kykum.'

Avgar could hear Marlvon suppress his raw emotions. *Did she give you hard proof?*

Marlvon shook his head. 'How could she?'

Perhaps it's my cynical mind thinking as of old, but would you still be coming on this mission if Islonda was still alive?

Marlvon's eyes flashed. 'Don't! Don't you dare give me hope that might be false... that she might still live. If I believe her to be alive and imprisoned, then I would have no choice but to free her. My love for her would not permit any other action.'

Avgar raised his hands in submission. *I'm sure you're right; Phlyte is an honourable woman; she would not use such dishonest means. I'm sorry for even raising the possibility.*

Marlvon closed his eyes and breathed slowly out of his nose. He bowed his head and rubbed his forehead in weariness.

I have taken enough of your time. I will take my leave. Goodnight.

Marlvon didn't reply and Avgar walked away from him and made his way in the dark to the side of the ship once more.

He glanced out over the black rolling seas. The moon was no more than a thin slither on her way to departing the night sky. The stars shone about her brightly and

Avgar lost himself in their beautiful multitudes. He didn't know how long he stood staring at the stars, but after quite a while, he felt a gentle hand on his shoulder.

'Looking at them always makes me feel so small; like I matter no more than a solitary ant.' Winter's voice sounded thoughtfully sad.

Avgar turned and looked at his son. Winter's orange hair was growing back quickly, but in the darkness, it looked brown against his pale face.

Seeing Winter stirred mixed feelings within Avgar. Pride followed disgust, love danced with loathing, and clarity mingled with confusion. Avgar shook his head to clear his thoughts and looked at Winter once more.

Compared to the stars or the ocean, we are small. Compared to each other and we are normal. Compare us to ants and we are giants. Through these different comparisons, our size does not change; just our importance.

Winter looked confused and Avgar sighed and kept his next thought internal. *He is not blessed with great intelligence.*

'Father, I have some news that I've been meaning to tell you, but the time does not seem right. It is not really of great importance, but I thought you would like to know.'

Avgar looked enquiringly at Winter.

'Before we left Myrth Isle, Phlyte came and visited me. You may remember, she took me away by myself. She led me to the armoury and bade me pick any weapon that I wanted. There were many wonderful swords and sharp axes. There were even war hammers, maces, spears, pikes and every other type of weapon that you can imagine. The choice seemed to be a hard one and many beckoned me to pick them up. But they never seemed to suit my hand. Until I found these.'

Winter brought forward a pair of sai. Avgar took the hard steel, three-pronged weapon from Winter and examined their make. The middle prong was sharp like a sword, and the very tips of the side prongs were as well. The handle was leather-bound and they were weighted perfectly.

The sai was your chosen weapon in Mirny. Your skill was excellent. You made a good choice. He handed the sai back to Winter, who took them and absentmindedly twirled them in his hands.

'They are not the same as those that were bound to me by my blood and your magic, but they will serve me well.'

Avgar nodded. *Have you had a chance to practice with them?*

'Only in the confines of my cabin. It has been many months since I last wielded the sai.'

May I suggest that tomorrow you seek out Marlvon and practice with him? He is a skilled swordsman and it will be good to remind your muscles how to fight.

'Thank you for the advice; I'll speak to Marlvon tomorrow.'

Avgar felt a sudden wave of tiredness wash through him. By the position of the moon, he supposed that half the night must have passed. *I am weary; it is time I were in bed. Goodnight, Winter.*

'Goodnight, Father.'

Avgar left Winter, who continued to look out over the ocean as his father had done only moments before.

The morning came and Avgar sat on deck, testing out his magic with simple tasks like buckling his boots. In practising, he hoped to improve his control over his energy flow.

The morning was still young when Winter came on deck with Marlvon trailing behind. Avgar looked closely and saw that they both carried their weapons. He quickly ceased curling a rope with his magic to focus on the two young men.

Winter looked as excitable as a puppy and Marlvon remained expressionless. As they got closer, Avgar heard what they were discussing. When Winter saw his father sitting there, he brought him into the conversation.

'Father, we're wondering how to protect ourselves from getting cut or skewered on the sharp blades. Can you do some of your magic to protect us or cover the sharp edges?'

Avgar thought for a while and then declined. *It would be possible, but I don't want to risk it. If I had my full powers, as of old, then I could do it in a heartbeat. You'll just have to be careful of each other.*

Marlvon frowned. 'Perhaps if we wrapped some leather or canvas around the blades… that might work.'

'Good idea. I'll see what I can find.' Winter scampered away.

Marlvon looked over at Avgar. 'You're not going to be much use fulfilling our task if you can't use your magic.'

Don't you worry, I can use it. It's just that the amount of energy that I expend is unpredictable and I would rather save the risk until it is absolutely necessary.

Marlvon nodded his understanding.

Winter returned promptly with a length of canvas fabric that would be used if a sail were to need repairing. 'This should do.' He also carried seven corks. 'I found these below deck in empty rum bottles. We can stick them on the ends.' He passed one to Marlvon who stuck his on the tip of his sword.

It didn't take long for the fabric to be cut to length and fastened with cord to the weapons. The two stood facing each other and Avgar thought that they looked ridiculous.

By this stage Ryde had woken from his late night and had come to watch the sparing. He spoke in a gruff voice. 'This will be over quickly.'

Winter stood with a sai in each hand and oozed excitement. Marlvon remained relaxed, but focused on his opponent. Avgar knew Winter would attack first and he did so, with a feign to the left and then a thrust with his right arm. Marlvon quickly deflected the blow, side-stepped and slapped Winter on the shoulder with the flat side of his sword.

Avgar knew from experience how much that would have hurt, but Winter showed no sign of the discomfort. The sorcerer watched when the two men faced each other again and saw Marlvon's mentality change to one of attack. Avgar could almost read Marlvon's mind as if it were written on a page. He quickly sent his thought to Winter. *He means to hurt you. He wants to do this to get back at me. You should cease this session.*

Winter flicked his eyes to Avgar. In that instant, Marlvon lunged with his canvas covered blade flapping in a short downward arc towards Winter's head. Winter raised his sai in a reflex and caught the blade between the prongs. He flicked his wrist at the same time as stepping to the side. Marlvon's sword was yanked out of his hand and clattered to the ground. Avgar wondered if Winter would take the advantage and strike Marlvon. He did not, but stepping back to let his opponent collect his weapon.

Ryde rubbed his hands together. 'Well, that was unexpected; this might get interesting after all.'

Avgar noticed that Marlvon's intentions changed to a more guarded approach. The two advanced simultaneously and again Winter bested Marlvon. Avgar felt a smug sense of pride at his son, although Marlvon did not look concerned. Winter danced with confidence and Marlvon swiftly put him in his place and sent him sprawling across the deck. Ryde laughed a deep bellied laugh at that.

The tension between Winter and Marlvon grew and the two fought back and forth. Then Avgar noticed that Marlvon began to dominate. *He's figured out how to fight Winter and the sai.* The more skilled warrior won time and time again until Winter was battered, bruised and bleeding. He eventually raised his hands in defeat. 'I concede.'

'You fought well, Winter. Surprisingly so, but you have much to learn.' Marlvon sounded tired, but not exhausted.

He's still got enough energy to go on for a lot longer. Avgar marvelled at Marlvon.

'Winter, we will repeat this tomorrow… and every day until we arrive at Nivera.'

Winter smiled. 'Thank you, that would be useful.'

Marlvon then pointed his sword at Avgar and Ryde. 'You two will join too. If we're to defeat Tunley, we all need to be sharp with a blade.'

Avgar saw reason in this. *I agree. Although as we get closer to Nivera we should not over exert ourselves so we may be fresh on arrival.*

'I am not foolish, Avgar. I will ensure that we are ready at the right time.'

Avgar nodded.

'Now, I'm hungry; I haven't eaten today and my stomach rumbles.'

The four men broke their fast together and Avgar felt for the first time that they were working together and not against each other. He smiled and thought that Phlyte would be pleased.

The following days were filled with aches and bruises for Avgar. His time in Headly had dulled his strength and stamina, but his raw talent and experience still remained. Aside from this, he was happy to see the four men working towards a single purpose, but he couldn't shake the negative feelings directed at him from Marlvon.

The party sailed for over ten days before they sighted land. Ryde advised that there was a bay to the east of Nivera that they could seek shelter in, but he recommended they sail a short way up the Sempa River and dock at Nivera's port. This way was more treacherous for many ships travelling together, but Ryde knew that a single boat could navigate the delta. Nivera's only port was in the Sempa and had been designed to prevent an attack from a fleet.

The delta of the Sempa shifted often, but there was one path that remained open at all times. This passageway was wide enough for a single vessel and only those who knew its secrets dared to sail it. Ryde had confidence in his ability to do so; he had used this way a handful of times during his service in the Outcast's navy.

The port itself sat well outside the city walls and, once docked, the four men had an uphill climb to reach the western city gate. As they reached the gate, Avgar noticed the wind swing around to a ferocious westerly and saw tall thunderheads marching across the sky towards them. He shuddered and was glad to be off the open water.

The four men were stopped at the gate by guards who lowered their pikes in defence. Avgar watched as Marlvon raised his palms outwards and spoke clearly. 'We are here to deliver an urgent message to the Lord of Nivera. We are friends and you would be wise to allow us entry.'

The two guards looked at each other uncertainly. 'How do we know that?'

'You don't, but we're willing to be accompanied to gaol cells for questioning.'

One of the guards nodded and called to another soldier who was in the guardhouse behind the gates. 'Ho, run and fetch a dozen more guards. We've got four men coming into prison.'

'Yes, sir.' The man ran off to bring reinforcements.

While they waited, Avgar peered behind the guards and into the fields of flowers beyond. He was surprised at this oddity; it seemed like such a waste of resources to create something that had no purpose past being nice to look at.

It was not long before the guards arrived and the four captives handed over their weapons reluctantly. 'Please ensure that these are cared for. They are highly valuable and will be put to good use to the advantage of Nivera in the days to come.' Marlvon pleaded with the soldiers.

They were led through the fields of flowers, then the city, and directly to the prison cells. As with all newcomers to Nivera, Avgar was taken aback by the inherent beauty of the artistically designed streets and buildings. By the time they arrived at the dungeons, the wind had whipped up into a frenzy and the first droplets of rain had started to fall. Avgar was glad to be moving under cover and was surprised to see that, unlike many cities, the gaol was not aligned with the citadel. Indeed, in Nivera there was actually more of a palace than a citadel, with lavish embellishments and many glassed windows. This, Avgar observed from a distance as he entered the much plainer stone prison.

The first thing that Avgar noticed inside was the stillness of the air after being out in the impending storm. The second thing he noticed was the warmness of the building. Most prisons were cold, damp and unpleasant places, whereas Nivera's prison appeared, at least at the entrance, to be warmed. The prisoners were taken down a hallway and shown through a small wooden door and into a holding cell. This may have been warm, but it was bare and dreary. A small slit window let a little light into the room, but also made an eerie whistling noise with the savage wind passing over it.

'You will wait here.' The guards departed and clanged the solid door shut. The room fell into dusk-like darkness and Avgar slumped his shoulders. Winter commented sarcastically that he was having fun and Marlvon and Ryde sat down to rest.

At least we're not outside. Avgar projected to everyone. The others agreed, but no more was said.

The rest of the day passed and the light faded quickly. Avgar felt his stomach rumble and hoped that some food would be brought to them. Winter complained repetitively and Marlvon had to threaten to gag him in order to get him to shut up. The storm continued to howl outside and once again, Avgar was grateful to be indoors.

The final light of day vanished and the cell was eased into complete darkness. Each of the men were silent, deep within their own thoughts, when a clank of a lock came from the door. They all stood and waited for the door to be opened inward. A guard bearing a flaming torch entered the room followed by a man of medium build wearing fine silk clothes and a smart leather cloak.

Avgar cringed from the relative brightness of the flame as the man looked about the four squinting men. The man then burst out in laughter and pointed at Ryde. He tried in vain to speak, but couldn't get a word past his laughter. Avgar was thoroughly confused and looked at Ryde for an explanation.

The man, who happened to be the Lord of Nivera, wiped his eyes then walked over to Ryde and gave him a forceful hug. 'Ryde, you old kraken! What a sight! How's the scar? I see that you haven't grown your eye back yet! Ha!'

'Xayre, I see that you still think you're a funny bastard. It's been such a long time; by the moon, you've aged a century.' Ryde retorted with a smile on his face.

'It must have been at least a quarter of that since I saw you.' Xayre looked about the room. 'I'm neglecting my duties now, aren't I? Still practising at high society, you see.' He smiled and Avgar couldn't help but smile back. 'I'm Xayre, the Lord of Nivera… just. Veltrene died not that long ago and I replaced him. I'm still a bit fresh, I'm afraid. But never mind that, who are your friends, Ryde?' He continued on without stopping for an answer. 'Ryde and I used to sail together when we were no more than young seamen. I was with him the day he got that little scratch on his face. That was a fierce battle, to be sure. But we won out and put our enemy to the sword… or rather, to the ocean floor. Then Ryde grew too good for his own boots and became a captain. Then I had to follow his orders. They were a few hard years; I can tell you. He even made me scrub the deck once just for putting a harmless sea-snake in his bed. Abuse of power, that was.' He clapped Ryde on the back. 'And now it looks like I'm ranked above you.' He trailed off, and Avgar saw the smile on Ryde's face flicker for just a moment.

Ryde looked about the room, clearly wanting to move on. 'Let me introduce these men. I have with me, Marlvon from Bankton, Winter and Avgar. Avgar can't speak, so no point in asking him anything, but we're here on a mission of great importance.' Ryde's voice grew stern and Xayre shifted his bearing to one of seriousness. 'The leader of Roasline, High Chancellor Tunley, has taken Fort Kykum.'

'This we know.' Xayre interrupted.

Marlvon cut in, knowing that Ryde would want him to do so. 'Well, he is on his way here with an armada. He will arrive within days. You would be wise to raise the city's defences and prepare for an ocean attack.'

Xayre clenched his jaw and turned grim. 'Are you absolutely certain of this?'

'Without an ounce of a doubt.' Marlvon replied flatly.

'Tell me everything you know.'

Marlvon divulged the information regarding Tunley and his impending attack on Nivera. Avgar listened and was impressed that Marlvon forgot nothing. The sorcerer had wondered if Marlvon would tell of their assassination plans and was pleased when he did. *With Xayre's connection with Ryde, we should be given free rein to do as we please.*

Once the discussions were over, Xayre turned to the guards. 'These men are free to go wherever they want. See that their weapons are returned to them and escort them to the palace for a meal and lodgings.'

The soldier nodded.

'It's good to see that you continue to get yourself mixed up in affairs that are outside your skills, Ryde. Ha!' He turned to Marlvon. 'Thank you for your information. I must go now and prepare what few defences this city has.' He nodded and left the cell.

A soldier guided the four men to the palace, where they ate supper before turning in for the night. Avgar was too tired to notice the lavish designs and furnishings of the palace and he fell asleep on a soft bed listening to the rain and wind lash the shutters that kept the warmth within his room.

A few days passed and Avgar grew concerned. While the innate structure of Nivera with her outer wall meant she could be defended relatively easily, there was a serious lack of troops. Those who had been left behind when Veltrene had sailed off to attack Roasline were not of the highest calibre and, despite Xayre's solid leadership, Avgar wondered how long the city would hold.

His other concern was that the four allies had failed to devise a plan on how to kill Tunley. They knew he would attack by sea, but could not for the life of them think of how they might reach his person. Avgar supposed they would just have to wait until he arrived and hope that an opportunity would present itself. He didn't much like leaving things to chance, and this put him in a foul mood.

Avgar was in one such foul temper when Tunley's fleet was first sighted far offshore. He hastened to see the ships for himself and was a little surprised that the fleet was not larger. Avgar was not aware that only those ships with oars had reached Nivera and that those without would join them in a day or two.

The city braced itself for the inevitable attack, and Avgar ensured that he remained well out of harm's way. This was not an act of cowardice, but rather one of strategy. He could offer little help to the defence from a ship attack, and it was important that he remained alive. Avgar was once more frustrated by his position and found himself wishing for his smoking herb.

Tunley's initial attack was soon over and Avgar was dismayed at the ease by which Nivera's cannons were destroyed. The city had even needed to call up their rickety old trebuchets to fend off the attack on the first night.

Tunley clearly did not recognise the dire state of the city's defences; he withdrew from pushing his advantage and seemed to be waiting for something. Avgar soon realised that Tunley was waiting for the remainder of his fleet. This looked much more impressive to Avgar, who was glad that Xayre had not ordered a sea-based attack. Avgar watched from the palace as Tunley's fleet divided and his ships attacked Nivera once more.

Avgar laughed when Xayre's repositioned cannons opened fire and demolished one of Tunley's ships. He could see the indecision in the fleet's movements and rubbed his hands together when the ships withdrew from Nivera.

Darkness fell and Avgar could no longer see the fleet's movements, so he sought out his bed. His instincts told him that he should rest while he could, for a time of high energy use was nigh upon him.

50

It was mid-morning and Marlvon walked in the flower fields that filled the space between Nivera's defensive wall and the city itself. The clouds above felt oppressive to Marlvon, but the blooms that surrounded him lifted his spirits. He wandered the meandering paths that wound their way subtly through the flowers, like a creek through a meadow. In the uniform light, the colours and hues seemed subdued, as if they were dozing and only half awake. He beheld their varying colours and saw potential lying in wait for a single ray of dazzling sunshine to fall upon their petals and rouse their beauty from its muted slumber.

While his eyes were delighted at the magnificence around him, his nose was equally intrigued. As he made his way along the paths, wafts of sweet scents of a nature that words could not describe hung heavy in the air and danced upon his senses. The spell of the flowers worked strongly upon him and he found his mind calmed and his thoughts limited.

Then, as slowly as the snail crawling across the path in front of him, Marlvon thought of Islonda. Tears welled in his eyes and flowed freely down his cheeks. He spoke sadly to the flowers that surrounded him, 'Islonda would have loved to have seen you.' He continued to think of her for several more moments and then he recalled his vow to himself to push his sorrow from his mind, until her death was avenged. *Why did you have to die?*

Marlvon looked about the flowers once more and their beauty seemed to lessen before his very eyes. He set his chin and looked over the flowers to the wall of Nivera that sat several hundred yards away. He made for it as directly as he could, but found the criss-crossing paths often led him astray.

He followed the wall eastward to a gate with adjacent stairs to the top of the fortification. The gate, he was pleased to see, was shut firmly and secured with thick beams of hardwood crossways and struts lodged into the ground that would prevent the gate swinging inward.

The young man mounted the stairs three at a time until he reached the top. He strolled across the dark grey wall and, not for the first time, marvelled at the two divots that ran the length of the fortification. He thought these to be an ingenious invention that allowed cannons or ballistae to be pulled by a team of oxen around the circumference of the wall on carts to their place of need where they were secured with chains to the parapet; preventing undue stress being placed on the cart's wheels when fired. This mobility had proved invaluable during Tunley's first attack on Nivera, allowing fresh cannons to be rolled into place after Tunley's initial barrage destroyed the larger, fixed cannons of the turrets.

Marlvon stepped over these tracks and took in the view away from the city. The ground ran from the wall in a gentle slope covered in tussocks of thick grass, hardy shrubs, and wild thistles. Some miles distant, Marlvon could make out a collection of tents and bivouacs. He knew that Tunley was camped there and was preparing his attack on Nivera. Although a small rise of land prevented Marlvon from seeing Tunley's ships, he knew that something was afoot by the constant line of horses, carts, and men. Marlvon could not see clearly what was being transported, due to the distance, but knew that whatever it was, would be to the disadvantage of Nivera.

The fighter looked over his shoulder at the flowers and contrasted it to the brewing doom of Tunley. A wave of confused thoughts then washed over Marlvon. *Islonda, if only you were here and we could escape this situation together.*

The solitary man drew out his new sword and lay it down upon the parapet. *Will it be you who slays that warmonger? Will it be by my hand that my love is avenged… revenged?* A tiny insect flew into his vision and landed on the thin blade. Marlvon looked closely at the red back with black spots and recognised it to be a ladybug. Marlvon smiled, *You're a pretty little thing.* His smile faded to a frown. *Do I really want to kill again? Is revenge really worth staining my hands with more blood? It will not bring Islonda back, that's for sure. Do I continue this cycle of death? Then, what happens after he's dead, will someone seek revenge on me, leading to more blood? Will the killing ever stop?*

The ladybug flew away and Marlvon watched it go. He spoke clearly to the void before him, 'Why could we not have just settled down for a peaceful life together?'

No response came.

Marlvon's heart felt heavy. *Without Islonda, what is the point of life; what is my point to living?* He looked over the wall to the ground many feet below. A depressing thought dawned on him and he spoke it to the world. 'It would be such a simple thing… to fall…'

He then thought inwardly. *Is that who I am? I don't want to seek revenge. I don't want to kill. I have the stain of countless deaths on my conscience. Perhaps… if I fell… the slate would be clean…* He looked over the edge once more. *Would that just make me a coward? Am I someone who abandons others in need… abandons his friends in need?* He opened his mouth and spoke firmly, 'No, I am not that man.' He smiled for the first time that morning. 'But, revenge… I will not kill

Tunley for revenge. Islonda wouldn't like that.' He breathed deeply and then saw a flicker of movement out of the corner of his eye.

Marlvon picked up his sword and swung to the left in one fluid movement. He stepped back in surprise, for standing before him was an image of Phlyte. He looked closely at her and thought that she looked to be made of flowing glass filled with a weak smoke.

'Hello Marlvon.' She smiled, guessing the reason for his surprise. 'This is how I appear when I show myself far from Myrth. If it were night, my likeness would be clearer and bolder.'

When she spoke, Marlvon heard her voice inside his head and not with his ears. It sounded distant, weak, and vulnerable.

Without thinking, Marlvon blurted out his resolution. 'I will not kill Tunley for the sake of Islonda's revenge.' Saying it aloud firmed his conviction.

'But you will still kill him?' An inkling of fear entered Phlyte's tone, 'Or at least help him be killed?'

Marlvon thought long and hard and did not rush to respond. When he did, his voice remained resolute. 'For the sake of all of the innocent lives throughout the land, I will see it done.' Marlvon felt within his being a truth and a purpose of direction. A great weight lifted from his shoulders.

Phlyte smiled, 'Thank you.' Her smile faltered. When she next spoke, she sounded hesitant 'I have something to tell you that will go straight to your heart. Almost a confession, you might call it.' She paused and appeared to bite her lip while Marlvon fidgeted and wanted her to get on with whatever she had to say.

'It concerns Islonda.' Marlvon's eye narrowed and he took a step towards Phlyte; a storm building within him. 'She is still alive; imprisoned within Fort Kykum.'

Marlvon felt blood rush to his face and the storm clouds parted. He wavered between being overjoyed and feeling furious for being lied to. In the end, his joy gained ascendency, but he did not let it overwhelm him for fear that there was some hidden trick lying in wait. He wanted to ask many questions, but the first one out of his mouth was a simple one of concern and love. 'Is she okay?'

'Both her and the baby within her are well enough, given the circumstances. Our spies could get little information, but they say that she longs for freedom and for you.'

Marlvon exhaled a long and slow breath. His thoughts and feelings were jumbled and Phlyte spoke before he could order them.

'I have no doubt that you will hate me for deceiving you so callously. I did what I felt was needed to secure your help. I did not enjoy doing it, but the cost was little compared to the benefits that would be reaped.'

Marlvon felt a sour taste in his mouth at Phlyte's lack of remorse. 'You were wrong to think that the best way to motivate me, and secure my allegiance, was through death and revenge. I am not that kind of man.' Marlvon felt dirty as he spoke, but cleaner for having stated his morality. 'Pleading with me the case of the innocent would have been a stronger argument to win me over. But the act is done. You have shown your colours and they are tainted, regardless of the purity of your goal.'

'I will not argue this point, except to say that when you have lived as long as I have, your perspective of the world changes.'

Marlvon cocked his head to the side and looked at Phlyte with questions in his eyes. 'How old are you, exactly? And your powers, they appear limitless. Surely you could devise an easier end to Tunley than the crude instruments of Avgar, Ryde, Winter and myself?'

'Phlyte looked into the distance as if remembering some distant past. 'My age… my best guess would be about five hundred years old.'

Marlvon felt gobsmacked.

'The years roll by but for all of those you saw in our meeting hall, we do not age. And yet, our existence is tainted; we are a shadow of our former selves.

'My kin and I sought to extend our life. The cost of which was for our bodies to remain within the same room forevermore. Outside that room we can see, smell and hear, but we cannot touch, never again can we touch.' Her voice was filled with sadness.

'At first, this did not bother us, for we could will our essence wherever we wanted. Over the years, however, our desire to feel the outside world grew and we began to loath our existence. They were bitter years indeed.

'But, as all winters pass, so did our selfishness. We emerged from the doldrums of self-pity with a newfound desire to help others and achieve peace over the lands. We reached out and made contact with people from the mainland. We directed many of them to Myrth and instructed them how best to rebuild the society there. Some of these we even taught the ways of magic, such as the swordsmith, Fec.

'For all we brought to Myrth Isle, we provided a safe haven to live in. We were open with our past so as not to be treated as gods.'

Phlyte looked at Marlvon with raised brows. 'You commented that our powers are limitless. In this, you are wrong. The powers that we wield today are a small fraction of those we had in the days of old. Indeed, the rate of our loss is accelerating so that each month that passes, we grow noticeably weaker. Many amongst us are joyful at this, for it means that our watch on the lands is coming to an end. I, myself, grow anxious that we will leave behind a world that is not at peace. Thus, I will do whatever I can to bring about peace, regardless of how dirty it makes me feel.' Phlyte looked sad once more. 'The sun might be setting on our time in this world, but it is a sunset that is long overdue.' Phlyte seemed to pass into a state of deep thought.

Marlvon too, was deep in thought. He found it hard to reconcile what he had heard with the world that he lived in and knew. *How can this be? This is both fantastical and saddening.* 'I do not know you well, but it grieves me to think that someone who has lived so long and has so much knowledge and experience will soon pass from the world.'

Marlvon shook his head and thought once more of Islonda. 'Enough of this. Tell me more about Islonda; where is she being held?'

Phlyte refocused her attentions to the present. 'She is a prisoner in the main gaol in Fort Kykum. Tunley's army holds the fort and there would be no way to reach her with Tunley still in command.'

I don't think she quite understands my skillset. 'Perhaps, but you have no need to fear that I will abandon this course that you have set me on. I said that I will see it done and so I will.'

Phlyte looked him up and down with her transparent eyes. 'I believe you.' Marlvon nodded. 'I'm sorry, but I simply don't have any more information about Islonda than that which I have already told you. I do, however, have a vital piece of information on the High Chancellor Tunley.' Marlvon cocked an eyebrow and indicated for her to continue.

'He has the Healer's protection. He is paranoid and tests this daily. There is only one person in all the lands who has the power to bestow and rescind the protection and that is the Healer Supreme; Lyafe. Avgar knows of him and can tell you more about the man, but Tunley keeps him prisoner close at hand. He will not be easy to reach or to influence; Tunley has him tamed with vicious threats of murder. More on the matter, I cannot say.'

Cannot or will not, I wonder. 'Thank you for the information, you have given me much to think about today.'

Phlyte crossed her arms and assessed Marlvon's strength. 'You're a good man, Marlvon, and I hope that we can talk more after all of this is over.'

'Perhaps, but I will have other priorities to attend to first.' Marlvon couldn't keep the sharpness out of his voice.

'So you do. I feel that my time here is drawing to an end. Goodbye and good luck to you in defeating Tunley.'

'Thank you. If you come across any other useful information, please show yourself again.'

'I will do what I can within the laws of our people... and within my abilities. Farewell.'

Without waiting for a reply, Phlyte shimmered before Marlvon's eyes and disappeared from his sight. He heard a passing whisper in his head as she vanished. 'Fight for Islonda and for the innocent many.'

Marlvon turned back to look over the wall at Tunley's distant camp. He held his sword up to eye height and pointed the blade where he imagined Tunley to be. *You are not long for this world, Tunley.*

He swished his blade down and realised once more that he did not yet have a name for his weapon. *I must name you.* Marlvon brought the blade up again and looked at it closely. The craftmanship was second to none and the flawlessness of the basket was beautiful. Marlvon found his eyes drawn to the stone in the hilt. Its yellow-brown colouring seemed to shift when he tilted it and he was reminded once more of a creature's eye.

He hadn't yet named the sword and now ran through a series of options in his mind, taking into account the stone, the blade's purpose, and the history of the metal. *Hammer's Eye, Peace-maker, Beast's Eye, Freedom, Skewer, Evil's Bane, Blacksmith and Bringer of Peace.* He rolled these around his mind like a cow chewing the cud. He spoke them out loud, but they simply didn't seem to do the rapier justice.

Marlvon looked at the blade again, then cast his eyes over the land before turning his thoughts inwards. *What is this sword? Steel from Jault's hammer and Myrth Isle, a stone and snapling leather. What is the purpose of this blade? To end this war by killing Tunley.* He tapped the tip lightly on the parapet. *It is a tool… a means to an end… nothing more.* He let that thought play about his mind for a few moments and then smiled. *Why do swords always have names? It is so that they may build a reputation of blood. So that others fear them and those who wield them. Fear, do I really want people to fear me? No, of course not.* Marlvon felt his mind was becoming resolute. *I will not name this instrument of death, regardless of the power that may lie within it. After its task is done, it will be no more than an ornament to remember Islonda's father by.* Marlvon felt satisfied within his being. *Yes, that is how it shall be; you will remain nameless.*

Marlvon felt as though the day had been long and weary and yet it was far from over. He left the wall and made his way back to the city proper to find food and report to Xayre and the others all that he had seen.

Two days passed and not much happened within the city of Nivera. Marlvon heard many of the frequent reports that came to Xayre of Tunley's movements, but little could be deduced as to where he might attack. Marlvon had also inspected the defences and given his advice, but he was not an expert in the defence of cities and left the task to Xayre's more capable captains.

Marlvon tried to find peace throughout this time, but found himself longing for Tunley to attack so that the wait might be over and Marlvon might be one step closer to his Islonda. He refused blankly the possibility that he might not make it through the fighting to see the mother of his future child; he simply could not allow that thought into his mind.

Marlvon often spent his time in the presence of Xayre, Avgar, Winter and Ryde and noted how each of the men dealt with the impending battle differently. Xayre was busy organising this or that for the city and seldom had time to rest. Avgar spent a lot of the time deep in thought or practising some form of weaponry. Ryde seemed unaffected and continued to tell Marlvon tales of his youth.

Marlvon was most surprised by Winter's response. Aside from consuming a huge amount of food, the young man seemed to be more serious and conducted himself with an air of professionalism. He complained little and practised with his sai often. Marlvon grew friendly with him and saw within him great potential; provided he continued to apply himself. In this new found intensity, Marlvon could see hints of Avgar coming through. He was sure that Avgar noticed this change as well.

Marlvon, Winter, Avgar, Ryde and Xayre were relaxing and having a late supper together in a small parlour when a hurried messenger came racing through the doorway. He spoke to Xayre without waiting for permission, 'Sir, Tunley is on the move. Torches can be seen moving westward around the wall.'

Xayre stood swiftly. 'This I need to see. You four, come with me.' He looked at the messenger. 'Thank you. You may tell your commander that the message has been received. Instruct him to await my orders.'

The messenger raced away once more and the five men hastened from the room. Xayre led them up a flight of stairs and along a windowed passageway before going through a heavy door and out onto a high courtyard. This was one such place that Xayre had ordered telescopic looking glasses to be positioned, so that he may easily see what was going on in multiple locations from a distance.

Xayre hastened to the cast iron railing and lifted a telescope. He peered into the blackness in many directions.

'What do you see?' asked Winter excitedly.

'Hhmm, the messenger was right. There is a line of torches several miles past the wall. They are moving slowly, but there is no mistaking that they're heading west.'

Marlvon enquired, 'Can you see how many men there are?'

Xayre didn't answer straight away, as he was straining his eyes to see. 'No, the blackness is too complete. But by the spacing and number of torches, I'd say most of Tunley's host.'

Marlvon felt uneasy. 'Why would he use torches?'

'To move his men in this darkness, you'd need something to follow.' Xayre passed the looking glass around, but no one could glean more than Xayre had. 'He must be going to attack at the west part of the city where the Sempa meets the wall. He could bring his ships upstream to create a coordinated attack. The wall there might be weaker due to the sandier soil.'

Marlvon narrowed his eyes, 'Something's not right. Those torches seem too evenly spaced to be a host of men.'

Xayre dismissed him, 'Nonsense, a well-organised army can march evenly. No, I'm convinced they'll be attacking from the west.'

Marlvon's heart sank. *It's just a bit too convenient.* 'My instincts say otherwise. You would do well to sure up the defences in the east part of the city.'

Xayre turned to Ryde. 'You've seen many battles. What would you advise, old friend?'

Ryde spat on the ground as he thought. After a short while, he spoke. 'If he had a bigger host, I would say that you're both right and Tunley would be attacking from both sides.' He thought some more. 'If I were this Tunley, I wouldn't have used torches. But torches at night are better to hide your numbers and intentions than marching in daylight. He might even have more soldiers than our sentries report. Whatever our decision, it's a gamble and no mistake.'

Xayre grew irritated. 'So, what would you do?'

Ryde looked at him sternly. 'I'd move the bulk of my defences west, but keep enough at hand to be able to hold off in case he attacks elsewhere.'

'You always did like to hedge your bets.' The stressed Xayre could not hide the derision from his voice. He looked through the glass once more. 'Very well, I will do as Ryde suggests. I have much to prepare.' He strode from the courtyard, caught up in his own thoughts.

'I will remain on the eastern side of Nivera, for I cannot disregard my instincts.' Marlvon made his position firm. *Where's Phlyte when we need her?* Marlvon looked over at Avgar. 'Can you use your powers to sense Tunley's intentions, or how many men are on the move?'

If I had my full powers, yes, but at the moment, the distance is too great. Marlvon heard Avgar's voice in his head and knew that the others did too. He couldn't help but wonder what help Avgar's powers would be able to provide, given he didn't have his *full* ability. He refrained from communicating this to Avgar and instead moved on. 'We should all stick together. Will you join me on the east side?'

Winter voiced his concern, 'But what if you're wrong and we miss the chance to kill Tunley?'

When no one else replied, Marlvon answered the young man. 'Tunley is no fool. He will not be in the vanguard, regardless of where his troops attack the wall. We will have time to manoeuvre to wherever he is… provided we stay alive.'

Winter spoke once more, 'Has anyone come up with a way to kill Tunley yet?'

Ryde answered first, 'Since Marlvon told us he has the Healer's protection, I've been givin' it some thought. I say we fill him with arrows from a distance.'

'Will that even work?' Winter asked promptly.

Yes, I believe it will. The Healer's protection only protects from direct attacks. The spell cannot tell who shot the arrow, so that should kill Tunley. Avgar's voice sounded in their heads. *I'm surprised I didn't think of that myself.*

Ryde grinned. 'Then all we have to do is wait for the scumbag to be in the open, we waltz on in and spike him full of shafts.'

Marlvon smiled too. 'Sometimes, the simplest plan is the best. I had been thinking about pushing a rock on him from a high window or having Avgar collapse a building on him, but I wasn't sure if that was within his powers.' Marlvon knew Avgar felt the barb.

'Very well, it is settled. We should all prepare ourselves for the battle ahead. Garb yourself with armour and weapons, then grab some food and drink. We will all meet in front of the palace when we're ready. Prepare yourselves for a long night. Gentlemen, I'll see you shortly.'

They all left the courtyard and made their own way to their quarters to prepare for battle. Marlvon opened a chest that was positioned at the foot of his bed. Within the first day of arriving in Nivera, he had sought out what he desired. He had not taken such protection from Myrth Isle as he had not envisioned being in a battle proper. He felt foolish at this assumption and chastised himself for being naïve.

From the leather-bound chest, he first drew a short hauberk. This mail shirt was fashioned with sleeves that ended at the elbow and a torso covering that stopped just below Marlvon's groin. It fit him well and he placed this over a leather shirt. Atop the hauberk, Marlvon placed a simple brown tunic made of light cotton, similar to what a farmer might wear. Marlvon knew that in battle, your enemy had but a moment to get your measure and if Marlvon looked like a man of no importance, he might catch his opponent off guard. Marlvon's skills at disguise were never far from the surface.

Marlvon slipped his hands into gauntlets that were leather on the interior of his hands and hard steel on the outside. He blackened these so that they wouldn't stand out and hoped that the basket on his sword would also protect his fingers.

On his forearms, Marlvon strapped flexible vambrace. These he hid beneath the long-sleeved shirt and he knew that he could use the vambrace to block a blow if needed, although this was not ideal. It was customary to wear greaves on the outside of his pants, but Marlvon elected to wear his underneath loose fitting simple trousers so as to hide his armour once more.

The brave man elected to wear nothing on his head, opting for clearer vision and swift reactions. He knew that not many people would choose to go helmless into open battle and smiled at his own arrogance.

On his feet, he placed his old soft leather boots. These would not hinder a blade at all, but he wanted to be comfortable. As Marlvon laced these tightly, he noted that he was not made for open battle, but rather was more suited to close, personal fighting.

Last of all, he strapped his Myrthian sword to his back where he could swiftly draw it at need. Marlvon then made his way down to the front of the palace via the kitchens to secure some food and the armoury to collect four bows and quivers. He was the first in the courtyard, but did not have to wait long before Avgar arrived. The old man was similarly armoured, but with plain leather gloves instead of the gauntlets that Marlvon wore. They nodded to each other and both munched an apple while they waited in silence.

The clouds overhead were low and the air felt thick to Marlvon. He finished his apple and tossed the core away. Shortly thereafter, came Ryde followed by Winter. Ryde greeted them as soon as he saw Marlvon and Avgar.

'I see that the two of you have similar battle wear as myself. Ha, what a rabble we are!' He laughed loudly and then pointed at Winter behind him with his thumb. 'This one is dressed as if he's going on parade.'

Marlvon looked and saw that Winter was almost wearing full plate armour. He had a burgonet on his head, allowing his pale face to be seen, an adorned cuirass protected his chest and back as well as gauntlets, greaves and vambrace on his hands, legs and arms.

Marlvon noticed Avgar was glaring at his son to which Winter replied with a firm voice. 'I'm strong enough to bear the weight, father.'

'Right, we're all here now. Let's go. We will head to the edge of the city, where the flower fields begin and find a building that we can see all directions clearly from. We don't know where Tunley's attack will come from, so we need to be ready to move at short notice.

'There is all likelihood that we will get entangled in the main fighting, but we need to remember that our aim is not to act like a common soldier. We must hold back and wait for a chance to kill Tunley. If we die, then hope for peace will be left to others; do you trust them?' Marlvon did not wait for a response before continuing. 'We are all skilled warriors, but in battle, numbers count for more than skill; do not throw your life away needlessly.'

As they walked, Marlvon looked at all of their faces. Ryde and Avgar looked serious, but relaxed, whereas Winter looked excited. He knew that Winter had great skill, but he was still young and had not been in many real fights.

'We need to stick together to be the strongest that we can. You all must follow my lead. I will keep Avgar close and use him to communicate to all of you, as he can speak in all of our minds. Listen to what he says, especially in the blood-lust of battle.'

'All right, Marlvon, we're all capable men. We know what to do.' Ryde's comment was intended to calm Marlvon.

'I know, Ryde, I know.'

After that, all conversation died and each man became lost in his own head. Marlvon thought largely of Islonda and how he longed to see her. He used this passion to fuel his energy, but kept it at bay, knowing that there may be a long wait before his sword was needed.

They arrived at the edge of the city and quickly found a two-story dwelling. They knocked and the door was answered by a kindly looking old man in a nightdress. Marlvon explained their business and the old man allowed them to climb onto his thatched roof to look over the surrounding lands. They could see little, for the darkness was complete. They listened hard and could hear nothing more sinister than an owl hooting in the distance and small creatures scurrying around in the thatch beneath them.

Marlvon appointed himself as the first watch and bid the others get some sleep in the attic below the roof while they could. He was met with no argument and before long he was alone with only his thoughts to keep him company.

51

A light drizzle on a dreary day fell on High Chancellor Tunley's head and shoulders as he stood outside his tent. In one hand, he held a chicken leg that he was eating and in the other, a mug of ale. He stared absentmindedly at the wall of Nivera sitting several miles away as he chewed his chicken.

Three days had passed since Tunley had come ashore east of Nivera. He had immediately ordered his troops to raid any nearby farms for supplies and capture any local inhabitants who had not sought refuge in Nivera. He was pleased when the reports came that the farms were well stocked and that it appeared as though the farmers had left in great haste. The chicken he was gnawing was from one such farm. As for inhabitants, only two such men had been captured. One was as old as old could be and was lame in his right leg. Tunley soon put him to the sword; one less mouth to feed. The other man was a stubborn serf who refused to be told what to do by the invaders. Tunley had him questioned for information on Nivera and her possible weaknesses. He was not forthcoming in answers, and those he did provide were of little value. As a reward, Tunley had decided to make a spectacle for his men to enjoy.

Tunley had his captains gather around a fenced pen. He ordered the man to be put in the pen and leapt in after him. He gave the man a blunt, rusty knife and chose a wooden club for himself. Tunley removed his shirt and imagined that he looked rather strapping. The High Chancellor failed to notice the captain's sniggers at his protruding belly.

The serf was bruised and battered from being questioned, and he watched Tunley suspiciously from the other side of the twenty-foot arena. Tunley looked straight back at him and smiled wickedly. 'Righto, man. You no doubt want me dead, and my men and I like a bit of sport. Come on and have at me; let's see if you're man enough to scratch me. Ha!'

The man smiled slightly and Tunley knew the serf thought he would be victorious. Tunley then focused on the man and held his club tightly. They began circling each other on the grassed soil. The man lunged at Tunley without warning, but Tunley was quicker than he looked and deflected the man's advance. They separated and faced each other once more.

The serf eyed Tunley with more concern in his eyes as he realised that you don't lead an army without being skilful in battle. But still, Tunley thought the serf to be over-confident. The High Chancellor was, after all, a strong young man.

This time, Tunley was the one to advance. He stepped into the man's range, caught his opponent's knife arm with his left hand and brought his club down on the man's forearm. He pulled the blow at the last moment, not wanting to break his arm just yet. *These farming folks really don't know how to fight very well.*

He stepped back and the man rubbed his arm. Tunley taunted him further. 'Come on, you can do better than that. You need to focus on why you want to kill me; let the hate fill you with strength, then attack me.'

Tunley watched as the man took his advice and his features became set with focus. He ran at the High Chancellor, who stepped aside. He lunged again, but for Tunley's other side. The High Chancellor misread his opponent and the rusty knife missed his neck by a hair's width.

The men watching grew silent and looked on with fearful anticipation in their eyes.

The serf grew in confidence and pressed his perceived advantage. Tunley began to step backwards as the younger man pursued him. Then Tunley stopped and held his ground. The serf saw his opportunity and stabbed Tunley forcefully in the guts. A roar of surprised pain ripped through the fighting pen and the two men fell apart with blood on both of their torsos. Tunley reached down and put his hand where the knife had made contact. He lifted his head and roared with laughter.

The serf was lying on the ground clutching his punctured stomach and groaning in pain. Tunley bent over him and held his club up high. 'At least you tried.'

The man's pleading eyes looked up at him, confused. 'What kind of a monster are you?' He managed to wheeze.

'A living one.' Tunley whispered to the man then brought the club down.

The High Chancellor stood over the corpse and laughed to the confused crowd around him.

'Gentlemen, the Healer's protection at work! Hahaha!'

The silence of the crowd was followed by forced cheering, which Tunley took to be overwhelming support for his cunning. *That was very exciting, I want to fight more men.* 'Any more locals that are found are to be captured for my use.'

The captains responded with agreement.

'Right, now that the fun is over, we have work to do. We're not going to break through that wall with our bare hands, so I want cannons. Each of you will be responsible for your own ships and I want all cannons that can be easily brought ashore to be done so. Have carts from the farms strapped to any of our horses or horses left behind by the locals to allow the cannons to be mobile.' Tunley looked about the men who wore grim faces.

'It won't be easy and many cannons will be too large to bring ashore without the proper equipment, but it needs to be done, so make it happen.'

'Aye, aye.'

'Dismissed.'

The sailors saluted Tunley then departed, whispering to each other. Tunley couldn't catch their words, but he supposed they were talking about his magnificent fight and clever plan with the cannons.

The High Chancellor stepped over the serf's corpse on his way out of the pen and made his way back to his tent for a well-earned drink.

Over the proceeding days, Tunley organised his attack on Nivera. He sent out scavenging parties and surrounded the city at a safe distance with troops. He knew Nivera would be able to last for many months under siege, but the High Chancellor simply didn't have the patience or the resources for such a wait. His immediate plan was to cut off any entry or exit from Nivera. He hoped that this would boost his men's morale and that of the city dwellers would be diminished.

Removing the cannons from the ships took longer than Tunley would have liked, with the main barrier being the inability to get the heavy pieces of metal off the boats. One of his captains, a clever man, rigged up a pulley system over a mast to allow the weapons to be lowered into rowing boats. These were precariously rowed ashore under gentle strokes. Only one cannon was lost in this process when a wave washed over the side of a low riding boat and sent her down to the ocean's floor.

Once the boats were beached, a team of draught horses dragged the boats further up the pebbly sand. The rowing boats were then tipped on their sides and the lumps of iron were rolled out. The horses were used once more to heave the cannons up the beach where another pulley system was constructed to lift the weapons onto carts. This was a lengthy process, and both beast and man had to rest regularly.

All in all, it took four full days to bring the cannons and munitions ashore and a further two to organise these so that they could be effectively used in an attack, but spread out enough to disguise where Tunley might want to attack.

The carts and wagons to move the cannons from their landing place were easy enough to source, but the horses to pull them were scarcer. Tunley eventually authorised the use of a few of the horses that had accompanied them, but only in numbers that would not leave his meagre cavalry sparse.

While the cannons were being arranged to be mobile, Tunley had sent out scouts and sailors with a background in building to review the wall and find its weakest section. While he waited for the scouts to return, he managed to find three more farmers to battle in his sadistic one-sided fights. Despite his assured victory, he found these bouts highly amusing and entertaining.

Since arriving at Nivera, Tunley's paranoia had been worming into his head and he visited Lyafe, whom he had brought along, and reminded him of his threat should the Healer's protection drop. He even went so far as to test the Healer's protection prior to each of his fights. The cowed Healer Supreme had not dared to deceive him.

Reports of Nivera's wall integrity finally returned to Tunley. The structure seemed robust in most places, especially around the gates, but there was a point of lesser strength a mile or so inland from the gate closest to the Rogaus. Mould had crept up the wall like a grasping hand and the mortar looked water-worn. This, his men could see using their looking glasses that they had brought ashore from their ships. Tunley was excited by this news, but then sobered when he learnt that the reason for this damage was likely due to damp soil and foundations underneath the structure. With the recent rain added to this, the best he could hope for was a muddy stretch of land. At the worst, a bog hiding underneath the low shrubs that grew there.

Tunley desperately wanted to send a man to test the footing, but sense pushed this from his mind. To show interest in that particular part of the wall would alert the Niverians to his intentions and allow them to fortify the structure or rally their defences to that point. No, he would have to risk the ground to gain the advantage of surprise.

Tunley ordered the cannons and men to be ready to attack the following day. As evening set in, so did heavy clouds. By the time all light was gone, a heavy rain began falling. Tunley knew that the rain would hamper his attack more than it would the defence of the city and decided early in the night to postpone the attack. He surprised himself at this decision and briefly pondered the possibility that he was losing his nerve. He dismissed this thought quickly.

The following day was bleak. By mid-morning the rain had ceased, but the clouds remained heavy. A chill wind blew that seemed to cut through Tunley's warmest clothes. His shivering limbs set his mind thinking and he longed to be distracted. An interesting thought struck him and he sought out Lyafe, the Healer Supreme.

The Healer was where Tunley had ordered him to be; secured to a tent pole with manacles about his wrists and feet in a simple tent. A guard stood out the front and reported that Lyafe had caused no trouble.

Tunley pushed back the tent flaps and found Lyafe sitting in the dirt looking like a filthy vagabond. The Healer looked up at Tunley with hollow eyes and a defeated expression on his face.

'Lyafe, how wonderful to see you again.' He stepped into the tent. 'It's not so wonderful to smell you though. Ha!'

'Mmmph.' Lyafe grunted in reply.

'I've been thinking about the protection that you have given me and its limitations. In a field of battle, it seems less useful than you might at first think. There are arrows, spears and all manner of things flying around on a battlefield, to which your protection offers no… well, no protection.'

'If you were worthy of the Healer's protection, then you would not seek to fight on a battlefield.'

'Don't interrupt me!' Tunley shouted at the sitting man. 'Surely though, throughout the years, the Healers attended battlefields to help the wounded. They must have had some protection. No?' Tunley finished his statement with a question.

Lyafe's eyes narrowed. 'The Healers do not, and never have, attended battlefields. There is no way to protect against what you *fear*.' Lyafe dragged out the word fear to emphasise its potency.

Tunley looked down his nose at Lyafe. 'You know nothing of my fears!'

'I know more than you think.' Lyafe sounded smug to Tunley. He wanted desperately to hit him, but knew that it would be he, Tunley, who would feel the blow.

'Your insolence has just cost the life of the first child I meet on entering Nivera. Ha, not so smug now, are you?' Tunley chortled.

A sorrowful expression filled Lyafe's face. 'Please, I'm sorry, I meant nothing by it.'

'Stop snivelling; it is done.' Tunley walked about the tent pole and came to face Lyafe once more. 'I'm bored and I would like to have some fun.' Lyafe looked apprehensive, but remained silent.

Tunley called in the guard. 'Send for the closest seaman you can find. And be sharp about it too.'

The guard saluted and left. 'After we've had our bit of fun, you're going to give the Healer's protection to as many men as you can until nightfall.'

Lyafe hung his head. 'As you wish.'

A young seaman presently entered the tent looking fearful. Tunley grinned at him and welcomed him in jovially. 'Sailor, sailor, welcome, welcome. You are going to have a great honour placed upon you. I've heard your captain speaks highly of your abilities and, as a reward, Lyafe here is going to give you the Healer's protection.'

The young man looked confused, but ecstatic. 'Thank you, sir, thank you very much.'

'Don't mention it. Now, Lyafe needs you to tell him your name?'

The sailor looked at Lyafe. 'Opit, sir.'

'A fine name for a sailor.' Tunley turned to Lyafe. 'Healer Supreme, I want you to give this man the Healer's protection… five times.'

Lyafe looked fleetingly confused, then sighed. 'Very well.'

Tunley watched as Lyafe mumbled many words interspersed with the seaman's name. After a few moments, he stopped. 'It is done.'

Tunley rubbed his hands together. 'Excellent, excellent. How do you feel, Opit?'

'The same as normal, sir.'

'That sounds in order then. Let's have some fun.' He beckoned Lyafe's guard in once more. 'Guard, I want you to strike this man across the jaw; he has been mouthy to me.'

Both seamen looked taken aback. Not one to shirk his duty, the guard shrugged his shoulders and struck the man. The guard cried out in pain and surprise and cradled his jaw in his hand. The young seamen smiled brightly though, untouched by the intended blow. 'Thank you, High Chancellor, sir.'

Tunley enjoyed the spectacle and laughed at the guard's shock. He ordered the older man back to his post and put his arm around the young seamen's shoulders. 'Let's go for a walk.'

Tunley led the man out of the tent and into the whipping wind. They made their way to an open expanse of grass on which the sailors had been sparing and practising their fighting skills. As Tunley approached the field, the sound of clashing blades abated and the only sound that could be heard was the whistling wind. The young sailor had a broad grin on his face. Never would he have thought of being given this great honour.

He's like an innocent lamb being led to the slaughter… but how thick will the lamb's wool be? Tunley thought.

'I'm going to blindfold you, then we'll have a bit of fun with some of the men. Your job is to keep as still as you possibly can.'

Opit nodded, still grinning excitedly.

Tunley covered Opit's eyes, then had him stand still. He quickly walked away and found an archer. The man saluted at his commander, but looked nervous and uneasy.

Tunley ignored that and murmured so that only the archer could hear. 'I order you to put an arrow through that man's stomach.'

The archer looked aghast, but drew an arrow nonetheless. He drew the string taut and with the slightest hesitation, released. The string twanged and the arrow flew through the air before striking true and imbedding itself in Opit's stomach. Opit let out an involuntary cry of shock and fell to his knees, scrabbling to remove his blindfold.

While this was going on, the archer yelped and collapsed to the ground, writhing in pain. Tunley prodded him with his foot and forced his hands away from his stomach. There was no sign of a wound or blood. *That's interesting.*

The large man then raced across the ground to where Opit was kneeling as pale as a bedsheet. His hands grasped feebly at the arrow shaft that was protruding from his gut. Again, no blood was present and Tunley squatted down in front of the man.

Opit looked up at him with big round frightful eyes. 'It doesn't hurt. Why doesn't it hurt?'

Tunley was excited by this development. He put a hand on the man's shoulder. 'You need to relax, Opit, I'm going to take the arrow out.'

Without waiting for a reply, Tunley clasped the arrow firmly and pulled it slightly. He immediately felt a sharp pain deep within his naval and released his hand. He looked about and called over the closest sailor.

'Seaman, pull this arrow out or I'll cut off your arm.'

The sailor balked at the prospect of such a punishment and quickly yanked the arrow out of Opit's stomach. The man cried out in pain and grabbed his stomach. *This is all very interesting and confusing.*

The High Chancellor had expected a spurt of blood to follow the arrowhead, but none came. He ripped the man's tunic apart and examined the wound. What he saw blew all of his expectations away: the clean wound left by the arrow was closing over before his eyes.

'How do you feel?'

Opit looked puzzled. 'It feels… odd. Not painful, just odd.'

Tunley smiled; the implications were enormous. His mind began to race. *What would happen if I chopped his head off? Could it be re-joined?* He then thought to himself. *What if I get Lyafe to give me the protection ten times… or one hundred… or even more?*

Tunley then looked down at Opit. *He's a risk. I'll have to get Lyafe to remove his protection.*

'Opit, you're free to go now. Prepare as best you may for the imminent battle.'

Tunley stood and left the happy sailor and the two writhing men behind. He made his hasty way back to Lyafe's tent, all the while rubbing his hands together in eagerness. When he arrived, he barged straight in. 'Lyafe, I want you to grant me the Healer's protection again. I want you to keep granting it until nightfall.'

'What of the other men you wanted me to protect?'

'Pfft. They'll be fine.'

Lyafe's answer came with scorn. 'You're such a selfless man, Tunley. That attribute must be the reason why so many people follow you.'

Tunley wanted to hit the Healer, but held off due to the Healer's protection. 'You can insult me all you want, for now, but I'm the one who is in command of the largest stretch of land that anyone has ever commanded before. And on that land are countless people willing to follow me freely. They see me as the light in the darkness of their miserable lives. They are like moths to a flame… except that they know that if they get too close to this flame, they will burn… and they fear my scorching heat, my limitless power and my exceptional brilliance. The warmth from my flame and the attack on the Outcasts has awakened a deep-seated beast-like desire for violence and blood within my people. *That* is why people follow me.'

Lyafe looked sadly up at Tunley. 'You're sicker than I first thought. Let me help you heal and you can live a long life with a sane head.'

'Ha! You jest, Lyafe; I've never felt stronger. Now, get to and start giving me more protection… and don't forget, I will be testing it and if it fails, then scores upon scores of children will be brutally killed.'

Lyafe bowed his head in submission. 'You had best leave me, so that I can begin this filthy task.' Tunley saw sense in departing and so left without further delay.

After finding a hunk of fire-cooked pork to eat, Tunley spent the rest of the day making the rounds and ensuring that preparations were completed for his attack on Nivera. The cloud cover remained all day and with evening came a deep darkness to the world; as if a god had thrown a soft blanket over the land. Sounds became muffled and sight was limited to that of a hundred yards or so. Tunley could not have been happier and immediately enacted his plan.

He first ordered fifty men to light torches and march around the perimeter of Nivera. These men were to be spaced out such that the Niverians would believe that many men were on the move. While this was going on, Tunley ordered the cannons to be brought within firing range of Nivera's wall and angled by the cannon-masters to cause maximum destruction of the wall. This process alone took most of the night, for the terrain was uneven and the lumps of metal hard to manoeuvre with the horses. But it got done, and Tunley was very well pleased.

In addition to the cannons, Tunley ordered his sailors to arrange themselves in preparation for attacking through the hole in the wall. These men were stationed behind the cannons to avoid collateral loss of Tunley's limited forces. The High Chancellor also sent a dozen ships to prepare a diversionary assault on Nivera.

Once the cogs of Tunley's plan were moving together, he made his way back to his tent and tried to sleep while he could. He tossed and turned on his stretcher until he eventually dozed off into a fitful sleep where his dreams were haunted by spectres and ghouls dancing around a green fire.

The High Chancellor of Roasline was woken well before dawn by one of his guards. He cursed at the man while rubbing sleep out of his eyes. He then jumped up and moved his limbs about to remove any stiffness from his joints. A smile spread across his face as he thought of the day ahead. *Today is a good day for a victory.*

He left his tent and ordered a sailor to bring him a cup of half strength wine and wedge of bread. The morning seemed chill and subdued to Tunley when he stepped outside. A small breeze blew in the darkness and Tunley walked with his hand on the pommel of his sword. He made his way to the cannons and greeted the men, who would fire the weapons, with muted excitement. They returned his greeting with clear tension in their voices and movements.

Tunley looked to the east and saw the very first hint of light underneath the clouds. He rubbed his hands together in glee. He turned to the men and ordered them to prepare themselves, but held off lighting any fires until the last possible moment.

A distance rumble suddenly echoed across the morning and Tunley's head snapped around. Excitement bubbled forth as he knew that his ships had started firing on Nivera. He waited until more light crept into the sky, but not so long as the sun was peaking over the horizon. His excitement could wait no longer and he ordered the cannons to begin their assault. It didn't take long before the first one boomed loudly and he breathed the burnt sulphurous smell deep into his lungs. *This is going to be a wonderful day.*

52

WAKE UP, WAKE UP! Avgar yelled in Marlvon's head. *Prepare for battle and come immediately.* Marlvon did as he was bid and his pulse thumped rapidly in his ears. Before he made it to the roof of their lookout, he heard the unmistakable distant *boom* of a cannon. He hastened further to strap on his armour.

The light of a new day was just caressing the sky when Marlvon scrambled onto the roof. Avgar was the only other one there and he pointed east to the Rogaus. *Ships are attacking over yonder.* Marlvon looked in the general direction, but could see little due to the wall blocking his view.

Suddenly, the roof shook and Marlvon was thrown to his knees. Enormous booms ripped through Marlvon's head and he tried to make sense of what he had just heard. He snapped his neck around to the south and was agape to see Nivera's wall crumbling into rubble.

'How could this happen?' Marlvon asked under his breath.

Avgar replied, *it sounded as though at least forty cannons all fired at once.*

Marlvon's thoughts raced as he realised Nivera's vulnerable position. Three score men had been left at the eastern gate to defend the city on Marlvon's advice, whereas the main bulk had been taken away west. *If Tunley plans it right, his men will be in the city before either force arrives. He has just won Nivera before a soldier even steps within the perimeter.*

Marlvon turned to Avgar, whose face was pale. 'Our mission does not change; we do not deviate from our path.'

Avgar nodded, *let us climb down and meet Ryde and Winter on the ground.*

The two men rapidly descended and arrived at the front door as the first sounds of Tunley's men breaching the wall were heard. Winter's face had blanched, and Ryde clenched his jaw.

Marlvon needed to take command quickly. 'We're not going to win fighting them in the open. We will need to stick together and fight in the close streets where their numbers will hold no advantage. Remember, we need to kill Tunley, not his soldiers, so the most important thing is to stay alive until we get our chance. You have to trust me when I tell you that we *will* get our chance.'

He looked about the men, who nodded in turn.

'Tunley will not enter with the first wave, if he has any sense, and may not at all until victory is assured. We need to keep our eyes open and find him as quickly as we can.'

Winter interrupted Marlvon, 'How will we know him? We've never even seen him. What does he look like?'

It was Ryde who answered. 'He is an arrogant pig. He will be well protected, but seeking his own kills. We will be able to recognise him.'

Marlvon continued, 'Ryde is correct; it's usually very easy to pick the commander of an invading force out from the crowd. Our hardest part will be finding him among the thousands of sword bearing soldiers.' He thought for a moment. 'Tunley will make for the palace. If his reputation is true, he will want to claim it quickly, so he may enjoy the spoils of his victory. We should lie in wait nearby. Not in the palace; he will be expecting some resistance in there, but nearby.'

Marlvon looked about the men once more. 'Let us go, before the city is overrun. And remember, stick together.'

The four men quickly glanced over the flowers and saw rank upon rank of Tunley's soldiers marshalling inside the wall. Marlvon saw a measly two score of defenders approaching from the east and knew that they would not last long against Tunley's superior numbers. Marlvon spat on the ground, picked up his bow and then beckoned to the others to follow him.

The men laboured up the slope through the chaotic streets. The inhabitants of Nivera had woken to the booming cannons and were racing around in a panicked frenzy. Marlvon knew that before long the streets and lanes would be deadly quiet as the locals sought refuge indoors.

Marlvon shook his head in sadness. *There will be many innocent lives lost today.*

They were halfway to the palace when the first clangs of swords and cries of pain washed over the city. The small defensive force had arrived to confront the invaders. Too soon the cries stopped and Marlvon knew that Tunley's soldiers would enter the streets at any moment. He quickened his pace.

Marlvon did not fear that the soldiers would overtake them, but rather feared that they would not be able to find a suitable point of ambush before the attackers advanced deep into the city.

When they were still a good distance from the palace, Marlvon noticed that Winter was lagging behind. *Curse his heavy armour. He's the youngest and should be able to keep up.* Marlvon slowed the pace so that they would remain together.

Shortly after, screams reached his ears and Marlvon turned to see smoke rising at the border of the city. It irked him greatly to flee from the fight and abandon the innocent Niverians to certain death. He vowed then and there to never forget their sacrifice.

Eventually they reached the palace and the four men stopped out of necessity to catch their breath and give their burning legs a moment to recover. Marlvon ensured that this rest was brief.

'Tunley will likely come up the main street.' Marlvon sucked deeply into his lungs. 'Seek out hiding places so we can evade his foot-soldiers long enough to await his arrival.'

The four men broke into two groups; Avgar and Winter, and Ryde and Marlvon. They searched the buildings on either side of the street for positions with good cover, that had a line of sight down the street. Even as they searched, Marlvon could hear Tunley's soldiers getting closer. He estimated they were halfway to the palace when the main body of Nivera's troops intercepted them from the west. When that happened, the screams in the air were drowned out by the clash of metal on metal; sword on shield.

Eventually, or so it seemed to Marlvon, Avgar's voice echoed in his head. *Come, we have found somewhere.* He told them directions and Marlvon and Ryde ran to meet him.

The building was an old dressmaker's shop that hadn't been used in years. The windows had been half boarded up and old moth-eaten dresses hung on wooden hangers. Cobwebs seemed to stretch everywhere and Marlvon wondered how such a decrepit store had been allowed to remain in Nivera when everything else spoke of freshness, cleanliness and beauty.

Marlvon quickly rifled through the back of the shop and found coats that would have been used for fine men trying to impress young girls. These did not fit any of the four, but Marlvon thought that all the better.

'If we are spied, it is better to seem like homeless men seeking to hide in an old shop than four armoured warriors waiting to ambush the invading commander.'

Everyone agreed and put the musty old garments over their clothes and armour. Winter removed his helmet and they all took up positions where they could see down the street without being seen within.

It didn't take long for Marlvon to see the first of Nivera's defenders retreating towards the palace. Ten or so warriors ran past and made a stand not far from the dressmaker's shop. Two dozen of Tunley's men came charging up the slope and battle ensued. Marlvon had to calm himself and steady the others in order to stop them running out to assist the defenders. He whispered hurriedly to them, 'We don't know who else is about to come up the hill. There could be an entire battalion of soldiers a few moments away. We need to stick to our plan.'

Let me see what I can do. Avgar communicated to the three other men. He scrunched up his face in concentration and Marlvon looked out the window.

One of the attackers called out in surprise,

'My eyes, what's happened to my eyes? I can't see!' His cries were cut off as a Niverian ended his life.

Three more soldiers met the same fate, but Avgar was breathing heavily. The numbers were down to eighteen against seven with the odds still favouring Tunley's men. Five of the attackers suddenly screamed in pain and grasped their necks before collapsing dead.

Avgar projected his voice in Marlvon's head once more. *The rest of Tunley's men have the Healer's protection; I can sense it. I dare not kill them directly, but I will try an indirect method.*

He concentrated once more and Marlvon saw one of the soldiers grasp his throat and try to breathe deeply. He was clearly distressed that he could not, but fought all the more vigorously until, after a few moments, he collapsed with his face turning blue.

Avgar let out a groan. Sweat beaded his brow and he looked exhausted. *That took more energy than it should have. I dare not attempt that again.*

With the numbers at twelve against six, the defenders saw little hope and tuned tail and ran for the palace. The attackers did not pursue, but instead retreated to the rest of their forces. Marlvon thought this interesting as the heat of battle had not clouded their judgement. Once they were gone, he looked about the other three. 'Avgar, how did you kill them?'

The body has several fragile parts in it. I learnt this during my time in Headly. Behind the eyes, there is a cord that connects to the brain. I used magic to cut that cord, leaving the soldier without sight. His opponents then do the real work of killing him. Another weak point is a blood vessel in the neck that goes to the brain. Again, a simple cut and a man is dead. If I had my full control over my powers, I could kill a dozen soldiers in a few heartbeats with this method.

'And what did you do to the last man?'

I knew I couldn't kill him in the same way without meeting the fate that I intended him to receive, so I placed an invisible barrier in his windpipe. Air could come out, but none could go in. My barrier did not harm him, but the lack of air did. This, as you saw, was a slower way to kill, and I lost control of my powers for a moment and felt my energy drain rapidly. In a few moments, I should be all right, but I don't fancy attempting that experiment again. As I rest, I will think of other ways to circumnavigate the Healer's protection.

'Thank you for what you did. I hope you can come up with something else useful.' Marlvon looked about and checked that each of the men had their bows ready at hand.

'When Tunley comes, we will shoot him through the windows before he even knows what's happening.'

The lull in the battle passed and the sound of killing intensified once again. More of Nivera's defenders retreated past the shop window towards the palace. *I suppose they'll make a stand in the courtyard.* Being a palace and not a structure of war, it would prove hard for the Niverians to defend the palace, but what choice did they have? Marlvon wondered.

In seemingly no time at all, the front of the battle approached. Two lines of Niverians faced many foes. Marlvon could see that they would be unable to win and wished that they would throw down their arms and surrender.

The forefront of Tunley's forces soon drew level with Marlvon and then passed them by. Stragglers of the advancing wave were going into each of the buildings to root out any hiding defenders. Marlvon was wondering how to act if their shop was broken into when Avgar's voice reached his mind. *When they search here, stay as still as you can. I will do everything in my power to prevent them from seeing us.*

It was not long before two soldiers wearing the blue sash of Roasline's navy kicked in the doorway and barged into the decrepit shop. They stood still and looked about closely.

'What a shit-hole!' one of them exclaimed. They took a few more steps into the shop and looked further into the darkness. One of the men stood no more than six feet from Marlvon and seemed to look straight through him. Marlvon held his breath and feared to move.

The other soldier wrinkled his nose. 'Smells like shit, too! Let's get out of here, there might be good loot in the next building.' The two hurriedly left and the four men heaved sighs of relief.

'You're quite useful to have around, Avgar. I especially liked your addition of the sense of smell.' Avgar nodded, clearly exhausted.

The four men watched numerous troops pass their place of hiding, but none even gave their shop a second look. The soldiers seemed relaxed and at ease, which Marlvon knew was not a good sign for the defenders of Nivera.

After a break in the passing soldiers, Marlvon heard the sound of hooves on cobblestones and well-ordered marching feet. Then, into his line of sight, came a light grey warhorse with a pompous looking man sitting astride him. The man wore solid looking armour, but lacked a helmet. In his hand, he held a long sword with blood on the blade.

'That's Tunley!' Ryde hissed.

'Wait until he's closer; we all need a clear shot.' Marlvon drew back his bow in preparation. He then noticed that stumbling behind Tunley's horse, but ahead of the host of marching troops, was Xayre. He had blood smeared down from where his left ear used to be and received continual prods from pikes of his guards. *Nivera is lost.*

Marlvon then spoke to the others. 'Nivera is lost, but we may still be victorious. Do not lose sight of the bigger goal.'

Tunley was now within firing range. All four men drew their bows and aimed at the High Chancellor of Roasline.

'Fire on three.' Marlvon felt excited yet resoundingly calm. 'One… two… thr—' *Stop!* Phlyte's voice shouted in their heads. *Do not shoot!* Marlvon relaxed his grip, but for Winter it was too late. He pulled his aim at the last instant and his arrow whizzed over Tunley's head.

Phlyte continued urgently, *Tunley has bastardised the Healer's protection. If you shoot him, it will only harm you!*

Marlvon felt a welling of oppression rise within him and he shouted back at Phlyte in his head. *The how can we kill him?*

I have walked the knife edge of our laws in telling you this much; I dare not say more… the others of my kind are watching. Marlvon felt Phlyte withdraw and he knew they were on their own again.

While this dialogue had been going on, Tunley had stood up in his stirrups and yelled to his men. 'Root out whoever's hiding in that shop! Do not kill them; I want to deal with them myself.'

Marlvon sensed his inevitable death approaching and he felt sad. Not sad that he was not long for this world, but sad that he would not get to see Islonda again. Sad that he would never meet his son or daughter and watch them grow. Sad that they would not get to know him and would have a fatherless life.

He then resolved not to go meekly and drew his rapier from its scabbard. The gentle scraping sound was one that Marlvon had heard many times in his life and believed that this would be the last time that he would hear it.

Marlvon stood to his full height and took a step towards the door. Avgar's voice suddenly sounded in his head. *Do not attack them! Many of the soldiers have the Healer's protection, but I cannot tell which ones do and which ones don't. You would only kill yourself if you attack.*

'Arrggck' Ryde spat. 'Cheating bastards.'

Marlvon sheathed his sword and awaited the soldiers.

Eight men smashed through the door and roughly pushed Marlvon, Avgar, Winter, and Ryde into the daylight. Marlvon squinted while his eyes adjusted to the light and he could feel Tunley staring at them.

'You dare to fire an arrow at me? Who do you think you are?'

To Marlvon, Tunley sounded neither angry nor concerned, but merely like a thespian putting on a show. Marlvon watched as Tunley looked at them one at a time. None of the men replied. Tunley seemed to smirk at the resistance and then his smirk flickered into a wicked smile.

'Ho, ho, ho, ho. Who have we got here? Can it possibly be the troublesome Captain Ryde from Roasline's dungeons?'

Marlvon looked from Tunley to Ryde and saw ice crystallise in the stare that Ryde gave the High Chancellor.

'You've come a long way from being Kathsum's obedient puppy. Still ugly though.' Ryde's voice was as icy as his stare.

'And you've come… well… nowhere. You're still no one who is going to die a painful and rather slow death.' Tunley smiled, clearly enjoying himself. 'But all this talk is slowing my victory of Nivera.'

Tunley's horse suddenly tossed his head violently. Tunley looked down uncertainly. The horse whinnied and neighed angrily and stamped his front feet. Marlvon looked to Avgar, who had sunk to one knee.

The grey stallion then screamed a blood-curdling scream, reared on his hind legs and bolted. Tunley flew off the back of the horse and landed in a crumpled heap on his head. Marlvon felt hope kindle in his heart until he heard the hideous screech of the horse who was thrashing around on the ground with the back of its head collapsed in.

Tunley stood and brushed some dirt off his armour. 'Someone silence that thing!' he roared. Two soldiers obeyed and when the horse was dead, an eery stillness seeped through the street.

Avgar's voice came panting in Marlvon's ears. *The barrier in Tunley's throat didn't work; it only choked me. I then blinded and spooked the horse. Tunley's protection must have detected that the horse had thrown him and inflicted the injury on the horse. I'm sorry… I'm out of ideas.*

'What a shit animal.' Tunley was unaware of Avgar's involvement. 'Someone fetch me another beast. I'll go on foot until it arrives.'

Tunley then turned to the soldiers standing either side of the four captives. 'Throw them in gaol; I want to deal with them personally… when I can take all the time that I want with them.' He cocked his head. 'But before you take them away… break Ryde's nose for me… for old times' sake,' Tunley cackled loudly.

Marlvon heard the crack of the broken nose and cringed. Ryde did not cry out, but just spat out a globule of blood. Marlvon then felt rough hands seize him and direct him out of Tunley's path. The High Chancellor rode on and Marlvon felt helpless and empty, seeing his mark slowly move freely up the hill.

53

Marlvon had hoped that he would never see the inside of a gaol cell again, but since the confrontation with Tunley, he had spent twelve days in such lodgings. The particular cell that he, Winter, Avgar and Ryde had been thrown in was more like a cage than a dungeon. The floor was hard stone, there was one solid wall with a thin high window and the other three walls were made up of iron bars. The advantages of this, were more air flow, the ability to talk with other prisoners, and it was lighter than in a closed dungeon. The disadvantages were that there was no privacy from the guards, a chill wind often passed through the room and you could easily see and hear others being tortured in adjoining cells.

Marlvon couldn't believe his luck when all four of the men had been locked in the cell together. He soon realised that this was because there were to be many other prisoners locked in the other cells. Regardless, he was grateful to have his friends as company.

High Chancellor Tunley had visited them only once and that was to gloat of his victory and the death of Xayre. On the same visit, he had taken meticulous pleasure in threatening to use a poison that he had once used on Ryde to paralyse him. Ryde had seemed unconcerned by the threats until Tunley left. Then he had confided in Marlvon that he would rather die than be subject to Tunley's torture. Marlvon had refused to kill Ryde and instilled hope in him that while they were still alive, there was a chance that Tunley could be killed. How this could happen, he did not know.

On the thirteenth morning in the gaol, Marlvon sat in the corner with his knees drawn up to his chest. His usually shaven face was covered in a growing beard. The cell next to his lay empty after its previous occupant was tortured to death the previous night. Marlvon had not slept after that ordeal and he had found himself comforting Winter, who had vomited at the violence.

Marlvon now dozed while thinking of Islonda and pondering why he had not seen or heard from Phlyte since their capture. The sound of booted footsteps startled him and he opened his eyes to see two soldiers enter the room with a defeated-looking man walking shackled in front of them. The guards unlocked the cell next to Marlvon and ushered the newcomer in without touching him.

The man went and sat with his back against the wall and put his face in his now free hands.

Avgar came over with an interested expression on his face and stood in front of Marlvon. He then banged hard on the bars in an attempt to get the attention of the new prisoner. The man slowly lifted his tired eyes and looked at Avgar, who smiled back.

The man's eyes then sprang wide and he stood quickly. 'Avgar! Well, this is a surprise.' He looked about the cell at the others. 'And Winter!' He looked closely at Marlvon. 'You look familiar, but I cannot remember your name,' he frowned. 'Yes, now I recall. I ordered you off Headly for killing Eyp.' He pointed at Ryde. 'And you as well.'

Marlvon finally recalled who the man was. 'Lyafe, the Healer Supreme. This is a turn of events.'

Avgar glared at Marlvon. *You killed Eyp?*

'Yes. Need I remind you whose deaths you're responsible for?'

The past is in the past. Avgar hurriedly added.

Lyafe was looking at Avgar. 'Did you figure out how to speak again?'

Avgar shook his head and Winter spoke for him. 'He still cannot talk, although he can send his thoughts to the three of us.'

Lyafe looked and sounded thoroughly interested. 'Can he indeed? That's amazing. Tell me, what has befallen you since we last met?'

Marlvon cut Winter off before he could continue. 'How do we know that we can trust you? Tunley has been given the Healer's protection and that must have come from you.' Marlvon tried to speak without accusation in his tone, but failed.

Lyafe's shoulders slumped. 'You are right, it did, and I cannot be trusted. If Tunley asks anything of me, I will give it.'

Ryde uttered under his breath, 'Coward.'

Lyafe looked at him with resistance in his eyes. 'If I don't do what he asks, then he will kill hundreds of innocent children. I will not be responsible for their deaths.'

Marlvon spoke evenly, 'It is hard to judge which is the greater evil: the death of those children or, by giving Tunley ultimate power, the death of unspecified others.'

'I know. Don't think that I don't know. It torments me. Every waking moment, it torments me.' Silence fell between them as they all thought of the difficult situation that Lyafe had been put in.

Marlvon wanted to move on, 'I will tell you what has happened to us, but will conceal information that might be dangerous for Tunley to have.' Marlvon then informed Lyafe of all that had befallen them. He was vague when it came to Myrth Isle and the powers of Phlyte and the other sorcerers who resided there. When he had finished, Lyafe reciprocated by telling them all that had happened to him. It was a much shorter tale and not a pleasant one to hear.

'Lyafe, we need to kill Tunley, but we cannot do so while he has the Healer's protection. Can you remove this hurdle?'

Lyafe looked dejected. 'I have the power, yes. But will I do so? No. Not unless you can guarantee his death.'

Winter blurted out, 'Why not? Surely you want him dead too.'

'He tests his protection regularly and randomly. If the protection does not hold, then he makes himself safe until it can be restored, and hundreds of children die. He has threatened this and he has made good on his threat... once... when I removed his protection as a test.'

Ryde spoke crudely, 'He has you firmly by the bollocks and, therefore, he has the entire population of the lands by the bollocks too.'

'Is there any way to kill someone who has the Healer's protection?' Marlvon enquired.

'Us Healers do not focus on killing each other! But, normally, yes. The protection will only stop direct attacks, however Tunley has taken the usual protection and amplified it. He is in uncharted territory and who knows if he can be killed or even if he will ever die. For all I know, he is now immortal.'

Ryde spoke again, 'All the more reason for you to remove his protection and sacrifice some children for the sake of many.'

Lyafe gave him a look that plainly dismissed the idea.

Marlvon had a thought. 'Is it possible to remove some of the protection, but not all of it? Say, not so much that when he tests it, he will believe that it is place, but enough that someone could shoot him with an arrow.'

'That is a risky move.' Lyafe thought. 'The problem is, that he has had me place so many layers of the protection on him, that I have no idea how many I would have to remove. And if I removed too many... then it could be disastrous.'

Just then, a guard walked past and clanged his truncheon on the iron bars. 'Enough yabbering from you lot.'

Marlvon suddenly realised that all that they had spoken may have been overheard by the guards. *We will have to be more careful next time.*

Lyafe went and sat by himself against the wall while the other four men stopped talking as instructed and paced gloomily through their cell.

The guard smiled unpleasantly. 'I hear that you're going to have a visitor today... and he has something special planned for you.'

A chill ran down Marlvon's spine. The way that the guard had said this made him think of naught else but Tunley.

The guard moved on to the next cell and told them to 'shut their traps' as well. Marlvon edged closer to Lyafe and whispered urgently. 'Lyafe, please can you remove some of Tunley's layers? At least a handful.'

Lyafe nodded curtly.

'And can you give the four of us the Healer's protection?'

Lyafe shook his head. 'He would know. As soon as he touched you. Then it would be worse for you and much worse for the children.'

Marlvon felt resigned to what might await him and the other four. 'Thank you, Lyafe.'

A noon meal of stale bread and thin broth came to the prisoners and they ate it ravenously. The plates were cleared and Marlvon was just settling in for a doze when authoritative footfalls echoed through the room.

Marlvon stood and waited impatiently for what was to come. He felt agitated that there was little he could do to direct his fate and felt at the complete whim of Tunley. *I suppose that's how he wants us to feel.*

The door to the large room opened and Tunley himself entered. The large man had his hair tied back in a slick ponytail. His clothes looked expensive, with gold stitching woven through the many folds of deep green fabric. He walked confidently over to the cell and leant against the bars.

'My, my, look at the four of you. A bit more bedraggled than when you stood so pompously in front of me. How have you been faring? Actually, don't answer; I don't really care.'

Marlvon thought of many expletives that he could use, but realised that he would just sound weak.

Tunley continued on. 'I've been having some interesting conversations with a few of the residents of Nivera. They have been most forthcoming and enlightening. It seems that I have landed quite a catch with the four of you.' He pointed first at Ryde. 'I've got Ryde here who will be my personal enjoyment.

'Then there's you, Marlvon, who I believe is the nephew of the once great Resvon. Quite the royalty.

'Then Avgar who, as I understand, briefly held the control of the Outcasts and who has some rather interesting powers. I'm very much looking forward to learning about these powers.'

The evil man grinned. 'And last and least, I have Winter, Avgar's son. You will prove the perfect leverage in getting Avgar to talk about his powers.'

Marlvon couldn't help but smile a little.

'What's so funny? Think you're too good for me?'

'You will never get Avgar to talk, no matter what you do to his son.'

'They all say that… at first.'

Ryde laughed too, clearly irking Tunley. 'You're slow on the uptake, aren't you? It seems your local gossipers aren't very informative. Bah, a thorn in your side, it will be.'

Tunley stood up straight with all mirth gone from his face. 'Enough, I did not come here to be mocked. I came here to tell you that tomorrow, Marlvon, you will meet your doom. Judging by the sword that you were carrying, you think you're good with a blade. Well, tomorrow, you will have the chance to go one-on-one with me in an arena. Publicly killing the nephew of Resvon will further solidify my claim over the Outcasts.'

Marlvon felt dumbstruck and could not think of how best to respond. 'I'll pass, thank you very much. I'm rather starting to enjoy my lodgings.'

'Ha, well you may enjoy them for this night only, then, you will be lodging under the ground.' Tunley left the prison laughing hysterically to himself.

Marlvon made his way over to Lyafe. 'You have to remove his protection before I fight him. If you do this, I can guarantee that I will kill him,' he whispered quietly.

'I cannot. He will test the protection before you start.'

'So, remove it once we've started fighting!' Marlvon was growing angry at the certainty and manner of his death.

'It would take too long. He had me spend much time placing protection after protection on him. To remove it would take a full day at least.'

Marlvon felt crestfallen. Then he had an idea. 'Can you give me the protection?'

'He will test it before you start as well.'

'Can you give me the protection after we start?'

'I could, but as soon as he finds out, he will have you killed with arrows… or worse.'

'But if he stabs me when I have the protection, then he will die.'

'That is not so certain. With his multi-layered protection, the magic might be redirected. I placed the protection on you and so it would be me who indirectly is killing him and therefore I would be killed. I just don't know what would happen.'

'Is it not worth the risk?'

Lyafe looked stern and thoughtful. 'Yes, perhaps it is. Very well, I will place the protection on you once you've started fighting. At least he won't be expecting that.' He closed his eyes and for a moment looked downcast. 'But how will I know when you've started?'

'Avgar can help with that. Using his powers, I will tell him when we've started.'

Lyafe nodded. 'That could work. You know, it will have to be a clean, definitive blow from Tunley to kill him. You're putting yourself at great risk.'

'Ha, no greater risk than if I had no protection.'

'Very true.'

A silence fell between them, which Marlvon eventually broke. 'Thank you, Lyafe. Together we can defeat Tunley.'

Marlvon left Lyafe and went to share his plan with the other three in the cell in hushed whispers. After which, he began preparing his mind and body for rest through the afternoon, before his final night in the cell.

At midmorning, a trio of guards came to collect Marlvon. At their appearance, his hands broke out in sweat and his heartbeat quickened. He stood and waited for the guards to open the cell. Lyafe, Winter and Ryde wished him luck and bid him farewell. Avgar reassured him that he would be with him the entire time relaying messages. This reassured Marlvon that their plan was a solid one.

He left the cell and followed the guards of the entrance to the gaol. There he met two more guards in full armour with one carrying a bundle. He threw this at Marlvon who clumsily caught it.

The guard spoke with a rough, but authoritative voice. 'The High Chancellor wants this to be a fair fight, so he's letting you have your mail shirt and sword back.'

Marlvon smiled and quickly donned the shirt and strapped the Myrthian blade across his back. Having these simple items filled Marlvon with confidence and all trepidation was swept away.

The guards surrounded him and led him from the prison towards the palace. This journey was not long, but Marlvon used it to channel the training of his youth and reignite the killer that he had been.

He ignored the bustling crowd and the smattering of cheers and jeers and soon arrived at the palace courtyard. Tunley's men had been busy in erecting a raised platform with room for crowds to gather around. Marlvon thought, *He sure likes to make a spectacle.*

Avgar warned Marlvon that he was about the take a risk with his powers and attempt to see through Marlvon's eyes. Marlvon's vision flickered black for a moment and then appeared normal once again. The young man heard Avgar's voice in his head. *That taxed me, and I only held the image for a moment. I may attempt that again, but only at great need. Instead, I will try to hear what you hear… it should require less energy. I have also relayed what I saw to Lyafe and he tells me that Tunley has hosted many such fights… always with the same winner.*

Marlvon blocked that from his mind as he stepped under a rope and onto the platform. Crowds were gathered all around, some overshadowed by the beautiful palace overlooking the arena. Marlvon noted that it would have been a lovely scene for a performing troupe of actors. He smirked to realise that he was perhaps no better than a puppet following a well-worn script. He hoped, however, to rewrite that script and become the puppeteer himself.

The crowd at the far end of the stage suddenly parted and striding along was High Chancellor Tunley. He was dressed in tightfitting leather clothes with a shiny mail shirt over his barrel-like chest. He climbed the steps to the platform and a servant lifted the rope for him to duck under. He raised his right hand and cheers rang out from the crowd. He looked at Marlvon and smiled.

Tunley turned to the crowd and urged them to be silent. Once they were, he spoke loudly and strongly. 'Ladies and Gentlemen, today you will witness the demise of a bygone era. Today I challenge Marlvon, the nephew of Resvon and his last living relative. Today, I will defeat Resvon's shadow and unquestionably be the ruler of the Outcasts!'

The crowd cheered and Marlvon doubted there were many Niverians in attendance.

Tunley continued loudly, 'You can see that he is armed with a sword; his very own sword no less, and I am armed likewise. This will be a fair match of skill and prowess. He may be younger, yet the fire of life burns stronger within me.'

Marlvon felt a slight nick on his shoulder and he turned to see that a guard had cut him slightly. He felt the pain and realised that this was the test to ensure that he did not have the Healer's protection. The guard nodded to Tunley, who smiled anew.

The High Chancellor then turned to a soldier and asked that the man do the same to him. He did and Marlvon saw the soldier flinch when he cut Tunley.

Marlvon quickly spoke to Avgar under his breath so that the sorcerer could hear through Marlvon's ears. *We have both been tested, tell Lyafe to give me the protection and start removing Tunley's.*

A short moment later, Avgar replied, *You now have the protection. I'm going to see if I can help Lyafe in removing Tunley's layered protection with my magic. I will not communicate further, unless I have something important to tell you. Happy hunting, Marlvon!*

Marlvon nodded to himself. *Right, the board is set. The odds are in Tunley's favour, but he does not know all that confronts him. I need to dance with this arsehole to give Lyafe as much time as I can. Then, when I can dance no more, he will strike me down and in doing so, strike himself down.* Marlvon was ready.

Tunley stepped into the centre of the arena and beckoned Marlvon to do likewise. Marlvon obeyed and, unsheathing his sword, held it firmly in the right hand. They stood face to face and Marlvon watched for the slightest move from Tunley.

The High Chancellor couldn't help himself and mocked Marlvon. 'I'm going to enjoy this, you worthless rat.'

Marlvon just smiled and kept his tongue behind his teeth.

Tunley lunged. Marlvon twisted to the side and Tunley's blade slashed at thin air. Marlvon brought up his sword and stabbed towards Tunley, being intentionally slow to allow Tunley to deflect his blow.

Marlvon went on the defence. Tunley advanced, slicing in all directions. After a few defending blocks, Marlvon knew he was the better swordsman by far, but his lack of food over the past fortnight or so, had made his arms feel slow and his blocks weak. The defender parried three more attacks and then something strange started to happen to Marlvon's vision: he saw a shadow of Tunley's attack a moment before it happened. This phenomenon threw him off balance and Marlvon only missed being cut in two by a mere inch as he fell to the ground.

Marlvon quickly rolled to the side and leapt to his feet. Tunley sneered at him and pressed his advantage. He swung at Marlvon's head and again Marlvon saw a vision of the attack a moment before it occurred.

Marlvon ran to the far corner of the arena and caught his breath. He looked down at his sword and the yellow-brown stone seemed to pulse with energy. A thought then occurred to him. *An eye! The sword is allowing me to see what's coming before it does. Ha! Thank you Fec and Phlyte, thank you.* With this knowledge, Marlvon more than easily evaded Tunley. He watched as the High Chancellor grew angry.

'You're good at evading me, but not very good at attacking me.'

Marlvon didn't reply with words, but attacked Tunley. He pulled his blows and hoped that Tunley wouldn't notice. Marlvon hit Tunley in the stomach with his fist, knowing full well that he himself would feel the blow. The last thing Marlvon wanted was for Tunley to grow tired of the fight and order his execution.

This dance continued and Marlvon realised that the time was approaching for him to allow Tunley to kill him. He knew what he had to do, but he couldn't quite bring himself to stick his neck out, knowing that his head might be chopped off.

He steeled his resolve and thought of Islonda. This flicker of a drop in his attention brought Tunley within his guard. The fat man struck and Marlvon only half deflected the blow to his left arm. Tunley's sword made contact with Marlvon's flesh and dug deep. Marlvon didn't feel a thing, but he knew instantly that Tunley had felt something. Not the full blow, but perhaps a shadow of it. Tunley stepped back and narrowed his eyes. 'That little weasel, Lyafe. He will pay for this.' Tunley retreated to the far side of the arena and shouted, 'Archers, this man is a cheat. Prepare to fire!'

Two things then happened in rapid succession. First, Marlvon heard the drawing of bow strings from the palace windows and second, he heard a whisper of Avgar's voice deep within his head. *We've done it… he… has… no… protec…* His voice then faded and through their connection, Marlvon felt Avgar had spent his last drop of energy and passed from the world.

Marlvon firmly clasped the snapling leather of his sword hilt in his right hand and sprang into a sprint towards Tunley. The High Chancellor held his hand up for the archers and then hesitated for a moment with a wicked smile on his face. He urged Marlvon on, 'Come to me; come to your doom.'

Marlvon knew Tunley thought that his protection would kill Marlvon when he struck and he felt elated. The avenging man leapt the final six feet and drove the point of his sword straight through the mail shirt and into Tunley's heart. The impact knocked the large man backwards and Marlvon rolled over the corpse, leaving his sword wobbling in the High Chancellor's chest.

He quickly sprang to his feet, turned and retrieved his sword, uncertain how the crowd would react. He looked earnestly from one side to the other.

Complete silence filled the courtyard. Nobody knew what to do. Marlvon had to take the initiative. 'I am Marlvon, nephew of Resvon. I claim leadership over the Outcasts as my uncle once did. He was a great leader who allowed the Outcasts to prosper and those across the Liagar live in relative peace. If any want to challenge me to the leadership, now is the time to do so! Let such men step forth.' He waited and no one moved or spoke. He waited a moment longer, then continued speaking. 'Tunley's reign is over. Let his forces withdraw from the city and make camp outside the wall.'

A rumbling of voices and movement broke out and Marlvon tried to gauge their mood. A Ship Master stepped boldly forward. 'I will not challenge you for the leadership of the Outcasts, but we have fought hard to take this city and I have an army behind me. What have you got?' He pointed his sword at Marlvon. 'I want Nivera!'

Marlvon could see the situation slipping away from him. A flicker of a reflection caught the corner of his eye and he scanned the faces of the crowd. He bluffed with a strong voice, 'I have the loyalty of the Outcasts and we are strong!'

The man took another step towards Marlvon. 'I could have my archers shoot you now.'

An old man stepped onto the platform and came to stand beside the new leader of the Outcasts. Marlvon looked at him in surprise. 'Well met, Guflinkov.'

Just then, a horn blew long and loud. It was distant, but not too distant. Marlvon thought it to be just outside the walls of Nivera.

Guflinkov spoke to the Ship Master gently, but firmly. 'The city is surrounded by Outcast cavalry. We are through the wall and ready to gallop up the streets and take Nivera back. We have also filtered through the crowd. There are now two Outcasts to every one of the Roasline troops. We do not want to shed more blood. But the question is, do you want to risk losing more lives, including your own, on a gamble?'

Marlvon pointed the tip of his sword at the man's chest. 'Concede and I promise, your entire force can leave in peace.'

The man hesitated, then scowled and threw down his blade. 'I concede.'

Marlvon breathed a huge sigh of relief. *It is done! Tunley is dead! But, I'm the Leader of the Outcasts. That's not what I wanted.*

Marlvon felt a wave of exhaustion settle over him. He knew that he couldn't rest, but he also knew that he couldn't do everything himself. He turned to Guflinkov. 'Can you see to the removal of Roasline's troops from Nivera?'

Guflinkov rested a warm hand on his shoulder. 'You've done well. The Myrthians will be pleased. Yes, I can see to their removal. You go and release your friends.'

Marlvon didn't question how Guflinkov knew about the others in gaol, but thanked the old man and left the platform. The crowd parted, with many of the Niverians thanking and congratulating him. He smiled and nodded in recognition, but did not slow his pace on the way to the gaol.

News of his victory had spread quickly and the Roasline guards had left their post, so Marlvon found the prison unguarded. He located the cell keys quickly enough, but only planned to release his friends and Lyafe. The other prisoners would plead with him, but he would ignore them. Without being certain who could be trusted, it was safer to have them remain in their cells.

When he got to his old cell, Winter was sitting on the floor with Avgar's head in his lap. Tears splashed freely down Winter's face onto the tattooed cheek of his dead father. Marlvon went to Winter first and squatted in front of him.

'Avgar gave his life to save countless others. What he did was a truly great deed.'

'I know, but he is still my father,' Winter sobbed.

'Aye, and a good man.' *In the end,* Marlvon couldn't help adding in his mind. Marlvon stood and embraced Ryde. 'It's over! We did it.'

Ryde held him at shoulders length. 'You mean, you did it.'

'If it wasn't for you, I wouldn't have made it out of Fort Kykum all those months ago.'

The corner of Ryde's mouth curled up. 'Speaking of which, I believe you owe me quite a large sum of money.'

'Ha, never fear, you will have it paid in full.' Marlvon knew Ryde was joking, but resolved to pay the man what he was due at a later date.

Marlvon made his way into Lyafe's cell and was greeted by the Healer Supreme weeping openly.

'Oh, Marlvon, beyond all hope, you have saved us and many others. I will forever be in your debt.'

'There is no debt to pay, for I am of a like mind.'

Lyafe smiled, 'If I may, there will be other Healers around who I should find. There will be many injuries to heal.'

Marlvon nodded and Lyafe left.

Together, Marlvon, Winter, and Ryde carried Avgar's body on a stretcher to the palace and laid him down where his body would be safe. Marlvon then told the other two all that had happened since he left the prison.

He had only just finished when Guflinkov entered the room. 'Marlvon, you are needed elsewhere. There will be time for your friends later,' he added kindly.

Marlvon left with the old man to see to the duties that were placed before him. Even as he walked from the palace, he couldn't help but smile; he now had the power to free Islonda.

54

The days that proceeded Marlvon taking on the mantle of the Leader of the Outcasts were too short for all that was required to be done. Marlvon was busy from dawn to dusk. He oversaw the withdrawal of the Roasline troops from Nivera and arranged for provisions to be supplied to enable the invaders to return via sea to Fort Kykum. He would have preferred them to return to Roasline, but the Ship Master appointed in charge was stubborn and refused to budge on the matter. Marlvon did, however, arrange for Islonda and all of the Healers to be freed when the Roasline navy arrived at Fort Kykum. He sent several Healers with the troops to ensure that this eventuated.

Once the Roasline navy had departed, repairs needed to be made to Nivera's wall and the city proper. There were many Niverians willing to help with this and good will spread quickly through the city. These repairs would take many months to complete and Marlvon hoped to be long gone before they were complete.

Amid the commotion of departing troops and reconstruction works, Marlvon ensured that there was an appropriate funeral for Avgar as well as all those who had died in the conflict. Avgar's funeral was a sombre affair with only Marlvon, Ryde and Winter present. His body was burnt and his ashes were scattered in a southerly wind over the Rogaus. This was what Winter wanted for his father.

On the fifth day since Tunley was defeated, a day of mourning was observed where all work stopped and everyone's thoughts moved to those whom they had lost. Marlvon distributed what drink there was in the palace cellars to those who wanted to celebrate the lives of those they had lost.

Throughout these days, Marlvon worked tirelessly with the knowledge that the harder and quicker he worked, the sooner he would get to see his beloved Islonda. He thought of her every moment that he could and longed to hold her in his arms. To this purpose, he interviewed many men and women who might be suitable to take over the mantle of being in charge of Nivera. Many came up short; being too weak, not compassionate enough, lacking experience, being power hungry or just plain ignorant to what was involved in running a city. In desperation, he sought out Guflinkov and begged the old man to take on the task until the people could vote for a leader. Guflinkov grudgingly agreed, arguing that he was not a leader at heart, but for the stability of the city, he would see it done.

Voting, that was something else that Marlvon wanted to bring to the Outcasts. He wanted the Leader of the Outcasts to be appointed by the people and not ascend to the title by brute force. He knew that it would be hard to change the Outcast's ways, especially those from Psymryte, but he wanted to try. Indeed, he wasn't even sure if Psymryte would recognise him as the Leader at all, let alone his desire to change how their system of government ran. He had sent an emissary to the city across the Sempa to investigate their position, but was yet to receive a response.

After many days of hard labour, both physical and mental, Marlvon dozed in an armchair in the palace library. Many shelves of books were stored here, but Marlvon had not had the time to even glance at the titles. Still, he found the room peaceful and calming. There was something about the smell and the feel of the room that settled him.

His head nodded to his chest when a soft knock tapped at the door. He shook the sleep from his mind and called for the person to enter. Lyafe walked into the room wearing clean white robes of wool. 'Good evening, Marlvon.'

'Good evening. I trust your pursuits are going well?' Marlvon knew that Lyafe had almost been as busy as himself. He had gathered what Healers had been with Tunley's navy and set about healing many wounds inflicted by the invading force.

'The pursuits still need pursuing… as they always will. But I come here not to report on my progress but to make a request.'

Marlvon lifted an eyebrow. 'Oh, what would you like?' he asked inquisitively.

'I would like the use of a ship to carry myself, and several fellow Healers, back to Headly. I say *use* of a ship, when really I mean ownership of a ship.'

Marlvon smiled, then frowned. 'Headly was burnt to the ground; there is nothing left of it.'

Lyafe looked downcast, 'I knew it was set ablaze, but had kept an ember of hope within my heart that some of the town remained.'

'Would you want to rebuild it?'

Lyafe looked about the room thoughtfully. 'The power of Headly was not in the buildings. If I'm speaking honestly, they were a bit on the old side anyway, but the power was rather in the Healers themselves and the land itself.' He rubbed his chin. 'I suppose we will have to rebuild Headly, but it is not a task that the Healers were made for. We rebuild bodies, not wood and stone structures.'

'Many people have been affected by Tunley's actions, Lyafe. Nivera has much to repair, but they could perhaps spare a handful of people, if they are willing.'

'Any help would be appreciated and I'm aware of the need for helping hands here.'

Marlvon thought for a moment, then had an idea. 'Perhaps there is another option. I have not fully told you the tale of how we came to Nivera, due to Tunley's control over you, but that danger is now gone. Living on Myrth Isle is a people both ancient and powerful.' He smiled out of the corner of his mouth. 'Their ancestors were the very ones who gave the Healer's their powers of protection and healing. I believe they would be willing to house you, if not forevermore, at least temporarily. Yes, I would advise you to seek your help from Myrth Isle.'

Lyafe smiled broadly. 'This is good news to hear.'

'Yes, and you can have your ship. I know just the one: *Hope*.'

'I like that. It will suit us well. Thank you.' It was said simply and Marlvon felt the conversation drawing to an end.

'Good night, Lyafe'

'Good night, Marlvon. May the moon shine brightly on the path before your feet.' Lyafe left the room and Marlvon was happy to be able to help the Healer Supreme.

Several more weeks passed, and Marlvon felt he would soon be able to leave Nivera. He was planning his departure with Guflinkov one bright late-winter morning when the door of their study was thrust open and in strode Sister Sor.

Guflinkov walked over to her and held both of her hands in his. 'Sor, it is a wonder to see you again.'

She beamed back at him with her eyes twinkling brightly. She looked over to Marlvon, 'It seems as though you have managed just fine without my help.'

'The miles between here and the Moaks are long. Much can happen while one is travelling them.'

'Yes, you are right. Although I feel a fool for having played no greater part in the demise of Tunley than being a burden for a horse.'

Marlvon could see her dissatisfaction at not being involved. 'Phlyte sent you on a mission to bring Olswerth to Nivera. You were then to bring the monks to our plight should the battle still be raging. No one could foresee the events that played out after we left Myrth. For all we knew, you were going to be the saviour of the lands, but alas, it was not to be.'

'Worse than that, Lunar and Solar refused to come. Since leaving Guflinkov, I've had nothing but disappointment and rejection.'

Marlvon was surprised at the monks' tone. 'Perhaps the gods did not wish them to come.'

She still looked irked when she glanced at Guflinkov. 'Have no women brought about the end of Tunley? Is it only *men* who have been pivotal?'

Marlvon felt taken aback, not defensive, but confused. 'It is not the task that picks the person, it is the person that picks the task.'

Guflinkov put a comforting hand on her shoulder. 'You're not thinking of the broader world, Sor. The overall desire has always been peace in the lands. Kathsum was the closest person to ever reach such a thing. She was even closer than we are now, for who knows who will take command of Roasline now that Tunley is gone. You also forget Phlyte, who has been the most pivotal person in seeking peace in the past century. And do not sell yourself short either. Yes, your trip to the monks was fruitless, but not so to Olswerth's domain. And not so your bringing of Winter safely to Headly. Without you, Winter would have died long ago. Furthermore, had Winter died, then Avgar may not have been willing to make the sacrifice that he did. Had Avgar not made that sacrifice, then Tunley would now rule over Nivera and perhaps Psymryte. One cannot predict what effect even our smallest actions will have.'

Guflinkov lifted Sor's chin. 'You are still young and there is still much work to do and a name to make for yourself. Indeed, I can think of the perfect task for you.' Guflinkov turned his head to Marlvon.

'In the next few days, Marlvon will leave Nivera with Ryde to travel to Fort Kykum to seek out Islonda, his fiancée. I was hoping to ask Winter to journey with him as protection, and now that you have arrived, I can think of no one better to join the troupe.'

Sor looked bemused.

'It will be dangerous. Marlvon is now the leader of the Outcasts and he will be diving headfirst into a city that is held by Roasline. Your fighting skills may be needed yet.'

Marlvon cut across Guflinkov with another thought. 'Past protecting me, I believe you would be the perfect emissary between myself and the new ruler of Roasline, whomever that may be. You have sound judgement, are quick at thinking, can be delicate and diplomatic when needed, not to mention that you're skilled at defending yourself physically.'

Sor smiled ruefully. 'That's more like it. You say that the person chooses the task… well, I choose this task.'

'Then it's settled. We will leave in two days' time.' Marlvon felt relieved to have Sor on board, she would prove invaluable in negotiating peace with the new Roasline ruler.

Marlvon had handed the management of Nivera over to Guflinkov and had set sail on a small, fast ship. The planned trip hugged the coastline to avoid the danger of the open sea. He took a crew to sail the boat with him and a small contingent of fighters. Marlvon could have taken a larger, more powerful ship, but he planned to enter Fort Kykum by stealth and didn't want to draw attention to his purpose.

As soon as he had left Nivera, the weight of leadership fell from his shoulders and he felt the free wind in his hair. He knew that he was a good leader; fair and just to all, but he did not enjoy the task. He longed to be free from the burden of other's responsibilities and sailing along the coast gave him that freedom.

He spent much of the voyage talking to Ryde; sharing tales of their youths. At other times, he thought of the future and his time with Islonda. As well as Ryde, the crew and the soldiers, Winter and Sor had accompanied Marlvon. These two were an interesting pair; they argued often, but continued to spend time in each other's company.

Eight days after leaving Nivera, Marlvon found himself standing aft looking over the ocean with Winter by his side. They stood together for a long while and simply looked out into the rolling swell of the Rogaus and said nothing.

Eventually, Marlvon broke the silence, 'Winter, what do you want to do with your life?'

The pale face of Winter turned and looked at Marlvon. 'What do you mean?'

'Well, you're a young man entering the physical prime of your life. You're a fine warrior, although I doubt your heart is in that. You're caring; you displayed that by looking after your father so passionately. You're inquisitive and have a thirst for new things. So, I was wondering if you've thought about what you want to do after our little visit to Fort Kykum.'

Winter turned back to the passing coastline. 'To be honest, I have not given it much thought.' Winter looked down. 'My mind has been too preoccupied with Sor.'

Marlvon could sense Winter had concerns that he wanted to share and remained silent to give the man the space he needed to find his words.

'When she cared for me at the monks, we became friends. On our journey to Headly, she wanted to be more than just friends, but my feelings did not match hers. We remained friends, but on Headly we grew apart. I lost interest in pursuing the Gods of Day and Night to focus on my father. She seemed to grow resentful of me and my choice.' He sighed. 'Then we had the falling out on Myrth and she left with Guflinkov. I thought that being thrust together on this ship might help us become friends again, but she still seems angry at me for choosing my father over her gods. Marlvon, I don't know how to win back her friendship.'

'Does it surprise you that after everything the two of you have been through, your rejection of her deepest beliefs has caused a rift between you?'

'I suppose not. But how do I fix it?'

'Always with the young, it is about having a solution, yet not the process of finding that solution.' Marlvon shook his head. 'Have you spoken to Sor about your thoughts? If you open up yourself to her, she might better understand you.'

'I suppose.'

'She is a compassionate woman. Yes, she can be quick to the defensive, but she has the training of the monks behind her; compassion is one of their core values. Approach it as if you are explaining your actions, not looking for her blessings. She may very well hate what you have done till the end of her days, but she is unlikely to hate you; Winter the man.' Winter continued to look absently to the horizon.

'You're a good person, Winter. And all good people do well to remember what it is like for the other person, in whatever situation that may be. Think of how Sor feels in her interactions with you. I see in her eyes that she still loves you. It would be a great burden to love someone, but detest the way that they have behaved. Deep in her heart, she will want to move past that detest and look kindly on you once more. Does that make sense?'

'I suppose.' He sighed. 'I just hope that we can be friends again, as we once were.'

'I have no doubt that you could be great friends in the future. Just have patience.'

'Hhmmm, you're probably right.' Winter looked over at Marlvon. 'You've been good to me since my father's death.'

'Perhaps I feel as though I owe you something. He did give his life to save mine.'

'And everyone else's.'

'True.'

'I'm going to find Sor. Thank you for your advice.'

Marlvon shook Winter's hand and watched the young man head towards the cabin. *The world is open at his feet.*

Marlvon was about to head indoors for a bite to eat when a shimmer to his left caught his eye. A gentle voice whispered in his ear, *You are a kindly man, Marlvon.*

'Phlyte.' He felt his mood harden. 'Show yourself, we have much to discuss.'

In the bright midday sunshine, Phlyte's outline appeared. Marlvon could barely see her, as she looked like no more than a shimmer of heat haze.

'You may say what you will to me, Marlvon, for soon the cares of this world will be of no concern to me.'

Marlvon was taken aback, 'How soon?'

'The winter is ending and spring is soon upon the world. I will not make it to the hot summer that is coming.'

Marlvon felt sad and all heat of an argument left him. 'Your absence will sadden the world.'

'Even though this will be the last time you see me, do not grieve for me.'

Marlvon nodded, 'As you wish.'

'Once we're gone, the burden will fall to others to ensure peace remains. First with you and the new leader of Roasline, whomever that may be, then with others once the mantle has been passed on. If I may be so bold as to make one final suggestion; when the new High Chancellor of Roasline is elected, send for Lyafe to organise a peace treaty with that country. He will be residing with us on Myrth Isle.'

Marlvon raised his eyebrows. 'You needn't worry. I desire peace as much as you and I had already planned to do as much.'

'Excellent. Then I will give you one last piece of information before I say my farewells. Islonda was released from prison and is living just outside the Keep to the east. She is residing in the only place that would take her in. You will know it by its red door.'

'Thank you.' Marlvon felt uneasy by the way that Phlyte had said 'the only place that would take her in'. Marlvon wanted to question her further, but Phlyte held up a hand.

'I will leave you. May your family prosper and you find the peace that you desire.'

'Farewell, Phlyte.' Marlvon nodded and said his final goodbye. Phlyte vanished with a gentle gust of wind. The wise sorceress was never seen outside of Myrth Isle again.

⁊

The days passed by like the coastline. Marlvon grew impatient at their slow pace, but there was little he could do to speed them along. His advice to Winter had proven sound, for he heard less bickering between the young man and Sor. Marlvon was pleased that they were friends once more and grateful for a more harmonious voyage.

As winter crept into spring, Ryde advised Marlvon that they were perhaps two days from Fort Kykum. Marlvon felt excited at the prospect and talked endlessly of how they should approach the city.

Despite the discussions, he kept coming back to two options. 'The way I see it, we can either sail in as bold as brass pretending to be traders, or come ashore outside the city's sight and enter over the land.'

'I know this, Marlvon. We have been through it time and time again. I swear, you'll drive me to the drink again with your repetitiveness.' Ryde slapped him on the back. 'I thought you were meant to be decisive.'

Marlvon ignored Ryde's boredom. 'The fortress is held by Roasline. We don't know how friendly they will be to new arrivals. But then it would be quicker to arrive by sea and I have waited so long to see Islonda again.'

'Yes, yes, and next you're going to say that you've waited so long, what's an extra night compared with being caught at the final hurdle?' Ryde sounded exasperated. 'You're like a little boy awaiting a present from a favourite uncle.'

Marlvon shut his mouth with a clomp. 'Nonsense, I'm just threshing out all of the possibilities.' He took a deep breath. 'Right, then, I will make a decision now and stick by it.'

'Thank the earth.' Ryde muttered.

'We are going to…' Marlvon paused, took another deep breath to decide and then spoke what deep down he knew to be the best course of action, 'land the ship and approach on foot.' He felt happy to have decided, but a little bit miffed that it was the cautious route and not the quick and bold passage.

'Well, that's a surprise,' Ryde rolled his eyes.

'There is much to prepare. You make the arrangements with the captain and I'll see to everything else. It all needs to be just right.'

The two men went their separate ways on the small ship to prepare for the danger ahead.

An old man and his grown daughter walked along a dirt road under a drizzling warm midday sun. They were garbed in simple clothes and the man wore a long, weather-worn coat. Underneath this coat he hid a sword of immense power. The two walked casually, but at a pace that saw the miles disappear behind them. They were headed to Fort Kykum to buy a new donkey for the farm, or so their story went.

Marlvon had chosen to go by the name of Mant, but Sor saw no reason for changing hers. When leaving Nivera, Marlvon had gathered a collection of items used to disguise their party. As he usually liked to do, Marlvon played an older man and had greyed his hair and added wrinkles to his face. He had changed little to Sor other than to cover her forehead moon tattoo and put a wig atop her head; short hair on women always drew attention.

There was quite a lot of traffic on the road for the start of spring, although Marlvon noticed that a lot of it was men wearing the uniform and green sash of Roasline's army. While he was glad to be back in the more familiar lands surrounding Fort Kykum, he was saddened to see the occupation by Roasline troops.

Marlvon and Sor blended in well with the non-military road users and Marlvon knew that Winter and Ryde, who were a few hundred yards ahead, would too. Behind him, two more warriors were hidden in disguises. His heart was against bringing anyone else along, but his head made him adhere to caution. Their plan was to meet up with Winter and Ryde once they reached the citadel and have the two soldiers shadow them to keep a watch from a distance.

As they walked along, Marlvon turned slightly and looked at Sor. Not bothering to change his voice yet, Marlvon asked, 'Why did you come back from the monks?'

'What do you mean?' Sor seemed to be taken away from her private thoughts by the question.

'Well, the monks refused to come to our aid. Your mission of turning Winter into a monk was foiled, you've dedicated your life to your Gods and the practice of your people is to worship them in the Moaks. There didn't appear to be a driving force to bring you back.'

'I had to get the message to you that the monks weren't coming.'

This sounded like a well-rehearsed response and Marlvon didn't believe it. 'Nonsense. What's the real reason?'

Sor bit her lip as if not wanting to continue, but did nonetheless. 'Lunar and Solar were… displeased… with my stance on their inaction. We had heated words.' She fell silent.

'Did they banish you?'

'Not exactly. I… I kind of banished myself.' She looked guilty and ashamed. 'I said that I would not return to the monks while I lived.'

Marlvon felt amazement; for Sor to go against her Gods was an incredible act.

She hastily added, 'Don't get me wrong, I still fervently believe in the Day and Night Gods and I still worship them. I just think that their will would be to seek peace at all costs. To this end, I will no longer only stay awake at night.'

Marlvon walked on in silence, then Sor continued. 'I have seen the world, Marlvon. I have seen good and evil and much in between. I realise just how much grey there is in the world. The dawn and dusk of good and evil is far longer than night and day, if you take my meaning.'

'I believe I do.'

'My sheltered upbringing has been unshielded and I have been exposed to a complex and colourful world.'

They walked on in silence for many yards before Marlvon asked another question. 'What will you do now that you've left the monks?'

Sor smiled, 'Winter said that you asked him that question too. I don't fully know. I do know that I will continue to worship the Gods. Perhaps, after I finished my appointed task of liaising with Roasline, I will bring the Gods out of the Moaks and educate any who are willing to listen and learn. Or perhaps I will go to the Healers and help in any way that I can. Perhaps I will reside for a time in Nivera and explore her beauty and secrets. Whatever I choose to do, it will not be an idle choice, but one full of purpose and meaning.' Sor sounded proud in her conviction.

Marlvon couldn't help asking another question, despite feeling as though he was prying a little. 'And what of Winter? The two of you have gone through much together.'

'That is true.' She looked out over the farmlands with their stone walls and grazing sheep. 'I don't know… my love for him has faded; I think. It was not to be. We are friends now. I enjoy his companionship, but would still be able to find ample meaning without him around. I think he needs to find a purpose that suits his needs and desires, not someone else's.'

'You're wise for your years.'

'Ha! Perhaps I've spent too long with you on the journey here from Nivera.'

'Perhaps.' They fell into an unspoken silence for the next mile or so, by which time they were approaching the gate to Fort Kykum. Marlvon slowed his walk and added a subtle limp to his stride. He hunched his shoulders and put an expression of long acceptance on his face.

Marlvon noticed the guards standing on either side of the open gate as they approached with caution. He needn't have worried, for the guards didn't look twice at them. *They feel comfortable in their dominance. And so they should. The Outcast's army is a shadow of its former strength. I wonder how far off the bulk of Roasline's army is… hopefully they're not too close.*

Marlvon and Sor seamlessly passed through Fort Kykum. In fact, Marlvon passed through more easily than he ever had in his life; there were no beggars or hawkers on the street to slow his progress and everyone seemed more interested in their own business than that of others. This pleased Marlvon greatly.

It was evening by the time they reached the west wall of the inner keep. Marlvon approached it from a small laneway and spied where Winter and Ryde were waiting for them. He made sure that no one was watching the two men before leaving the shadows and greeting them in the mock innocence of a chance meeting.

Ryde reported that their passage was equally straightforward and saw no suspicious activity. He followed up with a comment, 'Why should we be paid attention to? There are thousands of people here and we're unimportant nobodies.' He smiled. 'Well, at least three of us are.'

Marlvon felt the itch to continue. 'Let us go; I want Islonda securely with me before nightfall. Too many times I've been in Fort Kykum after dark, often with unpleasant experiences.'

Marlvon led the other three around the north side of the keep, ensuring to maintain a distance of several streets from the wall and gate.

They reached roughly the east side of the hill, and without stopping, Marlvon instructed them to search for a building with a red door.

'We'll start closest to the keep and work our way down the slope. We should all stick together; my hackles are prickling.'

Marlvon felt a sense of unease, but he could not locate its source. He feared an attack, but his feeling felt more a general sense of unease than something specific or obvious. *Perhaps, I am scared of what I might find when I discover Islonda.*

The four entered a skinny street down the hill that had an air of tension about it. The buildings were built close together and looked older than the up-hill streets. Most were two or three stories high and they seemed to loom over the street as Marlvon walked along it. Broad-shouldered men stood about the doorways of several of the buildings and many of the windows were boarded up. Two houses into the street, Marlvon's instincts told him that this was the street that he had been looking for. His heart quickened, and he loosened his sword in its scabbard.

The group instinctively bunched together. Strangers who passed them stopped talking and stared at them. Marlvon's eyes darted here and there looking for the red door or any threat to their safety.

Halfway down the street, Winter tapped Marlvon on the shoulder and pointed to a two-story house. Marlvon saw at once that the door had red peeling paint and an oil lamp dimly lit above it which cast moving shadows over the façade. The windows on either side were half boarded with the other half being covered inside by thick curtains. Out the front was a single man with bare muscular arms and a curved scimitar by his side. He had an evil look about him and a hard expression on his face. His beady eyes had already spied Marlvon and his friends, and he watched them intently.

Marlvon readied himself and approached the man as the last light of day left the sky, thrusting the laneway into dark shadows. Marlvon debated how to greet the man and had decided on honesty. Regardless, he didn't get the chance, for the henchman spoke first.

He pointed a long finger at Sor and spoke with a deep, halting voice. 'She cannot enter. You three can, if you have a copper piece each.'

Marlvon turned to Sor. 'We will be as quick as we can.' Then he whispered so that the man could not hear him. 'Remember, my soldiers are not far behind.'

She nodded and Marlvon got three copper pieces out of a leather pouch. He gave one to Ryde, but Winter refused. 'I'm not leaving Sor out here by herself. I'll stay with her.'

Sor glared at him, 'I can look after myself.'

'Stop this bickering, now. Sor, Winter will stay with you. If we need help, you will hear us and you can both come to our rescue.'

Sor seemed to bite her tongue, but nodded.

Marlvon and Ryde turned back to the man and paid the entrance fee. He stood aside and let them enter. They opened the red door slowly and entered a hallway. Marlvon's heart raced faster than if he had run a mile at full speed. They made their way down the hallway and peered into a room on the right. It was dimly lit, but Marlvon could see four men lounging on couches. Two of them smoked long thin pipes that gave off a sickly sweet smell. The other three seemed unconscious. It finally dawned on Marlvon that they were in a poppy den. These *establishments* had been springing up in the main cities over the past decade, and their reputation was not a good one. *At least it is not a brothel.*

'Ryde, somewhere there will be a head man who will try to sell us crushed poppy to smoke. If Islonda is here, he will know where she is.'

They continued to search the building, Marlvon getting more anxious with each footstep further into the house. They poked their heads into two more rooms with similar findings to the front room. They then came to a staircase with steps that were worn in the centre where people had walked for decades past. Down the stairs came a thin man wearing a garish purple cloak and shiny leather boots. He greeted Marlvon and Ryde warmly.

'Ah, welcome new-comers to my fine establishment. I take it you're looking for a taste of our finest product and a comfortable place to enjoy it.'

Marlvon saw the man's quick eyes look them up and down. Marlvon put on an aged voice to match his appearance. 'Alas, not just yet good man. I am looking for my niece and I heard that she could be found here.'

The man frowned and a flicker of annoyance crossed his face. 'No… no women here.' He smiled cheekily. 'The only mistress here is the beautiful poppy.'

Marlvon tried not to lose hope; he knew this type of man and doubted the truth of his words. *Phlyte would not have lied to me about this.*

'I'm sorry to hear that. I was willing to pay a gold piece to the person who had been caring for her while I've been away.'

Marlvon watched the man's eyes light up. 'One gold piece is not much good. It's so lonely without a brother to rub against.'

Marlvon could feel Ryde growing irritable, but his experience kept him calm. 'Hmm, that's an interesting thought. I think I would need my niece to be here, alive and well cared for, to pay a sum of two gold pieces.'

'That seems to be a reasonable request. I would ask you to come with me, but how can I be sure that you're good for your word?'

Marlvon pulled a single gold piece from his purse. He flicked it to the man. 'There you go. You will get another when I see she is safe and in health.'

'You know, it's just coming back to me now. We do have a woman here. She cleans the house and cooks for me. She should be in the kitchen now.' The man stepped off the bottom step and walked past Marlvon to go further down the passageway. As they walked, the man talked freely.

'Yes, my memory is all coming back to me. A few weeks ago, I had just finished sampling a new supplier and went outside for a breath of air. The poppy had put me in a good mood that afternoon. Out on the street, my joy was burdened, for I saw a young lady sitting in the gutter crying freely. Now here's a sad pretty thing, I thought and I went over to her to see if I could cheer her up. I sat down next to her and asked her to tell me her story. Through much sobbing, she told me a fanciful tale of being engaged to the nephew of the old leader, Resvon and how she had travelled across the Rogaus to the Healers, then back again as a captive of Tunley's navy.'

The man shook his head. 'I don't know if it was the way she told it or the joy of the poppy, but I was laughing enough to split my sides. Then she told me how she had nowhere to go and that seemed less funny. She turned to me and I saw, for the first time, that she was with child. My mind was made up and I decided to take her in and feed her. In return, all she had to do was clean and cook. She has stayed here ever since. She is an excellent cook and tells tantalising stories of this and that. She tells these to entertain my customers and they always want to hear more. Since she's come here, no one wants to leave.'

He scratched his chin and they arrived at a closed door. 'The baby will be a problem, but I think I know a man who will take it off my hands once it's born. I'll get a good price too.' Marlvon had a sudden urge to stick the bastard with his sword, but he restrained himself.

'She's good looking too, your *niece*.' He winked at Marlvon. 'Once the baby's gone, she might need to help keep my bed warm, you know, to repay the kindness I've shown her.'

Marlvon had to use his entire will power to hold his fist from striking the man. Ryde was bursting with anger beside him as well.

Marlvon forced himself to speak. 'Is she through here?'

The man went first and Marlvon followed with his heart in his mouth. He knew that he would have to be very careful how he played this; the man clearly thought he owned Islonda and would be loath to part with her.

The kitchen was no more than a small fireplace with a table for preparing food. Old banged pots hung off a rope in the corner. Marlvon didn't notice any of that though as his eyes went immediately to the woman bending over the table cutting carrots with a blunt-looking knife. She looked up as the door opened and Marlvon's heart caught in his mouth.

Islonda, after many months, he finally beheld her once more. 'Islonda,' was all he could croak out.

She looked quizzically at him, even hopeful. Marlvon then remembered his disguise. 'It's Mant, your uncle. I know it's been a while and I look older than last time we met, but surely you recognise me?' Marlvon tried to convey as much meaning as he could in his stare at her.

She slowly put down the knife and straightened up. Marlvon saw she was heavily pregnant and wanted nothing more than to take her in his arms and hold her forever. She looked thinner in the face than last time he had seen her, but she appeared healthy enough. Marlvon had always cherished her quick thinking and he was pleased to see she still kept this attribute, even though so much had happened to her.

'Uncle Mant, it has been too long.'

Her voice was music to Marlvon's ears, but he detected a hidden strain lying beneath her tone.

'Come and give your uncle a hug.'

'Not so fast.' The house owner stepped between them and held out his hand.

Marlvon took the meaning and handed him the gold piece.

'You may have a few moments with her and then you must leave. She has yet to prepare my meal and I'm hungry.' The man stepped out of the way and banged on the door thrice.

Islonda quickly made her way into Marlvon's arms and he held her close to him. The act filled him with joy and he felt like skipping around the room on tiptoes.

After a long while, she pulled apart and looked up into his eyes. 'I've missed you! Please tell me you've come to take me away.'

The fact that she doubted his intentions told him how much fear lay within her. 'Of course I have.'

As he turned to the house owner, two large men entered the small kitchen. Marlvon eyed them and did not miss the purpose of them being present.

'How much do you want for me to be able to take my niece with me, without causing any trouble?'

'Take her? Ha, she is far too valuable to me for you to take her away, old man.'

Marlvon felt the likelihood of bloodshed increasing and detested the thought. If it came to blows, he had no idea how many foes he would have to fight to be able to escape. And Islonda being pregnant posed the problem of mobility; she could hardly be expected to run away from pursuers.

Marlvon tried to keep the mood jovial. 'Then let's play a game; humour me. I have deep pockets.'

'I could not part with her for less than five hundred gold pieces.'

Marlvon knew that this was a ludicrous price. He clapped his hand on his belly and laughed, or pretended to laugh. 'You do humour me.' *Should I bluff and pull out? No, he wants her more than the money and won't bite.* 'Come on, can you be more reasonable?'

'Very well, four hundred and ninety.'

Marlvon's heart sank. 'If I carried that kind of money with me, then I would happily pay it. Perhaps there's another arrangement we can come to.' Marlvon spoke the words, but he held little hope in them.

'I think your time is up; it's time for you to leave, Mant.'

Marlvon moved slightly and gave himself a modicum of space in the small kitchen. 'One hundred gold pieces. I can give you that right now and I walk away with my niece and no one gets hurt.'

The man's eyes twinkled. 'I've got a better deal: you give me the coins and you leave with your silent friend here and your life. Or, these two gentlemen slit your throats and I take the coins off your corpse.'

Marlvon could see the arrogance in the man's face. He clearly thought that he was in a commanding position.

Why does everything have to end in violence?

Marlvon moved to be between Islonda and the men. Then, quicker than they could comprehend, he drew his hidden sword, flicked his wrist and in a single powerful cross-sweep, decapitated the two henchmen. The owner of the house's face dropped in recognition and Marlvon felt a flow of hatred towards the man sweep through him. The man scrambled towards the door, but Marlvon pushed past the dead bodies and drove his sword cleanly through the man's back. The man fell to the floor with a dull thud.

Marlvon could feel bile rising into his mouth, but he forced it down to deal with the situation. 'Ryde, find something flammable; we're going to burn this house down.'

He turned to Islonda and put his hands on her shoulders. 'Islonda.' He pulled her into a firm embrace. 'Islonda, is there a back door out of here?'

She replied in a shaky voice. 'Yes. The door over there leads to a dark laneway.'

'Good, can you go and wait by the door, please?'

While Islonda waited by the back door, Marlvon awkwardly moved the table to block the internal door. Ryde had found some oily lard and had drizzled it onto the dead bodies and around the room. When Marlvon was ready, he nodded to Ryde, who flicked a burning log out of the fire and onto the floor. The fat lit at once and Marlvon, Ryde and Islonda left via the back door before the smoke caught their throats.

They hit the cool night air and Marlvon breathed a sigh of relief. They were out of immediate danger, but far from safe. He started to plan their next movements. They would go the end of the laneway then he would send Ryde down the street to fetch Sor and Winter.

His thoughts were broken by Islonda clasping onto his hand tightly. 'Is it really you?' She managed to croak out.

'It is, my love. I am here and will never leave you again. We're in for a long night though; are you up to it?'

'Anything to get away from this place.' She shuddered.

'We will have much walking ahead of us. If you need to stop at any point let me know. It will not be easy.' Marlvon knew that the night was going to be hard for him, but couldn't imagine how hard it would be for Islonda at her stage of pregnancy. Regardless, he knew that she would grit her teeth and do what was needed to be done; it was just who she was, and he loved her for it.

At the end of the lane, Ryde went to collect Winter and Sor. Marlvon and Islonda just stood there hugging while they waited for the others to return. They didn't need to say anything, they just connected through the contact.

A few moments later, Ryde, Winter, and Sor returned. Ryde spoke in his gruff voice, 'All quiet down there. I reckon we got a bit of a spell before the fire is noticed.'

Marlvon nodded, glad of the news. 'Then let us make sure that we're far from here when the call goes up.'

Marlvon set off at the fastest pace that he thought Islonda could match. He shortly realised that he had misjudged and that Islonda was struggling to keep up. Yet it was Ryde who spoke up first.

'Marlvon, stop. We need to change our plan. If we keep at this pace Islonda will be on the ground before long.'

Marlvon stopped and Ryde continue to talk. 'It will take us most of the night to reach the gates and then we don't even know if they will be open. What would we do then? Camp by them like beggars?'

'No, that would not do.' Marlvon looked at Islonda. 'I'm sorry, in my eagerness to escape the city, my judgement was lost.' She smiled at him. 'We need to find somewhere safe to sleep the night. Ryde, do you know of any such places close by?'

Ryde scratched his chin. 'I believe I do. At first, I thought of my old house, but that is down nearer the docks and likely full of Roasline's sailors. However, my sister Prie's house might still be empty. It is a small two room place with only one small window. She would have locked the door before leaving it... for the last time.' Ryde coughed. 'Follow me. It is a short way down the hill.'

Ryde led at a slow pace that was comfortable for Islonda, and it wasn't long before they arrived at Prie's house. The one-eyed sailor had been right. The house was small and locked firmly. Marlvon had to splinter the door frame to force it open and the five people hurried inside.

The room was as dark as pitch, and it took a moment before Ryde could find something to light. Once a lamp was lit, they all felt more comfortable and were able to relax somewhat. The house was small with minimal furniture, but Marlvon ensured that Islonda was comfortable on the low bed. They all ate what little food they had carried with them, mainly dried grapes and nuts, before settling down for the night.

As well as looking after Islonda, Marlvon watched Ryde, whom a sadness of grief had fallen on. The old sailor went about the house feeling different objects and muttering to himself. Eventually, he seated himself in a stiff wooden chair by the window and closed his eyes, but clearly not to sleep.

Islonda fell asleep quickly in Marlvon's arms, but Marlvon could find no rest. His mind raced through the events of the evening and he couldn't get the images of the dead men out of his head.

At some stage past the middle of the night, Marlvon must have fallen asleep, for he was woken by Ryde as weak shafts of light filtered through the small window.

'It's time to get up,' Ryde croaked.

Marlvon roused himself and Islonda woke too. He found a dried chamber pot under the bed and offered it to Islonda, who gratefully used it. While she was busy relieving herself, Marlvon was thinking hard on how they would best escape Fort Kykum.

He eventually decided that the only option was to secure a horse for Islonda and leave by the gate as they had arrived. No one should be looking for them and there seemed to be minimal danger in the plan. Islonda would have to spend a long time in the saddle, but that could not be helped.

Marlvon gathered the small group together and told them his plan. They all seemed to agree, until Sor spoke up. 'While I'm no expert with women nearing childbirth, I do have some experience in the matter. Surely this will prove too much and the imminent birth will be brought on sooner. That's not to mention the discomfort that Islonda will be in, the frequent stops for her to, ahem, refresh herself and the harm that all of that jiggling might cause to the unborn child. There has to be another way. Could we get a trap for the horse?'

Marlvon felt crestfallen and turned to Islonda. 'Could riding a horse really hurt our baby?'

She replied with a shaky voice, 'I don't know. In Bankton, women rarely rode horses at all, and those at my stage usually did little physical work. But if there's a chance that it might… then we have to find another way.'

'I have not the money for a trap or a cart; I would only have enough for a horse. And I do not want to steal one either; that would be too hard. Oh well, it looks like it will be a slow journey of many days on tired feet.' His tone sounded deflated at the prospect.

Muffled silence filled the cramped room until Winter shifted uneasily. 'Perhaps, there's another way.' Marlvon looked at him hopefully and Winter continued, 'Could we secure a boat and sail out? It would be easier for all of us.'

Silence filled the room once more, but this time it was a silence of contemplation and hope.

Ryde spoke first. 'It's daring, to be sure, and there will be hurdles to jump.'

'Tell me what you're thinking.' Marlvon eagerly wanted more information.

'Well, first we need to get a boat. It wouldn't need to be a big one, but could we afford it? I'm not sure; it would depend on what's on offer. If not, we would need to resort to theft. Once we have a boat, I could sail it easily, but what armed security will be down at the docks? What with the Roasline occupation of the city and all. And by security, I mean access to the docks themselves, then clear water to sail in and finally leaving the water gate.

'I couldn't be certain, but I had a quick look over the water yesterday and the gate seemed to be all in ruin. Once we're on the open water, if we don't hit a storm, we should make it safely to our ship… if we're not intercepted.'

Everyone looked at Marlvon and waited for him to respond.

'I should have thought about this before we came here. The way I see it, the options are to sail out, with all the hazards that await us; walk out of the city, which would be the safest, but longest; or to find a horse and ride out and accept the risks.' He looked to Islonda. 'I just want to be safe and free of Fort Kykum.'

She put her hand on his. 'Me too.'

He looked back to the room at large. 'We will go down the path of sailing out. Winter and Ryde will go ahead to the docks and attempt to secure a vessel. Islonda, Sor and I will make our slow way down to the docks in preparation. Should obtaining a boat be too troublesome, then we will abandon this option.'

Everyone nodded in agreement. Marlvon stood and handed Ryde his money pouch. 'Spend what you need, but buy some food for the journey first.'

'Aye, and some cloth to keep us warm on the open water.'

Winter stood too and they went to the door. Marlvon caught Ryde on the arm as he was about to leave. 'We will meet you where the main road arrives at the docks. Ryde, take this too; its value might help secure a more appropriate vessel.' Marlvon handed the old sailor his Myrthian sword.

'Are you sure you want to part with this?'

'It is a tool. Yes, a very fine tool, but a tool nonetheless. If it helps Islonda reach safety, then that will be a worthwhile use of it.'

Ryde nodded and then left with Winter in tow.

Marlvon meticulously removed the remaining disguise from his face, which had smeared in the excitement of the previous night. Islonda was happy to see his true face once more, especially when he smiled at her. Once the others were prepared, they all left Prie's small house and headed down the hill to the docks.

Travelling down the hill was a slow process and Marlvon noticed a high presence of Roasline troops. Thankfully, these posed no issues for them and kept to themselves.

Marlvon, Islonda and Sor eventually reached the docks and Marlvon saw the full extent of the damaged gates. Chunks of large debris still lay in the water and construction was underway on building new gates. Marlvon was glad to see that these were not yet complete as it would make their exit from the Fort easier.

It was mid-afternoon when Ryde and Winter returned from their mission. Ryde was smiling ruefully, but Winter looked less certain.

'How did you fare?'

Ryde threw Marlvon's sword to him. 'We have a boat.'

'If you can call it a boat.' Winter mumbled under his breath.

'It is perhaps not as grand and you might hope for… or as big… and Winter and Sor will need to go by land.'

Marlvon's heart sank. 'What have you bought?'

'I have secured us a single sailed skiff. It will fit the three of us, but it won't be comfortable.'

Winter chimed in again. 'I don't envy you your journey in this boat. It is old and the sides are not far above the water.'

Ryde looked at Winter coolly. 'Due to the war, there were few boats at all, let alone ones for sale, as you well know. And besides, you underestimate my skill as a sailor.' He looked at Marlvon. 'She will not be fast, but will do the job.'

'The money has been spent and so she must. Let us go now, and sail from here so that we can put distance between us and Fort Kykum while there is still light.'

'That's the spirit.' Ryde sounded unnervingly excited.

They made their way to the poor end of the civilian dock and Ryde showed them their boat. The skiff was an off-white colour with flaking paint. A dull green word was written on the bow: *Pony*. There were two bench seats and a single mast with a furled sail. It was the sort of boat that young boys learnt to sail in and certainly wouldn't be taken out of the gates and into the Rogaus proper.

Marlvon felt apprehensive, but his adventurous side felt as excited as Ryde looked. 'You're a daring man, Captain Ryde.'

'Ha! If you're not daring in life, then when will you be?' He leapt into the boat and Winter passed him the provisions. He held his hand out to a pale Islonda. 'My Lady, dare you step onto my most excellent vessel?'

She smiled despite herself and took Ryde's hand to step onto *Pony*.

Marlvon clasped Sor by the arm firmly. 'Sister Sor, we will meet you where we first made land. Winter, good luck, you may be there before us.'

Marlvon leapt aboard and Winter untied the mooring. Ryde took up the two paddles and rowed them away from the dock. Once they were in clear water, he unfurled the sail and set the bow for the open Rogaus. 'Let us sail to the high seas and greet the adventures that await us.'

Marlvon settled in next to Islonda and longed to be alone with her in safety.

The journey to their ship took them three days. Ryde expertly hugged the coastline to ensure safety and aside from being incredibly uncomfortable, getting little sleep and longing for land, no ill befell them.

When they arrived at their ship, Winter and Sor were waiting for them. They climbed aboard and after quick greetings, Marlvon ordered that a course be set for Nivera, and that he and Islonda were to be left alone until the following morning.

Marlvon and Islonda settled into the bed in Marlvon's cabin and held each other closely without saying a word. They drifted into a happy sleep and Marlvon finally felt that the world was righting itself.

The journey back to Nivera was uneventful. Until Islonda started having birthing pains. She laboured for a full day, at the end of which a healthy boy was born. The parents agreed on a name that Marlvon had thought of and were proud to call their baby Jaultvon, in honour of Islonda's father and Marlvon's family.

Shortly after Jaultvon was born, Ryde, as a Captain, married Marlvon and Islonda. There was much merrymaking that night and all the way back to Nivera.

On arriving at the artisan city, Marlvon had much to attend to and saw little of Islonda and his new son. Every moment he spent away from them, he rued and worked all the faster to complete his tasks as quickly as possible.

After several months, a letter arrived from Lyafe of the Healers requesting a meeting between the Leader of the Outcasts, the Leader of Psymryte, Olswerth and the new High Chancellor of Roasline; Jaid. A peace treaty was to be negotiated on a newly rebuilt Headly. Marlvon at once agreed and he immediately set out with Islonda, Jaultvon, Ryde, Guflinkov, Winter and Sor.

The negotiations for peace took several days and exhausted Marlvon more than a raging battle. Sor proved pivotal in the discussions, and Jaid immediately took a liking to her. In the end, a deal was struck where the Liagar River was the boundary between the two peoples.

Jaid had argued stoically that Fort Kykum should remain in the control of Roasline as they had won it by force. Marlvon knew the Outcasts could do little to stop her from taking it as their army was decimated and, in the end, he conceded to her control of it.

At that point, Jaid had seen this as a pivotal moment and reneged on her claim in the interests of peace and the greater good, provided that a battalion of troops could be stationed there. Marlvon wondered if Sor had been working on Jaid behind the scenes to his favour and agreed to Jaid's generous concession.

The vastness of the Outcast territory had been troubling Marlvon. While the leaders were present, he gave Psymryte, and the lands leading up to Olswerth's borders, to the Leader of Psymryte to control as he saw fit. This annexation negated a potential threat of the people of Psymryte to claim ownership of the Leader of the Outcasts.

Marlvon also announced that one year from that day, he would step down from leading the Outcasts and be replaced by someone selected by the Outcast people. All present, except Islonda, were disappointed with this announcement as they knew Marlvon to be a skilled leader. Alas, he would not be convinced to remain leader, and he set about preparing what needed to be done to ensure a seamless transition. Guflinkov vowed to assist in this process.

Once the treaty was finished, Marlvon returned to Nivera with Islonda, Jaultvon, Ryde, Olswerth and Guflinkov while Winter and Sor joined Jaid's party in heading to Roasline.

Winter and Sor would spend several years in Roasline before travelling around different cities, towns and villages. Sor preached to all who were interested the ways of the Gods of Day and Night, while Winter was merely content to visit new places, meet with new people and learn all that he could about the world and the different ways that humans lived. They remained travelling friends until Winter passed away after his sixty-second birthday. After which, Sor returned to the Moaks and re-entered the monk's community.

Ryde remained in Nivera until the end of his days. Marlvon gifted him a house that overlooked the Rogaus and a small ship to call his own. He often sailed with a close crew, up and down the coast or across the water to visit Headly, and was content with his lot.

Guflinkov lived to see a new Outcast ruler; a sensible man with much vigour and progressive views. After the new leader was settled in, Guflinkov asked Ryde to sail him to Myrth Isle, where he spent his few remaining years in peace. He died a happy man with the knowledge that he had worked hard towards his goal and had achieved it.

Marlvon, Islonda and Jaultvon settled down on a large, but manageable, olive farm outside of Bankton. Islonda had two more children, both girls and Marlvon spoilt his offspring dreadfully.

Islonda found purpose in running the farm and quickly worked it into an efficient operation. She found harmony in the work and was able to move on from the horrors of her past.

Marlvon found peace less easily. He had recurring nightmares where he relived the crimes that he had committed as a younger man. At these times, Islonda was able to calm him, but a lingering feeling of sickness filled his mouth. As his children grew, he began to spend more and more time walking in a woodland on their property. He would listen to the birds and the wind in the leaves and nature calmed his mind.

Islonda saw his pain and wept many tears for his suffering. She spent much of her time with him and encouraged him to share his troubles with her. Sometimes he did and sometimes he did not. She knew not to press him at these times, but held him firmly instead.

The years passed by and Marlvon began to let Islonda into his torment more and more. It wasn't until their children were fully grown adults, that Marlvon happily smiled and said to Islonda, 'Here, with you in this world, I am at finally peace.'

Shawline Publishing Group Pty Ltd

www.shawlinepublishing.com.au